WHEN
YOU
READ
THIS

WHEN YOU READ THIS

A NOVEL

mary adkins

HODDER &
STOUGHTON

First published in Great Britain in 2019 by Hodder & Stoughton
An Hachette UK company

1

A CIP catalogue record for this title is available from the British Library

Hardback ISBN 978 1 473 67331 1
Trade Paperback ISBN 978 1 473 67330 4
eBook ISBN 978 1 473 67332 8

Printed and bound in Great Britain by Clays Ltd, Elcograf S.p.A.

Hodder & Stoughton policy is to use papers that are natural, renewable and recyclable
products and made from wood grown in sustainable forests. The logging and manufacturing
processes are expected to conform to the environmental regulations of the country of origin.

Hodder & Stoughton Ltd
Carmelite House
50 Victoria Embankment
London EC4Y 0DZ

www.hodder.co.uk

For Lucas and Finn

GOOGLING GRIEF

by Jade Massey

All the poems about grief

are wrong.

My grief is the

opposite

of a couplet.

It is not pretty.

It does not make room

for rhymes.

Here is my poem

about grief:

So this is pain.

This is what it was

all along.

SIMONYI BRAND MANAGEMENT
96 Morton Street, 9th Floor
New York, NY 10014

June 18

Dear Mr. Simonyi:

I came upon your company on the Stanford University Employers Forum, on which your firm is listed as a place where Stanford students have had positive internship experiences previously. Grace Wang ('16) wrote that she had a wonderful summer working with you and your colleague Iris. While "wonderful" is rather nebulous and uninformative, her point is well made. I see that you have not posted a fall internship opening, but I am writing to express my interest in interning for you come September.

I am a rising fourth-year with a deep and abiding commitment to public relations and communications work since the wee age of three and a half, at which time I launched my first promotional campaign for a line of children's toys created by my father, Carl Van Snyder Jr. My contribution consisted of conspicuously playing with the toys (which later became the award-winning ToddleGenius™ line) while at day care, in line with my father's at-home demonstrations. ;)

Since that time, I have established a proven track record of promotional success after promotional success. I am the youngest ever member of my fraternity to be elected social chair, and as such, I organized the Palo Alto chapter of the Race Against Alzheimer's this past spring, raising over $100,000 for the organization Don't Forget Us. I am also a Krav Maga black belt, nationally ranked chess player (12–15 age group), and founder of the online magazine *SHAVED*, devoted to topics of personal hygiene and masculinity's fluctuating contours.

I would be thrilled to join Simonyi Brand Management in New York City as a fall intern and am available to begin as early as August 24. Also, I would not require a salary, as this Urban Internship Semester must be in exchange for credit hours only.

My résumé is attached. In an attempt to be thorough, I have declined to be brief. Please let me know if you have a page limit, and I will do my best to trim it down to one (though the font size, of course, may have to decrease, which I'm aware can be a challenge to more mature eyes).

Sincerely,
Carl Van Snyder III

If you want to find out you're dying from a bot, I have a recommendation: Dr. Hsu at New York Presbyterian delivers death
warrants with the empathy of a salamander.

I should have expected nothing less, given that two weeks
ago, he informed me that a CT scan showed lesions on my lungs
by saying "This does not necessarily mean you have cancer."

I explained to Dr. Hsu that telling someone they don't necessarily have cancer is only good news if they already think they
have cancer. For those of us who believe ourselves to be healthy,
the correct phrasing is, "I have some bad news."

He thanked me for the suggestion.

Here's how it happened today. I arrived at the office around
8:30 as usual, before my boss as usual. I was reading news online. NASA reports that 25 million Americans have stockpiled
guns in preparation for doomsday. A man has spent $100,000 on
operations to become a real-life Ken doll. My phone buzzed, and
like that, I have lung cancer.

Dr. Hsu explained that not only are the lesions on my lungs
indicative of cancer, but they also mean that I will probably be
dying soon. He mentioned chemo, trying it, seeing what happens. But my cancer is special. It isn't referred to in stages like
other cancers. It only comes in two varieties: limited and extensive. Mine is the bad kind.

"I want to be honest with you. The prognosis is not good," he
said. I thanked him for his honesty, because that's what you do
when someone bothers to point out they're being honest.

"Death is a fact for us all," he went on, "but yours will most likely come in six months or sooner," like the end of my existence is a gestating baby, or the love of my life. Half a year. Twenty-four weeks. Before summer.

The call was short, just long enough for us to plan for me to go in Wednesday. At some point in the conversation my boss walked in, and I noticed my 98-cent deli coffee had tipped over. The puddle dripped off the desk onto the floor. "WE ARE HERE TO SERVE YOU," the paper cup promised, sideways.

As I told Smith that I have six months to live, I laughed, like it's a joke. Is it?

He hugged me. I can't remember if I hugged back. He smelled like the Ralph Lauren cologne I once bought for Daniel but then gave to him instead, after some fight Daniel and I had, of the dozens or hundreds. *Do you tell ex-fiancés you are dying?* The question flitted through my mind as a matter of etiquette, one my mother would have an answer to. Somewhere, on a shelf in Virginia, there probably is a well-worn book with a paragraph on what courtesy ex-lovers owe one another with regard to announcements of terminal illness.

For Smith's benefit—he looked like he might have a heart attack—I kept talking, explaining the series of increasingly ominous events that led to this morning. First came the chest pains, then the CT scan, the results of which were delayed because of Christmas. Then the biopsy. It felt like someone else was talking about me. The actual Iris had fled. She's already gone.

He asked how long "this" has been going on. I know now that by "this" he was referring to the tests—to my discovery of the disease rather than to the disease, itself. But I misunderstood.

"Who knows?" I said.

I realized on the train home he meant the tests. He meant:
Why didn't you tell me?

I didn't tell him, of course, because when you tell people
things, they treat them as real, and then you have to decide. I
had been hoping for the best. I have always been an optimist.

Neither of us knew what one does after being diagnosed with
cancer that will probably kill you. Certainly not resume business as usual. So I came back to my apartment, which I'm now
regretting. Maybe I'll go back to work. At least then he'd stop
texting to ask if I'm okay being alone.

Is that what people do? Avoid being alone with their new cancer? I could call Jade, but I'm sure she's in the kitchen with her
cell tucked away in a closet. Using my triannual call to my mom
to tell her I have cancer just seems cruel. And I'm not in the
mood for the baby mamas (my friends from my early twenties
who had babies in our early thirties and then ceased to be capable of talking about anything but their children, so we've drifted.
Plus, our friend Sabine, who was the glue keeping us together,
moved to California).

Frankly, I'm surprised this site made it to fruition. A year
or so ago the founders came to the firm looking for branding
assistance in exchange for equity in their "graphic storytelling
platform start-up." Todd and . . . Chad? Ethan? According to
Ethan/Todd/Chad, both people with terminal illnesses and stay-
at-home moms were itching to blog in triangles, arrows, and
colorful bar graphs. They had a colorful binder of demographic
research on target niches, and Smith had been intrigued, initially (I wasn't—they were both the same shade of too-tan and
talked about the future like it was a lottery they'd rigged). They
had originally called it a d-log (drawing log, like "vlog"), but that
didn't go over well in focus groups. Throughout the presentation,

Smith and I both fought to suppress our laughter. For days afterward, he and I came up with who else might like to make a d-log: geriatric clowns! Racist poets! Disgruntled ghosts!

Now, here I am, a data point come to life. Bravo, Chad. I have a heads-up, a full six-month lead. I get to sit with my impending death over coffee so we can make plans.

Things you don't think about dying, until it's happening: I will break my lease.

I was an assistant while I saved to open a bakery, which never happened. I wanted a family, too, but so much for that. I got skinny then fat then skinny again. I smoked then quit.

She was an admin who got skinny then fat then skinny then died.

Here's the thing I need to figure out. This whole time I thought my real life hadn't started yet. Turns out that was my life. I have six months or so to make that okay, somehow.

COMMENTS (10):

DyingToBlogTeam: Welcome! We see you've already begun sharing. Remember that commenting on other users' Exit Posts will bring more visitors to your own page. Dying to Blog is a community of members facing the same challenge, and we want you to get your Maximum Departure Value™ out of it!

BonnieD: hi I'm Bonnie. I like your blog. u have to use more graphics tho because this is a graphics site and posts that get on the Popular page are never ones like yours. no offense but it looks like a word document. but i stumbled on you and like u so i will follow u anyway.

IrisMassey: Thanks, Bonnie. Do you have a blog on the site?

BonnieD: no. my mom used to be on it.

BonnieD: hers was really good but it moved to the afterlife page.

BonnieD: they have to move them otherwise u'd just have a bunch of
corpse blogs and that would be depressing lol

IrisMassey: I'm sorry.

BonnieD: it happens

IrisMassey: Thanks for the tip.

Jan10101010101: buy Viagra buy romaine penis large buy not here
thank u for your excellent content

EIGHT MONTHS LATER

Friday, August 28 | Simonyi Brand Management

---

from: smith@simonyi.com
to: rosylady101@yahoo.com
date: Fri, Aug 28 at 10:55 AM
subject: Vandalism of your posters

Dear Rosita,

I got your message. I understand your concern, especially after, as you note, we spent so much time perfecting the subway ad, and I remain grateful for your patience and gracious spirit during the photo shoot—agreed, he wasn't the most professional photographer around (apologies again for the fingernail clipping on-site), and I know you weren't thrilled to learn that I plucked him off of Craigslist, but that says nothing of how much I value you both as a client and as my dentist.

Remember that a year ago, no one knew who you were, because no one knew Paula Abdul had a ghastly mouth as a child. But then we all learned, thanks to that intrepid *Post* reporter, that you built Paula's mouth chair-side. You *made* Paula. It is a phenomenal feat, and one for which I'm glad you're finally receiving the recognition you deserve. Since the news broke, we have done an outstanding job (if I say so myself) harnessing your initial publicity to develop a personal brand. The interviews, the book deal, the additional celeb endorsements. Now that the book's coming out, and our campaign targeting commuters in the region has finally launched, I need to warn you about something:

fame comes at a price. You will have haters. It is inevitable. My clients don't read the comments, don't read the blogs, don't read the tabloids. And in your case, they don't pay attention to a little graffiti on a few subway ads.

We knew (or at least I did, and perhaps should have made more clear) when we decided to place the posters in New York subway stations that they would be vandalized. If you spend much time riding New York City transit, you will notice that no advertisement is immune from the occasional mustache or profane smear. These interactions with the ads, I would suggest, aren't something to bemoan. On the contrary, they enhance the likelihood of people noticing and remembering your smoldering, shimmering grin! Rosita de Santiago, DDS!

This is the time to welcome attention in any form.

You reference with loathing the estimable Dr. Zizmor, New York City's first medical professional to take to in-motion, 2-D campaigning on the trains. Sure, his posters about getting rid of pimples rendered him the target of ridicule. He also now owns a yacht and three houses on two different coasts.

Relatively speaking, I think T-E-E-F-S neatly penned across your five front incisors is fairly innocuous.

Warmly,

Smith S. Simonyi

President

Simonyi Brand Management

from: YOPLAY <philgergel@gmail.com>
to: smith@simonyi.com
date: Fri, Aug 28 at 11:34 AM
subject: YOU WILL NOT BELIEVE THIS B AS IN BULL + S AS IN SATIRE

NOPE.

NOPE NOPE NOPE.

NOT AGAIN.

YES *AGAIN*.

GO TO YOUTUBE

SEARCH MY NAME PLUS RAPPER SO YOU DON'T GET THAT YOYO TRICK MAN

CLICK ON "IT'S NOT EASY HAVING GREEN—ORIGINAL VIDEO"

SURPRISE!

IT IS NOT MY ORIGINAL VIDEO *after all*. THE LADIES HAVE BEEN REPLACED WITH MUPPETS, AKA I HAVE A BEAST FETISH APPARENTLY WHEREIN THE BEASTS ARE MADE OUT OF CLOTH

NOTE, FURTHERMORE: THE MUPPETS I "KISS" IN THIS "PARODY" OF MY RAP ARE ALL "MALE," BUT DUMMY DIDN'T EVEN USE KERMIT

FOOL

SO WHAT ARE THEY TRYING TO SAY NOW—THAT I AM A SINGER *FOR CHILDREN?*

SMITH, I AM DONE. WITH. THIS. DRAMZ.

AFTER "RAIN ON ME, SIR JESUS"—ok GOSPEL WAS A BAD IDEA, NOT MY FORTÉ SO MUCH AS not my forté—I HAVE STRUGGLED TO ESTABLISH MYSELF AS AN ARTIST WITH RANGE DESPITE PRESSURE FROM THE MASSES

WHO NEED ME TO FIT INTO A NEAT AND APPROVED CATEGORY OF MUSIC. I SUPPOSE MY RECENT DIP INTO COUNTRY DIDN'T HELP. DO PEOPLE THINK I CAN'T MAKE UP MY MIND ABOUT TO WHAT GENRE I BELONG?

BUT I AM AN ARTIST, AND ARTISTS:

A. EXPERIMENT
B. UNDERSTAND THAT JUST BECAUSE YOU EXPERIMENT DOES NOT PLACE YOU INTO A CATEGORY
C. ARE SUBJECT TO SO MUCH SCRUTINY WE OCCASIONALLY OFF OURSELVES

I'M NOT GOING TO OFF MYSELF, BUT I do EXPERIMENT, AND AT THIS POINT IN MY CAREER, I DO NOT HAVE ANY INTEREST IN PRETENDING ONLY TO BE INTERESTED IN ONE FORM OF SELF-EXPRESSION JUST TO PROTECT MY "brand" LEST I BE ABANDONED BY MY FANS, AND MY CAREER END BEFORE I AM DECREPIT AND USELESS, SUCH AS AT AGE 45.

I AM A VERNAL 32 YEARS OF AGE. BUT AS A WHITE RAP ARTIST OF SHORTER STATURE CLIMBING AN UP-HILL HILL, I AM FATIGUED.

I AM SLEEPY.

EVER SINCE I WON *SARAN WRAP'S FREESTYLE SHOWDOWN* AND GOT MY FIRST RECORD DEAL FOR "DON'T WHIZ ON ME" FOUR YEARS AGO, I HAVE BEEN THE TARGET OF THOSE WHO WOULD WISH TO SEE ME SHRIVEL UP LIKE A MAN'S JUNK IN THE SNOW.

IT IS TIME TO END THESE JUVENILE ATTACKS ON MY

MUSICAL GENRE EXPLORATION ONCE AND FOR ALL.
HOW DO WE FIGHT BACK?
    AS THEY SAY: D.I.Y.D.D.Y.O.
    DO IT YOURSELF
    DON'T DO
    YOURSELF
    OFF
PLEASE ADVISE,
YO-PLAY/Phil

---

from:	smith@simonyi.com
to:	YOPLAY <philgergel@gmail.com>
date:	Fri, Aug 28 at 12:04 PM
subject:	re: YOU WILL NOT BELIEVE THIS B AS IN BULL + S AS IN SATIRE

I understand your frustration. I truly do. You are my most valued client, and I give you my true opinion, always.

I think we should ignore this video. It's nothing. "Fighting back" or responding in some way could be seen as thin skinned. You want to be perceived as having a sense of humor, right? Being playful, like your music?

Finally, remember what they say about all press?

SS

from:	carl@simonyi.com
to:	smith@simonyi.com
date:	Fri, Aug 28 at 12:09 PM
subject:	Today's Agenda

Good morning Boss!

Today's schedule:

~~10—Leah Rollins-Loebel (Prospective Client), Nutritionist to the Stars~~ (sorry—already passed)

1—Call with Phil Gergel (aka Yo-Play)

3:30—Proposed meeting with Carl, me, on the following action items:

A. The possibility of assigning me more tasks that utilize my strengths rather than tasks that a chimp could do

B. How one schedules a book tour when one doesn't agree with the premise of the book

Also, I took the liberty of cleaning out my desk a bit, as there were a few drawers on the bottom with contents, and I will be needing the storage space for my gym clothes, etc. I imagine these items belonged to your former employee who predated my tenure here at Simonyi Brand Management. Much of it appears to be trash (receipts, scraps, to-do lists), but I didn't toss anything, as there were some other items as well—a straightening iron, lip gloss, a few self-help books, an article torn from a magazine titled "Becoming Your Best Self" (what a bleak testament to the pressures of womanhood, this assortment—I might have to use it in a short story).

I have placed it all in crates I found in the lobby of the building, so if the super comes a-knocking, guilty as charged. They are stowed behind the conference table.

Oh, and there was also what appears to be a printout of a blog. It is titled "My Life's First Draft: A Blog Turned into a Book by Iris Massey." She seems to want you to publish it. (Side note: Based on this Post-it, I have inferred that this woman who last sat at my desk *died*? How recently?? Because fyi *that* is something I'm going to need some time to process . . .)

Off to lunch,

Carl Van Snyder

Associate

Simonyi Brand Management

---

from: smith@simonyi.com
to: carl@simonyi.com
date: Fri, Aug 28 at 12:11 PM
subject: re: Today's Agenda

Carl,

Thank you, but an agenda would be much more helpful if you would send it at the beginning, rather than the middle, of the workday.

Also, you are not an associate so please remove that from your email signature.

And what is this about Iris and a blog? I don't see it on your desk . . .

Thx,

SS

from:	smith@simonyi.com
to:	iris.a.massey@gmail.com
date:	Fri, Aug 28 at 12:58 PM
subject:	no subject

I wonder how many people continue to email other people after they die. That'd be an interesting radio story. Or just a depressing one.

I have a new intern who started this week, Carl. He fell out of the sky in June, and Richie convinced me to hire him since it's going on four months and I haven't been able to bring myself to look for your replacement. He is twenty-one and full of pep. I figure it might be nice to have someone around.

Meanwhile, a month after his spectacular "rap funeral," Phil—the one client making me any money at this point—has decided to return to rap, having discovered that country requires more of a "singing voice" than he's capable of. And of course the transition from "Yo-Play" to "Phil Gergel" did not go unnoticed by the tabloids. Now that he's done with country, he's pretending that he never left the hip-hop world, and we are continuing to pretend that he's straight.

His "funeral," your cannabis-induced brainchild (I am tempted to make a joke about how your death spared you from having to endure the execution of it), rivaled your original vision in its spectacle. Webster Hall was packed. His coffin was ushered in by six bodybuilding pallbearers in white tuxes as a gospel choir sang a funeral march. Dwarves in party hats distributed folded paper unicorns that looked more like horses wearing KKK gear, since the paper didn't take well to the horns. He retained your idea of being "reborn," emerging from the coffin via suspension cords, just like the best part of a community theater production of *Peter Pan*, and the crowd was delighted. It was exhausting, and far less amusing than if you had been around.

I am shocked by how much I miss you.

Every day, I knew you'd be here when I walked in, and every day, we would make fun of this absurd field we are in.

When I offered you the job, I was sure you'd leave it within six months, tops. I think we both did. This job was your bridge to your future.

But then a year went by, then two . . . should I have pushed you to leave? I didn't because I liked having you here. I was selfish.

Iris, I have no clue why you stuck around this place so long. But dammit, the best part of every day was making you laugh. I wasn't conscious of it as my goal, but it was.

The last time you and I spoke, it was about Richie, how happy you were with him. You sounded downright giddy about it. Then, you said that the night before, your sister had taken you dancing. To me these seemed like good signs.

I asked if you needed anything.

"Tell me something funny," you said, so I told you how Phil had adopted a guinea pig and named it Abraham Lincoln. Your laugh turned into coughing. And then we hung up, but first I made myself say that I missed you. You said it back. I think we both wondered if it was our good-bye, since you wouldn't let me come see you, but I told myself that that didn't make sense. You were dating my friend! And going dancing!

I waited for you to come back. And you didn't.

I'm in deep, Iris. I got in deep.

---

from: smith@simonyi.com
to: carl@simonyi.com
date: Fri, Aug 28 at 1:12 PM
subject: re: Today's Agenda

Carl,

Please be reminded that lunch is an hour. And what Post-it?
Thx,
SS

---

from: smith@simonyi.com
to: carl@simonyi.com
date: Fri, Aug 28 at 2:29 PM
subject: re: Today's Agenda

Carl,

I have looked everywhere and do not see a printout of anything. I know we haven't spoken explicitly about this, but it seems like a good opportunity to say that all files and other documents that are work-related should remain here at the office.

Additionally, assuming you haven't skipped town due to the monotonous tasks you feel you've been assigned, do let me know if you plan to be gone for more than three hours in the middle of a workday.

Thank you for so neatly packing away her things, by the way.

---

from: wally@homilypines.com
to: smith@simonyi.com
date: Fri, Aug 28 at 2:51 PM
subject: Checking in

Hiya Smith!

Hope all is well in the big apple. You are missing the start of a beautiful fall out here! Took your mom on a walk yesterday to enjoy the sunshine. She's not so much into leaving her room these days, so it was quite a feat to convince her to let me get her in the chair. I swear it feels like she stiffens up like a toddler resisting sleep when I try to move her (though I know that's impossible). I've taken to letting her have her way more times than not, lest I get verbally accosted. Calls it her "jail cell." You know how she can be. What a sense of humor she has!

I was thinking if you came for a visit that might give her some reason to smile. But I know you're busy.

Jillian asked me to remind you that your August bill is outstanding. I told her I was sure you didn't need reminding and it'll come in with your September payment. Your mom says hi.
Wally

---

from: smith@simonyi.com
to: richierich1000@gmail.com
date: Fri, Aug 28 at 3:08 PM
subject: Loan

Hey Richie,

Any chance I could borrow like two grand to help me make my mom's rent this month? I hate to ask given what I already owe you, but I lost two clients to a bigger firm in July, one of those corporate giants, and I haven't signed anyone in about six months. I'm working on it. Every time I sit down to write an email to a prospective client, it feels like I'm inhaling sand, but I'm working on it. If you are up for adding it to my tab, I'll pay you back as soon as I can. Beer later?

I was also wondering if you'd be down for putting me in touch with any of your smaller clients, like the guy downtown who got all of that attention for selling the quiche that induces labor? I forget the name of his café.

You know I wouldn't come to you unless I'd already tried everything I can think of.

Beer later?

Thanks man,

Smith

---

from:	Airbnb
to:	smith@simonyi.com
date:	Fri, Aug 28 at 3:12 PM
subject:	Your listing is UN-SNOOZED!

Hi Smith,

Congratulations, you have successfully un-snoozed your listing **Beautiful One Bedroom with Balcony on Upper West Side**. It is set to go live again tomorrow, Sat, Aug 29. This means that your listing will show up in search results, and guests can reach out to you to book.

Your date availability is listed as **all dates**, and your termination date is set to **no termination date**. To change the visibility of your listing, or to snooze again, go to Manage Listing.

Thanks,

The Airbnb Team

---

from: smith@simonyi.com
to: richierich1000@gmail.com
date: Fri, Aug 28 at 3:42 PM
subject: Thanks

Just saw the bank transfer. Thanks for handling that so fast.
    Beer? When is good?

---

from: carl@simonyi.com
to: smith@simonyi.com
date: Fri, Aug 28 at 4:21 PM
subject: re: Today's Agenda

Dear Smith,

    Of course I understand that lunch is not three hours!

    And LOL re the skipping town. Don't worry, I'm not that easy to get rid of. ;)

    Typing on my phone here—almost back to the office.

    The reason I was gone so long is that I intercepted the thieving of a lady's cell phone and found myself dozens of blocks north in pursuit of the thief. Fortunately, one of us (him) hasn't spent four years running Varsity track at the state level (gold medals in 2011, 2012, 2013). Still, he ran like a Kenyan. When I eventually managed to catch up, he had stopped to rest against the wall of a Spanish deli. I stealthily informed an unoccupied cop munching on a hoagie, who abandoned his sandwich to retrieve the phone with little fanfare. Of course I wasn't going to leave a person of color alone with a cop, perp though he was. I remained to legally observe.

    I have some internal conflict over the experience, to be honest. The owner of the phone hardly even thanked me. She seemed to think the officer had more to do with the recovery of her phone, never mind that I was the one who hurdled from the West Village to Midtown. Maybe she wanted a new phone anyway.

Gah. It's almost 5. Rats. I have to run to make my 6p hot yoga class because the 8p is canceled. The train takes longer than I expected from our office to my sublet in Brooklyn, where I'm living with three NYU students (*inventing* their own majors—give me a break) who literally don't believe in cleaning. I am not allowed to use Lysol lest they be poisoned from the noxious fumes. But, you know, dust mites and rat pellets I'm sure are fine.

I'll leave the book/blog/whatever on my desk for you because I just walked in, and you seem to be very focused working on something in there. I inadvertently took it with me to "lunch" (as if I had time to eat). In my altruistic lurching, I accidentally knocked over my Arnold Palmer, spilling it on the sticky note she put on top. It is . . . kind of legible still? Hmm. Maybe not. In case, here's what it said:

Smith,
If you think this is any good, feel free to publish it. No pressure just because I'm dead.
Iris

I thought that was cute! No pressure just because I'm dead!

I must go so not to get a shitty spot next to the smelly, hairy guy (good for him doing yoga, though), and/or miss Pranayama deep breathing.
Namaste,
Carl

from: UWinNao
to: smithsimonyi@gmail.com
date: Fri, Aug 28 at 5:11 PM
subject: Hey, it's okay!

We heard you had a rough go of it just now!

We get it. It stinks to lose. On the other hand, as Thomas Edison wisely said, "Many of life's failures are people who did not realize how close they were to success when they gave up."

To get you back in the game, we're rewarding you with **25,000 naoPoints**. Remember, you can use naoPoints to unlock new games or uncover strategy tips!

from: gamblersanon.org
to: smithsimonyi@gmail.com
date: Fri, Aug 28 at 5:29 PM
subject: We miss you at Gamblers Anonymous.

Psychiatrist Leonard Higgenbottom, MD, says that one reason we gamble is because we believe that we can, will, and probably should lose.

Is this you?

Come back to Gamblers Anonymous Online, where our fellowship of men and women faces our common problem, one day at a time. Together we can accomplish what we cannot alone.

BEFORE

December 30 | 1:32 AM

I used to think lungs look like this

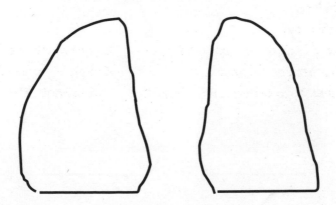

but they're flipped

Mine look like

Actually

(If you google pictures of your cancer,

beware of the ads.)

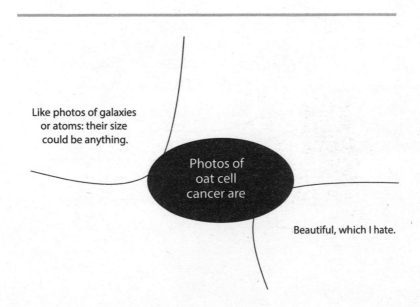

As I look at
them I think

As I look at
them I think

What is
microscopic
can appear
astronomical.

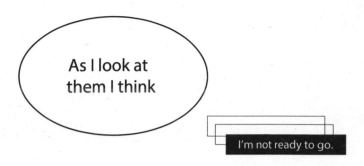

COMMENTS (10):

BonnieD: :-O!

ArduousArdvark: LOL that is fucking hilarious photos warehouse

BonnieD: hey arduous there are kids on this site, plz keep it klean

ArduousArdvark: like me u mean? i'm thirteen bitch

BonnieD: so. i'm 16.

ArduousArdvark: hot

BonnieD: watch ur mouth plz, thank u

ArduousArdvark: so I'm like dying too? so i think i won't? but thank YOU.

IrisMassey: Hey. Support each other, guys?

ArduousArdvark: LOL right

FRIDAY, AUGUST 28: JADE

AMAZON Review (1 of 141) of iRelaxx 100% Authentic Satin Bathrobe in Frisky Lavender
August 28, 4:40 a.m.
Jade R Massey: 4 Stars

I am a bit thick through the hips and bought this in a M.

Unlike other reviewers, I did not have a problem with the ripped seams or missing loops. It's a fucking bathrobe for $17.99. There are going to be some problems. Also it has the inner tie to make sure it doesn't come loose, so it's not like the outside belt is doing that much work, anyway. The knot holds if I tie it in a bow. If I loop it once it comes loose. To me this is common sense, however, so I disagree with Sharon M. that this is a fault of the robe. I believe it to be physics.

Finally, the material is indeed thinner than I expected, as most of the 140 people who have also reviewed this item note. Unlike many of you, however, I am not currently interested in seduction. Still, it's good for lying around in and doesn't feel too sticky on my skin.

from: kwaters@rmpofnewyork.com
to: jademassey@yahoo.com
date: Fri, Aug 28 at 5:30 AM
subject: How EGG-cited are we about your future?!

Dear Jade,

It's been nine months since you attended EGG FREEZING 101: TAKING CONTROL OF YOUR FERTILITY. We would love to hear where you are in the process of planning your future.

Let me know if you'd like to set up a follow-up appointment with our IVF coordinator.

Sincerely,

Karen Waterson

Marketing Director

Reproductive Medical Partners of New York

from: mail@rmpofnewyork.com
to: jademassey@yahoo.com
date: Fri, Aug 28 at 5:37 AM
subject: Your email preferences have been updated

You have been unsubscribed from our listserv.

We are always looking for ways to improve our service! If you are willing to share your reasons for unsubscribing, simply reply to this email.

---

from: jademassey@yahoo.com
to: mail@rmpofnewyork.com
date: Fri, Aug 28 at 5:46 AM
subject: re: Your email preferences have been updated

I'm dealing with a death in the family and not thinking about freezing my eggs right now.

Free tip—women who come to your seminar have not forgotten that our reproductive systems are aging. I am as aware that my eggs are thirty-seven as I was last year that they were thirty-six, when I attended your seminar. If I don't contact you it's because I have shit going on, or because I can't deal with trying to prolong my fertility window at the moment.

Please treat the women who are your prospective clients with a bit more respect. We are adults capable of contacting you when we're ready to move forward.

---

from: jade@barntherestaurant.com
to: marcus@barntherestaurant.com
date: Fri, Aug 28 at 7:28 AM
subject: Course 11

Dear Marcus,

During my time away I had an opportunity to reflect on our menu, and having now returned to work following my leave of absence, I've had some ideas. Please humor me.

The move to the tasting menu was difficult for me. You know my strong feelings about how undemocratic I find tasting menus. But I cooperated and threw the full weight of my support behind it, and of course early reviews seem to indicate that you were right. It was a positive move for us.

But especially after an encounter I had with a patron last night, I feel that if we are going to stick with the tasting menu, the final course must be cut. A tasting menu has an arc; it must. It tells a story. Otherwise, why does it exist?

The Dog Days theme that you created in my absence is lovely. For the most part. The silky Vermont curds. The fluke: A+. My favorite is the disguised balut, but of course it is—that's the greatest achievement of my career, I think. But at the conclusion of this harmonious succession of pure delight and surprise, guests are presented with . . . *an ice cream sandwich?*

Now, we both saw how many of those melted puddles of goo came back to the kitchen last night. And I haven't been around to know for sure, but I'll bet that has been the trend over these last couple of weeks that Dog Days has been live. You are probably working on a plan to retire the sandwich as we speak. But the sandwich itself is not the problem, and a replacement is not the solution. The problem is sugar.

I don't know if you know this about my sister, but the woman was baking up a storm until she could no longer stand upright. Sugar is fertilizer for cancer. And heart disease, and obesity. I realize we don't cook so people can eat. I realize that we are not Burger King, and our mission is not to feed or nourish but to pleasure. Still, there is gravity to every other dish on our menu; it has had a life. It is derived from the organic energy of the living. Ending a tasting menu with a course of refined sugar is blasphemy. It's tacky. It's unnecessary. And it discredits us with guests who may otherwise find that they both are thrilled during *as well as* after the meal, as it doesn't leave them bloated balls of gas one breath closer to a diabetes diagnosis.

I know you believe that we must at least give people the option of a sweet course at the end because that is what people expect. That without the option they will sense something missing, like a phantom limb. I just disagree. I think concluding with the seaweed mole pudding is classy, narratively intelligent, and most importantly, respectful to the guts of our patrons.

You are probably shaking your head, but I ask you only to consider it. I am happy to be the one to respond to pushback, though I doubt it will amount to much.

Finally—a reminder that I'll be in Virginia Monday and Tuesday next week, back Wednesday morning.

See you shortly,

Jade

---

from: jade@barntherestaurant.com
to: bernardhsu@newyorkpresbyterian.com
date: Fri, Aug 28 at 8:14 AM
subject: Concerning the treatment of your former patient Iris P. Massey

---

Dear Dr. Hsu,

Good morning. I am the elder sister of your former patient Iris Pamela Massey, who underwent chemotherapy in your office from January 6th to March 31st of this year. I am writing to express my deep concern over the treatment she received under your care. If my records are correct, her chemotherapy treatment consisted of Platibon and Topovesin. According to my research (see attached paper by Dr. Peter J. Lachow, MD, PhD, at the University of San Diego), the drug Avazumab has been found to increase the effectiveness of the cocktail when added to the mix. Was it not possible to adjust my sister's treatment in accordance with this up-to-date research?

Sincerely,

Jade R. Massey

Chef

Barn—"2 Michelin Stars for 5 Years and Counting"

from: jademassey@yahoo.com
to: winsomebeautydorothy@hotmail.com
date: Fri, Aug 28 at 8:43 AM
subject: Flight info

Mom,

I've changed my flight to Monday as you suggested, since you'll be at Bible study Sunday night. See below—I arrive at 8:40 Monday morning and leave at 6:30 Wednesday morning so I can get straight to the restaurant.

Things we'll need to get done while I'm there:

Monday

- Grocery shopping. Last I checked, all you had in your fridge was some brown asparagus and an expired carton of Greek yogurt. I know you don't believe in cooking, but we can at least get you some healthy snacks that you can munch on between cartons of pad thai. (Speaking of which, remind me to talk to you about MSG. There are a million reasons to request it without MSG, and your digestive tract will thank you.)

- Cleaning out the garage. The tower of Winsome products gathering dust is teetering on the brink of a full-blown avalanche. I worry you're going to hit it with your car one day, and then we'll really have a mess. I think we should just send them back. After 30+ years with the company, you are more than entitled to a refund on a few bottles of face serum and BB cream. And if or when you decide to resume selling, you can just reorder new product.

Tuesday

- Doctor's appt. I called Dr. Greenbaum and scheduled you for a physical. I know you don't trust doctors, but I don't think the pain you're describing in your neck and shoulder is normal. Nor do I think it's good to be taking Ambien every single night. According to drugs.com: *Ambien is for* <u>short-term use only</u> . . . <u>Do not take this medicine for longer than 4 or 5 weeks without your doctor's advice</u>.

· Oil change for the Buick.

Tuesday night I'll cook us dinner. I'm thinking either cauliflower bánh mì bowls or whatever the fresh catch is at the Publix. If neither sounds good we can do meatballs.

Love,

Jade

---

from: bernardhsu@newyorkpresbyterian.com
to: jade@barntherestaurant.com
date: Fri, Aug 28 at 11:40 AM
subject: DRAFT re: Concerning the treatment of your former patient Iris P. Massey

---

Dear Ms. Massey,

I appreciate your patience as this is my first week in the office of Dr. Hsu, and I am still familiarizing myself with office protocol and processes. In order to remain HIPAA compliant, I must ask that you please have your sister fill out the attached authorization form and return it to our office before I may release any details about her medical care to you.

Best,

Anna Truong

Office Assistant

---

from: jade@barntherestaurant.com
to: bernardhsu@newyorkpresbyterian.com
date: Fri, Aug 28 at 11:48 AM
subject: DRAFT re: Concerning the treatment of your former patient Iris P.
           Massey

Dear Ms. Truong,

How on earth am I supposed to do that given that my sister is

---

from: iris.a.massey@gmail.com
to: bernardhsu@newyorkpresbyterian.com
date: Fri, Aug 28 at 11:54 AM
subject: re: Concerning the treatment of your former patient Iris P.
           Massey

Dear Ms. Truong,

Please find attached authorization to discuss my medical treatment with my sister, Jade Massey.

Sincerely,

Iris Massey

---

from: bernardhsu@newyorkpresbyterian.com
to: jademassey@yahoo.com
date: Fri, Aug 28 at 2:50 PM
subject: re: Concerning the treatment of your former patient Iris P.
           Massey

Ms. Massey:

As your sister completed the release I am permitted to respond to your question.

I see in your sister's file that she declined the Avazumab on

January 2. I don't have any further notes. It is possible it was not covered by her insurance. Perhaps you should ask her directly? Anna

Friday, August 28
TherapistAwayNetwork™
Patient Name: Jade Renee Massey
AUTO PROMPT: **What small change can you make today?**

Dr. Zarchikoff,

I totally understand your decision to hike Machu Picchu on the eve of your 70th birthday. In fact, I'm inspired and awed by it. Good for you. Seriously.

I do, naturally, wish it wasn't happening the same week as I'm going back to work after my leave of absence. Regarding "a small change I can make," that certainly seems like a big enough one for the moment, given that (as you know) I've spent the last several months nocturnal, living on kale chips, red wine, and the home shopping networks. Tech from 8 to 10 is a drag, but beauty from 10 onward is calming. I appreciate that colors, regardless of the item and material, are named after food—licorice, mocha, tangerine. Sometimes I actually place an order—online, not by phone. (God, I'm not that far gone.) I wake up around four under green crumbs (green, the exception, is "grass"). I may or may not brush the maroon (actual Cabernet) stains off my teeth before getting into bed as the sky lightens behind my blinds.

Not anymore. Time to get my life back. I have *finally* finished sorting through Iris's things, and apart from the box of stuff I presume belongs to her Queens boyfriend, it all has a destination—

Virginia to my mom's, or Goodwill. Given that I lost my contacts when I dropped my phone in the toilet last month, I don't know how to find him. Do I even know his last name? Richie . . . Martin? No, that's a singer. I suppose I could go back into her email (I had to today . . . long story).

I also emailed Marcus my idea for cutting the dessert course. You will be glad to hear I'm trying to be more vocal about my needs there.

One thing that's bugging me—I learned today that Iris chose not to take the more effective chemo drug she was offered. Why would she do that? It could not have been cost. You know I got her savings. According to Google, Avazumab is pricey. That's apparently why some people don't take it. But that can't be the case for Iris. She had plenty to cover it out of pocket, even at the high end. It makes no sense, unless her doctor did not clarify for her the relative effectiveness of the drug. That would seem to be the only reasonable explanation. I imagine you're going to counsel me to "let it go," but truthfully I think this could be a claim for malpractice.

How long are you gone again? Two weeks? I fly to Virginia on Monday. Lord knows I'll be selected for extra screening at TSA with this case of turmeric. I figure it might relieve my mother's osteoporotic pain. (At your age, you should probably look into taking it, too.) Who knew it was possible for a person's health to deteriorate so rapidly in three months? That sounds callous. I'm just surprised by the physical and emotional toll this has taken on my mother given that she and Iris hardly spoke. Or maybe that's *why* it's so hard for her. Listen to me, I sound like you.

I hope you are enjoying your hike.

Dear JADE,

Thank you for your submission to TAN™. We will make sure your provider receives this message.

"Change" can be traced back to the Latin *cambire*, meaning "to barter." Often, the idea of changing sounds daunting to us, as if we are being asked to uproot our identities and start over from scratch. But most changes, even significant ones, need not be approached with such grandiosity. The simplest changes are like barters, decisions to forgo one thing in exchange for another. These small acts are, cumulatively, more significant than they often feel in a given moment.

TAN™ is not to be used in case of emergency. If you are in crisis, call 9-1-1.

Sincerely,

Your friends at TAN

SATURDAY, AUGUST 29

from: smith@simonyi.com
to: jademassey@yahoo.com
date: Sat, Aug 29 at 11:08 AM
subject: Hello

Dear Jade,

You and I met briefly at Iris's funeral. I hope you are doing well under the circumstances.

Are you still at Barn? Congratulations on the new Michelin star—saw the write-up in the *Times* last weekend. One of these days when normal folks like me can get a reservation, I look forward to making a visit.

I have some of your sister's things (the stuff she left behind in her desk). Barn isn't too far from my office at 96 Morton Street, 9th floor. Would you be able to swing by sometime?

Sincerely,

Smith S. Simonyi

President

Simonyi Brand Management

---

from: jademassey@yahoo.com
to: smith@simonyi.com
date: Sat, Aug 29 at 11:33 AM
subject: re: Hello

You can mail my sister's things to:

   Jade Massey

   93 Underhill Ave., Apt. 14

   Jersey City, NJ 07306

JM

---

from: smith@simonyi.com
to: jademassey@yahoo.com
date: Sat, Aug 29 at 11:35 AM
subject: re: Hello

Dear Jade,

   I figured you could sort through her stuff to see what you wanted to take and what you wanted to leave. There are four crates of items, much of which I believe is trash.

Sincerely,

Smith

---

from: jademassey@yahoo.com
to: smith@simonyi.com
date: Sat, Aug 29 at 11:37 AM
subject: re: Hello

I prefer to go through it in my own home rather than at your office with you standing over me. Please mail them, thanks.

JM

---

from: smith@simonyi.com
to: jademassey@yahoo.com
date: Sat, Aug 29 at 11:41 AM
subject: re: Hello

Tone can be difficult to decipher over email, but I am pretty sure I detect hostility in yours. I apologize if I offended you in some way by asking you to come by. I am trying to be helpful. I'll get the boxes in the mail to you as soon as I can.

I don't know if you were aware, but your sister was writing a blog at the time of her death. In boxing up her things, my intern came across a copy she left for me. Iris asked me to try to publish it. I figured you'd want to know about it if you didn't already. I'll put a copy in the mail along with the boxes.

---

from: jademassey@yahoo.com
to: smith@simonyi.com
date: Sat, Aug 29 at 11:48 AM
subject: re: Hello

So she wants you to publish her "secret blog."

Not to stomp on your publishing dreams, but thirty-something with cancer writes about her life as a secretary being cut short by the same thing everyone else dies of, too? That is not going to sell. And if it does, it will be to sentimental barbarians who want to read about someone else's illness so they can feel better about their own pathetic lives. She died so young! Before she ever even made anything of herself! Before she even got married! Thank my lucky stars I'm not her! I'M SO #BLESSED!

It's cancer porn.

Here, I'll give you the back cover: "She reminds us to act on our dreams before it's too late." Or how about "#YOLO."

You leave her funeral early like you have somewhere better to be, and now you want to make her blog into a book you can sell? Big celebrity-brand guy, or whatever it is you do? Show a little decency.

JM

---

from: smith@simonyi.com
to: jademassey@yahoo.com
date: Sat, Aug 29 at 11:49 AM
subject: re: Hello

So there's your beef with me.

I left the funeral early because I got a call from my mother's retirement home. My "something better to do" was seeing the area code 608 flashing on my cell, which tells me the call is from Homily Pines in Sun Prairie, Wisconsin, an institution with 24/7 medical professional care of the kind my mother requires. She is disabled over ten years now, and her prognosis was six. That week she'd had an adverse reaction to her medication and spent a couple of days in the hospital. I was afraid she had died, which is my fear every time I see that damn area code. But I am glad you feel like you know me well enough to assume I'm an asshole.

I haven't yet read beyond the first several pages of her blog, so I can't counter your assertion of what it contains. Still, despite apparent appearances to the contrary, I respected your sister. If she wanted to share what she wrote with a wider audience than only those who followed her blog back in the spring, my default response is going to be to honor that. Call me crazy.

And lest you think I am one of those people who treats the

dead as if they stick around as ghosts or spirits, dwelling just over our heads, surveying our actions, let me assure you that I'm not attempting to please some phantasmal version of her corpse. I don't believe Iris is watching, or that she is going to be angry at me if I *don't* publish it. Whatever energy moved in her has dispersed into a universe that is blind to our concocted narratives of "purpose." We are not special. We do not survive death. We only think we are, and do.

If I am wrong and she is assuming gold-tipped wings from a cherub as we speak, no matter. The nature of my interest is principle. She requested it. I'd like to honor that.
Smith

PS—The copy about the dreams isn't too bad (if clichéd), but "YOLO" is just tasteless. And she wasn't my secretary. She was my assistant, and would have been my associate if she'd ever been willing to accept the title.

---

from: jademassey@yahoo.com
to: smith@simonyi.com
date: Sat, Aug 29 at 1:19 PM
subject: re: Hello

Let me try again: my sister was very ill. As the person present in the weeks leading up to her death, I will assure you that cancer does indeed affect the mind as well as the body. So does chemo.

You may know that I took a leave of absence at Barn so I could stay with her for those last couple of months. I observed that as she was proceeding through the stages of grief, she took to writing to process. Apart from that fling she had with the heavy-set man from Queens whom I believe was a friend of yours, her days were spent baking sweets and then throwing them away—muffins, cupcakes, peanut brittle toppling out of the trash can. She said she was making things for people, but she never seemed to give any of it away. It all ended up in the garbage. Do you see what I am saying?

I am not insulting Iris. If she'd written something while she was healthy and alive that you happened upon—perhaps a novel?—that'd be different. This is not that. Lord knows if I was in her position, I'd likely deal with the situation in unhealthier ways than oversharing with strangers on the Internet and obsessive cookie baking. But I think you will find there is little in her blog by way of literary merit or commercial appeal. It was a diary, for fuck's sake. Of a sick woman on the decline.

Speaking of God, if your unsolicited atheistic diatribe was to goad me after my sister has just died, well done. It must feel good to be so much smarter than everyone else because you don't believe in an afterlife. Want to lecture me about evolution, too? Go ahead and start quoting Darwin to me like I don't know who he is. Give me a lecture on religion and be sure to use the words "opiate" and "Richard Dawkins."

You have made your views loud and clear. Here are mine; I'm not okay with you publishing, or seeking to publish, my sister's cancer blog. So no need to send it—I don't have to read it to feel entirely, unflinchingly certain of this.

I'm sorry about your mother.

JM

What the fuck is your problem? Were you raised to

---

from: jademassey@yahoo.com
to: smith@simonyi.com
date: Sat, Aug 29 at 1:22 PM
subject: re: Hello

I apologize for the text I inadvertently forgot to delete at the bottom of my email. Please disregard that part only.

---

from: smith@simonyi.com
to: carl@simonyi.com
date: Sat, Aug 29 at 1:25 PM
subject: Fwd: Hello

Carl,

See below. On Monday, please ship the boxes to her. Use the cheapest means—USPS ground or whatever.

And do include a copy of the manuscript, please. I'll leave one on your desk.

Thx,

SS

---

from: carl@simonyi.com
to: smith@simonyi.com
date: Sat, Aug 29 at 2:04 PM
subject: re: Fwd: Hello

Dear Boss,

In regard to your email just now, I am trying not to work weekends. It is important for boundary-setting for both my immediate and distant future, as studies show that if you start drawing boundaries early, you retain the skill throughout life—and if you don't, well. I'm not sure I'm to that chapter yet.

However, since we are now effectively in communication on a Saturday and the boundary has been crossed, I would like to use this opportunity to express my concern over the conversation in the email chain below. You might want to be a little nicer to her, because while I am not formally a lawyer, last spring I did audit an IP class at Stanford Law (ranked no. 1 in *US News*, tied with unnamed school that rhymes with "tail"). If you indeed decide to pursue publication of the book, I imagine you are going to need the sister, or at least the next of kin, on board as heir of the copyright. Should I email my professor to confirm? I don't mind. I have to keep in touch with him anyway so he will write me a LOR—that is, if I succumb to my parents' pressure and decide to go to law school after all. Lulz.

Now get off the computer and enjoy your weekend!

Carl

---

from: smith@simonyi.com
to: carl@simonyi.com
date: Sat, Aug 29 at 2:05 PM
subject: re: Fwd: Hello

Even if she left it for me, asking me to publish it?

What is an LOR?

---

from: carl@simonyi.com
to: smith@simonyi.com
date: Sat, Aug 29 at 2:06 PM
subject: re: Fwd: Hello

Letter of Recommendation.

¯_(ツ)_/¯

---

from: smith@simonyi.com
to: carl@simonyi.com
date: Sat, Aug 29 at 2:07 PM
subject: re: Fwd: Hello

I don't know what that thing means either.

---

from: carl@simonyi.com
to: smith@simonyi.com
date: Sat, Aug 29 at 2:09 PM
subject: re: Fwd: Hello

It's a shrugging guy!!!!!

Also remember that the words on the Post-it are smudged due to the Arnold Palmer, so that particular document probably wouldn't hold up in court. Sorry/not sorry. In the pursuit of justice spills will occur.

---

from: smith@simonyi.com
to: iris.a.massey@gmail.com
date: Sat, Aug 29 at 6:17 PM
subject: no subject

It's funny, you're gone, but reading your manuscript makes it seem like you're not.

You know, I think you're selling yourself short in this thing.

My dad, as you know, was not the greatest guy, especially toward my mom. If there is a person who died full of regrets, and probably hating himself, it was my father.

Whenever he pulled up to the house after being on the road for a while, and my mom came outside to greet him, he couldn't move fast enough. Not a small man, he would more or less fall out of the cab and jog over to her with so much effort that it was awkward to watch. He was like a giant kid, the clasps of his overalls jangling until they embraced. In those moments, they always looked in love. There were times when she actually squealed. It was a scene I came to associate with returns. Of course, returns require departures.

The year I turned nine was the first time she kicked him out that I remember, and the next few months were the most peaceful of my childhood. She started cleaning houses, and I'd occasionally go along to sit on other people's sofas and watch *The Price Is Right*. She'd flip the mops upside-down to transform them into mop creatures, and we'd crack up. I stopped being afraid to come home from school. We ordered a lot of pizza. But there was also something missing—him. She wasn't getting a boot thrown in her face or yelling so loudly I'd crawl in the shower and turn on the water, but she also didn't smile as much. She definitely didn't squeal.

When they eventually got back together, the happiness didn't last, of course. The next eight years went about the way I've described to you before. And I didn't understand that we were a stereotype. It felt like we were the first people to suffer, in secret, the confounding cycles of a rageful alcoholic who gets clean once in a while.

The spring I turned seventeen, she left a handful of times, disappearing with both her summer and winter clothes, leaving a big open space in the hall closet to make a point. But every time, she would return, and there was a moment when they looked in love again. For just a day, or even only a few hours, this fleeting euphoria would exist between them. Eventually I realized they were probably both trying to get that feeling back all the time. It was why she had to keep going, and why he had to keep giving her a reason to go: so that she could come back.

Even for him, a miserable asshole, there were still these kind of . . . redemptive, I guess, flashes that squeaked through the expanse of shit. There was joy in the crevices. I witnessed it.

I find myself hoping as I turn the pages that you came to this understanding about your own life, that for any regrets you may have had, you recognized there were joyous parts. You certainly created them for others.

I don't care what your sister wants. You wanted this manuscript published, so that's what I'm going to do.

---

from:	smith@simonyi.com
to:	sheryl@berringerpress.com
date:	Sat, Aug 29 at 6:49 PM
subject:	Congratulations! And a question

Hi Sheryl,

What a delight to receive your wedding announcement! I had no idea that you and Steve were even a couple!

I have a half-baked idea for Berringer to throw your way. I know you'll be frank with me because you always are, in that college-roommate's-college-girlfriend way. It concerns my former colleague, who tragically passed in May at the age of thirty-three. During the last six months of her life, she authored a blog that received considerable attention online. My office is currently working to determine the copyright situation with this "manuscript," so to speak, but as a preliminary matter, I'm just curious—what do you think of it? In terms of its publishability, assuming the copyright is a nonissue? As you may recall, she and I were close, and I find myself wanting it to be more widely available, but I don't know what that would look like.

Linking to it below.

Congrats again,

Smith

---

from: jillian@homilypines.com
to: smith@simonyi.com
date: Sat, Aug 29 at 7:02 PM
subject: Aug + Sept Rent

Dear Smith,

We still have not received payment from you for either August or September. Please remit payment at your earliest convenience. Jillian

---

from: smith@simonyi.com
to: richierich1000@gmail.com
date: Sat, Aug 29 at 7:14 PM
subject: re: Loan

Hey Richie,

You around? Thanks again for helping me out. Want to get a beer?

---

from: UWinNao
to: smithsimonyi@gmail.com
date: Sat, Aug 29 at 8:19 PM
subject: YOU WON!

Congratulations! You just won **$1,740** at UWinNao! For being one of our favorite players, we are rewarding you with **50,000 naoPoints**.

Visit us again soon . . . how about *nao*?!

---

from: Bro-vado
to: smithsimonyi@gmail.com
date: Sat, Aug 29 at 9:21 PM
subject: Your account has been deactivated

To reactivate, simply log back in.

Please complete the following brief survey to help us better serve you. You have chosen to deactivate your account because:

     A. You prefer a competitor site
     B. You are taking a break from gaming
     C. You had a specific problem arise with Bro-vado

Come back and we'll start you off with a courtesy **$25** deposit to jump-start your winning!

---

from: Bro-vado
to: smithsimonyi@gmail.com
date: Sat, Aug 29 at 10:14 PM
subject: Your account has been reactivated

If your account was reactivated in error, please contact customer service at the number below. It will now be 7 days before you can deactivate again.

How to find out you're about to die

Answer the
phone.

How to find out you're about to die

Answer the
phone.

Everything and
nothing changes.

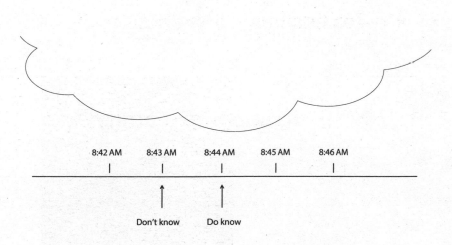

How to face death

☒ Try to imagine eternity

☒ Read books on dying

"We die as we lived,"
some guy wrote.

But how did I live?

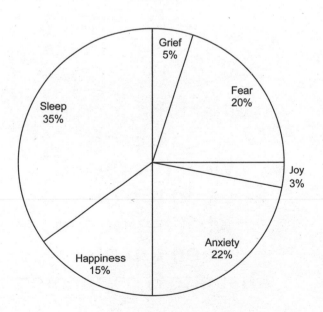

I estimate

But probably more like

■ Grief

■ Fear

□ Joy

▨ Anxiety

▨ Happiness

▨ Sleep

what is happening
on top of
what happened
on top of
what happened
on top of
what else is happening

There wasn't an arc

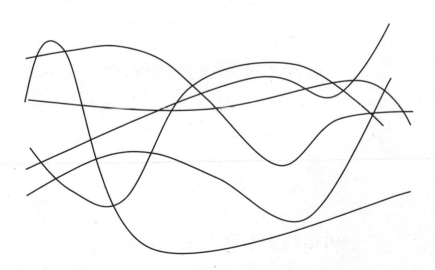

Or a bunch

It was more

dots

The dots look different close up

NONE OF IT
MATTERS AND I

NEVER WANT IT
TO END

COMMENTS (12):

BonnieD: S

ArduousArdvark: since when is a triangle a dot

ArduousArdvark: or a square

ArduousArdvark: it's called geometry

BonnieD: I know what she means.

BonnieD: don't worry, Iris

ArduousArdvark: what

BonnieD: some experiences feel like circles and some feel pointy. and some have extra sides

ArduousArdvark: a circle doesn't have sides

BonnieD: sigh

ArduousArdvark: what

BonnieD: you're tedious

MONDAY, AUGUST 31

Monday, August 31
TherapistAwayNetwork™
Patient Name: Jade Renee Massey
AUTO PROMPT: **What have you lost?**

My mind.

It is 5:00 a.m. My flight leaves in three hours, and I just received an email from Marcus, which he must have sent on his way home (could he have bothered to give me more notice?). He says I can't go to Virginia. I quote:

You just returned from a month leave, which turned into a two-month leave, which turned into a five-month leave. The only reason you still have a job is that you're competent. I can't keep finding ways to cover for your absence. You are a chef, and you work in a restaurant that is not an average restaurant. It is a restaurant where chefs all over the world dream of working. The fact that I even granted you a leave of absence would shock people. Now that you're back, I need you around. Your call.

Maybe I shouldn't be blindsided, but I am. Sure, it was a startling act of kindness that he allowed me time off in the first place.

I did not expect that kind of generosity from Herr Marcus. And that's why I have thanked him a zillion times. But to threaten me like this—yes, Barn is *the* Barn, but does he remember why Barn is the Barn? He needs me, and he knows it. If I leave, it will be his loss, not mine. Who is he going to run recipes by—Enar, the Nordic dishwasher? He's extremely ripped, but come on.

Which is why I don't think he'd do it. Fire me. He's all talk.

But what if he does? Fuck.

What do I do.

My mom needs me. That much is clear. And there's more. Last night, I logged into my sister's email again. I just wanted to know why she didn't go with the better chemo. I only searched for "cancer," "chemo," and "treatment." (Okay, yes, I searched "Jade," but then I logged out before I saw anything. And I did discover that her old boss is still emailing her, which makes me feel bad for being so rude to him as he's clearly in love with her.) Though I found nothing on the chemo, I did learn she was on weed. She was ordering "Cannabis Tincture" from some distillery in Seattle. Lord knows how that might have impacted the efficacy of the chemo. So now I have more work cut out for me if I'm going to pursue this possible malpractice claim, which I think I owe it to her to look into.

It appears I know what I have to do. But I will not give Marcus the satisfaction of firing me. I may have lost my sister, but I haven't lost my goddamn dignity.

Dear JADE,

Thank you for your submission to TAN™. We will make sure your provider receives this message.

Did you know "loss" is of Germanic origin, derived from *los*, meaning "destruction of an army?" As you move through your day, consider what army you are mourning the destruction of. What officers were in its ranks? What were they defending you against?

TAN™ is not to be used in case of emergency. If you are in crisis, call 9-1-1.

Sincerely,

Your friends at TAN

---

from: smith@simonyi.com
to: rosylady101@yahoo.com
date: Mon, Aug 31 at 8:43 AM
subject: re: Vandalism of your posters

Dear Rosita,

I assure you with utmost sincerity that in none of the graffitied ads, despite the black markings concealing your teeth, do you appear toothless. Dashing, yes. Glowing, yes. Professional, yes. Toothless, no. If you do not see a spike in bookings this month, I will eat my words, but I would put money on it. Hang tight!

Best,

SS

---

from: smith@simonyi.com
to: mdublin@forwardchartersairline.com
date: Mon, Aug 31 at 9:10 AM
subject: Great to meet you

Michael,

Fantastic to meet you the other night. I am, as promised, writing to introduce myself more formally. I am aware that Forward Charters has had a challenging last year, what with the missing bridal party, the charred wedding dress, and the rumors about the pilot's drinking. I invite you to view this as an opportunity to create a revitalized face for the airline. Four years ago I assisted Tiny Planet Airlines in rebranding in the wake of its public image crisis after it crashed into that pile of medieval ruins outside of Budapest. Today, its ridership is at a peak since the early '00s.

I'd love to chat further.

Best,

Smith S. Simonyi

President

Simonyi Brand Management

---

from: mdublin@forwardchartersairline.com
to: smith@simonyi.com
date: Mon, Aug 31 at 9:12 AM
subject: re: Great to meet you

Who put you up to this? Listen, my wife is not the president of the airline. *I* am. You can tell her that. Actually, you can tell her I said to go to hell, because I *did* sleep with that agent in Chicago, and it was hot as fuck!

---

from: smith@simonyi.com
to: mdublin@forwardchartersairline.com
date: Mon, Aug 31 at 9:15 AM
subject: re: Great to meet you

I see you've got it covered. Thanks for getting back to me!

---

from: smith@simonyi.com
to: contact@lassimariset.com
date: Mon, Aug 31 at 9:30 AM
subject: Congratulations!

Dear Lassi,

I first want to congratulate you on your incredible achievement this weekend at the Continental Cup! You are a regular Olaf Rye (the first ski jumper!), and at only thirteen!

I was so pleased to come upon the news of your win in the International Skiing Federation journal online.

Lassi, as the youngest winner in a decade and a competitor for the World Cup later this fall, you are going to be acting on the world stage from this moment on. Are you ready?

I am a celebrity brand manager with a background working with athletes competing at the international level, as well as other stars and thought leaders. If you are interested in ensuring that your remarkable success and talent open as many doors as possible, not only for promotion of your brand but for engagement across media platforms (the sky's the limit!), please give me a call.
Sincerely,
Smith S. Simonyi
President
Simonyi Brand Management

---

from: sheryl@beringerpress.com
to: smith@simonyi.com
date: Mon, Aug 31 at 9:55 AM
subject: re: Congratulations! And a question

S—

Where is MS? Attached? Yes okay.

College roommate's college girlfriend! Ha! Indeed! What memories we share. My, time. My, time, time, time.

You had no idea about Steve and me, right? You and everyone else we were in school with. It's a huge surprise to many of our colleagues, as well, but we've actually been fucking for years. HR knew, of course.

Here's the other thing that will knock your socks off: we're hyphenating our names. Gritten-Barrett! Like grin and bear it! Ha! I know! With names like those, how could we not?

That's my go-to.

I will have my intern Brutus review. That's a girl. I thought it was a boy till she came in for the interview. Females are now named Brutus in the world and girls are boys and boys are girls. I cannot keep up, nor do I give a fuck.

And I'm glad to hear from you, actually, because I have an author for you. Memoirist with a DISGUSTING rags-to-riches story. I mean it's DISGUSTING. Literally born in the trunk of a taxi, went to Yale, and wound up in the goddamn Musée d'Orsay. People fucking love art. Also her art isn't even about her shitty homeless childhood. How transcendent is that? The most beautiful goddamn thing ever. Her name is Zahara Ferringbottom. Let me know and I'll put you in touch.

xSheryl

---

from: YOPLAY <philgergel@gmail.com>
to: smith@simonyi.com
date: Mon, Aug 31 at 9:59 AM
subject: re: YOU WILL NOT BELIEVE THIS B AS IN BULL + S AS IN
          SATIRE

IT CAME TO ME.
A PARODY OF THAT PARROT-Y

SHOW THEM I AM TRULY A MAN OF PLAY

WE REPLACE MY FACE WITH MISS PIGGY'S FACE

GET IT? SHE IS CHEATING ON KERMIE WITH ALL THOSE CLOTH BETAS

DO YOU THINK THAT'S FUNNY OR IS IT JUST CALL-ING MYSELF A LADY PIG?

PS—I WAS READING IN THE AIRPLANE MAGAZINE THE OTHER DAY ABOUT RETIREMENT, WHICH IS WHEN YOU HAVE TO STOP WORKING BECAUSE YOU GET SO DAMN OLD NO ONE WANTS TO PAY YOU TO HEAVE YOUR WRINKLED ASS OUT OF BED. WHAT AM I SUP-POSED TO DO IF I HAVE NOT SAVED ENOUGH MONEY TO SUSTAIN MY LIFESTYLE, COME SUCH A DAY?

I GOT AN ACCOUNTANT SO I DON'T GO BROKE PRIOR TO THESE ALLEGED "GOLDEN YEARS." I TOLD HIM HOW WE WORK IS THAT YOU JUST HOLD MONEY AND THEN TAKE IT OUT WHEN YOU EARN IT. HE SAID THAT IS UN-USUAL BUT I SAID THAT'S HOW WE'VE DONE IT SINCE THE BEGINNING SO. HOW MUCH IS IN MY ACCOUNT? TWO GRAND? EIGHTY? I HAVE NO CLUE. AS I HAVE, IN HIS WORDS, "NOT BEEN ATTUNED" TO MY SPENDING. PLEASE SEND HIM RECORDS SO HE CAN FIX WHAT MY INNER CHILD HAS DAMAGED

THANKS MUCH AS ALWAYS YOURS,

YO-PLAY/Phil

---

from: smith@simonyi.com
to: YOPLAY <philgergel@gmail.com>
date: Mon, Aug 31 at 10:03 AM
subject: re: YOU WILL NOT BELIEVE THIS B AS IN BULL + S AS IN
SATIRE

Phil:

I can have my intern get on the video right away.

What exactly does your accountant need from the account, what sort of records? He must mean invoices. I can send those over now.

---

from: YOPLAY <philgergel@gmail.com>
to: smith@simonyi.com
date: Mon, Aug 31 at 10:05 AM
subject: re: YOU WILL NOT BELIEVE THIS B AS IN BULL + S AS IN
SATIRE

HE IS RIGHT HERE. HE SAYS NOT JUST INVOICES, ALL RECORDS, SUCH AS BANK STATEMENTS

HE SAYS I AM AN EMOTIONAL SPENDER.

BUT I DON'T KNOW WHY THAT IS A BAD THING WHEN IT SOUNDS SO GOOD

WHEN CAN THE VIDEO BE READY?

---

from: smith@simonyi.com
to: YOPLAY <philgergel@gmail.com>
date: Mon, Aug 31 at 10:06 AM
subject: re: YOU WILL NOT BELIEVE THIS B AS IN BULL + S AS IN
SATIRE

I'm swamped today, but I'll get the documents over to you as soon as I can, and I will make the video a priority.

---

from: carl@simonyi.com
to: smith@simonyi.com
date: Mon, Aug 31 at 10:06 AM
subject: Paging Benjamin Franklin!

Call me crazy, but I think I just had a very good idea for the United States Postal Service. They need to do pickups where they actually come in and box up your stuff for you. Because while I do believe in patronizing the USPS, figuring out how to pack and transport this much stuff is *not* a strength of mine. On a scale of 1 to 10, I am a zero.

You know, it probably makes most sense if I just call a courier company that does this sort of thing and have them come do it.

---

from: smith@simonyi.com
to: carl@simonyi.com
date: Mon, Aug 31 at 10:08 AM
subject: re: Paging Benjamin Franklin!

Carl,

I recall from your résumé that you're adept at video editing, correct? Please see the request below from Phil and get started right away. Instructions for what he wants should be clear. We can talk more in a bit if you have questions, but right now I have to run an errand.

Set aside the packing and whatever else you're working on in order to get started on this video project. Phil is a very important client.

---

from: smith@simonyi.com
to: richierich1000@gmail.com
date: Mon, Aug 31 at 10:10 AM
subject: re: Emergency

Just left you a message—it's an emergency. I need to borrow some money. And I may need a lawyer. I'm on my way to your office to see if I can catch you in person.

---

from: carl@simonyi.com
to: smith@simonyi.com
date: Mon, Aug 31 at 10:11 AM
subject: re: Paging Benjamin Franklin!

No problem at all! I love comedy, videos, and creating comedic videos. I look forward to reading what he has in mind, but first, since it sounds like you're in a hurry—does this mean I'm merely *postponing* packing up all this crap to send to Jade Massey of Jersey City, or am I allowed to outsource it?

---

from: smith@simonyi.com
to: carl@simonyi.com
date: Mon, Aug 31 at 10:12 PM
subject: re: Paging Benjamin Franklin!

Just set everything else aside and focus on this.

from: smithsimonyi@gmail.com
to: richierich1000@gmail.com
date: Mon, Aug 31 at 10:33 AM
subject: re: Emergency

Me again. Just left you another message. Call when you can?

from: YOPLAY <philgergel@gmail.com>
to: smith@simonyi.com
date: Mon, Aug 31 at 10:37 AM
subject: re: YOU WILL NOT BELIEVE THIS B AS IN BULL + S AS IN
          SATIRE

WE ARE WAITING FOR RECORDS. PLEASE SEND SO
HE'LL LEAVE ME ALONE. I TOLD HIM I WANT TO GET
IT OVER WITH now SO I DON'T HAVE TO COME BACK
AGAIN
   HE IS SO MEAN
   SO I BOUGHT SOME GOATS ONCE SO WHAT??

from: smith@simonyi.com
to: richierich1000@gmail.com
date: Mon, Aug 31 at 10:56 AM
subject: re: Emergency

You here? Ringing your buzzer.

---

from: carl@simonyi.com
to: smith@simonyi.com
date: Mon, Aug 31 at 10:57 AM
subject: re: Paging Benjamin Franklin!

Good news! I know you said to set it aside, but Deshi from GiveUsYourWork is on his way to pack up the boxes, and he's only charging $10 plus shipping costs. (How does he even make ends meet? I'm really beginning to see what my Social Contracts in the Modern Age professor meant when he bemoaned the booming freelancer economy. Still, for our immediate purposes, #worthit.) (Omg, how quickly I became #partoftheproblem . . . so many feelings . . .)

But BACK TO IT (banality of evil, ugh)—fastest method, you said, right? I'll tell him FedEx Overnight.

Oh, he's already here!

---

from: smith@simonyi.com
to: richierich1000@gmail.com
date: Mon, Aug 31 at 11:05 AM
subject: re: Emergency

At coffee shop across the street. Your office light isn't on.

Are you getting my texts? Will wait here till you're back.

from: carl@simonyi.com
to: smith@simonyi.com; YOPLAY <philgergel@gmail.com>
date: Mon, Aug 31 at 11:29 AM
subject: Regarding the video assignment

Dear Smith and Phil,

As a (relatively) straight man, I have long been troubled by my possible role in perpetuating homophobia. This current assignment raises ethical concerns for me. I have been charged with creating a video in which I replace male-to-male amorous activity with female-to-male amorous activity. Yes, they are Muppets. But as Muppets, they are gendered. The goal of this video is, apparently, to dial back the suggestion that Phil is gay. But the underlying message of this project is homophobia.

After a thoughtful twenty minutes of self-struggle, I have determined that I cannot complete this project while maintaining my integrity. I am, however, attaching an article on the historically disproportionate distribution of male vs. female characters among the Muppets, which began to be remedied in the 1990s and yet remains unequal even today.

Sincerely,

Carl Van Snyder III

Senior Intern

Simonyi Brand Management

---

from: smith@simonyi.com
to: carl@simonyi.com; YOPLAY <philgergel@gmail.com>
date: Mon, Aug 31 at 11:32 AM
subject: re: Regarding the video assignment

Carl (and Phil),

While I understand your concern, we can deal with homophobia another time. This is important to Phil.
Thx to both of you,
Smith

---

from: smith@simonyi.com
to: carl@simonyi.com
date: Mon, Aug 31 at 11:33 AM
subject: re: Regarding the video assignment

Carl,

(Took Phil off) Please *do not* communicate with clients without my permission apart from scheduling appointments. This is very important.

---

from: carl@simonyi.com
to: smith@simonyi.com
date: Mon, Aug 31 at 11:44 AM
subject: re: Paging Benjamin Franklin!

Boss,

It's fine! He already wrote back, and you won't believe it, but he had *no idea* the video was speculation about his sexual orientation! In fact, he seems to be completely in the dark re: all those memes about him being closeted. What bliss, to be so naïve! I almost hated to tell him.

But he took it like a true ally. He is not upset, and he agrees that we should abandon the video, as he does not want to be affiliated with bigotry. What a relief—that Phil Gergel is so decent!

Honestly, there's another reason it's best to forgo projects like this one for the time being. Did you know Mercury is in retrograde, so it's a dangerous time to be technologically innovative? Things made of technology tend to break down out of nowhere. Last night my roommate broke his phone by dropping it onto his *own face*. Probably his head didn't give way much due to the fact that his pillow is memory foam. (Those make me sweat, do they you??)

By the way, Phil also asked me to send over some bank records. So he gives you an account and you can just access it as needed? How convenient. Looks like the log-in is saved on this computer, too! Consider it done.

PS—Did you sleep in the office last night? Just wondering because when I arrived there was a blanket bunched up on the bottom of the lobby couch. And if that's an option, I'm definitely interested. My roommates are now into assigning chores to one another and policing the hell out of the chore sheet. I just don't have it in me, not this summer.

---

from: smith@simonyi.com
to: carl@simonyi.com
date: Mon, Aug 31 at 11:45 AM
subject: re: Paging Benjamin Franklin!

Carl,

Wait.

Do not send any financial files or information until I return.

from: YOPLAY <philgergel@gmail.com>
to: smith@simonyi.com
date: Mon, Aug 31 at 11:53 AM
subject: re: YOU WILL NOT BELIEVE THIS B AS IN BULL + S AS IN SATIRE

DID YOU KNOW PEOPLE THINK I'M GAY?????

from: YOPLAY <philgergel@gmail.com>
to: smith@simonyi.com
date: Mon, Aug 31 at 11:55 AM
subject: re: YOU WILL NOT BELIEVE THIS B AS IN BULL + S AS IN SATIRE

I SPEND BECAUSE I CARE
   I HOPE
   NO I DO
   I DO
   I LOVE THAT CARL BY THE WAY
   HE SAYS YOU ARE OUT N ABOUT SO HE IS GOING TO
SEND THE FILES

from: carl@simonyi.com
to: smith@simonyi.com
date: Mon, Aug 31 at 12:00 PM
subject: re: Paging Benjamin Franklin!

Uh-oh. Did I do something wrong? Was just trying to be helpful . . .

---

from: YOPLAY <philgergel@gmail.com>
to: smith@simonyi.com
date: Mon, Aug 31 at 12:06 PM
subject: re: YOU WILL NOT BELIEVE THIS B AS IN BULL + S AS IN
          SATIRE

SMITH WHAT IS BARRY SAYING TO ME RIGHT NOW
I CANNOT BELIEVE MY EARS AND HEARING

---

from: smith@simonyi.com
to: YOPLAY <philgergel@gmail.com>
date: Mon, Aug 31 at 12:09 PM
subject: re: YOU WILL NOT BELIEVE THIS B AS IN BULL + S AS IN
          SATIRE

I am going to pay it back. I can explain. I am very sorry, but it isn't what it looks like.

---

from: YOPLAY <philgergel@gmail.com>
to: smith@simonyi.com
date: Mon, Aug 31 at 12:12 PM
subject: re: YOU WILL NOT BELIEVE THIS B AS IN BULL + S AS IN
          SATIRE

YOU STOLE FROM ME?
ET TU, BRUTE?

---

from: YOPLAY <philgergel@gmail.com>
to: smith@simonyi.com
date: Mon, Aug 31 at 12:13 PM
subject: re: YOU WILL NOT BELIEVE THIS B AS IN BULL + S AS IN SATIRE

STOP CALLING MY PHONE I CANNOT FACE YOU IN THIS MOMENT

---

from: smith@simonyi.com
to: YOPLAY <philgergel@gmail.com>
date: Mon, Aug 31 at 12:16 PM
subject: re: YOU WILL NOT BELIEVE THIS B AS IN BULL + S AS IN SATIRE

I did have to move some money around to cover my mother's rent. I am going to pay you back right away. Today if possible. I have a new prospective client—huge—an author—I just need a day or so to sign her. I promise it will work out if you'll just trust me.

---

from: YOPLAY <philgergel@gmail.com>
to: smith@simonyi.com
date: Mon, Aug 31 at 12:34 PM
subject: re: YOU WILL NOT BELIEVE THIS B AS IN BULL + S AS IN SATIRE

WITHDRAWALS WITH NO FEES INVOICED, BARRY SAYS
  SUMS MISSING, GONE
  FOR MONTHS NOW
  AND YOU BLAME IT ON YOUR MOTHER? ISN'T SHE A
CRIPPLE?

so

low

A CRIPPLE

YOUR ASS SHOULD BE IN A MANILA FOLDER ON THE DESK OF A KHAKI DETECTIVE THIS INSTANT

MY ACCOUNTANT WANTS ME TO PRESS CHARGES!!!

BARRY SAYS WHAT YOU DID IS CRIMINAL.

AGAINST THE LAW.

HOW CAN YOU STEAL FROM ME AFTER ALL THIS TIME? I AM IN GOOD MIND TO SUE BUT AM WILLING TO TALK FIRST TO HEAR YOUR SIDE OF THE STORY, MOSTLY CAUSE I NEED THE KARMA

HOWEVER YOU AND I ARE THROUGH

FOR GOOD

JUDAS

I only tried to see the good in you.

---

from:	smith@simonyi.com
to:	YOPLAY <philgergel@gmail.com>
date:	Mon, Aug 31 at 12:35 PM
subject:	re: YOU WILL NOT BELIEVE THIS B AS IN BULL + S AS IN SATIRE

I'm sorry. I don't know what else to say.

---

from:	carl@simonyi.com
to:	smith@simonyi.com
date:	Mon, Aug 31 at 12:44 PM
subject:	re: Paging Benjamin Franklin!

Oh no. What have I done. Am I fired?

from:	jade@barntherestaurant.com
to:	marcus@barntherestaurant.com
date:	Mon, Aug 31 at 12:49 PM
subject:	Goodbye, Marcus

Marcus,

Thank you for the clarity of your email this morning.

Please consider this email my resignation.

Jade

from:	richierich1000@gmail.com
to:	smith@simonyi.com
date:	Mon, Aug 31 at 12:53 PM
subject:	re: Emergency

dude I was at the gym. u ok? whats going on

I did a little research into how memory works. Turns out when you remember something, what you're remembering is the last time you remembered it. So every time you do, it's different.

Happens.

New layer of detail

When you remember it

Then you remember it again

And again

And again

And if you don't remember it

It shrinks up

●

Like a muscle

_____

●

Or old love

Until eventually what you remember

is pretty much all memories of memories.

I am writing down dots

The mangled dots.

COMMENTS (49):

BonnieD: Told u pics get u on the popular page, congrats! now watch out u are famous lol

HarryBeastMan: tits tits titties tits tits titties

GloriaGlowing: @moderator see above

HarryBeastMan: u want me glowbird u know it

Moderator: User has been removed. Apologies for the insensitive remarks. As you were!

Click to see 43 more . . .

BigJessBarbs: This blog reminds me of my knitting days!

TUESDAY, SEPTEMBER 1

from: Bro-vado
to: smithsimonyi@gmail.com
date: Tue, Sep 1 at 4:49 AM
subject: WHO'S THE MAN?

YOU ARE! Here's a breakdown of your most recent session:

High: $32,319

Low: $0

Walkaway: $0

ProTip: End your session while you're up . . . then come back with more to play with the next time.

from: smith@simonyi.com
to: iris.a.massey@gmail.com
date: Tue, Sep 1 at 7:50 AM
subject: no subject

It's ruining me, and yet I go to it. I go to it because . . . what was the email I received the other day? I believe that I "can, will, and probably should lose."

I don't know if that's true. But when I read it, I think of something Clementine said to me once.

Clementine was hung up on one thing that happened early in our relationship, long before we were married. We met on a Monday, and ten days later, on a Thursday, my dad died. I was twenty-eight, and she and I had been on two dates when I got the call. I told her I was going home for a bit but left out the details—that I was going to bury my dad, and that my mom was in the hospital. As I later tried to explain to Clementine, I didn't know how bad my mom's injuries were when I left. No one did, not even the doctors.

I flew to Wisconsin and handled everything—buried him, got her set up in a long-term care unit . . . Then I came back to New York, and Clementine and I continued to date. But still I didn't tell her what had happened. What was the point? So she could comfort me? We hadn't even had sex yet. Of course, she found out eventually that he was dead, and that my mom was disabled. And at that point, fine, I did sort of lie—I claimed the "accident" had happened earlier in the year, and that my mom had *fallen* down the stairs. I implied that these were separate incidents.

But we'd been dating for four months. I was supposed to bare my soul?

The problem was, I suppose, that I never corrected either of these white lies. The night before we were getting married, she learned the real story from Richie, who inadvertently filled her in on the true version of events after she interrogated him. The way she looked at me—like I was a con.

Over the two years we managed to stay married, she would lob comments at me here and there, like, "I shouldn't be surprised to feel invisible to you. Men always end up treating their wives like they treat their moms."

"You mean how I support you both?" I only said once.

"You really think that's what love is?" she said back. It wasn't a question. It was an accusation. Like whatever respect for me she'd maintained was now gone. Like she understood me better than I did myself, and was disgusted by what she knew.

That is how I feel now. That low.

---

from: jademassey@yahoo.com
to: smith@simonyi.com
date: Tue, Sep 1 at 8:08 AM
subject: Apology

Dear Smith,

I'm sorry for my attitude last week. I was unnecessarily rude to you. Thank you for mailing my sister's things. I appreciate you reaching out about them, and for taking care to get them to me.

I hope your week is going well.

Sincerely,

Jade

PS—Speaking of things that need returning—am I remembering correctly that you're a friend of Richie, whom my sister was seeing this spring? Might you have his contact info? I lost it.

from: smith@simonyi.com
to: jademassey@yahoo.com
date: Tue, Sep 1 at 8:20 AM
subject: re: Apology

No worries. I apologize, too. I got a bit defensive when you implied that I didn't care enough about your sister to stay through her funeral.

The boxes should arrive today. My intern sent them overnight delivery yesterday afternoon via FedEx.

Richie's email is richierich1000@gmail.com. If he doesn't respond right away, don't be surprised. He's really busy at the moment.

from: jademassey@yahoo.com
to: smith@simonyi.com
date: Tue, Sep 1 at 9:23 AM
subject: re: Apology

I'm in Virginia. But I'll be back later this week and can let you know that they made it.

And he's already written back, thanks!

from: smith@simonyi.com
to: jademassey@yahoo.com
date: Tue, Sep 1 at 9:26 AM
subject: re: Apology

What's in Virginia? No pressure to respond.

---

from: jademassey@yahoo.com
to: smith@simonyi.com
date: Tue, Sep 1 at 9:29 AM
subject: re: Apology

My mother. She's struggling.

---

from: smith@simonyi.com
to: jademassey@yahoo.com
date: Tue, Sep 1 at 9:40 AM
subject: re: Apology

Ah.

---

from: jademassey@yahoo.com
to: smith@simonyi.com
date: Tue, Sep 1 at 9:58 AM
subject: re: Apology

She's doing better than she was. Right after Iris died, she disappeared for ten hours, which may not sound like very long, but was
long enough to freak me out. I found her in the freezer section of
Costco in Queens, with no idea how she'd gotten there from the
hospital. After the funeral, she headed back to Virginia. I came
down a month or so later to check on her.

My mother, a proud Baptist all of her life, joined her local
church choir when she moved to Virgina years ago and has been
super active at the church since. Well, after Iris died, she quit
going. To Sunday services or choir practice. It was a concern for
all of us since singing is her favorite thing these days (she's also
been director of her local social club's "Gray Lady" chorus of
geriatric women for several years). In July, the choir director and

I convinced her to go back. But apparently she showed up and started telling everyone that God doesn't exist. He said it was like she wanted someone to correct or stop her, but no one did. This happened a few weeks in a row. Finally, one week, they were rehearsing some song, a mass—and I'm not sure what happened. She didn't give me details. But when the song was over, she believed again.

The choir leader and I were relieved for different reasons. He was glad she wouldn't be showing up lecturing everyone on God's nonexistence any longer. I was glad because she had her community back.

So now she's at church regularly again, and that's good since the people there seem to take care of her. But between the Costco situation and the 360 on God, I'm nervous. The disappearing and not remembering it especially freaked me out.

Sorry. Don't have many people to talk to down here. I'm rattling on.

---

from: smith@simonyi.com
to: jademassey@yahoo.com
date: Tue, Sep 1 at 10:32 AM
subject: re: Apology

When my dad died, I would sit for hours staring into space, unaware that I was doing nothing, or that time was even passing. I fantasized about how it happened, and how I might have stopped it had I been there. But mostly I just stared.

Maybe the Costco situation doesn't need to be concerning. It sounds pretty normal.

I'm sure she's grateful to have you there. And it's good you're able to take time off work!

from: jademassey@yahoo.com
to: smith@simonyi.com
date: Tue, Sep 1 at 10:40 AM
subject: re: Apology

Well, I quit. Or was fired for wanting time off. Guess it depends on how you look at it.

Let me know if you know of anyone hiring!

from: smith@simonyi.com
to: jademassey@yahoo.com
date: Tue, Sep 1 at 10:42 AM
subject: re: Apology

That's too bad. Okay, I'll keep an ear out. On? Out.

from: jademassey@yahoo.com
to: smith@simonyi.com
date: Tue, Sep 1 at 10:44 AM
subject: re: Apology

You mean an eye out? Thanks.

Oh, and—I am a bit embarrassed to tell you this, but I shouldn't be, because I had a good reason. I needed to log into my sister's email earlier in order to check something about her medication, and I saw that you had emailed her. I didn't read anything, don't worry. I'm not a snoop. But I think you should know that I saw it, and I may have to get back in there as needed.

---

from: smith@simonyi.com
to: jademassey@yahoo.com
date: Tue, Sep 1 at 10:47 AM
subject: re: Apology

Talk about embarrassed.

---

from: jademassey@yahoo.com
to: smith@simonyi.com
date: Tue, Sep 1 at 10:53 AM
subject: re: Apology

Don't be.

So that you don't think less of me—I am trying to figure out if her doctor has perhaps committed malpractice by not putting her on the more effective chemo drug, or by not telling her that it was the more effective drug. I did learn from her email history that she was taking weed this spring, unbeknownst to me, and, I imagine, unbeknownst to her doctors. I have no idea if it was for pain or what. At least now I know.

---

from: smith@simonyi.com
to: jademassey@yahoo.com
date: Tue, Sep 1 at 11:14 AM
subject: re: Apology

She was on a cannabis-based regimen she found online. It wasn't for pain though. She was convinced it could cure her cancer. It was why she acted so loopy sometimes. Our client—former client, rather, who you may know as Yo-Play—decided in the spring that he was going to leave rap in order to become a country music artist. Terrible decision. But Iris, high on her "tincture," wrote out a fantastical "rap funeral" plan for him, which she didn't run by me before emailing to him. The cosmic joke was that I had to go through with it in June.

At least those were some fun days. In a relative sense. You know what I mean. If she was going to be at work with cancer, at least she was laughing.

"Taking" weed, ha. Aren't you in the restaurant business?

---

from: jademassey@yahoo.com
to: smith@simonyi.com
date: Tue, Sep 1 at 11:27 AM
subject: re: Apology

Oh. Well, she never told me about it.

People in my industry, at least in the back of the house, aren't big drug users. Front of house is another story. But in the kitchen we stick to cigarettes (not me). I have never even tried marijuana. I don't plan to. I have no interest. And I'm certain, without even having looked into it, that it doesn't cure fucking cancer. Good grief, I could have told Iris that much if she'd bothered asking. I used to be married to a doctor for pete's sake.

I have to go. Thanks for sending the stuff.

Jade

---

from: carl@simonyi.com
to: smith@simonyi.com
date: Tue, Sep 1 at 11:32 AM
subject: An idea

Hi Boss,

I woke up in the middle of the night last night with two ideas to run by you.

First, while the name Simonyi Brand Management has its own . . . special quality, I am wondering if you've considered a more current moniker for the firm, something fresh like BRAND-AID, or BRAND CENTRAL (since we're in New York!). Lately when I tell people where I work, they (a) don't understand what "Simonyi" is ("a Hungarian soup?"), and (b) don't understand how to pronounce it. They spend all their time focused on your last name when what they *should* be asking is what the firm can do for them!

Two, Iris's book—I've finally gotten a chance to read it. Defining audience is so important. Who are we selling it to? Who actually has an interest in this stuff? Thus, I can see it being repurposed as a children's book (what with all the illustrations), à la GOODNIGHT MOON: **GOODNIGHT, IRIS.**

What do you think?

Carl

---

from: smith@simonyi.com
to: carl@simonyi.com
date: Tue, Sep 1 at 12:01 PM
subject: re: An idea

I don't think a pun is the way to go with firm name. And a children's book feels off.

---

from: smithsimonyi@gmail.com
to: horn@horncriminaldefense.com
date: Tue, Sep 1 at 12:56 PM
subject: Inquiry

Dear Mr. Horn,

I came across your ad online and am reaching out because I find myself in a position in which I may need an attorney. This is a somewhat humiliating and delicate situation, thus I prefer not to reach out to any of the attorneys I know socially—you understand, I hope.

I left you a voicemail a few minutes ago with the details.

Is this the kind of thing you could help me with?

Best,

Smith

---

from: horn@horncriminaldefense.com
to: smithsimonyi@gmail.com
date: Tue, Sep 1 at 1:10 PM
subject: re: Inquiry

Don't talk to anybody about anything. Don't say what you said on this voicemail for fuck's sake. Can you come in on Friday? First hour is $525. $10K cash retainer.

---

from: smithsimonyi@gmail.com
to: horn@horncriminaldefense.com
date: Tue, Sep 1 at 1:14 PM
subject: re: Inquiry

Well, that makes sense except that I've already admitted to all of it.

---

from: horn@horncriminaldefense.com
to: smithsimonyi@gmail.com
date: Tue, Sep 1 at 1:15 PM
subject: re: Inquiry

---

how? where? in person? phone?

---

from: smithsimonyi@gmail.com
to: horn@horncriminaldefense.com
date: Tue, Sep 1 at 1:17 PM
subject: re: Inquiry

Over email. He wouldn't answer my calls.

---

from: horn@horncriminaldefense.com
to: smithsimonyi@gmail.com
date: Tue, Sep 1 at 1:19 PM
subject: re: Inquiry

---

of course. fucker wanted it in writing. can you do Friday or not

---

from: smithsimonyi@gmail.com
to: horn@horncriminaldefense.com
date: Tue, Sep 1 at 1:22 PM
subject: re: Inquiry

I don't have $10K right now.

from:	horn@horncriminaldefense.com
to:	smithsimonyi@gmail.com
date:	Tue, Sep 1 at 1:26 PM
subject:	re: Inquiry

well when you do, you have my number. no more talking to any-one about this. And no talking to your former client at all. Got it?

I've been thinking about love lately. When did I first experience it?

It was my second week of public school, and Jade and I were
on the bus in the town in Alabama where we'd just moved, the
last town we'd ever live in for more than a few months, though of
course I didn't know that at the time. I was six and she was ten.
My shoe had come untied, and I was standing in the aisle of the
bus tying it. Because I was looking down, I didn't see that I was
blocking the path of a giant fifth-grader named Lance. Everyone
was scared of Lance. He terrorized the school bus so viciously
from the back that kids scrambled to sit at the front. Sometimes
we squeezed three to a row up there, risking reprimand by the
driver, just to avoid him.

Lance had just boarded, but I was tying my shoe.

"Move, fatty!" he yelled, and his friends all laughed. My Polly Pocket backpack suddenly felt really stupid, as did everything else about me: my ponytail, the ribbon in it, my shorts with the orange zebras. As I started to cry, crawling into the seat with Jade, she looked up at this bully, who was a full year older than her, and said, "Real brave to pick on a first-grader. You must feel super proud."

No one had ever stood up to Lance before. No one until Jade. He didn't know what to say back. He muttered something about me being in his way and walked away.

Over the years, when I hear the term "tough love," I think of my sister. That's her. Love in Teflon form.

COMMENTS (1):

DyingToBlogTeam: Here's a friendly tip from your friends at DyingToBlog! Try posting at the same time every day. When users know when to expect your post, they're more likely to pay you a visit!

FRIDAY, SEPTEMBER 4

---

from: jademassey@yahoo.com
to: smith@simonyi.com
date: Fri, Sep 4 at 11:49 AM
subject: no subject

Are you sure all of this is hers?

---

from: smith@simonyi.com
to: jademassey@yahoo.com
date: Fri, Sep 4 at 12:16 PM
subject: re: no subject

It should be. Why?

---

from: jademassey@yahoo.com
to: smith@simonyi.com
date: Fri, Sep 4 at 12:17 PM
subject: re: no subject

It's just a lot of entrepreneurial books and stuff. It doesn't seem like her.

from:	smith@simonyi.com
to:	jademassey@yahoo.com
date:	Fri, Sep 4 at 12:19 PM
subject:	re: no subject

Because of the bakery.

from:	jademassey@yahoo.com
to:	smith@simonyi.com
date:	Fri, Sep 4 at 12:20 PM
subject:	re: no subject

Bakery?

from:	smith@simonyi.com
to:	jademassey@yahoo.com
date:	Fri, Sep 4 at 12:28 PM
subject:	re: no subject

BAKED. Or HYBRID. She went back and forth on the name. When I met her at the incubator at Tufts four years ago it was HYBRID. Back then all the items were going to be hybrids. But the restriction of only selling cross-breed pastries (à la the cronut) eventually felt stifling to her, plus the name is not very appetizing, so BAKED became the leading contender until she realized it was taken.

We came up with a bunch of marketing copy like: What happens to a cream deferred?

I'll be here all week.

---

from: jademassey@yahoo.com
to: smith@simonyi.com
date: Fri, Sep 4 at 12:33 PM
subject: re: no subject

Cream deferred? I don't get it.

---

from: smith@simonyi.com
to: jademassey@yahoo.com
date: Fri, Sep 4 at 12:36 PM
subject: re: no subject

Cream, like dream. The Langston Hughes poem?

---

from: smith@simonyi.com
to: jademassey@yahoo.com
date: Fri, Sep 4 at 12:40 PM
subject: re: no subject

Shit. I just realized that joke is just sad under the circumstances.

---

from: jademassey@yahoo.com
to: smith@simonyi.com
date: Fri, Sep 4 at 12:43 PM
subject: re: no subject

What is an incubator?

---

from: smith@simonyi.com
to: jademassey@yahoo.com
date: Fri, Sep 4 at 12:48 PM
subject: re: no subject

Boot camp for entrepreneurs. Four days of lectures and workshops. I was there to restructure my business because I was spread thin and needed to make a conscious decision about my focus. Iris had come up with the idea for her bakery, but once she got there she decided she wasn't ready. She had just left her retail job—a makeup store or something? Anyway, she needed something to tide her over. And I needed an assistant.

---

from: jademassey@yahoo.com
to: smith@simonyi.com
date: Fri, Sep 4 at 12:58 PM
subject: re: no subject

I see.

Friday, September 4
TherapistAwayNetwork™
Patient Name: Jade Renee Massey
AUTO PROMPT: **What is difficult for you to talk about?**

Iris was planning to open a bakery and didn't tell me, her chef sister. I worked five blocks away from her for crying out loud.
   I am in the restaurant business.
   She hoarded piles of cutouts of cakes and pies stapled to recipes stapled to seasonal theme ideas stapled to sketches of storefronts and interior layouts. She and Smith Simonyi met at some

"incubator" she never mentioned. They wrote business plans. She told him and not me. Just like she left this online journal for him and not me.

Did she think I'd be overbearing? Take over?

Is it the same reason she didn't tell me about her blog or the weed?

I suppose I did sort of know about the blog. There was a day last spring. I had been living there for three weeks, ever since she called to ask if I'd stay a night or two in case she needed help getting to the bathroom. She had entered a phase in which she loathed any comment or expression that resembled pity.

"Act normal," she begged. "*Please* act normal."

But what was normal about the two of us living together in her one-bedroom apartment as adults? What was normal about her being so sick she had trouble standing on her own at times? Every so often she'd take out her laptop and type. I assumed she was emailing someone. I wondered if maybe it could be Daniel, her ex.

I asked.

"It's a blog," she said. "Dying people write about dying on it," she said.

"Sounds uplifting," I said.

She shrugged. "It's the only place I feel understood now."

I started to tear up.

"Dammit, Jade," she yelled, "stop it!" Then she went to her room to take a nap, leaving me crying alone like an asshole, the one who *wasn't* dying of cancer.

So I take it back: she did tell me about her blog.

∎

Dear JADE,

Thank you for your submission to TAN™. We will make sure your provider receives this message.

Did you know "difficulty" is derived from the Latin *dis*, meaning "reversal," and *facultas*, meaning "ability or opportunity." When we think of a difficulty as a reversal in opportunity, it becomes possible to see it in a new light. Difficulties are about shifting the frame of reference from old abilities to new opportunities. Today, ask: What is my difficulty inviting me to experience?

TAN™ is not to be used in case of emergency. If you are in crisis, call 9-1-1.

Sincerely,

Your friends at TAN

---

from:	wally@homilypines.com
to:	smith@simonyi.com
date:	Fri, Sep 4 at 3:22 PM
subject:	Checking in

Hiya Smith,

So sorry about this but we got your check and can't cash it. I got the rates off! I knew they went up but I was thinking they'd gone up $200, to $7,185. Turns out it's a $400 increase for residents with single rooms, so that's $7,385. I don't know if you want to consider moving your mom in with a roommate. I don't know if she would like that or not, to be honest. On one hand I think the company could be good for her, and on the other she's kind of an introvert and likes her shows the same every day so sharing the TV with another person might make her pretty unhappy, since that's the thing she looks forward to. I think it'd be good if you were able to come up with the $200 extra, I guess is what I'm saying.

Let me know. Apparently energy costs went way up because the local energy company changed ownership and we were all underpaying or some hogwash.

Hey, you know what, I'll go ahead and cash this check and just front the $200 for now and you can pay me back.

Holler when you can make it out for a visit! We'd love to see you.

Wally

---

from: Airbnb
to: smith@simonyi.com
date: Fri, Sep 4 at 3:40 PM
subject: BOOKING INQUIRY for "Beautiful One Bedroom with Balcony
          on Upper West Side" for Sat, Sept 5—Thurs, Sept 10

Hi,

My name is TRAVEL MAN2,

I am looking for a house to stay in right away starting tomorrow with my girl for five nights and five days after those nights.

We will use very cleanly. Actually we are students. So we don't have enough budget. Could you make it cheaper????

If this message makes you feel bad, please disregard!

Many thanks!

from: sheryl@berringerpress.com
to: smith@simonyi.com
date: Fri, Sep 4 at 4:12 PM
subject: no go

S—

Just got a chance to discuss your colleague's blog with my interns. Brutus was ambivalent. Willow's assessment is that no way should you attempt to do anything with this. "Plenty of people die with books or poems or drawings lying around in some drawer. It's sad, but it doesn't mean we should publish them. The work has got to stand on its own."

A little jaded for a twenty-year-old, I thought. But given that this thing has a millennial feel, I take her point.

Glad you want to take on Zahara Ferringbottom. She is truly a remarkable person, and you will thank me.

xSheryl

from: smith@simonyi.com
to: cfournier@treblepublishing.com
date: Fri, Sep 4 at 4:38 PM
subject: Manuscript of note

Dear Christian,

I hope you are enjoying the final days of summer.

I am writing to let you know about a manuscript authored by a colleague who passed in May. During the last six months of her life, Iris wrote a blog that I can see working as a Treble self-help title. I am linking to it below.

I look forward to hearing your thoughts!

Let's get Campari soon,

Smith

January 13 | 5:13 AM

A symptom of cancer appears to be insomnia. Unless insomnia is just a symptom of dying. Here's how I always felt about the chicken vs. egg conundrum: who cares? They come as a pair.

I am sort of dating someone. Richie. He makes coffee sleeves for coffee shops. Everyone loves his coffee sleeves because they have quotes on them, like "The only thing we have to fear is fear itself." And they're made out of recycled litter he finds around New York City.

Our first date was New Year's Eve, right after I got my diagnosis. Smith had set us up. At the end of November, he gave my number to Richie and let me know I might receive a text or call, but it took us another four weeks to get a date on the calendar. We thought it would be funny, and maybe fun, to have our first date on New Year's Eve. This, of course, was before I'd gotten the news. I gave him an out due to my suddenly having cancer, but he ignored it. We met at the office to watch the fireworks from the window because it's a great view of the Hudson, and he brought pizza and wine. I wasn't sure if his nonchalance about my cancer was charming, or just bizarre, but now I find it refreshing not to be coddled.

Even though I've only known I'm dying for two weeks, Jade has already taken to policing my intake of all things, as well as monitoring my daily schedule, medical plan, and "questions list" for my doctor, which she keeps telling me needs to "remain living." I know she means I need to add to it as I think of things, but it sounds like it's the list we're trying to keep alive, not me.

Jade is also not happy that I haven't yet told our mom that I have cancer. I think I'm still hoping I won't have to. I've started chemo. If the cancer goes away, it'll be a conversation we never have to have. I know it's wishful. But I'm in the wishful thinking business. This is what I've spent four years doing for people—dreaming big, or "DB," as Smith my boss calls it. I have seen how it can work for others. Now it's time for it to work on my fucking cancer.

COMMENTS (13):

ArduousArdvark: DB = lame

ArduousArdvark: DB = dying 2 blog lol

BonnieD: my mom didn't tell me for a long time and when I found out I was mad

BonnieD: I found it patronizing

BonnieD: also if I had known I could have cheered her up and stuff

IrisMassey: what would you do to cheer her up?

BonnieD: tell jokes about skinny women who used to be fat

BonnieD: she loved making fun of those women because their per-
sonalities always changed once they got skinny.

BonnieD: she was fat and fine with it

IrisMassey: what kind of jokes?

BonnieD: like walk around and be like, "this lettuce juice that I made
in a blender is even more delicious than French fries, I have
soooooo much energy! I looooove cucumber juice"

IrisMassey: Haha. Get some sleep! It's late no matter where you are.

BonnieD: Colorado. it's 3 in the morning here but I don't really
sleep. ok nite

SATURDAY, SEPTEMBER 5

from: smith@simonyi.com
to: cfournier@treblepublishing.com
date: Sat, Sep 5 at 9:02 AM
subject: re: Manuscript of Note

Dear Christian,

I'm so thrilled to hear that you're interested in my former assistant's manuscript. In response to your question, I am in the process of ensuring we're clear on the copyright front.

I'll be in touch soon.

Best,

Smith

from: smith@simonyi.com
to: carl@simonyi.com
date: Sat, Sep 5 at 9:10 AM
subject: Copyright

Carl,

Please check out Dying to Blog and suss out if, as a contributor, Iris signed away the copyright to her posts.

And would you begin Monday researching imprints that might be appropriate for her manuscript? At the moment, I'm drawn to self-help, but there could be other takes on it I'm sure. I mean frankly, we aren't even strapped into publishing. Given the interest you've expressed in alternative approaches to presenting her blog, perhaps you'd like to explore various platforms on which we might distribute it. Something tech-y? An app? Feel free to think creatively.

I know this past week was a difficult one for both of us. I am glad to have you as an intern, and I hope we can find a way to work together in a way that makes use of your skills and caters to your interests. But, of course, as we spoke about on Tuesday—it is very important that you check with me *before* sharing any materials with clients.

Have a good weekend.

Thx,

Smith

---

from: carl@simonyi.com
to: smith@simonyi.com
date: Sat, Sep 5 at 9:45 AM
subject: re: Copyright

I'm SO BAD at this boundaries thing. A workaholic on a Friday is a workaholic on a Saturday and Sunday. And FYI, Monday is Labor Day, so I will be in the Hamptons at a SHAVED cookout.

Okay, I will reach out to them, but remember what I said about the sister? I think that's going to matter as well.

See you Tuesday!

from:	smith@simonyi.com
to:	carl@simonyi.com
date:	Sat, Sep 5 at 9:47 AM
subject:	re: Copyright

I'll deal with the sister. Thx.

from:	smith@simonyi.com
to:	jademassey@yahoo.com
date:	Sat, Sep 5 at 11:02 AM
subject:	re: no subject

Did you really not read the emails I sent to Iris?

from:	jademassey@yahoo.com
to:	smith@simonyi.com
date:	Sat, Sep 5 at 11:28 AM
subject:	re: no subject

Emails, plural? I only saw one. (And I didn't read it.)

from:	smith@simonyi.com
to:	jademassey@yahoo.com
date:	Sat, Sep 5 at 11:31 AM
subject:	re: no subject

How are you doing?

---

from: jademassey@yahoo.com
to: smith@simonyi.com
date: Sat, Sep 5 at 11:45 AM
subject: re: no subject

I'm okay. Focused on getting my life back on track. Today I'm sending out résumés and cleaning my apartment. And I'm going to look up the malpractice claim and what all it entails.

How are you?

---

from: smith@simonyi.com
to: jademassey@yahoo.com
date: Sat, Sep 5 at 6:44 PM
subject: re: no subject

That's good.

Me? Oh, at rock bottom. No big deal.

---

from: smith@simonyi.com
to: jademassey@yahoo.com
date: Sat, Sep 5 at 6:45 PM
subject: re: no subject

Joking.

---

from: jademassey@yahoo.com
to: smith@simonyi.com
date: Sat, Sep 5 at 8:20 PM
subject: re: no subject

Um, ha?

from: smith@simonyi.com
to: jademassey@yahoo.com
date: Sat, Sep 5 at 8:27 PM
subject: re: no subject

Things are not great. I messed up with a pretty big client so I'm dealing with that. But it's nothing you want to hear about.

from: jademassey@yahoo.com
to: smith@simonyi.com
date: Sat, Sep 5 at 8:33 PM
subject: re: no subject

Were you in love with her?

from: smith@simonyi.com
to: jademassey@yahoo.com
date: Sat, Sep 5 at 8:38 PM
subject: re: no subject

The client? It's a he. I can't say his name. And no, I wasn't . . .

from: jademassey@yahoo.com
to: smith@simonyi.com
date: Sat, Sep 5 at 8:41 PM
subject: re: no subject

I mean Iris.

---

from: smith@simonyi.com
to: jademassey@yahoo.com
date: Sat, Sep 5 at 8:44 PM
subject: re: no subject

What makes you think that?

---

from: jademassey@yahoo.com
to: smith@simonyi.com
date: Sat, Sep 5 at 8:48 PM
subject: re: no subject

You wrote it. In the email you sent to her.
 (I did read it. Sorry.)

---

from: smith@simonyi.com
to: jademassey@yahoo.com
date: Sat, Sep 5 at 8:50 PM
subject: re: no subject

I wrote that?

---

from: jademassey@yahoo.com
to: smith@simonyi.com
date: Sat, Sep 5 at 8:53 PM
subject: re: no subject

It was heavily implied. You talked about how much you miss her.

---

from: smith@simonyi.com
to: jademassey@yahoo.com
date: Sat, Sep 5 at 9:04 PM
subject: re: no subject

I don't think I was in love with her. I do miss her a lot.

---

from: jademassey@yahoo.com
to: smith@simonyi.com
date: Sat, Sep 5 at 9:42 PM
subject: re: no subject

You know those cartoons where a giant boulder falls out of the sky and flattens the coyote or bunny or guy with the beard? That's how it feels to me. Like I don't even have the choice to care about anything, because I've been flattened. Just eyeballs staring up into nothing.

Sometimes I cry as hard as I can for as long as I can, as if eventually I'll be finished. Like grief is a marathon and I just have to log enough miles. I wake up looking like I was in a boxing match in the night. People talk undereye bags, but do you know how much your eye*lids* can swell from crying?

I tell myself to get out of bed, but then I think, why bother? Doing anything. We are alive then we aren't. The world is indifferent to whether we're here. What's there to be other than indifferent back?

---

from: smith@simonyi.com
to: jademassey@yahoo.com
date: Sat, Sep 5 at 9:50 PM
subject: re: no subject

I think you should give yourself credit for feeling that way and still getting shit done. You feel like *that,* and yet you're looking for a job and flying back and forth to Virginia to care for your mom? That's impressive as hell.

---

from: jademassey@yahoo.com
to: smith@simonyi.com
date: Sat, Sep 5 at 9:54 PM
subject: re: no subject

Well. Thank you, I guess. I've also started writing poetry, which is weird. I wrote that to you a moment ago and deleted it because it sounds stupid. But since nothing matters, neither does that.

Speaking of moms, how's yours?

---

from: smith@simonyi.com
to: jademassey@yahoo.com
date: Sat, Sep 5 at 9:56 PM
subject: re: no subject

My mom? Why do you ask?

---

from: jademassey@yahoo.com
to: smith@simonyi.com
date: Sat, Sep 5 at 10:04 PM
subject: re: no subject

You told me she wasn't doing well. That's why you left the funeral.

---

from: smith@simonyi.com
to: jademassey@yahoo.com
date: Sat, Sep 5 at 10:38 PM
subject: re: no subject

Right. She's okay. I mean, she's still paralyzed. Ha.
    Can I read your poetry?

---

from: jademassey@yahoo.com
to: smith@simonyi.com
date: Sat, Sep 5 at 10:47 PM
subject: re: no subject

Glad to hear it. Well, I'm falling asleep. Good night.

---

from: smith@simonyi.com
to: jademassey@yahoo.com
date: Sat, Sep 5 at 11:00 PM
subject: re: no subject

Good night.

I have been thinking about when I started baking, and it was right after the fire. The fire that I probably started.

I was twenty-seven and still at Nose, the perfume shop where I worked for two years between my consulting job and my current job. I was happier at Nose than I had been at Propel, but that's not saying much. It was retail, after all.

I'd also started dating Daniel, which both excited me and made me anxious all the time. My feelings for him kept me alert, on my toes, a constant buzz that fed my nicotine addiction. My smoking had escalated. Before Daniel, I'd gotten it down to one cigarette a night, but it had climbed to three, then eleven or twelve. I was going through three or four packs a week.

That night, we all stood outside the building, those of us who lived in it, and watched the smoke pour out of Mrs. Freder's on the first floor. I had just had a cigarette in my bedroom window an hour earlier. I was pretty sure I had fully extinguished it before dropping the butt down the fire escape, where it would have bounced like a Plinko game onto the littered alley below. (I had no qualms littering back then, though I should've, given my Smokey the Bear exposure as a child.) Of course I had extinguished it. I had squashed it on the ledge and then dropped it below like a million times before. But maybe I'd been too careless, too hungry to light my next. Maybe I'd neglected to notice the trace of a glow at the tip.

Mrs. Freder was crying and meth-head Ernie from upstairs had his arm around her.

When the smoke thinned and we were allowed back inside, we passed through the remains of her ground-level one-bedroom. It was soggy and black, like drenched burned toast, minus a few objects that had survived the rapture. A toaster. The porcelain base of a lamp styled as the figure of a Victorian lady. A red rubber plunger.

I listened as a bulky fireman asked Mrs. Freder if she had left her stove on, perhaps. The stove sat by the window, now open, below my own. Could it have been open before? It was late April and possible.

Tom the landlord, who was always way too nice to be a New York landlord, let her stay in the empty unit across the hall while her unit was being cleaned up. Ernie brought her a small TV with an antenna, and I brought other things: towels, plates and pans, cups and napkins, a lamp, the quilt Daniel's grandmother made for him that he'd brought over after my radiator temporarily broke. When her daughter and son came from Chicago and Miami, she invited me down to meet them. They thanked me for all the dinners I'd delivered to her since the fire.

I couldn't smoke in my window again after that. And since

public smoking never appealed to me, I was left with little choice but to quit.

I started baking because I was restless without cigarettes. I noticed a recipe book with a cheesecake on it in the window display of a bookstore and decided to make that cheesecake. It took me three hours because I fucked it up with too much sugar, nine if you count the cooling period, and by the time that was over, I realized I hadn't craved a smoke.

I learned how to make raspberry tarts and lavender sea salt ice cream, blueberry crème brûlée with lemon glaze, and honey pistachio biscotti. I shared it all with Mrs. Freder and Ernie and then everyone else. I decided I wanted to bake for people and that, if I saved enough money, I would open a bakery. It was the first career idea I ever got really excited about.

All of this is to say, I have mixed feelings about what I did. I'm sorry that I might have burned your apartment up, Mrs. Freder. But I'm also glad it led me to start making people things.

COMMENTS (1):

ChristmasWasMyFavorite: Lavender in ice cream? I'd rather eat pine straw! Or hay! Lol

SUNDAY, SEPTEMBER 6

---

from: jademassey@yahoo.com
to: smith@simonyi.com
date: Sun, Sep 6 at 8:13 AM
subject: no subject

Why don't you think she told me? About the bakery?

---

from: smith@simonyi.com
to: jademassey@yahoo.com
date: Sun, Sep 6 at 11:55 AM
subject: re: no subject

Maybe she thought it was your territory. You're the chef.

---

from: jademassey@yahoo.com
to: smith@simonyi.com
date: Sun, Sep 6 at 12:29 PM
subject: re: no subject

But I don't even like sweets. She knows that. I hate pastries. With a passion. Actually that's not entirely accurate. What I hate are *desserts*. You've just had this beautiful meal, the arc of it has left you perfectly satiated and grateful and complete, and then out comes a dish that invariably contains something red or pink, and quivering—you're going to close this culinary experience with a *sugar bomb*. It's repulsive. A sloppy, sentimental epilogue to a book that had a suitable ending.

---

from: jademassey@yahoo.com
to: smith@simonyi.com
date: Sun, Sep 6 at 12:32 PM
subject: re: no subject

Hmm. Actually, maybe she thought I would judge her.

---

from: smith@simonyi.com
to: jademassey@yahoo.com
date: Sun, Sep 6 at 1:30 PM
subject: re: no subject

What you're doing right now? That's the worst part, for me, about losing someone. They are no longer around for you to know what they think, or thought. You don't get to assume you know what they'll say and then be surprised when you're wrong. There's no tension. All conversation is imaginary, confined to the echo chamber of your own mind.

I always hated hearing people talk about the dead as if, suddenly after death, their desires became transparent. "She would have wanted you to do this." "He would have wanted that." Who knows what they would want if they were still alive? Isn't that the terrible thing? You have no idea, and you can't ask. You can't rehash the past, or say you're sorry. You can't even tell them you're mad.

My ex-wife used to imply she knew what my dad would want or do even though she never met him. She felt permission to say things like, "What would your dad think?" in this tone like she knew the answer.

---

from: jademassey@yahoo.com
to: smith@simonyi.com
date: Sun, Sep 6 at 2:15 PM
subject: re: no subject

That's not the worst part for me. (Isn't THIS a fun conversation!) The worst part for me is thinking about how now she's just a bunch of memories. What happens when they go?

My mother has always been fond of beautiful things. Fashion and makeup are her food and water. After my father died when I was seven and Iris was three, she started working for Winsome Beauty Brands, a pyramid-style marketing enterprise that she diligently rose to the heights of in the late 1980s. By the time I was twelve, she'd been promoted to national director status. As a national director, she was charged with traveling all over the country leading seminars, and of course we were dragged along. For the next six years (ten for Iris) we lived in Ramada Inns. Always Ramada.

Last night I remembered how in the early Ramada Inn days, Iris and I would camp out in ladies' bathrooms at the hotels, or nearby shopping malls—anywhere with public restrooms—and peek over the stalls to watch grown ladies pee. At twelve, I was too old for it and knew it was dumb, but I liked seeing how happy it made Iris to misbehave in this harmless way, how much delight she got out of being naughty.

Once her foot slipped into the toilet, soaking her sneaker and sock. Our mother's temper was our greatest fear. Terrified, we hurried back to our room and tried to blow-dry her sock and shoe. Our mom was freakishly observant, and I was sure she'd notice. At minimum she'd detect the guilt on our faces. But when she jangled in from work, a cloud of perfume as always, she didn't make a single comment or interrogate either of us. We'd gotten away with it. And that night, we were so proud of ourselves. I remember thinking, Iris and I could get by if we ever needed to run away. We could make it as a team.

What happens when I can't remember our shared life anymore? What becomes of it?

---

from: smith@simonyi.com
to: jademassey@yahoo.com
date: Sun, Sep 6 at 2:28 PM
subject: re: no subject

Would it really be so terrible if you forgot the memory where, as a child, you thought you might have to run away?

---

from: jademassey@yahoo.com
to: smith@simonyi.com
date: Sun, Sep 6 at 2:35 PM
subject: re: no subject

You left out the important part—knowing we could survive together.

---

from: smith@simonyi.com
to: jademassey@yahoo.com
date: Sun, Sep 6 at 2:41 PM
subject: re: no subject

You could write them down like she did. I understand what you mean though. I think it's why I kept her stuff in here for months. I didn't want to move it, because once I did, it felt like erasing her from this place.

---

from: jademassey@yahoo.com
to: smith@simonyi.com
date: Sun, Sep 6 at 2:44 PM
subject: re: no subject

"Here"? At work on a Sunday, huh?

---

from: smith@simonyi.com
to: jademassey@yahoo.com
date: Sun, Sep 6 at 3:01 PM
subject: re: no subject

Yeah.

I mean, you've been through this before, right? With your dad?

---

from: jademassey@yahoo.com
to: smith@simonyi.com
date: Sun, Sep 6 at 3:19 PM
subject: re: no subject

Our dad's death was different. Iris doesn't even remember him. I remember him well from when he was alive, but his death I remember mostly in images of my mother grieving. And as the origin of my, shall we say, preoccupation with health concerns (fine, I'll say it: hypochondria).

---

from: smith@simonyi.com
to: jademassey@yahoo.com
date: Sun, Sep 6 at 3:38 PM
subject: re: no subject

I don't know if this happens with your memories of your dad—but I won't have thought about something for years, then out of nowhere it will percolate. I'll find myself smack in the middle of it again.

When I was a kid, my dad warned me that if I forgot to say grace before bed, I'd turn into a cow in my sleep.

"Do you want to wake up a cow?" he'd say, and I'd press my hands together and close my eyes.

My whole childhood I believed that if I didn't pray before I went to sleep, I'd wake up a farm animal. I'd completely forgotten this until last year, when I saw a cow on a billboard in Midtown. I saw that cow, and it returned to me vividly, including the prayer: *Bless my mom. Bless my pop. Grant us mercy until we plop.*

from: jademassey@yahoo.com
to: smith@simonyi.com
date: Sun, Sep 6 at 3:43 PM
subject: re: no subject

Until we *plop*?

You called him Pop? Were you close?

from: smith@simonyi.com
to: jademassey@yahoo.com
date: Sun, Sep 6 at 3:51 PM
subject: re: no subject

No, I called him Dad.

Yeah, it's ridiculous. He wrote it. And was probably drunk when he did.

Were we close? I mean, he was my dad, so sure. But he drove, so he was gone a lot.

from: jademassey@yahoo.com
to: smith@simonyi.com
date: Sun, Sep 6 at 3:54 PM
subject: re: no subject

Drove? Like as a trucker?

from: smith@simonyi.com
to: jademassey@yahoo.com
date: Sun, Sep 6 at 3:55 PM
subject: re: no subject

Yes.

---

from: jademassey@yahoo.com
to: smith@simonyi.com
date: Sun, Sep 6 at 3:58 PM
subject: re: no subject

Oh, gotta run. I have a call about a possible job. I lost track of time!

    Thanks for talking.

---

from: smith@simonyi.com
to: jademassey@yahoo.com
date: Sun, Sep 6 at 3:59
subject: re: no subject

Good luck!

Well, I told my mother I have cancer. My sister made me. She arrives Tuesday.

It has left me thinking about family.

I discovered thrift shops in Somerville, Massachusetts, during my freshman year of college. They were miraculous. I had no idea how I had lived eighteen years without being inside one. I had heard of them, of course. I'd just never been to one, and it was astonishing: you could get barely used, gorgeous items for single digits!

I would cash my paycheck from restocking books at the campus library and go straight to Summer Street Seconds. I bought what I felt like wearing, the things I wasn't allowed to buy as a kid and teenager, things my mother would have vetoed with disgust. I mixed black and brown. I wore hot pink tights. White after Labor Day! Open-toed sandals with "stockings"—lacy ones, no less!

My favorite shoes ever were a pair of violet kitten-heel boo-ties that I wore on my first college date. He was my Philosophy 101 TA, a senior. He had eyelashes so long that one girl changed sections because she claimed she got dizzy whenever she looked at him. He called me quirky, and said he had assumed from my style that I was gay. He smoked Black & Milds and didn't believe in a distinction between art and life. He explained postmodernism to me like this: *The Simpsons*. I pretended to un-derstand. Our mom had not allowed us to watch *The Simpsons*, as she felt it "glorified mediocrity." Also, that Bart disrespected his parents—"Honor thy father and mother" was one of her fa-vorite lines of scripture.

Those heels stayed with me for eight years. I wore them studying abroad in Paris, walking through the Latin Quarter, pretending to be French. As a consultant, I wore them to bars and clubs and rooftop parties in Manhattan and Brooklyn. When I was twenty-six, they finally wore out. The heel snapped, and the cobbler on Flatbush Avenue near my apartment scoffed at my plea to save them.

"These shoes were not made to last this long," he said in a thick Italian accent. "You have done more in them than they were meant for already."

But my love of thrift shops did not subside. One afternoon a few years ago, I wandered into a Goodwill to browse. In the corner, I found a pile of camouflage bags, stuffed full and worn. The bags, a troubled Goodwill employee told me softly, were the unclaimed belongings of soldiers who had died while deployed. They were unclaimed because there was no one to take their stuff after they were gone. Their last names, as always, were stitched onto the bags in block lettering. She told me this as if she needed to get it off her chest. She wasn't comfortable with the bags being up for grabs like that.

I read through the names, feeling for each one, but the bag I'll never forget, the bag that still haunts me, was the one belonging to W. Shone.

SHONE, W.

Once, he had shone. Now, here he was. The poetry of it broke my heart.

I have a mom. A mom who may hate my sense of fashion, but who is coming on Tuesday nonetheless. I will do my best to remember that there is a kind of blessing in that.

COMMENTS (1):

ChristmasWasMyFavorite: Isn't the past tense of shine SHINED?

MONDAY, SEPTEMBER 7

from: carl@simonyi.com
to: smith@simonyi.com
date: Mon, Sep 7 at 9:18 AM
subject: Hi! Please Do NOT Take Personally

Happy Labor Day from Montauk!

I forgot that sand makes me anxious, so I've retreated to a café to familiarize myself with our client list. Question: is this a *normal* number of clients who aren't making us any money? I am confused about how this industry works. It seems like we have a lot of clients who are dormant, and very few who are actually worth our time.

I am very excited about our new client Zahara Ferringbottom, however. How does this look for bio copy on our site:

In the lineage of Serbian performance artist Marina Abramović, Zahara Ferringbottom, author of the forthcoming memoir <u>Art Precedes Life</u> and internationally renowned performance artist, relentlessly pursues walls while clad in shapewear. Her work invites the audience to consider how we limit our souls in service *of our bodies. In other words, she wears a leotard and runs at walls . . . and you can't look away.*

See you tomorrow!
CVS

---

from: smith@simonyi.com
to: carl@simonyi.com
date: Mon, Sep 7 at 9:24 AM
subject: re: Hi! Please Do NOT Take Personally

Doesn't she run UP walls?

I don't know what list or other records you took with you to Montauk, but a reminder (again) not to take documents from the office, please?

To your question, we're definitely in a bit of a slump, yes.

---

from: carl@simonyi.com
to: smith@simonyi.com
date: Mon, Sep 7 at 9:30 AM
subject: re: Hi! Please Do NOT Take Personally

Her publicist wrote "up" walls, but I figured that was a typo because of gravity.

As for the slump, perhaps it would be useful to revisit this idea of renaming.

What about: RAISIN' BRAND

---

from: smith@simonyi.com
to: carl@simonyi.com
date: Mon, Sep 7 at 9:31 AM
subject: re: Hi! Please Do NOT Take Personally

No puns, remember?

It's a good idea to check on the ZF question later this week.

---

from: contact@lassimariset.com
to: smith@simonyi.com
date: Mon, Sep 7 at 10:19 AM
subject: re: Congratulations!

---

can u get me on tv or . . .

---

from: jademassey@yahoo.com
to: smith@simonyi.com
date: Mon, Sep 7 at 10:20 AM
subject: no subject

Do you think it's stupid that I quit my job?

---

from: smith@simonyi.com
to: jademassey@yahoo.com
date: Mon, Sep 7 at 10:55 AM
subject: re: no subject

I'm not sure I know enough about the situation to weigh in.

---

from: jademassey@yahoo.com
to: smith@simonyi.com
date: Mon, Sep 7 at 11:18 AM
subject: re: no subject

You know that I was a chef at a Michelin restaurant. Two star. Which I left without another job to replace it. To spend some time with my mom, who isn't like yours. My mom can walk, and feed herself, and even drive. She'd manage without me.

I mean, she'd struggle.

You deal with careers, right? Do you think it was stupid?

---

from: smith@simonyi.com
to: jademassey@yahoo.com
date: Mon, Sep 7 at 11:40 AM
subject: re: no subject

It was bold. Rash, perhaps. But you're obviously talented. You'll land on your feet.

---

from: jademassey@yahoo.com
to: smith@simonyi.com
date: Mon, Sep 7 at 11:44 AM
subject: re: no subject

My mother and I don't even get along.

---

from: smith@simonyi.com
to: jademassey@yahoo.com
date: Mon, Sep 7 at 12:00 PM
subject: re: no subject

Oh? Why is that?

---

from: jademassey@yahoo.com
to: smith@simonyi.com
date: Mon, Sep 7 at 12:05 PM
subject: re: no subject

Did Iris talk about her?

---

from: smith@simonyi.com
to: jademassey@yahoo.com
date: Mon, Sep 7 at 12:06 PM
subject: re: no subject

Not much. No, really not ever, actually.

---

from: jademassey@yahoo.com
to: smith@simonyi.com
date: Mon, Sep 7 at 12:40 PM
subject: re: no subject

Let me think of an example.

Okay, the reason we lived in Ramada Inns specifically is because my mom's boyfriend—the one she had after our father died—owned a slew of them, and so we lived there for free. His name was Donovan, he was married, and she would fly out to LA once a month for a weekend to visit him. Sometimes he would come visit us in one of the towns where we were living, but he wouldn't stay at the Ramada. Mom would leave us there and go meet him at a Hilton or a Hyatt or a W, or some hotel we didn't know the name of. We just knew it was fancier.

Those weekends, Iris and I would dress up in her clothes and put her makeup on each other. This wasn't out of admiration. It was a game: who could make the other one look the most like her, strike the closest balance of gaudy and clownish, apply the bright fuchsia lipstick outside the lines of the lips in the precise way that she did to "enhance" the shape of "the lip," mimic the orange streaks of blush on the cheeks just under the bones (early contouring—if you know what that is—though not called that then, and definitely the wrong shade for it). After you finished applying makeup on your subject, you spun her around to face the mirror, and she would give you a ranking from one to ten. Ten meant you looked just like our mom. One would mean you looked nothing like her, but we never gave ones, or anything lower than a six for that matter.

Then we'd pretend to be her, prancing around the room casting about insults, complaining about the quality of the food and the watered-down iced tea. ("This watery tea is inexcusable!" she'd exclaim at the counter of a Wendy's, as if it were the Rainbow Room.) We'd laugh our faces off and then try to find free Pay-Per-View on TV. (Occasionally, the Ramada rooms in those days had cable that had been misconfigured such that the porn channels would come through in patches here and there.)

Then we'd take off the makeup and dresses and pantyhose, and return everything to its proper place, double- and triple-checking to make sure we'd put everything back in its exact spot, carefully removing any of our strands of hair from her brush, all within at least an hour before she was due to come home (though she never did, not those nights), just in case, for once, she kept her promise and returned. We would close the door behind us quietly and retire in one of our rooms, usually mine, where we'd find a movie on TBS or a talk show and leave the TV blaring until we fell asleep in the same double bed. In every hotel in those years, even when we got our own rooms, we only ever slept in one room, in one bed.

One time, she came home early. Way early. By her smeared mascara, I gathered that she and Donovan had had a fight. When she walked in, Iris had one leg in her pantyhose, one leg out, and I was zipping up a pencil skirt. She beat us with her hairbrush.

She's not as bad now. Not nearly. She hasn't been for years, since Iris and I both moved away. But of course I have resentment from childhood, yada yada.

---

from: smith@simonyi.com
to: jademassey@yahoo.com
date: Mon, Sep 7 at 12:54 PM
subject: re: no subject

I understand. I also grew up in an abusive household.

---

from: jademassey@yahoo.com
to: smith@simonyi.com
date: Mon, Sep 7 at 1:20 PM
subject: re: no subject

Whoa, there. I don't know if I'd call it abuse (or a household, for that matter). The hairbrush thing was . . . it was what it was. She wasn't typically physical. So at least, not in that sense.

Emotionally, maybe. Our mom thought it was "creepy" that we always shared a bed.

"Girls, that's creepy," she'd say over a Styrofoam cup of hotel-lobby coffee as we followed her out to the car, our book bags dangling from our right shoulders. (Carrying a book bag on one shoulder, as opposed to on both, was in style in those days in most towns, though not all of them; you couldn't be sure if the one-shoulder hang was going to be in or out, so you had to study the crowd from a distance on your first day and switch it up if you'd bet wrong.) "You're both teenagers. Sleep in your own beds."

But Iris wasn't a teenager, yet. I would wonder if my mom just forgot. Once, I dared to remind her: Iris was twelve.

"I'm rounding," she said. From then on, she rounded Iris's age up, I guess to prove herself right.

So yeah, maybe.

The weird thing is—since Iris died, she's been completely different in a way that is alarming. I mean, I don't want her to be *mean*. But she's not herself, and not just in the sense that she's suddenly scribbling notes in the margins of her Bible. She's this ghost of a person who just moves about with no opinions on anything. She lets me make all the decisions. She checks out. I have to repeat myself several times to get a response from her. Last week, the cat ate half of her plate of spaghetti while she was sitting there, and she didn't notice until he started puking it up on the table. I came out of my room to find Mistoffelees hacking up a hairball covered in tomato sauce while my mom wondered aloud why the hairball was red. I actually find myself missing the old her.

from: jademassey@yahoo.com
to: smith@simonyi.com
date: Mon, Sep 7 at 1:30 PM
subject: re: no subject

God, I just realized I must sound terrible. Your mom is paralyzed and I'm complaining about how mine gets easily distracted and is much nicer than she used to be.

from: smith@simonyi.com
to: jademassey@yahoo.com
date: Mon, Sep 7 at 1:35 PM
subject: re: no subject

Apples and oranges. I'm not offended.

from: jademassey@yahoo.com
to: smith@simonyi.com
date: Mon, Sep 7 at 1:46 PM
subject: re: no subject

So you *don't* think I'm stupid for quitting necessarily? As a data point, I also didn't get along very well with the head chef.

from: smith@simonyi.com
to: jademassey@yahoo.com
date: Mon, Sep 7 at 1:52 PM
subject: re: no subject

I suppose my first question is, can you afford to be unemployed? I'm assuming the answer is yes.

from: jademassey@yahoo.com
to: smith@simonyi.com
date: Mon, Sep 7 at 2:04 PM
subject: re: no subject

For now. I have savings. And Iris left me hers, not that I would dip into that unless it was for something really important.

from: smith@simonyi.com
to: jademassey@yahoo.com
date: Mon, Sep 7 at 2:18 PM
subject: re: no subject

Honestly? I think it's nice you are devoted to your mom despite the fact that it isn't easy. So devoted that you quit your job. I admire it.

from: jademassey@yahoo.com
to: smith@simonyi.com
date: Mon, Sep 7 at 2:37 PM
subject: re: no subject

If I didn't, I'm afraid I'd regret it.

from: smith@simonyi.com
to: jademassey@yahoo.com
date: Mon, Sep 7 at 2:56 PM
subject: re: no subject

I'm not sure I believe in regret. Everyone has regret, but that doesn't mean the choices we made were mistakes, or that we even could have acted differently. It just means we look back and *feel* like we could have.

I think regretting is a way to believe (incorrectly) that we have control over life. We get to feel like if we had done something differently, things might have turned out better. But that's just as easily not the case. Maybe if we'd done something different, things would be even worse.

---

from: jademassey@yahoo.com
to: smith@simonyi.com
date: Mon, Sep 7 at 2:59 PM
subject: re: no subject

Okay, fine. But you also care for your mom.

---

from: smith@simonyi.com
to: jademassey@yahoo.com
date: Mon, Sep 7 at 3:19 PM
subject: re: no subject

I haven't seen her in four years.

---

from: jademassey@yahoo.com
to: smith@simonyi.com
date: Mon, Sep 7 at 3:20 PM
subject: re: no subject

Wait, really?

---

from: smith@simonyi.com
to: jademassey@yahoo.com
date: Mon, Sep 7 at 3:22 PM
subject: re: no subject

Yeah.

from: jademassey@yahoo.com
to: smith@simonyi.com
date: Mon, Sep 7 at 3:30 PM
subject: re: no subject

What's the deal? You don't get along?

from: smith@simonyi.com
to: jademassey@yahoo.com
date: Mon, Sep 7 at 3:48 PM
subject: re: no subject

Not that. She was a good mom. The kind who made me pancakes in the shape of snowmen for no reason. When I turned sixteen, despite the fact that I'd hardly ever talked to a girl for longer than ten seconds, she slid a condom into my wallet "just in case." But the accident didn't just break her back. It affected her brain (though the doctors claim it didn't, they are wrong). It made her feistier, I guess is how I'd put it. More irritable. She is quicker to anger. Long story short, we haven't been as close in a while.

from: jademassey@yahoo.com
to: smith@simonyi.com
date: Mon, Sep 7 at 3:50 PM
subject: re: no subject

Did you say she's paralyzed?

---

from: smith@simonyi.com
to: jademassey@yahoo.com
date: Mon, Sep 7 at 3:52 PM
subject: re: no subject

She is quadriplegic.

---

from: jademassey@yahoo.com
to: smith@simonyi.com
date: Mon, Sep 7 at 3:54 PM
subject: re: no subject

God, that's sad. I'd be angry, too.

That must be so depressing for you to watch. Is that why you don't go see her?

Gotta run—have a consultation with a med mal lawyer about Iris. Talk later!

---

from: smith@simonyi.com
to: jademassey@yahoo.com
date: Mon, Sep 7 at 3:55 PM
subject: re: no subject

And I should probably get some work done today now that we've spent the majority of it rehashing our childhoods.

---

from: jademassey@yahoo.com
to: smith@simonyi.com
date: Mon, Sep 7 at 3:56 PM
subject: re: no subject

Working on Saturday *and* on Labor Day? Lawyers are one thing, but I didn't know the world of branding was so intense . . .

---

from: smith@simonyi.com
to: jademassey@yahoo.com
date: Mon, Sep 7 at 4:08 PM
subject: re: no subject

Ha. Well, I have nothing else to do.

Hey—do you want to have dinner tomorrow? No pressure. I know you're not into publishing your sister's blog, but maybe we could talk about ways we could honor her memory in some other way. (To be clear so that it's not awkward, not as a date.)

---

from: jademassey@yahoo.com
to: smith@simonyi.com
date: Mon, Sep 7 at 4:27 PM
subject: re: no subject

Sure. I don't know what that would be. It's not like we're going to erect a statue or something. (Thanks for not pushing me more on the blog, by the way. I'm relieved that's off the table.)

I'm also fine just talking about Iris with someone else who misses her. That sounds kind of nice.

But I can't do dinner. I don't eat at restaurants. Unless it's dim sum. Sorry. I'll be too distracted assessing the food to be a good dinner partner.

Maybe we could just go on a walk on the High Line or something? I'm trying to get out into nature more. (High Line = New York version of nature.)

---

from: smith@simonyi.com
to: jademassey@yahoo.com
date: Mon, Sep 7 at 4:33 PM
subject: re: no subject

A walk it is.

Richie and I decided to go upstate this weekend, and as a life-time New Yorker who grew up jumping turnstiles in the Bronx, he doesn't drive—never even got his license. So today I had to renew mine, which I'd let expire because I also don't drive in New York. (The irony of needing to renew my license right now I won't even bother to point out.)

I was in line at the DMV and cranky like everyone else. It didn't help that the guy in front of me was getting a vanity plate, and couldn't understand the process for doing so.

The DMV employee was telling him he had to submit up to three choices, and this confused him. He didn't understand if that meant he could submit only one, or if he *had* to submit three.

"So I can submit one?"

"No, three."

"You said up to three."

"You can submit one, but you may not get it. Write down your choices here." She slid a piece of paper to him through the window. The woman behind me cursed under her breath, and I consciously fought turning around to commiserate. I took a deep breath as the man wrote on the paper and then slid it back under the window.

"Sir, I said eight characters."

"Oh, come on!" another man hollered from several feet back. But then he started to count his letters, saying them out loud.

"F."

"O."

"R."

"G."

"I."

"V."

"E."

"M."

"E . . . oh. That's nine."

Then he said, how about the number 4? 4-give-me. She typed for a second, consulted the screen, and told him it was taken. So was 4giveMe with no spaces. She offered 4giveYou, 4giveUs, or 4giveme with 3s for the E's. She wrote it down for him.

"That doesn't look right to me," he said, and the guy behind me yelled "Come on!" again. The man interested in forgiveness finally seemed to understand that the people behind him had grown impatient.

"How about 4giveRJ?" he said. It was available.

COMMENTS (1):

BigJessBarbs: Fun Fact: If you write "I am a horrible person with no
interpersonal skills" on the DMV application, you automatically
get the job!

TUESDAY, SEPTEMBER 8

from: Chad Wotherspoon
to: carl@simonyi.com; smith@simonyi.com
cc: Todd Kohlstedt
date: Tue, Sep 8 at 9:03 AM
subject: re: Copyright Inquiry re: blogs on site

Dear Carl et al,

AMAZING that we're hearing from you on this. Amazing.

No, she didn't sign anything; we ask our contributors solely for license to publish their content on our site. However, her blog was actually just pulled by our new marketing gal Margaux as a potential part of an upcoming promo campaign, so it's serendipitous you reached out! We couldn't find a contact for her, which was a real downer because we need to make sure *we* have the copyright to reproduce it as an e-book for download! Ironies.

Might you be able to put us in touch with next of kin? Was she married? Kids?

Cheers,

Chad

from: carl@simonyi.com
to: Chad Wotherspoon
cc: Todd Kohlstedt; smith@simonyi.com
date: Tue, Sep 8 at 9:14 AM
subject: re: Copyright Inquiry re: blogs on site

Hi Chad,

What an utterly exciting and record speed response!

She died without a husband or kids, but we are in touch with her sister, so checking with her should not be a problem. Smith, thoughts?

More soon,

CVS

from: smith@simonyi.com
to: carl@simonyi.com
date: Tue, Sep 8 at 9:31 AM
subject: no subject

Carl, I just wanted you to stealthily figure it out, not alert them.

from: carl@simonyi.com
to: smith@simonyi.com
date: Tue, Sep 8 at 9:40 AM
subject: re: no subject

Wait, what about this isn't great?

---

from: smith@simonyi.com
to: carl@simonyi.com
date: Tue, Sep 8 at 10:18 AM
subject: re: no subject

I don't know. It feels different. Icky in some way.

---

from: Chad Wotherspoon
to: carl@simonyi.com; smith@simonyi.com
cc: Todd Kohlstedt
date: Tue, Sep 8 at 1:21 PM
subject: re: Copyright Inquiry re: blogs on site

Super! It's a bit late because the others are scheduled to go to press at the end of the month, but we can push it through if we enter it into Habitat soon—can Daryl's team get on that, Todd? We can go ahead and start production. Smith, I'll take you off from here. We'll work on it with Daryl's team—if you could just handle the IP question by EOB on 10/23 at the latest, that'd be fantastic. Does that give you enough time? I can put you in touch with legal to find out exactly what we need from you.
Cheers,
Chad

---

from: smith@simonyi.com
to: carl@simonyi.com
date: Tue, Sep 8 at 1:25 PM
subject: re: no subject

Carl,
    I'll handle it from here.
Thx.

from: jademassey@yahoo.com
to: donnalionschef@gmail.com
date: Tue, Sep 8 at 1:30 PM
subject: Hello!

Hi Donna!

It's been too long! Hard to believe that it's been twenty years since we were babies just starting school.

How is it going at 85 Cherry? Are you still there?

I left Barn recently and am putting out feelers for what may come next. I'd love to get together for coffee if you have a free moment.

Jade

from: Barnes & Noble [bn.com]
to: jademassey@yahoo.com
date: Tue, Sep 8 at 1:51 PM
subject: Your Order Is on Its Way!

Dear Jade,

The following order(s) has shipped and is on its way:

The Year of Magical Thinking (9.99)

H is for Hawk (12.99)

Grief for Dummies (14.99)

Fertility after 40 (15.99)

The Ghost Womb Myth Revisited (4.99)

Subtotal: $58.95

Visit <u>Order Status</u> to track your order. Thanks for shopping at BarnesandNoble.com!

---

from: HelloCupid
to: jademassey@yahoo.com
date: Tue, Sep 8 at 2:02 PM
subject: SEAFARER1980 is looking at your profile!

JadeJadeJava,

It's been 6 months since you logged in—have you found a match? Let us know! Hearing that we've helped you find love makes our heart go pitter-patter.

And if not, why not come back and visit? People are checking out your profile. Here's a sneak peek at the latest messages you've received:

From SEAFARER1980:

JadeJadeJava,

Nice name. I am, too, a fan of the caffeinated beverage.

A bit about me: I am currently exploring the 112 meditation techniques of Vigyan Bhairav Tantra. Growing my law practice keeps me busy, but I'm always down for exploring ancient spiritual systems.

Speaking of, I like sex—and I don't just mean the act but also the nuances of it, the power exchange that makes people crazy, the quid pro quo.

Shoot me a message if you are intrigued . . .

From DAWGONNIT:

sup

ps write me back if you want a real man and WILLNT USE ME FOR FREE RIDES IT WILLNT WORK

Tuesday, September 8
TherapistAwayNetwork™
Patient Name: Jade Renee Massey
AUTO PROMPT: **What secret question do you hold?**

Tonight I am taking a walk with my sister's former boss, but I need to be certain that it's not a date. He says it's not.

Smith is pleasant enough to talk to. But if I recall correctly, he is short, so it wouldn't work out anyway. Plus I haven't even seen his hands. They could be monstrous.

All of this—and something else. I reached out to Henry today. I know. But I wanted to ask him about whether he thought I have a case against Iris's doctor. He suggested that I drop it and move on, which, if I'd thought about it for five seconds, I could have predicted. He's a doctor, so of course he is going to be on the side of medicine. Like you would be, I imagine, if you were here. Actually, if you were here, you'd say: Why did you *actually* email Henry?

I don't know. Partly what I just wrote. But I guess I also . . . why do I feel like I'm supposed to tell him that I might have a date with someone? It's not a date. Even *Smith* said it's not a date. And I'm not with Henry anymore. There is no reason to think I need to talk to him first. I owe him no heads-up. I don't want to be with Henry anymore . . . do I?

∎

Dear JADE,

Thank you for your submission to TAN™. We will make sure your provider receives this message.

Did you know "secret" is derived from the Latin *secretus*, meaning "separate" or "apart"? When we hold secrets from others, we are keeping them at a distance. Sometimes, by exploring the nature of that distance, we can figure out how it is serving us. Once we understand its purpose, we can ask ourselves—am I still the person I was? Do I really need this secret any longer?

TAN™ is not to be used in case of emergency. If you are in crisis, call 9-1-1.

Sincerely,

Your friends at TAN

---

from: smith@simonyi.com
to: iris@simonyi.com
date: Tue, Sep 8 at 11:59 PM
subject: no subject

Emailing you at your work email since your sister is apparently dipping into your Gmail.

I spent some time with her tonight. Based on her emails, I got the impression that in person she'd be chatty and open, but when she showed up, she was guarded and on edge. (It may have been because she was flustered. I'd suggested we meet at the corner of Twenty-Third and Tenth since she'd be taking the PATH train in from Jersey, but she'd thought I'd said Twenty-Fifth and waited there for fifteen minutes before rechecking her email.)

We met at five. It was a hot day for September, and she kept her arms crossed for the first half hour or so of our walk along the Hudson. But as I spoke about you, she began to relax. Not like it made her happy to discuss you, more like it reminded her that she was sad, and she forgot to be as closed off.

She told me that in the boxes of your things from work she'd found a scarf that belonged to Daniel—evident because his name was stamped on the tag like a child's. She wondered if you'd kept it because you intended to give it back, or because of nostalgia. I told her I'd seen you wear it regularly in the winter, and maybe you simply liked that it was a well-made scarf.

I told her I'd set up you and Richie, and that he was my first roommate in New York. I found myself telling her how he used to sneak into NYU real estate classes to learn how to be a broker until he became one. She looked skeptical, but then when I told her about the coffee sleeves venture and making a killing, she seemed less so. She liked the part about them being environmental.

"He is not who I'd have thought she'd like," she said, "but she seemed to enjoy him." She suggested that sisters never think the men their sisters choose are good enough. (I wasn't sure if she knew about your feelings toward her ex-husband, which of course fall in line with her theory, so I didn't mention them.) I felt a little defensive of Richie. I told her that whatever it was you and Richie had there at the end, you did one over on him. That he spent a full month after you died cocooned on my couch.

"It hasn't been easy for anyone, I guess," she said.

Jade is preoccupied with not forgetting you, worried that she won't remember who you were. In an attempt to reassure her, I said, "Look at how much Iris managed to recall about the past, including the distant past, when she sat down to write. Jade didn't like this."

"Can we not talk about the blog?" she said. "I'm working on feeling better, not worse." She laughed. It seemed forced.

I told her I don't find it sad. I asked if that's why she doesn't want it published.

She said, "We're not ready," meaning, I assume, her and your mom. I dropped it.

She asked more about my business, what I do day to day, and I got the sense that her questioning was more about you than me. She wanted to learn what your daily life had been like.

I didn't plan to spend six hours roaming southern Manhattan with your sister, but neither of us made a move to leave until she started falling asleep on a bench in Union Square Park. The first hour we spent talking about you, but then we turned to other things. Our marriages. Our childhoods.

When I described the night as "shiny," she called me poetic. I've never been called poetic before.

She asked me at some point what my vice is. Maybe because she told me hers is working too hard and drinking red wine, I actually told her the truth. I gamble. (I told her I haven't in a while. I didn't say: a week ago.)

She asked if I do it every day.

I said no, mainly during a crisis. When things are already going badly.

"That makes sense," she said, which surprised me, because it never made sense to me at all. Why on earth would that make sense? "If things are already bad, you blow things up so they can't get worse." A fog had settled around us, which made the West Village streets feel like a stage with no one on it but us.

I like her, Iris. Is it because she reminds me enough of you that it feels familiar? Or could it be more?

At your funeral, the only other time I've ever seen her, I was struck by the way she commanded the room, her generous energy as she hosted people like it was a dinner party. She appeared a person who takes charge.

But I'm seeing another side of her now. She is afraid. She's searching. And she misses you more than she thinks she lets on.

Tuesday, September 8
TherapistAwayNetwork™
Patient Name: Jade Renee Massey

UPDATE to Most Recent Post. *Please enter additional text below. It will appear at the bottom of your post.*

His hands are fine.

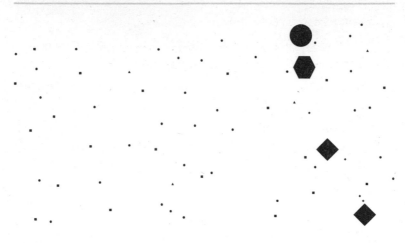

THE DANIEL DOTS

At night my dreams take me places I can no longer go in real life. I am with Daniel again. He is lying next to me, spindly and warm. In last night's dream, I used to be sick but now am not, and we are relieved, and we are in love again. Even in the dream, I scold myself: *Things will shift. It is never too good for too long.* But my reservation scatters and fades while the thing that sticks, that weighs me down upon waking, sweaty against my pillow, is the loss.

In the morning light the ache lingers. The cruelty isn't that it's fantasy, but that it's over. I am hungover from a recollection.

Does time forget to put a check on our dreaming? I haven't been with Daniel in three years, can safely say I haven't loved him in nearly two, but last night, I did, and so this morning, I feel the sting of loss again.

Sometimes I wonder how much of this is my cancer mind, my neurons scrambling to make sense of what is happening as malignancy ravages me from the inside out and the drugs ravage me from the outside in.

When I was younger and stupider and loved him despite the signs I shouldn't . . . well, I have done a fine job of writing off that gal as a fool, and in turn, how I felt about him. He didn't deserve my love. Once I figured that out, I scrubbed it clean from my heart. It took time, of course. But sometimes, after I've closed my eyes, the love comes back in full. I awake with the heart of that girl, swollen with hope and belief in a soul she fears will never belong to her completely, which only makes her want it more.

It didn't go as planned.

Daniel was at the foot of our bed wearing my one-piece, palm trees stretched over his rippled chest, distorted.

"What do you think?" he asked. We were packing for a trip to the beach with my friend Sabine and her husband, and my antidepressant had assembled twenty pounds onto my butt, thighs, and stomach, hence the purchase of the conservative, ruffled one-piece, a hideous tribute to the tropics that I only bought because it was the most flattering among the selection at Macy's, and there was no way I was going to a *second* store to stare at my pale, dimpled skin under fluorescent lighting. Apparently, the swimsuit I selected also fit my boyfriend.

"It looks better on you. Great," I said.

"I guess I'm wearing it, then, and you're wearing mine." He threw his bright green surf shorts at me. I batted them away and pulled the sheet up around my thighs. Then he was on top of me, pushing his shorts onto me over the lacy underwear I still wore in those days before I realized that my thumbs are too opposable to wear lacy underwear without ripping holes in it. He pulled the swim trunks up my legs all the way to my waist as I fought, wriggling and winded and hideously conscious of every roll, every lump of flesh. Finally I gave in, a limp seal. My nightgown was twisted around my breasts, and his shorts tangled up in my legs.

"I'm out of breath from four seconds of exercise," I said, panting.

"You put up a good fight," he said from behind me.

I started to cry.

"What's so funny?" he asked, then realized I wasn't laughing.

"Hey," he said, pinching my ass. "You are beautiful." And I cried more because he was being so sweet, but mostly because I felt fat.

Three years later, I was hunched over a toilet in Café Frida west of Central Park. My crinkly peach wedding dress, vintage from a secondhand store on MacDougal, was all bunched up in Sabine's hands as I vomited mucus. Clutching it, she kept telling me to be careful, like I could control the trajectory of my bile.

I was to marry Daniel in a couple of hours because I loved him enough to get married. Loved him so much, in fact, that I was marrying him despite the arguing.

We hadn't gone a day without a fight that I could remember. We'd been to therapy. We'd been on a couples' retreat where we stared into each other's eyes, not blinking, for long stretches. We'd traded a journal back and forth in which we wrote each other letters in an attempt to cut through our defense mechanisms. We set aside one day a week where we were only allowed to enjoy each other's company: Fridays were for being happy; no arguments allowed. Like addicts, we never once made it through a Friday without spiraling into heated tension.

We could scream for hours, tormenting neighbors I'm sure. We were so adept at pressing each other's buttons, we were like two organists playing each other with all four limbs, blasting furious energy through empty space at a moment's notice. We were wildly in love, and because of it, we made each other miserable. It was my wedding day, and I was as sad as I'd ever been.

Plus—and this I never told a soul—I'd begun having feelings for someone else, someone who didn't drain me. It was new, and nothing, but enough of a contrast that I wondered: maybe there's a better way.

Sabine helped me up, and we backed out of the stall. She checked for spots and pronounced me clean. I washed my hands. We made eye contact in the mirror. She asked my mirror self if I was okay. My mirror self nodded, yes.

She gave my mirror self a weird look.

"What are you doing?" I asked.

"I'm sending you a message with my eyes," she said.

"It's not translating," I said.

"You can back out. It's not too late."

She laid out how it would happen. I would tell Daniel that I wasn't ready, that I needed to postpone. She was careful not to use the words "cancel" or "break up." She would tell the guests that I wasn't feeling well enough for the ceremony. I didn't have to face anyone but him. It didn't have to be a humiliating nightmare.

Hearing it spelled out like that, I could picture it, and it wasn't insurmountable. Perhaps if I'd had to face our friends and family members (only twenty or so of them, but still), I'd have been too afraid. But Sabine's offer to handle the logistics, via a watered-down version of the truth that I could wrap my mind around, allowed my gut to prevail. And so I did it. I fucking backed out of my wedding on my wedding day. Like some goddamn Lifetime movie.

It was strangely seamless. Sabine told the guests to go home. Later I slept in her bed, in her pajamas. I had spread my dress neatly across her love seat, as if I might wear it again one day.

Emotionally, however, it was worse than I could have imagined. Later that week, sharing the last meal I'd ever have with Daniel, I wondered, as I would again and again, how I'd ever feel anything but sorrow over choosing not to be with the person I loved most in the world.

It wasn't ever cracked

I had to pull it apart

like the saddest fucking
wishbone ever

COMMENTS (3):

BonnieD: :(

ChristmasWasMyFavorite: You should write a romance novel!

BigJessBarbs: News Alert!!! Men you didn't marry don't matter at
the end of your life, sweetheart!

WEDNESDAY, SEPTEMBER 9

from:	winsomebeautydorothy@hotmail.com
to:	Junior League Singers Full List
date:	Wed, Sep 9 at 5:17 AM
subject:	"Hands that Work, Hearts Full of Joy" Concert Follow-up + Some News

Dearest Fellow Singers,

Congratulations on a truly spectacular performance at the Evergreen Community's Labor Day "Hands that Work, Hearts Full of Joy" on Monday. Judith, our contact at Evergreen, called me this morning to let me know that the residents are still talking about how much they enjoyed hearing the love songs of their youth, which they seldom get to experience in their golden years. Bernice's solo in "I Could Write a Book" was of particular charm to several of the more senior gentlemen. I understand that Judith has received a handful of requests for Bernice to be invited back soon! Just wait until they hear your sheep solo in "Christmas Barnyard Sampler" come the holidays!

And now this email takes a turn, for I have a favor I must ask as director of the Gray Lady Chorus. My eldest daughter (the former chef) is arriving back into town today. I would appreciate your patience at choir practice tomorrow evening, as she does seem to enjoy attending our rehearsals when she is visiting. I understand that some of us, particularly Loretta and Eunice, are not crazy about having an audience when we are in the "learning" stage of our music, but my daughter is single (at thirty-seven), unemployed, suffering from a jaundiced complexion, and in need of positive female role models such as yourselves. I do not imagine it will be forever, but for the immediate future I just need to remind myself that she is trying to feel useful, and allow her to be a "help." Your cooperation is greatly appreciated!

In other news, KellyAnne Smithies has volunteered to host this year's fall cookie baking party. Thank you, KellyAnne!

Sincerely,

Dorothy

---

from: gamblersanon.com
to: smithsimonyi@gmail.com
date: Wed, Sep 9 at 7:03 AM
subject: You're on a streak

Dear Smith,

You have attended Online GA Meetings 7 days in a row.

That's a winning streak. Keep up the good work, and reap benefits you didn't know were possible.

On your team every step of the way,

Gamblers Anonymous

---

from: smith@simonyi.com
to: Airbnb GUEST EMAIL
date: Wed, Sep 9 at 7:30 AM
subject: re: BOOKING EXTENSION INQUIRY for Thurs, Sept 10—Mon, Sep 14

Hi Travel Man2,

I'm glad to hear that you're enjoying New York enough that you want to extend your stay! You're welcome to stay in my apartment through Monday. One favor—if anyone asks, please just tell them you're my cousin. Just gets a little messy with the co-op board sometimes.

Best,

Smith Simonyi

---

from: carl@simonyi.com
to: zaharaferringbottom@zaharaferringbottom.com
date: Wed, Sep 9 at 9:05 AM
subject: Clarification

Dear Zahara,

My name is Carl and I'm assistant to Smith. I am writing to clarify a preposition for your biography, which I'd like to post on the Clients page of our site.

Do you run UP walls or AT walls? I'm having difficulty tracking down this information, since your performances are undocumented and no one at MoMA PS1 will get back to me. It *does* seem like an important distinction.

Thanks in advance,

CVS

from: jademassey@yahoo.com
to: smith@simonyi.com
date: Wed, Sep 9 at 9:42 AM
subject: ☺

Good morning.

from: smith@simonyi.com
to: jademassey@yahoo.com
date: Wed, Sep 9 at 9:50 AM
subject: re: ☺

Good morning.

from: jademassey@yahoo.com
to: smith@simonyi.com
date: Wed, Sep 9 at 9:51 AM
subject: re: ☺

Best memory. Go!

from: jademassey@yahoo.com
to: smith@simonyi.com
date: Wed, Sep 9 at 11:02 AM
subject: re: ☺

Don't think so hard. Some of us don't* have all day.

*Do, but who's checking?

---

from: smith@simonyi.com
to: jademassey@yahoo.com
date: Wed, Sep 9 at 11:04 AM
subject: re: ☺

My best one is tied up with a bad one is the problem.

---

from: jademassey@yahoo.com
to: smith@simonyi.com
date: Wed, Sep 9 at 11:05 AM
subject: re: ☺

Of course it is.

---

from: smith@simonyi.com
to: jademassey@yahoo.com
date: Wed, Sep 9 at 11:11 AM
subject: re: ☺

What does that mean?

---

from: jademassey@yahoo.com
to: smith@simonyi.com
date: Wed, Sep 9 at 11:12 AM
subject: re: ☺

You're a bit of a pessimist is all. Best/worst memory, go!

from: smith@simonyi.com
to: jademassey@yahoo.com
date: Wed, Sep 9 at 12:29 PM
subject: re: ☺

All right, here goes. For a while, my dad drove for a company called FasTrans. But the summer before I started second grade, Oscar Mayer, which was based in Madison, expanded its Wienermobile fleet, and my dad became one of a hundred hotdoggers hired to drive the wieners around the Midwest. As a kid I thought it was the coolest thing, of course. For the last three weeks before the start of the school year, he and I handed out wiener whistles (plastic whistles that, you guessed it, were shaped like wieners) at diners, Wal-Marts, 7-Elevens. I was living with my dad in a wiener with a RELSHME plate! I missed my mom, of course, but it was all so new and adventurous that I didn't think of her much. We were just two guys having a blast, living in a hot dog. I'd never been happier.

Then one day I woke up to a man angrily knocking on the window. We weren't supposed to be living in the wiener. My dad told me to clean up the inside, then climbed out and shut the door. While I gathered up scratch-offs and napkins and rock-hard stray French fries in the grocery bag we used for trash, the man yelled at him. My dad stood next to the car in the parking lot of the rest stop, taking it, while I walked the bag of trash across the lot to a dumpster. I understood that what we'd done was shameful because we'd done it to save money.

I found a spot on the curb on the other side of the lot, and as I shimmied the change I'd collected from the wiener in the belly of my T-shirt, I dreamed of hurling it in the man's face. He'd ruined our trip, when all we'd done wrong was sleep.

Driving home, I could tell my dad was embarrassed in front of me. That killed me.

from: jademassey@yahoo.com
to: smith@simonyi.com
date: Wed, Sep 9 at 1:27 PM
subject: re: ☺

Well, I'm glad you have the good part at least? (Not being sarcastic.)

Here's mine. It was a New Year's, and Henry (husband at the time) had insisted we do the "polar plunge": a January 1st collective dip into the Atlantic Ocean at the Jersey Shore with a bunch of other wack jobs who thought this was a good idea.

We'd just run in and run right back out, he said, promising that it would be thrilling and a hearty shock to the circulatory system.

So we drove to the shore wearing our swimsuits under our layers of winter clothes. It was icy even in the car, in the dry heat. For the full hour-long drive I dreaded the "plunge" part, but once we arrived, the energy of the crowd gathered on the beach was infectious.

"One, two, three, go!" a thick, beer-gutted man hollered, and over a hundred of us, middle-aged adults mostly, ripped off our coats and pants and sweaters and socks. In a mad dash we rushed into the surf. Some, including Henry, immediately ducked their heads under, but I hurried in only up to my waist and splashed water onto my chest and arms before darting back onto the sand to fetch my towel.

It was enough. Henry was right—the shock was electric. I ate a hot dog, a delicious hot dog, feeling powerfully, unflappably alive.

It was a great day.

from: smith@simonyi.com
to: jademassey@yahoo.com
date: Wed, Sep 9 at 1:39 PM
subject: re: ☺

You eat hot dogs?

from: jademassey@yahoo.com
to: smith@simonyi.com
date: Wed, Sep 9 at 1:42 PM
subject: re: ☺

Right? I did that day.

from: smith@simonyi.com
to: jademassey@yahoo.com
date: Wed, Sep 9 at 1:46 PM
subject: re: ☺

The reason I told you last night wasn't a date is because in the spring your sister told me you were dating your ex-husband again. I wondered if you still were.

from: jademassey@yahoo.com
to: smith@simonyi.com
date: Wed, Sep 9 at 1:59 PM
subject: re: ☺

That was out of nowhere.

Yes, we were. And Iris would have loved to know it ended. Again. Ended again. She was not a fan, as you probably are aware, since you apparently have heard about him.

---

from: smith@simonyi.com
to: jademassey@yahoo.com
date: Wed, Sep 9 at 2:04 PM
subject: re: ☺

She may have mentioned that she wasn't crazy about Henry 4, as she called him.

---

from: jademassey@yahoo.com
to: smith@simonyi.com
date: Wed, Sep 9 at 2:18 P
subject: re: ☺

Technically he was Henry 3. He was my third Henry to date. But then we broke up for a short time when he felt like he might prefer to date a nurse he worked with, and then changed his mind so we dated again, upon which he became Henry 4. (If you're thinking that I should have seen the pattern, I agree.)

Then we got married, then divorced two years ago. And then, last spring, we briefly dated again. Which I guess would make him also Henry . . . 5?

Let's just say it took me a while to realize it wasn't going to work.

Get this—now he's angling to get together again. Sometimes he does this when he's bored.

I'm surprised to hear that she called him Henry 4. I thought her nickname for him was Only Henry, based on the time he got frustrated at being referred to by her as "Henry 3" and lost his temper.

"There is one Henry now! I am Only Henry!" Iris found the tantrum hilarious.

from: smith@simonyi.com
to: jademassey@yahoo.com
date: Wed, Sep 9 at 2:24 PM
subject: re: ☺

Ah. That explains our favorite drink: the Only Henry, made to perfection by the bartender at Doyle's Bar and Grill on the corner: 1 part whiskey, 2 parts ginger beer, and a squeeze of lime juice. Iris told us she'd invented it but didn't explain the origin of the name.

from: jademassey@yahoo.com
to: smith@simonyi.co
date: Wed, Sep 9 at 2:28 PM
subject: re: ☺

Wow, thanks, sis.

from: smith@simonyi.com
to: jademassey@yahoo.com
date: Wed, Sep 9 at 2:30 PM
subject: re: ☺

Why did you get back together with him so many times?

from: jademassey@yahoo.com
to: smith@simonyi.com
date: Wed, Sep 9 at 2:37 PM
subject: re: ☺

I suppose because I had regrets (even though you don't believe in them ;)). And the regrets made me think I'd made a mistake.

---

from: smith@simonyi.com
to: jademassey@yahoo.com
date: Wed, Sep 9 at 2:39 PM
subject: re: ☺

Is that not what regrets mean? (I do believe they *exist*, I just don't know if we should make decisions in an attempt to avoid future ones.)

---

from: jademassey@yahoo.com
to: smith@simonyi.com
date: Wed, Sep 9 at 3:00 PM
subject: re: ☺

Maybe there's a distinction between regret and nostalgia that I now understand. I miss him sometimes. But that's different from regret. I'm nostalgic for my twenty-three-year-old metabolism, too. Do I wish I was twenty-three again? Lord, no.

Anyway, now that my ex-husband is also my ex-boyfriend, I get to say "How many times does it take a prefix to stick?" That's my new joke.

---

from: smith@simonyi.com
to: jademassey@yahoo.com
date: Wed, Sep 9 at 3:03 PM
subject: re: ☺

Have you considered stand-up?

---

from: jademassey@yahoo.com
to: smith@simonyi.com
date: Wed, Sep 9 at 3:09 PM
subject: re: ☺

Does it pay, and can I start tomorrow?

---

from: smith@simonyi.com
to: jademassey@yahoo.com
date: Wed, Sep 9 at 3:22 PM
subject: re: ☺

Haha. How did it end this last time? With Henry 3/4/5/Only?

---

from: jademassey@yahoo.com
to: smith@simonyi.com
date: Wed, Sep 9 at 3:37 PM
subject: re: ☺

Oh, man. Let's see. Iris had died a week earlier. It was the middle of the night. I was lying next to Henry. And I had the sensation that I'd been falling into a deep well for a long time with him, and that I had just hit the bottom with a thud. I wish I could say it was a dream, but I was awake. And so I couldn't write it off as my asleep brain. I lay there thinking about how I knew everything about him I could know, understood everything we were capable of being. I saw our future stretched out thirty or fifty years, and it was not my future.

I suppose the clinical way of putting it is that we had different ideas of what we wanted out of our lives.

You know I'm about to ask you about your divorce now, right?

---

from: smith@simonyi.com
to: jademassey@yahoo.com
date: Wed, Sep 9 at 3:42 PM
subject: re: ☺

Mine was entirely run-of-the-mill. Woman leaves man because he isn't emotional enough: a classic, cautionary tale.

---

from: jademassey@yahoo.com
to: smith@simonyi.com
date: Wed, Sep 9 at 3:44 PM
subject: re: ☺

All right, I won't press.

---

from: smith@simonyi.com
to: jademassey@yahoo.com
date: Wed, Sep 9 at 3:47 PM
subject: re: ☺

Funny—you and me, both divorced, with no kids and deceased fathers. Real portraits of the American dream.

And Iris, too!

---

from: smith@simonyi.com
to: jademassey@yahoo.com
date: Wed, Sep 9 at 3:48 PM
subject: re: ☺

(Kidding. I think that came across ruder than I intended.)

---

from: jademassey@yahoo.com
to: smith@simonyi.com
date: Wed, Sep 9 at 3:50 PM
subject: re: ☺

I want children. I just wasn't ready before the last year or so, which was a point of contention with Henry. But I've always wanted them. Do you not?

---

from: smith@simonyi.com
to: jademassey@yahoo.com
date: Wed, Sep 9 at 3:53 PM
subject: re: ☺

Depends. Not at the moment, no.

---

from: jademassey@yahoo.com
to: smith@simonyi.com
date: Wed, Sep 9 at 3:56 PM
subject: re: ☺

And Iris wasn't divorced, you realize.

---

from: smith@simonyi.com
to: jademassey@yahoo.com
date: Wed, Sep 9 at 3:59 PM
subject: re: ☺

She left someone at the altar. That's pretty close.

---

from: jademassey@yahoo.com
to: smith@simonyi.com
date: Wed, Sep 9 at 4:01 PM
subject: re: ☺

Were you there for the non-wedding? I don't remember meeting you.

---

from: smith@simonyi.com
to: jademassey@yahoo.com
date: Wed, Sep 9 at 4:11 PM
subject: re: ☺

No. I was wooing a prospective client in Nashville, a singer-songwriter who'd just won a Golden Globe for his score of that TV miniseries *The Underlings*. I really wanted to sign the guy (which didn't happen). And Iris and I had only been working together a year, so I kinda figured she'd invited me out of obligation. The next morning I texted her congrats, and when she didn't respond, I assumed she was having a great time honeymooning in Madrid. I was in Nashville through Monday.

On Tuesday I showed up, and there was a note on my desk. She wrote that she hadn't gone through with it, and so no Spain, but she still needed the couple of weeks off. She didn't respond to my texts later that week, or the following. Two weeks later she was back, saying she didn't want to discuss it.

I always found it odd she came into the office to leave the note instead of just emailing me.

from: jademassey@yahoo.com
to: smith@simonyi.com
date: Wed, Sep 9 at 4:24 PM
subject: re: ☺

I wasn't there, either. I mean, I was *there*—in the park for the wedding. But I wasn't *there* there. I was distracted by some kitchen drama from earlier that morning at the restaurant, wrapped up in my own world. I didn't think to check on Iris beforehand. Until her friend—Nadine, something, maybe?—came out and announced that there would be no wedding, I had been entirely preoccupied. Who knows what the issue even was, surely something to do with my boss, Marcus.

It doesn't surprise me that she left you that note. Was it handwritten? She was oddly fond of handwritten notes.

from: smith@simonyi.com
to: jademassey@yahoo.com
date: Wed, Sep 9 at 4:30 PM
subject: re: ☺

Yes.

from: jademassey@yahoo.com
to: smith@simonyi.com
date: Wed, Sep 9 at 4:53 PM
subject: re: ☺

When she was in sixth grade, we moved midyear (not uncommon for us). We started at a new school just in time for the science fair. The winner got a year of free admission to the science museum, which was a big deal because there was an exhibit where you could make your own candy. Or was it your own soda?

Anyway, Iris really wanted to win, but she was insecure about coming up with a project. She was convinced she'd make a fool of herself. (When you move mid school year as a kid, especially multiple times, there are whole units of knowledge that you miss. In one state, US history is covered in fourth grade, but in another, it's third, and so all the kids already know it—I made it to adulthood thinking the Boston Tea Party was an actual tea party.) It never bothered me that much to be behind in some subjects. We were ahead in others. But Iris got so embarrassed when gaps in her education were exposed—she was always bringing up that she never learned the US presidents, state capitals, or animal classifications, for instance. And this was pre-Internet, so it wasn't like we could just look stuff up. Point is, she wanted me to come up with a science project for her. We made clouds.

And she won!

Which I learned . . . in a handwritten note.

That was the point of this long story.

---

from: smith@simonyi.com
to: jademassey@yahoo.com
date: Wed, Sep 9 at 4:57 PM
subject: re: ☺

What are animal classifications? You *made clouds*?

---

from: jademassey@yahoo.com
to: smith@simonyi.com
date: Wed, Sep 9 at 5:00 PM
subject: re: ☺

You know, like animal kingdoms. Genus. Order.

Making clouds is less complicated than it sounds. It involves an empty glass bottle (my mother's Perrier), steam, and an ice cube.

---

from: smith@simonyi.com
to: jademassey@yahoo.com
date: Wed, Sep 9 at 5:02 PM
subject: re: ☺

I am 100% sure I never learned the animal kingdoms either.

"Making clouds" is kind of beautiful. When do I get to read some of your poetry?

---

from: jademassey@yahoo.com
to: smith@simonyi.com
date: Wed, Sep 9 at 5:06 PM
subject: re: ☺

Ha.

---

from: smith@simonyi.com
to: jademassey@yahoo.com
date: Wed, Sep 9 at 5:10 PM
subject: re: ☺

"Ha" is progress! Last time I asked, you just ignored me.

---

from: jademassey@yahoo.com
to: smith@simonyi.com
date: Wed, Sep 9 at 5:12 PM
subject: re: ☺

[You never hear from me again.]

---

from: smith@simonyi.com
to: jademassey@yahoo.com
date: Wed, Sep 9 at 5:13 PM
subject: re: ☺

☺

---

from: smith@simonyi.com
to: jademassey@yahoo.com
date: Wed, Sep 9 at 9:43 PM
subject: re: ☺

Did I say something?

---

from: jademassey@yahoo.com
to: smith@simonyi.com
date: Wed, Sep 9 at 10:59 PM
subject: re: ☺

Sorry, I was on a flight.

---

from: smith@simonyi.com
to: jademassey@yahoo.com
date: Wed, Sep 9 at 11:02 PM
subject: re: ☺

Where to?

from: jademassey@yahoo.com
to: smith@simonyi.com
date: Wed, Sep 9 at 11:09 PM
subject: re: ☺

Back to Virginia. Just for two days.

    I wonder what would have happened between her and Richie.

from: smith@simonyi.com
to: jademassey@yahoo.com
date: Wed, Sep 9 at 11:17 PM
subject: re: ☺

Me too.

from: jademassey@yahoo.com
to: smith@simonyi.com
date: Wed, Sep 9 at 11:19 PM
subject: re: ☺

How is he doing?

from: smith@simonyi.com
to: jademassey@yahoo.com
date: Wed, Sep 9 at 11:25 PM
subject: re: ☺

He still isn't really getting back to me, so I don't know.

---

from: jademassey@yahoo.com
to: smith@simonyi.com
date: Wed, Sep 9 at 11:27 PM
subject: re: ☺

Is that normal?

---

from: smith@simonyi.com
to: jademassey@yahoo.com
date: Wed, Sep 9 at 11:30 PM
subject: re: ☺

Not really. Anyway, you've had a lot of change these last few months. Sister. Job. Re-re-break up.

---

from: jademassey@yahoo.com
to: smith@simonyi.com
date: Wed, Sep 9 at 11:34 PM
subject: re: ☺

And I dyed my hair this morning. I'm a redhead now. It's possible I look like a Disney witch, given that a few minutes ago, my mother described it as "purple."

---

from: smith@simonyi.com
to: jademassey@yahoo.com
date: Wed, Sep 9 at 11:43 PM
subject: re: ☺

I liked your hair color before. But I'm sure it looks lovely now, too.

from: jademassey@yahoo.com
to: smith@simonyi.com
date: Wed, Sep 9 at 11:49 PM
subject: re: ☺

Thanks. That's nice of you to say. Time for bed. G'night.

from: smith@simonyi.com
to: jademassey@yahoo.com
date: Wed, Sep 9 at 11:54 PM
subject: re: ☺

Good night, Disney witch.

I'm in love. It hit me this weekend. I didn't see it coming. For, well, a number of reasons. First of all, he's beefy. Hugging him is like holding four people crammed into the skin of one human. He gels his hair, reads Nicholas Sparks novels, and believes in *The Secret.* And yet every day, he surprises me. He's a power-lifter passionate about global warming. He's thoughtful in small ways, like noticing I've stopped putting lemon slices in my water (because of mouth sores, a fun chemo side effect). He smells like a combination of mint and that body spray teenage boys wear—but I actually *like* it.

It feels like it did when I was fourteen: I miss him after forty-five minutes; I read and reread his texts. His arrival is an event I prepare for, my preparation a ceremony. For once, lately, it's not a ceremony of death, but a ceremony of life.

And even though I have the mouth sores, and I'm self-conscious my hair has finally started falling out, and I have no idea why he's attracted to me at the moment, we're happy.

This past weekend we went upstate. For years I've slept with my suitcase by the wall next to my bed, rather than stowed. The reason in my consulting days was that I always figured that I'd soon be packing it again, so why bother? But the habit stuck even after the traveling stopped, and for years now it's sat collecting dust. Last weekend, however, it finally got some use. I lugged it down my building's four flights even though we were only going for three nights. My few outfits and bag of toiletries/meds slid around inside.

I returned from our trip upstate with four dresses, two skirts, a faux fur shrug, and a pair of sequined stilettos. It's possible that I will never wear much, or any, of this outside my apartment. These days I don't have much energy to get out, apart from work. (If Jade had her way I wouldn't still be going to work at all—I've tried explaining to her that I actually like it, and besides, I'm only part-time since chemo started.) I won't be showing up to either of those in glamour wear. But when Richie and I found ourselves wandering into a thrift store in Saugerties, New York, and I started ogling garments, he convinced me that only-inside-my-apartment is good enough. Later that night, we said the L word. And who knows, maybe I have a whole lifetime of parties ahead of me. I haven't given up yet. So, $113 poorer, here I sit, wearing pink fur and sequins, typing on my couch.

I left for Saugerties with a half-empty suitcase and a fling, and came back with one full of shiny things and a boyfriend. Not bad for a weekend, I think.

COMMENTS (2):

DyingToBlogTeam: Happy Groundhog Day!

AnikaMommyof3: Iris, we've been calling you. No need to hide, we know about the cancer. Clara ran into Jade at Whole Foods, and then someone in Morgan's Facebook mommy group posted a link to your blog as the Friday Morning Gratitude Read. Imagine Morgan's surprise when she saw it was by you, and it was about having cancer, not mono. Point being, we are here for you and praying for you, sweetie. And can't wait to meet the new beau! Xo

THURSDAY, SEPTEMBER 10

from: harvwashburn55@hotmail.com
to: smith@simonyi.com
date: Thu, Sep 10 at 10:12 AM
subject: A "Hairball" Idea: Grooming Salon for Pets and Their Humans

Dear Sir or Madam,

I am writing with an idea that I am 100% confident will revolutionize the grooming industry. This is your one and only opportunity to be a part of it, should you so choose.

Picture: A salon . . . for both pets, and the humans they call parents.

How often is it that you want to get a haircut but you also need to get your dog groomed, and you feel you must choose? No longer.

At *The Groom Room* we will do both, simulcraneously.

I have some investment already. Sure, I need more. I've applied to be on *Shark Tank*, and that will prove helpful once I'm cast.

Please respond at your earliest convenience, as this is not the kind of idea one should "sit" on. I must establish a brand and identity.

Harvey Washburn
Bloomington, Indiana

---

from: carl@simonyi.com
to: smith@simonyi.com
date: Thu, Sep 10 at 10:15 AM
subject: Fwd: A "Hairball" Idea: Grooming Salon for Pets and Their
            Humans

Morning, Boss!

What do you think? "Hairball" indeed, but not all hairball schemes are bad . . . I once shoved a futon out of a second-story window to spare my father from having to haul it down the excessively narrow stairwell of my dorm. Given that he was later diagnosed with a triple hernia after merely transferring some urns of sweet potato vine from our east veranda to our west, it was clearly the right choice.

CVS

---

from: smith@simonyi.com
to: carl@simonyi.com
date: Thu, Sep 10 at 10:20 AM
subject: re: Fwd: A "Hairball" Idea: Grooming Salon for Pets and Their
            Humans

Absolutely not. Don't respond.

from: carl@simonyi.com
to: smith@simonyi.com
date: Thu, Sep 10 at 10:25 AM
subject: re: Fwd: A "Hairball" Idea: Grooming Salon for Pets and Their Humans

Now that I think about it, the fact that the futon didn't break is sort of a miracle. But truthfully—can we really afford to be turning down work right now?

from: jademassey@yahoo.com
to: smith@simonyi.com
date: Thu, Sep 10 at 12:11 PM
subject: Divorce

I take it back. I *am* going to press you on it. I'm too curious.

from: smith@simonyi.com
to: jademassey@yahoo.com
date: Thu, Sep 10 at 12:14 PM
subject: re: Divorce

About?

from: jademassey@yahoo.com
to: smith@simonyi.com
date: Thu, Sep 10 at 12:17 PM
subject: re: Divorce

What was your relationship with your ex-wife like?

from: smith@simonyi.com
to: jademassey@yahoo.com
date: Thu, Sep 10 at 12:21 PM
subject: re: Divorce

Oh, boy.

from: jademassey@yahoo.com
to: smith@simonyi.com
date: Thu, Sep 10 at 12:33 PM
subject: re: Divorce

No rush. I'm here all day. Just driving my mom around . . .

from: jademassey@yahoo.com
to: smith@simonyi.com
date: Thu, Sep 10 at 1:40 PM
subject: re: Divorce

Scratch that: I'm bored and refreshing my email incessantly, so anytime now . . .

from: smith@simonyi.com
to: jademassey@yahoo.com
date: Thu, Sep 10 at 2:20 PM
subject: re: Divorce

Maybe I should just see if my old therapist will send me her notes, and you can read those. She was always scribbling away. I'm sure they're juicy.

from:	jademassey@yahoo.com
to:	smith@simonyi.com
date:	Thu, Sep 10 at 2:24 PM
subject:	re: Divorce

You really don't want to talk about it, huh?

from:	smith@simonyi.com
to:	jademassey@yahoo.com
date:	Thu, Sep 10 at 2:29 PM
subject:	re: Divorce

Just don't tell me what they say.

from:	jademassey@yahoo.com
to:	smith@simonyi.com
date:	Thu, Sep 10 at 2:30 PM
subject:	re: Divorce

All right, all right. I'll drop it.

from:	smith@simonyi.com
to:	jademassey@yahoo.com
date:	Thu, Sep 10 at 2:34 PM
subject:	re: Divorce

I'm struggling with how to describe it. Maybe I'll just tell you a story.

---

from: jademassey@yahoo.com
to: smith@simonyi.com
date: Thu, Sep 10 at 2:36 PM
subject: re: Divorce

That works.

---

from: smith@simonyi.com
to: jademassey@yahoo.com
date: Thu, Sep 10 at 3:00 PM
subject: re: Divorce

The day before Clementine left me, I came home to find her on the balcony clutching a shimmery silver envelope and screaming, "FLY, DAMMIT!" at the ground. Next to her foot was half a butterfly. Or rather, a whole butterfly, folded. It wasn't moving. Inside the envelope, she showed me, were dozens more, also folded. "Hibernating," she explained. The butterflies, according to the company she'd purchased them from, were supposed to awake upon being flung, and fly away.

She has a slight accent from growing up in East Texas, which gets stronger when she gets mad.

"FLY, FUCKER!" she was yelling in her twang, so full of rage at the poor insects that I suspected (correctly) it had something to do with me.

"Maybe they're just hibernating better than they're supposed to," I said. I'd never heard of hibernating butterflies. I pulled out a third and mimicked her technique. It fell. I asked what they were for.

She told me she wanted to release them at a baby shower for her friend who was having her "rainbow babies," a set of twins. I didn't remember anything about such a person, or what rainbow babies meant. This astounded and irritated her.

"The IVF one?" she said. "She's had a bunch of miscarriages, and so these twins are a godsend? We talked about rainbow babies for, like, half an hour the other night."

I still didn't remember. Weary of me, she reached into the pocket of her sweater, and I noticed a box of Marlboros peeking out of it. I had never seen her smoke. I didn't know she did. She lit a cigarette and sat in one of the patio chairs her mother had given us for Christmas. I sat in the other, wondering if I was allowed to ask when she started smoking. But she beat me to the questioning.

"Why did you marry me?" she asked.

I told her because I loved her, obviously. I asked back: why did she marry *me*?

"You weren't a dick. That's rare here," she said, referring to New York City. She said she found it attractive that I'd come from nothing, made myself successful. And that when she'd learned I'd lost my dad and was taking care of my mom, she saw me as a kind of hero.

"But?" I said, because it was clear one was coming.

"But you're more stoic than heroic."

It stung, and I told her so. Then I asked when she started smoking. She looked at me, disgusted, and said that she'd been smoking since I met her.

"You couldn't smell it on my breath?" She seemed to suggest that me not knowing she was a smoker was a metaphor for much more. I wasn't observant enough or something.

The next morning before work, I had an impulse to go to the window and check the ground. The folded-up butterflies were gone.

---

from: jademassey@yahoo.com
to: smith@simonyi.com
date: Thu, Sep 10 at 3:08 PM
subject: re: Divorce

What do you make of this story you chose to tell?

---

from: smith@simonyi.com
to: jademassey@yahoo.com
date: Thu, Sep 10 at 3:12 PM
subject: re: Divorce

I was fantastic at disappointing her, and she was fantastic at making me feel disappointing. And even fucking butterflies couldn't get off the ground in our presence.

---

from: jademassey@yahoo.com
to: smith@simonyi.com
date: Thu, Sep 10 at 3:20 PM
subject: re: Divorce

Did you really not know she was a smoker?

---

from: smith@simonyi.com
to: jademassey@yahoo.com
date: Thu, Sep 10 at 3:21 PM
subject: re: Divorce

I really didn't.

---

from: jademassey@yahoo.com
to: smith@simonyi.com
date: Thu, Sep 10 at 3:33 PM
subject: re: Divorce

She must not have smoked *that* much then. Did you know Iris was a smoker?

---

from: smith@simonyi.com
to: jademassey@yahoo.com
date: Thu, Sep 10 at 3:35 PM
subject: re: Divorce

By the time I hired Iris, she had quit. I never knew she smoked till I read her blog. How long, do you know?

---

from: jademassey@yahoo.com
to: smith@simonyi.com
date: Thu, Sep 10 at 5:10 PM
subject: re: Divorce

The first time I saw Iris smoking, she was thirteen. We were living in Little Rock, and I found her squatting behind a dumpster in the parking lot, her arms wrapped around her bony little knees, puffing on a Camel. She frantically put it out and begged me not to tell our mom, but of course I wouldn't have. It was two against one.

I told her smoking was stupid, but that's all I said. I could have told her to give me the pack.

In my mind, I was already on my way out, counting down the months until I could start culinary school, move to one city and stay there, with my own room that wasn't a hotel room. Iris, though, was a little kid when we became transient. The bulk of her childhood was spent on the move. It's hard to have no friends and live on pizza and Chinese takeout and cold cuts on white bread that you eat on hard, scratchy sofas. Changing schools every few months, in a new town in a new state with people who have known each other for years and have their cliques and norms and inside jokes. Trying to break into that again and again, withstand the awkwardness, the discomfort—no wonder she started smoking. It gave her something to do with her hands, if nothing else. *I* certainly never got used to the conversation:

"What do you mean, you live in a hotel?"

"Have you heard of Winsome Beauty Brands? Our mom is a national director, and so we move around a lot."

"But why do you live in a hotel?"

So I joined her behind stinky dumpsters along highways, and later, once Mom finally settled down in Virginia, behind the toolshed where she stored all of our stuff from childhood that she hadn't thrown away—our drawings and certificates and diplomas all became stiff and blurred in the first winter's snow. I didn't smoke with her, but I sat.

One time I *almost* scolded her. I was twenty-four. She was twenty. We were at this club in Soho, talking to some guys, and I went to the bathroom. When I came back out, they were all gone. I figured she'd stepped outside for a cigarette. But it was February in New York, when "freezing" is an understatement. (These were the days before cell phones were ubiquitous, and though she had a flip phone, I didn't.)

I passed by the bouncer and coat check where our coats were—Iris had the tag—letting him stamp my hand so I could get back in. Shivering in my dress, I scanned the sidewalk and spotted the front tips of her heels poking out from the other side of the building, a poof of smoke rising against the blue Manhattan skyline.

"Dammit, Iris, it's freezing!" I yelled. I hurried over, preparing to tell her once and for all that her smoking had gotten out of hand because she had scared me, and it was fucking cold, but when I reached the corner she was crying.

I asked her what was wrong. She didn't answer. I put my arm around her, holding my breath and trying not to lose my temper as she took drag after drag until all that was left was the butt.

"Do you want to talk about it?" I finally asked, relieved we could go back inside. She shook her head.

As we hobbled back—I could no longer feel my toes—she said "Thanks for not getting mad at me." And I was glad that I hadn't, after all. We both were so conditioned to brace ourselves for anger, stiffening up like abused cats. We tried to give each other understanding.

But if I *hadn't* let it go, if I'd been a bossier big sister—would she have continued? Would she have gotten lung cancer?

I just made this about me. Sorry.

---

from: smith@simonyi.com
to: jademassey@yahoo.com
date: Thu, Sep 10 at 5:24 PM
subject: re: Divorce

Are you kidding? I would much rather talk about you than me.

I don't think you should blame yourself. One conversation, or even two, would not have changed things.

---

from: jademassey@yahoo.com
to: smith@simonyi.com
date: Thu, Sep 10 at 6:10 PM
subject: re: Divorce

If you say so.

---

from: smith@simonyi.com
to: jademassey@yahoo.com
date: Thu, Sep 10 at 6:12 PM
subject: re: Divorce

Let's get back to the lighter stuff. If you lived on cold cuts, how on earth did you end up a chef?

---

from: jademassey@yahoo.com
to: smith@simonyi.com
date: Thu, Sep 10 at 6:22 PM
subject: re: Divorce

I guess because I used to cook with my dad. But that wasn't when I knew I wanted to be a chef.

---

from: smith@simonyi.com
to: jademassey@yahoo.com
date: Thu, Sep 10 at 6:25 PM
subject: re: Divorce

When did you know?

---

from: jademassey@yahoo.com
to: smith@simonyi.com
date: Thu, Sep 10 at 6:38 PM
subject: re: Divorce

South Carolina. Tina Christine DuPree's house. My one friend during the six months we were there. Her mom taught me how to cook country fried steak by slapping two bloody filets on the counter, guzzling what remained in a bottle of red wine, and handing the empty bottle to me to pound the steak flat. I was eleven, and hooked.

---

from: smith@simonyi.com
to: jademassey@yahoo.com
date: Thu, Sep 10 at 6:40 PM
subject: re: Divorce

God bless bloody filets and Tina Dupree's mom.

---

from: jademassey@yahoo.com
to: smith@simonyi.com
date: Thu, Sep 10 at 6:44 PM
subject: re: Divorce

Damn right.

    My mom's choir practice is starting. Talk later.

I love to bake but am not a big cook. Like my mom, I prefer order-ing in to having to construct a meal on the fly. Tonight I decided to pick up sushi on my way home from work, and as I waited for my order at Abi Sushi, my favorite Japanese takeout restaurant in my neighborhood, "Fast Car" by Tracy Chapman came on the restaurant's scratchy speaker.

It took me back to 1999, the summer before my senior year of high school. My mom, sister, and I were driving down a South-ern California highway in the apple-red '99 Camry my mom re-ceived as a job perk earlier that year. We were in the silent part of an argument I don't remember—the pause between accusa-tions and defenses over something petty. Who got what room in the apartment my mom's boyfriend Donovan had rented for us for the summer so we could be closer to him (and his wife and children).

We each raged out a separate window—Jade in the back seat, me in the passenger seat (my perk of being the one who still "lived there"), my mom staring ahead. Jade had a quick vacation from culinary school for the month of August and, upon hearing that my mom and I were now in the beautiful land of SoCal, decided to join us for the month and sublet her room in New York rather than attempt to live on the fumes of her student loans.

And I was still mad at her for leaving me alone with our mom four years earlier. It's not that she had done anything wrong. I would have done the same thing. I think I missed her more than I was willing to acknowledge.

After a few minutes, Jade passed up a CD and asked me to put it in the Toyota's player. It was Tracy Chapman. I had never heard of Tracy Chapman. It took only a minute or so for her voice to mesmerize me, for her low, gravelly tone to disarm me completely.

Later that week, I read up on her at a computer in the complex's business center. She grew up in Ohio, and her parents divorced when she was four. She lived with her mom and older sister in poverty until she escaped, thanks to a need-based scholarship to a fancy private high school in the Northeast. At one point, she told a reporter, "The idea of being famous doesn't appeal to me because I hate parties and it seems like it might be one big party."

My dad died when I was three. But to me, the idea of life being one big party sounded fantastic.

I applied to Tufts, where Tracy Chapman had gone to college, and wrote my admissions essay about my nomadic existence. I'd managed to get all As throughout high school, and to my shock, I was admitted with a full-tuition merit scholarship. I fled to Medford, Massachusetts.

At Tufts, I majored in English because it was the most interesting, and took my career counselor's advice senior year, accepting a job in consulting. Consulting had been pitched to me as "problem solving." I'd wanted a job that would make me feel useful, and problem solving sounded like such a thing. (In fact it was capitalized: Problem Solving.)

Turned out that the other aspects of the job were what defined it. The travel was familiar, but the rest was new to me: business-class everything, carefree spending (all travel being expensed), colleagues who bought $6,000 watches. I had gone to Tufts in search of myself, then gone into consulting in search of a purpose, but at twenty-two I felt less real than ever before. At least growing up in hotels, I could feel the earth beneath me. Now, I lived a life in which all anyone talked about was credit card points: at dinner, we'd order one of everything and battle to get the bill for the points. It turned into a game. Everyone guessed the size of the bill, and whoever was closest won the check. We abandoned the leftovers.

As one year turned into two, and two into four, I became more integrated into the realm of people who fancy themselves immune to the grit of surviving. I'd fled that grit, leaving my mother with it in Arizona. But I found that I preferred it to a life of needs manufactured out of excess. I was haunted by the feeling that my life was inconsequential, perhaps because there were, literally, no consequences. Money, it turned out, was like the hot boyfriend who is appealing until you discover the toll that being with him takes on you as a person. I remember one day wandering into a bookstore in some city where I'd been flown in to Problem Solve, and spying a copy of *The Unbearable Lightness of Being* on a table of Must-Reads. The title alone brought tears to my eyes. My life had become so unbearably light. Was I even there? I was a guest at one big party, and Tracy Chapman was right—it wasn't what I wanted.

The day I spent $1,500 on a trench coat—Burberry, on sale—was the day I knew I had to get out, or whatever incipient me existed somewhere inside, the me I had yet to discover, would die. That purchase was proof that I was starving her. I sold it to the highest bidder on eBay and wrote my letter of resignation.

The job at Nose was my lifeline. Jade thought I'd lost my mind, giving up a prestigious partner-track position to work the counter at a perfume shop in the Village. She interpreted it as some kind of Stockholm syndrome, my return to the beauty industry, the bane of our upbringing.

Who knows? Maybe it was. But the way I saw it, I needed a hands-on job—a *human* job—to pull me back to reality, and the listing that caught my eye at that exact moment happened to be one for which I was qualified thanks to my experience with my mother's company. (I left consulting off my résumé, of course, for fear of being deemed overqualified.)

My first task was to stand on the sidewalk and spray perfume in the air just before people approached. It earned me more looks of disdain, anger, and annoyance than I could track in a given week. It also made me feel like I was reconnecting to the planet. People cursed at me! Shoved me aside! I was alive again.

I stayed at Nose, riding life like a tube down a river, and driving my sister crazy in the process, for two years. Until I discovered baking. When I quit, I used some of my savings to attend the Tufts Entrepreneurship Incubator, where I met Smith, my current boss. And I didn't leave the earth again.

Now, sixteen years later, Tracy Chapman made me nostalgic for that SoCal drive that would come to define my future. I sit here watching towers of snow form in the dark yard behind my fire escape, and yet I'm in that Toyota, basking in the luxury of our rage. The closeness of our bodies, their warmth and infuriating connection. The horizon that, though I was passive toward it, seared its blue-on-blue line onto my memory. The bright hunger I felt as a teen. The sharpness of my mind that loathed its own sharpness.

Even then, I was aware that one day I would be grateful for that moment. And here I am.

COMMENTS (7):

BigJessBarbs: That Tracy Champer sure does have a deep voice for a woman!!

AnikaMommyof3: Thanks for returning my text, Iris. I understand if it's easier right now for you to talk to strangers, but just reminding you that we are here if you need us: Lesley, Clara, Morgan, and me.

ClaraWaters: Yes, me, too!

MorganKip-Hamp: If not for Propel we all wouldn't have met, though! S S

AnikaMommyof3: Not the time or place, Morgan.

ClaraWaters: Morgan can we push playdate tomorrow to 10:15? Saunders is still awake and I swear he's going to be napping by 9.

MorganKip-Hamp: Sure, just text me.

MONDAY, SEPTEMBER 14

from: smith@simonyi.com
to: jocelynvoight@greenberrymurder.com
date: Mon, Sep 14 at 9:06 AM
subject: Letter from a fan!

Dear Ms. Voight,

I was thrilled to learn recently of your "murder mystery week-end" series from a friend who was a passenger on the Grand Star DEATH LIVE! Cruise. The notion of live, interactive entertainment sustained by a cast in character for over forty-eight hours, including through six gourmet meals, is stunning, and she tells me that you pulled it off with incredible skill. To think that you scripted the entire thing! To be performed on a boat, no less! I had to read the brochure several times to believe it.

If I may, I think you are selling yourself short in your current branding and marketing approach. For instance, "Mingle with murderers" is cute, but it sounds a little bit like you're bringing in a theater group from the local prison. Same with "If you're lucky, you'll come out alive." I'm envisioning being chased around by a gaggle of actors, and frankly, that sounds a little tiring. The reference to the "bloody deck" leading you to "lose your lunch" is quite evocative—of seasickness.

Would you be interested in having a conversation about some ideas for taking your brand to the next level? (Or should I say— deck? ;))

Sincerely,

Smith Simonyi

President

Simonyi Brand Management

---

from: carl@simonyi.com
to: smith@simonyi.com
date: Mon, Sep 14 at 9:45 AM
subject: re: Today's Agenda

Boss,

What do we think of Iris's book as a quiz in a women's magazine? "Live Your Best Life!" kind of thing?

Or even a listicle! "10 Ways to Improve Your Life at Its Conclusion."

CVS

---

from: smith@simonyi.com
to: carl@simonyi.com
date: Mon, Sep 14 at 10:07 AM
subject: re: Today's Agenda

No.

from: carl@simonyi.com
to: smith@simonyi.com
date: Mon, Sep 14 at 10:22 AM
subject: re: Today's Agenda

In that case, here's what I've got. My fraternity brother Stephen Ferrano who is now working at Walrus Press (indie house—v. small) is willing to read Iris's manuscript.

He does express concern that it is the length of a novella but no one reads novellas, especially not ones by dead people. Plus, this isn't even fiction. Do you remember the memoir by the guy who BLINKED THE WHOLE THING BECAUSE HE COULDN'T MOVE? That's the only memoir he could think of that's so short. And he had an excuse for it being so short, which is that he was BLINKING IT. AND he was almost dead.

Iris could still type, so one could make the argument that she should have typed more pages.

I'll let you know what he says, but it sure would be exciting if we had multiple publishers interested! We could do the thing, what's it called, when they have to bid for the book? An auction! Carl

from: zaharaferringbottom@zaharaferringbottom.com
to: carl@simonyi.com
date: Mon, Sep 14 at 11:24 AM
subject: re: Clarification

In regard to prepositions.

Thank you for your email.

Up or at walls.

As my senior thesis in art school, I chiseled a hole through the wall of the art building. No, it was not legal. No, my adviser didn't know. Night after night, I burrowed with my tools in the dead hours of the morning, destroying the exalted stone bearings of Arthur K. Billingsley Memorial Hall, circa 1892.

Up?

Or at?

I subvert.

---

from: carl@simonyi.com
to: smith@simonyi.com
date: Mon, Sep 14 at 11:31 AM
subject: Fwd: re: Clarification

Boss,

Just forwarding so you are aware that our new client is a bat-shit lunatic. That's all for now! Off to Kundalini lunch hour.

Tootles.

MESSAGES
Mon., Sept. 14, 11:40 AM

JADE: I've got it! I'm going to open her bakery. What do you think?

SMITH: That you hate desserts.

JADE: True. However: 1. Baked goods are not necessarily desserts. They can (and should) stand alone. THAT I'm fine with.

JADE: 2. I don't have a job right now.

JADE: 3. She left me her savings, with which she was going to open a bakery.

JADE: 4. I know how to cook.

JADE: 5. You can help me brand it (please?).

SMITH: Those are not bad reasons. Of course I will help you.

It's happened—my tumors have shrunk dramatically. The lesions are nearly invisible.

They can't call it "remission" yet, or "NED" (no evidence of disease), because my particular cancer is very responsive to chemo in the short term but does often come back once chemo stops. Dr. Hsu says that for this reason, I shouldn't get too excited. But he also says it's definitely a sign in the right direction, and that, if anything, it means I will probably live beyond the original sell-by date he gave me in December.

I admit I'm surprised. I was hopeful, but not especially optimistic. Everyone but Richie seems surprised, too. Richie says he always knew I would get better. Jade has already started talking about plans for an "Iris Beat Cancer" party. I told her not to jinx it.

But I *do* feel like something is changed. Here—God willing—on what may be oh-my-god-is-it-the-other-side-of-cancer, I feel different.

My whole life I have been focused on how I should change, searching for what I can do to become better in some way. I've devoted thousands of hours to working on my flaws in my head, entertaining a perpetual roster of hypotheses: *What if I meditated—would I be less anxious? What if I cut dairy, wheat, or sugar? If I became a marathoner, or volunteered, or studied Buddhism, or became a blonde, would the dissatisfaction that eats away at me from the inside finally go away?*

I'd try a new diet. Or kind of yoga. Or self-help book. And if it resonated in some way, I'd see myself from a new perspective:

Me

Also me

Also me

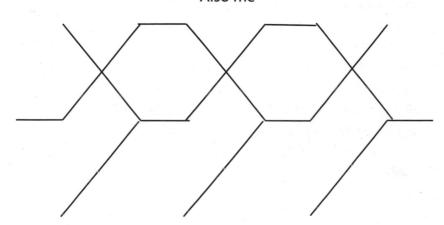

But no matter how far I stepped back or how wide the frame, what I saw wasn't enough. There was always more room to improve, more to be done to uncover that superior, elusive "me" out there, waiting. She was made up of the same pieces, maybe, but in a different pattern:

Me

Doesn't / line up

Pointless space

Better

Dying has turned out to be the world's fastest-acting perspective check.

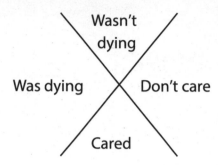

I don't care that I can't meditate. I don't care that I fucking love sugar, and that I have the thighs to show it, even with cancer. I don't care that I curse too much, and don't always vote, and once kissed my friend's boyfriend, and liked *The Fountainhead*, and don't recycle when it's inconvenient, and lied one time to a cop by telling him I was heading to tutor poor kids to get out of a speeding ticket. I don't care that my teeth are crooked because I never had braces, and that the birthmark on my right eyebrow makes my face look sort of lopsided (Christ, I don't even have hair now).

Because I'm here. I'm *still here*.

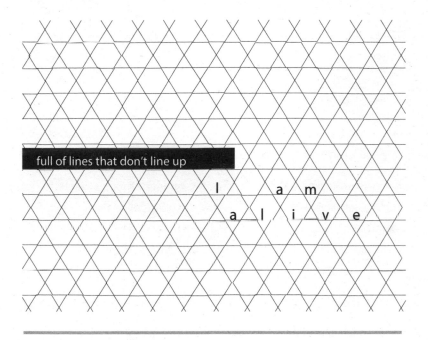

full of lines that don't line up

I am
alive

I can fall asleep

and wake up.
wake up.
wake up.

COMMENTS (5):

DyingToBlogTeam: May you march forth on March the Fourth!

BonnieD: HOORAYYYYYYYY!!!!

GloriaGlowing: Wow, this is heartening. I didn't think chemo could work so well. Thanks for sharing.

IrisMassey: Gloria: like I said, my particular kind of cancer (small cell) is especially responsive to it at first. But also to be honest it may have been more than just the chemo . . . alternative medicine kind of thing. If you want to hear more give me your email and I'll message you privately. ;)

ArduousArdvark: sell by date lulz

ONE MONTH LATER
MONDAY, OCTOBER 12

---

from: wally@homilypines.com
to: smith@simonyi.com
date: Mon, Oct 12 at 11:03 AM
subject: Checking in

Hiya Smith,

Hope you're doing well. Your mom asked me to get in touch due to things aren't going so hot with the new roommate Martha Stevenson. I guess she isn't all that new anymore, given it's been over a month they've shared a room. She and Martha can't seem to agree on who chooses what goes on the TV, and since Martha is the one who *can*, well, she ends up commandeering the remote for the most part. Not that your mom lets her be a channel tyrant without a fight. She hollers until Martha changes it back. And then she falls asleep and Martha switches it and the cycle repeats.

I worry the stress isn't good for either of them, and I even tried instituting a rule where every other hour is Martha's, and every other hour is your mom's, but then somebody has a nap and the schedule gets off and the fighting starts up again. Maybe she'd listen to you? It could be a good time to come out, you know, if you want to see the new room and meet Martha and talk to your mom about how cooperating is better for her health and frankly for all of us.

Let me know what ya think,

Wally

---

from: sandra.p.willoughby@thelanding.com
to: smith@simonyi.com
date: Mon, Oct 12 at 11:22 AM
subject: Issue of concern

Dear Smith:

A concern has been raised that there has been a great deal of traffic in and out of your unit recently. While co-op guidelines permit sublets of greater than 30 days subject to board approval, shorter stays as well as guests whom the board has not approved are not permitted.

I trust that you will see to this matter promptly and cease whatever operations seem to be taking place in 12D, as The Landing is neither a hotel nor a hostel but a reputable community that is home to 40 upstanding New York residents such as yourself.

Please let me know if you have any questions.

I am,

Sandra Willoughby

President

The Landing Co-operative

from: hbclark@bellemagazine.com
to: smith@simonyi.com
date: Mon, Oct 12 at 11:31 AM
subject: Your message

Smith,

I got your message. No hard feelings at all about the past. Yes, I was Clementine's friend first, but I still consider you my friend as well. Divorces happen, especially at our age. Clementine is doing great as far as I know, and I hope you are, too. (I haven't kept in super close touch with her over these last few years.) Would it be weird if you had reached out to me to, say, ask me out? Sure. I'd obviously have to say no. But solely in a professional capacity? Of course I'm up for discussing your new client.

A chef! I'd love to hear more about her decision to leave a restaurant as prestigious as Barn to embark on an unknown future, particularly in something as quaint as baking.

I'd be interested to see a draft of an essay on her decision to start her sister's bakery. <800 words, first person, not too heavy on the death stuff? Can I get a draft end of week?

xo

Hadley

from: jademassey@yahoo.com
to: smith@simonyi.com
date: Mon, Oct 12 at 11:32 AM
subject: Thank you . . . again

Hey Smith,

Thank you for coming with me (again) to check out the space in Chelsea (both times), but I've decided to keep looking. It just didn't give me a good vibe. It was the same problem with the Battery Park one, but different. Like something bad had happened in there or something. Maybe someone was killed there, I don't know.

Does it feel like we're moving fast on this? It feels extremely fast to me. Are we still on for dim sum later?
Jade

---

from: smith@simonyi.com
to: jademassey@yahoo.com
date: Mon, Oct 12 at 11:34 AM
subject: re: Thank you . . . again

I believe that if someone is murdered in a property that is up for sale, it has to be disclosed.

---

from: jademassey@yahoo.com
to: smith@simonyi.com
date: Mon, Oct 12 at 11:39 AM
subject: re: Thank you . . . again

Butchered nonfatally, then. Stabbed and survived. I understand that no one "disclosed" anything, but I get a queasy feeling in there.

What is happening with Richie? Is he going to give the green coffee sleeves to us for free, since it was Iris's dream and he was sleeping with her before she died?

from: smith@simonyi.com
to: jademassey@yahoo.com
date: Mon, Oct 12 at 11:46 AM
subject: re: Thank you . . . again

Isn't the priority to find a space, get permits, and then, well, figure out what this bakery *is*?

from: jademassey@yahoo.com
to: smith@simonyi.com
date: Mon, Oct 12 at 11:50 AM
subject: re: Thank you . . . again

FYI, I meant "green" as in environmentally friendly, not green like the color. Or are they also *not* green in that sense? I thought you said they were recycled from local trash. That was my interest. Now I can't remember if that's true or not. If they aren't, I'm not interested and we should go back to the drawing board on coffee sleeves.

from: smith@simonyi.com
to: jademassey@yahoo.com
date: Mon, Oct 12 at 11:59 AM
subject: re: Thank you . . . again

The sleeves are recycled, yes, though again, I don't think that's our focus right now.

MESSAGES

Mon., Oct. 12, 12:06 PM

JADE: Switching to text bc on my way to Pilates. Are you still gambling online? What, poker?

SMITH: Where did that question come from? Did you get my email about the essay in Belle? It would be great press for the bakery.

JADE: Oh, right. Opening email now . . .

JADE: Her name is HADLEY? Is she a grown-up, or six?

JADE: Wait, she's hitting on you! Your ex-wife's friend is begging you to ask her out.

SMITH: She explicitly says that if I asked her out, she would say no. How is that begging me to ask her out?

JADE: Telling you not to ask her out is her way of screaming ASK ME OUT.

SMITH: This essay opportunity is a really easy way to get the word out about the bakery. Two words: free publicity. Plus I think it pays. By the end of the week can you have something?

JADE: I don't know if I have time to write an essay. I don't know what I would write. I'm not a writer. I'm not even a baker, yet. I still have that to figure out. And I have to go back down to Virginia Thursday because my mom decided to host her entire church congregation at her house this weekend and somehow thinks this is something she can manage on her own.

SMITH: Oh come on.

JADE: "Come on" re: her wanting to date you, or the essay?

SMITH: Both!

JADE: Okay, I'll try to put together something.

SMITH: Jade, I wouldn't ask someone out right now, when you and I are kind of . . . you know. Dim sum sounds good, let me put it that way.

JADE: Why did you say my name like that? And why wouldn't you ask
    someone out right now?

SMITH: Is this a trick question? Are you trying to get me to say that
    we're dating? Fine, we're dating.

JADE: We're not dating. We can't be dating.

JADE: ARE we? We only kissed once.

SMITH: Twice. So glad they were memorable.

JADE: You don't want kids. That won't work for me.

SMITH: Can we talk about this later?

JADE: So it's true! You don't want kids!

SMITH: I never said that! I said it depends!

JADE: On?

SMITH: The person! The future! I don't know. You won't even say we're
    dating!

JADE: Pilates is starting. I have to go.

JADE: I'm just saying there's no point in us dating if you don't want
    kids, so we can save ourselves the trouble.

1:32 PM

JADE: I can't believe you didn't write me back during all of Pilates.

JADE: I can have something to you by the end of this week, fine.

SMITH: Thank you.

JADE: And yes to dim sum. See you at 6.

from: smith@simonyi.com
to: iris@simonyi.com
date: Mon, Oct 12 at 4:19 PM
subject: no subject

Richie is still avoiding me. Does he suspect the gambling? I don't gamble money I borrow from him. I've barely logged on in the last few weeks.

I know money is money, and the reason I need to borrow is because I keep losing what I have, but I didn't borrow *in order* to gamble is the point I think I need to make clear to you.

To me. The point I need to make clear to myself.

God, I'm so full of shit.

On a Saturday morning six weeks after my wedding day that wasn't, I still hadn't returned a single gift. They sat piled in a corner of my studio, mostly wrapped. I was wandering home in my clothes from the night before. Unable to be with either of the men I cared about, I'd gotten smashed and slept with the bartender. At the corner of Ninth and Court Streets, a block from my place, a little boy manned a lemonade stand. He held out a paper cup to me, but all I had on me was a credit card. I said sorry. He told me I could have it, anyway. The gesture gutted me. I took it from him, but when I got to the end of the block, I dropped it into the trash can, full, because I couldn't bear it.

I wish I could go back and talk to that girl. I wish I could grab her and say, "You're not a bad person. You're not a failure. Now, drink the fucking lemonade because that kid can still see you."

COMMENTS (1):

SP2004: you are not a bad person just for cursing but cursing IT-SELF is bad because it is toxic and spreads to babies

FRIDAY, OCTOBER 16

---

from: smith@simonyi.com
to: jademassey@yahoo.com
date: Fri, Oct 16 at 8:56 AM
subject: hi

Good morning. How's it going in Virginia? How was your trip
down yesterday?

---

from: jademassey@yahoo.com
to: smith@simonyi.com
date: Fri, Oct 16 at 9:17 AM
subject: re: hi

Okay. I made my mother the best omelet of my life this morning
(I sampled it) (ate half). In my industry, we say that there are
two options for an omelet: transcendent, and tastes like eggs.
Today's was the former. That is more difficult than it sounds. I
mean, there are entire books written on eggs. Not cookbooks.
Philosophical *treatises*. To me, the perfect omelet is made with
nothing but a fork. But there are people who would argue that
a spatula is acceptable. Others would say it's too violent, on par

with tongs. You don't know violence until you've watched delicate greens quiver under giant metal teeth.

---

from: smith@simonyi.com
to: jademassey@yahoo.com
date: Fri, Oct 16 at 9:29 AM
subject: re: hi

You were going to get me the draft by today?

---

from: jademassey@yahoo.com
to: smith@simonyi.com
date: Fri, Oct 16 at 9:36 AM
subject: re: hi

Shit.

---

from: jademassey@yahoo.com
to: smith@simonyi.com
date: Fri, Oct 16 at 9:38 AM
subject: re: hi

I can have something to you by this afternoon.

---

from: smith@simonyi.com
to: jademassey@yahoo.com
date: Fri, Oct 16 at 9:55AM
subject: re: hi

Jade, you haven't even started? What did you do Wednesday night when you left the bar to write?

---

from: jademassey@yahoo.com
to: smith@simonyi.com
date: Fri, Oct 16 at 10:01 AM
subject: re: hi

Packed! I said I was leaving to write *and* pack.

I also binge-watched this web series called *The Uncertain Detective*. This woman is concerned because her dog doesn't recognize her, so she thinks her dog is a clone. But it turns out the reason her dog doesn't recognize her is that *she* is the clone. You should check it out.

I'll have something to you by this afternoon. I'm writing RIGHT NOW.

---

from: ronaldglass@apexunitedcitizens.com
to: smith@simonyi.com
date: Fri, Oct 16 at 10:20 AM
subject: Re-branding

Dear Mr. Simons,

My name is Ronald Glass. I am the founder of Apex United Citizens. You may have heard about Apex in the media as of late, but I ASSURE YOU THAT THESE RUMORS ARE FALSIFIED.

Apex is a community of individuals seeking to expand their minds and hearts through the Apex curriculum, which I have recently revamped in light of rumors THAT ARE WHOLLY AND FULLY UNTRUE.

I am seeking assistance in re-branding Apex, and would welcome a meeting with you per this matter.

As a token of my appreciation, I am providing below a "glimpse" of what is in store for anyone (you?) who chooses to join Apex. It is a pearl of wisdom that, this time, is for free! There is more where it came from.

Sincerely,

Ronald P. Glass

The Meaning of Life in Less Than 300 Words
BY RONALD P. GLASS

So I hear you wish you had a different breakfast cereal in the cabinet. I hear you wish you had a different couch, such as the one possessed by your neighbor, with the reclining option and the flap that folds up to expose a convenient and reliable cup holder for containers of all sizes. You are tired because you are sick, born with an illness you have no control over. It is called being a *Homo sapiens*.

But I will tell you a secret. Here are three ways to make your own nature work for you not against you, such as in the style of "judo."

1. If you had those other things or if you were as healthy as a robot-human, you would still wish you had something different. It is the human condition to wish for "the Different." Pretend you are someone else wishing they were you, and you will begin to see "the Positive" aka "the bright side" because you have taken on a new perspective of another envious, unsatisfied human except that human is looking at you!!!!!!
2. Or you can just try to focus on the good things.
3. **Best Way** In the style of "smile and you will be happier" and also "the power of positive thinking," think of yourself as happy and you will be. <u>This is my favorite of the methods.</u>
    a. We create reality with our beliefs.

b. If you visualize yourself as happy you become it.

c. The same applies to eternity.

d. If you believe in eternity, it exists. If you don't, it doesn't.

e. So visualize happiness and eternity and you'll be happy for eternity! Or don't, and you won't. But whatever you do, don't visualize unhappiness and eternity!

---

from: carl@simonyi.com
to: smith@simonyi.com
date: Fri, Oct 16 at 10:28 AM
subject: Fwd: Re-branding

Boss,

I just googled Apex. Let me put it this way:

"Oxygen restriction," and "twelve missing people."

I feel this is truly an ethical conundrum for us. On one hand, this man seems truly terrible. On the other, we need the business.

Thoughts?

---

from: smith@simonyi.com
to: carl@simonyi.com
date: Fri, Oct 16 at 10:43 AM
subject: re: Fwd: Re-branding

Absolutely not. Don't respond.

And while we're on the subject, because this seems to keep coming up, please remember what I said about communicating with clients without my approval. This includes both prospective and former clients as well.

---

from: carl@simonyi.com
to: smith@simonyi.com
date: Fri, Oct 16 at 10:50 AM
subject: re: Fwd: Re-branding

Got it. Quick question: Does "former clients" include Phil?

---

from: smith@simonyi.com
to: carl@simonyi.com
date: Fri, Oct 16 at 10:53 AM
subject: re: Fwd: Re-branding

Yes. It includes Phil.

---

from: carl@simonyi.com
to: smith@simonyi.com
date: Fri, Oct 16 at 11:58 AM
subject: re: Fwd: Re-branding

I understand. But there is going to be a wee problem with that policy, given that Phil has just hired me. We've sort of been in touch. But don't worry, I will only do my work for him during lunch hours and weekends, and I am sure we will get him back to SBM in no time.

I remain your loyal intern M-F, 9–5. Despite what others are saying, I'm sure you had a good reason for doing whatever you did.

Please don't fire me. I need this internship and a subsequent LOR.

Carl

---

from: smith@simonyi.com
to: carl@simonyi.com
date: Fri, Oct 16 at 12:08 PM
subject: re: Fwd: Re-branding

Seriously, Carl??

---

from: carl@simonyi.com
to: smith@simonyi.com
date: Fri, Oct 16 at 12:17 PM
subject: re: Fwd: Re-branding

I suggest we focus on the silver lining: so far I have picked up on no plans of his to sue you. Yay?

---

from: jademassey@yahoo.com
to: smith@simonyi.com
date: Fri, Oct 16 at 6:31 PM
subject: My Essay

BELLE COLUMN: *CAREER CHANGERS*

"GARNISH WITH SALT"

by Jade Massey, Owner of _____[Name of Bakery TBD]

I don't actually like pastries, which you would think would be an issue when opening a bakery. But listen to my story, and you might understand where I am coming from.

Not long ago I was working 15-hour shifts seven days a

week at one of New York City's most demanding restaurants. I loved cooking, but I was tired.

Last winter my younger sister by four years was diagnosed with terminal cancer and died in May at age 33.

Several months later, I stumbled on a dream of hers about which I hadn't known. She had been an administrative assistant by day, but a baker by night. She had dreamt of opening a bakery. And she'd never told me.

First, the obsessing commenced: *Why* hadn't she told me about her dream? Images of my flawed sister-ing took over my brain as I recalled the incidents that might have inspired her to withhold her aspiration from me. Was I too bossy? Too opinionated? Did I make her feel, in some way, like she couldn't achieve her goal?

Then came the curious thought, a natural one given my circumstances and my sister's—should I try to fulfill her dream, the one she didn't have time to complete? She was gone. And, of course, I am a chef. It almost made too *much* sense.

But there was a problem. I loathe pastries. I don't like sweets, in general, particularly when they are baked and involve flour. Since I was a small child I've preferred salt to sugar. Bitter cocoa I can stomach; milk chocolate just tastes cloying. Flaky crust, to me, was never a delicacy; it was decay. I saw the feathering not as light and airy but as the peeling off of layers of skin. It didn't help to learn the extent to which refined sugars and flours (paired with trans fats, no less) destroy our insides.

My sister could see the beauty in them nonetheless, and while I admired that in her, I didn't share it. Until I realized that perhaps I could by sheer will.

Just over a month ago I began pursuing my sister's dream. I am using this opportunity to explore what I think of as the "anti-pastry"—it satisfies many of the same desires as the traditional pastry, but is different, as well. It contains less sugar than the traditional pastry. It is safe for those with common food allergies—all of my pastries are gluten-free, and some are dairy and nut free. And every (okay, maybe not every, but most) pastry is garnished with my personal favorite ingredient of all time: salt.

Jade's Light-as-Air Brazilian Cheese Popovers

Despite the fact that these require you to bake with tapioca flour, which is the glitter of the kitchen in that it gets absolutely everywhere, I think you'll find that they're worth the mess.

INGREDIENTS

1 cup almond milk (or substitute coconut)

2 tablespoons olive oil

1½ cups tapioca flour

2 egg whites

¼ cup shredded Parmesan

¼ cup shredded cheddar

2 teaspoons salt

Yield: 6 popovers

Preparation time: 30 minutes

Preheat oven to 400 degrees. The rack should be on the middle setting. Generously grease a bouchon pan with butter or canola oil.

In a saucepan, mix the milk and olive oil. Bring to a boil.

Combine the mixture in a bowl with the tapioca flour. Mix,

either with a hand mixer or a spoon—beware, the mixture is hot! Add the egg whites, cheeses, and salt. Mix until the dough contains only small lumps. It will be sticky and a bit runny.

Place the pan in the oven for two minutes to heat it up.

Spoon the dough into six cups of the pan so that each cup is full.

Cook for 20 minutes, or until the tops are plump and tinged golden. <u>Do not check on the popovers by opening the oven until at least 18 minutes have passed.</u> This could cause them to collapse.

Serve warm. They don't save well. If you store them, you'll be disappointed.

Enjoy!

---

from: smith@simonyi.com
to: jademassey@yahoo.com
date: Fri, Oct 16 at 6:48 PM
subject: re: My Essay

What's the name of the bakery? I can't send this over with blank lines where the name of the bakery should be.

And what's a bouchon pan?

---

from: jademassey@yahoo.com
to: smith@simonyi.com
date: Fri, Oct 16 at 7:20 PM
subject: re: My Essay

Can you write TBD?

Same as a mini popover pan.

from:	smith@simonyi.com
to:	jademassey@yahoo.com
date:	Fri, Oct 16 at 7:32 PM
subject:	re: My Essay

No, I can't write TBD.

Is that something people own? Can they just use a muffin tin?

from:	jademassey@yahoo.com
to:	smith@simonyi.com
date:	Fri, Oct 16 at 7:34 PM
subject:	re: My Essay

No. It needs to be a bouchon/popover pan. The wide bottom of a muffin pan will cause the bottoms to burn before the middle is done, and you'll wind up with gooey blobs.

Fine. The name of the bakery is SALT.

from:	smith@simonyi.com
to:	jademassey@yahoo.com
date:	Fri, Oct 16 at 7:35 PM
subject:	re: My Essay

SALT? Really?

from:	jademassey@yahoo.com
to:	smith@simonyi.com
date:	Fri, Oct 16 at 7:37 PM
subject:	re: My Essay

You don't like it? It's, like, the anti-bakery name. Salt.

---

from: smith@simonyi.com
to: jademassey@yahoo.com
date: Fri, Oct 16 at 7:41 PM
subject: re: My Essay

Okay. Salt.

Also—not to be too nitpicky, but are these really a pastry you're going to be able to serve at the bakery? If they need to be served warm?

---

from: jademassey@yahoo.com
to: smith@simonyi.com
date: Fri, Oct 16 at 8:09 PM
subject: re: My Essay

I never said *I* was going to serve them. If that was a condition, you should have said so. Fine, here's a more traditional baked good:

Jade's Orange-Kissed Chocolate Chip Cookies

INGREDIENTS

$1^1/_2$ sticks of butter, melted

1 cup brown sugar, packed

$^1/_2$ cup granulated sugar

2 large eggs

1 egg yolk

2 teaspoons vanilla extract

1 teaspoon orange extract

$^3/_4$ cup coconut flour

1 teaspoon baking soda

1 cup chocolate chunks

A bit of orange zest

A bit of salt

Yield: 12 jumbo cookies

Time: 30 minutes

Preheat oven to 325 degrees. Grease two baking sheets or line with parchment paper.

In a large bowl, whisk together melted butter, brown sugar, and granulated sugar. Mix in the eggs and yolk, vanilla, and orange extract.

Add the flour and baking soda.

Add the chocolate chunks and orange zest.

Place up to six golf-ball-size balls of dough far apart on one baking sheet—only six because they will spread.

Bake 20 minutes or so.

Allow to cool fully—if not adequately cooled, they may crumble. Once cooled, however, they will hold. Have faith.

Sprinkle with sea salt.

---

from: smith@simonyi.com
to: jademassey@yahoo.com
date: Fri, Oct 16 at 8:23 PM
subject: re: My Essay

Does this work with the last part of your essay? About the sugar?

---

from: jademassey@yahoo.com
to: smith@simonyi.com
date: Fri, Oct 16 at 8:29 PM
subject: re: My Essay

Look, baked goods have sugar, okay? Or they suck. You wanted something fast. I can't come up with the perfect recipe in a week. It's not *that* much sugar. It's less sugar than many cookie recipes.

But you're right, it's probably not in the spirit of the bakery. Maybe this essay is a bad idea . . .

---

from: smith@simonyi.com
to: jademassey@yahoo.com
date: Fri, Oct 16 at 8:35 PM
subject: re: My Essay

I don't care if it has sugar. I just didn't know if we should cut the line about the sugar if it's going to be followed by a recipe with sugar. If it's less sugar than normal, that seems fine.

---

from: jademassey@yahoo.com
to: smith@simonyi.com
date: Fri, Oct 16 at 8:39 PM
subject: re: My Essay

Cut the line, I don't care.

---

from: smith@simonyi.com
to: jademassey@yahoo.com
date: Fri, Oct 16 at 8:42 PM
subject: re: My Essay

Nope! Looks great! Sending as is.

I've been thinking about how brief life is, even for those who get to live the longest. Say each year of your life gets a dot. If you survive to age ninety:

That's it. Your ninety years fit easily on an index card.

Before my diagnosis, I had sort of figured that I'd be a fortu-nate one, that I had around this many left:

Then I found out I didn't have any left.

Then I found out I *might* have some left.

Who knew dying would be so much like a finicky lightbulb.

A woman I knew once said she feared she was addicted to starting over. That seemed so sad to me at the time. Now it seems less sad than not starting at all. I decided to open a bakery but never made it out of the planning stage. I wanted a family. I always wanted to go on a cruise, of all things, and never went.

If I have more dots left, I will start over. I will open my bakery. I will try to have a kid. I will take the tackiest, most garish cruise I can find.

Please let me have them. Please.

COMMENTS (1):

BigJessBarbs: Do NOT book a cruise on Princess Ocean Adventures, I swear to God I got thrown off that boat during a storm in '88 do NOT get me started.

MONDAY, OCTOBER 19

from: smith@simonyi.com
to: jademassey@yahoo.com
date: Mon, Oct 19 at 11:49 AM
subject: Hello?

Did you get my texts?

from: jademassey@yahoo.com
to: smith@simonyi.com
date: Mon, Oct 19 at 12:08 PM
subject: re: Hello?

Sorry, swamped. The all-church supper was last night and I had to cook for one million church ladies. Then today I had to clean up after one million church ladies, plus talk with another attorney about the suit against Jade's doctor. He *also* says I don't have a case, but I don't buy it. So many of these guys are only in it for the money. If they don't think they can earn enough to make it worth their time, they'll tell you that you have no case. On top of all this, my mother has decided to start selling Winsome again because she is feeling better, which means I'm going to have to start driving her around door to door since there is no way I'm letting her behind a wheel after she knocked over her neighbor's trash can on our way to the grocery store.

What's up? Oh, also, can we plan to go look at this new space I found when I'm back on Friday? It's a newly renovated former vegan sandwich shop in Greenpoint. Apparently a benefit of taking over a lease from a former food service business is that you can inherit permits. That would be a huge load off, given that I already feel lost in the labyrinthine bureaucracy of that nonsense, and I've hardly glanced at it. But even apart from the administrative convenience, I think this spot could be The One. I have an exceptionally good feeling about it. And if it is, we'll need to have everything ready to go—deposit and so forth—so I may have to ask you to run to the bank for me sometime between tomorrow and Thursday. Would you mind?

---

from: smith@simonyi.com
to: jademassey@yahoo.com
date: Mon, Oct 19 at 12:50 PM
subject: re: Hello?

Belle doesn't want the essay. The editor doesn't think it works.

---

from: jademassey@yahoo.com
to: smith@simonyi.com
date: Mon, Oct 19 at 12:54 PM
subject: re: Hello?

What do you mean? What doesn't work about it for Hadley? It was the sugar? I'm such a hypocrite. I took the easy way out.

from: smith@simonyi.com
to: jademassey@yahoo.com
date: Mon, Oct 19 at 1:00 PM
subject: re: Hello?

It wasn't the sugar. She feels the essay lacks authenticity.

from: jademassey@yahoo.com
to: smith@simonyi.com
date: Mon, Oct 19 at 1:14 PM
subject: re: Hello?

Um, excuse me—this is coming from a *women's* magazine?

from: smith@simonyi.com
to: jademassey@yahoo.com
date: Mon, Oct 19 at 1:15 PM
subject: re: Hello?

I mean, you did sort of dash it off very quickly, right? This can't
be that surprising?

from: jademassey@yahoo.com
to: smith@simonyi.com
date: Mon, Oct 19 at 1:20 PM
subject: re: Hello?

If it's that bad, why didn't you say so? I could have worked on it
more!

---

from: smith@simonyi.com
to: jademassey@yahoo.com
date: Mon, Oct 19 at 1:28 PM
subject: re: Hello?

You didn't have time to work on it.

If I may be frank, I think it's going to be hard for you to launch a bakery in New York when you're spending much of your time in Virginia.

---

from: jademassey@yahoo.com
to: smith@simonyi.com
date: Mon, Oct 19 at 1:58 PM
subject: re: Hello?

If *I* may be frank, I don't think how much time I spend in Virginia is any of your business.

---

from: smith@simonyi.com
to: jademassey@yahoo.com
date: Mon, Oct 19 at 1:59 PM
subject: re: Hello?

Let's just talk later.

---

from: ronaldglass@apexunitedcitizens.com
to: smith@simonyi.com
date: Mon, Oct 19 at 4:11 PM
subject: Follow-up on Re-branding Request

Dear Mr. Simons,

Ronald Glass, again, founder of Apex United Citizens. I wrote to you on Friday but haven't heard back, yet. I'm not blaming you—if you are hesitant or preoccupied, that's my fault for not having adequately inspired you!

In order to motivate a response, here is a second teaching from the pages of Apex:

Drama Is Evolution's Downfall
BY RONALD P. GLASS

WAH! WAH! WAH!

Everywhere you look, people in the industrialized world are creating fake stakes and crying over them. This is an outgrowth of the fact that we used to have real stakes, such as predators. Also, a high likelihood of dying during childbirth. And cholera.

Now that we privileged folks don't have cholera or tigers chasing us, and we wash our hands and rule the planet, our brains, still stuck in the Pleistocene, i.e. "stone age," seek out things to worry about and, finding nothing, stir up problems.

Husband cheating on you? Oh, well. Find another one.

Out of money? I say to that: Are you breathing? Then you're fine.

Legs too short, nose too crooked? Tell me this: If you were running from a cheetah across the plain, would you care about your facial dots and dents?

For fifth-grade picture day, my mother blanketed my head in hot rollers and covered my face in her gooey orange founda-tion, then pasted fake lashes onto my lids that I tried to pull off on the bus because the glue stung my eyes, tugging at them as gently as I could. But they wouldn't break free, and I was terri-fied they'd be stuck there forever. No one else wore makeup yet, except Casey Fredericks, who also owned a garter belt and was usually on a diet that only allowed her to eat uncooked pasta.

When I walked into the cafeteria where the children were herded prior to the first bell, Austin Quattlebaum yelled, "Clown!" I ran to the bathroom, filled my hands with sticky pink soap, and scrubbed. I couldn't see to find the paper towels and, standing there by the sink with my eyes on fire, I decided that I hated her.

The dynamic between my mother and me was rooted in fear for as long as I can remember. She was a screamer. A shamer.

It shaped me into a little girl who walked on eggshells, awaiting the worst. But that day in fifth grade, something shifted; I went on the offensive. No longer would I allow her to terrorize me without fighting back.

After that, our relationship remained strained, but less one-sided. I would do something to anger her, like deciding I didn't believe in thank-you notes or meaningless greetings like "How are you?," and she would whine that I was such a difficult child and talk about me to others as if I wasn't there. I became a vegan because she didn't know what that meant and because it was inconvenient. When I was seventeen, I told her I was interested in girls, also a lie. It worked. My God-fearing mother—with the married boyfriend—slapped me.

When I got on a plane in Phoenix, headed to college, and hugged her good-bye, I remember being stunned that she teared up, because I felt nothing but relief.

For the next ten years we saw each other once a year or so. Then came the Thanksgiving we spent in Atlantic City, where she lived at the time. It was the last holiday we all spent together as a family.

My sister's husband Henry showed up to the house my mother had rented, armed with a turducken—which, in case you don't know, is a turkey stuffed with a duck, stuffed with a chicken.

I had never liked Henry all that much, but I didn't yet loathe him at that point. It was fairly normal for me not to be crazy about Jade's boyfriends. We had different taste in men. I liked the charmers, the sociable doers. She liked the wounded, brooding academics, people who needed her emotional guidance.

Henry was a successful doctor, but he was always blaming Jade for something in a calm, distant way that gave his criticism a false air of objectivity. Her work schedule wasn't conducive to their marriage (even though his was at least as grueling); her ambition didn't leave room for kids (even though he had known about her ambition before they married). He would undercut her with remarks like "Jade doesn't have time to accompany her husband to Italy, but makes time for book club."

I told myself I didn't know the inner workings of their relationship. Maybe they were just a standard, if sad, kind of couple, struggling to stay connected. But the fundamental incompatibility between them could not be buried forever. Jade's finger is still crooked from the time a cast-iron skillet fell on it, breaking it, at which point she ignored the pain and finished her shift. Her hands are covered in faint red streaks left by slippery knives, her forearms stacked with horizontal oven burns. Henry, meanwhile, once said to me of her cooking, "It's a great skill she can use at home with the kids."

Perhaps he thought cooking was a phase she would outgrow.

The Thanksgiving of the turducken, he boasted of its inevitable deliciousness, as if he himself had invented the novelty, while taking over the stove in the tiny kitchen of my mother's rental. Then he got drunk on the cooking wine, fell asleep watching football, and forgot about his turkey-duck-chicken, roasting away.

As Jade and I sat in the kitchen drinking another bottle we'd opened, she said, "You may have noticed we aren't getting along very well." She confided that he'd given her an ultimatum. If she didn't leave her job so they could get started with kids, he was going to divorce her.

I asked what she was going to do. She said, beg him not to.

And if that doesn't work? I asked.

"I guess I'll probably quit," she said. "What am I supposed to do? I love him."

The turducken burned. It was inedible. He blamed Jade for

not keeping an eye on what he had established as his masterful undertaking. My mother, who had been spritzing her orchids, offered us all Vicodin.

Jade and Henry stuck it out, but I drove my rental car back to my Brooklyn apartment that evening and downloaded a stack of self-help books on living with crazy families, and skimmed them late into the night, taking from all of them a single idea that resonated as both wise and comforting: I was allowed to draw a line in the sand. I was allowed to stop involving myself in their drama. And so that's what I did.

Jade and Henry stayed together four more years. She didn't quit her job, but he didn't divorce her. I imagine each was waiting for the other to push things over the edge.

She finally left him two years ago because she was so miserable that something had to give. And she knew that it wasn't her job that was the problem—it was him. (Deep down I think we always know when it's a Him.)

Henry, meanwhile, has not accepted the divorce. He has petitioned Jade ever since to get back together with him. Does the man love misery? Is he a masochist? Who knows how love works. Until now, to my knowledge, she has resisted. Until now. Because now, they're dating again. She doesn't know I know.

But I also have an "until now" with my own mother.

Does the looming prospect of death open us up? Does it bring out the magnanimity in our souls, because all we want is to connect with the people we connected to once upon a time, imperfect as they are, hurtful as they can be?

Today, chemo was unusually quiet. Normally the room is boisterous—far more than I ever would have guessed. It's full of spouses, children, and grandchildren all on their best behavior, working hard to lift the spirits of the dying. But today, apart from a grandchild handing out construction-paper shamrocks, there was little to distract me from my thoughts, which, as they often do these days, turned to my own family.

I found myself deciding that I don't blame Jade for re-dating Henry, and I no longer blame my mother for making our lives what they were. My mother made me stretch every night to have long legs. She asked every morning if I'd washed my face and accused me of lying if I had a zit. She once whipped me with a belt for coming home from a slumber party with a temporary tattoo of a starfish. She showed me where to place the tip of the nail polish brush for a smooth finish and made me practice until I left no trace of color on my skin. She weighed me on Fridays.

I always viewed the shoving of her crushing ideals onto me as her way of telling me I wasn't good enough. But my mother shaped her entire life around beauty. I see that now. She was loving me the way she loved herself.

COMMENTS (5):

DyingToBlogTeam: Happy St. Patty's Day!

ChristmasWasMyFavorite: We moms don't get any credit!! Cut us some slack!!

BonnieD: Chemo? Are you still doing that? I thought your cancer was almost gone.

IrisMassey: Still have to keep up the chemo for now, BonnieD.

BigJessBarbs: What time is it there? I'm in China and it's dinner time!

THURSDAY, OCTOBER 22

from: jademassey@yahoo.com
to: smith@simonyi.com
date: Thu, Oct 22 at 7:20 AM
subject: ONE more BIG favor?

Argh. I'm not going to make it back by tomorrow after all. It's a long story involving my mom's Winsome products not arriving in time and our needing to drive to the HQ in Richmond and pick them up. I realize I'm sort of proving your point here, and I know I have been asking you for too many favors, but like I said, this is important—would you go to the open house for me? Pretty please?

Don't text me, I won't get it. My mother microwaved my phone, so it's fried. (She was "trying to warm up" my sweater for God knows what reason, and it was in the pocket.)

from:	carl@simonyi.com
to:	jademassey@yahoo.com
date:	Thu, Oct 22 at 10:32 AM
subject:	Good news!

Hi Jade!

Just got to the office and saw you called a few times. Is everything okay? Smith is in a meeting right now with a new client. I'm sure he'll be glad to give you a call as soon as he's out.

While I have you on the line, good news! As I assume you know, we've been trying to place your sister's MS (that's industry-speak for "manuscript" ;)) with a publisher for a while now. I cannot even begin to tell you how difficult it has been for us to find someone interested in your sister. Several editors wrote back that Iris has no platform or is a nobody (my word—I believe the actual quote was "not famous"). Others found it a problem that she is no longer alive for edits. My former fraternity brother Stephen Ferrano, who is now an editorial assistant at an indie house, was open to pursuing her blog as a self-help title, but his coworkers seem to have persuaded him that since she is deceased, no one will want to self-help with it. There's a Harvard transfer/ Lit major for you.

All of which is to say, I was thrilled when Todd and Chad, the founders of the site on which your sister wrote, said they are interested in using her blog as part of their upcoming campaign for the site! Has Smith talked to you about that? Jeez, hopefully it isn't too late. I think they were under time pressure. We will have to check with them to find out if it's even still an option. Fingers crossed! I'll reach out to them today and keep you posted.

Carl

from:	jademassey@yahoo.com
to:	carl@simonyi.com
date:	Thu, Oct 22 at 10:40 AM
subject:	no subject

Smith,

I don't know what's going on, but we need to discuss this ASAP.

Jade

from:	carl@simonyi.com
to:	jademassey@yahoo.com
date:	Thu, Oct 22 at 10:49 AM
subject:	re: no subject

Still Carl. You emailed me by accident. Can I help?

from:	jademassey@yahoo.com
to:	carl@simonyi.com
date:	Thu, Oct 22 at 10:52 AM
subject:	re: no subject

Please have Smith email me as soon as he is available, thank you.

from:	wally@homilypines.com
to:	smith@simonyi.com
date:	Thu, Oct 22 at 11:05 AM
subject:	Thanksgiving

Hiya Smith,

I was wondering, given that it's just about four weeks from Thanksgiving, if you might try to come down for it this year.

Each of the past three, we've had a very good time enjoying a full holiday spread cooked by the lady parishioners of Sun Prairie Methodist. Your mom has threatened to skip this year due to she claims there's nothing interesting there and she'd rather nap. I would hate for her to miss it, though, especially since it's been such a challenging fall for her with the move into the same room as Martha.

Speaking of which, that does seem to be going better since we Facetimed with you last week. I think it helped her to understand that it's a financial decision you will remedy if you can, and that she will need to be patient and make the most of it if she doesn't want to upset you. Or maybe she was just happy to see your face, even over video.

Let us know. I can't vouch for the turkey because I've gone vegetarian, but the pumpkin pie last year was out of this world. Wally

---

from: jademassey@yahoo.com
to: smith@simonyi.com
date: Thu, Oct 22 at 11:48 AM
subject: no subject

I can't believe you went behind my back.

---

from: smith@simonyi.com
to: jademassey@yahoo.com
date: Thu, Oct 22 at 11:49 AM
subject: re: no subject

Hi. Is your phone dead?

from: jademassey@yahoo.com
to: smith@simonyi.com
date: Thu, Oct 22 at 11:51 AM
subject: re: no subject

Yes. My mom fried it. But it's not like I could talk to you without screaming, anyway.

from: smith@simonyi.com
to: jademassey@yahoo.com
date: Thu, Oct 22 at 11:52 AM
subject: re: no subject

What? How did she fry your phone?
   Why screaming?

from: jademassey@yahoo.com
to: smith@simonyi.com
date: Thu, Oct 22 at 11:52 AM
subject: re: no subject

Don't bother feigning cluelessness. You have been pitching her book behind my back. I told you I'm not okay with it. I was SO clear. I COULD NOT have been clearer.

---

from: smith@simonyi.com
to: jademassey@yahoo.com
date: Thu, Oct 22 at 11:53 AM
subject: re: no subject

I only put out some feelers. I figured we could talk if I got a bite. Can we talk on the phone please? Don't you have a landline there? Or a phone you can borrow?

---

from: jademassey@yahoo.com
to: smith@simonyi.com
date: Thu, Oct 22 at 11:53 AM
subject: re: no subject

Feelers?? Well, it sounds like you got one. The Dying to Blog guys, Smith? Seriously?

---

from: smith@simonyi.com
to: jademassey@yahoo.com
date: Thu, Oct 22 at 11:55 AM
subject: re: no subject

Carl told you about that. That—we should talk about that. I am ambivalent about it, too, to be honest. I think I would much prefer us going with my friend and the press where he works. Can we talk about this in person when you're back?

---

from: jademassey@yahoo.com
to: smith@simonyi.com
date: Thu, Oct 22 at 11:55 AM
subject: re: no subject

"To be honest"? Is that what you've decided to be NOW? That you're CAUGHT?

WE HAVE ALREADY TALKED ABOUT THIS.

---

from: smith@simonyi.com
to: jademassey@yahoo.com
date: Thu, Oct 22 at 11:56 AM
subject: re: no subject

You haven't even read it! How can you be opposed when you haven't even read it?

---

from: jademassey@yahoo.com
to: smith@simonyi.com
date: Thu, Oct 22 at 11:57 AM
subject: re: no subject

Another lie. I told you I've read it!

---

from: smith@simonyi.com
to: jademassey@yahoo.com
date: Thu, Oct 22 at 11:57 AM
subject: re: no subject

You said you've read "most" of it. Months ago, when you found it on her computer while snooping.

---

from: jademassey@yahoo.com
to: smith@simonyi.com
date: Thu, Oct 22 at 11:58 AM
subject: re: no subject

YOU are criticizing ME?

Reminder: *You* betrayed *my* trust. I haven't done anything wrong here.

---

from: smith@simonyi.com
to: jademassey@yahoo.com
date: Thu, Oct 22 at 11:58 AM
subject: re: no subject

I didn't lie to you. I just didn't want to ignore the one thing your sister asked me for before she died. And I figured you would come around. I'm guilty of that much, sure.

---

from: jademassey@yahoo.com
to: smith@simonyi.com
date: Thu, Oct 22 at 12:00 PM
subject: re: no subject

She had CHEMO BRAIN. What she came up with while she had CHEMO BRAIN doesn't COUNT. What SHE wanted was to open a bakery. Which is why that's what I'm doing!

from:	smith@simonyi.com
to:	jademassey@yahoo.com
date:	Thu, Oct 22 at 12:03 PM
subject:	re: no subject

I don't think it has anything to do with her being on chemo. I think you don't like the parts about you. You don't like how you come across. That's why you stopped reading. And you know what's ironic about that? If you actually finished it, I think you'd feel differently.

from:	jademassey@yahoo.com
to:	smith@simonyi.com
date:	Thu, Oct 22 at 12:08 PM
subject:	re: no subject

Are you kidding? Do you know when I stopped reading? When her cancer came back. Because it was fucking devastating. I'm glad to know you think so highly of me, though, a person you claimed to be dating. Why would you even want to date me if I were actually that narcissistic??

from:	smith@simonyi.com
to:	jademassey@yahoo.com
date:	Thu, Oct 22 at 12:09 PM
subject:	re: no subject

Ha! Claimed! I did, yes, until you clarified that we aren't.

---

from: jademassey@yahoo.com
to: smith@simonyi.com
date: Thu, Oct 22 at 12:11 PM
subject: re: no subject

I said I didn't KNOW if we were dating.

It doesn't matter. Betrayal is betrayal.

---

from: smith@simonyi.com
to: jademassey@yahoo.com
date: Thu, Oct 22 at 12:12 PM
subject: re: no subject

Since we're being frank, I will say that I find the idea that *you*, in fact, are the one executing her wishes to be a stretch.

---

from: jademassey@yahoo.com
to: smith@simonyi.com
date: Thu, Oct 22 at 12:14 PM
subject: re: no subject

EXCUSE ME?

---

from: smith@simonyi.com
to: jademassey@yahoo.com
date: Thu, Oct 22 at 12:16 PM
subject: re: no subject

Will you stop shouting? To say that you're dragging your feet on the bakery is an understatement. You spend all your time traveling back and forth to Virginia to parent your mom, and researching this "malpractice" claim that isn't going anywhere.

from:	jademassey@yahoo.com
to:	smith@simonyi.com
date:	Thu, Oct 22 at 12:18 PM
subject:	re: no subject

What do you know about the malpractice claim? We haven't even talked about it. You know nothing about it. And things in law move slowly. Everyone knows that.

from:	smith@simonyi.com
to:	jademassey@yahoo.com
date:	Thu, Oct 22 at 12:19 PM
subject:	re: no subject

I think you don't actually want to open the bakery. She wanted it, and so you feel like you're supposed to do it. But you don't actually want it, so you're stalling.

from:	jademassey@yahoo.com
to:	smith@simonyi.com
date:	Thu, Oct 22 at 12:19 PM
subject:	re: no subject

Armchair diagnosing me now!

from:	smith@simonyi.com
to:	jademassey@yahoo.com
date:	Thu, Oct 22 at 12:20 PM
subject:	re: no subject

You hate desserts!

---

from: jademassey@yahoo.com
to: smith@simonyi.com
date: Thu, Oct 22 at 12:25 PM
subject: re: no subject

Well, I think you're a jerk for not going to see your mother.

---

from: smith@simonyi.com
to: jademassey@yahoo.com
date: Thu, Oct 22 at 12:26 PM
subject: re: no subject

I see. Okay.

---

from: jademassey@yahoo.com
to: smith@simonyi.com
date: Thu, Oct 22 at 12:30 PM
subject: re: no subject

I think it bothers you that I "PARENT" my mother because it makes you feel guilty!

---

from: smith@simonyi.com
to: jademassey@yahoo.com
date: Thu, Oct 22 at 12:33 PM
subject: re: no subject

Anything else?

from:	jademassey@yahoo.com
to:	smith@simonyi.com
date:	Thu, Oct 22 at 12:36 PM
subject:	re: no subject

THAT'S why you don't like that I'm in Virginia all the time. It reminds you of where you AREN'T. As for the malpractice claim, which I am only looking into, if *your* sister died, you'd want to know why, too.

from:	smith@simonyi.com
to:	jademassey@yahoo.com
date:	Thu, Oct 22 at 12:37 PM
subject:	re: no subject

She died because she had cancer, Jade. That's the reason.

from:	jademassey@yahoo.com
to:	smith@simonyi.com
date:	Thu, Oct 22 at 12:42 PM
subject:	re: no subject

I do want to open the bakery. More than anything. Just not with your help.

from:	smith@simonyi.com
to:	jademassey@yahoo.com
date:	Thu, Oct 22 at 12:43 PM
subject:	re: no subject

Got it. Good luck.

from: jademassey@yahoo.com
to: smith@simonyi.com
date: Thu, Oct 22 at 12:51 PM
subject: re: no subject

You want to read my poetry?! Here's one. It's a haiku:

> If you meet a Smith
> Simonyi: KEEP YOUR DISTANCE.
> Liar! Asshole! PRICK!

An update.

This update concerns a review of my latest CT scans by a doctor I have never talked to or heard about until today: Dr. Allison. Dr. Allison is a radiologist. Unlike my oncologist Dr. Hsu, this other doctor, in reviewing the scans, spotted a mass on my liver.

The day before yesterday, Dr. Allison and Dr. Hsu found mutual free time in their busy schedules to chat and figure out why their opinions on the scans differ. And once Dr. Hsu took a closer look, he had to agree with Dr. Allison that there is possibly something "of concern" on my liver. He doesn't know why he missed it before, he says, except that he does not spend as much time looking at scans as Dr. Allison, and therefore isn't an expert.

Ah. Well, that might have been nice to know.

The question of whether I now have cancer on my liver will need to be addressed via follow-up scans on Friday.

Fortunately Smith was out of the office when he called. I tore up papers. I threw a stapler. I screamed till my throat hurt. I didn't feel sad until I thought of telling Richie.

It's like I'm on the subway and I can't make out the garbled, scratchy announcement, which could be that the train is going out of service, or being rerouted, or just that there's a slight delay. Do I stay on or do I have to get off here?

Do I have cancer or don't I? Someone, please, for God's sake. Tell me what is happening so I can decide how to feel.

COMMENTS (2):

BonnieD: No! ☹☹ Doctors suck!

ChristmasWasMyFavorite: Didn't this blog used to have pictures?

---

from: smith@simonyi.com
to: iris@simonyi.com
date: Thu, Oct 22 at 8:44 PM
subject: no subject

I've managed to isolate myself from everyone in my life. Phil fired me. Your sister hates me. My mother is mad at me. Wally thinks I'm a bad son. Richie is clearly avoiding me because he's sick of feeling like an ATM, and sick of me. *I'm* sick of me.

The other day, I was remembering that game we used to play. I think we called it "Either/Or." The one where you pick between two things: one you get to keep, and the other you lose forever?

You might start with, say, Muffins or soda?

I'd definitely pick soda since I don't eat muffins. Then it would be my turn to come up with a contender for soda: Soda or movies?

That's not a great one because it's too easy. Obviously movies. You'd pick movies, for sure, then go for something like, Movies or music? That's harder.

And the game would go on until we were living in a world without muffins, soda, movies, socks, the color red, cell phones, air travel, and toothpaste, and our choices would reach the level of abstraction: Love? Sex? Family? I was always amused that, eventually, regardless of the path the game had taken, our choice would come down to some version of the same dichotomy—life without the myriad things that make life tolerable, or death?

I always chose death, because at that point, who wants to live? You've lost everything worth living for. But you, every time, would find the one good thing that was left and keep going back to it: "But did we get rid of friendship?"

"No, but we lost love, sight, creativity, joy, and hamburgers."

"But we still have friendship . . ."

You always clung to reasons not to choose death.

I feel like I'm at the end of that game, and all the reasons for living are gone, but you're the one who died, and I get to stick around.

I remember once reading a news story about an Irishman who was sentenced to death, and over the two years he spent on death row, he made peace with it. Though he maintained his innocence, he came to terms with the fact that his life was ending.

But then something happened: his sentence was converted to life in prison. Suddenly he had before him decades of life to go, years of time he'd already given up on. I was struck by what he said in his interview about it later, after he was exonerated—he said that when his sentence was converted, he wasn't relieved. He was afraid. He'd made peace with death, but he had no idea how to face more life.

How did you find your way to the kind of peace you reached? Is it because you were dying? How do I do that, but with more life to go?

---

from: Bro-vado
to: smithsimonyi@gmail.com
date: Thu, Oct 22 at 11:58 PM
subject: GET IT, MAN

You walked away with cold hard cash!

Here's a breakdown of your most recent session:

High: $482

Low: $14

Walkaway: $234

ProTip: Setting yourself a time limit can prevent you from developing a problematic habit and ensure that you continue to enjoy Bro-vado for the healthy form of leisure that it is!

Thursday, October 22

TherapistAwayNetwork™

Patient Name: Jade Renee Massey

AUTO PROMPT: **What do you fear?**

Dr. Z, thank you for your email. I'm very sorry to hear about the giardia. I knew you could acquire it from drinking contaminated water in South America, but I had no idea the parasite could have such a long incubation period. I hope you recover quickly. No pressure to read this, by the way. I just need to process.

I was sort of falling for Smith Simonyi. I liked that talking came naturally, that I didn't have to work to fill the silence. I liked how he would find excuses to put a hand on my back or arm. I liked his surprisingly wide smile. I liked that he never seems nervous but doesn't seem arrogant, either. I like that I found it easy to trust him.

We were spending time together every other day or so, Dr. Z.

Whenever I was in town, we'd get lunch or coffee. A beer, dim sum. Take a walk. Often under the pretense of working on the bakery, but we both knew it was more than that.

But this whole time, he was going behind my back to try to get my sister's book published despite the fact that I've made it quite clear to him that I'm not comfortable with it. He isn't who I thought he was. And he put her wishes over mine (which I feel like answers the "was he in love with her" question). He claimed he was going to tell me eventually . . . but when?

He also said some nasty things about my plan to open the bakery, how he thinks I'm dragging my feet because I don't actually want to do it.

It's not true. It really isn't. I do want it. It's really important that I do this for her.

The other day at a hair salon I was trying out on a Groupon (I made a poor decision last month to dye my hair red and suddenly needed it fixed, ASAP), a dad walked in with his sons, who looked around nine and eleven. The smaller one took the chair. The dad said to the stylist, "He wants a Mohawk." Then he said to his son, "Show him the picture on your phone."

"Why does he want that?" the older one asked the dad, peering over his brother's shoulder at the screen.

"I don't know," the dad said. "Ask him." But the younger one said nothing, just smiled at his reflection in the mirror.

"It's not going to look just like that," the older one said, panicking. "I don't think you should do it." And I got that kid. So much. He was used to being the one who charts a new path, who does the daring thing. Here was his younger brother, stepping out to make his own way, and it scared his older sibling, who was probably more nervous about his kid brother making a mistake than he was about making a mistake himself.

She wanted to open a bakery, and regardless of my own wishes, I have the ability to do that for her.

Smith says that she also wanted her book published, but that just feels like it can't have been important in the same way. To air her anguish to the world? Her regrets about the life she didn't get to live? How is that going to honor Iris—the real Iris, before she was sick? How is that going to help us heal?

■

Dear JADE,

Thank you for your submission to TAN™. We will make sure your provider receives this message.

The origin of the term "fear" is linked to the root of "revere," which, of course, is related to "reverence." Sometimes what we fear is also what we hold the deepest respect for. When we recognize this, we can often reconcile our fear and admiration into a single source of power, allowing the truth contained within to inspire bravery we didn't know we had.

TAN™ is not to be used in case of emergency. If you are in crisis, call 9–1–1.

Sincerely,

Your friends at TAN

MONDAY, OCTOBER 26

from: rsstein@rssteintherapy.com
to: smith@simonyi.com
date: Mon, Oct 26 at 8:43 PM
subject: re: Hello

Dear Smith,

Good evening. Normally I would not provide these. It's not exactly standard practice in my profession to share my process notes with clients. But in your case I am willing to make an exception in hope that they offer some illumination.

I sincerely hope you are doing well. Please call if you have any questions about them or wish to talk.

Warmly,

Raquel

ATTACHMENT (1)
eNoteTherapy—*Revolutionizing Therapy Notes One Note At a Time*

DR. RAQUEL S. STEIN, LCSW
SESSION 1

Patient name: Smith Seymour Simonyi
Patient DOB: 3/22/76
Month_Day: April 22, Fri
Referral: Beth Israel Hospital ER
Intake Notes:

Patient arrived in acute distress, reporting that wife had left him "out of the blue" one week ago. He arrived home to find that she had moved out while he was away on business. Patient repeatedly asserted that there were no prior signs.

Patient reported he has been sleeping in shower, and that he suffered a panic attack during which he went to ER thinking he was having a heart attack.

After some probing, patient added that he drove to a casino in Connecticut over the weekend, where he gambled and lost much of his savings.

I suggested that the betrayal seemed to have triggered a PTSD episode and inquired if it reminded him of any past events.

Patient stated that he knew what it was but saw no point in revisiting it.

"This is why I never came to therapy before."

He reported that he grew up in a household in which his father was physically and verbally abusive toward the patient's mother in the patient's presence. Patient left home at 18. When he was 28, he was living in New York when his mother killed his father by pushing him down a flight of stairs. He pulled her with him. She survived and is now quadriplegic, living in a facility outside Madison, Wisconsin. He expressed that he blames himself for not being there, but also her, for killing his dad, and he feels he shouldn't. He has not seen her in several years and pays for her care. He stated that discussing these feelings does not seem to make them any less painful.

"Life is hard, and these are just sad things."

We discussed coping mechanisms. He shared that he probably gambles too much but is not convinced this was a response to his upbringing, though his affect was flat and removed. He said he planned to try hot yoga, which seemed to work well for his admin.

I asked what he misses about his wife. He stated that he misses her being around. I asked what they did together. "Normal stuff." Did they ever fight? "A normal amount."

When I inquired as to the subject of their most recent argument, he presented as hostile. He stated that I was trying to figure out what he had done wrong to make her leave.

"I'm not a bad person," he stated at a heightened volume.

He then explained that he and his wife had fought over getting a dog. She'd wanted one. He had resisted. This upset her. I asked why he had been opposed. He said because it would die before him. He had tried to explain to her that anticipating the death of the dog, he would not even be able to enjoy having it.

"Do you think she left me because of the dog?" he asked, distressed. I told him I didn't know. I asked his wife's name, which he still had not spoken. Clementine.

I asked if he had any thoughts of hurting himself, and he said no.

We concluded the session with a mantra should the panic attacks resume: It's distress, not danger.

Patient scheduled to return in four days, on Tuesday.

RS Stein

CSW

Dr. Raquel S. Stein, LCSW

SESSION 2

Patient name: Smith Seymour Simonyi

Month_Day: April 26, Tues

Time since last appointment: 4 days

Patient presented as if in dissociative state. Superficially high spirits. Initiated conversation by announcing a turnaround: "A full 180." Stated that he had a productive weekend, making a great deal of money, more than enough to compensate for his losses the previous week at Mohegan Sun.

As to how he had made the money, "a combination of things." I asked how he was sleeping, given he had previously reported sleeping in his shower. He said he was "back in bed and everything."

He had spoken to his wife. She had told him she was leaving because, if she had to pin it on one thing, it was that he cannot express his feelings, to the point that she can't tell if he has them, and she is lonelier living with him than without him. I asked what he thought of it.

"If she wants a crier, I'm sure she can find a crier." His affect was briefly sad.

Buoyant once again, patient then thanked me for my time and told me that he would no longer be needing my services. He had gone to hot yoga two days in a row with his secretary and was finding in it the catharsis he required. He had only come in to tell me as much and to thank me for helping him through his crisis.

I wondered aloud why he had not just told me as much over the phone. I asked if he was sure he wanted to cease his treatment—otherwise, why had he shown up for it? He had not needed to end our treatment in person.

He appeared rattled, stated that he was certain, and left 20 minutes prior to the scheduled end of the session.

DISPLAY: **PROCESS FlagNotes™**: Initial diagnosis is unprocessed guilt and grief manifested in impulsive behavior; defensive stoicism; and pathological avoidance of relationships that he believes will lead to pain. Hypothesis: continues to stoke anger toward mother in hope that if he remains angry, her eventual death will hurt less than his father's did when he was in his mid-20s.

Dr. Raquel S. Stein, LCSW

SESSION 3

Patient name: Smith Seymour Simonyi

Month_Day: May 25, Mon

Time since last appointment: 4 years, 29 days

Patient arrived in acute distress, having recently experienced the death of his colleague. He professed concern that his distress would trigger an uncontrolled bout of gambling, and said that he was seeking help in order to prevent a "spiral" such as the one he experienced following his divorce, which was also the last time he visited this office.

I affirmed his choice to preemptively seek treatment in an effort to avoid what he felt was his typical, destructive response to grief. We spent the remainder of the session allowing him space to express his feelings, as he seemed eager to do.

We discussed the colleague (Iris), whose presence in his life seemed to be that of a sort of surrogate partner.

He left by stating that he doubted he would return to my office, given his general "distaste for therapy," but that, once again, he appreciated my willingness to see him in his current crisis. I made it clear that he should call without fearing I will bully him into committing to a regular therapeutic schedule. Given his previously sporadic interest in clinical work, this seemed the safest approach.

End of all entries for patient.

from: smith@simonyi.com
to: iris@simonyi.com
date: Mon, Oct 26 at 11:32 PM
subject: my dad

"He touched many lives and will be dearly missed."

The last line of my father's obituary, still available on the *Sun Prairie Star*'s website, was written by a woman who worked for the paper, after she told me that the obit I submitted was too short.

Touched many lives. What a load of shit.

When I buried him, I've never felt so alone, or so adult. Overnight, roles had switched. My dad was gone, my mom was in the hospital, barely conscious, and there were decisions to be made and bills to be paid. I picked out a casket. I signed papers listing fees for things I didn't know existed—body prep, body transport, insurance for if there's a flood at the cemetery. It cost everything I'd saved in my twenties. Did you know you can skip embalming? Or even the coffin altogether, if you're down for a "natural burial"? But not knowing if he wanted these or not, I wasn't going to cut corners. Not on my own father.

Neither of my parents had thought ahead to anything about dying or getting injured. They didn't have wills or life insurance. She sure as hell didn't have any kind of long-term disability. I bought a plot in the cemetery in the middle of town. The burial was minutes long. I stood there next to my great-aunts as a guy around my age, mid-twenties, shoveled clumps of dirt that trickled over the glossy black box. Then he picked up speed, and the dirt piled up until there was nothing but a freshly tilled rectangle of soil bigger than my dad.

And all I kept thinking that night was, sure, it was bad before.

They had their issues. But she'd made it infinitely worse. She'd ended the bad, but she'd ended the good, too. Now we had nothing.

So yes, I'm mad. I'm angry she didn't stand up for herself sooner, so it didn't have to end that way. I'm angry she let him treat her how he did, and I feel guilty about that, but I do, because I don't get to be angry at him anymore. He's gone. There's no one but her to be fucking angry at. I'm mad she got dragged into it. I'm mad she's paralyzed, and that I wasn't there to stop it. I'm mad at us both, and it may not be fair, but, fuck, I am.

---

from:	Bobbles Internet Hosting
to:	smith@simonyi.com
date:	Mon, Oct 26 at 11:33 PM
subject:	AUTOMATIC RESPONSE—YOUR EMAIL WAS NOT DELIVERED—DO NOT REPLY TO THIS EMAIL <<my dad>>

SIMONYI.COM Administrator,

Because this account was not renewed, it has been discontinued per the user agreement, which states that 90 days following failure to renew the address, it will become defunct. If you would like to restore the email address **iris@simonyi.com** please contact Bobbles Customer Care. Note that per the user agreement, email previously sent to and from this address cannot be restored even if the address is reactivated.

---

from:	smith@simonyi.com
to:	iris.a.massey@gmail.com
date:	Mon, Oct 26 at 11:35 PM
subject:	Fwd: my dad

For you, below.

TUESDAY, OCTOBER 27

---

from: jademassey@yahoo.com
to: smith@simonyi.com
date: Tue, Oct 27 at 6:17 PM
subject: no subject

Still emailing Iris, I see. Why'd you forward it?

---

from: smith@simonyi.com
to: jademassey@yahoo.com
date: Tue, Oct 27 at 8:59 PM
subject: re: no subject

I figured if any server reaches beyond this life, it's Google.
   Still checking her email, I see.

---

from: jademassey@yahoo.com
to: smith@simonyi.com
date: Tue, Oct 27 at 9:45 PM
subject: re: no subject

Trying to figure out what she wanted.
   I read your email. Sorry. I think I miss talking to you.

---

from: smith@simonyi.com
to: jademassey@yahoo.com
date: Tue, Oct 27 at 10:13 PM
subject: re: no subject

Doesn't matter.

---

from: jademassey@yahoo.com
to: smith@simonyi.com
date: Tue, Oct 27 at 10:30 PM
subject: re: no subject

Sounds like you're going through some shit.

---

from: smith@simonyi.com
to: jademassey@yahoo.com
date: Tue, Oct 27 at 10:35 PM
subject: re: no subject

We don't need to talk about it.

---

from: jademassey@yahoo.com
to: smith@simonyi.com
date: Tue, Oct 27 at 10:41 PM
subject: re: no subject

Is that why you email this stuff to someone who is dead? So you don't have to talk about it? You can just share into the void and not hear back what you don't want to hear?

---

from: smith@simonyi.com
to: jademassey@yahoo.com
date: Tue, Oct 27 at 10:42 PM
subject: re: no subject

Jade, please? I know I'm a fuckup.

---

from: jademassey@yahoo.com
to: smith@simonyi.com
date: Tue, Oct 27 at 10:50 PM
subject: re: no subject

Just go see your mom, Smith. Fuck your whole regrets theory. That's not why you need to go.

It's back. Rather, it was never gone. Just migrated south a bit, to my liver.

And this time, in its new location, it isn't likely to be responsive to chemo. So today I told Smith that this week will be my last of work. Richie, Jade—they can handle it. But I'm not sure Smith can. It's time to go before I begin to disappear.

As of Monday, my existence at Simonyi Brand Management will be no more than an absence. Then this will be true of my apartment. Then it will be true everywhere.

Could my absence on this earth do some good? Is it possible? (Apart from the obvious, that there is one fewer person on the planet consuming resources.)

At the high school where I spent my twelfth-grade year, we had Sharing Is Caring Day, a fundraiser for the school's special ed program. For us students, it meant a day full of games and prizes, the last of which was a scavenger hunt. My team consisted of six kids in a pickup, three in back, three in front. Our acquisitions included:

- A photo of a live chicken
- A helium balloon
- A round of gin rummy with a retirement home resident
- A whole tub of movie popcorn, consumed
- A lock of someone's hair
- Documentation of the biggest bubble blown by any team member
- A school T-shirt from five or more years ago

Still to go: a dad's joke.

In the McDonald's parking lot, we shifted our focus from person to person.

"Can't help."

"Not me."

"Mine's dead."

None of us had dads. All six of us, and not a single dad.

We could ask a dad of somebody on another team, someone suggested, but the consensus was that that would be uncool.

"Mr. Morris is a dad," one person pointed out. No one jumped at the idea because the thing was, our principal Mr. Morris's son had died a few years earlier. But if we asked him, at least there wasn't the issue of trespassing on another team's turf.

We headed to Mr. Morris's. When we got there, he was in his pajamas. You could see his wife through the window, watching TV. We told him we were doing the Sharing Is Caring scavenger hunt and needed a dad joke, but none of us had dads.

"How do you know a wildcat from a bobcat?" he asked.

"How?" we all yelled.

"One answers to Bob and the other doesn't!"

At first no one laughed. It was so awful. Then we all did, including Mr. Morris. He didn't have a son anymore, and we didn't have dads anymore, and here we all were because of it, laughing about a bobcat.

Maybe once I'm gone, the fact that I'm missing will bring people together, too.

COMMENTS (1):

BigJessBarbs: I would have used a mom for the joke and said TAKE THAT sexist pigs!

FRIDAY, OCTOBER 30

from: ronaldglass@apexunitedcitizens.com
to: smith@simonyi.com
date: Fri, Oct 30 at 9:02 AM
subject: Third and Final Contact

Dear Mr. Simons,

I write for a <u>third and final time</u> to offer you the opportunity to benefit from the teachings of Apex by working with me on my brand. Also I am willing to pay you. Was that not clear before? Who among us does not like money?

I eagerly anticipate your enthusiastic, though delayed, response.

Sincerely,

Ronald P. Glass

Why You Should Not Care About Time

BY RONALD P. GLASS

Tick tock! Tick tock!

Clocks lead us to believe that time exists.

However, they are pointing us wrong, as hands often do.

Time is as stretchy as a wad of Silly Putty. Don't believe me?

Just send your twin into space! She will come back dewy and elastic, while you've pruned up like a thumb in a tub.

If you cling to the view that time matters, it will.

If you understand that a minute can hold all the wonder of an hour or week or lifetime, you will leap like a man on the moon.

---

from: carl@simonyi.com
to: smith@simonyi.com
date: Fri, Oct 30 at 9:15 AM
subject: You won't believe this

Boss,

I have some news.

Iris almost quit her job three years ago.

How I know this is—long story short, the bottom left drawer in my desk has been stuck since Day 1. It won't go in all the way and drives me nuts because of my #ocd. So this morning I decided to fix it, finally. I removed it from its base, and, lo and behold, there were some papers stuck back behind the track. They were drafts that Iris wrote telling you she was going to quit, dated three years ago. Maybe you knew this? Hopefully not so I can feel valuable and my ego will get the same shot of dopamine it does when I meet a deadline or get an A! Just kidding!

How was BRANDISH doing three years ago?

---

from: smith@simonyi.com
to: carl@simonyi.com
date: Fri, Oct 30 at 9:28 AM
subject: re: You won't believe this

Huh. Well, I can't say I'm surprised.

It wasn't about the firm flailing, though. Three years ago we were doing well. The only thing I can think of that happened around that time is that Iris was supposed to get married.

And our name isn't BRANDISH. Nice try.

---

from: carl@simonyi.com
to: smith@simonyi.com
date: Fri, Oct 30 at 9:32 AM
subject: re: You won't believe this

Oh. Oh boy.

---

from: smith@simonyi.com
to: carl@simonyi.com
date: Fri, Oct 30 at 9:34 AM
subject: re: You won't believe this

What? Carl, you know how I feel about cryptic emails. Almost at front of line at Starbucks, I'll be there in 10 or so.

---

from: carl@simonyi.com
to: smith@simonyi.com
date: Fri, Oct 30 at 9:35 AM
subject: re: You won't believe this

Do you want me to lie or do you want the truth?

---

from: smith@simonyi.com
to: carl@simonyi.com
date: Fri, Oct 30 at 9:36 AM
subject: re: You won't believe this

For fuck's sake, Carl.

from: carl@simonyi.com
to: smith@simonyi.com
date: Fri, Oct 30 at 9:39 AM
subject: re: You won't believe this

Backstory of the last ~15 minutes: I thought it was weird that this never came up in her blog. And then I thought, well, maybe she had posts she wrote and didn't publish. That happens, you know? So I logged into her dyingtoblog.com account (she should have known better than to keep a document on the desktop titled PASSWORDS—she wasn't 85). And . . . she did. Have unpublished drafts.

from: smith@simonyi.com
to: carl@simonyi.com
date: Fri, Oct 30 at 9:40 AM
subject: re: You won't believe this

Carl! That's not okay!

from: carl@simonyi.com
to: smith@simonyi.com
date: Fri, Oct 30 at 9:41 AM
subject: re: You won't believe this

I know. I feel terrible.

from: smith@simonyi.com
to: carl@simonyi.com
date: Fri, Oct 30 at 9:41 AM
subject: re: You won't believe this

None of this is any of your business. Log out immediately.

from:	carl@simonyi.com
to:	smith@simonyi.com
date:	Fri, Oct 30 at 9:42 AM
subject:	re: You won't believe this

You're right. I'm signing out immediately and sharing nothing further.

If you want to know what's there, you will have to log in and read it for yourself.

Username: Irismassey

PW: cAramelTw1g

from:	smith@simonyi.com
to:	carl@simonyi.com
date:	Fri, Oct 30 at 9:44 AM
subject:	re: You won't believe this

Never do that again. This is unacceptable behavior. We will discuss it when I return. Waiting on my coffee, back in a second.

from:	smith@simonyi.com
to:	carl@simonyi.com
date:	Fri, Oct 30 at 9:46 AM
subject:	re: You won't believe this

Anyway, I imagine she was going to quit because she was planning to marry and didn't need the job anymore. She didn't wind up getting married, so she stayed.

---

from: carl@simonyi.com
to: smith@simonyi.com
date: Fri, Oct 30 at 9:46 AM
subject: re: You won't believe this

Nope.

---

from: carl@simonyi.com
to: smith@simonyi.com
date: Fri, Oct 30 at 9:52 AM
subject: re: You won't believe this

WHAT IN THE HECK KIND OF LATTÉ DID YOU ORDER, TRIPLE PUMPKIN SPICE??
 Count the cups in front of yours—is it more than 2??

---

from: carl@simonyi.com
to: smith@simonyi.com
date: Fri, Oct 30 at 9:55 AM
subject: re: You won't believe this

SHOULD I BE WORRIED YOU GOT HIT BY A BUS?

---

from: carl@simonyi.com
to: smith@simonyi.com
date: Fri, Oct 30 at 9:56 AM
subject: re: You won't believe this

I can't hold it in any longer: Boss, she was going to quit because she was in love with *you*.

from: jademassey@yahoo.com
to: winsomebeautydorothy@hotmail.com
date: Fri, Oct 30 at 1:33 PM
subject: Plan for the weekend

Mom,

I'm just going to take a cab from the airport. Please don't come get me. I'll see you in the morning. I'm hoping that we can tackle the following projects tomorrow:

- Shower clog. The fact that four bottles of Drano haven't done the trick means we have to try something else. I'll go to Lowe's in the morning and see what the man there recommends.

- Add a ramp to the porch so you don't keep tripping. Next time it could be your hip. Do you know what happens to women your age who break a hip? I don't think I need to tell you. Sam from your church says he can help us build it. He is a woodworker or something.

- Clean out the pantry. It's sweet that you offered to help that mentally handicapped lady—what's her name, Rose?—can peaches, but the jars are putrid. I don't think she screwed them on tight enough. I think we should throw them out and get her decent peaches at the farmer's market or something. Will she even know the difference, truly?

- Buy some fruit in case you get trick-or-treaters. Do you ever? It would be a shame to disappoint them by having nothing on hand to give out.

See you tomorrow (don't come get me!),
Jade

---

from: winsomebeautydorothy@hotmail.com
to: jademassey@yahoo.com
date: Fri, Oct 30 at 1:45 PM
subject: re: Plan for the weekend

ENOUGH IS ENOUGH. I will have no such eyesore gracing the likes of my front porch. Do not talk to me about Sam being a woodworker, he built a set for the Christmas pageant last year that COLLAPSED during the birth of Christ. INWARD. Mary and Joseph each broke a bone. Wrists, fingers, or both. He will be building me no ramps, at least insofar as you are not secretly *hoping* for my death by fall.

And we will <u>not</u> be giving the sweet children who come to my door *fruit* when they have gone to the trouble of donning costumes in exchange for something respectable like chocolate, nor will we be moving Rose Larrimore's peaches anywhere. If you don't like the smell, you will just need to keep the pantry door closed when you're here.

Of course I'm picking you up from the airport. I'm not decrepit or blind yet, for heaven's sake.

Mom

---

from: smith@simonyi.com
to: richierich1000@gmail.com
date: Fri, Oct 30 at 1:45 PM
subject: Apology

Hi Richie,

Just dropped a check by your office. Sorry for being such a money pit for so long. I know it was frustrating. I won't be asking to borrow from you anymore. Lame as it sounds—I do just miss hanging out.

Smith

---

from: richierich1000@gmail.com
to: smith@simonyi.com
date: Fri, Oct 30 at 2:02 PM
subject: re: Apology

---

what the hell is this?

---

from: smith@simonyi.com
to: richierich1000@gmail.com
date: Fri, Oct 30 at 2:14 PM
subject: re: Apology

I finally signed a new client and can pay you back. Sorry again.

---

from: richierich1000@gmail.com
to: smith@simonyi.com
date: Fri, Oct 30 at 2:30 PM
subject: re: Apology

MESSAGES

Wed., Mar. 25, 10:00 PM

IRIS: Hey. What's up?

RICHIE: well well well look who lives

IRIS: I'm sorry? Sorry.

RICHIE: is miss snappy gone? is it safe to speak freely?

IRIS: yeah

RICHIE: kidding. left you alone because you told me to.

IRIS: How've you been?

RICHIE: ok. little lonely

RICHIE: my girlfriend dumped me

RICHIE: she has cancer and SHE dumped ME

IRIS: I didn't dump you!

RICHIE: yeah ok

RICHIE: How are you?

IRIS: I'm feeling better today. My mom is back in town.

RICHIE: oh cool

IRIS: She arrived last night and already feels neglected.

RICHIE: want me to entertain her? i'll take her on the staten island ferry and everything

IRIS: Are you scared of dying?

RICHIE: and a full 180

RICHIE: honesty ok hmm

RICHIE: less than i'm scared i'll go crazy and wind up living with a bunch of feral cats and never showering

IRIS: Are you scared of ME dying?

RICHIE: of course

IRIS: I'm scared.

RICHIE: i want to hug you right now so bad

IRIS: I feel like I'm not supposed to be scared at this point. I'm supposed to be at acceptance

RICHIE: i don't think there's a way you're supposed to feel. u feel scared. that seems totally natural

IRIS: Thanks

RICHIE: hey question. do u believe in heaven?

IRIS: Like a happy place in the clouds? No.

RICHIE: more like life after death. like it keeps going

RICHIE: didn't mean to freak you out. sorry.

IRIS: I don't know. Do you?

RICHIE: yeah

IRIS: That's nice. That seems like it would be comforting.

RICHIE: ok this is getting too depressing. let's look on the bright side. what are we going to do when you DON'T die?

RICHIE: let's start planning

IRIS: Ha. Okay. Well I've still never been to Coney Island, so that

RICHIE: done

IRIS: I've always wanted to do that thing where people fish for
     mussels or clams . . . shellfish I mean. What is that called?

RICHIE: clamming? no clue. but sounds easy enough. what else

IRIS: I want to wake up on a Saturday morning with you and lie in
     bed all day and watch movies and drink mimosas.

RICHIE: but NOT Pulp Fiction

IRIS: I told you, I don't get into gangsters.

RICHIE: you got into this one ;) ;)

IRIS: Looking like one doesn't make you one.

RICHIE: yeah yeah. movie day we can make happen

RICHIE: what else

RICHIE: where'd u go

IRIS: I got sad.

RICHIE: why? we can do stuff. be optimistic.

IRIS: Richie, I'm going to die.

IRIS: I don't want to. And I don't want you to be sad. That's why I
     don't think we should do this fantasizing stuff. It would all be
     wonderful, sure. But I don't see things going that way.

RICHIE: i understand.

RICHIE: i am trying to.

IRIS: I'm going to sleep. Good night. Hugs.

RICHIE: night girl. giant hug all night long

---

from: smith@simonyi.com
to: richierich1000@gmail.com
date: Fri, Oct 30 at 3:00 PM
subject: re: Apology

---

what is this?

---

from: richierich1000@gmail.com
to: smith@simonyi.com
date: Fri, Oct 30 at 3:03 PM
subject: re: Apology

---

what does it look like

---

from: smith@simonyi.com
to: richierich1000@gmail.com
date: Fri, Oct 30 at 3:06 PM
subject: re: Apology

I get that it's messages between you and Iris. Did you mean to forward it to me?

---

from: richierich1000@gmail.com
to: smith@simonyi.com
date: Fri, Oct 30 at 3:08 PM
subject: re: Apology

---

u are so fuckin dense man

---

from: richierich1000@gmail.com
to: smith@simonyi.com
date: Fri, Oct 30 at 3:17 PM
subject: re: Apology

---

im not mad cuz u keep asking for money. u can gamble all u want. its your fuckin life. im mad cuz u kept asking me about money and not how i am doing. am i ok

---

from: smith@simonyi.com
to: richierich1000@gmail.com
date: Fri, Oct 30 at 3:24 PM
subject: re: Apology

How did you know about my gambling?

---

from: richierich1000@gmail.com
to: smith@simonyi.com
date: Fri, Oct 30 at 3:28 PM
subject: re: Apology

---

see? making this about yourself
    everyone knows dude
    addicts don't hide their shit they just think they do

---

from: smith@simonyi.com
to: richierich1000@gmail.com
date: Fri, Oct 30 at 3:33 PM
subject: re: Apology

Are you not okay? I know you miss her. I do, too.

---

from: richierich1000@gmail.com
to: smith@simonyi.com
date: Fri, Oct 30 at 3:40 PM
subject: re: Apology

---

u don't fucking get it. i know you miss her but it was different.

---

from: smith@simonyi.com
to: richierich1000@gmail.com
date: Fri, Oct 30 at 3:42 PM
subject: re: Apology

I know it's different. You guys were dating.

---

from: richierich1000@gmail.com
to: smith@simonyi.com
date: Fri, Oct 30 at 4:04 PM
subject: re: Apology

---

dude i loved her. i fell in love with her

---

from: smith@simonyi.com
to: richierich1000@gmail.com
date: Fri, Oct 30 at 4:10 PM
subject: re: Apology

Have I not been understanding enough of that?

from: richierich1000@gmail.com
to: smith@simonyi.com
date: Fri, Oct 30 at 4:12 PM
subject: re: Apology

no dude. not even close

from: smith@simonyi.com
to: richierich1000@gmail.com
date: Fri, Oct 30 at 4:15 PM
subject: re: Apology

I'm sorry.

from: richierich1000@gmail.com
to: smith@simonyi.com
date: Fri, Oct 30 at 4:20 PM
subject: re: Apology

i just miss her dude
u have no idea

MONDAY, NOVEMBER 2

Monday, November 2

TherapistAwayNetwork™

Patient Name: Jade Renee Massey

AUTO PROMPT: **What do you have to gain?**

Well, TAN, now that Dr. Z. has announced his retirement, it's just you and me.

My mother has kicked me out. She doesn't want me to come back down for at least six weeks. I have a feeling she only said six weeks because of Christmas, or it would have been longer. She's sick of me apparently, and has been for a while. The reason she looked catatonic? Was me. I was wearing her out.

I suppose I should feel grateful that she's back to her old "self" again, but what I'm really thinking about is how it is that everyone but me is moving on. My mom. Smith.

I don't get it. What magic reliever of pain has touched them but not me?

The last time Iris went to the hospital, my mom and I went, too. It was so clear it was the end. I hadn't realized how clear it becomes at some point.

My mom kept herself busy, alternately weeping in the corner while typing on her phone and scolding the nurses for various things she objected to in the room.

Then Iris said, "Leave." She mumbled, but we both heard it.

The nurse heard it, too. She had been changing Iris's pillow, which had become soaked with sweat and saliva and whatever other mysterious, viscous fluids the body releases as it goes.

The nurse gestured for my mom and me to follow her into the hall.

"It's hurtful, I know, when they do that," she said to my mom in a hushed tone. "They often lash out at someone near the end. It isn't personal." Then she told us stories of patients cursing at husbands, fathers, and mothers, of the most cruel accusations and name-calling flying from the mouths of people with one foot in and one foot out of this world. This seemed to make my mother feel worse, and not long after, she returned to her hotel for the night.

A little after 5:00 a.m., Iris died. I had dozed in stints and was caffeinated into that fuzzy, limbo state, teetering on the brink between sleep and wakefulness, unable to relax into either. She had been making these sounds—these sort of monstrous gasps for air, almost like coughs, but not.

I googled them. The first hit contained the words "death rattle."

Google was right. When it finally stopped, only a couple of minutes passed before she was gone.

"Bye, Jade," she said, like she was just falling asleep, and I was leaving for work, and we'd meet back up in the evening.

"Bye, Iris," I said.

I miss her as much today as I did the day after she died. No ounce of it has subsided. Time has done nothing to make it better. These months might as well have never even happened.

What do I have to gain? Anything to make it better than this. But unlike everyone else, I have no idea how.

■

Dear JADE,

Thank you for your submission to TAN™. We will make sure your provider receives this message.

"Gain" is a noun as well as a verb. As English speakers, we tend to rely excessively on nouns to convey meaning, and in doing so, restrict ourselves to ideas that already exist, rather than opening our imaginations to ideas that have yet to be named.

What if today you focused on "gain" as a verb, and allowed the noun that follows to remain inchoate, finding comfort in the mindset of gaining without knowing exactly what it is that lies before you? Perhaps—just perhaps—it is so large, you can't possibly begin to know what it's called yet.

TAN™ is not to be used in case of emergency. If you are in crisis, call 9-1-1.

Sincerely,

Your friends at TAN

UNPUBLISHED DRAFT
Last opened October 30, at 9:20 AM

The first morning of the incubator, I was late and slid into a row near the back next to a blond man in dark-rimmed glasses. Like me, he appeared a little older than most of the early-twenties crowd. At the front of the auditorium, someone was giving a speech about how we, as entrepreneurs, were the pioneers thrusting society forward in a bunch of ways that ended in -ly: technically, economically, socially.

I was thinking *I just want to start a bakery* when my neighbor leaned over and whispered, "I'm in PR." Then he paused before adding, "Thrusting us forward."

We spent the next five days quietly mocking the program and skipping sessions to drink at a local bar while getting to know each other. It wasn't romantic—I was with Daniel, and Smith had only just gotten divorced—but it was intimate. We were the bad kids at incubator camp. I'm sure for me, the rebel behavior was at least in part a defense mechanism. It was clear from day one that I wasn't ready to open a bakery. Market research, business plans—the terms thrown around made me want to take a nap. Our incubator taught me that I needed a lot more incubating.

It only made sense that I'd go to work for him. I needed a job for the time being, and Smith needed an assistant. We toasted glasses of Guinness and Stella. And that night I lay in my bed at the Hyatt and felt a sense of fate at work, as if this is what was meant to be, silly as I knew it sounded: another job for which I was overqualified, in a random field. But it wasn't the field that pulled me in. It was Smith.

He made it so easy to feel seen and heard. He listened. He laughed at my jokes. He seemed hungry for what I might say next.

Was I attracted to him? I asked myself this question hundreds of times over the years. Only a handful of them was the answer yes. The rest of the time, it felt past that . . . less urgent than romance.

Of course I was a little bit in love with him. He calls wine openers "chickens" with a straight face and can recite the US presidents in order if he sings them. He has never once treated me like I'm anything less than the smartest person in the room.

But only once did it really blossom into something like a crush, an actual infatuation. A little over a year after I began working for him, a couple of months after my thirtieth birthday, Daniel and I were engaged. I faced that spring that I had feelings for Smith, strong enough that I had to do something about them. What I wound up doing was making a mess by leaving Daniel the day of our wedding.

There were good reasons we shouldn't marry, but what had triggered my willingness to face them finally? From where did that strength surge? From wanting someone else. Feelings for Smith nudged me into action, and yet I wasn't ready to pursue those, either (part of me still thought Daniel and I might make it in the end). And thus, I would also need to quit my job.

The Monday after my failed wedding, I knew Smith wouldn't be at the office because he was in Nashville. I drafted my resignation letter several times before I realized that I couldn't do it. I didn't want to. I wanted to stay for the same reason I had needed to quit, and the same reason I'd taken the job in the first place. I liked being around him.

Soon it passed back into what we had originally, what Smith

and I were destined to amount to: friends. The fire wasn't there—not enough of one. It was more like a pilot light, a perpetual option neither of us was ever willing to ignite. Our hesitation wasn't out of fear, I don't think. It was an understanding that we didn't need more between us.

What we had—people didn't understand it. Maybe we didn't even understand it. But apart from the critical flash when I needed it to be more, it was platonic, and real, and it fed me.

---

from: smith@simonyi.com
to: carl@simonyi.com
date: Mon, Nov 2 at 5:01 PM
subject: re: You won't believe this

Carl, she was not in love with me.

---

from: carl@simonyi.com
to: smith@simonyi.com
date: Mon, Nov 2 at 5:09 PM
subject: re: You won't believe this

You caved!

Aren't you glad you read it? Don't you feel warm inside? Might as well read the other drafts while you're in there! ;) (Warning: some of them are really loopy. Was she *often* high at work?)

---

from: smith@simonyi.com
to: carl@simonyi.com
date: Mon, Nov 2 at 5:11 PM
subject: re: You won't believe this

No, I'm not glad. I feel like a creep for reading it behind her back.

March 30, 5:39 PM

Chemo makes your hair fall out slower and faster than you want. It took mine a month to start, but once it did, it released itself in clods, each fistful a reminder that I wasn't just poisoning the cancer. I was poisoning myself.

I took the plunge and shaved my head one afternoon in early February. A blizzard had just come through New York. Gray slush piles clogged the street corners, and the wind felt like it had mass. As I dove into it, my hair blew into my mouth and eyes, and I was annoyed until I realized it would be the last time that ever happened.

I had bought several scarves—a Cubist one from the MOMA store, another with daffodils, and one with Sylvia Plath's poem "Cinderella" printed on it in dark loopy cursive: *Amid the hectic music and cocktail talk, she hears the caustic ticking of the clock.*

I took them all to my hair guy Tim and laid them out like precious vintage garments, or wares for sale.

He grabbed the Plath scarf.

"You will be stunning," he said, which was a sweet lie. Then we washed my hair one last time and he wrapped a towel around it and brought out a bottle of Veuve. We toasted in silence, and I could tell he wished he'd thought of what to say.

I've been going to his little studio on St. Mark's for eight years. It only has four chairs, and as I took a seat in one, he locked the door and drew the curtains, which only closed partway. Every now and then a passerby would peek through the glass storefront, but otherwise, it was just the two of us and the music from the coffee shop next door. The coffee shop and the salon shared a wall.

We're going hoppin'. We're going hoppin' today.
Where things are poppin' the Philadelphia way.

He turned the chair to face away from the mirror so I couldn't watch. But in one of those big metallic holiday balls still hanging from his ceiling, my warped reflection nonetheless made clear what was happening, and I consciously chose not to look at it. He pulled the razor over my skull in measured strips, and I kept my eyes on the gray wall that was also a coffee shop wall, as we played Remember When.

Remember when you failed your driver's test twice at the age of twenty-five?

Remember when you showed up covered in paint? (I'd tripped into a paint can while passing by a construction site.)

Remember the party clown who showed up at your apartment by mistake and then asked you out?

When he was almost done, I stopped him. Above my head the razor buzzed, chopping the air where all my Remember Whens were bobbing, tearing them apart.

Tim placed his big callused hands on my head like he was a priest blessing me. They felt rough and warm on my fresh scalp. He slid a sharp edge over the skin around my left ear, the last final bit of my future, and then he took the poem scarf and wrapped it around and tied it. He turned the chair to the mirror, and I saw myself without hair. It wasn't how I thought I'd look, but it wasn't worse, either.

He raised his glass again. I lifted mine for his benefit and then brought it back down. I couldn't.

"To midnight!" He tapped his glass to the scarf on my head. "When the party gets good."

COMMENTS (4):

BigJessBarbs: Tell me about it. I lost my hair in two hours. And I mean ALL of it.

BonnieD: Did you see Ardvark died?

IrisMassey: Oh no.

BonnieD: Yes. ☹

FRIDAY, NOVEMBER 6

from: carl@simonyi.com
to: smith@simonyi.com
date: Fri, Nov 6 at 4:14 PM
subject: An honest chat

Boss,

I hope the shoot with ZF is going well!

Here are a couple of important thoughts before I take off for the weekend.

First, the good news. As of last week, Phil is off to an ashram for six weeks, which will allow me more time/emotional energy to dedicate exclusively to our work.

Next, an attempt at radical transparency. While I'm thrilled that we signed Zahara Ferringbottom and very excited about her despite the fact that she is literally insane, I have concerns about the status of BRANDISH (how does that not work?). I meant to tell you this last night, but I lost my nerve. Rosita called yesterday afternoon and said she is going with another firm. She didn't want to wait for a call back to tell you herself, and she wouldn't say which one. She says it is one that doesn't "make [her] the laughingstock of the New York dentistry community and then charge [her] for it."

(Sidenote: I know you said not to, but I did end up responding to Ronald Glass the cult leader just to get him off our backs. It was a mistake. Now he keeps inviting me to his center for a free mental health–replenishing treatment involving slugs. I think we made the right call in declining to take him on.)

But without Phil, our firm just feels a bit . . . like losers. We are a loser firm.

I am trying to remain optimistic that we can recover. After *Belle* declined to publish Jade's essay, it hit me—what if we submit something inspired by the *other* Massey sister? Thus, I am authoring the listicle I previously suggested, inspired by Iris. The good news is that it poses no copyright issues due to the fact that it's only inspired by her and not by-by her.

More soon.

CVS

PS—This afternoon I took the liberty of installing my high school friend Gus Martin's app OOF! (beta) on our computers. It does a bunch of things that don't matter, but the reason I downloaded it is that it slightly delays emails after you press send, so that you have a couple of minutes to recall them if necessary. (His motto is "Rescind to Resend"—cute, I think!) I figure it would have been useful (read: lifesaver) back in September when I accidently dispatched *the* email that shall not ever be mentioned again. So far I like OOF! Maybe we can give him a blurb for his splash page?

Sent with OOF!™ beta

from: smith@simonyi.com
to: IRIS
date: Fri, Nov 6 at 7:50 PM
subject: no subject

I can't stop thinking about that spring three years ago. Did I suspect how you felt?

I think I could sense it. I also think I sensed your reluctance about it. You were engaged. You'd chosen someone else. I wasn't going to put you in a position to question that, if that was what you wanted. I was glad you were happy. I thought you were happy.

With Richie, though, you actually were. You two had the thing.

You and I—could we have had it?

I didn't let myself fall in love with you . . . I didn't dare.

He's right. I don't get it. I never got there. I was a coward.

from: Your Steps Tracker
to: jademassey@yahoo.com
date: Fri, Nov 6 at 8:15 PM
subject: You've logged 60 Miles in 5 days!

Congratulations! You set a record this week of **60 miles in 5 days**!

Did you know that walking can reduce the risk of heart disease?

Keep steppin'!

Your steps are logged automatically. You are receiving this email as a T-Mobile customer.

Friday, November 6
TherapistAwayNetwork™
Patient Name: Jade Renee Massey
AUTO PROMPT: **What gives you hope?**

I've been walking a lot.

And thinking.

I am wondering if Smith may have been on to something. Maybe the blog freaks me out because of what it says about me. In any case, I've started reading it again.

This morning I got to the part about how I made her feel invisible. That was a doozy.

But I didn't have to read it to know it.

That day that Iris won the science fair, we probably ate takeout and watched TV and did our homework as usual. But the next morning, when I got to class, there was a note in my backpack: *I won the science fair.*

Somehow it made it worse that she included "the science fair." Not even just *I won.* As if I may have even needed to be reminded what it was she was competing in, despite the fact that I had helped her heat up the water in the microwave, then place it under the ice cube as I'd seen Ariella Franklin do at my previous school the spring before. I had helped her draw pictures of evaporation and paste them on the three-panel cardboard our mom was willing to buy for the occasion. I had done all of this, but in the end, I'd forgotten to ask how it went.

I had a million things on my mind. I'd just started at a new high school. I had boys on the brain, as well as who I was going to be, what kind of person. Would I pass my driver's test? How and when would I ask my mom to teach me? Would there be any guys at my new school willing to take a chance on the new girl with no social status? There were so many unknowns. It was remarkably easy for Iris to slip off my radar.

But it wasn't just that time. So many others—her wedding. Her school dance. From childhood to adulthood, all the moments I could have noticed Iris but didn't, because I was preoccupied with Jade.

I've tried to make it better. To do what she would want, now that she's gone.

Maybe this is my mistake—trying to fix it at all. The world is different now. She left with a part of me that isn't coming back.

I miss Smith.

Henry is now doing some sleuth work for me on the malpractice claim. Sort of—he thinks we should sue the cannabis company that sold her tinctures with promises of recovery. The things he'll do for me when he's hungry for reconciliation.

I don't know . . . I'm sort of over the whole lawsuit thing. I owe Henry details on the pot company, though. It's nice of him to look into it for me. I don't remember what it was called—I'll have to go back into her email to get it.

But if this angle at the suit is also a nonstarter, I'm done. Okay, universe? I'll be done.

Dear JADE,

Thank you for your submission to TAN™. We will make sure your provider receives this message. As Pablo Neruda says, "You can cut all the flowers but you cannot keep spring from coming."

TAN™ is not to be used in case of emergency. If you are in crisis, call 9-1-1.

Sincerely,

Your friends at TAN

SATURDAY, NOVEMBER 7

---

from: smith@simonyi.com
to: MOM
date: Sat, Nov 7 at 12:00 PM
subject: DRAFT no subject

Dear Mom,

    I'm sorry that I've resented

---

from: smith@simonyi.com
to: MOM
date: Sat, Nov 7 at 12:04 PM
subject: DRAFT no subject

Dear Mom,

    As your son, I maybe should have been more understanding of

from: smith@simonyi.com
to: MOM
date: Sat, Nov 7 at 5:55 PM
subject: no subject

Dear Mom,

When you read this, we'll have seen each other. I'm bringing it with me next time I come.

I am sorry that I've struggled to talk to you about what happened.

I miss Dad a lot. I did right away. I didn't know how to deal with that and also have a relationship with you. Like I wasn't supposed to love both of you. Like I had to choose between loving you and missing him. I didn't have a choice, though, because I did miss him, as dumb as it seemed to miss someone who made our lives so hard. I still do.

Now I realize you must have missed him, too—in ways I can't understand.

I want us to have a relationship again. I'm sorry.

Love,
Smith

from: smith@simonyi.com
to: wally@homilypines.com
date: Sat, Nov 7 at 5:59 PM
subject: Thanksgiving

Hi Wally,

I think I'll be there prior to Thanksgiving, actually. I'm going to come visit Mom next weekend.

Would you mind letting her know?

See you soon!
Smith

---

from: wally@homilypines.com
to: smith@simonyi.com
date: Sat, Nov 7 at 6:13 PM
subject: Thanksgiving

Of course. Great to hear. I'll tell her in the morning, and she'll be thrilled. She's just sleeping off some congestion. See you in a week!

---

from: postmaster@simonyi.com via BOXITWEB
to: smith@simonyi.com
date: Sat, Nov 7 at 6:27 PM
subject: UNDELIVERABLE: no subject

The e-mail address you entered "MOM" could not be found. Please check the recipient's e-mail address and try again to send your message. If the problem continues, please contact your help-desk for troubleshooting.

---

from: smith@simonyi.com
to: carl@simonyi.com
date: Sat, Nov 7 at 6:31 PM
subject: urgent

Carl,

I know it's a Saturday and you're probably at an ayahuasca ceremony or something, but what does this app you installed do besides delay emails? Tell me it isn't doing what I think it's doing.

---

from: carl@simonyi.com
to: smith@simonyi.com
date: Sat, Nov 7 at 6:39 PM
subject: re: urgent

Hmm. What might that be? I need a bit more direction.

Also, I don't do ayahuasca. I've watched YouTube videos of people doing it, and the vomit deters me. Plus they all seem to be dummies.

On the other hand, I *do* like the idea of sensing an overwhelming, universal love . . . pros and cons!

---

from: smith@simonyi.com
to: carl@simonyi.com
date: Sat, Nov 7 at 6:42 PM
subject: urgent

I think it's sending my drafts. I drafted a letter in my email account that I never meant to send. It just bounced back because I hadn't even included a real email address. So OOF! must have sent it?

---

from: carl@simonyi.com
to: smith@simonyi.com
date: Sat, Nov 7 at 6:43 PM
subject: re: urgent

I know it autofills based on your recent email history . . . but no, it's not supposed to automatically send drafts after it autofills. That would be a horrible feature of a product! Are you sure you didn't send yourself?

from: smith@simonyi.com
to: carl@simonyi.com
date: Sat, Nov 7 at 6:44 PM
subject: urgent

Yes. I just looked. It not only autofills . . . the fucking thing is sending my drafts to the *people* it autofilled. Every draft I've written since you installed it has been sent.

from: carl@simonyi.com
to: smith@simonyi.com
date: Sat, Nov 7 at 6:50 PM
subject: re: urgent

Yikes! That's a HUGE bug. I'll let Gus know.

Ugh, he's going to be so bummed about this. I didn't mention this before, but he's having a rough year. Would you know, Gus Martin is one of the most coveted names by criminals? He's only twenty-two and his identity has been stolen six times. Right now some car thief in Sacramento has his SS# pinned for $45K in CC debt.

AND he's got shingles.

from: smith@simonyi.com
to: carl@simonyi.com
date: Sat, Nov 7 at 6:56 PM
subject: urgent

Can you get into Iris's Gmail account? How do I do it? I need to delete something.

from: carl@simonyi.com
to: smith@simonyi.com
date: Sat, Nov 7 at 6:57 PM
subject: re: urgent

Um, Boss, that's illegal.

from: smith@simonyi.com
to: carl@simonyi.com
date: Sat, Nov 7 at 6:59 PM
subject: urgent

You do it all the time!

from: carl@simonyi.com
to: smith@simonyi.com
date: Sat, Nov 7 at 7:02 PM
subject: re: urgent

I go IN. I don't DELETE. That's a *traceable* crime.

from: smith@simonyi.com
to: carl@simonyi.com
date: Sat, Nov 7 at 7:04 PM
subject: urgent

Carl, give me the fucking password.

---

from: smith@simonyi.com
to: carl@simonyi.com
date: Sat, Nov 7 at 7:11 PM
subject: urgent

Now!

---

from: carl@simonyi.com
to: smith@simonyi.com
date: Sat, Nov 7 at 7:12 PM
subject: re: urgent

Do you have snapchat? I'd feel safer snapping you.

---

from: smith@simonyi.com
to: carl@simonyi.com
date: Sat, Nov 7 at 7:13 PM
subject: urgent

I'll delete the text, Carl. For fuck's sake.

---

from: carl@simonyi.com
to: smith@simonyi.com
date: Sat, Nov 7 at 7:15 PM
subject: re: urgent

Fine. Texted.
   I've never seen you like this!

from: carl@simonyi.com
to: smith@simonyi.com
date: Sat, Nov 7 at 7:59 PM
subject: re: urgent

Well??? How did it go? Did you delete? I'm trying not to ask questions, but I am *so* curious what's going on!

I will uninstall OOF! first thing Monday morning.

from: smith@simonyi.com
to: carl@simonyi.com
date: Sat, Nov 7 at 8:39 PM
subject: urgent

I didn't get there in time. It's already marked as read.

from: carl@simonyi.com
to: smith@simonyi.com
date: Sat, Nov 7 at 8:45 PM
subject: re: urgent

What??? She's DEAD. Who else is in there??

from: smith@simonyi.com
to: carl@simonyi.com
date: Sat, Nov 7 at 8:47 PM
subject: urgent

Doesn't matter. It's too late.

Saturday, November 7

TherapistAwayNetwork™

Patient Name: Jade Renee Massey

AUTO PROMPT: **What is a first step you can take?**

Ha. Joke's on me. What I get for checking her email.

Of course he loved her. Or at least wishes he'd "let himself," whatever that means.

I was the next closest thing.

Shouldn't be surprised, I guess, given I suspected it all along.

. . .

Dear JADE,

Thank you for your submission to TAN™. We will make sure your provider receives this message.

In baseball, first base is a position on the field that requires an elite player, because it is the critical point where a run is determined possible or impossible.

Where does the ball get thrown more times than anywhere else? That's right: first.

There is a reason for the saying that the first step is the hardest one, and it is the same reason that the ball is thrown more often to first base than other bases. When you start a journey, that's when you're most vulnerable. Make it past first, and you've survived the worst. (We didn't mean for that to rhyme, but we like it.)

TAN™ is not to be used in case of emergency. If you are in crisis, call 9-1-1.

Sincerely,

Your friends at TAN

Since I don't think I'll have time to finish writing out my dots, this week I made a list of a hundred memories and sorted them:

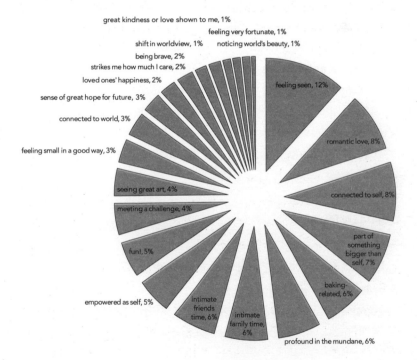

Feeling Seen. That's what I remember best.

Which I guess means most of the time I felt unseen.

For my eighth-grade school dance, I wore a cream dress that I inherited from Jade. It had peach polka dots and satin buttons down the back. It was the first time I remember feeling pretty.

I was sitting in the hotel lobby waiting for my mom to finish getting ready so she could drive me to the dance when Jade came in on her way out for the night. She was seventeen and a senior in high school. I waited for her to notice how I looked, but she didn't even glance at me. She looked beautiful, even in jeans.

"Bye," I said.

She didn't even say it back as she left.

The next year I got my first tattoo and dyed my hair hot pink, but by then Jade was in culinary school, and when she came "home" for break (I forget what hotel we were living in, maybe one in Kansas), all she said was "Rebel phase, I see."

I always wanted my sister to think of me as a real person. But I was her little sibling: part nuisance, part confidante when she needed one, part forgettable much of the time.

It's nice that she sees me now. Even if it's because I am sick.

COMMENTS (3):

TigerSashRox: I see you, girl!

BonnieD: we're here for you!

SP2004: might I recommend "Without a Pit, It's Not a Cherry?" You must love yourself before others can love you is the message.

MONDAY, NOVEMBER 9

from: jademassey@yahoo.com
to: smith@simonyi.com
date: Mon, Nov 9 at 8:30 AM
subject: Sorry

Dear Smith,

I apologize for saying what I did about you and your relationship to your mother. It wasn't fair. I was lashing out. These things are hard to navigate, and I was acting like they aren't. I know you had feelings for my sister (sorry for looking, but I'd rather know, and am glad I do now).

I just want you to know that I hold no hard feelings and wish you the best. Thank you for the conversations over the last couple of months. They've helped me.

Sincerely,

Jade

from: carl@simonyi.com
to: jademassey@yahoo.com
date: Mon, Nov 9 at 10:09 AM
subject: re: Sorry

Hi Jade,

Carl here, managing Smith's email. Very sad news. His mom died last night. He's in Wisconsin. Apparently she caught a case of pneumonia and it did her in. Poor guy. :'-(

But while I have you on the line, I have some *good* news. After we turned down Todd and Chad at Dying to Blog, I reached out to our *Belle* contact Hadley to see if she'd be interested in a listicle based on Iris's blog. Turns out she's more interested in running an excerpt or two from the blog itself. Anyway, since I have actually been putting in the sweat hours on the following listicle, I figure I will share it with you. I plan to submit it to Hadley this week just to see what she thinks. Or if you think we should stick to selecting a post or two from Iris's blog, I suppose we could do that, too.

I tried to keep it light, as we both know readers of *Belle* are unlikely to be voracious consumers of the somewhat . . . grim reflections penned by your sis. (No offense, I'm sure she was a hoot in real life.)

What do you think?

Talk soon,

CVS III

Title: 10 Ways to Improve Your Life at Its Conclusion

BY CARL VAN SNYDER III

When New York resident Iris Massey died at age 33 earlier this year, she left behind a dream, a career in stagnation, and an empty cradle. But she also left behind a blog. Through rigorous toiling through grueling questions, Iris dared to face what many of us ignore every day of our lives: the fact that sometimes our life doesn't amount to what we thought it would.

Inspired by Iris but not stated by her directly, thus not a copy of her expression of any ideas, here are 10 ways that you, too, can discover the latent potential in your own life before the guillotine comes crashing down.

1. **Indulge happy memories.** We all like to remember the good times, but sometimes we feel like we aren't supposed to be nostalgic, that it's a waste of time and what we're really supposed to be doing is working as hard as we can night and day, studying and getting all As and setting ourselves apart so that in the end, we can have whatever career we want and live the American dream at its most prestigious. But the rat race might as well be called "fatigue central." What's so bad about lying back and recalling your happiest times? An occasional bout of fantasizing about the past can be good for you, reactivating neural pathways that make those happy memories more robust and therefore easier to recall in the future when you need a "pick-me-up."

2. **Take up drawing.** Who among us did not at one point wish to be Van Gogh with his starry, swoopy sky, sans missing ear?

3. **Find an online community.** Do you live in the Middle of Nowhere, South Dakota? Do you feel like no one around gets you because you do not conform to the standards they set for their lives, such as what kind of person you are allowed to love? In that case, I have good news for you: get online! Everyone is online, mostly, except for in the dirt-poor parts of the world, and probably even there by now. That means you have about seven billion people to choose from for your new friends. Find people who get you, whether those are people who fall in love with goats or people who are also dying.

4. **Don't put off your dreams.** The disappointment of failure beats the disappointment of never trying. Fail to win. Win to fail. Etc. (Note to editor: This one might need a bit of work from someone else because I do not relate to it.)

5. **Break up with the capital-L "Loser."** Does your partner make you feel worse more often than he (or she or they) makes you feel better? If so, dump their ass. You get to live once. Don't spend your time with a lover who makes you yell all the time.

6. **Study science.** You don't know how big the universe is until you find out. And you don't find out until you ask, or go to a planetarium, or watch a free documentary on your laptop about the cosmos. It is really big. This will make you feel small, but in a good way, which will make you humble and want to not take yourself as seriously as you have a tendency to do. Or it will just make you respect nature, which is very important due to global warming.

7. **Do things for others, such as baking for them.** (Note to editor: cut? This one is boring to me, I'm half asleep just writing it.)

8. **Read books about dying.** You can never be too prepared for dying. It is happening to all of us as we speak. Therefore, in order to face death with grace when it descends upon you out of

nowhere, whether it is your own death or the death of another, best be ready by educating yourself in advance.

9. **Start a blog.** We all must express our feelings or else they get jammed up in our necks and threaten to burst forth in a scream or a stabbing. Don't explode. Rather, vent in a productive and socially acceptable way—by blogging or vlogging or tweeting or snapchatting or using insta. And if you do not want people to read your blog or tweets, you don't have to worry. They won't! There are too many out there to choose from anyway, which means it'll be mostly like a diary and you need not harbor performance anxiety.

10. **Try a crazy hairstyle.** Heck, go bald! What is life unless you're willing to tackle a little adventure, including new looks? Plus, hairstylists are notoriously eager to chat. If you are someone who has a hard time making friends, the salon is not a bad place to hit, as they are required to converse with you whilst you are in their swivel chairs.

MESSAGES

Mon., Nov. 9, 10:14 AM

Jade: Oh no. I'm so sorry, Smith.

My tenth-grade physics teacher Mr. Neely wore a toupee and smelled like mothballs. But Mr. Neely also knew about quasars.

Quasars are the brightest objects in the universe, brighter than stars by multitudes. They're anywhere from 500 million to 29 billion light-years away. Or were. Because by the time their light reaches earth, most of them don't exist anymore. The day I learned about them, I'd never heard anything so miraculous.

Mr. Neely assured us that they're too far away to be observed with the naked eye. You need a telescope. But I was always searching for them anyway, my eyes to the sky, eager to spot something that no longer existed.

Now I wonder if maybe I already sensed that one day I'd be gone and wanted to know that when it happened, I'd still be somewhere.

COMMENTS (2):

BonnieD: over my head!

BigJessBarbs: Math. 500-100 = 400 mil yrs too late. Go pick up a math book!

WEDNESDAY, NOVEMBER 11

from: jademassey@yahoo.com
to: henrystewartmd@gmail.com
date: Wed, Nov 11 at 2:20 PM
subject: Dinner

Hi Henry,

Sorry I hadn't yet responded to your messages. About the lawsuit—you can forget it. I'm not going to pursue it.

As for "us" . . . to be honest, it seems dumb to try again, right? I mean truly stupid, to be clear. But my friend's mom just died. And all of this death lately is making me think about how short life is. So . . . on the other hand, what's really to lose?

We can have dinner, sure. Let me know when and where is good for you.

Jade

MONDAY, NOVEMBER 16

---

from: Delta
to: smith@simonyi.com
date: Mon, Nov 16 at 8:00 AM
subject: It's time to check in for your flight to NYC-LaGuardia!

You may now check in for Delta Flight #2880 from Madison, Wisconsin, to New York, New York, at 8:00 AM on Tuesday, November 17.

---

from: YOPLAY <philgergel@gmail.com>
to: smith@simonyi.com
date: Mon, Nov 16 at 9:20 PM
subject: DAMMIT YOU

I JUST LANDED AT LAGUARDIA AND CARL TOLD ME ABOUT YOUR MOM

I HAVE BEEN TWO WEEKS ON AN ASHRAM INSTEAD OF SIX BECAUSE IT WAS THE MOST BORING TWO WEEKS OF MY LIFE AND YET IT TAUGHT ME PATIENCE AND UNDERSTANDING

I BELIEVE THAT PRIOR TO MY ASHRAM STAY I WAS LOOKING ONLY AT THE BOTTOM LINE AKA CAPITAL-ISM AND THAT IS NOT THE WAY TO WIN IN THE END

AKA NOW I FEEL BAD

YOU AREN'T A TOTAL FUCKUP, OKAY, YOU ARE A MODERATE ONE

HANG IN THERE SMITH

YOPE

---

from: YOPLAY <philgergel@gmail.com>
to: smith@simonyi.com
date: Mon, Nov 16 at 10:26 PM
subject: ME AGAIN

CARL SAYS I NEED TO BE CLEAR THAT I AM NOT REHIR-ING YOU

I'M JUST SAYING I FORGIVE YOU

OK BYE

---

from: carl@simonyi.com
to: smith@simonyi.com
date: Mon, Nov 16 at 11:17 PM
subject: Phil

Boss,

I assume you're still awake since it's an hour earlier over there. I hope you're hanging in.

When you come up for air, can you do me a favor and write back to Phil? He's worried about you. And nagging me. You know how he gets obsessed with one thing and can't get off it due to his ADHD.

Also, just putting a bug in your ear—have you considered reading any more of Iris's drafts? Specifically her *last* draft? Because I can see that the last time it was opened was on October 30th, which was when I opened it. And I suggest you read it. I think it's important you read it.

TUESDAY, NOVEMBER 17

---

from: carl@simonyi.com
to: smith@simonyi.com
date: Tue, Nov 17 at 10:10 AM
subject: Returned

Boss,

I see you have landed. Praise Delta email confirmations.
Does this mean you're coming back tomorrow?

---

from: Domino's
to: smith@simonyi.com
date: Tue, Nov 17 at 12:04 PM
subject: Your delivery is on its way!

We'll be at your door in 45 minutes or less! Click here to track
your pizza!

WEDNESDAY, NOVEMBER 18

---

from: contact@lassimariset.com
to: smith@simonyi.com
date: Wed, Nov 18 at 3:22 AM
subject: re: hi

---

hi again

    do you think you could get me on Netflix or Hulu . . .

---

from: Domino's
to: smith@simonyi.com
date: Wed, Nov 18 at 11:19 AM
subject: Your delivery is on its way!

We'll be at your door in 45 minutes or less! Click here to track your pizza!

---

from: Domino's
to: smith@simonyi.com
date: Wed, Nov 18 at 8:12 PM
subject: Your delivery is on its way!

We'll be at your door in 45 minutes or less! Click here to track your pizza!

THURSDAY, NOVEMBER 19

---

from: rosylady101@yahoo.com
to: smith@simonyi.com
date: Thu, Nov 19 at 12:08 PM
subject: You are un-fired and re-hired

Smith,

Rosita here. I would like to reacquire your services immediately, as I have been even unhappier with my current management team than I was with you. They are insisting that I be marketed as a "Mouth Artist." I cannot stand the word "mouth" or the word "artist."

Please consider yourself re-employed by me, effective immediately. Are you available to chat in 5 minutes? I have an agenda I'm just finishing up that I can shoot over once I add a couple of items to the last page.

Rosita

---

from: Domino's
to: smith@simonyi.com
date: Thu, Nov 19 at 4:10 PM
subject: Your delivery is on its way!

We'll be at your door in 45 minutes or less! Click here to track your pizza!

FRIDAY, NOVEMBER 20

from: sandra.p.willoughby@thelanding.com
to: smith@simonyi.com
date: Fri, Nov 20 at 8:01 AM
subject: Issue of concern

Dear Smith:

At our November board meeting last night, a concern was raised that there has been a great deal of traffic in and out of your unit recently. While co-op guidelines permit deliveries of pizza, we are writing to inquire about the volume of pizza deliveries. Specifically, we will be direct and ask: Is it plausible that one person would order this much pizza?

We are grateful that you promptly resolved the short-term sublet problem back in September. By consensus we request that if there is something nefarious at play with regard to these "pizza men" arriving at all hours of the day and night, you resolve it as quickly. Please let me know if you have any questions.

I am,

Sandra Willoughby

President

The Landing Co-operative

from:	Domino's
to:	smith@simonyi.com
date:	Fri, Nov 20 at 9:22 PM
subject:	Your delivery is on its way!

We'll be at your door in 45 minutes or less! Click here to track your pizza!

SATURDAY, NOVEMBER 21

from: carl@simonyi.com
to: smith@simonyi.com
date: Sat, Nov 21 at 12:07 PM
subject: Things are looking up!

Hi Boss,

Great news—Jade emailed me that she's fine with the excerpt! Do you know what I'm talking about or have I not filled you in?

Belle is going to publish a portion of Iris's blog. Which is good because Hadley was not a fan of my listicle, so this really does feel like our last shot, no pun intended.

Jade also sent some flowers for you. They are yellow with orange centers. I have <u>not</u> read the card. They are very pretty. I am attaching a photo.

Also Rosita has decided to rehire us—a plot twist that I will openly admit I find *bittersweet*.

Also my parents are interested in investing in Jade's bakery given that she is a former Barn chef. Do you want me to tell her the good news or do you want to?

Carl

MESSAGES—DRAFTS

Sat., Nov. 21, 12:55 PM

Smith: Hi Jade. Thank you for the flowers. I think maybe you misunderstood—

from:	jademassey@yahoo.com
to:	ENTER RECIPIENT'S ADDRESS
date:	Sat, Nov 21 at 2:03 PM
subject:	DRAFT no subject

Smith,

I wish I never read the

In the end it's not only everything we remember but what we don't, too. The moments that passed unobserved, not cele-brated or noted, just lived. We scold ourselves: *I failed to ap-preciate so much as it was happening! I wasn't paying attention!*

But to be bothered by that is only time playing tricks on a mind that thinks itself smaller than it is.

Don't try to appreciate it. You can't do it by trying. Don't try to do anything.

If anything, try not to try.

The thing is, there isn't one meaning that you remember or don't. It was what it was and is what it is, both simultaneously, along with every version it evolved into along the way, and will, the million iterations all stacked on top of each other like cans.

And what about the moments we forget? They are there, too, needles in our haystack-selves, a part of us even though we may never find them again and wouldn't know where to look. They prick us every now and then so we know they're there.

COMMENTS (1):

HarryBeastMan: I liked this blog more when it was less preachy. ☹

SUNDAY, NOVEMBER 22

from: carl@simonyi.com
to: smith@simonyi.com
cc: YOPLAY <philgergel@gmail.com>
date: Sun, Nov 22 at 11:34 AM
subject: An Intervention

Dear Boss,

This is an intervention from me and Phil.

You have been home for one week and have been responsive to nothing and have eaten Christ knows how much pizza. While this is perfectly acceptable for a limited period, we agree that one full week is enough for this particular phase of grieving. It is now time for you to enter a new phase. You can still sulk and mope and so forth, but we feel this new phase should involve coming to work at least because I am completely worn out from doing both of our jobs. Remember that I am ONLY A COLLEGE STUDENT!

Also we are going to Sonoma later this week for Thanksgiving to spend it with my family.

Please advise.

Carl

---

from: smith@simonyi.com
to: carl@simonyi.com
cc: YOPLAY <philgergel@gmail.com>
date: Sun, Nov 22 at 3:24 PM
subject: re: An Intervention

Wait. You're *both* going to California to see your family?

---

from: YOPLAY <philgergel@gmail.com>
to: smith@simonyi.com
cc: carl@simonyi.com
date: Sun, Nov 22 at 4:04 PM
subject: re: An Intervention

HE'S ALIVE!

YES

WE ARE BOTH GOING TO CALI

I AM GOING TO MEET CARL'S PARENTS WHO

HE DESCRIBES AS PINK

---

from: smith@simonyi.com
to: carl@simonyi.com
cc: YOPLAY <philgergel@gmail.com>
date: Sun, Nov 22 at 5:06 PM
subject: re: An Intervention

I'll be back to work tomorrow. Thanks for carrying the load, Carl. I'm really grateful. I'll write you the best "LOR" anyone's ever seen. And thanks, Phil, for forgiving (but not rehiring) me.

from:	carl@simonyi.com
to:	smith@simonyi.com
cc:	YOPLAY <philgergel@gmail.com>
date:	Sun, Nov 22 at 5:12 PM
subject:	re: An Intervention

(*^_^*)

PS—Since I know you will ask, that's bashful face.

from:	carl@simonyi.com
to:	smith@simonyi.com
date:	Sun, Nov 22 at 5:40 PM
subject:	re: An Intervention

Hi Boss,

Taking Phil off for this thread because it doesn't seem professional to loop him in on this.

Soooooo this morning I accidentally spilled coffee on the card from Jade that came with the flowers she sent, which is super weird because I *never* spill. The last time I spilled was the first week of my internship (I was so young!), when I was at lunch and drenched the Post-it from Iris in Arnold Palmer. Remember that?

I didn't want it to become saturated to the point of incoherence, so I did open the card. It reads:

I'm sorry. You were right.

What do you think she means? Right about *what*?

So cryptic!

I am also attaching to this email a screenshot of Iris's last draft for your information and well-being.

Carl

Attachment (1)

http://dyingtoblog.com/irismassey

UNPUBLISHED DRAFT

Last opened November 22, at 5:22 PM

Tonight I am going to the office to print this blog and leave it for Smith to publish. Guessing he'll have to get in touch with my sister at some point. And then, who knows?

I was here

And I remember some of it

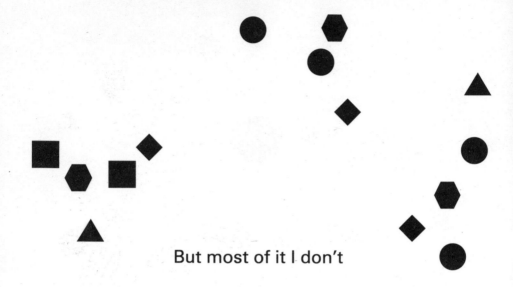

But most of it I don't

Between what I do

And what I don't

And loved.

COMMENTS (2):

DyingToBlogTeam: Happy National Pretzel Day!

BonnieD: :) this made me cry a little bit

MONDAY, NOVEMBER 23

MESSAGES

Mon., Nov. 23, 9:42 AM

SMITH: Thank you for the flowers.

JADE: How are you?

SMITH: Saddest I've ever been.

JADE: I hope that doesn't mean you've gambled away everything you own.

SMITH: No. I'm just getting fat on pizza.

JADE: Sounds reasonable.

SMITH: How are you?

JADE: I'm okay.

SMITH: Is it true—you're fine with Hadley publishing an excerpt of Iris's blog?

JADE: I said I'm okay with Belle publishing it. I still have mixed feelings about an adult named Hadley.

SMITH: Yes, I recall.

SMITH: Why the change of heart?

JADE: I read it. The whole thing. I finished it.

JADE: I gave the link to my mom to read, too.

SMITH: Wow.

JADE: I'm not saying you were right to go behind my back.

SMITH: I know. I owe you an actual apology.

JADE: But I'm not opposed to the idea of people reading it now. And you're right—I'm glad I read to the end.

SMITH: I'm sorry I went behind your back.

JADE: It's okay.

SMITH: What else is going on?

JADE: I got the space. The one in Brooklyn.

SMITH: Congratulations.

JADE: Thanks.

SMITH: Did Carl tell you his parents want to invest?

JADE: Yeah. Ha.

SMITH: Does that mean you aren't interested?

JADE: My plans have changed.

SMITH: Oh?

JADE: I don't know. I might open a restaurant or something.

SMITH: I imagine his parents would be into that as well.

JADE: You really aren't gambling, or was that a lie?

SMITH: I found this video online called *The Easy Way to Stop Gambling*. The whole time it didn't need to be a struggle, I was just making it a struggle. It seems to have worked. Go figure.

JADE: Is this a joke?

SMITH: Nope.

JADE: *The Easy Way*? Don't recruit me for your cult please.

SMITH: Or maybe you were right earlier in the fall when you said I do it to make things worse before they can get worse on their own. Things got as bad as they could get. There's no "worse" now.

JADE: I said that?

SMITH: Yes.

JADE: Were you able to see your mom before she died?

SMITH: No.

JADE: She knew you were coming.

SMITH: So what kind of food are you going to serve in your restaurant?

JADE: Good question.

SMITH: We should probably get to work. Dinner at 6?

JADE: I'm supposed to see Henry tonight for dinner.

SMITH: I see.

JADE: I could cancel.

SMITH: Cancel.

JADE: Okay.

SMITH: Go ahead and cancel all of Henry's upcoming appointments.

JADE: Okay.

SMITH: Dude got his shot. It's over.

---

from:	smith@simonyi.com
to:	rosylady101@yahoo.com
date:	Mon, Nov 23 at 12:44 PM
subject:	re: Dancing with the Stars

Dear Rosita,

You certainly make a case for joining the cast of DWTS—quite impressive, that video of your latest merengue competition. Such footwork!

Unfortunately, I don't think our continuing to work together is meant to be. Best of luck to you, in mouth artistry, merengue, and beyond.

Sincerely,

Smith S. Simonyi

President

BRANDISH

My sister has been staying with me. A few days ago she was going to spend a night back in Jersey so she could swap out her clothes and water her plants. She asked what needed to be done before she left. I said go dancing but I was kidding. Then I took a nap.

I woke up to her putting makeup on me: rubbing eye shadow on my lids, stroking mascara onto the tops of my lashes, dabbing lipstick onto my chapped lips. Of course, I didn't have any hair to do, and the wigs had started itching, so she tied on a scarf. I'm not sure which one. She put me in black pants and a gauzy, fitted blouse I wore when I was younger and hotter. I had saved it thinking that maybe, one day, I'd become thin enough to wear it again. In fact, I had.

She hailed us a cab and still wouldn't tell me where we were going.

"It's a surprise," she kept saying. We had to stop twice so I could throw up. The driver seemed annoyed the first time, but when I got back in, I could tell Jade had told him what was going on, because in the rearview mirror he stared at me with pity. The third time I threw up into a grocery bag he passed back. Finally, the car stopped in front of Rinse, the club where Jade and I went sometimes in our twenties when we wanted to get wasted and dance.

There was a bearded, husky man in all black standing outside, waiting. He shook Jade's hand and introduced himself to us as Pete, the guy she'd spoken with on the phone. Pete let us into the empty dance hall. The strobe light was already on, and Beyoncé's "Best Thing I Never Had" was playing. The dance floor looked enormous without anyone on it, and stepping onto it was strange, like going out into a snowy field that no one has walked on yet.

We danced by ourselves. I forgot I was sick. I forgot it was ending. I just danced with my sister, and it was the best. The very best. I can't even think of the words for how good it was.

Thank you, Jade. Thank you, thank you, thank you.

COMMENTS (122):

BonnieD: RIP Iris

XYZLots: just found this blog! sad too late. rip

BigJessBarbs: This was my favorite blog!

TigerSashRox: are we sure she's rip?

BonnieD: I think so? Iris u there?

Click to see 116 more . . .

WinsomeDorothy: Dear Everyone on this Blog, Yes, Iris is RIP. Thank you for your support of her, on behalf of Dorothy Massey, her mother. We miss you down here, girlie. Love, Mom.

EPILOGUE

from: carlvansnyder@gmail.com
to: jademassey@yahoo.com
date: Fri, May 13 at 12:34 PM
subject: OUR WEDDING CAKE

Dear Jade,

I hope you are doing well! I hear from Smith that restaurant plans are going well. Please keep me posted on the date of the launch, as I would love to come if I am available. I will be moving back to New York at the end of the month, after graduation.

Smith has warned me that you might say no given that you hate sweets, but I have an enormous favor to ask that would mean so much to Phil and me. Would you be willing to make our wedding cake? You have until October!

I know there are probably people we could find who would make better cakes, but since Smith is officiating the wedding, it feels very much like a family affair.

Reasons I think you should do it:

1. You will be anxious waiting for Iris's book proofs in November, and this will be a welcome distraction.

2. It will mean a lot to Phil and me.
3. It's good for the mind to try out new things. Our brains crave plasticity, longing to be exercised in fresh capacities in order to prolong mental acuity. In a way, we're doing YOU a favor!
4. Today is Friday the 13th. I don't know if you're one of the 21 million people who suffer from *paraskevidekatriaphobia*—fear of this day in the Gregorian calendar—but if so, it certainly wouldn't hurt to summon good energies your way by doing friends a favor. (They say that once you can pronounce *paraskevidekatriaphobia*, you're cured, though I can't test this claim myself, as I find the fear to be irrational and thus unrelatable.)

In exchange, I offer my services as an Elite Yelp reviewer four years and counting. Have you seen the Yelp page for BRANDISH recently? It's a masterpiece. When your restaurant launches, I will promptly post a rave review and recruit the like from my Yelp compatriots (we do that for each other).

What do you think?

Carl

---

from: HelloCupid
to: jademassey@yahoo.com
date: Fri, May 13 at 4:27 PM
subject: MANOFLAMANCHA is looking at your profile!

JadeJadeJava,

We can't believe it either! It's been over a year since you logged in—and people are checking out your profile! Here's a sneak peek at the latest message you've received:

From NOTABRIT:

Hi! I am a freelancer living in Crown Heights, just arrived from Chicago where I dwelled for 15 years. Before that, I grew up in Evanston, Illinois. But I won't blame you for thinking me an Englishman, as I suffer from FAS (Foreign Accent Syndrome), which has caused me to speak with a British accent since falling victim to a ferocious migraine in the spring of 2010. Don't worry, I've been assured it's of the posh variety.

Or maybe it even makes me MORE sexy to you???

How about you, Java, where are you from?

---

from:	HelloCupid
to:	jademassey@yahoo.com
date:	Fri, May 13 at 4:33 PM
subject:	PROFILE DELETED

Your profile has been deleted. Please help us improve our product by telling us your reason for deleting your profile. Simply check one of the boxes below.

Thanks,

The HelloCupid Team

_____ I am using another dating site.

_____ I had an unpleasant experience.

_____ I prefer to remain single.

__x__ I met someone.

ACKNOWLEDGMENTS

I am forever indebted to my agent, Claire Anderson-Wheeler. I am so grateful to the universe for bringing me to you. The same goes to my editor, Emily Griffin. I felt it was fate when we first talked about running long distances and being miserable about it. Working with you has been a daily privilege ever since. Melissa Cox and Elinor Cooper in the UK—it has likewise been a joy.

My friends who read this book when it was a first draft, Rina Goldfield and Emily Wulwick, thank you for being that kind of friend. Sarah Stone, you are the writer whisperer. Kimberlee Auerbach Berlin and Victory Matsui, thank you for your early insights as well.

My writing group helped raise this book through its challenging toddler and teenage years. Joselin Linder, Kate Tellers, Joanne Solomon, Nicole Solomon, Christine Clarke, T. J. Wells, Jorge Novoa, Jessica Mannion, Sam Ritchie, Alex DiFrancesco, Gabra Zackman, and Natalia Kislitsina—thank you for being this novel's favorite aunts and uncles. I don't know what I did to wind up among you other than knowing Kate Tellers, but as with many good things, that's probably all it was. I cherish our Tuesdays of hummus, overpriced red, and "what-ifs." May we remain compatibly deranged for many years.

And to the rest of my writer family—Haley Hoffman, Rachel Abramowitz, Greg Marshall, and my partner in most crimes, Lucas Schaefer—thank you for the endless supply of inspiration, commiseration, and laughs.

To Lee Shapiro, Chibuzo Enemchukwu, Israt Pasha, and Derek Frankhauser, thank you for your generosity as experts where I'm clueless.

Writing takes up a lot of space sometimes. I'm grateful to Audrey and Hal Krisbergh, and to Justin Ahren and the Noepe Center, for generously offering me a place to work.

Dr. Z., you're out there somewhere, raising your one eyebrow and probably giving me an "8" on this. Thanks for being my most irreverent and passionate English teacher, apart from Mrs. Chancy. Everyone, go find Diane Chancy and take seventh-grade English from her if you want to make the rest of your life better.

My sister, Katie Beth Ongena, is the kind of sibling who made me want to write a novel about sisters. Thank you for being as wonderful as it gets. Clista and Glen Adkins, thank you for being parents who pushed us to do what we love, to be creative, and to live lives we want to wake up to in the morning. You may have questioned that choice once or twice upon receiving phone calls about quitting jobs and dropping out of law school, but I'm so grateful for it.

Lucas, thank you for being my frequent editor and daily reminder to laugh at myself. I love spending this life with you.

Finn, I was putting the final touches on this manuscript while you were the size of a kumquat. As I write this, you're the size of a jalapeño. I hope this book doesn't embarrass you one day, but if it does, you can use it in your stand-up.

TRANSWORLD PUBLISHERS
61–63 Uxbridge Road, London W5 5SA
www.penguin.co.uk

Transworld is part of the Penguin Random House group of companies
whose addresses can be found at global.penguinrandomhouse.com

First published in Great Britain in 2013 by Doubleday
an imprint of Transworld Publishers
Corgi edition published 2014
Corgi edition reissued 2017

A CIP catalogue record for this book
is available from the British Library.

ISBN
9780552173612

Typeset in 12/14pt Minion by Falcon Oast Graphic Art Ltd.
Printed and bound by Clays Ltd, Bungay, Suffolk.

Penguin Random House is committed to a sustainable
future for our business, our readers and our planet. This book is made from
Forest Stewardship Council® certified paper.

1 3 5 7 9 10 8 6 4 2

RAISING STEAM

A Discworld® novel

Terry Pratchett

CORGI BOOKS

INTRODUCING DISCWORLD

The Discworld series is a continuous history of a world not totally unlike our own, except that it is a flat disc carried on the backs of four elephants astride a giant turtle floating through space, and that it is peopled by, among others, wizards, dwarfs, policemen, thieves, beggars, vampires and witches. Within the history of Discworld there are many individual stories, which can be read in any order, but reading them in sequence can increase your enjoyment through the accumulation of all the fine detail that contributes to the teeming imaginative complexity of this brilliantly conceived world.

BOOKS BY TERRY PRATCHETT

———————— The Discworld® series ————————

———————— **Other books about Discworld** ————————

TURTLE RECALL: THE DISCWORLD COMPANION . . . SO FAR
(with Stephen Briggs)

NANNY OGG'S COOKBOOK
(with Stephen Briggs, Tina Hannan and Paul Kidby)

THE PRATCHETT PORTFOLIO
(with Paul Kidby)

THE DISCWORLD ALMANAK
(with Bernard Pearson)

THE UNSEEN UNIVERSITY CUT-OUT BOOK
(with Alan Batley and Bernard Pearson)

WHERE'S MY COW?
(illustrated by Melvyn Grant)

THE ART OF DISCWORLD
(with Paul Kidby)

THE WIT AND WISDOM OF DISCWORLD
(compiled by Stephen Briggs)

THE FOLKLORE OF DISCWORLD
(with Jacqueline Simpson)

THE WORLD OF POO
(with the Discworld Emporium)

MRS BRADSHAW'S HANDBOOK
(with the Discworld Emporium)

THE COMPLEAT ANKH-MORPORK
(with the Discworld Emporium)

THE STREETS OF ANKH-MORPORK
(with Stephen Briggs, painted by Stephen Player)

THE DISCWORLD MAPP
(with Stephen Briggs, painted by Stephen Player)

A TOURIST GUIDE TO LANCRE – A DISCWORLD MAPP
(with Stephen Briggs, illustrated by Paul Kidby)

DEATH'S DOMAIN (with Paul Kidby)

THE DISCWORLD ATLAS
(with the Discworld Emporium)

A complete list of Terry Pratchett ebooks and audio books as well as other books based on the Discworld series – illustrated screenplays, graphic novels, comics and plays – can be found on
www.terrypratchett.co.uk

—————————— **Non-Discworld books** ——————————

THE DARK SIDE OF THE SUN

STRATA

THE UNADULTERATED CAT (illustrated by Gray Jolliffe)

GOOD OMENS (with Neil Gaiman)

—————————— **Shorter Writing** ——————————

A BLINK OF THE SCREEN

A SLIP OF THE KEYBOARD

SHAKING HANDS WITH DEATH

—————————— **With Stephen Baxter** ——————————

THE LONG EARTH

THE LONG WAR

THE LONG MARS

THE LONG UTOPIA

THE LONG COSMOS

————— **Non-Discworld books for young adults** —————

THE CARPET PEOPLE

TRUCKERS

DIGGERS

WINGS

ONLY YOU CAN SAVE MANKIND

JOHNNY AND THE DEAD

JOHNNY AND THE BOMB

NATION

DODGER

JACK DODGER'S GUIDE TO LONDON

DRAGONS AT CRUMBLING CASTLE

THE WITCH'S VACUUM CLEANER

To David Pratchett and Jim Wilkins, both fine
engineers who taught their sons to be curious.

It is hard to understand nothing, but the multiverse is full of it. Nothing travels everywhere, always ahead of something, and in the great cloud of unknowing nothing yearns to become something, to break out, to move, to feel, to change, to dance and to experience – in short, to *be* something.

And now it found its chance as it drifted in the ether. Nothing, of course, knew about something, but this something was different, oh yes, and so nothing slid silently into something and floated down with everything in mind and, fortunately, landed on the back of a turtle, a very large one, and hurried to become something even faster. It was elemental and nothing was better than that and suddenly the elemental was captured! The bait had worked.

*

Anyone who has ever seen the River Ankh sliding along its bed of miscellaneous nastiness would understand why so much of the piscine food for the people of Ankh-Morpork has to be supplied by the fishing fleets of Quirm. In order to prevent terrible gastric trouble for the citizenry, Ankh-Morpork fishmongers have to ensure that their suppliers make their catches a long, long way from the city.

For Bowden Jeffries, purveyor of the very best in seafood, the two hundred miles or more which lay between the fish docks at Quirm and the customers in Ankh-Morpork was a regrettably long distance throughout the winter, autumn and spring and a sheer penance in the summertime, because the highway, such as it was, became a linear furnace all the way to the Big City. Once you had had to deal with a ton of overheated octopus, you never forgot it; the smell lasted for days, and followed you around and almost into your bedroom. You could never get it out of your clothes.

People were so demanding, but the elite of Ankh-Morpork and, indeed, everyone else wanted their fish, even in the hottest part of the season. Even with an ice-house built by his own two hands and, by arrangement, a second icehouse halfway along the journey, it made you want to cry, it really did.

And he said as much to his cousin, Relief Jeffries, a market gardener, who looked at his beer and said, 'It's always the same. Nobody wants to help the small entrepreneur. Can you imagine how quickly strawberries turn into little balls of mush in the heat? Well, I'll tell you: no time at all. Blink and you miss 'em, just when everybody wants their strawberries. And you ask the watercress people how difficult it is to get the damn stuff to the city before it's as limp as a second-day sermon. We should petition the government!'

'No,' said his cousin. 'I've had enough of this. Let's write to the newspapers! That's the way to get things done. Everyone's complaining about the fruit and vegetables and the seafood. Vetinari should be made to understand the plight of the small-time entrepreneur. After all, what do we occasionally pay our taxes for?'

Dick Simnel was ten years old when, back at the family smithy in Sheepridge, his father simply disappeared in a cloud of furnace parts and flying metal, all enveloped in a pink steam. He was never found in the terrible haze of scorching dampness, but on that very day young Dick Simnel vowed to whatever was left of his father in that boiling steam that he would make steam his servant.

His mother had other ideas. She was a midwife, and as she said to her neighbours, 'Babbies are born everywhere. I'll never be without a customer.' So, against her son's wishes, Elsie Simnel decided to take him away from what she now considered to be a haunted place. She packed up their belongings and together they returned to her family home near Sto Lat, where people didn't inexplicably disappear in a hot pink cloud.

Soon after they arrived something important happened to her boy. One day while waiting for his mother to return from a difficult delivery, Dick walked into a building that looked interesting, and which turned out to be a library. At first he thought it was full of poncy stuff, all kings and poets and lovers and battles, but in one crucial book he found something called mathematics and the world of numbers.

And that was why, one day some ten years later, he pulled together every fibre of his being and said, 'Mother, you know last year when I said I were going 'iking in thè mountains of Uberwald with me mates, well, it were kind of . . . sort of . . . a kind of lie, only very small, mind you.' Dick blushed. 'You see, I found t'keys to Dad's old shed and, well, I went back to Sheepridge and did some experimenting and . . .' he looked at his mother anxiously, 'I think I know what 'e were doing wrong.'

Dick was braced for stiff objections, but he hadn't reckoned on tears – so many tears – and as he tried to console her he added, 'You, Mother, and Uncle Flavius got me an education, you got me the knowing of the numbers, including the arithmetic and weird stuff dreamed up by the philosophers in Ephebe where even camels can do logarithms on their toes. Dad didn't know this stuff. He had the right ideas but he didn't have the . . . *tech-nol-ogy* right.'

At this point, Dick allowed his mother to talk, and she said, 'I know there's no stopping you, our Dick, you're just like your stubborn father were, pigheaded. Is that what you've been doin' in the barn? Teck-ology?' She looked at him accusingly, then sighed. 'I can see I can't tell you what to do, but you tell me: how can your "logger-reasons" stop you goin' the way of your poor old dad?' She started sobbing again.

Dick pulled out of his jacket something that looked

like a small wand, which might have been made for a miniature wizard, and said, 'This'll keep me safe, Mother! I've the knowing of the sliding rule! I can tell the sine what to do, and the cosine likewise and work out the tangent of t'quaderatics! Come on, Mother, stop fretting and come wi' me now to t'barn. You must see 'er!'

Mrs Simnel, reluctant, was dragged by her son to the great open barn he had kitted out like the workshop back at Sheepridge, hoping against hope that her son had accidentally found himself a girl. Inside the barn she looked helplessly at a large circle of metal which covered most of the floor. Something metallic whizzed round and round on the metal, sounding like a squirrel in a cage, giving off a smell much like camphor.

'Here she is, Mother. Ain't she champion?' Dick said happily. 'I call her Iron Girder!'

'But what is it, son?'

He grinned hugely and said, 'It's what they call a pro-to-type, Mother. You've got to 'ave a pro-to-type if you're going to be an engineer.'

His mother smiled wanly but there was no stopping Dick. The words just tumbled out.

'The thing is, Mother, before you attempt owt you've got to 'ave some idea of what it is you want to do. One of the books I found in the library was about being an architect. And in that book, the man who wrote it said before he built his next big 'ouse he always made quite tiny models to get an idea of how it would all work out. He said it sounds fiddly and stuff, but going slowly and being thorough is the only way forward. And so I'm testing 'er out slowly, seeing what works and what doesn't. And actually, I'm quite proud of me'sen. In the beginning I made t'track wooden, but I reckoned that the engine I wanted would be very 'eavy, so I chopped up t'wooden circle for firewood and went back to t'forge.'

Mrs Simnel looked at the little mechanism running round and round on the barn floor and said, in the voice of someone really trying to understand, 'Eee, lad, but what does it *do*?'

'Well, I remembered what Dad said about t'time he were watching t'kettle boiling and noticed t'lid going up and down with the pressure, and he told me that one day someone would build a bigger kettle that would lift more than a kettle lid. And I believe I have the knowing of the way to build a proper kettle, Mother.'

'And what good would that do, my boy?' said his mother sternly. And she watched the glow in her son's eyes as he said, 'Everything, Mother. *Everything*.'

Still in a haze of slight misunderstanding, Mrs Simnel watched him unroll a large and rather grubby piece of paper.

'It's called a blueprint, Mother. You've got to have a blueprint. It shows you how everything fits together.'

'Is this part of the pro-to-type?'

The boy looked at his doting mother's face and realized that a little more exposition should be forthcoming. He took her by the hand and said, 'Mother, I know they're all lines and circles to you, but once you have the knowing of the circles and the lines and all, you know that this is a picture of an engine.'

Mrs Simnel gripped his hand and said, 'What do you think you're going to do with it, our Dick?'

And young Simnel grinned and said happily, 'Change things as needs changing, Mother.'

Mrs Simnel gave her son a curious look for a moment or two, then appeared to reach a grudging conclusion and said, 'Just you come with me, my lad.'

She led him back into the house, where they climbed up the ladder into the attic. She pointed out to her son a sturdy seaman's chest covered in dust.

'Your granddad gave me this to give to you, when I thought you needed it. Here's the key.'

She was gratified that he didn't grab it and indeed looked carefully at the trunk before opening it. As he pushed up the lid, suddenly the air was filled with the glimmer of gold.

'Your granddad were slightly a bit of a pirate and then he got religion and were a bit afeared, and the last words he said to me on his deathbed were, "That young lad'll do something one day, you mark my words, our Elsie, but I'm damned if I know what it's going to be." '

The people of the town were quite accustomed to the clangings and bangings emanating every day from the various blacksmith forges for which the area was famous. It seemed that, even though he had set up a forge of his own, young Simnel had decided not to enter the blacksmithing trade, possibly due to the dreadful business of Mr Simnel Senior's leaving the world so abruptly. The local blacksmiths soon got

used to making mysterious items that young Mr
Simnel had sketched out meticulously. He never told
them what he was constructing, but since they were
earning a lot of money they didn't mind.

The news of his legacy got around, of course – gold
always finds its way out somehow – and there was a
scratching of heads among the population exemplified
by the oldest inhabitant, who, sitting on the bench outside the tavern, said, 'Well, bugger me! Lad were blessed
wi' an inherited fortune in gold and turned it into a
load of old iron!'

He laughed, and so did everybody else, but nevertheless they continued to watch young Dick Simnel slip
in and out of the wicket gate of his old and almost
derelict barn, double-padlocked at all times.

Simnel had found a couple of local likely lads who
helped him make things and move things around. Over
time, the barn was augmented by a host of other sheds.
More lads were taken on and the hammers were heard
all day every day and, a bit at a time, information trickled into what might be called the local consciousness.

Apparently the lad had made a pump, an interesting
pump that pumped water very high. And then he'd
thrown everything away and said things like, 'We need
more steel than iron.'

There were tales of great reams of paper laid out on
desks as young Simnel worked out a wonderful 'undertaking', as he called it. Admittedly there had been the
occasional explosion, and then people heard about
what the lads called 'The Bunker', which had been useful to jump into on several occasions when there had

been a little . . . incident. And then there was the un-familiar but somehow homely and rhythmic 'chuffing' noise. Really quite a pleasant noise, almost hypnotic, which was strange because the mechanical creature that was making the noise sounded more alive than you would have expected.

It was noticed in the locality that the two main co-workers of Mr Simnel, or 'Mad Iron' Simnel as some were now calling him, seemed somewhat changed, more grown-up and aware of themselves; young men, acolytes of the mysterious thing behind the doors. And no amount of bribery by beer or by women in the pub would make them give up the precious secrets of the barn.* They conducted themselves now as befitted the masters of the fiery furnace.

And then, of course, there were the sunny days when young Simnel and his cohorts dug long lines in the field next to the barn and filled them with metal while the furnace glowed day and night and everyone shook their heads and said, 'Madness.' And this went on, it seemed for ever, until ever was finished and the bang-ing and clanging and smelting had stopped. Then Mr Simnel's lieutenants pulled aside the double doors of the big barn and filled the world with smoke.

Very little happened in this part of Sto Lat and this was enough to bring people running. Most of them arrived in time to see *something* heading out towards

---

* There were some salacious comments about this, but it appeared, alas, to the local and as yet unmarried girls that Mad Iron Simnel and his men had found something more interesting than women and apparently it was made of steel.

them, panting and steaming, with fast-spinning wheels and oscillating rods eerily appearing and disappearing in the smoke and the haze, and on top of it all, like a sort of king of smoke and fire, Dick Simnel, his face contorted with the effort of concentration. It was faintly reassuring that this *something* was apparently under the control of somebody human – although the more thoughtful of the onlookers might have added 'So what? So's a spoon,' and got ready to run away as the steaming, dancing, spinning, reciprocating engine cleared the barn and plunged on down the tracks laid in the field. And the bystanders, most of whom were now byrunners, and in certain instances bystampeders, fled and complained, except, of course, for every little boy of any age who followed it with eyes open wide, vowing there and then that one day *he* would be the captain of the terrible noxious engine, oh yes indeed. A prince of the steam! A master of the sparks! A coach-man of the Thunderbolts!

And outside, freed at last, the smoke drifted purposefully away from the shed in the direction of the largest city in the world. It drifted slowly at first, but gathered speed.

Later that day, and after several triumphant turns around the short track in the field, Simnel sat down with his helpers.

'Wally, Dave, I'm running out of brass, lads,' he said. 'Get your mothers to get your stuff together, make us some butties, bring out the 'orses. We're taking Iron Girder to Ankh-Morpork. I 'ear it's the place where things 'appen.'

* * *

Of course Lord Vetinari, Tyrant of Ankh-Morpork, would occasionally meet Lady Margolotta, Governess of Uberwald. Why shouldn't he? After all, he also occasionally had meetings with Diamond King of Trolls up near Koom Valley, and indeed with the Low King of the Dwarfs, Rhys Rhysson, in his caverns *under* Uberwald. This, as everybody knew, was politics.

Yes, politics. The secret glue that stopped the world falling into warfare. In the past there had been so much war, far too much, but as every schoolboy knew, or at least knew in those days when schoolboys actually read anything more demanding than a crisp packet, not so long ago a truly terrible war, the last war of Koom Valley, had *almost* happened, out of which the dwarfs and trolls had managed to achieve not exactly peace, but an understanding from which, hopefully, peace might evolve. There had been the shaking of hands, *important* hands, shaken fervently, and so there was hope, hope as fragile as a thought.

Indeed, thought Lord Vetinari as his coach rattled along towards Uberwald, in the rosy afterglow that had followed the famous Koom Valley Accord even goblins had finally been recognized as sapient creatures, to be metaphorically treated as brothers, although not necessarily as brothers-in-law. He reflected that, from a distance, the world might conceivably look to be at peace, a state of affairs that always ends in war, eventually.

He winced as his coach hit another most egregious bump on the road. He'd had the seats supplemented with extra mattress padding but simply nothing could turn the journey to Uberwald into anything other than a penance at every pothole, leading to fundamental discomfort. Progress had been very slow, although stops at clacks towers along the route had allowed his secretary, Drumknott, to collect the daily crossword puzzle without which Lord Vetinari considered the day incomplete.

There was a bang from outside.

'Good grief! Must we hit every pothole on the road, Drumknott?'

'I'm sorry, sir, but it appears that her ladyship cannot even now control the bandits around the Wilinus Pass. She has a culling every so often, but I'm afraid this is the least dangerous route.'

There was a shout outside, followed by more banging. Vetinari blew out his reading lamp moments before a ferocious-looking individual pushed the point of a crossbow bolt to the glass of the carriage, which was now in darkness, and said, 'Just you come out here with all your valuables or it'll be the worse for you, okay! No tricks now! We're assassins!'

Lord Vetinari calmly put down the book he had been reading, sighed and said to Drumknott, 'It appears, Drumknott, that we have been hijacked by *assassins*. Isn't that . . . nice.'

And now Drumknott had a little smile. 'Oh, yes, how nice, sir. You always like meeting assassins. I won't get in your way, sir.'

Vetinari pulled his cloak around him as he stepped out of the coach and said, 'There is no reason for violence, gentlemen. I will give you everything I have . . .'

And it was no more than two minutes later that his lordship climbed back up into the coach and signalled for the driver to carry on as if nothing had happened.

After a while, and out of sheer curiosity, Drumknott said, 'What happened this time, my lord? I didn't hear anything.'

Beside him, Lord Vetinari said, 'Neither did they, Drumknott. Dear me, it's such a waste. One wonders why they don't learn to read. Then they'd recognize the crest on my coach, which would have enlightened them!'

As the coach got up to what might be considered an *erratic* kind of speed, and after some thought, Drumknott said, 'But your crest, sir, is black on a black background and it's a very dark night.'

'Ah, yes, Drumknott,' Lord Vetinari replied, with what passed as a smile. 'Do you know, I hadn't thought of that.'

There was something inevitable about Lady Margolotta's castle. As the great wooden doors slowly opened, every door hinge creaked. After all, there was such a thing as socially acceptable ambience. Indeed, what kind of vampire would live in a castle that didn't creak and groan on cue? The Igors wouldn't have it any other way, and now the resident Igor welcomed Lord Vetinari and his secretary into a cavernous hall with spiders' webs hanging pendulously from the ceiling. And there was a sense, only a sense, that down in the basement somewhere, something was screaming.

But of course, Vetinari reflected, here was a wonderful lady, who had made vampires understand that returning from the grave so often that you got dizzy was rather stupid and who somehow had persuaded them to at least tone down their nocturnal activities. Besides which, she had introduced coffee to Uberwald, apparently exchanging one terrifying craving for another.

Lady Margolotta was always short and to the point, as was the nature of the conversation that followed a splendid dinner a few days later. 'It is the grags. The grags again, yes, Havelock? After all this time! My vord, even vorse, just as you, my dear, prophesied. How could you have foreseen it?'

'Well, madam, Diamond King of Trolls asked me the very same thing, but all I can say is that it lies in the indefatigable nature of sapient creatures. In short, they can't all be satisfied at the same time. You thought the bunting and fireworks and handshakes and pledges after Koom Valley was signed and sealed was the end of it, yes? Personally, I have always considered this a mere interlude. In short, Margolotta, peace is what you have while incubating the next war. It is impossible to accommodate *everyone* and twice as impossible to please all the dwarfs. You see, when I'm talking to Diamond King of Trolls he is the mouthpiece of the trolls, he speaks for *all* the trolls. Sensible as they are, they leave it all to him when it comes to the politics.

'And then, on the other hand, we have yourself, dear lady: you speak for all your . . . folk in Bonk* and most agreements made with you are, well, quite agreeable . . . But the dwarfs, what a calamity. Just when you think you're talking to the leader of the dwarfs, some wild-eyed grag will pop out on the landscape and suddenly all bets are off, all treaties instantly become null and void, and there is no possibility of trust! As you know, there is a "king" – a *dezka-knik†*, as they call him – in every mine on the Disc. How does one do business with people like this? Every dwarf his own inner tyrant.'

'Vell,' said Lady Margolotta, 'Rhys Rhysson is managing quite vell in the circumstances and ve in higher Uberwald . . .' now her ladyship almost whispered, 'are *very* much on the side of progress. But, yes, how can vun vin vunce and for all, that is vhat I vould like to know.'

His lordship set down his glass carefully and said, 'That, alas, is never totally possible. The stars change, people change, and all we can do is assist the future with care and thoughtful determination to see the world at peace, even if it means ushering some of its worst threats to an early grave.

'Although I'm bound to say that subtlety and careful interrogation of the things the world puts in front of us suggest to me that the Low King – whom, as protocol dictates, I called upon before coming here to meet you – is forming a plan right now; and when he makes his

---

* Correctly pronounced Beyonk.
† Literal translation: 'chief mining engineer'.

play we will throw everything in to support him. He is taking a very big gamble on the future. He believes that the time is right, especially since Ankh-Morpork is now well known to have the largest dwarf community in the world.'

'But I believe his people don't like too much modernity. I must admit, I can see vhy. Progress is such a vorrisome thing when one is trying to maintain peace in the vorld. So ... unpredictable. Can I remind you, Havelock, that many, many years ago, an Ephebian philosopher built an engine that vas very powerful, scarily so. If those people had persevered with the engine powered by steam the nature of life now might have been very much different. Don't you find that vorryink? How can ve guide the future when von idiot can make a mechanism that might change *everything*?'

Lord Vetinari dribbled a last drop of brandy into his glass and said cheerfully, 'Madam, only a fool would try to stop the progress of the multitude. *Vox populi, vox deorum*, carefully shepherded by a thoughtful prince, of course. And so I take the view that when it's steam engine time steam engines will come.'

'And what do you think you're doing, dwarf?'

Young Magnus Magnusson didn't pay much attention at first to the senior dwarf whose face, in so far as it could be seen, was definitely grumpy, the kind of dwarf that had apparently never himself been young, and so he shrugged and said, 'No offence, O venerable one, but what I think I'm doing is walking along minding my own business in the hope that others would be minding their own. I hope you have no rat with that?'*

It is said that a soft answer turneth away wrath, but this assertion has a lot to do with hope and was now turning out to be patently inaccurate, since even a well-spoken and thoughtful soft answer could actually drive the wrong kind of person into a state of fury if wrath was what they had in mind, and that was the state the elderly dwarf was now enjoying.

'Why are you wearing your helmet backwards, young dwarf?'

Magnus was an easy-going dwarf and did the wrong thing, which was to be logical.

'Well, O venerable one, it's got my Scouting badge on it, you know. Scouting? Out in the fresh air? Not getting up to mischief and serving my community well?'

This litany of good intentions didn't seem to get Magnus any friends and his sense of peril began belatedly to function much faster. The old dwarf was really, really unhappy about him, and during this short exchange a few other dwarfs had sauntered over to them, looking at Magnus as if weighing him up for the fight.

It was Magnus's first time alone in the twin cities of Bonk and Schmaltzberg and he hadn't expected to be greeted like this. These dwarfs didn't look like the ones he had grown up with in Treacle Mine Road and he began to back away, saying hurriedly, 'I'm here to see

---

* Humans might have said 'beef' at this point, but not many dwarfs have a taste for cow, whereas rat is perennially dependable.

my granny, right, if you don't mind, she's not very well and I've come all the way from Ankh-Morpork, hitching rides on carts and sleeping out every night in haystacks and barns. It's a long, long way—'

And then it all happened.

Magnus was a speedy runner, as befitted the Ankh-Morpork Rat Pack,* and as he ran he tried to figure out what it was that he had done wrong. After all, it had taken him for ever by various means to get to Uberwald, and he was a dwarf, and they were dwarfs and . . .

It dawned on him that there had been something in the newspapers back home saying that there were still a few dwarf societies that would have nothing to do with any organization that included trolls, the traditional and visceral enemy. Well, there were certainly trolls in the pack back home and they were good sports, all of them, a bit slow mind you, but he had occasionally gone to tea with some of them and vice versa. Only now he remembered how occasionally old trolls and older dwarfs were upset for no other reason than that after hundreds of years of trying to kill one another

---

* Scouting for trolls, dwarfs and humans was brought in shortly after the Koom Valley Accord had been signed, on the suggestion of Lord Vetinari, to allow the young of the three dominant species to meet and hopefully get along together. Naturally the young of all species, when thrown together, instead of turning against one another would join forces against the real enemy, that is to say their parents, teachers and miscellaneous authority which was *so* old-fashioned. And up to a point, and amazingly, it had worked and that was Ankh-Morpork, wasn't it? Mostly, nobody cared what shape you were, although they might be very interested in how much money you had.

they, by means of one handshake, were supposed to have become friends.

Magnus had always understood that the Low City of the Low King was a dark place, and that was okay for dwarfs as dwarfs and darkness always got on well together, but here he sensed a deeper darkness. In this trying moment it seemed that here he had no friends apart from his grandmother, and it looked as though there was going to be a lot of trouble between him and the other side of town where she lived.

He was panting now but he could still hear the sounds of pursuit, even though he was leaving the deeper corridors and tunnels behind him and heading out of the underground city of Schmaltzberg, realizing he would have to come back another day . . . or another way.

As he stopped briefly to get his breath back, a guard on the city gate stepped into his path with a certain greedy expression.

'And where do you think you're going in a hurry, Mister Ankh-Morpork? Back to the light with your troll friends, eh?'

The guard's spontoon knocked Magnus's feet from under him and then the kicking started in earnest. Magnus rolled to get out of the way and as a kind of reflex shouted, 'Tak does not want us to think of him, but he does want us to think!'

He groaned and spat out a tooth as he saw another dwarf coming towards him. To his dismay the newcomer looked middle-aged and well-to-do, which certainly meant that there would be no friendship here.

But instead of administering a kicking, the older dwarf shouted in a voice like hammers, 'Listen to me, young dwarf, you must never let your guard down like this . . .'

The newcomer smacked his original assailant to the ground with commendable ferocity and a gloriously unnecessary display of violence and as the guard lay groaning he pulled Magnus upright.

'Well, you can run, kid, much better than most dwarfs I know, but a boy like you should know that Ankh-Morpork dwarfs are not in favour at the moment, at least not around these parts. To tell you the truth, I'm not that happy about them myself, but if there's a fight it must be a fair one.'

At that he kicked the stricken guard very hard and said, 'My name is Bashfull Bashfullsson. You, lad, better get yourself some micromail if you're going to come calling on your granny looking all Ankh-Morpork. And it is ashamed I am that my fellow dwarfs treat a young dwarf so badly just because of what he wears.' And the full stop to that rant was yet another blow to the recumbent guard.

'I'll hand it to you, lad, I really have never seen a dwarf that can run as fast as you were doing! My word, you can run, but it might now be time to learn how to hide.'

Magnus brushed himself down and stared at his saviour, saying, 'Bashfull Bashfullsson! But you're a legend!' And he took a step backwards saying, 'I've read all about you! You became a grag because you don't like Ankh-Morpork!'

'I may not, young dwarf, but I don't hold with killing in the darkness like those bastard deep-downers and delvers. I like a stand-up fight, me.'

Saying this, Bashfull Bashfullsson kicked the fallen guard heavily yet one more time with his enormous iron-clad boot.

And one of the most well-known and well-respected dwarfs in the world held out his hand to young Magnus, and said, 'Now let your talent take you to safety. As you said, Tak does not require us to think of him, but remember that he does require us to think and you might want a thought or two about adjusting your attire when you come back to visit your granny again. Besides, she might not appreciate Ankh-Morpork fashions. Nice to have met you, Mister Speedy, and now get your sorry arse out of here – I might not be around next time.'

Far away and turnwise of Uberwald, Sir Harry King was pondering on the business of the day. He was widely known as the King of the Golden River because of the fortune he had made minding other people's business.

Harry was normally a cheerful man with a good digestion, but not today. He was also a loving husband, doting on Euphemia, his wife of many years, but alas, not today. And Harry was a good employer, but also not today, because today his stomach was giving him gyp by means of the halibut to which the phrase *long time no see* could not happily be applied. He hadn't liked the look of it when it was on his plate, halibut being a fish which tends to look back at you reproachfully, and for the last few hours he had envisaged the damn thing looking at the insides of his stomach.

The problem was, he thought, that Euphemia still remembered the good old days when they were poor as church mice and therefore necessarily frugal with their money, and such habits bite to the bone, very much like the inadvisably digested fish which had been swimming somewhere in the vicinity of Harry's bowels and threatening to swim a lot further.

Regrettably, Harry was a man brought up to eat everything that was put in front of him and that meant *everything* eaten up. When he had finally exited from the privy, where he fancied the damn fish had been watching him from the bowl, he had pulled the chain with such vehemence that it broke, causing the woman whom he sometimes called the Duchess to have words with him. And since words tend to lead to more words, nasty, spiteful little words flew on both sides, words that if Harry could help it would be flung back to the wretched fish which had started it all. But instead he and his wife had had what they had known all of their lives as an up-and-downer. And, of course, Effie, born in the next-door gutter to Harry, could give at least as good as she got in such situations, especially when armed with a quite valuable and decorative jug. Effie had a voice on her that at times could make a barrow boy blush, and she had called Harry the 'King of Shit', causing him to do what he never, ever wanted to do, which was to raise his hand in anger, especially since the jug with which his wife was now armed was also quite a heavy one.*

Of course it would blow over, it always did, and genuine marital harmony would drift into its accustomed place in the household. But nevertheless, all afternoon Sir Harry prowled around his compound like an old lion. *King of Shit*, well, yes, and because of him the streets were clean, or at least considerably cleaner than they had been before what might be called the Harry King dynasty. He mused, as he wandered, that his work was all about those unimaginable things that people wanted to leave behind them. And therefore there wasn't much for him on the top table of society. Oh, yes, he was *Sir* Harry, but he knew that Effie really wished they could leave behind the whole stinking business.

'After all,' she said, 'you're as rich as Creosote as it is. Can't you find something else to do – something that people actually *want* rather than need?'

Generally speaking, Harry was not very good at philosophy. He was proud of what he had achieved, but a tiny part of him was agreeing with Effie that surely there was something better for him than chasing the pure† and making certain the unreliable septic tanks of the city didn't overflow. Somebody had to do it, of course – and it wasn't as if it was actually Harry himself, not for many years, since he paid the gongfermors,

---

* Besides being from the McSweeney dynasty and therefore frighteningly expensive. Although, he thought, when he looked at the porcelain shards on the floor, they didn't look *that* expensive.*

† A term, technically speaking, for dog muck, much prized by the tanneries.

dunnykin divers and now a whole army of goblins as well to do the dirty work. Still, what he needed now, he thought, was an occupation that was manly without being despicable.

Absent-mindedly, he sacked his latest lawyer, a dwarf who had been caught with his nasty little fingers in the till, and managed to do it without actually throwing the little bugger all the way down the stairs.

Unusually despondent, Harry prowled on, seeking to calm his nerves. At the edge of his compound he sniffed the air, so far as he dared. There was a wind blowing from the hub and he turned to face it and caught a tantalizing smell: a manly smell, a smell with a purpose, a smell that wanted to take him places, and it said *promise*.

The relationship between Moist von Lipwig and Adora Belle Dearheart was firm and happy, quite possibly because they didn't see each other for substantial periods of time, since she was immersed in the running of the Grand Trunk and he was dealing with the Bank, the Post Office and the Mint. Despite what Lord Vetinari *thought*, Moist *did* have proper work to do at these institutions and that was, in his own mind, called holding it all together. Things worked, in fact they worked very well, but they worked, Moist thought, because he was always seen in the Bank or the Mint or the Post Office being Mister Bank, Mister Post Office and Mister Mint.

He chatted to people, talked to them about their work, asked how their wives and husbands were, having memorized the names of all the family members of the person he was talking to. It was a knack, a wonderful knack, and it worked a treat. You took an interest in everybody and they took an interest in their work and it was vitally important that he was always around to keep the magic flowing.

As for Adora Belle, the clacks were in her bones, it was her legacy and woe betide anyone who got between it and her,* even if that anyone *was* her husband.

Somehow the system worked as hard as they did and so they could afford Crossly, the butler, and Mrs Crossly too.† Their house in Scoone Avenue had a gardener too, who appeared to come with the territory. Crisp‡ was also a decent handyman and quite talkative, although Moist never understood a word he said. He came from somewhere in the Shires and spoke using a vocabulary that was theoretically Morporkian, but in reality had lots of straw in it with the syllable 'ahh' working hard in every conversation. He made cider in his shed at the bottom of the garden, utilizing the apple trees that the previous owner had carefully cherished. He also, as a matter of course, cleaned the windows,

---

* Unless they were a golem. During the dark days when the family clacks company had been usurped by *businessmen*, Adora Belle had diverted her energies into golem emancipation. She was still involved with the Golem Trust, but the pace of change in Ankh-Morpork, she was pleased to notice, meant that the golems were quite happily trusting themselves.
† Adora Belle was, as even she knew, a creatively bad cook, mostly because she thought cookery a waste of time for a woman with even half a mind; and since Moist took pretty much the same stance when it came to manual labour, the arrangement seemed to suit all parties.
‡ Which was his *only* name.

and with the help of an enormous box full of every type of hammer, saw, drill, screwdriver and chisel, bags of nails and a number of other items that Moist could not recognize, and moreover did not wish to, made Moist's life easy whilst making Crisp possibly the richest handyman in the neighbourhood.

Moist von Lipwig had done some heavy work once and couldn't see any future in it, but he could look at it for hours, provided other people were doing it, of course, and clearly some of them liked what they were doing, and so he shrugged and felt happy that Crisp was happy being a handyman whilst Moist was happy not picking up anything that was heavier than a glass. After all, his work was unseen and depended on words, which were fortunately not very heavy and didn't need grease. In his career as a crook they had served him well and now he felt somewhat smug at using them to the benefit of the citizenry.

There was a difference between a banker and a crook, there really was, and although it was very, very teeny Moist felt that he should point out that it did exist and, besides, Lord Vetinari always had his eye on him.

So everybody was happy and Moist went to work in very clean clothes and with a very clean conscience.

Having washed and dressed in said clothes in his private bathroom,* Moist went to see his wife, practising his smile on the way and endeavouring to look cheerful. You never knew with Adora Belle.† She could

---

* Separate bathrooms of course being the key to any happy marriage.
† 'Spike' to her fond husband. Her brother had called her Killer, but he meant it in a nice way.

be quite acerbic. After all, she ran the whole clacks system these days.

She also liked goblins, which was why there were some living behind the wainscoting of the house and others in the roof. They smelled, but the smell wasn't, once you got over the shock, all that bad. The compensation was that the goblins had taken the clacks into their scrawny hearts, one and all. The wheels and levers fascinated them. Moist knew that generally goblins hid out in caves and insalubrious places that humans didn't bother about, but now, when suddenly they were being treated as people, they had found their element which was generally the sky. They could scramble up a clacks tower faster than any man could run, and the rattling, back-and-forth clanking and relentlessly busy machinery of the clacks had them in its grip.

Already, after only a few months in the city, the goblins had improved the efficiency of the clacks across the Sto Plains threefold. They were creatures of darkness, but their perception of light was remarkable. There was a whole malignity* of goblins up on the roof, but if you wanted your clacks to fly fast, you didn't use the term out loud. The villains of the storybooks had found their place in society, at last. All it needed was technology.

When Dick Simnel walked into Sir Harry King's compound he wasn't at all certain how you spoke to grand folk. Nevertheless, he managed to talk his way through

---

* The official collective noun for a bunch of goblins.

the people in the front office, who had a rather jaundiced look and appeared to consider it their duty to ensure that no one should ever get to see Sir Harry King, especially greasy-looking young men with wild eyes trying hard to look respectable despite their extremely old clothing which, these gatekeepers thought, needed something, possibly a bonfire. However, Dick had the persistence of a wasp and the sharpness of a razor blade, and so eventually he ended up deposited in front of the big man's desk like a supplicant.

Harry, red-faced and impatient, looked over his desk and said to him, 'Lad, time is money and I'm a busy man. You told Nancy down on Reception that you've got something I might like. Now stop fidgeting and look me in the face square like. If you're another chancer wanting to bamboozle me I'll have you down the Effing stairs* before you know it.'

Dick stared soundlessly at Harry for a moment, then said, 'Mister Sir King, I've made a machine that can carry people and goods just about everywhere and it don't need 'orses and it's run on water 'n' coal. It's my machine, I built it and I can make it even better if you can see your way clear to advance me some investment.'

Harry King reached into his pocket and pulled out a heavy gold watch. Dick couldn't help but notice the famous gold rings that he had been told Sir Harry always wore, possibly as an ensemble of socially

---

* The wonderfully colourful oak wood of the Effing Forest was much in demand for high-class joinery.

acceptable and extremely valuable knuckledusters.

'Did I hear you right? It's Mister Simnel, isn't it? I'll give you five minutes to catch my fancy and if I think you're just another thimblerigger on the slant you'll go out of here rather more quickly than you came in.'

'My old mother always said seeing is believing, Mister King, and so I've come prepared. If you can give me some time to get t'lads and t' 'orses . . .' Dick coughed and continued, 'I have to tell you, Mister Sir Harry, I took the liberty of parking them right outside your compound, 'cos I talked to people and they said that if Harry King wants something to start happening it 'as to 'appen fast.' He hesitated. Was that a glint in Harry's eye?

'Well,' the magnate grumbled rather theatrically. 'Young man, even though time is money, talk is cheap. I'll come out in five minutes and you'd better have something solid to show me.'

'Thank you, Sir King, that's very kind of you, sir, but we'll have to get t'boiler warmed up first, sir, and so we'll have 'er throbbing in no more than two hours, sir.'

Harry King took his cigar out of his mouth and said, 'What?! Throbbing?'

Dick smiled nervously. 'You'll see, sir, you'll see.'

Very shortly afterwards, and just in time, smoke and steam enveloped the compound and Harry King saw and, indeed, was amazed.

And Harry King really *was* amazed. There was something insect-like about the metallic contraption, bits of which were spinning incessantly while the whole thing was shrouded in a cloud of smoke and steam of its own making. Harry King saw purpose personified. Purpose, moreover, that would be unlikely ever to ask for a day off for its granny's funeral.

Over the noise he shouted, 'What did you say this thing is called, my lad?'

'Iron Girder, sir. An engine that uses the expansion or rapid condensation of steam to generate power. Power for locomotion – that is to say, movement, sir. And if you'd allow us to lay down her rails, sir, we can really show you what she can do.'

'Rails?'

'Aye, sir. She runs on an iron road, you'll see.'

Suddenly there was the sound of a banshee on heat as Wally moved a lever.

'Sorry, sir, you 'ave to let t'steam out. It's all about 'arnessing t'steam. You heard her singing, sir, she wants motion, power is going to waste while she's just sitting here. Give me time and allow me to put a test track around your compound. We'll have 'er running very soon, I promise you.'

Harry was uncharacteristically silent. The thrumming of the machine was like a kind of spell. Again, the metal voice of steam rang out over the compound like a lost soul and he found himself unable to leave. Harry wasn't a man for introspection and all that rubbish, but he thought that this, well, *this* was something worth a closer look. And then he noticed the faces of the crowd around the compound, the goblins climbing up to gawp at this new raging devil which was nevertheless under the control of two lads in flat caps and very little to speak of in regard to teeth.

Getting his thoughts lined up properly, Harry turned to Dick Simnel and said, 'Mister Simnel, I'll give you two days, no more. You have your chance, mister, don't waste it. I am, as I say, a busy man. Two days to show me something that astounds me. Go on.'

Dwarfs and men sat and listened intently to the old boy sitting in the corner of the Treacle Miner*, human, possibly, but with a beard any respectable dwarf would have coveted, who had decided to share with them his knowledge of the treacle-mining world.

'Gather round, lads, fill my pot and I'll tell you a tale that's dark and sticky.' He looked meaningfully at his empty tankard and there was laughter as it was replaced by some well-wisher and, as he sipped his ale, he began his tale.

Years back, unexpected deep treacle reserves had been discovered under Ankh-Morpork, fathoms down, and as every treacle miner knew, the lower the treacle, the better the texture and therefore the better the taste. In truth, and in Ankh-Morpork at least, there was very little friction between dwarf clans on this matter, and the question of who would be allowed to mine the discovery was amiably dealt with by the old boys, dwarf and human.

Everyone conceded that when it came to working underground there was nothing like the dwarfs, but, to the dismay of the older miners, very few of the dwarf

---

* Known by habitués as the Sticky Head.

youngsters of Ankh-Morpork were at all interested in mining under any circumstances. And so the grizzled old boys welcomed any local miners of any species to work under the venerable streets of Ankh-Morpork, for the sheer pleasure of seeing treacle being properly produced again, and the miners, whoever they were, went about their sticky business in the search for the deep shimmering treacle.

And something happened, somewhere up near the Shires, where the dwarf miners had been working a reasonable seam, part of which was under land which at that time belonged to the Low King of the Dwarfs. In those not too distant days political relationships between human and dwarf were somewhat nervy.

On the day when things came to a head there had been a sudden fall of dark toffee, extremely precious and very unusual, but feared by every treacle miner because of its tendency to spontaneously collapse into the tunnels. According to the eyewitnesses, both humans and dwarfs were mining underground while politicians argued on both sides of the political divide. And this fall was mostly on the human side of the seam, with many men trapped in a deluge of un-relenting stickiness.

He hesitated for a moment and said, 'Or it might have been the dwarf side, now I come to think about it . . .' He looked embarrassed, but continued. 'Well, it doesn't really matter now who they were, it was a long time ago anyway. The miners working the seam from the other side of the fall heard that there were many miners down there, trapped and drowning in refined sugar derivatives, and said, "Come on, lads, get the gear together and let's get them out of there."'

The old boy hesitated a further moment, possibly for effect, and said, 'But of course that meant that they had to enter territory that required going through two bloody security barriers manned by armed guards. Guards, moreover, who were not that bothered about miners and were certainly not going to let any of the enemy down into *their* sovereign soil.'

Another significant pause, then the tale raced on. All the miners had piled up against the barriers. Someone said, 'We can't tackle them, they've got weapons!' and they looked at one another in what is known as wild surmise, and then another voice yelled, 'But so have we, when you look at it the right way, and ours are bigger!' And the speaker waved his enormous fist and said, 'And we're mining every day, not standing around and looking smart.'

And so as one dwarf, or possibly human, they rushed the barricade and the guards, realizing they were failing to frighten people, ran for cover as the miners with the picks and shovels came down on them at speed and sixty miners were saved from a very sticky situation on both sides of the seam.

Nothing official happened afterwards because officialdom didn't want any part of the shame of it.

The old boy looked around and glowed as if he himself had been one of those miners and, quite possibly, he might have been, and his tankard was topped up once again and he said wistfully, 'Of course, that was the old days. I wish it still was.'

* * *

It was just short of the end of the second day when Simnel and his lads had Iron Girder chuffing slowly and purposefully along a short circular track in Harry's compound.

And Harry couldn't help noticing that the look of the engine had changed and it now seemed somehow . . . smoother than before. In fact, he thought, he had been ready to say *sleek*, though it was hard to think of what looked like fifty tons of steel as sleek, but yes, he thought, why not? It shouldn't be beautiful, but *she* was. Stuttering, stinking, growling, smoking, but so very beautiful.

Dick said cheerfully, 'We're taking it slow, Mister Harry. We need to put down some *real* ballast before we can let 'er rip, but she grows on yer, don't you think? And when we've built 'er up, and added on wagons and suchlike there'll be no stoppin' 'er.'

And there it was again. It really ought to be a he, Harry mused, but somehow the 'she' stuck relentlessly.

And then Harry's rather crumpled brow furrowed even further. This young lad clearly knows his stuff, he thought, and he said his machine could carry people and goods . . . but who'd want to ride on this clanking great monster?

On the other hand, the compound smelled of steam and coal and hot grease – manly, healthy smells . . . Yes, he'd give them that little bit longer. Perhaps another week. After all, coal wasn't expensive and he wasn't paying them anything. Harry King realized he was feeling unusually happy. Yes, they could have a little more time. And the smell was good, unlike those he and Effie had put up with over the years. Oh, yes, they could definitely have their time, though he'd need to keep the lads on their toes. He looked up and the clacks towers blinked relentlessly and Harry King saw the future.

The wind above the clacks towers was blowing from the hub, cool and purposeful, and Adora Belle Dearheart fancied she could see the edge of the world from here. She cherished moments like this. They reminded her of when she was young, really young, when her mother would hang her cradle from the top of a tower while she was coding, leaving her daughter cheerfully making baby noises several hundred feet above the ground. In fact, her mother said her very first word was 'checksum'.

And now she could see, clearly out of its mists, the mountain Cori Celesti glittering like a great green icicle. She sang as she tightened up the spinners on the upper gallery. She was out of the office, as far from it as was possible, and it felt good. After all, she could even see the office from up here. In fact, she could probably see *everybody*'s office from here, but right now she sorted out the delicate little mechanisms and savoured a world where she could reach out and touch the sun, well, metaphorically at least. This reverie was broken by one of the tower's goblins.

'I am bringing twenty spinners and a flask of coffee, very hygienic, I cleaned the mug myself with my own hand. Me. Of the Twilight the Darkness,' he said proudly.

Adora Belle looked down at a face that would take a frantic battalion of mothers to love, but nevertheless she smiled and said, 'Thanks, mister. I must say you've really got acclimatized for somebody who has spent most of their life in a cave. I can't believe you don't even worry about heights, that never ceases to amaze me. And thanks again, it really is good coffee and still warm, too.'

Of the Twilight the Darkness shrugged as only a goblin could shrug. The effect was rather like a parcel of snakes dancing.

'Missus Boss, goblins no stranger to acclimatize. Don't acclimatize, don't live! And anyway, things going well down there, no problems. Goblins got respeck! And how is Mister Slightly Damp?'

'*Moist* is fine, my friend, and surely you know my husband doesn't like the name you goblins have given him. He thinks you're doing it on purpose.'

'You want that we stop doing it?'

'Oh, no! It teaches him a lesson in humility. I think he needs to go to university on that score.'

The goblin grinned in the way of a conspirator, and he could see Adora Belle trying not to laugh, while overhead the clacks continued sending its messages to the world.

Adora Belle could *almost* read the messages simply by watching the towers, but you had to be very, very fast; and the goblins were even faster than that. And who ever would have thought their eyesight was so discerning? Using the new augmented colour shutter boxes after dark, most human clacks spotters could separate about four or five or maybe even six colours on a very good clear night, but who could have imagined that goblins, fresh out of their caves, would be uncannily able even to identify puce as opposed to pink, while most humans didn't have a clue what a damn puce was if they saw it?

Adora Belle glanced at Of the Twilight the Darkness and once again acknowledged to herself that goblins were the reason why clacks traffic was so much faster, more accurate and streamlined than ever before. And yet how could she reward them for the increased efficiency? Sometimes the goblins never even bothered to take their pay. They liked rats, of which there was never a shortage, but because she was indeed the boss* she felt it incumbent on her to persuade the little nerds that there were, indeed, many other things you could be doing apart from coding and deciphering clacks messages. She almost shivered. They actively, obsessively liked to work, all day and all night if possible.

She knew if the name on the door said 'Boss' then in theory she had to think about their welfare, but they weren't interested in their own welfare. What they wanted to do was code and decipher, pausing only when the lady troll with the rat trolley came round. Honestly! They liked their work and not just liked it, but lived it. How many bosses had had to go all around the workplace telling people they really had to stop

---

* If you could give that name to somebody who had to deal every day with forms to sign, go to far too many meetings *about* meetings and handle the most petty of correspondence.

working now and go home? But then they didn't go home, they wanted to stay up in their clacks towers, and in the small hours of the night chat by clacks to goblins elsewhere. They would rather chatter than eat, it seemed, and even slept on the tower, dragging in little straw beds for when they were forced by nature to take a nap.

Adora Belle had insisted to the trustees that there should be a foundation set up, against the day when goblins and their children might want to move further into society. So a scant while after the remarkable musical talents of Tears of the Mushroom had been so spectacularly unveiled to Ankh-Morpork high society, the goblins had become people, strange people, yes, but people nevertheless. Of course, there was the smell, but you couldn't have everything.

Novelty went around Ankh-Morpork just like an embarrassing disease, thought Sir Harry King the following afternoon as he looked down on to the compound where people were peering through the gates and fencing in a great susurration of speculation. Harry knew his fellow citizens from the bottom up, as it were, willing slaves to novelty and the exotic, rubber-neckers all of them. The whole crowd were turning their heads as one to keep track of Iron Girder, like a flock of starlings, and all the time Iron Girder was chuffing away with Dick waving from the footplate, the air still full of the smuts and smells. And yet, he thought, it's all approval. No one's disagreeing, no one's frightened. A beast from nowhere. A fiery dragon, all smoke and cinders, has appeared among them and they hold up their children to look at it, waving as it goes past.

What strange magic—? He corrected himself; what strange *mechanics* could have achieved this? There was the beast and they were loving it.

I'll have to get familiar with these words, Harry thought as he left his office: 'footplate', 'boiler', 'reciprocal', 'molybdenum disulphide',* and all the tiresome but fascinating language of steam.

Having noticed that Harry was watching them, Dick Simnel allowed Iron Girder to slow down gently until, with an almost imperceptible bump, she came to a halt. Dick jumped off the footplate and strolled towards him, and Harry saw a triumphant look in his eye.

Harry said, 'Well done, lad, but be careful, be very, *very* careful. Be careful of everything right now. I've been watching the faces of them people with their noses pressed up against my fence, their little faces all corrugated, as it were. They're fascinated, and fascinated people spend money.

'The most important thing in business is to work out who gets that cash and it's like this, my boy, it's a jungle out there and I'm more than a multi-millionaire, much more. I know that while happy handshakes are very pleasing and friendly, when it comes to business you can't do without bloody lawyers because in this jungle I'm a gorilla! It's best you tell me the name of yours and

---

* This black crystalline compound was widely used by troll women as an anti-ageing cream. Dick Simnel had been thorough in his research and it was, apparently, a very efficient lubricant.

I'll get my lawyer to get in touch so they can talk all lawyer-to-lawyer while totting up their dollars. I don't want no one to say that Harry King fleeced the lad who tamed the steam.

'For what it's worth I'll fund you up to a certain point, no doubt about that, because I think this engine of yours has real possibilities, huge possibilities. So now you've got my interest and by the time the papers find out about this you'll have *everyone*'s interest.'

Dick shrugged and said, 'Well, Sir Harry, it's great that you're giving me a chance, so anything you suggest'll be okay by me.'

Harry King almost screamed, 'No, no, no! I like you, I like you a lot, but business is, well, *business is business*!' Harry's face was now puce with anger. 'You don't go and tell anyone that you'll take whatever they want to give you! You bargain, lad. Don't get starry-eyed! You bargain. You bargain hard.'

There was silence and then the lad said, 'Mister King, before I decided to come to Ankh-Morpork I talked about things with me mother, a very shrewd lady – she 'ad to be, what with me dad being somewhere out there in the ether, if you catch my drift. And she said if some-one wants to do business in the big city, Dick, make out that you're simple and see 'ow they treat you. If they treats you properly, simple as you are, then it's likely you can trust them. And then you can show them how smart you really are. And well, sir, it seems to me you're as straight as lunchtime. I'll go and find a lawyer right now.' He hesitated. 'Er, where can I find a lawyer I can trust? I might not be as clever as I think I am.'

Sir Harry laughed heartily. 'It's a tough call, lad, and a question I've lately needed to ask myself, as it happens. My friend Mustrum Ridcully over at the University told me about one only yesterday: a lawyer so straight he could be used as a crowbar. Why not let your lads go on showing Iron Girder to the crowd, and come with me in my carriage, although it's not a patch on the one you brought here, eh? Eh! Come on, lad, let's go, shall we?'

At his office in the Lawyers' Guild building, Harry King and Dick Simnel met Mr Thunderbolt, surprisingly large and, surprisingly, a troll. A troll with a voice like gently flowing lava.

'You will wish to know my credentials, gentlemen. I am a member of the Ankh-Morpork Guild of Lawyers and served my articles here under Mister Slant,' said Mr Thunderbolt. 'As well as my Ankh-Morpork practice I am the only troll to have, moreover, accreditation as a lawyer in the realm of the Low King. Apropos of nothing, Sir Harry, I am also the nephew of Diamond King of Trolls, although, of course, I must add that the nature of troll families is such that the mere word "nephew" does not do the situation justice.'

The voice was the voice of a professor, but one who had chosen to speak in an echoing cave. The features were more or less like those of all trolls, unless you looked for the giveaway signs and recognized the careful masonry work, the richness of the plant life in the visible cavities and, not least, that elusive shine, and possibly shimmer, which caught the light so delicately; not boldly in your face, but irresistibly there.

'And yes, I am diamond through and through and therefore I cannot tell lies for fear of shattering. Furthermore, I have no intention of trying to do so. It appears to me, gentlemen, from what you tell me, that the two of you are in accord, neither wishing to play unfairly and both of you wishing to act decently with one another and so, on this occasion, much as my Guild colleagues might disapprove, I suggest I act as mediator and lawyer for both of you. Troll justice is remarkably straightforward – I only wish that this could be the case everywhere else. However, should you fall out then I would not undertake work from either of you subsequently.'

Thunderbolt smiled and little sparkles flashed around the room like a firework display.

'I will put together a short document which might, in other places, be called an agreement to agree. And I am the judge not on the side of you individually but on the side of you both. I am diamond and I cannot allow injustice to happen. I suggest, gentlemen, that you continue with your project, which seems to me remarkable, and leave the paperwork to me. I look forward to seeing you at the compound tomorrow.'

Harry and Dick were silent in the coach until Dick said, 'Weren't he nice? For a lawyer.'

By the time they got back to the compound the goblin Billy Slick, who had worked for Harry for many years, was in a tizzy – although he didn't know that, not knowing the word existed – and he was at the gate waiting for them when the carriage drew up.

Frantically, he said, 'I closed the gate, Sir Harry, but it looks like they'll climb over anything to see this ... this ... this *thing*! I keep telling 'em we ain't running no fun house here.'

The light was fading and yet still the eyes of the onlookers were following Iron Girder as she travelled around the track while Simnel's team put her through her paces, throwing off sparks in the twilight like signals to the universe that steam was here to stay. And when most of the sightseers had reluctantly left to go home for their supper, some of Harry's goblins slunk into the compound to see the marvel of the age. They did indeed slink, Harry thought, not exactly like a burglar, but simply because the average goblin carcass was born slinking, except that right now they were dancing around Iron Girder, and the lads had their work cut out to keep skinny little goblin fingers out of dangerous places.

Iron Girder sat and occasionally gave out a puff of steam or smoke while all the time, in the twilight, Harry heard tiny staccato voices interrogating the engineers: 'What does this one do, mister?', 'What happens if I push this, mister?', 'I see, mister, that this one connects to the blastpipey armature.'

Harry and Dick joined Dave and Wally as they stood by Iron Girder answering the barrage of questions. To Harry's surprise, instead of the complaints he was expecting to be issuing from the lads' mouths, he saw they were smiling happily.

'They seem to get it, sir! Oh, aye!' said Wally. 'They're into everything! We're 'aving to keep an eye on them, but they seem to understand without being told, can you believe that?'

And Harry marvelled. He quite liked the little buggers, as any employer would quite like somebody who worked hard, but how does a goblin get the understanding of steam engines? It must be something in their nature. Their scruffy little faces were wreathed in smiles at the sight of something metallic and complicated. It was a sign of the times, he thought, and it looks like time for the goblins.

Simnel was silent for a moment as if waking up the internal steam for the next thought, then said, in a careful kind of voice, 'You really would think they were born to it!'

'I can't say I'm surprised, Dick,' said Harry. 'The clacks people say the same thing. It's uncanny but it seems that they automatically understand mechanisms, so be careful as they like to take things apart on the fly just to see what they do. But once they understand how whatever it is works they seem to put it all back together again. There's no malice, they just like to tinker with the best and, you know what, sometimes they improve things. How can you explain that? But if I was you I'd have one of you three sleeping under Iron Girder of a night just so they don't get creative.'

The following day Moist von Lipwig was gently awakened by Crossly, who as yet had failed to grasp his master's attitude to sleep, a fact which was reinforced by Moist turning over in bed and saying, 'Mumble mumble grunt mumble groan mumble off!' The sequence was repeated three minutes later, with the same response, this time with the emphasis on the last syllable, uttered three times with increasing volume.

Subsequently – in fact and to be precise, fifteen minutes later – Moist von Lipwig was pulled out of the arms of Morpheus by the none too gentle prodding of a blade belonging to one of the Ankh-Morpork palace guards, a species he didn't like very much in any case because they were stolid and dumb. Admittedly, so were the majority of the City Watch, in Moist's opinion, but at least *they* were *by and large* creatively and, at least, humorously dumb, which made them a lot more interesting. After all, you could talk to them and therefore confuse them, whereas with the palace guards, well, all they knew was how to prod, and they were quite good at it. It was wise not to put them to any trouble, and so Moist, fully conversant with how this sort of thing worked, dressed grumpily and followed them to the palace, and undoubtedly an audience with Lord Vetinari.

The Patrician was, unusually, not at his desk, but paying attention to something on the large polished table that filled one half of the Oblong Office. He was, in fact, playing. It seemed ridiculous, but there was no denying it: he was watching a children's toy quite intently, a little cart, or trolley of some sort, on a little metal rail, which allowed it to scuttle continuously in a circle for no readily apparent reason. He straightened up after Moist coughed loudly and said, 'Ah, Mister

Lipwig. It's so kind of you to come ... *eventually*. Tell me, what do you make of *this*?'

Somewhat perplexed, Moist said, 'It looks like a children's plaything, sir.'

'In fact it is a very well crafted model of something much bigger and far more dangerous.' Lord Vetinari raised his voice and said, as if talking not only to Moist but to the world in general, 'Some might say that it would have been easy for me to prevent this happening. A stiletto sliding quietly here, a potion dropped into a wine glass there, many problems solved at one stroke. Diplomacy, as it were, on the sharp end, regrettably unfortunate, of course, but not subject to argument.

'People *might* say that I wasn't paying attention and through neglect of my duties allowed the poison to seep into the imagination of the world and change it irrevocably. Perhaps I could have taken some action when I first saw Leonard of Quirm doodle something very much like this little toy in the margins of his drawing of the "Countess Quatro Fromaggio at her Toilette", but of course I would rather shatter the most priceless antique vase than see any harm come to one hair on that most useful and venerable head. I thought it would go the way of his flying machines, nothing more than a toy.

'And now it has come to this. One simply cannot trust the artificers; they design some terrible things for the sheer love of doing so, without wisdom, foresight or responsibility, and frankly, I would like to see them chained up where they can do no harm.'

And here Lord Vetinari paused and added, 'And I could have made that happen in an instant were it not for the fact, Mr Lipwig, that the wretches are so damn useful.'

He sighed, causing Moist to worry. Moist had never seen his lordship so discomfited, staring intently at the little truck as it went round and round on its little rails and filled the room with a smell of methylated spirits. There was something hypnotic about it, for Lord Vetinari, at least.

A silent hand dropped lightly, and eerily, on to Moist's shoulder. He turned around quickly and behind him was Drumknott, smiling gently.

'I suggest you pretend you didn't hear anything, Mister Lipwig,' he whispered. 'It's the best way, especially when he has one of his, er, sombre moments . . .' Still whispering, Drumknott continued, 'A lot of this is to do with the crossword, of course. You know how he is about that. I intend personally to write to the editor. His lordship considers elegant completion to be a test of his integrity. A crossword is meant to be an engaging and educational puzzle.'

And then, his normally pink face reddening, Drumknott added, 'I'm sure it's not intended to be a form of torture, and I'm certain that there is no such word as *lagniappe*. However, his lordship has terrific powers of recovery, and if you care to wait while I make you some coffee I'd wager he'll be his old self again before you can say "death warrant".'

In fact, Lord Vetinari stared at the wall for only eight minutes more before he appeared to shake himself down. He beamed at Drumknott and, less warmly, acknowledged the presence of Moist, who had been surreptitiously looking at the unfinished crossword lying prominently across the table.

Moist said, brightly but with the best of intentions, 'My lord, I'm sure you know that *lagniappe* is spelled differently than it sounds. Just a thought, of course, only trying to be helpful, sir.'

'Yes. I know,' said Lord Vetinari, in dark tones.

'Can I be of any *other* assistance, my lord?' said Moist, reckoning that he hadn't been prodded out of his bed for an undone crossword, or to admire a child's toy.

Lord Vetinari looked down his nose at Moist momentarily and said icily, 'Since you have *finally* decided to join us at this difficult time, Mister Lipwig, I will tell you that there was once a man called Ned Simnel who made a mechanical device, propelled in some arcane way, for taking in the harvest. The present difficulties might have begun there, but fortuitously his device didn't work, tending, apparently, to explode and burst into flames, and so the balance of the world was maintained. But, of course, the men who are drawn to tinkering continue to tinker in their little sheds! And not only that, they find ladies, good sensible ladies, who inexplicably agree to marry them, thus breeding a race of little tinkerers.

'One of them, a scion of the aforesaid Simnel, has apparently been scratching about in his father's shed and most certainly wondered if *he*, with his infinite curiosity, could achieve what his father, alas, had not.

And now this young man has created a machine which devours wood and coal and spews out flames, polluting the sky, undoubtedly scaring every living creature for miles around, and making the gods' own noise. Or so I am told.

'Finally, young Mister Simnel has found his way to our good friend Sir Harry King. And apparently the two of them are now dreaming up an enterprise, which I believe is called . . . the rail way.'

Vetinari paused only briefly before continuing. 'Mister Lipwig, I feel the pressure of the future and in this turning world must either kill it or become its master. I have a nose for these things, just as I had for you, Mister Lipwig. And so I intend to be like the people of Fourecks and surf the future. Giving it a little tweak here and there has always worked for me and my instincts are telling me that this wretched rail way, which appears to be a problem, might just prove to be a remarkable solution.'

Moist looked at the Patrician's grey expression. He had articulated the term 'rail way' in something like the voice of an elderly duchess finding something unmentionable in her soup. It had total disdain floating in the air around it. But if you watched the weather of Lord Vetinari, and Moist was an expert in the Patrician's meteorology, you would notice that sometimes a metaphysical cloudburst might very shortly turn into a lovely day in the park. He could almost smell his lordship coming to terms with the reality in front of him: tiny movements of the face, changes of posture and the whole litany of Havelock Vetinari thinking suddenly delivered one of those smiles which Moist knew suggested that the game was afoot, and the mind of Lord Vetinari was running and well oiled.

Vetinari said, getting more cheerful at every word, 'My coach is waiting downstairs, Mister Lipwig. Come.'

Moist knew that any kind of argument was useless, and he also knew that Lord Vetinari most definitely knew that too; but there was such a thing as pride, and so he said, 'My lord, I must protest! I have a lot of work to be done. Surely you are aware?'

Lord Vetinari, his robe fluttering behind him like a banner, was already halfway to the door. He was a long-boned man and Moist had to run to keep up, occasionally hopping down the stairs two at a time, with Drumknott in pursuit.

Ahead of him his lordship said, over his shoulder, 'Mister Lipwig, you *don't* in fact have a great deal of work to do. In fact, as Postmaster General, Deputy Chairman of the Royal Bank of Ankh-Morpork* and, of course, Master of the Royal Mint, you employ on *our* behalf a great many extremely clever people, who work very hard, that is true. Your strange camaraderie, your skill at getting people to like you against all the evidence and amazingly *continue* to like you, makes you a very good boss, it must be said, with staff who are very loyal to you. But ultimately all *you* really need to do in the way of desk work is a little light auditing every so often.'

Lord Vetinari stepped up his pace and continued,

---

* The actual chairman being, in point of fact, Mr Fusspot, chairdog.

'And what is it that we can take away from all this, I fail to hear you ask? Well, I shall tell you. What the wise man will take away is a certainty that any favour is worth doing for a good boss, and I, Mister Lipwig, am a most exemplary and forbearing employer. This is apparent from the circumstance that *your* head is still clearly resting on *your* shoulders despite the fact that it might possibly be in, oh, so many other places, as it were.'

The country of Llamedos prided itself on being *sensibly* dwarfish. In truth, there were as many humans as dwarfs who called Llamedos home but since most of them were miners, and, as a rule, were either small or almost permanently concussed, you really would have to look carefully to tell the species apart. Therefore, given that practically no one was bigger than anybody else, there was a general amiability in the area, especially since, although this wasn't generally talked about, the Goddess of Love saw to it that her spell covered all alike. And because nobody talked about it, well, nobody talked about it, and so life moved on with the mining for gold – what little there was of it by now – iron ore, such zinc and arsenic as could be teased out of the unforgiving rock and, of course, coal. All this was supplemented with fishing on the coast. The outside world was involved only occasionally, when something of *real* importance happened.

That was yesterday. Today, it happened.

The ship arrived at the dock in Pantygirdl, the largest town in Llamedos, just after lunch. The arrival of the grags on board, who had come to preach the truth of pure dwarfishness to the people of the town, would have been welcomed had they not come with delvers, the shock troops of the grags, who had never before been seen above ground. Until then, the people of Llamedos were quite happy that the grags were doing whatever it was they did in the realm of the spirit and the observances thereof, keeping things done properly so that everybody else could get on with the unimportant things like the mining and the fishing and the stonework up in the hills.

But today it all went horribly wrong, because Blodwen Footcracker was getting married to Davy Counter, an excellent miner and fisherman and, importantly, a human, although the importance of this fact did not seem to most people locally to be, well, important. Just about everybody in Pantygirdl knew them both and considered them a sensible match, especially as they had known one another since they were toddlers. And while they were growing up people wondered, as people did, about the chances of a dwarf and a human conceiving a child and considered it a long shot to say the least, but then they satisfied themselves by telling one another that, after all, love was certainly there in abundance and, besides, whose business was it anyway? He and she were compatible and loving and, as the mines and the boats took their toll of miner and fisherman alike, there were always plenty of orphans anxious for a new home in their own country. And everybody in Pantygirdl agreed that the situation, while not as it might have been, was nevertheless satisfactory to the kind of people who minded their own business, and they wished the happy couple, who were, it must be said, very nearly the same size, all the very best.

Alas, the grags and the delvers must have thought otherwise, and they broke down the doors of the chapel, and since people in Llamedos didn't go armed to their weddings the grags had it all their own way. And it might have been a complete massacre were it not for old Fflergant sitting hitherto unnoticed in the corner, who, as everyone ran for shelter, threw off his cloak and turned out to be exactly the kind of dwarf who *would* take heavy weaponry to a wedding.

He swung a heavy sword and axe together in a wonderful destructive unison, a whirlwind of fighting, and in the end there were only two casualties among the wedding party. Unfortunately one of those was Blodwen, killed by a grag whilst clinging on to her husband's arm.

Covered in blood, Fflergant looked around at the shocked wedding guests and said, 'You all know me. I don't like mixed marriages, but like you I can't abide those bloody grags, the bastards! May the Gap take them!'

Lord Vetinari's coach spun through the streets of Ankh-Morpork, and Moist watched the traffic scatter around them until they reached the River Gate and were out of the city proper. The coach bowled quickly along the road as it followed the Ankh downstream, towards Harry King's Industrial Estate, a world of smokes, steams and, most of all, undesirable odours.

Ankh-Morpork was cleaning up its act. It had been a good act, full of spices, plagues, floods and other entertainments. But now the Ankh-Morpork dollar was rising high, and so was the price of property. Amazingly, a great many people wanted to live in Ankh-Morpork, as opposed to somewhere else (or quite possibly as opposed to being *dead* in Ankh-Morpork, which was always an optional extra). But, as everybody knew, the city was gripped in its ancient stone corsetry, and nobody wanted to be there, metaphorically speaking, when the stays burst.

There was overspill, and my, how it was spilling. Farming land around the city state, always at a premium, was now full of speculative building.* It was a wonderful game, and Moist, in a previous life, would undoubtedly have joined in and made a fortune, several fortunes in fact. And indeed, while Lord Vetinari was looking out of the window, Moist listened to the sirens and their beguiling songs of money to be made

---

* A term meaning that the builder speculates about how far away he can be, and with how much money, before the buyer finds that the footings have, in fact, no feet, the septic tank is one foot deep with a tendency to flow backwards, and the bricks owe a lot to that most organic and venerable of all building materials, cow shit. The whole business traditionally begins with a plot, in every sense of the word. Entire suburbs were being built with such beguiling names as Nightingale Valley and Sunflower Gardens which had never heard a nightingale or seen a sunflower in bloom, but nevertheless were on the market with CMOT Dibbler Practically Real Estate and Associates, currently doing a roaring trade.

by the right man in this right place and the entrancing vision hung in the air for a tantalizing moment.

Ankh-Morpork was surrounded by clay, easily dug up, so if the cow shit ran out there was the material for your bricks, right there in front of you, with timber easily available from the dwarfs, delivered to your site by water. Soon you'd have a terrace of bright new homes available to the rising and aspirational population anxious to buy, and then all you needed was a shiny billboard, and, most definitely, an exit strategy.

The coach passed by many buildings of this sort, which would no doubt be little palaces to the occupants, who had escaped from Cockbill Street and Pigsty Hill and all the other neighbourhoods where people still dreamed that they could 'better themselves', an achievement that might be attained, oh happy day, when they had 'a little place of their own'. It was an inspiring dream, if you didn't look too deeply into words like mortgage and repayments and repossession and bankruptcy, and the lower middle classes of Ankh-Morpork, who saw themselves as being trodden on by the class above and illegally robbed by the one below, lined up with borrowed money to purchase, by instalments, their own little Oi Dong*. As the coach rumbled past the settlements, known together as New Ankh, Moist wondered whether this time Vetinari, in allowing all these lands to be colonized in such a way, had been very stupid or indeed very, *very* clever. He plumped for 'clever'. It was a good bet.

---

* Oi Dong being not dissimilar to Shangri-La.

Eventually they arrived at the first outpost of the complicated, stinking, but ultimately most profitable, wire-netting-fenced compound of Sir Harry King, sometime tosher and rag-and-bone man, now believed to be the richest man in the city.

Moist liked Sir Harry, he liked him a lot, and occasionally they shared the wink of men who had made it the hard way. Harry King had indeed come up the hard way and those who got in his way went down the hard way too.

Most of the area before them was full of the products of Harry King's noisome profession, conveyor belts coming and going from who knows where, being loaded and unloaded and sorted by goblins and free golems. Horses and carts went past loaded with even more grist for that particular mill. At the far end of the compound was a collection of large sheds, and in front of them a stretch of surprisingly clear space. Moist suddenly noticed the crowd outside the compound fence, pressing up against every inch of wire netting, and felt their expectancy.

As the coach stopped, he smelled the acrid scent of coal smoke cutting through the general fetor, and heard what sounded like a dragon having difficulty sleeping, a kind of chuffing noise, very repetitive, and then suddenly there was a scream, as if the biggest kettle in the world had got very, very angry.

Lord Vetinari tapped Moist on the shoulder and said, 'Sir Harry tells me that the thing is quite docile if handled with care. Shall we go and have a look? You first, of course, Mister Lipwig.'

He pointed to the sheds, and as they got nearer the smell of coal smoke got thicker, and the almost liquid chuffing noise got louder. Moist thought, well it was a mechanism, that's what it was, wasn't it? Merely a thing like a clock, yes, just a mechanism, and so he straightened up and walked fearlessly, on the outside at least, towards the door where a young man with a greasy hat and an even more greasy overall was beckoning with a greasy grin like a fox looking speculatively at some chickens. It seemed they were expected.

Harry came bustling out and said, 'Greetings, my lord . . . Mister Lipwig. Please come and meet my new associate, Mister Dick Simnel.'

Behind them, inside the shed, was the shuddering metallic monster, and it was alive. It really was alive! The thought lodged instantly in Moist's brain. He smelled its breath and heard its voice. Yes, life; strange life but nonetheless life of a sort. Every part of it was subtly shaking and moving, almost dancing by itself, a thing alive, and waiting.

Behind the beast, in the shed, he saw wagons, presumably ready to be towed, and he thought, yes, it's an iron horse. All around it were acolytes: men working on lathes, hammering on metal, running backwards and forwards with buckets of grease and cans of oil and occasionally pieces of wood which, right now, looked out of place amongst all the iron. And there was a strong sense of purpose that meant *we want something done and we want it done fast.*

Dick Simnel smiled broadly from behind a mask of grease and said, ''ow do you do, sirs. Well, 'ere she is!

Nowt to be afraid of! Her name, technically, is Number One, but I call 'er Iron Girder! She's my machine. I made her, every little bit: nuts, bolts, flanges and not to forget each and every rivet. Thousands of 'em! And all the glasswork too. Very important, your sight glasses and gauges. Had to design everything meself because no one has ever done it before.'

'And when you give her rails she'll move more freight than a battalion of trolls, and get there much faster to boot,' said Sir Harry, standing behind Moist. And he added, 'It's true. I swear that young Simnel tinkers with Iron Girder all the time: tinker, tinker, tinker. An overhaul every day.' He laughed and said, 'I wouldn't be surprised if he eventually got her to fly.'

Mr Simnel wiped his hands on his greasy rag, causing them to get even more greasy, and then proffered one to Lord Vetinari, who gently waved it away, saying, 'I would prefer it if you dealt with Mister Lipwig, Mister Simnel. If I decide to allow you your fascinating . . . experiment, it will be to him that you answer, in the first part. Personally, I treasure my ignorance of how machinery works, although I am well aware that this is something of great interest to some people,' he added, in a tone of voice that suggested he meant strange and secret people . . . busy people, excitable people, fiddling people, tinkering and volatile people. A kind, alas, who would say something as innocent as, let's give it a try, it can't hurt, surely? We can always hide under the coffee table.

'*My* interest,' continued Lord Vetinari, 'lies in ways

and means, opportunity, danger and consequences, do you see? I am given to believe that your remarkable engine is propelled by steam, heated until the boiler almost, but doesn't quite burst. Is that not the case?'

Mr Simnel gave the Patrician a cheerful smile and said, 'That's about it, gaffer, and I've blown up one or three in testing, I don't mind telling thee! But now, sir, we've got it right, sir. Safety valves! That's the ticket! Safety valves made out of lead, bungs that melt if the fire box gets too hot so the water comes down and extinguishes the fire before the boiler blows.'

Simnel carried on, 'Live steam is *very* dangerous, of course, to them that don't have the knowing of it, but to me, well, gaffer, it's as playful as a puppy. Sir Harry has allowed me to build a demonstration track, sir,' and he gestured to the rails that led out of the shed and wound round the perimeter of the compound. 'May I ask if you gentlemen would care to come for a little spin?'

Moist turned to Vetinari and said, with a flat face, 'Yes, how about it . . . gaffer?' And got a look like a stiletto. A look that said, we'll have words about this later.

Vetinari turned to Simnel and said, 'Thank you, Mister Simnel. I think on this occasion I will give that honour to Mister Lipwig. And I dare say Drumknott will be eager to accompany *him*.'

This was said brightly, but Drumknott looked anything but delighted at the opportunity, and frankly neither was Moist overjoyed, remembering too late that he had put on an expensive new jacket.

Moist asked, 'Mister Simnel, why does your contraption need to run on rails, please?'

Dick Simnel smiled the expansive smile of a man who really, really wants to talk about his wonderful pet project and is now keen to illuminate every bystander to the point of boredom, and in the worst cases suicide. Moist recognized the type; they were invariably useful and in themselves amiable and quite without malice of any sort, but nevertheless they were implicitly dangerous.

And right now, Mr Simnel, happy as a clam and greasy as a kebab, said, speaking earnestly, 'Well, sir, steam likes it smooth, sir, and the countryside is full of ups and downs, and steam and iron are heavy, and so putting all this together back at Swine Town we found it much more sensible to lay down what we call t'*permanent way*, it's a kind of road wi' tracks, or rails, just for the engine to run on, as it were.'

'*Railway*'ll do fine for the punters, though,' said Harry. 'I keep telling the lad – short and snappy, that's the kind of name people remember. Can't expect them to ride on something they can't spell.'

Simnel beamed, and suddenly his genial face seemed to fill the world. 'Now then, Iron Girder is greased, in steam and all fired up for you, gentlemen. Who's ready for a little ride?'

Drumknott had not uttered a word, and remained staring at the dribbling engine like a man looking at his doom. Moist, taking pity on the little clerk for once, half pulled him, half helped him up into the small open cabin of the metal beast, while Mr Simnel fussed around, tapping mysterious brass and glass items, and the fire in the belly of the beast burned hotly, and filled the place with yet more smoke.

And suddenly there was a shovel in Moist's hand, put there by Simnel so fast that Moist couldn't avoid it. The engineer smiled and said, 'You can be t'stoker, Mister Lipwig. If she needs stoking you'll need to open up t'fire box when I tell you. Ee, we'll 'ave some fun.'

Simnel looked down at the stunned Drumknott and said, 'Er, as for you, sir, well, I'll tell you what. You, sir, you can blow t'whistle, by means of this chain here. And as you see, gentlemen, this is by way of being a working prototype, with not very much of the comforts of home, but 'old on and you'll be fine, so long as you don't stick your head *too* far out. We'll be pulling a fair few ton today. Sir Harry were interested to see what she were made of, and so, er, Mister Drumknott, blow the whistle, if you please!'

Speechlessly, Drumknott yanked on the chain, and shuddered as a banshee scream came from the engine. And then, well, thought Moist, there was not very much, just one chuff, a jerk, another couple of chuffs, and another jerk, another chuff, and suddenly they were moving, not only moving but accelerating as if the end of Iron Girder was trying to be out in front.

Through roiling clouds of steam Moist looked behind at the loads they were towing in the creaking carts, and he could *feel* the weight, and yet still the engine with its train was gathering speed and momentum. Mr Simnel was placidly tapping his dials and shifting levers, and now here came a curve, and the train chuffed, and every truck followed the curve like ducklings following their dear old mum, rattling a little, certainly creaking, but nevertheless being one big moving *thing*.

Moist had travelled fast before. Indeed, a golem horse, that rare creation, could have easily outpaced them. But this, well, this was machinery, handmade by men: wheels, bolts, brass knobs, dials, gauges, steam and the grunting sizzling fire box, beside which Drumknott was standing now, hypnotized and pulling the chain that blew the whistle as if performing a holy duty, and everything shook and continued to shake like a red-hot madhouse.

Lord Vetinari and Harry came into view as the train raced towards them on its first lap. And they disappeared behind Moist into the cloud of smoke and steam left hanging in the air. Then, as Iron Girder plunged on, it broke through into Moist's consciousness that this wasn't magic, neither was it brute strength, it was, in fact, *ingenuity*. Coal and metal and water and steam and smoke, in one glorious harmony. He stood in the fierce heat of the cabin, shovel in hand, watching and wondering about the future, as the train of carriages bumped round once more, screeching slightly on the second curve. Then, with the sound of tortured metal, it slid to a stop a few feet away from the watchers in front of Iron Girder's shed.

Now Mr Simnel was all arms and business, shutting things down and turning things off as the wonderful engine died. Moist corrected himself: not died –

she was sleeping but still dribbling water and hissing steam and, inexplicably, she was very much alive.

Simnel dropped down from the cab on to a makeshift wooden platform and looked at his enormous stopwatch, glanced at the dial and said, 'Not bad, but I couldn't really open 'er up round here. On the test track over at Swine Town I got her going at almost seventeen miles an hour, and I can swear that she could go *much* faster if I could lay down a longer track! And she moved reet wonderfully, didn't she, gentlemen? With all that load, tons of it.' This was said to his fellow engineers.

'Aye, what is it?' And this, in fact, was directed to a small wide-eyed urchin, who seemed to have miraculously appeared by the side of the track. Simnel looked on gravely as the urchin took out a very small notebook from his jacket pocket and meticulously wrote down the numeral *1* as if it were a command.

And Moist, for some reason, couldn't help himself from saying, 'Well spotted, young man, and you know what? I rather feel that you're going to need a much bigger book before long.' And the certainty hit him that, although Lord Vetinari's face was as impassive as ever, those of Harry King and some of the other onlookers were gleaming in the smoky light of the future to come. Given the numbers already lining the fence, straining to watch the train on its circuits of the compound, the news was out and flying.

Harry King said, 'Well, gents, is this iron horse not amazing? She seems to be able to move *anything*, I assure you. Now, there's a nice lunch awaiting us in my

boardroom, gentlemen. Shall we go up there? ...
There's some cracking good beef.'

Lord Vetinari broke his silence. 'Certainly, Sir Harry,
and perhaps in the meantime someone could locate my
secretary?'

They turned to look at the engine, which had come
to a stop in a kind of human way, not all at once, but
settling down like an old lady making herself comfortable in a favourite armchair, except that at that
moment Iron Girder blew out a hissing stream of
shining water vapour, which does not normally happen
with old ladies, at least not in public.

Drumknott, up in the cabin, was still desperately
pulling the chain for the next whistle, and he seemed to
be weeping like a toddler bereft of a favourite toy as the
sizzling got fainter. He caught their gaze, carefully relin-
quished the chain, climbed down from the footplate
and almost tiptoed through the sizzling steam and the
occasional unexpected mechanical creak, as the metal
cooled. He walked gingerly over to Dick Simnel and
said, hoarsely, 'Could we do that again, please?'

Moist watched the Patrician's face. Vetinari seemed
to be deep in thought, then he said breezily, 'Very well
done, Mister Simnel, an excellent demonstration! Am I
to believe that many passengers and tons of freight
could be carried by means of this ... thing?'

'Well, yes sir, I see no reason why not, sir,
although of course there would have to be some additional work, decent suspension, and properly
upholstered seats. I'm sure we could outdo the stage
coaches, which are a right pain in the arse, sir,

and no mistake . . . if you would excuse my Klatchian.'

'Indeed I will, Mister Simnel. The state of our roads and therefore of our horse-drawn carriages leaves much to be desired. A journey to Uberwald is a penance without a cause and no amount of cushions seem to help.'

'Yes, my lord, and riding on sleek steel rails in a well-sprung carriage would be the height of comfort. So smooth!' said Moist. 'Perhaps people could even sleep in a suitable carriage, if there was such a thing?' he added. He was surprised that he'd said this out loud, but, after all, he was a man who saw possibilities, and now he was seeing them in spades. And he saw the face of Lord Vetinari brighten considerably. Iron Girder had ridden her tracks much better than the post horses managed with the flints and potholes of the high roads. No horses, thought Moist, nothing to get tired, nothing that needs feeding, just coal and water, and Iron Girder had pulled tons of weight without a groan.

And as Harry led the Patrician towards his office, Moist ran his hand over the warm living metal of Iron Girder. *This* is going to be the wonder of the age, he thought. I can smell it! Earth, air, fire and water. All of the elements. Here is magic, without wizards! I must have done something good to be in this place, here today, at this time. Iron Girder gave a final hiss, and Moist hurried after the others heading for their lunch and the future of steam.

In the plush comfort of Harry King's boardroom, all mahogany and brass and extremely attentive waiters, Lord Vetinari said, 'Tell me, Mister Simnel, could your engine go all the way to, let us say, somewhere like Uberwald?'

Simnel appeared to cogitate for a moment and then said, 'I don't see why not, your worship. It might get tricky round about Skund and, of course, it gets a bit steeper further on, but I'd say the dwarfs know how to knock damn great 'oles in t'scenery when they want to. So yes, sir, I'm certain it's possible, in time, with a big enough engine.' He beamed and said, 'If we have t'coal and t'water, and t'tracks, a locomotive engine could take you anywhere you wanted.'

'And is it open to anyone to build an engine?' said Vetinari suspiciously.

Simnel brightened up and said, 'Oh, aye sir, they can try, but they ain't had none of my secrets, and we Simnels've been working on steam for years. We've learned by our mistakes. *They* can learn by theirs.'

The Patrician smiled faintly. 'A man after my own heart, though laminating oneself to the roof of one's workshop is such a finite lesson!'

'Yes, I know, but if I might be so bold, sir,' Simnel continued, 'I'd like to bid for t'Post Office work, right here and now. Strike while t'iron's hot, that's always been the Simnel motto. I know the clacks can send a message as fast as lightning, but it can't do parcels and it can't do people.'

Lord Vetinari's face gave nothing away, and then he said, 'Oh really? *I* strike when I like, but never mind, Mister Simnel. I will not stand in the way of your exploring possibilities with Mister Lipwig, but I suggest we must also consider the position of the coachmen and farriers in this time of change.'

Yes, Moist thought, there would be changes. You'd still find horses in town and Iron Girder couldn't plough, although for a certainty Mr Simnel could make her do so. 'Some people will lose out and others will benefit, but hasn't that been happening since the dawn of time?' he said out loud. 'After all, at the beginning there was the man who could make stone tools, and then along came the man who made bronze and so the first man had to either learn to make bronze too, or get into a different line of work completely. And the man who could work bronze would be put out of work by the man who could work iron. And just as that man was congratulating himself for being a smarty-pants, along came the man who made steel. It's like a sort of dance, where no one dares stop because if you did stop you'd be left behind. But isn't that just the world in a nutshell?'

Vetinari turned to Simnel. 'Young man, I must ask you, what do you intend to do next?'

'There's that many people wanting to see Iron Girder up close like, I thought mebbe I'd hitch up t'wagons and put in some little seats, and offer them all the chance of a ride behind her. If Sir Harry's agreeable, that is.'

'There is of course the question of public safety,' said Vetinari. 'Did I hear you say earlier you have blown up . . . "one or three" I think was the phrase?'

'I made those explode a-purpose, to see exactly how it 'appened. That's the way to get the knowledge, you see, sir.'

'You take your work very seriously, Mister Simnel. And have any other engineers evaluated your findings? What I'm asking, Mister Simnel, is what is the judgement of your peers?'

Simnel brightened up. 'Oh aye, sir, if you mean Lord Runcible, sir, he's our landlord over at Sto Lat, but when I asked him, he laughed a lot and said it were amazing what people got up to and told me just not to run Iron Girder in the pheasant season while they were mating.'

'Indeed,' said Vetinari. 'If I might rephrase my question, what is the verdict of other engineers who have seen your wonderful machine working?'

'Oh, I don't think *anyone* calling 'imself an engineer, except me and my lads, has ever seen Iron Girder, although I've heard that over in Nothingfjord a couple of lads've made a damn good steam pump for getting groundwater out of mines and suchlike. All very interesting, but not as interesting as Iron Girder herself. I'd like to go visit them for a pint and a chat one day, but as you can see I'm busy, busy, busy all the time.'

'Your lordship,' said Harry, 'I respect Mister Simnel because I've seen that he's one of those men who tuck their shirt into their trousers and that says *dependable* to me. Now, there's a line of people out there who really want to whizz about behind the lad's ... er ... locomotive. I reckon they'll pay top dollar for taking a ride on the very first one of its kind. And the people of Ankh-Morpork are so thirsty for novelty that the whole city is, you might say, hurrying the future along for the sheer joy of watching its progress. So I'm thinking that every man and boy and possibly even their ladies would like to have a ride on this wonderful machine.'

'And should we count the risk, when simply to live in Ankh-Morpork is to shake hands with risk every day of the week?' murmured his lordship. 'Mister Simnel, you have my goodwill, such as it is, and I can see a twinkle in the eye of Sir Harry, a man who, if I may say so, looks like someone who intends to be an investor, although, of course, that is entirely up to him and you. I am no tyrant . . .'

There was a moment of hushed silence around the table and Lord Vetinari continued, 'That is to say I am not a tyrant stupid enough to take a stand against the zeitgeist, but, as you know, I am the man who can steer it with care and consideration. That is why I intend to speak to the editor of the *Times* this very evening to leave him, as he would say, in the loop. He always likes to be consulted, it makes him feel important.'

His lordship smiled and said, 'Amazing, how *do* we think up these things? I wonder, indeed, what will come next.'

The atrocity of the attack on the clacks tower at Sto Kerrig, which had so recently been a lifeline to the world for the people in the town, shocked everyone. As Adora Belle Dearheart looked at the wreckage in the gathering dusk, she was not surprised to see a very large and handsome wolf approaching at speed and, unlike most wolves, carrying a package between its jaws. The wolf disappeared behind a haystack, and shortly afterwards out of the haystack came a handsome female, only marginally dishevelled, wearing the uniform of the Ankh-Morpork City Watch.

Captain Angua, the most notable werewolf in the Watch, said, 'Oh my, they've certainly made a mess, haven't they? And are you sure that only one of your people was hurt?'

'Two goblins, captain, but they bounce well. Quick-witted, too. Can you imagine, they managed to send out a final message saying that their tower was under fire from dwarfs before they legged it. Very conscientious, the goblins, when it comes to machinery. They are always better on the night shift. Can I say, captain, when you find out who did this I'll press charges and press them very hard indeed, to a point when a police officer like yourself would have to look away for fear of seeing something they didn't want to.'

'I wouldn't worry about that, Miss Dearheart. His lordship takes the view that to interfere with the clacks is to interfere with the proper running of the world. Treason not only to one's own state, but to all.'

'At the moment, my friend Shatter of the Icicle, the lead goblin on this tower, has a bit of a battered arm, but he'll certainly assist in finding the dwarfs who did this. However, I don't know where Shine on the Moon has got to.'

'I'll prowl the area until my back-up gets here. I'm expecting the cart and Igorina for the forensics,' said Angua. 'If you hear something screaming it might be me, but don't worry. Commander Vimes has no time for senseless saboteurs.'

There was a pause, and Adora Belle said gravely, 'There's something I think you ought to see. Look under this pile of timber: this dwarf looks very, very dead and horribly mutilated. I assume he probably tripped and fell when he was setting fire to the tower. What do you think, captain?'

Carefully, Captain Angua looked at the corpse and said, 'He's lost an ear.'

Adora Belle said, 'Well, apropos of nothing at all, I understand that when goblins get truly riled up they go all frisky and look for souvenirs.'

'But I'm quite certain, of course, that none of your clacks goblins would be getting up to anything like that, right?' Angua asked.

Distantly, Adora Belle replied, 'Yes, having been almost burned alive by dwarf extremists would be shrugged off as another day in the office and not something to get very excited about.'

She looked at the captain quizzically, who said, 'Quite so. Undoubtedly any injuries were caused by the incompetence of the terrorists themselves.'

'Why, yes, indeed, yes,' said Adora Belle.

'Wasn't it amazing how one of them managed to chew his own ear off?' Angua observed.

'So, can Shine on the Moon come out of hiding now?'

'I'm sorry,' said Angua carefully, 'I didn't hear what you said over the cracking of the tower.'

The silence in Lord Vetinari's study was absolute.

Nevertheless, the tread of Drumknott's approach contrived to make it even more silent as the secretary handed his lordship a little slip of paper and told him that a second clacks tower had been torched by people calling themselves, in translation, 'The Only True Dwarfs'.

Drumknott waited while not a muscle moved in Lord Vetinari's face before he said, 'Let it be known that enemy action on the clacks system will be followed by the death of not only those who did it but also those who ordered it to be done, whoever they are. Send this to every embassy, consulate and head of state. Action this night, please.'

Still speaking calmly, Lord Vetinari continued, 'It is also time, I think, to let the dark clerks deal with the more unusual suspects. I'm sure your concludium has given you some clues, Drumknott, and of course we will assist in any way possible. The Low King must be . . . unhappy about this. Although the stricken clacks tower was ours, we know that the impact of this problem falls in the last event on the King himself. Therefore, send him a message on the black clacks and let him know that I myself and, undoubtedly, Lady Margolotta will support any new plan he chooses to make. The grags have once again broken a solemn accord and *that*, Drumknott, batters the pillars of the world and not inconsiderably. After all, if you can't trust governments, whom can you trust?'

There was a subtle cough from Drumknott and his smile at that point was more like a grimace. Before the secretary was released to his private office and its other intrigues, Lord Vetinari continued fishing in his own stream of consciousness, and said, 'I seldom get angry, Drumknott, as you know, but I am angry now. I should be grateful if you would send for Commander Vimes in his other incarnation as Blackboard Monitor Vimes. I require his assistance and I don't think he will be a happy man – which, from my point of view, has no downside in these circumstances. Please put the message out to Mister Trooper that this is not the time to be a nice person.'

He went on, 'This isn't war. This is a crime. There will be a punishment.'

Rhys Rhysson, Low King of the dwarfs, was a dwarf of keen intelligence, but he sometimes wondered why someone with that intelligence would go into dwarfish politics, let alone be King of the Dwarfs. Lord Vetinari had it so easy he must hardly know he was born! The King thought humans were, well, reasonably sensible, whereas there was an old dwarf proverb which, translated, said, 'Any three dwarfs having a sensible conversation will always end up having four points of view'.

It wasn't quite as bad as all that, but it was near enough these days, he told himself, as he looked over at the assembled members of his council in which, according to the rules, he was the first among equals. He had read somewhere in the scrolls that they owed him fealty, whatever that was. It sounded like a kind of porridge.

When his secretary, Aeron, had returned from a

recent visit to Ankh-Morpork, he had described a foot-the-ball game he witnessed, which had, at its centre, a referee. Right now, Rhys was feeling something of what the referee had to go through since all the balls were kicked right at him. How could you be the Low King in a realm where even the factions had factions and those factions had microscopic factions? He envied, oh how he envied, Diamond King of Trolls who, apparently, gave instruction and advice to his myriad subjects. After which they said *thank you*, something that the Low King didn't hear very often. Diamond King spoke for *all* trolls *everywhere*. The dwarfish race, however, had fractured now almost to the point of disarray and all of this ended up as a problem the Low King had to deal with.

There was today, obviously, an agenda or, rather, a regrettably large number of agendas, one for every faction. Glumly, Rhys wondered what the word was for a large number of agendas, and decided that the term should be a *living death of agendaritis*. It was the deep-down grags that gave him nightmares because, well, there was something offensive about those thick leather clothes and conical hats. After all, he thought, we're all dwarfs together, are we not? Tak never mentioned that dwarfs should cover their faces in the society of their friends. It struck Rhys that this practice was deliberately provocative and, of course, disdainful.

Now, on the everlasting agenda, dwarfs from every mine were grumbling about the exodus of the young to the big cities. And, of course, they all had reasons for why this might be the case, all of them wrong. Anyone who wasn't a dwarf who preferred to live in darkness, in every meaning of the word, knew that the reason the younger generation was now overwhelming Ankh-Morpork, for example, was simply down to those very same grumblers and their activities. On the other hand, those he thought of as progressive dwarfs, the type who would quite happily have a troll as a friend, were bearing down on *him*, the King, about their race's tendency to drive itself into a kind of purdah.

There was a great cloud of misunderstanding in the Low King's hall, which on every side appeared almost wilful, as if any dispute, however insignificant, had to be thrashed through to the bitter end. It was something in the dwarf psyche. We spend too much time indoors, Rhys thought. He sighed when he realized that Ardent, whose voice had become unbearably loud, now had the floor.

Ardent was a dwarf that the King would have liked to see present at a mine disaster, preferably underneath it. However, Ardent had followers, stupid followers, and he also had powerful friends. And that was it. Politics. Politics was like those little wooden sliding-picture games for children: you had to move all of the pieces in the hope of finding a place where the whole picture slotted together.

At the moment Ardent was insinuating that, in truth, the mining of fat in the Schmaltzberg fat mines was not truly dwarfish, a comment which led an elderly dwarf, whom the King recognized as Sulien Heddwyn, to get to his feet.

Heddwyn put his hands on his axe and said, 'My

father was a fat miner. My grandfather was a fat miner. And so was my grandmother, she was a *very* fat miner and I was a miner when I was a minor. My mother gave me a tiny pick as soon as I was old enough to hold it. Every one of my relatives back to the dive of the Fifth Elephant was a fat miner and I'll tell you, the export income from the Plains for our purest fats is what keeps this town running. So I won't take an insult like this from a *b'zugda-hiara** too afraid to look at the sunshine.'

The sound of metal on metal echoed around the hall, followed by silence, with everyone waiting to see what was going to happen next. And that meant Rhys Rhysson had to break that silence. After all, he was, was he not, the Low King, the Low King of all the dwarfs?

He smiled, well aware that one wrong word from him would send shock-waves around the cavern and the result, whatever it was, would be his fault. Such is the fate of those who work only for the propagation of peace over warfare, and the way of the conscientious facilitator is a path strewn with thorns.

He looked at the angry councillors brandishing weapons around the huge table. It was as if being a dwarf meant that you lived in a permanent state that the term 'grumpiness' simply couldn't convey. A conference of dwarfs was, in their language, a confusion of dwarfs.

His voice low, Rhys spoke. 'For what purpose am I King? I will tell you. In a world where we formally

* 'lawn ornament'

recognize trolls, humans and, these days, all manner of species, even goblins, unreconstructed elements of dwarfdom persist in their campaign to keep the grags auditing all that is dwarfish.'

He looked sternly at Ardent as he continued, 'Dwarfs from every area where dwarfs live in sufficient numbers have tried to modernize, but to no avail apart from those in Ankh-Morpork, and the shame of it is that often those determined to keep dwarfkind in the darkness have somehow inculcated their flocks into believing that change of any sort is a blasphemy, no specific blasphemy, just a blasphemy all by itself, spinning through the cosmos as sour as an ocean of vinegar. This cannot be!'

His voice rose and his fist crashed down on the table. 'I am here to tell you, my friends and, indeed, my smiling enemies, that if we do not band together against the forces that wish to keep us in darkness dwarfkind will be diminished. We need to work together, talk to one another, deal properly with one another and not spend all our time in one enormous grump that the world isn't entirely ours any more and, at the finish, ruin it for everyone. After all, who would deal with such as us in a world of new choices? In truth, we should act as sapient creatures should! If we don't move with the future, the future will twist and roll right over us.'

Rhys paused to accommodate the inevitable outburst of *Shame!* and *Not so!* and all the other detritus of rotted debate, and then spoke again. 'Yes, I recognize you, Albrecht Albrechtson. The floor is yours.'

The elderly dwarf, who had once been favourite to

win the last election for Low King, said courteously, 'Your majesty, you know I have no particular liking for the way that the world is going, nor some of your more modern ideas, but I have been shocked to discover that some of the more headstrong grags are still orchestrating attacks on the clacks system.'

The King said, 'Are they mad?! We made it clear to this council and all dwarfs, after the message we received from Ankh-Morpork about their clacks being attacked, that this stupidity must cease at once. It's even worse than the Nugganites,* who were, to be sensible about this, totally and absolutely bloody insane.'

Albrecht coughed and said, 'Your majesty, in this instance I find myself standing shoulder to shoulder with you. I am appalled to see things go this far. What are we but creatures of communication and communication accurately communicated is a benison to be cherished by all species everywhere. I never thought I would say this, but the news I am hearing lately, and am expected to delight in, makes me ashamed to call myself a dwarf. We have our differences and it's right and proper that we should have them, and discourse and compromise are cornerstones in the proper world of politics, but here and now, your majesty, you have my full and unequivocal support. And as for those who stand in our way, I call down a murrain on them. I say, a murrain!'

---

* Not to be confused with the fabled Nougat Knights, famed in dwarfish mythology as the ancestors who, at the beginning of the world, created the treacle mines and other subterranean sweets.

There are uproars and there are uproars and this uproar stayed up for a very long time.

Eventually Albrecht Albrechtson brought his axe down on to the table, splitting the wood from top to bottom, bringing terrified silence across the gathered dwarfs, and said, 'I support my King. That is what a King is for. A murrain, I said. A murrain. And a Ginnungagap for those that say different.'

Rhys Rhysson bowed in the direction of the old dwarf. 'I thank you, my old friend, for your support. You have my undying gratitude and you leave me in your debt.'

Then, to some onlookers, the Low King might have looked a little taller. Over the hubbub, and there is no hubbub as bubbling as a dwarf hubbub, the King felt strangely buoyant, lifted, like the strange gases found around the crater of the Fifth Elephant. It seemed to the King that some of his councillors were suddenly thinking, actually thinking, and they had listened, actually listened. And now they were trying to think creatively.

Rhys continued, 'Not for nothing is Ankh-Morpork the residence of even more dwarfs than live here in Uberwald; and we now know that quite a large number of our dwarfs are emigrating to the lands of Diamond King of Trolls. So it is that our traditional enemy is now a friend to the many fleeing from the agents of the grags.'

As he expected, the hubbub bubbled even more: wilful bubbled hatred, bubbled misunderstanding, bubbled spitefulness.

He said, 'I tell you now that history will run straight over us squabbling dwarfs and I will not stand by and allow that history to end with our race brought down to the status of angry *b'zugda-hiara*! I am the King, by right, duly elected with all the proper observances. I was anointed on the Scone of Stone in accordance with traditions going back to the time of B'hrian Bloodaxe and I will serve the sacred duty by all means necessary. I declare these grags and their puppets are *d'hrarak* and I will not suffer their pernicious doctrines any more. I am the King, and I will be King!'

The uproar returned, as it always did, but Rhys thought he could see some comfort in the faces around the table and then his gaze ran into Ardent and triumph wobbled a little and he thought softly: sooner or later, my friend Mister Ardent, I will have to deal with you.

Lord Vetinari's expression did not alter as he read the headline in the *Ankh-Morpork Times*: 'LOCOMOTIVE PROJECT DANGEROUS FOR HEALTH' followed in a much smaller font by 'SO IT IS CLAIMED'. And it wouldn't alter until he had had a word with the editor. Of course, the Patrician knew that any change was an affront to somebody, and quite clearly the proposed locomotive undertaking couldn't hope to be anything other than a target.

'Apparently,' Vetinari remarked to Drumknott, 'the pounding rhythm of the railway wagons will lead to immorality. This from a Mister Reginald Stibbings of Dolly Sisters.' He signalled to one of the dark clerks.

'Geoffrey, what do we know about this Mister Stibbings? Does he have a particular *expertise* in immorality?'

'The one at Loose Chippings, my lord? I am informed that he has a very young mistress, sir. A young lady formerly employed at the Pink PussyCat, and very highly thought of there, I believe.'

'Does he? An expert indeed, then.' Vetinari sighed and continued, 'Though of course I do not imagine it is in my remit to monitor the private doings of my people.'

'My lord,' interjected Drumknott. 'As a tyrant that is, in fact, exactly what you do.'

Vetinari gave him a look that did not actually employ a raised eyebrow but which implied that one might be forthcoming if the recipient of the look pushed his luck. He shook the paper in front of him and continued. 'A Mrs Baskerville from Peach Pie Street says that young ladies travelling on the train might find any kind of gentlemen sitting next to them.' He thought for a moment and said, 'In this city, expecting to encounter any kind of gentleman seems somewhat optimistic. But perhaps she has a point. It might be prudent to have compartments for ladies only. I rather think that Effie King would approve that.'

'Excellent idea as always, sir.'

'And what do we have here? A Captain Slope is very concerned about noxious gases around the lines of the railway.'

Lord Vetinari snapped his paper shut and exclaimed, 'The people of Ankh-Morpork are already at home to noxious gases. It's their birthright. Not only are they at home with them, they quietly persist in making more. It seems that Captain Slope is one of those people who won't like the railway at any price. Suggesting that sheep will miscarry and horses will run until they die of exhaustion ... Indeed, it seems that Captain Slope thinks the railway will be the end of the world. Well, Drumknott, you know my motto: *vox populi, vox deorum.*'

Curious, the Patrician thought, as Drumknott hurried away to dispatch a clacks to the editor of the *Times*, that people in Ankh-Morpork professed not to like change while at the same time fixating on every new entertainment and diversion that came their way. There was nothing the mob liked better than novelty. Lord Vetinari sighed again. Did they actually think? These days *everybody* used the clacks, even little old ladies who used it to send him clacks messages complaining about all these new-fangled ideas, totally missing the irony. And in this doleful mood he ventured to wonder if they ever thought back to when things were just old-fangled or not fangled at all as against the modern day when fangled had reached its apogee. Fangling was indeed, he thought, here to stay. Then he wondered: had anyone ever thought of themselves as a fangler?

However, on the other hand, his lordship quite saw the point of the coach drivers and the others who even now, according to the *Times*, could see their business falling away if the railway were to be introduced, and he pondered, in such circumstances, what is the careful prince to do?

He thought, how many lives had been saved by the clacks, and not just lives: marriages and reputations and possibly thrones? The clacks towers now spanned the continent this side of the Hub and Adora Belle Dearheart had provided evidence that the clacksmen had several times spotted nascent fires, and on one occasion, outside Quirm, a shipwreck a little way out to sea – when they had clacksed that information to the nearest harbour master, saving all hands.

There was nothing for it but to follow the wave. New things, new ideas arrived and strutted their stuff and were vilified by some and then lo! that which had been a monster was suddenly totally important to the world. All the time the fanglers and artificers were coming up with even more useful things that hadn't been foreseen and suddenly became essential. And the pillars of the world remained unshaken.

As a responsible tyrant, Lord Vetinari regularly audited his actions fearsomely and without favour. Trolls in Ankh-Morpork were rarely talked about these days because, amazingly, people barely thought of them as trolls any more, just as, well, large people. Much the same, although different. And then there was the position of the dwarfs, the Ankh-Morpork dwarfs. Dwarfish? Yes, but now on their own terms. The Low King was certainly aware that in Ankh-Morpork there was a large population of dwarfs that had taken a look at the future and decided to grab a slice of it. Tradition? they had thought. Well, if it suits us then every so often we'll have a parade of all things dwarfish. Sons and daughters of our parents but, as it were, augmented. We have seen the city. The city where almost anything is plausible, if not possible, including, for the ladies, a better class of lingerie.

Far away in a small mine at Copperhead, Maelog Cheerysson the cobbler put down his hammer and tacks.

'Look here, my boy,' he said to his son, who was leaning on his work bench. 'I've heard what you said about the grags being the salvation of dwarfs, and this morning I found this: it's an iconograph of me in Koom Valley. The last time. Oh, yes, I was there, nearly everybody was there. We'd been told by the grags that the trolls were our enemies and I thought of them as nothing more than nasty big lumps of rock out to crush us! Well, we were all lined up facing the buggers, and then somebody shouted, "Trolls, put down your weapons! Dwarfs, put down your weapons! Humans, put down your weapons!"

'And there we stood and we could all hear other voices in different languages and right in front of me there was this bloody big troll, oh my! He had his great big hammer ready to pulverize me. That was not to say that my axe wasn't about to take his bloody knees off at the same time, but the voices were so loud that everybody stopped and looked around and he looked at me and I looked at him and he said, "What's happening here, mister?" and I said, "I'm damned if I know!"

'But I could see the other side of the valley and there was a great big kerfuffle between the top brass, all screaming about dropping our weapons, and I looked at the troll and he looked at me, and he said, "Are we going to have a war, or what?" and I said, "Oh, and I'm pleased to meet you, my name is Maelog Cheerysson," and he sort of grinned and said, "They call me Smack, and I'm pleased to meet you."

'And all around us people were wandering around and asking one another what the hell was going on and were we fighting or were we not fighting and if we were fighting what were we fighting for? So some of the lads sat down and lit a fire for a brew-up, while at the other end of the valley the flags were fluttering and everybody was walking around like it was a holiday or something.

'And then a dwarf came up to us and said, "Good fortune, lads, you're going to see something that no one else has seen for millions of years," and we did, I reckon. We were some way away from the front of the queue because trolls and humans and dwarfs were coming back out of the cavern, and every single one of them going past us looked as if he'd been hypnotized.

'Now, I've told you about the miracle of Koom Valley before, my lad, but you haven't seen this iconograph of me and Smack. It was took at the time just after we realized we weren't going to be fighting that day and we all went in ones and twos into that cavern and saw the two kings: the king of the dwarfs and the king of the trolls, entombed in shining rock, playing Thud! And we saw it! And it was true! They'd been friends in death. And that gave us the signal that we needn't be enemies in life.

'And that was it until later Smack and me tried to find something both of us could drink. A lot of the people were doing the same thing, but the potion he gave me nearly blew my bloody head off. It certainly made my boots burn. Smack has got two kids now, you see, doing all right, working in Ankh-Morpork. Trolls ain't all that good at writing, but I think of him and I think of Koom Valley every day.'

The old cobbler looked sideways at his son's face and said, 'You're a smart boy. Smarter than your brother was . . . and I reckon you've got a question to ask me.'

The boy coughed and said, 'If you saw them playing Thud, Dad, can you remember which one was about to win?'

The old dwarf laughed. 'I asked that when I met Commander Vimes, and he wouldn't tell me. We reckoned he probably broke a few pieces off so no one knew who the winner would be so some curious little fellow like you wouldn't go off and try to start the whole damn war again.'

'Commander Vimes? The Blackboard Monitor?'

'Yes, it was him all right. Shook my hand. Shook both our hands.'

The boy's tone was suddenly reverential. 'You actually shook hands with the actual Commander Vimes!'

'Oh, yes,' said his father nonchalantly, as if meeting the famed Blackboard Monitor was all in a day's work. 'I suspect you have another question, my lad.'

And the boy frowned. 'So, Dad, what's going to happen to my brother?'

'I'm sorry, I don't know. I sent a petition to Lord Vetinari, saying that Llevelys is a good lad who got into bad company. And I received a reply, and his lordship said that a young dwarf set fire to a clacks tower while people were working on it. And his punishment will be at his lordship's leisure. And so I sent him another letter, saying that I had fought at Koom Valley. And I received another reply, and his lordship said that he understood that I *didn't* fight at Koom Valley because fortunately nobody did, but he understood that I must do what I can for my eldest son, and as his lordship said, he will cogitate.'

The old dwarf sighed. 'I'm still waiting, but as your mother says, while we're not hearing anything, then he's still alive. Now don't tell me, my lad, that the grag extremists are on our side, because they ain't. They're the ones that'll tell you that the dead kings have been made up in Ankh-Morpork and were dummies and so were we if we thought they were real. And, my boy, the dumb believe it! But I was there. What I touched I felt, and so did everybody else on that day and that's why I get angry when the grags start preaching about the horrible humans and the terrible trolls.

'They want us to be frightened of one another, thinking there must be an enemy, but the only enemy now is the grags and those poor fools like your brother, who set fire to a clacks tower and got badly burned for his trouble. They are the victims of the sneaking bastards in the darkness.'

Far away in the Oblong Office Drumknott put the

midday edition of the *Times* in front of Lord Vetinari and looked down at Mr Cheerysson's latest frantic petition, saying, 'They've torched two more clacks towers, my lord, but so far no one has died. Except on their side, of course. Young dwarfs, badly advised. They should have known better.'

The silence enveloped Lord Vetinari. 'Indeed,' said his lordship, 'but it is easy to be an idiot when you are seventeen and I would warrant that the grags who put them up to it are much older. There is no sense in breaking the arrow if, by acting sensibly, you may capture the archer. I'll leave the Cheerysson boy thinking about his fortune in the Tanty for a while and will make a note to have him brought over to talk to me in a month or two. If he's clever, his parents won't be grieving, and I'll have a number of names and, above all, the goodwill of his parents. Always worth thinking about, don't you agree, Drumknott?'

'Damage to property,' said Drumknott speculatively.

'Yes,' said Lord Vetinari. 'That's it.'

A few days later, Crossly quietly entered the master bedroom of the house in Scoone Avenue, nudged Moist, and, when that had no effect, finally pinched his ear in order to get his attention.

He whispered, 'Excuse me, sir, but his lordship requires your presence at the palace *immediately*, and I am sure that neither of us would like to see the mistress troubled at this time, yes?'

At home and, for once, in bed at the same time as

Moist, Adora Belle Dearheart was gently snoring, although she was certain that she did not.

Moist groaned. It was the crack of seven and he was allergic to the concept of two seven o'clocks in one day. Nevertheless he dressed with a speed and silence trained by experience, walked noiselessly downstairs, left the house and got a trolley bus to the palace. He ran up the steps to the Oblong Office, reflecting that, day or night, he had never seen it empty. This time Lord Vetinari was at his desk, looking, if the word could be applied to Lord Vetinari, chipper.

'Good morning, good morning, Mister Lipwig! Rather speedier than last time, yes? I imagine you haven't had time to look at your newspaper today? Something rather droll has happened.'

'Is it something interesting to do with the railway, perhaps, my lord?'

Lord Vetinari looked puzzled for a moment and then said, 'Well, there is something, yes, since you ask.'

He sniffed as if what he was dealing with was not in the great scheme of things all that important and continued, 'I am being told that everybody is going to Harry King's compound to see the marvel of the steaming train, which seems to have caught the public fancy. I understand that Sir Harry, with his usual business acumen, is already turning this into a commercial enterprise.

'Of course, that is news, but when you do indeed get hold of a newspaper you might notice a small apology from the editor of the *Times* to the effect that the crossword has been removed, as the compiler is stepping down for a while owing to the pressures of keeping up the standard of achievable games that are nevertheless sufficiently taxing. Of course, as a rule I do not gloat, but I fear she has met her match. I shall ask Drumknott to arrange for a box of chocolates to be sent to her, from a secret admirer. After all, I am generous in victory!'

Lord Vetinari cleared his throat again and said solemnly, 'Alas, Drumknott has taken the morning off to go and have another look at the engine. A morning off. Whoever heard of such a thing? I have to say that I'm somewhat surprised, as the only other time he has ever requested time away from my service was to attend the paperclip, stapler and desktop aids symposium three years ago. He got very excited about that one, too. One wonders what the attraction of this engine can be. Does it not seem rather strange to you?'

Moist was a little nervous of the use of 'strange' and 'Drumknott' in the same sentence, and instead volunteered to visit the site of the train to escort Drumknott back to the palace.

'Since you will be there, Mister Lipwig, I shall be pleased to hear your . . . impressions on the economic opportunities for my city.'

Ah-ha, thought Moist, so that's why he's dragged me out of bed . . . again. Nothing to do with the crossword, nothing to do with Drumknott, but *everything* to do with *his* city getting an interest in the railway.

His lordship gave Moist a brisk nod and waved the paper, suggesting that it was time for him to be on his way.

* * *

It took Moist a long time to push his way through the throng anxious to see the modern miracle of the age. Harry King's business compound was at the very end of the queue that seemed to straggle halfway back to the city. There was no sign of Drumknott but Moist wasn't surprised. When Drumknott was standing in front of you, he was so retiring as not to be there.

There were guards on the gates all round the compound, Harry's own and City Watch, watching like hawks as one by one the citizens queueing up parted with a whole dollar a time to ride behind the locomotive. And a dollar was a dollar, possibly a day's food for a family, and yet, as far as Moist could ascertain, flying over the rails on the wonderful train was worth tightening your belt for. It was better than the circus, better than everything, to be speeding along with the wind in your face and black smuts that made the eyes water, but were, well, the badge of the train riders, who nevertheless didn't seem to notice it, given the amount of unpleasantness that could slap, splat, spit or fly into your face when you stepped into the street, or even when you walked into your own house, if you lived anywhere near the Shades.

Moist was well versed in the people of Ankh-Morpork's love of novelty, and, he had to admit it, Iron Girder, pulling her train like the queen she was, was novelty in the extreme. She came trundling around the corner with people in the carts behind screaming and waving to friends still waiting in the queue. And as a connoisseur of the madness of crowds he watched carefully, and noted that some passengers disembarked and scuttled away to the man who was handing out little tokens in exchange for another dollar, and then ran all the way to the back of the very, very long queue for another go.

There was a click near by and then a flash, and he turned to see the perennially cheerful face of Otto Chriek, lead iconographer of the *Ankh-Morpork Times*, who gave him a friendly wave.

'Vell now, Mister Lipvig, surely you're behind zis in your cheeky little vay?'

Moist laughed and said, 'No, not me, Otto, but it's *very* popular, isn't it!' And I want to be at the very centre of it all, he said to himself.

He noticed that periodically the man collecting the money hurried away carrying huge leather pouches, with a troll bodyguard fore and aft, and was instantly replaced with another showman ready for the moneys of the mob. And so Moist, as he told himself in his own cheeky vay, followed the money. He followed it in between the great noisome heaps and stinking lagoons of Harry's empire until the man with the large pouches of coin walked into a large shed. He followed him inside and froze, because he was immediately surrounded by the kind of men who have their noses splashed against one side of their face, little in the way of conversation and, he noticed now, very bad halitosis.

Fortunately, the shed also contained Sir Harry, who was bright enough to wave a hand in the air and say, 'Okay, boys, loosen those sphincters. It's only Mister von Lipwig, my old chum and bank manager. He's practically one of us, ain't you, Moist?'

Moist grinned, thankful that sphincters were, right now, not in play, and said, 'Well now, Harry, you know, as your bank manager I of course make it my duty to look after your interests, and I gather that you're looking after the interests of Mister Simnel too?'

That hung in the air like a sickle, a sharp one at that, and he watched Harry's face, which hadn't moved one single muscle. And then, abruptly, Harry burst out laughing and said, 'Oh my, Mister Lipwig, I always said you was a sharp card and, if it comes to that, a card sharp!'

He nodded to his bodyguards and said, 'Go and have a little break, lads. Me and my old friend here'll be having a little chinwag, such as old friends do. Go on, bugger off, the lot of you.'

And indeed they did, all except one, the very largest, a troll who glittered strangely and was watching Moist most intently, but not as intently as Moist watched him. And, Moist thought, the troll was . . . a gentleman. He couldn't think of him in any other way; he was well dressed, which was remarkable in itself as most trolls viewed clothes as optional.

Somewhat embarrassed at this interest, Moist felt rude enough to say, 'Okay, Harry, but there's one bodyguard still here. D'you think I'm going to try anything?'

Harry King guffawed. 'That, Mister Lipwig, is my lawyer. His name is Mister Thunderbolt, got the letters after his name and everything, ain't you, Thunderbolt?'

Lawyer! Bingo!

Harry was laughing all the way from his belly now

and said, 'Mister Lipwig, the look on your face! Don't worry, though. Mister Thunderbolt takes everybody that way. That isn't to say I ain't glad to see you, but you could be of service to both me and our friend the engineer. Shall we go somewhere a bit more private? Coffee?'

Harry waved at a clerk, who bustled away swiftly, and then ushered Moist and Thunderbolt up to his office overlooking the compound. Harry sat down and beckoned to Thunderbolt and Moist to do the same.

'Now then, you know me, Mister Lipwig, like I know you. We're a pair, eh? Not exactly crooks, not exactly, well, not now anyway, 'cos we've grown up and know how to do business properly, don't we?' He concluded with a wink. 'And we both know a once-in-a-lifetime deal when we see it, I'm sure. Tell me if I'm wrong, yes?'

There was somebody who was a lawyer in the room, moreover a lawyer who could presumably kill you with one punch, and it was always worth thinking about anything that you were going to say in front of a lawyer because you never knew if you really could trust the weasels, but Moist nodded at Mr Thunderbolt and said, with careful diction, 'Sir Harry, Lord Vetinari has set me the task of assessing this wonderful new invention on behalf of the city.'

Harry King opened a box of big cigars, sniffed them and chose one before proffering the box to Moist and Thunderbolt. The troll declined, of course, but Moist was never one to turn down one of Harry King's finest cigars. They came from far-off places and were truly excellent. Harry puffed out a big cloud of smoke, leaving him for a moment looking just like Iron Girder, and it occurred to Moist that Harry, who knew that symbols were important, was definitely hoping to be the first railway baron.

'Mister Lipwig, Iron Girder is peacefully, for want of a better word, transporting eager citizens around the track regular as clockwork. Round and round they go, happy as you like, you must agree? Mister Simnel says he built her as a proof of concept and he needs a lot of money to build a full-size version that can pull even more people and, above all, freight, because he reckons that's where the money is to be made, although looking out of the window at all those smiling faces I'm not so sure of that.'

Sir Harry sent another plume of smoke into the air and looked smug, which, Moist considered, was probably the case, before adding, 'Since I know you, Mister Lipwig, and I know that you can read me, yes, I'm prepared to bankroll the lad in exchange for a slice of the profits, a *big and fair* slice. I understand that he's now all but skint, totally boracic, with the arse nearly out of his trousers, and if he's ever going to get his ambition to run bigger trains to here, there and bloody everywhere then he needs a partner with experience of the world, and I have that experience from the bottom up, as it were.

'But, you know how it is, gents . . . when a man gets older and he's made his pile he starts caring a bit more about what people think about him, so I ain't no dwarf, I won't steal an advantage on a young man with prospects. That's why I'm happy to say that with the help of Mister Thunderbolt here I've struck a fair deal with the young lad. Ain't that so, Mister Thunderbolt?'

The air seemed to glitter as the troll stood up, shimmering as he spoke. His voice appeared to come from twilight canyons far away. It wasn't just sound, it had a presence in its own right.

'Yes, that is so. Sir Harry, I suggest now that even though you have a handshake deal with Mister Simnel, there should be three shares in this enterprise, to avoid deadlock, with the third and very small share in the hands of the city, to wit, Lord Vetinari. The purpose of the arrangement is in case Mister Simnel and you, Sir Harry, are unable to agree on a matter connected with what we are all calling the "railway". Lord Vetinari will have the casting vote to end that deadlock. But the city will not take any dividends; its income will come, as always, from straightforward taxation, which I am sure Lord Vetinari will consider an important part of this enterprise.

'The small print will be a little more complicated, and of course if Mister Simnel's locomotives catch on there will be opportunities to sell extra shares in the future. If you both agree, gentlemen, I will deal with that aspect and you may be certain that in compliance with Sir Harry's instructions Mister Simnel and his family will have a significant share in the business.'

As slowly as he had stood up, Mr Thunderbolt sat down again, and Moist von Lipwig and Sir Harry King looked at one another.

Harry, beaming, said, 'I suppose I'd better get the lad in, then,' and nodded to Thunderbolt to open the door.

A few minutes later Dick Simnel sat uncomfortably in his seat, trying not to make anything greasy, without much hope and even less success.

Harry appeared not to notice and said cheerfully, 'Now then, lad, it's like this. You reckon that with enough money you could make engines larger and more powerful than Iron Girder, right? And with long enough, er, rails, you could get to all the other cities? Well, lad, I'll bankroll you in this enterprise until you're in a position to prove that this is possible.'

He stopped talking for a moment, looked at the ceiling and said, 'Tell me: how long d'you think that'll be?'

The engineer looked thoughtful and somewhat baffled and said, 'I couldn't rightly say, sir, but the more the money jingles the faster the wheels'll turn. I mean, if I can hire the best skilled workers and, well, sir, I've made my calculations, done a lot of testing and I reckon I could have a new engine ready for . . .'

Moist held his breath.

'One thousand dollars.'

Moist glanced at the face of Harry King, who flicked the ash from his cigar and said, in a deadpan way, 'A thousand dollars? And how soon can you have it on the rails, lad?'

Simnel took his small sliding device out of his pocket, played with it for a minute or so and said, 'How about two months?' He fiddled with the device again and added, 'Around teatime.'

Moist was fidgeting at this point, and he chimed in with, 'Excuse me, I know you said that Simnels have been working on steam for years and that other people might have been too, but do you know if anybody else has anything like this? Might they steal a march on you even if they don't have your secrets?'

To his surprise Simnel said cheerfully, 'Oh yes, sir, about four or five of them, but none of them have yet produced even a working concept like Iron Girder. They're making all t'mistakes my dad did, and making a few others of their own an' all, from what I hear. Superheated steam doesn't give you a chance. Get it wrong and it'll tek t'flesh off your bones. Now me, sir, well, I'm a stickler for measurements, tiny teeny weeny measurements. They ain't very exciting but that's the soul and centre of being an engineering artificer.

'Unfortunately, my granddad and my dad were a bit slapdash about them, seeing as they didn't have the proper knowing of them, but measurements is your saving grace if you want to raise steam. Me mum paid for me to get a better learning, being as 'er side of the family had money from . . .' he paused, 'fishing, and one of my uncles made theodolites and other delicate instruments, and I thought to meself, well, this is very helpful, especially when he taught me 'ow to blow glass, and what I need glass for is my own little secret . . .'

Simnel looked anxious for a moment and said, 'I'll need a shedload of iron, especially for t'tracks themselves. And, of course, then there's the question of laying t'tracks through people's land . . . someone'll have to talk to the landowners. I'm an engineer, always will be, and I'm not sure I know how to 'aggle with the big nobs.'

'Ah, as it happens we have a born haggler with us

right now,' said Harry. 'What do you say, Mister Lipwig? Do you want to be a part of it?'

Moist opened his mouth to speak.

'There you are, then, young Dick. We'll use Mister Lipwig for any negotiations. He's the kind of man who'd follow you into a revolving door and still come out in front. And he speaks posh, when necessary. Of course, he's a bit of a scoundrel, but aren't we all in this business?'

'I don't think I am, sir,' said Simnel cautiously, 'but I know what you mean. If you don't mind, I'd like to suggest that my first track is laid all the way back to Sto Lat. Well, not exactly Sto Lat, it's a place on the out-skirts called Swine Town, there being so many pigs in the area. That's where the rest of my gear and machinery is stored.'

Simnel looked nervously at Sir Harry, who was pursing his lips. 'It's a long way, lad, must be twenty-five miles or more, and you'd be right out in the sticks there.'

Moist couldn't hold his tongue. 'Yes! But they wouldn't be the sticks for long, would they? Try and get fresh milk in the city . . . it's always bad cheese by the time it gets to you, and then there are things like straw-berries, watercress, lettuce, you know, everything with a limited shelf life! The areas that have the railways'll be more prosperous than those that don't! It was the same at first with the clacks. Everybody said they didn't want the towers, and now anybody who's anybody wants one at the bottom of their garden. The Post Office'll be on your side too, moving the mails faster and all that, and

I can assure you that the Royal Bank will be right behind you, and indeed, Mister Simnel, I'll invite you to join me in my office as soon as possible to discuss our *special* banking facilities . . .'

Harry King slapped his thigh and said, 'Mister Lipwig, didn't I say it: you're a man who sees an opportunity when it's in front of him!'

Moist smiled. 'Well, Harry, I think it's in front of all of us now.'

In fact, in his mind's eye Moist could see *lots* of opportunities and plenty of room for problems, and here right in the middle of it all was Moist von Lipwig. It couldn't get better than this! His smile widened, inside and out.

It wasn't about the money. It had never been about the money. Even when it was about the money, it wasn't entirely about the money. Well, it was *slightly* about the money, but most of all it was about what the dwarfs called the *craic*. The sheer pleasure about what you were doing and where you were doing it. He could feel the future catching him up. He could see it beckoning. But, of course, sooner or later someone would try to kill him. That usually happened, but you had to take the chance. It seemed to be a necessary part of the whole thing, whatever the whole thing actually was. You *always* had to take the chance. Any chance.

Harry gave Moist a sideways glance and said, over his shoulder, 'Mister Simnel, if you've got a lot of your valuable stuff in a shed up there in Pig City or wherever, would you mind me sending a couple of my . . .' Harry paused, seeking for a genteel wording,

'. . . my *useful* gentlemen to keep an eye on the place for you?'

Simnel looked puzzled and said, 'It's really a quiet old place, sir.'

Harry moved into what might be called his avuncular persona and said, 'That might very well be so, my lad, but I think that you and me are going to a place where there'll be a lot of money, and where there's a lot of money there are a lot of people trying to take it off you. I'd like to think that if anyone broke into your big shed to fossick around for any interesting bits of machinery or clues as to how you build your engines, they might find themselves having to explain their interest to Snatcher, Stiletto Dave and Grinder Bob. They're all good lads, kind to their old mums and wouldn't hurt a fly. Call it, well, call it . . . *insurance*. And if you can be good enough to let them have a key, I'll send them up there right now. Mind you, if you can't find a key I'm sure they'll find their way in. They're very versatile in that respect.'

Young Simnel smiled and said, 'That's very thoughtful of you, Sir Harry. Perhaps I should give them a message to take to my mother. She'll show them where everything is. My dad said always put a few nasty little booby traps around the place before you lock up and then after that owt they can steal from you they're welcome to, if they've still got their arms to carry it away, that is.'

Harry laughed out loud and said, 'Sounds to me like your old dad looked at things just the way I do. What's mine is mine and what is mine is me own.'

* * *

When Moist and Mr Thunderbolt stepped out into the compound Moist saw that people were *still* queueing up for a ride on the train, which was waiting like a queen while Mr Simnel's lads filled her bunker full of coal, and oiled and greased everything again, including themselves. They tapped her wheels and polished everything that could be polished, once again including themselves, while just about every little boy in the city, and, amazingly, most of the girls, stared at her in awe, worshipping at her shrine. And then it came back to him: earth, air, fire and water, the sum of everything! The goddess had found her worshippers.

There was a sound like thunder, but it was only Mr Thunderbolt clearing his throat to say, 'Remarkable, isn't it, Mister Lipwig? There appears to be what one can only call a *presence* of sorts, a hint, as it were, that life turns up in many different guises, perhaps? Just a passing thought.'

Moist had never heard such clear diction from a troll, and it must have shown, because Thunderbolt laughed, saying, 'A touch of diamond does the trick, Mister Lipwig, and I will endeavour to draw up contracts that suit all parties, you need not worry.'

Just then Moist beheld Drumknott, greasy and cheerful and covered with smuts, stepping off the engine and regretfully handing a hat and a very grubby jacket to one of Mr Simnel's lads. Moist grabbed the little secretary by one arm.

'Where did you get to, Mister Drumknott? I've been

looking for you *everywhere*,' he lied. 'His lordship is expecting you back any time now.'

Moist wasn't sure he liked Drumknott, but it wouldn't do to have him as an enemy, being so close as he was to the engine that drove Ankh-Morpork, and so he cleaned up the little man as best he could and flagged a coach back into the city, noticing, as they travelled along the busy towpath, that the major traffic was still going the other way.

Moist knew about the zeitgeist, he tasted it in the wind, and sometimes it allowed him to play with it. He understood it, and now it hinted at speed, escape, something wonderfully new, the very bones of the land awakening, and suddenly it seemed to cry out for motion, new horizons, faraway places, *anywhere that is not here*! No doubt about it, the railway was going to turn coal into gold.

'Excuse me, young man.'

Sergeant Colon and Corporal Nobby Nobbs, who had taken it upon themselves to patrol the line of expectant sightseers queueing for a ride on the train, looked around uncertainly. It had been a long time since Sergeant Colon had been a young man, and as for Nobby Nobbs, although it was generally agreed that he was the younger of the two, there was some doubt about whether the term *Homo sapiens* could be applied to him; the jury of Ankh-Morpork was out. Colon and Nobby were supposed to have been on the beat in the Shades, but Colon had delegated that task to a couple of new recruits. 'Good experience for 'em, Nobby. And it's likely to be a dangerous business, this streaming engine. Needs someone to have a look-see – a couple of experienced coppers, let's say, prepared to put therselves in harm's way for the public good.'

'Young man . . . excuse me,' came the voice again. The speaker was a harassed-looking lady with two boys at heel, who weren't at all at heel and were expressing their frustration at having to wait for the promised ride on the train in the supremely annoying ways that only small children can manage. In a desperate attempt to distract them from their contest to inconvenience as many people in the queue in front of them as possible, their mother had seized on the first official-looking people who might be able to entertain her offspring with some interesting facts.

'We were just wondering if you could tell us how this locomotive goes?' she asked.

Fred Colon took a deep breath. 'Well, missus, there's the boiler, you see. It's like a kettle.'

This was not enough for the smaller child, who said, 'Mum's got a kettle. That doesn't go anywhere.'

His mother tried again. 'And how does this "boiler" work?'

'Well, you see, it sends the hot water to the engine,' said Nobby hurriedly.

'Right,' said the lady, 'and then what happens?'

'And then all the hot water goes into the wheels.'

The elder boy looked sceptical. 'Really? How's that done?'

Nobby, cornered, said, 'I think the sergeant can tell you that.'

A little bead of sweat appeared on Colon's face and he was aware that the two children were looking at him as if he were some kind of exhibit. 'Ah, well, the water is magnetic, right, because of all that spinning,' he said.

The elder boy said, 'I don't think it works like that.'

But Colon was on a roll and ignored him. 'The spinning causes the magnetism and that's what makes the water stick in there. Lots of iron in train wheels, stands to reason. And that's what keeps the train on the iron road, magnetism.'

The smaller boy changed tack. 'Why does the engine go *chuff*?'

'That's because it's chuffed,' said Colon with a sudden flash of inspiration. 'See, you've heard of "*chuffed*". That's where it comes from.'

Nobby looked at his friend in admiration. 'Is that why, sarge? I never thought of that!'

'And when it's had enough of a chuffing, there's enough magnetism to hold the train on the iron road, see?'

The last phrase was delivered in a rush in the hope that no more questions would be forthcoming. But it doesn't work like that with children. The elder boy had had enough and decided to show off the knowledge gleaned from friends who had been there earlier in the day. 'Isn't it to do with reciprocating motions?' he said, with a glint in his eye.

'Ah, well, yes,' blustered Colon helplessly. 'You've got to have your recip-roca-tory motions to get the right *kind* of chuff. And when everything is chuffing and reciprocatoring, away we go.'

The smaller child was still puzzled, as well he might be. 'I still don't understand, mister.'

'Well, perhaps you're too young to know,' said Colon, taking refuge in the excuse used by exasperated adults through the millennia. 'Very technical stuff, your chuffing. Probably shouldn't even be trying to explain it to children.'

'I don't think I understand either,' said the mother.

'You know clockwork?' said Nobby, coming to the rescue again. 'It pretty much goes like clockwork, only bigger and faster.'

'How's it wound up?' asked the boy.

'Ah yes,' said Colon, 'that chuffing noise, of course, is the winding up. And when it's wound up, then off it chuffing goes.'

The smaller boy held up a clockwork engine and said, 'He's right, Mum, you wind them up and away they go.'

Bemused, the lady said, 'Right . . . well, thank you, gentlemen, for a comprehensive little talk. I'm sure the boys were fascinated.' And she handed Colon several coins.

Colon and Nobby watched the happy family as they climbed on to the cart behind Iron Girder. And Nobby said, 'It's a nice feeling, isn't it, sarge? Being helpful to people.'

Moist's cab halted at the palace, and he helped an exhausted Drumknott up the stairs. Amazingly he was beginning to feel sorry for the little chap, who was looking like a lotus eater who had run out of lotuses.*

Moist very carefully knocked on the door of the Patrician's office, which was opened by one of the dark clerks. The clerk stared at Drumknott and looked askance at Moist, as Lord Vetinari himself stood up in surprise, leaving Moist impaled between two askances. So he saluted smartly and said, 'I beg to report, sir, that Mister Drumknott very gallantly and fearlessly and at some personal cost has helped me form an opinion as to the practical aspects of the new-fangled train, risking his life *repeatedly* in so doing, and for my part I have seen to it that your government has a suitable measure of control over the railways. Sir Harry King is funding further research and trials, but personally, my lord, I believe the new railway will be a winner. I'm convinced that this prototype can pull more stock than dozens of horses. Mister Simnel seems to be very thorough in his work, extremely meticulous and, above all, the people appear to have taken the train to their hearts.'

Moist waited. Lord Vetinari could outstare a statue and make even a statue start to feel nervous and confess. Moist's counter was a fetching grin, which he knew annoyed Vetinari beyond measure, and there was absolute silence in the Oblong Office while blank stare and cheery grin battled it out for supremacy in some other dimension, which ended when his lordship, still staring fixedly at Moist, said to the nearest dark clerk, 'Mister Ward, please take Mister Drumknott to

---

* Moist wondered whether it should be loti, but thought, well, what the hell.

his rooms and clean him up, if you would be so kind.'

When they had departed, Lord Vetinari sat down and drummed his fingers on his desk. 'So, Mister Lipwig, you believe in the train, do you? It certainly appears that my secretary is impressed. I have never seen him so excited by something that wasn't written on paper, and the afternoon edition of the *Times* seems to be in agreement with him.'

Vetinari walked over to the window and stared down at the city in silence for a moment and continued, 'What can a mere jobbing tyrant achieve in the face of the even greater, multi-headed tyrant of public opinion and a *regrettably* free press?'

'Excuse me, sir, but if you wanted to you could shut down the papers, couldn't you? And forbid the train and put anyone you like in prison, yes?'

Still staring down at the city, Lord Vetinari said, 'My dear Mister Lipwig, you are clever and certainly smart but you have yet to find the virtue of wisdom, and wisdom tells a powerful prince that firstly he shouldn't put just anyone he likes in prison, because that is where he puts the people he *doesn't* like, and secondly that mere unthinking dislike of something, someone, or some situation is no mandate for drastic action. Therefore, while I have given you permission to continue, the train does not have my wholehearted approval. Neither does it have my curse.' The Patrician seemed to consider for a moment and added, 'Yet.'

He walked up and down again for a second or two and then, as if the thought had only just struck him, said, 'Mister Lipwig, do you think it a possibility that a train *could* in fact get all the way to, say, Uberwald? That journey is not only extremely slow, tedious and uncomfortable by coach, but it is fraught with many . . . ah, perils . . . and traps for the unwary traveller.' He paused and added, 'And indeed the unlucky bandit.'

'Oh, yes, that's where Lady Margolotta lives, isn't it, sir?' said Moist breezily. 'But it would mean negotiating the Wilinus Pass, sir. Very dangerous up there! Bandits have been known to knock out coaches by throwing down rocks from the crags.'

'But there is no other way without a very lengthy detour, Mister Lipwig, as you probably know.'

'In that case, my lord . . . I think it might be possible to construct such a thing as an armoured train,' said Moist, inventing furiously. He was gratified to see that Lord Vetinari brightened when he heard that, repeating the words 'armoured train' once or twice more.

Then his lordship said, 'Can it *really* be possible?'

And in the squirrel cage of Moist's mind, he thought, Can it? Can it really? It must be more than twelve hundred miles! It takes well over two weeks by coach and that's if you don't get hijacked, but who was going to try to hijack an armoured train? The engine would be wanting water frequently and is it possible that it could carry enough coal for the whole journey? The numbers rolled in his head. Stopping places, troughs for water, mountains, gorges, bridges, marsh land . . . So many things, any one of which could scupper the project . . .

But going to Uberwald would mean passing through so many other places on the way and all of them could be opportunities to make money. The demons of critical path analysis swarmed around his brain. There was always something that you had to do before you could do the thing you wanted to do and even then you might get it wrong.

To Vetinari he said cheerily, 'Well, sir, I don't see why not. And, of course, for such a long journey it should be possible to sleep on the train and for heads of state to occupy a complete suite of carriages, if not the whole train. Surely that could be arranged?' Moist held his breath.

After a few seconds his lordship said, 'That would be appropriate, but, Mister Lipwig, I am not *entirely* bribed. The train must prove itself both financially *and* mechanically. However, I look forward to its success. It seems, Mister Lipwig, that you are using your extra-cheery voice and so once again you find yourself in your own chosen environment, that being the centre of everything. But tell me: where do you think will be the destination of the first commercial train? Quirm?'

'Actually, sir, that has been discussed and it looks as if it's going to be Sto Lat, because that's where Mister Simnel has his machine tools and a large stock of materials that he would need to transport to Ankh-Morpork. Besides, that place is a nexus for the Sto Plains, and nexus means—'

Lord Vetinari raised a hand and said, 'Thank you, Mister Lipwig. I do know what a nexus is.'

Moist smiled and headed for the door, showing his panic only on the inside, and as his hand reached the doorknob Vetinari's voice behind him said, 'Mister

Lipwig, you surely realize that a thoughtful prince, a prince who wishes to keep his throne for some time and is shrewd in the ways of people, would not travel in a thrilling armoured train . . . He would put somebody *else* on that train, somebody expendable, having himself travelled the previous day in a suitable disguise. After all, there are such things as very, very large boulders, and most definitely there are a great many spies. But I shall consider your idea. It has a beguiling ring to it.'

Over the next few weeks more and more people heard about Iron Girder and even larger crowds passed through Ankh-Morpork to see the new marvel of the age, including delegates, ambassadors and representatives from most of the towns across the Sto Plains. And, of course, there were the *other* artificers and freelance tinkerers, inspecting everything they could see and trying to find out everything they could about what it was they weren't being allowed to see.

Every night Iron Girder was driven along a set of rails into a locked shed on the compound where she would be safe from interference due to the presence of Harry's most fearsome attack dogs and also two golems, brought in by Harry because, unlike dogs, they couldn't be killed by a meal laced with poison poked under the door. They patrolled the huge shed, sometimes with members of the City Watch just for the look of the thing.

Moist spent a lot of time in and around the compound in his not very official but somehow understood role as the grease in the outfit's management, as essential as the buckets of the stuff that seemed to be required in everything to do with the railway. He had, after all, a stake in the railway's fortunes as head of the Royal Bank of Ankh-Morpork, where money was starting to go in and out faster than a revolving door as Harry wrote cheques for iron shipments, timber and extra metalworkers, many of whom were from the company of Free Golems: every one of them his own man, albeit one made of clay.

And grease was definitely needed here. There was a mountain of paperwork already being generated by the railway, which Moist skilfully passed along to Drumknott, whose passion for paperwork was not quite yet eclipsed by his new passion for the railway. The little pink man was in hog heaven.

Surveyors had been called in to work on a route. They were everywhere with their little theodolites. They treated Dick Simnel as one of them, only different. Moist was pleased about that. Dick had friends now, and if they didn't understand all of his language they did indeed recognize it as bona fide language somewhat similar to their own and therefore they gave him respect. After all, these other people, in a way, did what he did only in different shapes, stresses, curves, loads, tolerances and substances, and thus where it counted were brothers under the skin. And like Dick, they worked by numbers and knew the absolute necessity of getting them right, and especially they knew the absolute requirement for precision.

In the compound the sound of metal on metal filled the air, and on every flat surface in Harry King's offices maps were laid out, and they were good maps.

'Lads,' Dick Simnel had said to the theodolite men, 'Harry King is a good gaffer who pays top dollar for a top-rate service. He's chancing everything to get the locomotives running, so I want you to make it easier for him. Iron Girder can take some slopes, and by 'eck she'll take more before I'm through, but for now, what I'm telling thee is to keep t'permanent way as level as possible. And I know that there are such things as tunnels and bridges, but they take a lot of time and are flippin' expensive! Occasionally a little detour might save us a lot of money, which is to say your wages. But think on, and I know it's obvious, but do not go any-where near swamps and other shaky ground. A locomotive with its coal tenders, carriages and crew is reet, *reet* 'eavy and the last thing we want to be learning is 'ow to pull a bogged-down locomotive out of t'quicksand.'

And off they'd gone. The men with clean shirts every day. The men of the sliding rule. Moist liked them because they were everything he wasn't. But maybe he should teach them about being a scoundrel. Oh, not about taking money from widows and orphans, but about being aware that many people weren't as straight as a theodolite.

The surveyors proved only too happy to agree that the area around Sto Lat was the gateway to the Sto Plains, so now all they needed to do was get the people with, as it were, the keys to the gate to understand this, a job that everybody was extremely happy to turn over to Mr Moist von Lipwig.

As it turned out, there were a great many landowners between Ankh-Morpork and Sto Lat, and any number of tenants. Nobody minded a clacks tower near by. Indeed, often these days they demanded one, but, well, a mechanical thing chuffing through your cornfields and cabbage plantations spewing out smoke and cinders, well, *that* was a different matter, which would be the kind of problem that could be settled only by the application of that wonderful lubricant known to every negotiator as warm specie.*

The aristocrats, if such they could be called, generally hated the whole concept of the train on the basis that it would encourage the lower classes to move about and not always be available. On the other hand, some were of a type that Moist recognized: shrewd old buffers who'd lead you to believe they were harmless and possibly slightly gaga and then, with a little twinkle in their eye – BANG! – squeeze more money out of you than a snake, twinkling all the way.

Lord Underdale, one such gentleman, had plied Moist with an indecent amount of gin and brandy while naming his terms: 'Now see here, young man – *twinkle, twinkle* – you can take your tracks across my land if we can agree a route and it won't cost you a penny if you will firstly carry my freight for nothing

---

* The term 'specie' requires the person asking for it to rub their thumb and forefinger together in a *knowing* way, if you know what I mean, guvnor?

and secondly put a loading station just where I want it so that I can also travel anywhere I want merely by flagging down one of your locomotives. Do you see, young man – *twinkle, twinkle* – I go free and my freight goes free. Do we have an accord?'

Moist looked out of the wonderful mullioned windows at the smoke beyond the ancient trees and said, 'What exactly *is* your freight, sir?'

The old man, all beautiful long white hair and ditto beard, said, 'Well, now, since you ask, it's iron ore with a certain amount of lead and zinc. Oh dear, I see your glass is empty again. I must insist you have another brandy – it's such a cold day, is it not? *Twinkle, twinkle.*'

Moist smiled and said, 'Well, your lordship, you are a tough bargainer and no mistaking – *twinkle, twinkle, TWINKLE.* Since our project is *very* heavy when it comes to metals, we could perhaps do business? That is to say if our surveyors don't come up with any problems, such as swampy ground and suchlike.'

'Well, Mister Moist, since you have drunk every last drop of brandy I have pressed on you without appearing to be the least bit intoxicated, I must consider you a man after my own heart – *twinkle, twinkle.*'

And here Moist definitely detected the subtle signs of intoxication as the old man said, 'I have to tell you that yesterday I was contacted by a man who said he represented the up-and-coming Big Cabbage Railway Company.'

Moist knew about them, yes, they were a company all right, but they didn't yet have a single engine or anybody as skilful as Simnel to tame the raw steam. He rather suspected that a lot of money would go their way from the gullible and then, when there was enough, the bright office would be empty and the gentlemen concerned, with different moustaches, would be legging it somewhere else to start up *another* railway company. Part of him longed to be one of them and then he thought, I *am* one of them, only this one has to work.

'Apparently,' continued Lord Underdale, 'they are going to build a far superior engine to the one being demonstrated in Ankh-Morpork.' The old man laughed at Moist's almost total lack of expression and said, 'You told me that you represented a railway company, Mister Lipwig. Well, now your company has . . . *company*!'

Moist belched forensically, very carefully choosing his time. 'This may be the case, sir, but we have – *hic!* – a working engine, which is . . . the toast of Ankh-Morpork!' And here Moist allowed a certain slur to enter his voice and continued, 'And now, why don't we, as gentlemen, cut a deal and shake hands on it like gentlemen so we both know where we stand?' He stood up and stumbled a little, saw the extra *twinkle* in the old man's face, and rejoiced.

Later, in the stables, as he saddled up to go home, Moist audited his afternoon's work. This was a game he knew all too well. He had seen the trap and had been prepared, and thus the side deal for iron-ore shipments and railway access was a sensible one but slightly more beneficial for the railway, in recognition of the fact that elderly gentlemen shouldn't try to get impressionable young men drunk, especially when they own more land than any reasonable person could ever need. Yes, Moist thought, moral compass? He smiled.

Before he mounted up, Moist carefully removed from about his person two hot-water bottles and a rubber pipe. He very carefully stowed both bottles in a large padded saddlebag, smiling as he did so. The old boy really shouldn't have tried to make him drunk. It was so . . . unethical.

When Moist eventually got back to the city, he went straight to the centre of Harry King's compound, ran up the stairs to Sir Harry's great big office, and dropped yet another portfolio, prepared by Mr Drumknott, of all the contacts he had dealt with, the rents, the routes agreed.

'These are for your lads, Harry, and this is for you.' He set down very carefully a large crate containing a number of bottles.

Harry stared at him and said, 'What the hell are these for!'

Moist shrugged and tapped his nose. 'Well, Harry, it's like this. A lot of the people I have to deal with are elderly men who think they're cunning and try to fill me with expensive alcohol in the belief that they can get the better of the deal and no mistake. Of course, I drink every drink put in front of me! No! Don't look like that! I really can hold my drink. In fact I can hold a great deal of drink, and I'm pleased to report that rubber doesn't detract from the taste of whisky, very fine brandy or Jimkin Bearhugger's best gin.'

'Well done, Mister Lipwig. I've always known you're a man to watch *extremely* carefully and I do so like to see a master at . . . *work*. Now follow me, Mister Lipwig, and try not to slosh, will you?'

In a few weeks the compound had changed beyond recognition: the big drop forges that used to thud behind Quarry Lane had been moved wholesale out of the centre of the city and enormously augmented their rate of hammering with the rhythms of the railway factory.

Harry seemed very proud of it, considering that if muck was brass, a thump of the hammer was pennies from heaven. As they walked through the cacophony he shouted, 'Great lads, the golems! They're always punctual, and they don't get ill. Most of all, they just *like* working! And I like anyone who likes to work: goblins, golems, I don't care what you are if you're a good worker.' He thought for a moment and added, 'As long as you don't dribble too much. Just look at the way those lads hammer things with their fists. I wish I could get more of them, but you know how it is.'

Moist looked around the fiery hellhole that was the ironworks. In the satanic air he could just about tell the golems from the human workers in their leather overalls, because the golems were the ones walking around holding pieces of red-hot iron in their bare hands. The furnaces illuminated the grey sky, and always and forever the clanging went on. And the pile of fresh new rails got bigger and bigger.

He nodded, since normal speech was clearly out of

the question among the clanging and the banging. Indeed, he knew how it was. In short, the citizens of Ankh-Morpork who might be expected to fill the heavy-lifting trades, such as the golems and the trolls, were increasingly realizing that just because they were big and tough did not mean they had to do a big tough job if they didn't want to. This was, after all, Ankh-Morpork, where a man walked free even if he was not, strictly speaking, a man.

The problem, if you could call it that, had been building up for some time. Moist had first noticed what was happening when Adora Belle said that her new hair stylist was a troll, Mr Teasy-Weasy Fornacite*, and, as it turned out, a pretty good hairdresser, according to Adora Belle and her friends. And there it was: the new reality. If all sapient species were equal, that's what you got: golem housekeepers and goblin maids and, he thought, troll lawyers.

Harry King was rumbling on as they emerged back into the open: 'It's a bugger! Now they're free, you can't get the golems! Ask your missus! They're all off doing landscape gardening and suchlike daisy rubbish, and I reckon I'm paying every human ironworker in the damn city double the odds, and only twenty-one of them heavy boys. It's such a shame, such a shame.'

'I don't know, Harry, you seem to be moving phenomenally fast.'

---

* The moment Moist heard the name he went for the dictionary and was relieved to find that fornacite was a rare lead, copper chromate arsenate hydroxide mineral. The troll was a lovely bluey green colour.

Harry nudged Moist and said, in a conspiratorial tone, 'I'll have you dumped in the river if you tell anybody this, but I'm loving it! I mean, most of my life has been, not to put too much of a fine point on it, shit, honest to goodness shit, not to mention of course piss, which has also been a very good friend to me, but you see all *that* is just moving stuff about, not actually *making* something. And it gets better because, you see, it's something me and the Duchess can talk about in polite company. Oh, of course, I'll still be maintaining the night-soil business and all of that . . . it is, after all, my bread and butter, so to speak, which, to tell you the truth, is more like steak and all the trimmings nowadays, but right now my heart is in the iron. And who can say that ain't beautiful, Mister Lipwig? I mean, daffodils, well, I quite like them, but look at the sheen on the steel, the sweat on the men; the future being made one hammer blow at a time. Even the slag is beautiful in a way.'

Iron Girder passed by on her everlasting journey around the compound and Harry said, 'What we need is the right class of poet.' He flung out a hand towards the admirers with their notebooks and all the others who clung to the railings. 'Look at them all! They're looking for miracles. And you know what? They'll get them.'

It started to rain, but the onlookers, especially the train spotters, with their very useful clothing, just stood there, watching Iron Girder kick up a mist into the air.

It seemed to Moist that for a moment Harry King was somehow different, even more alive than usual, and Harry, it had to be said, was pretty vital in any case. And now Harry King, Cess Pit Man, was metamorphosing into a National Treasure.

Bedwyr Beddsson tried to get his boots off. After a night in the mines it was amazing what you found in your boots, some of it alive. When the boots were off, not without a struggle, he took the harness off Daisy the pit pony and watched her sniff the clean air and canter into the little field near the entrance to the mine. It did your heart good to see her. There were times when Bedwyr would have liked to do the same thing. His mother had told him, you can't change your stars, meaning, presumably, this is your life and you have to live it. Now, as he stepped inside his living quarters, he wondered if Tak might let him try again.

He loved Bleddyn, his wife of many years, and his children were doing just fine in the school in Lancre, but today he was troubled. The grags had called and were quite polite this time, although neither he nor Bleddyn really cared for politics. How could they mean anything when you've spent your life sweating down in the mines? His pony was now free, but he was at the end of his tether. He just wanted to provide for his family as best he could. What was a dwarf to do?

Bedwyr wanted his children to do better than him, and it looked as though they would. His father had been annoyed about this. Bedwyr was sorry that the old boy was dead, but the world kept turning and the Turtle moved. New things were being done in new ways. And it wasn't that the grags were holding hard to yesterday; they hadn't even got as far as this century.

Bleddyn had cooked a good rat supper and was upset when she saw his face and said, 'Those damn grags again! Why don't you tell them to put their nonsense where the light shines too much!'*

Bleddyn didn't usually swear, so that surprised him, and she continued, 'They had a point once. They said that we were being swallowed up by the humans and the trolls, and you know it's true, except that it's the wrong kind of truth. The kids've got human friends and one or two trolls as well and nobody notices, nobody thinks about it. Everyone is just people.'

He looked at her face and said, 'But we're diminished, less important!'

But Bleddyn was emphatic and said, 'You silly old dwarf. Don't you think the trolls consider themselves diminished too? People mingle and mingling is good! You're a dwarf, with big dwarf hobnail boots and everything else it takes to be a dwarf. And remember, it wasn't so long ago that dwarfs were very scarce outside of Uberwald. You must know your history? Nobody can take that away, and who knows, maybe some trolls are saying right now, "Oh dear, my little pebbles is being influenced by the dwarfs! It's a sin!" The Turtle moves for *everybody* all the time, and those grags schism so often that they consider everyone is a schism out there on their own. Look it up. I've cooked you a lovely rat – nice and tender – so why not eat it up and get out into the sunshine? I know it isn't

---

* Humans would have said, 'Put it where the sun don't shine.'

dwarfish, but it's good for getting your clothes dried.'

When he laughed she smiled and said, 'All that's wrong in the world is that it's spilling over us as if we're stones in a stream, and it'll leave us eventually. Remember your old granddad telling you about going to fight the trolls in Koom Valley, yes? And then you told your son how *you* went back to Koom Valley and found out the whole damn business was a misunderstanding. And because of all this, our Brynmor won't even have to fight unless someone is extremely stupid. Say no to the grags. Really, they're bogeymen. I've spoken to all the women round here and they say exactly the same thing. You're a dwarf. You won't stop being a dwarf until you die. And you could be a clever dwarf or you could be a stupid dwarf, like the ones who knock down clacks towers.'

Bedwyr very much enjoyed the rat, which had been nicely seasoned, and, as a wise husband does, he thought about things.

Two days later, coming back from Blackglass, where he had gone to buy a load of candles, Bedwyr found two dark dwarfs setting fire to the base of a clacks tower. All he had on him were his tools and it was amazing how useful a simple miner's tools could be. A number of clacksmen and goblins joined him hastily in putting out the fire, and they had to stop Bedwyr from using his heavy boots to show his disdain for those who resort to arson. He told them, 'My brother's daughter, our Berwyn, she works on the clacks down in Quirm . . . All this stuff you don't notice until it's on your doorstep, and now I think I've woken up.'

Bedwyr didn't kill the delvers, he just, as it were, disabled them. But when he left hurriedly to go home, he noticed that the goblins were . . . busy. From the point of view of people working in an undefended clacks tower in the wilderness, the world was seen as black and white, and for these delvers it went black.

Railway fever, already red-hot, was becoming incandescent, at least across the Sto Plains. Would-be investors clamoured for a stake in the Ankh-Morpork and Sto Plains Hygienic Railway.* There were swamps to drain, bridges to reinforce and so theodolites twinkled in the sunshine.

But even with Vetinari's support and Harry's millions, it was a slow business. Every piece of track had to be laid with care and tested before anything could be run along it – let alone a train. Moist had expected that Harry would want to get things done fast at any cost with little thought of safety all round. Oh yes, he shouted a bit when the surveyors took up too much time, but the grumble remained a grumble. The same picture kept coming back into Moist's mind: Harry King already had the money, lots of it, but the railways were going to be his legacy. No more the King of the Midden. A Lord of the Smoke was better any day and so while he screamed that he was being sent to the poorhouse he nevertheless signed the paperwork promptly.

---

* There had been some discussion about the word 'hygienic', and Moist had lost. Hygienic, everyone else thought, gave the project a certain tone, a sort of *je ne sais quoi*. Lady King said this herself and who was going to argue with the Duchess?

To Effie, now definitely a Lady,* her husband the railway entrepreneur at last had a job that his wife liked to talk about. And Effie didn't just like to talk about it, she got involved with it and increasingly often was to be found in Harry's office. As it happened, it was Effie who came up with the idea of the moving gangs. And so trail after trail of wagons were working their way through the countryside, in which working men and surveyors could sleep and take their meals anywhere the railway wanted them to go rather than wasting time going home at night.

The track-laying was now pressing hard at Moist's heels as he dealt with the multiplicity of landowners along the route. And that was a painfully slow business too, every one of them exercised by the internal conundrum: if you held out for too much then there might just be somebody reasonably close by who would welcome the train for a pittance, if he was stupid enough, but then of course he might be clever and he would get his perishable produce to market before you could, and there you would be: with all the dust and all the noise and all the smoke and *none* of the money.

In the interests of keeping things moving as quickly as possible, the Patrician had allowed Moist to requisition one of the city's few golem horses. The horses were notable for their indefatigable galloping and also for turning your pelvis into jelly if you didn't pad up

---

* Although in the eyes of her spouse she had always been the Duchess, a pet name he reserved for just her.

extremely well, but even with all the multiple layers Moist was just about rattling when he got back to the city after weeks of negotiations.

Exhausted, and in defiance of custom and practice, health and safety – but, on the other hand, with all the glory of the gods of style – to the dismay of the palace guards he rode the golem horse all the way up the steps to the door of the Oblong Office. There he was pleased to see Drumknott, who deftly opened the door and stepped backwards so quickly that Moist, by ducking, managed to trot neatly to within a foot of Lord Vetinari's desk.

Unruffled, the Patrician lowered his coffee mug and said, 'Mister Lipwig. It is customary to knock before entering my office. Even, and especially, when entering on horseback. You may thank the gods that Drumknott had the presence of mind to disable our . . . little alarm system. How many times must I tell you?'

'Every time, sir, I'm sorry to say, because you see, sir,' said Moist, 'if I'm to be of any use to you I have to be Moist von Lipwig, sir, and that means, I'm afraid, sir, that I have to find the edge of the envelope and put my stamp on it, sir, otherwise life wouldn't be worth dying for.'

Moist could see Drumknott wincing at the concept of anyone stamping on any stationery whatsoever and continued, 'It's in my blood and frankly, sir, I'm fed up with dealing with old codgers who think they can get the better of Moist von Lipwig, and the cunning and the unpleasant and the stupid and the clever and the greedy . . . sometimes all wrapped up in one man.

After all this, I think my soul needs a bit of a wash and brush-up, sir.'

'Ah, soul!' said Lord Vetinari. 'I didn't think you had one, Mister Lipwig. Well, I live and learn.' He steepled his fingers. 'Mister Lipwig, Mister Simnel's activities have drawn the eyes of the world. Of course one could not expect that every country, sizeable town and great city would *not* start thinking about the railway. It is a weapon, Mister Lipwig, a mercantile weapon. You may not know this because you don't live in *my* world. Young Mister Simnel came to Ankh-Morpork because this dirty old town, for all its faults, is the very place upon which this world spins, the place where history is changed, where because of an enlightened and caring government – which is to say *me* – every man, child, dwarf, troll, werewolf, vampire and even zombie and yes, goblin, can call themselves free; free of any master, save the law, which applies to everybody equally whatever their species and status in life: *Civis Ankhmorporkianus sum!*'

There was a thump as Lord Vetinari banged his fist on the table. 'Ankh-Morpork, Mister Lipwig, is not to be outdone! Now, I know you have been spending a lot of your time these days in making sure that the first fully commercial and grown-up train will indeed have a railway upon which it can run, and when it does it will be the wonder of the world. But all things move on, and it is for us to keep our city in the forefront of that movement.

'No doubt you, Mister Lipwig, Sir Harry and Mister Simnel are already thinking ahead. May I suggest that a daily railway service to and from Quirm could only set the seal on the usefulness of the railways. While a more efficient way to get to Uberwald is eminently desirable, alas I fear it must wait. I am naturally being badgered by all the other governments to bring the railway to them, but Quirm is our neighbour and an important trading partner and' – he lowered his voice – 'perhaps we could get our fresh seafood before it walks to Ankh-Morpork on its own. Agreed?

'You may leave the final details of the negotiations for the line to Sto Lat to Drumknott,' Vetinari continued. 'He has my permission to call upon the services of one of the dark clerks . . . The talents of Mister Smith would be eminently suitable for sorting out any . . . recalcitrant landowners, I think.'

Moist noticed that Drumknott's eyes had an unusual gleam in them, although the little secretary said nothing.

'You may go, Mister Lipwig, and may I counsel you that riding a golem horse in here again will be a *very* dangerous errand and may result in you having kittens.' His lordship smiled nastily and continued, 'Cedric is always waiting – *twinkle, twinkle.*'*

---

* The feared kitten torture was actually one dreamed up by Moist, and Vetinari had been impressed. In the dungeons of the palace there was a large iron maiden, seldom used. In these modern times the kitten torture regime was the punishment that would cause the miscreant to pause before doing anything that would place them in the dungeon again. The mechanism and the kittens were presided over by Cedric: not clever, but grateful for the pay packet every month, and he was very fond of kittens, with which the streets of Ankh-Morpork were overflowing. The kittens would be placed in the iron maiden in large numbers, along with the

Leading the golem horse from the office, Moist thought, '*Twinkle, twinkle?* Oh, gods, it's catching.'

Mustrum Ridcully, Archchancellor of Unseen University, was held up on his walk across the University's Great Hall by Barnstable, one of the Bledlows.

The man touched the brim of his bowler hat in traditional salute, coughed politely and said, 'Mister Archchancellor, sir, there's a . . . person who wants to see you, and he won't take no for an answer. A very sorry-looking cove, sir, looks like he never had a decent meal in his life, sir. And personally, sir, I reckon he's just after a handout. Bit of an undesirable, sir, and he's wearing a kind of a dress. Shall I show him the door, sir?'

The Archchancellor thought for a moment and said, 'This man, does he smell like a badger?'

'Oh yes, sir, you got it in one!'

Ridcully smiled. 'Mister Barnstable, the old man to whom you refer is a master of every martial art ever conceived. In fact he conceived most of them himself and he is the only known master of déjà fu*. He can

miscreant who could just about sit. At the bottom was a little hatch, large enough to push through a sizeable saucer of milk. Every time a kitten was in distress and made its distress noticeable, Cedric would open up the maiden and give the victim a whack with his cudgel, the amount of cudgelling being contingent on the state of upset of said kitten. There were some idiots who thought this laughable, but it worked, and after a certain amount of cudgelling visitors were said to be amazed at the general atmosphere of happiness inside the iron maiden, where the purring was so loud it resonated throughout the dungeon.

* A discipline where the hands move in time as well as in space, the exponent twisting space behind his own back whilst doing so.

throw a punch into the air and it'll follow you home and smack you in the face when you open your own front door. He is known as Lu-Tze, a name that strikes fear in those who don't know how to pronounce it, let alone spell it. My advice is to smile at him and, with great care, deliver him to my office.'

Lu-Tze looked carefully at the range of brandies on the Archchancellor's heaving, creaking drinks trolley and sat back. Ridcully, his pipe smoking like the funnel of Iron Girder, said, 'How nice to see you, my old friend. It's all about the locomotion, yes?'

'Of course, Mustrum – is there anything else to talk about? The Procrastinators are grinding and everybody in Oi Dong is fearful of the Ginnungagap . . . the darkness at the end of the world before the new world takes its place, hmm? Although personally, I think it's a jolly good idea, what with this one being all battered about and unkempt and uncared for. The only problem I have yet to solve is how to get from the dying world into the new world. *That* is a bit of a puzzle. But even the Abbot is disturbed about the arrival of steam engines when it isn't steam-engine time.'

Ridcully poked at his pipe with a pipe cleaner and said, 'Ye-es, that is a conundrum. Surely the steam engine *cannot* happen before it is steam-engine time? If you saw a pig, you would, I think, say to yourself, well, here's a pig, so it must be time for pigs. You wouldn't question its right to be there, would you?'

'Certainly not,' said Lu-Tze. 'In any case, pork gives me the wind something dreadful. What we know is that the universe is a never-ending story that, happily, writes itself continuously. The trouble with my brethren in Oi Dong is that they are fixated on the belief that the universe can be totally understood, in every particular jot and tittle.'

Ridcully burst out laughing. 'Oh, my word! You know, my wonderful associate Mister Ponder Stibbons appears to have fallen into the same misapprehension. It seems that even the very wise have neglected to take notice of one rather important goddess . . . Pippina, the lady with the Apple of Discord. She knows that the universe, while it requires rules and stability, also needs just a tincture of chaos, the unexpected, the surprising. Otherwise it would be a mechanism – a wonderful mechanism, ticking away the centuries, but with nothing *different* happening. And so we may assume that the loss of balance will be allowed this time and the beneficent lady will decree that this mechanism might yield wonderful things, given a chance.'

'For my part, I would like to give it a chance,' said Lu-Tze. 'Serendipity is no stranger to me. I know the monks have been carefully shepherding the world, but I rather think they don't realize that the sheep sometimes have better ideas. Uncertainty is always uncertain, but the difficulty with people who rely on systems is that they begin to believe that nearly everything is in some way a system and therefore, sooner or later, they become bureaucrats.

'And so, my friend, I think we say hail Pippina and the occasional discord. I'm sure the rest of the circle will be of the same mind, to judge by their activities.

After all, it's as clear as the nose on your face: here is a steam engine. Ergo, it *is* steam-engine time.'

'Hurrah!' said Ridcully. 'I'll drink to that.'

'Why, thank you. I'll have a tincture of brandy with my tea, to keep out the cold, if you don't mind,' said Lu-Tze.

Moist sat at his desk, his mind churning over how best to introduce the matter of Quirm to Sir Harry. He blankly registered a ... substantial ... gentleman in front of him saying, 'Mister Lipwig? I have a pro-position to—'

Moist laughed. 'Sir, anybody who has a proposition for me these days will get a maximum of five minutes, one of which has already passed. What is it?'

'I'm not just anybody, Mister Lipwig,' said the man, drawing himself up to his full height, which was in fact slightly less than his full girth. 'I am a chef. Perhaps you've heard of me – All Jolson. I understand from certain sources* that any day now your wonderful locomotives will be going to and from Sto Lat. I wonder, have you thought about what the people on board will eat? I'd like to bid for the franchise to sell food on the trains and possibly in the waiting rooms as well. Small snacks, and more substantial servings for the long-distance passenger. There's nothing like a pot of my slumpie to lift the spirits of a weary

---

* All's mastery of artery-clogging cuisine had made him a number of friends in interesting places – trading sources for sauces had turned out to be very good business practice.

traveller. Or Primal Soup – very warming, that. I've been experimenting with serving it in cups, with little lids on, 'cos there are things in that soup that, to be honest, you wouldn't want to spill on yourself.'

Moist caught the essential words like a trout catching a newborn mayfly. Food on the trains! Waiting rooms, yes! Places where people would want to spend their money. Once again he remembered that the railway was not just about the rails or the steam.

And as Jolson handed over a slightly lard-stained calling card Moist let his mind fill with ancillary possibilities. Yes, you would definitely need a place to stay while you were waiting for your train, somewhere dry and warm with something to drink and even, heaven forfend, a sausage inna bun that actually had seen a pig. And yes, since Dick had said he'd be quite happy for a locomotive to travel at night, then at the destination there might be railway hotels, as swish as the railway carriages and sprightly, because people would be coming and going at all times of the day or night. It would seem as if the whole world were on the move.

Restless himself, he went out into the compound and crossed to the great shed. Having thought that young Simnel was happily living every dream he had ever had, he was surprised to come across the engineer sitting beside the throbbing Iron Girder, alone and, there was no other word for it, glum.

Moist automatically stepped into his position as the oil that greased the wheels of progress and said, 'Something wrong, Dick?'

As if beset by unseen demons, Simnel said

sombrely, 'Well, it's like this, Mister Lipwig. I were invited along to t'Guild of Cunning Artificers last week, to see Mister Pony, and do you know what? He told me I should get apprenticed to somebody! Me! The lads are coming on fine and should be *my* apprentices, but it turns out that I'm not a master and so 'ave to be indentured for four years to a *real* master and then I might just about make a journeyman after a little while. But I told them, I never had indentures, never 'ad a master, because, d'you know for why? I haven't been an apprentice because there were no one to teach me all the stuff I know. I 'ad to work it out for meself!

'And then I read about those old guys in Ephebe who once built a little steam engine which worked ... and then exploded all over them, although nobody got 'urt, and any road, they were saved because their steam engine were a kind of boat and they all ended up in the water wi' soggy togas. And then I thought to meself, well, those old guys must've known a trick or two and so I got another book about them from t'library in Sto Lat, and you know what, Mister Lipwig? All those old boys wi' their togas and sandals, they also invented the sine and cosine, not to mention your tangent! All that mathematics, which I love. And then there's your quaderatics. Can't get anywhere without quaderatics, can you?

'And any road, they looked like a bunch of old guys who you'd think would do nowt more than lie about arguing about philosophy and then it turns out that all along they knew just about everything about, well, everything and just wrote it all down. Can you believe it? They 'ad it in their 'ands. They could've built a proper steam engine, and steam boats that didn't explode. That's academics for you. All that knowing and they went back to discussing t'beauty and truth of numbers and missed the fact that they'd discovered summat reet important. Me? If I want beauty and truth I look at Iron Girder.'

Dick slapped his fist down on the metal carapace and said, '*There's* beauty. *There's* truth, right there. And they had all that knowing 'iding away. Look at 'er! My machine! I built her! Me! And I'm not even good enough to be an apprentice.'

He paused for breath and continued, 'Now don't get me wrong, Mister Moist, I know it's just words but, you see, it's come home to me that, since I've never done me indentures, I can never be a *master* because there's nobody who knows more about what I'm doing than, well, me. I've looked in all t'manuals and read all t'books and you can't be a master until all the other masters say you are a master.'

Simnel looked even more haunted while Moist stood with his mouth metaphorically open and listened to the meticulous Mr Simnel blaming himself for being a genius.

He continued, 'The lads, as I call 'em, could never 'ope to be masters neither because they won't have been taught engineering by a master! It's flaming ridiculous!'

Moist burst out laughing and put his hands on Dick's greasy forehead, carefully turning the lad's head around to face the length of the compound and the huge ever-present queues for the train ride, and he said quietly, '*They* all know you're a master and Iron Girder is your masterpiece. What boy would not wish to be you, Mister Simnel, a manmade masterpiece yourself. Do you understand?'

Simnel looked doubtful, possibly still hankering after letters after his name and a certificate for his old mother to hang on her wall.

'Yes, but with all due respect, the people aren't authorities on the taming of steam. I mean no offence, like, but what do they know?'

Moist snapped and said, 'Dick, in some respects down there somewhere is the soul of the world, and they know everything. You'll have heard of Leonard of Quirm. There are some masters who make themselves and you have, you've made yourself an engineer and *everybody* knows it.'

Simnel brightened and said, 'I don't intend on starting me own guild, if that's what you're thinking, but if some young lad comes to see me and wants to learn the way of the sliding rule then I'll do him right. I'll make 'im an apprentice the old-fashioned way and his hands'll never be clean again. And I'll give him indentures until they're coming out of his flaming teeth, all writ down on vellum, if I can find any. That's how it should go, and he'll work for me until I reckon he's done enough to be a journeyman. That's how you do it. That's how you make your trade.

'When I saw you first, Mister Lipwig, I reckoned you were all mouth and no trousers. And I've watched you running around hither and yon and being the grease for the engine of the railway. You ain't so bad, Mister Lipwig, ain't so bad at all, but you'd look better with a flatter cap.'

Iron Girder let out a sudden hiss of steam, and the two men, laughing, turned to look at her. There was something new about the engine. Hang on, Moist thought, her shape has changed, hasn't it? She looks . . . bigger. I know she's the prototype and Simnel is forever tweaking things, but somehow I don't think I ever see the same engine twice. She's always bigger, better, sleeker.

As Moist was pondering the question he became aware of Simnel beside him shifting from foot to foot. At last Dick said hesitantly, 'Mister Lipwig, you know that girl with the long blonde hair and pretty smile who sometimes comes into the compound? Who is she? She acts as if she owns the place.'

'That,' said Moist, 'is Emily, Harry King's favourite niece, not married yet.'

'Oh,' said Simnel. 'The other day she brought me out tea – and a bun!'

Moist looked at the worried face of Dick Simnel, who was suddenly in a place where the sliding rule couldn't go. No, this was a different kind of rule, and so he said, 'Would you care to take a walk with her, Dick?'

Simnel blushed, if a blush could actually be seen under all the grease. 'Aye, I really would, but she's all smart and dandy as a daisy and I'm—'

'Stop right there!' said Moist. 'If you're going to say that you're just a bloke in greasy dungarees I'd like to draw your attention to the fact that you own a very big slice of all the revenue the railway is ever going to make. So don't go around saying "Oh dear me I'm too poor to even think about making advances to a nice young lady," because you're the best catch that any young lady in Ankh-Morpork could ever find, and I imagine that even Harry, in the circumstances, wouldn't throw you down the stairs as he did with the swains who were the suitors of his daughters. If you'd like to go walking out with Emily I'd say go to it and I'm sure her uncle and parents will be overjoyed.'

To himself, Moist thought: in fact, Harry would love it because it'd keep the money in the family. I know Harry King, oh, yes. 'What's more,' he added, 'she's a lawyer in the making: understands the legalities of running a business. You should get on like a house on fire.'

In the voice of a man encountering new territory, Dick said carefully, 'Thank you for the information and advice, Mister Lipwig. Mebbe one day when I've got meself clean I might get meself the courage to knock on 'er door.'

'Well, don't wait too long, Dick. There's more to life than the sliding rule.'

The Grand Opening of the Ankh-Morpork and Sto Plains Hygienic Railway brought the international press out in droves.

Dick Simnel had always intended that the first *serious* public railway journey would start from Sto Lat, putting the old town on the map as it were. Sir Harry was somewhat dismayed by this:* a true denizen of Ankh-Morpork, he tended to get a little disorientated when outside the city. Still, as Moist had pointed out, after an outward journey by road the guests would find the return rail trip with refreshments all the more impressive.

When their coaches eventually arrived at what the gold-edged invitation had described as the 'Sto Lat terminus', the journalists and other invited guests discovered that terminus apparently meant a work in progress: which is to say most of it wasn't there yet (being full of workmen, human, troll and goblin, labouring at cross purposes just like on every big construction site anywhere) but nevertheless a sympathetic eye could arrive at the conclusion that something rather good was being built here.

The guests were ushered on to a long raised platform, standing above gleaming steel rails that ran off into the distance, the tracksides crowded with onlookers. In the other direction the rails led to a very large barn, where Dick's apprentices, recently scrubbed, were lined up on either side of the closed doors, along with a brass band that could hardly be heard above the noise of the workmen.

Moist von Lipwig was, of course, master of ceremonies, there to welcome them with Harry King and Effie by his side. Lord Vetinari too was there, as holder of Ankh-Morpork's guardian share in the

---

* A dismay shared by many of the journalists, who worried they would get mud on their new shoes and be attacked by pheasants.

railway, accompanied by Drumknott, who wouldn't have missed the occasion for a big clock. And Queen Keli of Sto Lat* was present to give the occasion the royal seal of approval, with the Mayor by her side looking stunned by the circus that appeared to have taken over his town.

As always in these matters, everything had to wait until everything else was ready. That seemed to have been anticipated, judging by the door with a neat label WAITING ROOM, alongside the entrance to the platform.†

And then the waiting was over. At Moist's invitation Queen Keli stepped forward to drive in the golden spike, the last one on the line, signifying it was now open for business. The chuffing sound that was the signature tune of the railway got louder and more expansive, the crowd of bystanders thronging the sides of the track waved their colourful little flags and cheered with increased enthusiasm, and two apprentices opened the gates of the barn. To a metaphorical drumroll Moist announced: 'Ladies and gentlemen, Mister Dick Simnel and Iron Girder!'

Leading the dream of steam, Dick Simnel, in pride of place on the footplate, beamed an unmissable look of *I told thee so.*

Behind the engine ten carriages bumped along and,

* Proctector of the Eight Protectorates and Empress of the Long Thin Debated Piece Hubwards of Sto Kerrig.
† There were in fact two waiting rooms, one for men and families and the other for single ladies; as predicted, Effie was very firm that all aspects of the railway should be clean and wholesome, indeed hygienic, something she was very keen on.

glory be, some of them even had a roof! The icon-
ographers' flashes popped and, very gently, Iron Girder
moved along the track and stopped beside the
platform.

Moist waited until the applause faded away and said,
'Ladies and gentlemen, you may safely climb aboard.
There will be refreshments, but first may I invite you to
inspect the carriages.'

Now Moist needed to be everywhere at once.
Anything to do with steam and locomotives was news
and news could be good news or news could be bad
news, or occasionally news could be malicious news.
Dick just loved talking about Iron Girder and everything else to do with locomotion, but he was a
straightforward man and the press of the Sto Plains
could eat up for lunch a straightforward man if he
wasn't careful. Moist, on the other hand, in the
vicinity of the press, was as straightforward as a
sackful of kaleidoscopes. While the chattering was
going on, he did his best to hover around Dick Simnel
like a wet-nurse.

The *Ankh-Morpork Times* wasn't bad, and the *Tanty
Bugle* was mostly interested in 'orrible murder and the
more salacious aspects of the human condition, but
Moist's heart sank as he realized that Dick, temporarily
off the reins, was now talking to Hardwick of the
Pseudopolis Daily Press, who was adept at getting
the wrong end of the stick very much on purpose and
then hitting people over the head with it. And
Pseudopolis disliked Ankh-Morpork with a sullen
and jealous vengeance.

As Moist executed the world's fastest nonchalant walk, he heard Hardwick saying, 'What do you say, Mister Simnel, to people who are upset because the noise and the smoke will cause their horses to bolt and their cows and sheep to miscarry?'

'I don't rightly know,' said Simnel. 'Never had a problem here on the Plains. When I were doing me tests the horses in the next field would try to outpace Iron Girder, racing her, as it were, and I reckoned they thought it was fun!'

But Hardwick wasn't to be thrown off. 'You must admit, Mister Simnel, that the train is inherently dangerous? Some people have said that your face melts if you reach speeds greater than thirty miles an hour!'

It seemed to Moist that everyone else who had been chattering away in the vicinity went silent to listen as one person, and he knew that if he intervened at this point things would get worse, and so all he could do was hold his breath, just like everybody else, to see what the solemn country boy would say.

'Well now, Mister 'ardwick,' said Simnel, sticking his thumbs into his belt as he always did when broaching long sentences. 'I think many things are inherently dangerous: such as wizards, and trees. Dangerous things, trees, they could fall down and drop straight on your 'ead without you knowing it. And boats are dangerous an' all, and other people might be dangerous and you, Mister 'ardwick, you've been talking to me for five minutes now, 'oping that a country lad like me might be tempted into saying summat I shouldn't.

'So I'll tell you this: Iron Girder is my machine, I

made her, every single bit of her. I tested her and every time I find a way to make her better and safer, I do it. But, oh aye, *you*, Mister 'ardwick, you might be dangerous! Power is dangerous, all power, yours included, Mister 'ardwick, and the difference is that the power of Iron Girder is controllable whereas you can write whatever you damn well like. Do you think I don't read? I've read the rubbish you spout in your paper and, Mister 'ardwick, a lot of what you write is flamin' gristle, Mister 'ardwick, total stinking made-up gristle, meant to frighten people who don't know owt about steam and power and the cosines and the quaderatics and tangents and even the sliding rule . . . but I hope you enjoy your journey anyway, Mister 'ardwick. Now, if you don't mind, I've got to get in t'cab. Oh, and I've had Iron Girder up to more than thirty mile an hour and all I got were sunburn. Good day to you, Mister 'ardwick. Enjoy your ride.'

And then, reddening as he registered the hush all around him, Simnel said, 'Apologies to all the ladies here for my straight language. I do beg your pardon.'

'No apologies necessary, Mister Simnel,' called out Sacharissa Cripslock, reporter for the *Times*. 'I believe I speak for all the ladies present when I say that we appreciate your candour.' And since Sacharissa was not only respectable in the same way that other people are religious, but was also invariably armed with highly sharpened pencils, the rest of the crowd suddenly found that they too had the greatest admiration for Mr Simnel and his plain talking.

On board, there were many marvels to show off,

including the lavish lavatories, apparently another brainchild of Effie, which came as a surprise even to Moist. He wondered what the press would make of Effie's gift to railway travel. Sometimes the art editor of the *Ankh-Morpork Times* could be quite creative.*

'This is as good as those they have in the poshest hotels,' Moist said privately to Sir Harry, who emerged from the cubicle flushed with pride.

Harry beamed. 'You should look in the ladies, Mister Lipwig! Scent, cushions and real cut flowers. It's like a boudoir in there!'

'I suppose the, er, waste can be dropped straight down on to the tracks, eh, Harry?'

Harry looked shocked. 'Oh, some people would do that, but not Harry King! Where there's muck there's money, lad, but don't tell the Duchess. There's a big cistern under one of the carriages. Waste not, want not . . .'

Questions were coming thick and fast from all sides. For those people who hadn't already taken a ride behind Iron Girder in Harry King's compound, the matter of railway etiquette loomed: could you stick your head out of the window? Could you bring your pet swamp dragon if it sat on your knee? Could you go and talk to the driver? On this occasion, Moist was pleased to say yes; the editor of the *Ankh-Morpork Times* being selected for this accolade. The smile Mr de

---

* The caption as it turned out was '*Let the train take the strain*'. It appeared that Mr de Worde and his wife were very impressed with the toilet facilities.

Worde gave as he stepped from the platform on to the footplate cemented this moment on to the front page, assuming this journey was a success – although you had to be aware that it would also make the front page if the engine blew up. Journalism was, well, after all, journalism.

The train pulled away with a whistle and a cloud of smoke and everything was moving along nicely, especially when the trolley with the refreshments rattled through the carriages. Harry and All Jolson were in complete agreement about what made a good meal – namely, calories – and had not stinted. There was enough butter on the slumpie to regrease Iron Girder from top to bottom. The scenery flew past, to the guests' well-oiled admiration and gasps of awe, until the train approached the first bridge.

Moist held his breath as the train slowed down almost to a halt. There was a troll and he waved a big red flag and cheerfully announced* that he and his gang had worked on this bridge and were so pleased to see it being used and thank you for coming ladies and gentlemen. There was laughter, assisted most certainly with alcohol, but nevertheless there was laughter and it was genuine. Moist let the breath go. He supposed few of the passengers could remember the days when to see a troll was to be frightened (or, if you were a dwarf, want to kick his ankles in). Now here they were, building the railway, quite at home.

Moist looked across the First Class carriage to where

* And when a troll announces, you really are announced at.

Lord Vetinari was seated. He had openly commended Effie on her part in the planning and design, and given his usual urbane, anodyne answers to journalists looking for a quote, but Moist couldn't help but notice that the Patrician was smiling, like a granddad at a newborn grandchild. Moist caught his eye and thought he saw his lordship wink with the speed of a cyclone. Moist nodded and that was that, but he hoped that it might be at least one sin forgiven. Three deaths in one lifetime would definitely be over-egging it.

But it was a nice day, the sun was shining, and as Iron Girder raced along the track a couple of horses in the field alongside tried to catch up with her. So much for Mr Hardwick, and poo to him again because Iron Girder chugged her way down through gentle slopes to the township of Upunder where they stopped to allow the passengers to enjoy the very best of brassica hospitality.

After that it was a short run down to Ankh-Morpork itself, which was beckoning with long smoky fingers. They crossed the new iron bridge over the Ankh and wheezed on to Harry King's compound, where a brass band was playing the national anthem, 'We Can Rule You Wholesale', to the cheers of the waiting crowd.

At the banquet that evening the rail travellers were joined by other Ankh-Morporkian and Sto Plains dignitaries. And in the peroration of his address Sir Harry announced that the next city to receive the magnificent railway would be Quirm, it was hoped very shortly. In the thunder of applause, Harry toasted the Quirmian ambassador, Monsieur Cravat, and this was followed by more toasts, including one to Iron Girder herself. Lord Vetinari opined that it had been a very helpful day; and the unknown quantity of sphincters that had been tightened once again relaxed somewhat.

When the party broke up, some of the guests were walking sideways or hardly at all. Dick, seeing a familiar face swim into his happy world of coloured lights, said, 'Ee, that were champion, Mister Lipwig! All those tiny places in the distance all along t'track . . . I were thinking that the railway could be like a tree: you know, one big trunk and then all branches . . . You'd make 'em cheap and small but I reckon people'd like 'em . . . Make folks' lives easier if they could get a train from *anywhere*—'

Moist, resolutely ignoring the beckoning possibilities, cut him short. 'Steady on, Dick. First we have to get to Quirm.' And then drive that express train route to Uberwald, he added to himself . . . His lordship was so very keen on international relations.

Later that night, Fred Colon and Nobby Nobbs proceeded in a policeman-like fashion around the railway compound. After all, they bore the Majesty of the Force and therefore had a right to be absolutely anywhere they liked, looking at anything they wanted to.

And as their boots swung in unison, Fred Colon said, 'I hear they're taking the railway all the way to Quirm. My old woman's always going on at me about us taking a holiday down there. You'll know about that, Nobby, now you're practically married and got responsibilities. But you know me, I'm allergic to all that avec, and I hear you can't get a good pint there for love nor money.'

'Actually,' said Nobby, 'it ain't all that bad. When I was working the rota last week on the goods yard there were a load of cheeses that got broken open by accident, as it were. Of course, they couldn't be sent back and it's amazing what Shine of the Rainbow can do with cheese. It's good stuff, especially with snails.' Nobby realized he was talking treason and so hurriedly added, 'Their beer is still like piss, though.'

Fred Colon nodded. All was what it should be. He glanced back at his friend and said, 'If the railway works properly, things are going to be quite different. I hear telling the train'll be going very fast and that means if a bloke does a robbery and then goes and catches the train, he could be away on his toes long before we could ever catch up with him. Maybe the railway will need policemen. You never know! It's like old Stoneface said, wherever you get people, you'll get crime and then you'll get policemen.'

Nobby Nobbs considered this information like a goat chewing the cud, and said, 'Well, you go and tell old Vimesy that you want to be the first railway policeman, eh? I'd love to see his face!'

Billy Slick surveyed the very large person at the front of the queue and sighed.

'Look,' he said, 'you can't all be train drivers. We've got lots of train drivers right now and it takes time to work your way up to being a driver. Ain't there anything else you can do?'

'Well,' said the crestfallen lad in front of him, 'my mum says I'll make a very good cook one day.'

Billy smiled and said, 'Might have something for you then, we need cooks.' He pointed out another recruiting table a bit further along and said, 'Get yourself over to Mabel. She's looking for catering staff and that sorta thing.'

The young man's face lit up with excitement and he hurried off to a future which almost certainly included unsociable hours and hard labour in cramped conditions but, most importantly, unlimited free rides on the wonder of the age.

'I'm a painter, mister,' said the next man in Billy's line.

'Excellent! Sure you don't fancy being a train driver?'

'No, not really. I've always been a good painter and I expect the locomotives need painting.'

'Great!' said Billy. 'You're hired. Next!'

When Billy looked up from his clipboard he found the craggy figure of a young troll looming over him.

'Man said der's a job wiv a shovel and tons of coal. Could do dat,' the troll said, adding a hopeful 'Please?'

'A stoker?' Billy guessed. 'Blimey, you're a bit big for the footplate, but we could use you around the place and no mistake. Put your mark here.'

The table shook as the troll's thumb hit the form and cracked his clipboard.

'Good man – I mean, troll,' Billy said.

'Nuffin' to worry about. Get dat all der time.'

The troll rumbled away in the direction of the coal

store and his place in front of Billy was taken by a smartly dressed young lady with an air of authority.

'Sir, I think the railway is going to need a translator. I know every language and dialect on the Disc.' Her voice was firm but there was a glint of excitement in her eyes as she looked at Iron Girder and the other engines in the compound and Billy knew she was hooked. He also knew that 'translator' was not on his list of vacancies and sent her off to Sir Harry's office, while he returned to his search for shunters, tappers and other workers. And so the line moved on again. It seemed everybody wanted to be part of the railway.

It felt to Moist, bumping in the saddle as the golem horse bore him back towards Ankh-Morpork, that he had been talking for years with greedy landowners who were asking for enormous rents even if it was achingly obvious that the railway would benefit the whole area, and this time, to reach Quirm, there was going to be more than eight times the length of route to cover. And when he wasn't talking to landowners, he was talking again to the surveyors, who were not greedy but were definitely horribly *precise*. They rejected proposed routes as too steep, too waterlogged, crumbling, or occasionally flooded and, in one case, full of zombies. Acceptable routes might just as well have been drawn by a snake snaking around the landscape from suitable ground to suitable ground. And everybody wanted the railway close, oh yes please, but not so close that they could hear it or smell it.

And that was the Sto Plains in a nutshell, or, if you

like, a cabbage bucket. Everybody everywhere wanted the benefits of steam but not the drawbacks. And no city on the Plains wanted the Big Wahoonie to get more than its fair share.

It took the diplomatic genius of the Patrician to set the record straight, reminding them that although the railway was being built initially in Ankh-Morpork, if other cities and towns wanted to partake of its useful-ness, well, yes, in a sense it would be theirs because what goes down on the up line must go up on the down line.

Politics? Vetinari loved it. This was the ocean in which he swam. But assuredly you never crowed, just showed the world the tired visage of a conscientious civil servant, doing things cheaply and with the minimum of fuss. He had long ago perfected the art of giving way with a smile when engaged in complex negotiations, but Lord Vetinari's smile was that of a man who knows that his opponents have yet to find, metaphorically speaking, and despite their cleverness, that their underpants are now down around their ankles and their backside on show for all to see.

Ankh-Morpork to Sto Lat was becoming a regular journey, and it was *working* now. Moist had written the slogan, '*You don't have to live in Ankh-Morpork to work in Ankh-Morpork*' and properties in Sto Lat were becoming quite sought after. The idea of a little place in the country away from the big city, but with acceptable communications to Ankh-Morpork, suddenly looked *very* inviting.

The hours of travel on the golem horse were proving

altogether conducive to creative thought. His mind was filling up with the world of locomotive possibilities at the speed of a hamster *really* at odds with its treadmill. Another synapse in Moist's head flashed; the trains were just the start! The railway now, he knew, was something in the ether, floating over the whole world. An *idée fixe*, if he would excuse his own Quirmian.

Nevertheless, the engines remained important. Dick Simnel's workshops at Swine Town had been turning out many marvels, carefully placed on wagons behind the never-tiring Iron Girder. She now shared the big shed with two newcomers that Simnel had called the Flyers, which made the regular run to Sto Lat and back, while Iron Girder herself had gone back to giving rides around the Ankh-Morpork compound, extended with a short loop along the river to show off the new bridge. The small but growing band of patient train spotters had written down a number two in their little books, then a number three.

Within minutes of his arriving back in Ankh-Morpork, Moist was borne off by an ebullient Harry to see the latest development. Dodging sparks, they arrived at the doorway of the monstrous engine shed guarded by one of Harry's heavies, who glared even at his employer. He looked human, or at least humanoid, and Harry introduced him merely as 'Trouble'. Trouble, glaring at Moist, moved away from the door so that Moist and Sir Harry could go inside.

Moist could feel Trouble's glare on the back of his neck as he walked through, and asked, 'Harry, does Trouble have an official Watch record?'

Harry King stared for a moment at Moist and said, 'Of course he's got a Watch record! He's a *security guard*! And I need him. People have been hanging around, trying to break in, especially at night, and the *official* security – the Watch, the golems and guard dogs – generates a whole lot of paperwork whereas Trouble deals with trouble. Don't trouble Trouble and Trouble won't trouble you, as my granny always said.' Harry chuckled and added, 'Don't you worry, Mister Lipwig, I've expressly told him not to kill you . . . today.'

Moist took this under advisement and turned for a last brief look at Trouble, who made up a new scowl just for him, a reminder that there were oh so many painful things you could do to a person without actually killing them.

Harry nodded to the giant, who began to pull at a large tarpaulin in the middle of the floor – and clearly when Trouble pulled something it definitely remained pulled – to reveal an engine much larger than Iron Girder or any of Simnel's creations Moist had so far seen.

Harry slapped Moist on the back and said, 'Well now, Mister Lipwig, while you've been wining and dining with the nobs and diddling them out of their fortunes, I, and of course Mister Simnel, have been very busy boys, oh yes indeedy! The lad is up finishing off in the drawing office right now, but this new engine is the bee's knees, I don't mind telling you.'

'It's not exactly fun, what I've been doing—' began Moist indignantly, but Harry cut in.

'Yes, I know, we're all doing our bit towards Vetinari's

dash for Quirm, although personally I don't have much time for the lobsters; but I can see it's showing the flag of Ankh-Morpork and all that, and of course, if we can get really fresh fish and seafood into the city, then we'll be on the hog's back or, as they'd say, "the snail's shell". And Dick says this new baby,' he slapped the gleaming sides of the new engine as though it were a prize race-horse, 'will haul more freight and get there more quickly than any of the others!'

Moist thought about this and said, 'You know what, I bet you that as soon as our boy Simnel finishes this new Flyer he'll make sure that Iron Girder goes just that little bit faster. Harry, he's not going to let her be eclipsed even if it means constant tinkering until she's up to scratch. There's so many workers on the job these days, he spends most of his time on her in any case. She's the prototype of all of them, and he keeps changing the prototype.'

'And he wants to walk out with our Emily! Well, he's a smart lad and she'll always know where he is.'

The thought flitted across Moist's mind *I wonder what Iron Girder thinks about that.* And even as he dismissed the ridiculous notion he fancied he could hear a slight hiss.

Harry was still admiring the latest locomotive. 'I reckon the lobsters will be like chiens with deux tails to be the first real foreigners to have the famous railway. And our Emily tells me that the Quirmian for "railway" means "card game" so that would be right up your ruelle, yes? Make sure you keep an ace up your manche, Mister Lipwig, okay?'

'Manche?'

'Effie is learning me to talk lobster, she thinks it's a lovely and romantic language.'

Moist was moved to point out that he had hardly seen his own wife in the last month and had completed over fifty complex negotiations just to get to the border with Quirm.

'Capital, so you've really got your eye in now, yes? Anyway, Quirm ain't so far away and you'll enjoy the sunshine when you get there. And I tell you what! Before you go you can have a day off in lieu! And I don't say that to many people.'

Moist cleared his throat. 'Actually, er, Harry, you don't in fact employ me. The city does.'

'Does that mean I can't sack you?'

'I'm afraid so, Harry.'

Harry snorted with laughter. 'I hate having people around I can't sack. It's unnatural.'

It had been a long day after some long weeks and even longer months and that evening Moist was grateful to step into his own house, looking forward to his big four-poster bed which had a mattress that wasn't stuffed with straw, and pillows – actual pillows! Very few of the hostelries that Moist had stayed at during his travels considered pillows necessary or useful. Right now, metaphorically singing, he let himself in before Crossly could get there, and went not into the main part of the house but into the little corridor that led to Adora Belle's study, where his beloved was talking to Of the Twilight the Darkness.

The clacks was an equal opportunities employer, especially when it came to people who could swarm their way up the skeletal ribs of a clacks tower *and* once at the top sit down in a little chair and code like a demon, without actually being one, despite their appearance.

Adora Belle was going through clacks reports with a suspicious eye while the goblin crouched like a nightmare on the end of her desk. She waved her fingers to indicate that she couldn't afford to let go her concentration, then rolled up a script, handed it to the goblin and snapped, 'Get that out *now*, please, to tower ninety-seven. Someone there isn't coding accurately. Might be a trainee. I want to know, okay?'

The goblin snatched the scroll in a claw, sprang off the desk like a frog, headed for a little door near the floor and disappeared through it. Moist could hear rattling all the way up the wall as the goblin clambered up the panelling and scuttled to the private clacks tower on the roof. He shuddered, but before he could say anything Adora Belle looked up and said, 'Look, he's punctual, fast, reliable and codes more accurately even than me and all he wants from us is to be allowed to live with his family on the roof. Now don't you give me all that again about being traumatized by seeing the picture of a grinning goblin in that children's book when you were little, okay? Get over it, Moist. The goblins are the best thing that has happened to the clacks since, well, you know – us! They *love* running it and, what's more, with them around the place we don't have those nasty rat and mouse infestations that we used to have.'

Adora Belle stood up, walked around the desk to Moist and gave him a big kiss, and said, 'How was your latest marathon, mister? I got reports of your progress throughout, of course, as you may imagine.'

Moist took a step back. 'Reports? How?'

Adora Belle laughed. 'What is a clacks tower but an enormous watchtower? And every clacksman has a very expensive pair of Herr Fleiss's binoculars, made using the very best in Uberwald technology. There are lots of towers, so I made certain they kept a friendly eye on you – well, a lot of friendly eyes on you. After all, every clacksman knows your face and even the top of your head, and I thought it was my duty as a wife . . .'

'What, spying on your husband! Supposing I was messing about with other women?'

'That's all right, I know you weren't and if you had been I'd have had you killed – no offence meant – but you didn't and so I didn't and so everything is all right, yes? Mrs Crossly is doing a wonderful beef and oyster pie. See? Aren't you glad I knew exactly when you were coming home?'

Moist smiled, and then the smile broadened as he realized what it was he had been told, and he added thoughtfully, 'Are you telling me, my love, that you could spot and follow *anybody*?'

'Oh yes, probably, if they walk around a lot. The lads and lasses often peek when they have some down time. They just do it, there's no harm in it. The other day when you were heading home I was at the Grand Trunk office and was privileged to get a report of you bobbing up and down on your golem horse ... *very* fetching, they said.'

Adora Belle stared at her husband and added, 'Do you know that when you've found out something amazingly interesting and useful your eyes light up like a Hogswatch decoration? So stop glittering right now and go and smarten yourself up before we sit down to a proper dinner.'

It was a rule of Moist and Adora Belle's household that the evening meal, if at all possible, was sacrosanct. No eating at their desks, no rush, but candles, and silver-ware, as if it were always a special occasion. And a special occasion it was: the only time they could sit down face to face and just, well, be at least moderately married to each other.

However, Adora Belle couldn't conceal her dismay about losing her husband again for yet another pro-longed absence in a foreign country.

'Quirm isn't that far away,' Moist soothed. 'And once I get the local lads on side it won't be too bad.'

Adora Belle cleared her throat. 'Garçons. If they're lobsters, your lads will be known as garçons.'

'What?'

'Garçons. It's Quirmian, but don't worry, most of them speak Morporkian. And you know why? Because none of us can be bothered to learn Quirmian.'

'Well, no matter what they're called. Once the rail-way line's built I'll probably be able to come home more often.' He paused to take another mouthful of pie. 'By the way, Harry's just had a clacks from the King of Lancre asking if we could eventually run a line all the way to his kingdom so that, and I quote, "Lancre can take its rightful place on the world stage".'

'Don't underestimate that place,' said Adora Belle. 'They've got witches up there. They fly up to the clacks towers and scrounge coffee off the lads – well, at least one of them does, especially when the lads are young and the goblins aren't on shift. And then there are all the dwarf mines up at Copperhead. I'm sure they could find a use for the railway.'

Moist made a face. 'The lads say no way. It's too steep, and anyway, the Lancre bridge wouldn't take the weight of the engine. Sorry. But I suppose we could tell his majesty that we'll send surveyors to take a look once the Quirm line's complete.' Moist put down his fork. 'But here we are, and it looks like for the first time in ages we have an evening free. What shall we do? Perhaps it might be a good idea to give the staff the rest of the evening off . . .'

And Adora Belle replied with a smile, 'Yes . . . What shall we do?'

'It's simply mechanical,' said Ponder Stibbons over tea in the Uncommon Room at Unseen University. 'It just *looks* magical.'

'Shouldn't be allowed, then,' said the Senior Wrangler, spearing a whole pie with his fork. 'Looking magical is our business.'

'Well,' said Mustrum Ridcully, pointedly ignoring him, 'you can't stand in the way of progress, so why don't you hitch a ride on it? Does anyone else want a train ride? It gets so stuffy in here and I'm sure we don't want people thinking of us as being stick-in-the-muds.'

'But we are stick-in-the-muds,' said the Lecturer in Recent Runes. 'I treasure the fact.'

'Nevertheless, it's time we looked the railway in the face. Mister Stibbons will lead the way.'

The wizards left the University in a small fleet of coaches which caused quite a stir when they appeared at the Ankh-Morpork terminus. Stibbons, knowing his fellow wizards, had made arrangements beforehand and a special train had been laid on for the occasion, with particularly well cushioned seats.

'You will of course travel First Class, gentlemen,' said the station master, who had been well primed by Stibbons. 'But if you wish, some of you might be able to ride on the footplate.' He hesitated and said, 'Although I'm not sure those robes would be safe.'

The Archchancellor burst out laughing. 'Young man, a wizard's robe is impervious to fire. Good grief, if they weren't we'd be burned alive every day before elevenses!'

Stibbons, who had already had several rides with Iron Girder over the previous weeks followed by some intense conversations with Dick Simnel, had got the hang of the business and took some pleasure in seeing the best minds in the University coming to terms with their first railway ride.

It was a short journey to Upunder and back, including a dinner at the halfway mark which lasted longer than the train ride itself. On the homeward stretch, the Chair of Indefinite Studies was allowed to operate the emergency brake to the envy of the rest of the wizards, and there was a certain amount of waving of flags, blowing of whistles, and slamming of doors at each stop for the wizards to try their hands at. Iron Girder was in full steam and the fireproof wizards taking their turn on the footplate stared into the fire box and approved.*

Replete and tired on their way back to Ankh-Morpork, they considered this new form of locomotion as a phenomenon. The Senior Wrangler thought about objecting again, but was too full.

'Amazing, people waving at you as you go past,' said Ridcully. 'I've never seen that before. Who'd have thought it? Machinery making people smile. What are you writing down, Mister Stibbons?'

Blushing, Stibbons said, 'I like to spot an occasional train, you know ... I'm just interested in them ... It's like watching the future go past.'

The Archchancellor smiled and said, 'Then perhaps we should be the ones who are minding the doors, not to mention the gap, because the future is coming down the track fast. And who knows what is going to arrive next.'

It was a wonderful sunny day. Skylarks sang in the deep blue sky. It was a great day to be alive. Moist, needing a

---

* Even Professor Rincewind, who spent most of the journey hiding under his seat in the firm belief that locomotion was exactly the kind of thing that usually led to certain death, conceded that trains could come in very handy when one wanted to get somewhere, or, more importantly, *away* from somewhere, quickly.

change of air, walked away from the compound with a spring in his step, a little way along the railway track.

And right there on this perfect day . . . yes, there out of sight of anyone excepting, of course, the ambling Moist himself, on the rail that Iron Girder would have to travel along as soon as she came around the bend on to the little incline leading to the station, were two small . . . creatures. Rabbits, his common sense tried to tell him, plenty of them around here . . . even the compound was riddled with them. And, for a moment, the whole world stopped right in his face, leaving him spinning slowly in a little world of his own, looking out on to the real one.

There were the main engine sheds, over there was the crowd queueing for their rides, and there on the track was the future of the railway. It was one perfect moment where time stretched out, and Moist the only witness to this terrible tableau. It was like a strange game of high-speed chess unfolding before his eyes.

And then, suddenly, his legs took off from under him and he ran and ran, too breathless to shout, towards the two children who had hunkered down with their ears pressed against the rails, giggling because the vibrations were at times funny and bouncy and loud and . . .

RIGHT HERE, RIGHT NOW!

And . . . gone . . .

Moist woke up, which could be interpreted as a good thing. First time round, Iron Girder was over him and he was dead, but his next careful waking was in a white room that smelled of camphor wood and other disinfectants, sharp and reassuring smells: tangible proof that he had a nose at least, because he couldn't really feel anything else.

After a while subtle little noises grew into louder ones, coming closer and forming words, loudly reassuring and somewhat hearty words that crystallized into an individual in a white coat saying, 'Well, madam, he keeps going up and down, but with fewer downs and a welcoming parade of ups. He's getting more stable all the time and nothing's broken, although he's ruined a decent pair of boots – and, may I say, madam, that even here in the hospital there are already people organizing a whipround to replace them.'

Moist made a mighty heave, fought his way out of unconsciousness and arrived back in the here and now – a place where *everything* hurt. On the plus side, Adora Belle was looking at him, while looming behind her, in a white coat, was a large and expansive man of a sort that had played many rough competitive games when he was younger and wished he could do so now, if only the belly were smaller and the limbs willing.

Moist's wife was regarding her husband carefully, as if checking that all the bits were there in their rightful places, at which point the doctor grabbed his hand and boomed, 'Somebody up there must be watching over you, Mister Lipwig. How do you feel? As your physician I must tell you that jumping in front of railway trains is not recommended by medical practitioners, but acts of mindlessly idiotic bravery most certainly are, and can be applauded!'

Dr Lawn looked carefully down at Moist and said, 'You don't know what you did, do you, Mister Lipwig? Just you come along and we'll see if you can walk.'

Moist could walk and wished he couldn't. The whole of him felt as if it had been smacked very hard, but the nurses helped him upright and led him carefully to the ward next door, which contained, as it turned out, among the noise, two families; and there were small children and parents weeping. Bits of the past slammed into place in Moist's memory and got bigger and more horrible as once again he felt the breath of the engine as it sailed over the top of him, a toddler under each arm. No, it couldn't have happened like that – could it?

But clamouring voices were telling him otherwise, with women trying to kiss him and holding up their offspring to do likewise, their husbands at the same time trying to shake his hand. Bafflement filled him up like smoke and now in front of him Adora Belle was looking at him with a funny little smile, such as only husbands know of.

When they were at last able to disembogue themselves of the crowd of happy parents and somewhat sticky children, Adora Belle still had her faint smile. 'Well now, my dear, didn't you once say that a life without danger is a life not worth living?'

Moist patted her hand and said, 'Well, Spike, I married you, didn't I?'

'You couldn't resist it, could you? It's like a drug. You're not happy unless someone is trying to kill you, or you're in the centre of some other kind of drama, out of which, of course, the famous Moist von Lipwig will jump to safety at the very last moment. Is it a disease? Some kind of syndrome?'

Moist put on his meek face as only husbands and puppies can do and said, 'Would you like me to stop? I will if you say so.'

There was silence until Adora Belle said, 'You bastard, you know I can't do that. If you stopped all of that you wouldn't be Moist von Lipwig!'

He opened his mouth to protest just as the door opened and in came the press: William de Worde, editor of the *Ankh-Morpork Times*, followed by a porter and the ubiquitous Otto Chriek, the iconographer.

And, because Moist would never stop being Moist von Lipwig until he died, he smiled for the iconograph.

He reminded himself that this was only the start. All the rest would be along soon . . . but no matter, he had danced this fandango many times before, and so he maintained his best boy scout face and smiled at Mr de Worde, who started off by saying, 'It appears that you are a hero *again*, Mister Lipwig. The driver and the stoker say that you ran faster than they could brake the train, picked up the children and jumped to safety just in time. Safety, at that precise moment, being *under* your Iron Girder. It was a miracle that you were there, wasn't it?'

And so the dance began.

'Not at all. We make a point of keeping an eye on the visitors at all times, of course. The children were outside the compound and, strictly speaking, the responsibility of their parents, but we'll be putting up barriers along that stretch of the line immediately. You have to understand, people are flocking here. They seem to be irresistibly drawn by the novelty of live steam and speed.'

'And a very dangerous novelty, would you not say, Mister Lipwig?'

'Well now, Mister de Worde, everything old was once new and until explored was unfamiliar and dangerous, and then, as sure as night follows day they become just part of the scenery. Believe me, sir, that'll happen here with the railway, too.'

Moist watched the journalist painstakingly taking down his words and was ready when the man said, 'I've heard from elderly people all across the Sto Plains who're frightened of the noise and speed. And the trains leave smoke and cinders ... Surely that's dangerous for our fine city?'

Moist flashed his grin once more, thinking, here we go again.

'This place you choose to call "our fine city" is almost all smoke and cinders, and a lot else besides. The trials of Iron Girder have impressed everybody with her ability to carry heavy loads safely and at speed. Let's not forget that speed is essential when dealing with certain goods: your newspaper for one – no one wants to get their news late – and there's my Post Office parcels for another. We can get your first printing on the breakfast tables at Sto Lat. And as for scaring the elderly, well, one old lady recently told me that we should have waited until all the old people were dead before starting up with the railway, and I think you'd agree that that might be a very long time!'

Moist saw the journalist's face break into a smile, and knew he had a result. He continued, 'People often use the excuse that old people won't understand something when, in fact, they simply don't want it or understand it themselves. Actually, old people can be quite gung-ho about risk, and very proud of it.'

And here, for dramatic effect, he looked serious. 'Regrettably, prototype work cannot provide guaranteed safety; it's hard to make things safe until you know they're dangerous. Do you understand? I'm absolutely certain that one day the train will save many, many lives. In fact, I guarantee it.'

As soon as the excited press had got its quotes and pictures of the hero of the hour, and Moist had submitted to a final check by Dr Lawn, he said goodbye to Adora Belle and caught a cab to the compound. Once there, he barged into Harry King's office without even knocking.

'There should have been someone else on duty, Harry!' he shouted, banging a fist on the desk. 'If you have any sense, you'll put proper guards around the track close to the compound to keep an eye on people when the trains are running! I pulled your chestnuts out of the fire this time!' he screamed. 'But I'll tell you this, Harry. A couple of dead toddlers in a front-page story would've shut the railway down before we've hardly got started! Vetinari would do it, believe me. You know his distrust of mechanisms, and I doubt he'd lose much in the way of popularity if he told Mister Simnel to put his toys back in the box. It'd be a great shame, but people mustn't die just because of a bloody engine!'

Moist stopped. He was panting and out of breath, and Sir Harry King, whose expression had hardly changed during the diatribe, now had a face of flaming red.

In the silence Moist thought he heard a curious sizzle, like the sound made by Iron Girder when she was relaxing after a heavy day on the straight and curves. You could perhaps call it a kind of metal purring, but it had now gone, leaving doubts that it had ever been there.

Harry looked Moist up and down and said gravely, 'They said you flew under the train, holding two little kiddies in your arms. Did you?'

'You know, I have absolutely no idea. I *did* see the kids with their heads on the tracks, listening to the funny noises on the rails, and I distinctly remember myself saying Oh bugger! Then something whacked me on the side of the head and I don't remember a thing until I woke up in the Lady Sybil, on a bed, and that's the truth. I *am* a liar for the purposes of amusement, publicity, trivial one-upmanship, personal profit and the gaiety of nations, but I'm not lying to you now.'

There was silence, broken when Harry said hoarsely, 'You know I'm a granddad, don't you? A little boy and a little girl, courtesy of my eldest, and I don't often shiver, my friend, but I'm shivering now.' Harry stood up, with eyes running tears, and said, 'You're the man for this, Mister Lipwig, so you tell me what I should do, please.'

Moist hadn't expected this, but he managed to catch

the metaphorical ball. 'Clean up your act, Harry,' he said. 'Engineers and suchlike know all about hot steel, high speeds and wheels spinning fast, right! For most people, exhilarating speed is a runaway horse. Many people get hurt in this city every year when dear old Dobbin the dray horse suddenly feels his oats and heads for pastures new down the middle of the road.

'My advice is to shut down the Iron Girder rides for a week, for "maintenance". Tidy up, keep all the sharp stuff out of the way, stick up some barriers and have a few lads wandering around in uniform looking like they mean business. You know the kind of thing. Make a show of being safe.'

And now Moist heard the little sizzle again, and it seemed to sizzle in his soul, filling him with ideas, and in the theatre of his head he sat up in the gods, watching the stage of his imagination, agog to see what he came up with next.

'It's not just around the compound that there could be incidents like this, Harry – we need to keep an eye on the whole line. Someone to spot if there are kids on the track, or cows, or a train going the wrong way.' He saw Harry blanch at the thought of all the things that could go wrong, but he was in full flow now. 'They'll need a good view – some kind of watchtower would do the trick, with a clacks attached to signal to the drivers . . . Ask Dick – that brain of his is coming up with new designs faster than his hand can get them down on paper.

'And here's a tip: do something about those greasy old cattle wagons you're running behind Iron Girder. They're okay for a circus ride, maybe, but all of your rolling stock should be as good as the special ones we're using on the Sto Lat line.' *Sizzle*. 'Yes! More posh carriages for the nobs, and . . .' here Moist saw the money smile and continued, 'here's a thought, for those who aren't quite nobs but aspire to be like them, well, why not give them carriages that are not *quite* so plush, but visibly better than the very cheapest coaches which are, perhaps, open to the weather. That would give them something else to yearn for, and you'll have made yet another money pump.'

Moist now found himself caught in the glare of one of Harry King's most dangerous expressions.

'Mister Lipwig, damn me if you ain't a most dangerous man, yes indeed! You're inciting people to have ideas above their station, and that sort of thing makes people suspicious and anxious and, above all, very, *very* nervous.'

To Harry's surprise, Moist almost sprang into the air, spinning. 'Yes! Yes! That's the way! Lord Vetinari's way, too. He believes that people should strive to be better in every respect. I can see it now, Harry. Picture a young man taking his young lady on the train and hazarding an extra sixpence to go in the better-class seats. Well, he's no end of a swell, and he'll look around him and think, This suits me down to the ground and no mistake, I could do with more of this.

'And when he goes back to work he'll strive, yes, strive, to become a better, that's to say, *richer* person to the benefit of both his employer and himself, and not, of course, neglecting to thank the owner of the railway, to wit, your good self, who allowed him to have ideas above his railway station. Everybody wins, nobody loses. Please, please, Harry, allow people to aspire. I mean who knows, they might have been in the wrong class all this time. Your railway, my friend, will allow them to dream, and once you have a dream you've got somewhere closer to a reality.'

Throughout all this Harry stared at Moist as if he'd just seen a giant tarantula, but he managed to say, 'Mister Lipwig, a little while ago you were under a railway engine with fifty tons of rolling stock going past your ears and now you spring up like a jack-in-the-box, full of vim and vigour and schemes! What is it you've got? And how can I get some of it?'

'I don't know, Harry, it's just me being normal. You just keep going, whatever happens, and you never stop. It works for me. And remember: clean up your act – our act – to make sure that the public don't get caught up in the mechanisms.'

The sister state of Quirm comprised, like Ankh-Morpork, a major city, several theoretically autonomous satellites each vying with all the others for advancement, any number of squabbling townships, all bloated with self-importance, and a vast number of homesteads, parishes, farms, vineries, mines, hamlets, bends in the road that someone had named after their dog, and so on, and indeed, so on again.

Around the edges of the Ankh-Morpork hegemony* it was quite possible these days for a small

* Which, it has to be noted, included a certain amount of hinterland, as with most city states.

farmer on the hypothetical outskirts of all that could be called Ankh-Morpork to lean over his own hedge and chat with a Quirmian farmer who was most definitely in Quirm at the time, without in any way considering that this was a political matter. The conversation would generally be about the weather, the abundance or otherwise of water and the uselessness of the government, never mind which kind, and then happily they would shake hands, or give a little nod, and one would go home to drink a pint of home-made beer after such a busy day, while the other would do likewise with a decent home-made wine.

Occasionally the son of one farmer would go to the hedge and see the daughter of the other one, and vice versa and that was why, in a few – but very interesting – places along the boundary, there were people who spoke in both tongues. This sort of thing is something that governments *really* hate, which is a very good thing.

Technically speaking, Quirm and Ankh-Morpork were bosom friends, after centuries of conflict mostly about things that turned out to be inessential, inconsequential, untrue or downright lies. Yes, you used to need a passport to travel in either direction, but since Lord Vetinari had taken office nobody really looked at them any more. Moist had been there many times in his younger days and in different guises and under different names and, on one very memorable occasion, a different sex.*

---

* The jailers couldn't understand how he'd escaped until they realized they weren't getting their washing back.

Moist mused for a moment as that triumph came back to him. It had been one of the all-time great scams, and, although there had been a large number of other fruitful escapades, he had never dared try it again. The nuns would have got him for sure.

But now, as the coach to Quirm finally reached the border, the only obstacle was a gate, theoretically locked and manned by a couple of officers, one on each side. However, such was the nature of inter-state relations that they were quite often asleep or, if not sleeping, were happily cultivating their little gardens on either side of the border. Some might ask what was the point? Everybody smuggled and, after all, the smuggling went both ways, and so a pragmatic approach was floating in the zeitgeist.

And today Moist had a list of people to see, oh yes, he always had a list. He knew that Quirm itself desperately needed the railway as it had lots of produce to sell or be left with heaps of stinking fish, and so Moist was expecting a happy week dealing with the lobsters,* but right now he was dealing with people far from the coast who considered their tiny patches of ground to be sacred. Yes, they wanted the railway, but if it went across *their* land they wouldn't have any land left that wasn't railway.

Moist was assisted in his negotiations in Quirm by Acting Captain Haddock of the Ankh-Morpork City

---

* He knew he couldn't use that colloquial term around there, of course, but after all, the people of Quirm called the people of Ankh-Morpork *sphincters*, mostly in fun. Mostly.

Watch, presently seconded to the Quirmian force, who had learned the lingo, in an Ankh-Morpork kind of way. Acting Captain Haddock explained the dilemma created by Quirmian traditions of landownership over a pint of very weak beer.

'It's all to do with something they call *le patrimony*. It means that all the kids have to get something when mum and dad pass over. A big farm might have to be split into two or even three or more so everyone can get their share. Even the government knows this is stupid, but no one in Quirm takes any notice of what the government says. So it's up to you, Mister Lipwig, to get them to understand, but that's it, I'm afraid.'

Well, Moist tried, he really did, and after a frustrating fortnight haggling over every handkerchief-sized plot, he was ready to give up and head back to Ankh-Morpork. Harry wasn't going to like this, he thought, and, worse still, neither was Vetinari, but he could probably talk his way out of it, possibly.

His gloomy mood was lightened when he reached a small but prosperous estate belonging to the Marquis des Aix en Pains, a well-known wine grower. The Marquis was one of the last landowners on Moist's list. He had married a girl from Ankh-Morpork and was apparently extremely keen to have his very fine wines conveyed to customers as soon as possible with a minimum of jolting, which had a deleterious effect on the wine. Currently the coach journey, littered with potholes, required the wines to lie down in a dark cool cellar to settle for months afterwards.

The Marquis had invited Moist for lunch, which

turned out to be something he called *fusion cuisine*, with pâté devoid of avec, a main course of lobster and mash, followed by a most excellent spotted dick, a combination of dishes that you would expect to live long in the annals of gastronomic infamy but which wasn't too bad, especially when consumed in conjunction with the remarkably good house wines.

The Marquis was young and forward-looking and clearly taken with the idea of the railway, not only for the wine trade but also as a means of bringing people together. He winked at his wife as he said so, with the definite implication that getting people together was something very close to his heart; and he believed that the more people knew about one another, the better they got along. His views on Quirm's curious and slightly bucolic attitude to the division of wealth after the death of the parents were of great interest to Moist.

'Everyone wants to sell their wine and cheese and fish to Ankh-Morpork, zat is certain, but *nobody* wants to lose land. We all like our slice of Quirm: it's *real* real estate, something you can pick up and crumble in your fingers, something zat you can fight for. It's old-fashioned, I know, and of course its continued existence leaves the government exasperated, which, as a true son of Quirm, I consider perfectly acceptable.

'However, for you, my friend, zis is difficult because we don't sell our birthright unless, that is, the price is extremely 'igh. And, when the news gets out about the railway the price will be *extremely* 'igh: you will, as my wife says, 'ave to pay "*dans le nez*". I think, my friend, you will 'ave to find another route from here to Quirm

City if you want to get ze job done before *les poules auront des dents.*'

He hesitated for a moment and said, 'Come with me to ze library. I want to show you some maps.'

In a large and ornate room, filled with the heads of many stuffed animals – or at least *probably* stuffed – and a stench of old formaldehyde, Moist pored over a large map which the Marquis had pulled out of an old chest.

Pointing to what seemed to be a rather empty part of the map, the Marquis said, 'Most country *'ere* is worthless land, maquis all the way, nothing to mine except ochre, and precious little of zat too. It's more or less a wasteland, covered in scrub zat would tear your boots off and with nothing to induce people to be zere. Badlands, you might say, 'ome to rogues on the run, highwaymen, bandits and occasionally smugglers, all of them extremely nasty and armed to ze teeth. Oh, the government makes a play of getting rid of them every so often, but that isn't all. There are goblins and zey know nothing about land rights.'

'We've now come to terms with goblins in Ankh-Morpork,' said Moist quickly. 'It's a matter of finding something for them to do that they really like doing and are good at and, of course, after that it's just a case of remembering their names and refraining from kicking them. They can be extremely helpful if unkicked, although not necessarily likeable.'

'I wish *we* could get on decent terms with zem,' said the Marquis wistfully, 'but these, you must understand, are *Quirm* goblins, and therefore extremely argumentative and intractable and on top of it, often drunk. They brew their own wine for 'eavens' sake.' He thought for a moment and then corrected himself, 'Or, rather, a wine-like substance.'

'That doesn't sound so bad, does it?' said Moist.

'Really? They brew ze wine from snails. From the fruit of the wall, as you call it in Ankh-Morpork. It makes zem *extremely* rowdy, but zey would probably be okay if it wasn't for the bandits, who 'unt them for fun.'

'So do the *bandits* own the maquis?' said Moist.

The Marquis hesitated. 'No, it is indeed no man's land. I suppose if we talk to lawyers, they will say it's owned literally by ze state of Quirm in its entirety.'

'Well, sir, since it appears that the state of Quirm is gagging to have the railway, even if the landowners aren't, and if you can assure me of the land rights issue, I'll be very happy to do them a favour.'

The Marquis grimaced. 'Unfortunately, it's not as simple as zat. We are not difficult people, but the government drags its feet when it comes to cleaning out ze bandits, because, as you understand, bandits and governments 'ave so much in common that they might be interchangeable anywhere in the world . . . I see you smiling, Mister Lipwig. Is something amusing?'

'Many bandits?'

'A considerable amount. This whole area is rather spoiled by them – unpleasant bandits who would cheerfully commit murder if and when zey think zey can get away with it. I 'ave to tell you that if you are in a 'urry to clear the maquis of bandits, I'm afraid, Mister Ankh-Morpork, you might 'ave to do it yourself. And I see you are *still* smiling! Will you be so good as to share ze joke? The well-known so-called Ankh-Morpork sense of 'umour does not translate very well here, I'm afraid.'

'Don't be,' said Moist. 'When the humours were handed out, Ankh-Morpork got the one for joking and Quirm had to make do with their expertise in fine dining and love-making.'

He held a beat and said, 'Would you fancy a trade?'

The Marquise giggled into her wine, smiled at Moist and winked, while her husband grinned and said solemnly, 'I think, monsieur, we prefer the status quo.'

And Moist, who had almost but not totally embarrassed himself, said, 'Sir, apart from the goblins, do *any* decent people live in those badlands?'

The Marquis shook his head. 'No, certainly not, they're as dry as dust.'

Moist looked thoughtful for a while, then stood up, bowed to both of them, kissed the hand of the Marquise and said, 'Thank you so much for your hospitality and your help and information. I should get away now if I'm to make the overnight coach back to Ankh-Morpork, but I have a funny feeling that happier circumstances will soon prevail. In fact, I can feel them just floating in the air.'

Ankh-Morpork was full of dwarf bars, big and small, accommodating all comers. The gloom of the Dirty Rat was particularly popular with those who preferred a traditional style of establishment and a definite lack of umbrellas in their drinks.

'Knocking down clacks towers. What good does that do us? My old granny lives under a clacks tower and the lads let her send clackses for nothing.'

In the shadows somebody said, 'You shouldn't allow her to do that. The clacks is for humans.'

And then the quarrel began.

'You've got to admit the clacks is useful sometimes. It'd save a ship at sea, I heard. And anyway it helps you keep in touch with your friends.'

The voice from the dark corner said again, 'Don't touch the clacks towers, then. There are other ways. I've seen the locomotives. It should be easy enough to turn one over on the rails.'

'Oh yeah? And why d'you want to do that?'

'It'll show that us dwarfs are not to be trifled with and anyway, I'm hearing that dwarfs aren't being allowed to work on the railway.'

'I hadn't heard that. That's discrimination.'

'No, that's because silly buggers have been chopping up clacks towers, isn't it? It's what you get if you go around doing things like that. No wonder at all.'

'That's as may be, but the railway employs lots of trolls and even goblins . . . I mean, goblins! Filth! We're being pushed aside. The Low King has sold his soul to bloody Vetinari and the next thing you know they'll have built a railway line to Uberwald and all our mines will be full of stinking goblins . . . unless we stand up for ourselves now!'

'Yeah! Bloody goblins. All over the place!'

The conversation was punctuated by the sound of

much quaffing and the subsequent cleaning of the tables.

'Not that a true dwarf would *want* to work on the railway, mind you,' said the soft voice that hadn't yet identified itself.

'No! You're right. I'd never work on the railway. It's an abomination! It should be stopped!'

'They're laying tracks to Quirm from Ankh-Morpork. It would make a statement if we got in the way,' the voice from the shadows continued.

Someone thumped a hand on the bar and said, 'We must show them that dwarfs are not going to be pushed around any longer!'

'We could smash up those bloody water towers and steal the coal,' another suggested. 'That wouldn't hurt anyone but it would mean they'd have to walk.'

'That's not big enough. They'd just rebuild and carry on, like they've done with the clacks. We'd need to do something really big. Something that would make people pay attention.'

There was the sound of people thinking who didn't think very much. Somebody said, 'You mean killing people?'

'Well, you know, you have to make a stand. And later on, when people find out, we'll be the heroes.'

And then the barman, who had been keeping an eye on the group, said pointedly, 'It's closing time, gentlemen, ain't you got no holes to go to?' And shooed them out on to the street.

Ardent walked confidently away. After all, there was another dwarf bar a few streets away and the poison could drip so gently. Amazing how simple people could be manipulated by the right voice at the right time. And after that they did it for themselves with vocabulary like 'stands to reason' and 'they're up to something', little caltrops on the road to interspecies misunderstanding.

When Moist finally arrived back in Ankh-Morpork around breakfast time, he hurried to Harry King's house. It was unusual to see Harry being, as it were, just Harry King, family man. He was even wearing carpet slippers. Effie fussed about with the servants for more coffee while Moist made his report to her husband.

'Sir, we have a little problem down in Quirm. To put it bluntly, some unpleasant gentlemen are getting in the way of the success of our railway.'

Moist explained the land-rights situation to Harry and proposed that since the rolling acres of maquis didn't belong to anybody it belonged to everybody and he could put the railway line straight through. There was just the little matter of the bandits to be dealt with. The look on Harry's face would have warmed the cockles of any heart, especially if it was the heart of a shark, and really Moist didn't need to say much more, but did so anyway.

'It would be very helpful, Harry, if I could go back there one night soon with some of your golems and possibly some of your . . . security men, your *specialist technicians*, as it were. The kind of gentlemen who are adept at resolving conflict. Of course, I'll need to commandeer a coach.'

The expression on Harry's face changed like a

kaleidoscope until at last he said, 'Do you mind if I come too?'

And Effie shrieked, 'Harry King! At your age you're going to be doing nothing more than stopping home!'

'Oh, come on, my love, the man said these are bandits. It's my duty as an honest citizen. After all, I'm Harry King, the man who does business, and *this*, well, this is my business and I'm going to take care of it.'

'Harry, please! Remember your position in life!'

'A man makes his own position in life, Duchess, and this is business and I'm going to sort it and it will be the last time, okay?'

'Oh, all right ... but you mind and take notice, Mister Lipwig. And Harry, you do what Mister Lipwig tells you, he's a very sensible young man,' said Effie. 'And there's to be no alcohol and, Mister Lipwig, make certain he's wrapped up nice and warm because of his bladder, er, thing, you know. He's not as young as he thinks he is.'

And Harry roared. 'Yes, Effie! But right now I reckon I'm ready for anything. I'll get the word out to my lads and my golems, Mister Lipwig, and I'll see you back here tomorrow morning. Seven o'clock sharp.'

At home, Adora Belle said, 'It's a harebrained idea, of course, otherwise *you* wouldn't have had it, would you?'

'Actually, my sweetness, the raid was Harry's idea,' Moist lied. 'I think he thinks of it as his last grand hurrah, but he really had to twist my arm, I promise you, or my name isn't Moist Lipwig. You should have seen the look on his face!'

'Yes, you *are* Moist von Lipwig and you are really looking forward to this, aren't you? You have that look about you.'

'Not exactly,' said Moist. 'But it'll be a moonless night, and it might be instructive to see Harry and his chums having one of their little parties. Of course, *you* don't know anything about this, okay?'

Adora Belle's face went delightfully blank. 'This what? But just you remember, Moist, if it's going to be a mêlée do try to come back with all your bits in their rightful place.'

The following morning, two large coaches were waiting outside Harry King's house with a crew of Harry's chums on board. Moist wondered how Harry could gather them together so quickly and then thought about all the things Harry used to do back in the bad old days that he now fondly remembered as being so good. Actually, it was no surprise that the man could assemble an army to settle a little dispute about who owned the streets.

They were all on their best behaviour now and almost all of them didn't spit and there was no cursing, because the Duchess was looking out of the window, ready to wave them off.

Before the coaches departed, Harry addressed his team. 'It's like this, lads: this isn't exactly a killing job, unless they tries to kill you first. These ain't our streets, but they're bandits all the same. You could say we're making the world better for decent people, like what we are, and we're cleaning up the mess like we've always done.'

Moist looked at the faces of Harry's associates. Some had gold teeth and some had no teeth, but all of them had the surreptitious look of gentlemen that mostly go abroad after dark. And if you looked with an experienced eye, bits of them bulged, indeed one of them was holding a toolbox and an eager expression, clearly a man who wasn't for half measures.

Harry had made it clear that there was to be no alcohol, at least until the homeward stage, and so it was a subdued journey through the day. By mid-afternoon they came to the edge of the maquis. The country that lay before them was clearly no place for coaches, with the road petering out into a vague track amid the scrub. Harry ordered the drivers to halt at a spot that offered some grazing and water for the horses, where the coaches would be screened from view, and sent his associates to scout the maquis ahead.

Moist had never before travelled with such silent men; they seemed to absorb all noise and as they jumped down from the coaches with flannel feet they melted instantly into the landscape. Content to leave this part to the specialists, Harry and Moist settled back to wait.

It was a black night, and the whole party had made its stealthy way to the edge of the bandits' camp. They were now in the depths of the wretched wilderness of the Quirmian maquis, a nightmare of dense blackthorn that could strip the skin from your bone. It was a garden from hell, especially in the darkness. They could see the fitful flames of the cooking fires and hear the unmistakable sound of alcohol-assisted snoring. These outlaws ought to be ashamed, Moist thought, not one single lookout!

With his associates strategically deployed around the perimeter, Harry made his way quietly into the centre of the camp.

'Good morning, gentlemen! We are the Goblin Preservation Society and all of yous has got two minutes to get up and be out of here. Got it? Nice and smart, chums!'

A bandit stumbled out of his tent and sneered, 'We don't care who you are, and you can shove all of that right up your jacksie, monsieur.'

And Harry said, 'Good! We like shoving it anywhere! Go on, lads, but no goblins get hurt, okay?'

Moist took a careful step backwards and watched. Harry had stipulated that murdering people wasn't really on the cards tonight, but most of the bandits were either lying on the ground or running away within a couple of minutes of Harry's chums being unleashed. It was gang warfare, but one gang had no sense of strategy. Harry's men were surgical and methodical and very, very professional, even somewhat sombre. This was a job of work and they did it with care and precision. It was what you did, didn't you, and they were flattering themselves that for once they were the good guys, an experience, Moist thought, that they seldom ever had.

Harry took a look around the battleground to assure

himself that nothing more than a little concussion and the occasional broken leg had been achieved and was satisfied on all points.

'What do you plan to do with them?' Moist asked.

'Deliver them to the local justice, like the honest citizens we are. I suppose that'll be your Marquis.'

'Very good, but can I suggest we leave one or two behind, to make sure the rest of the bandit population get to hear what happens if they make honest citizens upset?'

'Suppose so,' Harry grunted. 'But I'll get the lads to do a few further . . . excursions in the area first, see if we can't mop up some more of 'em. Actions speak louder than words, Mister Lipwig.'

At the chateau later that night the Marquis emerged in his dressing gown to receive them, accompanied by two servants.

'Monsieur Lipwig, *mon ami*, what an unexpected pleasure to see you again so soon. And with companions.'

Harry stepped forward before Moist could speak and said, 'We've a parcel of miscreants here we've brought to you, my lord, since I reckoned you were the closest figure of authority in these parts.'

The Marquis cast a bright eye over the prisoners. 'I see at least two appear to 'ave "'ARRY KING" stamped across the temples. Can it be I 'ave the 'onour to address Sir 'arry King in person? Don't be surprised. My wife has told me much about ze King of ze Golden River, including his famous rings. You are most welcome, monsieur, and I 'ope we will be doing much business together. May I offer you some refreshment?'

''scuse me, sir, but what d'you want done with this lot?' said the toolbox-holding associate.

'Put them in the oubliette, if you would be so kind, we'll fish them out sooner or later.'

'What's an oubliette, sir? Is it like a privy?'

'Yes,' the Marquis laughed, 'I suppose it is in this instance! These garçons 'ave been a thorn in our side for quite a while, but I don't think we'll be getting any further trouble from *them*.'

When Moist, Harry and associates reboarded the coaches in the small hours and started on the long journey home, this time the crates of beer were brought out for the victors.

'Well done, lads,' Harry boomed as he cracked the top off a bottle. 'You did all I expected and more, gentlemen. And you know Harry King is a generous man and so I look forward to working with you again soon. You can rely upon it.'

He lay back on the seat and started smoking one of his cigars, every so often chatting to one or other of his chums about the escapades they had had long ago when the Watch was a laughing stock.

Adora Belle eventually woke Moist with a cup of tea around about four o'clock in the afternoon. As he supped the tea his wife puffed up his pillows and said, 'Come on, then, tell me, how did it go? I wasn't woken by any big bangs last night, which I consider a result, don't you?'

'Well, it wasn't a massacre and it wasn't a lot of smacked bottoms, as far as I could tell, but the good guys won, well, to a given value of good guy. Harry King's cronies are very sprightly for old guys, and devious as well.'

Placing a tray of food on his knees she said, 'I suppose breakfast in bed just can't present the same frisson for Mister A Life Without Danger Is A Life Not Worth Living, yes?'

Puncturing a sausage, Moist said, 'How well you know me, Spike. Now listen, it seems there are a lot of goblins in the maquis and the people of Quirm haven't found out yet how useful they can be even though they apparently do a good line in wine made from snails.' Moist grimaced and continued, 'Do you mind if I take Of the Twilight the Darkness to Quirm with me?'

His wife looked astonished. 'I didn't think you liked him?'

'Well, he grows on you, you know, like a fungus, and there's going to be a lot of puzzled goblins around now so they might like to see a friendly face.' He hesitated. 'If you can call it that.'

In darkness far from Moist in just about every sense that could be imagined, including the metaphysical, deliberations were taking place in a cavern that was paradoxically glittering and dark when tested by a different eye. It *was* illuminated, in so far as there was illumination, by one solitary candle, whose light was, as the saying goes, just there to show you the darkness. Nevertheless, its trembling little light was refracted in a veritable hoard of gems, the like of which, if you added up the sad little glimmerings, gave off entirely less light than could be delivered by a humble tallow candle.

It was, in short, a light that hid from light, and it had a reason to hide. Just as the unfortunate dwarf now sitting uncomfortably in the centre of the cavern had reason to wish to be elsewhere. Elsewhere, he thought, was the operative word; anywhere would surely be a better place than here.

On the other hand, he was under a religious obligation. He had first heard it on his father's knee, or possibly his mother's, because he had never seen or heard either of them clearly and their voices were always muffled, because silence was as much of a virtue as darkness among the grags, and as he recalled the undeniable fact, he almost tried to cut and run, stopping himself in a nanosecond because there was nowhere to hide. He was in it too high!* Never a good place to be for a dwarf, and the grags had the measure of him.

It was said that they had many ways of killing in the darkness and even had ways of moving from darkness to darkness without being apprehended by the intervening light. Oh, so much was said of them, although generally it was whispered. And he had done *so many* bad things, like eating beef and buying his wife colourful earrings and, worst of all, he had become friends

* For humans he would have been in too deep. Way too deep.

with Rocky Debris who was, horror of horrors, a troll, and also quite a decent bloke, who he quite often sat next to when they were going to work and who, like him, was a supporter of Dolly Sisters United and generally went with him when there was a match on, and surely anyone who cheered for your side was a friend, wasn't he?

And yes, he was, but down in the base of his brain was the bogeyman of his childhood, and subtle whisperings, curdled fragments of old songs sung on special occasions, little observances made holy by repetition with the right people sitting at the same fireside, in those cosy days when you were not really old enough to understand and didn't have your wretched brain stuffed full of ideas that part of you thought you shouldn't *ever* obey, like not shaking hands with a troll *and now he had been seen* and now they had him and now they stood between him and his chances of a new life after death. They held the keys to the next world and, on a whim, could have him floating in the ultimate darkness of the Ginnungagap where there were ... things, tormentors, creatures of indefinite invention and patience.

He shifted because of the cramp in his legs, and said, 'Please, I know I've got into bad ways and I've strayed from the path and indeed may be unworthy to call myself a dwarf, but if you allow me I can make recompense. Please, I'm begging you, remove my shackles and I promise to do whatever you ask.'

The silence in the room grew thicker, more dense, as if it was pulling itself together. How long had he been in here now? It might as well have been years, or merely seconds ... That was the difficulty about darkness; it encompassed everything, turning it into an amorphous substance in which everything got twisted, and remembered and then lost.

'Very well,' said the voice. 'We have looked into your wretched soul and are minded to give you one last chance. Be aware there will be no other.' The voice softened a little and said, 'Tak is watching you. Now you can eat your meal, which is right in front of you, and go from this place and be assured that Tak will be with you. Remember, for those who turn away there is no redemption. And when Tak needs you, you will be contacted again.'

After a rare, well-earned evening with his wife, Moist set off the next day on the golem horse with Of the Twilight the Darkness clinging on behind him.

As they galloped along, there was something about the golem horse that was troubling Moist von Lipwig. A golem horse was incredibly useful if you needed to get somewhere fast, that is if you liked a ride where you spent a lot of the time finding that stirrups just didn't do the job. You merely hung on until you got there, it was as simple as that. No need to steer, NagNav did the trick: if you told it where you wanted to go it took you there. The creature made no sound, required no water or oats and simply stood patiently when it wasn't in use.

And then it dawned on Moist what the problem was. It was all give and no take. Generally speaking, he didn't have much to do with the concept of karma, but he had heard of it and felt that a ton of it was dropping on him right now. The horse was all give and he was all take ... But that was nuts, he told himself. A spoon doesn't want you to say please and thank you, does it? Ah yes, he thought, but a spoon is a piece of metal and the golem horse is a horse. He hesitated, pondering. And thought, *I wonder* ...

Shortly before the border crossing they reached the head of the finished railway track. He and the goblin thankfully slid off the horse and a sudden impulse prompted Moist to ask the creature a question.

'Can you speak?' he asked, feeling more than faintly ridiculous.

And the answer came back out of the air rather than from the horse's mouth, as it were.

'Yes, if we want to.'

The goblin sniggered. Moist ignored him and pressed on with his line of inquiry.

'Ah, we're getting somewhere. Would you like to run around in meadows and generally cavort in pastures and so on?'

Out of nowhere came, 'Yes, if you wish.'

Moist said, 'But what do *you* wish?'

'I don't understand the concept.'

Moist breathed in and said, 'I saw a little stream not far back, and some green pastures and, for the sake of my soul, I would like you to go over there and gallop in the meadows and enjoy yourself.'

'Yes, enjoy myself, if you want me to.'

'For heavens' sake, this is manumission we're talking about here!'

'That would be horseumission, sir. And I must point out that I don't need to enjoy myself.'

'Well, do so for my sake, will you, please? Roll around on the flowers and neigh a bit and gallop about and have some kind of fun. If not for your own pleasure, then for my sanity, please.'

He watched the horse disappear into the meadow.

Behind him Of the Twilight the Darkness cackled. 'What a piece of work you are, Mister Slightly Damp, freeing the slaves and all. What you think his lordship will say about that?'

Moist shrugged. 'He might be acerbic, but a little acerbic isn't all that bad. He's quite a one for freedom is Vetinari, though not necessarily mine.'

Turning his attention to the railway, Moist was pleased to see that the work gangs, under the tutelage of Mr Simnel's young men, were evidently making steady progress laying down the next stage of track towards Quirm.

To travel onwards, Moist and Of the Twilight the Darkness hitched a ride on a handcar operated with gusto by two young railway workers, a curiously amusing contraption whose wheels ran along the newly laid rails still waiting to be fully bedded in.

They passed the border with only a brief stop to deal with the formalities which were, in fact, nothing more than nodding at the guards and saying, 'Is it okay if we cross, lads?' Whereupon they briefly stopped digging their respective allotments and waved him through.

Where the handcar ran out of track, they found an old man with a horse and cart waiting, as arranged, to take them the rest of the distance to the chateau. He was clearly very sniffy about having a goblin in his nice clean vehicle, even though it was only a cart.

The Marquis was waiting for them at the chateau and beamed at Moist. His nose wrinkled at the sight of Moist's companion.

'Who is this?' he asked in a tone a society lady might take upon finding half of something bristling in her soup.

'This is Of the Twilight the Darkness.'

Of the Twilight the Darkness gave the Marquis a smart salute. 'Of the Twilight the Darkness, Mister Mar-keee. Nice place you got here. Veeery nice. Don't worry about smell. I'll get used to it.'

After an awkward silence, the Marquis said, '*Mon Dieu.*'

'Not a god, Mister Mar-keee,' said Of the Twilight the Darkness, 'just goblin, best there is, oh yes. Very useful, you know.' The goblin continued in ringing sarcasm, 'And not only that, Mister Mar-keee, I'm real. If you cut me, do I not bleed? And if you do, I bleeding well cuts you too, no offence meant.'

The Marquis's laughter bounced off the scenery. There was no doubt about it. The goblin knew how to break the ice. Even an iceberg.

The Marquis held out a hand and said, '*Enchanté*, Monsieur Of the Twilight the Darkness. Do you drink wine?'

The goblin hesitated. 'Are there snails in it?'

As they climbed the wide stone steps up to the terrace, the Marquis said, 'Regrettably we don't include snail. I know your people like snail wine but I'm afraid I 'ave none to offer you.'

'Never mind, squire, will have it as it comes, please. And for record, Mister Mar-keee, they ain't my people, they your people. I'm an Ankh-Morpork lad. Have seen the big horse* and all that stuff.'

The view in the late afternoon sun over the maquis from the terrace was wonderful.

'You have many goblins in Ankh-Morpork, Mister Lipwig?' the Marquis asked as he poured Moist a glass of chilled wine. 'I've 'eard, of course, of Milord Vetinari's famous melting pot. And yet I am informed zat many people in Ankh-Morpork still feel very unsure about them and think that getting involved with goblins shows that ze owner is dirty! So much for the prejudices of your countrymen who are, one 'as to say, a fairly dirty lot in any case. Whereas 'ere in Quirm *notre logique* points out that we are cleaner. After all, Quirm is the 'ome of Monsieur Bidet! Yet another apparatus for keeping clean and yet *you* in Ankh-Morpork sneer at *us* for being dirty.'

'Yes, I know, it's deplorable,' said Moist. 'I did meet Monsieur Bidet, although regrettably I didn't shake

---

* An Ankh-Morpork citizen will never yield to the idea that there are other cities at least as good as their own and treat the concept that there could be with humorous disdain. The phrase originated when an Ankh-Morpork citizen was shown an equestrian statue in Pseudopolis and when faced with the beast, said, 'Maybe it's a Big Horse I'm Morporkian', an incident that gave rise to a popular bar room song.

him by the hand. Excuse me? Is something wrong?'

The Marquis suddenly looked preoccupied. 'Someone was watching us from the tree over zere. I must 'ave spoken too loudly because 'oever it is has made 'aste to get down to the cover of the ground. He's small, but larger than a goblin; you 'ardly ever see *zem* in ze trees.'

There was a movement in the air as Of the Twilight the Darkness vaulted over the parapet and disappeared into the landscape below. He reappeared almost as quickly, saying, 'Dwarf bugger. Have it away on toes. I spit me of him!'

The Marquis topped up Moist's glass and said, 'A dwarf? Something to do with you, Mister Lipwig? Industrial espionage? One would expect the dwarfs to be keen on something like a railway . . . they are, after all, metalworkers and traders in ore.'

'I don't think so,' said Moist. 'The clacks saw a bit of trouble a few months ago with extremist factions knocking down some of their towers, but that seems to have died down now. And there don't seem to be many dwarfs interested in working on the railway. Something to do with the grags, I expect. The grags don't seem to like anybody of importance in Ankh-Morpork.'

'Oh, yes,' said the Marquis. 'The famous Koom Valley Accord and all zat business. I believed it to be sorted out.'

'So did everybody else. You must know how it is. Can't please absolutely everybody. And you certainly can't please the grags, however hard you try.'

Fully refreshed, Moist and Of the Twilight the

Darkness set off into the maquis to find the goblin denizens, who even if they did not, strictly speaking, own the land through which the railway would go, needed to be informed and consulted. As squatters on unclaimed land, Moist thought, they surely must have some claim to it.

As they made their way into the scrubby and thorny landscape, Moist pondered the significance of the dwarf who had been spying on *him*, right here in Quirm, where you didn't normally see dwarfs. This meant he had been followed, and that almost surely meant more than one person. During his misspent youth and, not to put too fine a point on it, his largely misspent early middle age, he'd reckoned to be conversant with the methodology of spying, and one person alone couldn't ensure reasonable tracking of the target. What was the dwarf doing there? Where had he come from? And, more important, where did he go?

His reverie was interrupted when Of the Twilight the Darkness stopped suddenly by a rocky outcrop which, as far as Moist could tell, was indistinguishable from several other similar outcrops they had passed already. It was hot. Very hot.

'Wait here,' said the goblin. 'Will be back in a shake.'

In fact it was another sweaty hour and the sun was beginning to dip below the horizon before the goblin came back along the track, trailed by a large crowd of Quirmian goblins, their numbers swelling all the time as even more of them emerged from the undergrowth.

When it came to looks the Quirm goblins seemed

exactly the same as the ones over the border in Ankh-Morpork. However, unlike the Ankh-Morpork goblins, the Quirmian goblins were dressed in a way that could only be called snazzy. They had a certain panache unavailable to their Ankh-Morpork brethren, and a whiff about them of what was probably eau de snail.*
Admittedly, the materials on show were effectively the same – bits of animal skin or indeed the animals themselves, birds, feathers – all embellished with sparkling stones. It was as if goblins had discovered taxidermy, but hadn't *quite* got the important, nay, *essential* point of scooping out the messy bits first. But trust Quirm goblins to make their own *haute couture.*

Moist smiled. He could see that somehow the goblin lads here in Quirm were trying to do it *better*, possibly because they had a better class of shaky swagger and a certain cheerful *up yours* look in their eyes.

Nevertheless, they looked like a people who had been hammered hard on the anvil of fate and had been laminated with a natural bravado, which did not entirely hide their wounds.

Moist was glad he had Of the Twilight the Darkness on his side, because the goblins of this part of the maquis clearly had no liking for humanity. Of the Twilight the Darkness now sidled up to him in his bandy-legged and sneery little way and said, 'These people hurting oh-so bad it is. People gone. Little ones gone. Pots gone. Gone. But put big faces on it, yes. Can

---

* Which instead of masking the ubiquitous goblin smell merely lent it an extra piquancy.

no more be truly goblin. Hurt. Hurt. Hurt. Now I give speech.'

Of the Twilight the Darkness turned out to be the goblin equivalent of Moist himself.

Moist wasn't fluent in goblin, but you didn't need to know what was being said as you watched the faces and the way Of the Twilight the Darkness waved his hands. He was, in fact, doing a number.

Moist couldn't make out the words, but assumed it was something like, 'New life in Ankh-Morpork with all the rats you want *and* wages.' For there they were, ideas and promises curving through the air.

And so certain was Moist that he had picked up what was going on that he leaned down and said, 'Don't forget to say that in Ankh-Morpork goblins are now citizens with *rights*.'

Moist was extremely pleased to see the goblin pause and look at him. 'How you know I was talking of Ankh-Morpork, Mister Lipwig?'

'Takes one to know one.'

While Of the Twilight the Darkness delivered his speech, the goblins stared at Moist. As stares went, their eyes were not baleful or angry, they were just . . . hopeful, in the grudging way of people who had had to learn pessimism as a survival tactic.

One of the goblins then stepped forward and beckoned, clearly wanting to show him something. Of the Twilight the Darkness was also nudging him to follow. As Moist gingerly threaded his way through the network of almost invisible paths in the wasteland of thorns, pools of poisonous water and occasional blockages caused by old rock falls, he noticed a crackling underfoot. Bones, he realized – mostly small bones – and in his ear were the words of Of the Twilight the Darkness: 'Young goblins! Veeeeery tasty! A lot of good eating. Bandits thought so. But we hang, Mister Lipwig, we hang. We hang on.'

The horror tripped its way icily over Moist's backbone. Of the Twilight the Darkness continued.

'Those bandits was hungry. Small goblins. Easy to catch.'

'Are you saying they were *eating* the goblins?'

The vehemence of Moist's cry was picked up by Of the Twilight the Darkness immediately.

'Sure. Easy meat. The bandit men eat anything they can catch. Rats. Moles. Shrews. Birds. Even stinky bird like raven. Eat it up. Yum. Yum. Shit out nasty poisonous stuff. Goblin meat like chicken. Miracle of nature may be not, but no use to goblin when bandits around. They don't want much, mister, and good job, 'cos they don't get, but like me will do any job in free air. Place to live not being killed. Yes! Hunky-dory. And no need food in Ankh-Morpork. Big Wahoonie! Rats *everywhere*!'

'Okay, Mister Twilight, where do we go from here?'

The goblin gave Moist a cynical look, something which is very easy to do when you're a goblin, because you learn cynicism early and you learn it fast.

'You give me half name, Mister Damp. I forgive, have mercy. This time. I ask you. *Don't* do again. Is very important. Half name is shame. Challenge to fight. Know you hasty. No understanding. Will forgive you.

Will forgive once, *Mister Lipwig*! This by way of friendly information. No charge incurred.'

Whatever Moist von Lipwig was, he knew the use of the right word at the right time.

'Mister Of the Twilight the Darkness, thank you for your forbearance.'

It was beginning to rain. Sticky, lazy rain but the goblins seemed to be oblivious to it. These people are the world's most stoical of stoics, Moist thought, albeit with a sting in their tail. I wonder what they are like when they decide, and they will decide, not to take everything on their greasy chins.

Of the Twilight the Darkness grinned at Moist again and declared, 'Hey you, mister big hero, mighty warrior, except, hah, these dumb buggers really think you is bee's bollocks, think sun percolate out your arse.'

Moist realized that Of the Twilight the Darkness's presentation to the goblins of the delights of Ankh-Morpork and his status in the city might have been somewhat exaggerated.

'What did you say to make them think that?'

'These goblins need hope, Mister Lipwig. You ain't genuine good guy, but you can pretend like no bees' nest. I have already explained to them that you are great citizen of Ankh-Morpork and dreadful fighter.'

'Well,' said Moist, 'at least you got one bit right. But the bandits have surely been scared off now. The goblins can stay here, can't they? There'll be jobs on the railway when it comes through here. They'd like that, wouldn't they?'

'Bandit men come back in time. Always is bandits.

These goblins can't fly, Mister Soggy. Long way back to Ankh-Morpork line! Looks for you to get them out of here. Me? I ain't just fallen off Hogswatch tree. You don't carry knife, and now it night-time and you are still in maquis. Worse here than just bandits! Bad worse! Everything bad end up in the maquis and you *still* with no weapon. What are your orders, Mister Big Man?!'

Moist hesitated. He had a feel for this sort of thing, he was sure, and it hardly ever let him down.

'Okay. We'll take them with us. But first you must get us out of here.'

'No, Marvellous von Lipwig is going to take the people out. Plucky goblin sidekick just bring up the rear.'

'Really? Okay, then. Just point me in the right direction.'

There was a track of sorts, and myriad little pathways in every direction. Moist and his unhappy but hopeful band were shepherded surreptitiously from behind by Of the Twilight the Darkness, who was becoming a great lieutenant, despite the fact that he brazenly considered Moist to be a bit of a tit. But a useful tit all the same.

As they struggled back to what, in a fair wind, might have been called a proper track, Moist told himself that while it was true that Commander Vimes was the man who had been most prominent in the manumission of the goblins, he, Moist, could at least give them a job; you couldn't have a profession as *goblin*, now could you? It just made no sense. And yet if there were such a thing as a professional goblin, then it was definitely Of the Twilight the Darkness, who was so goblin that you could imagine that other goblins would tap one another on the shoulder and say, 'Blimey! Look at that goblin! Doesn't he look like a goblin to you?'

But jobs got things going, got *people* going, and raised their self-esteem. After all, goblins, quite apart from now being ubiquitous in the clacks industry, were also doing very well and picking up serious folding money in the ceramics business. Goblin pots were beautiful, extremely fine and as iridescent as a butterfly's wing.*

Moist's reverie was broken by Of the Twilight the Darkness. 'These poor herberts behind us think you need to know that dwarfs been asking after you, like sneaky one up tree I saw off. My, can't the greedy buggers shift when need. Don't like good flint edge! But still are some around. Reckon they waiting until we get to railway. Right place for ambush.'

Moist had devoted considerable energies to being a non-combatant, words being his weapon of choice, but when words weren't enough, in extremis he could deliver telling blows with his fists and feet. Right now he was wondering whether to surreptitiously drag said feet a little so that he would be surrounded by the band of goblins if there was an attack. After all, they all had

---

*Unggue pots, as they were called, had a major and sacred part in goblin society. In Ankh-Morpork sensible goblins were making quasi unggue pots for sale, looking like the real thing, Adora Belle said, but with the magic taken out and the wonderful sparkle left in. However, it helped if you didn't pay too much attention to what the pots *traditionally* held . . .

stone weapons, didn't they? And he didn't, did he? Goblins acquired a fighting spirit with their mothers' milk, if indeed their mothers *had* milk.*

They continued cautiously into the ever-deepening dusk, now moving as silently as they could manage. Even the goblin toddlers were quiet as they walked towards the promised land.

They skirted the grounds of the chateau and moved on through the woods in the direction of the railhead. A while later there came a crushed-gravel whisper at Moist's elbow from Of the Twilight the Darkness.

'I sending out some of swifter lads to scout ahead. Something not right at railhead. Couldn't get close enough to see but says at least dozen dwarfs in the woods up there, maybe more. Could hear the buggers clanging. They trying to be surreptitious, but dwarfs has not first idea of surreption. It's all been hammer and tongues to dwarfs. Could try go round 'em – but the buggers might try go round us same time. Best, I say, to deal with bogeys today, right? No worry, some these lobster lads know how to fight and they proud you leading them . . . ain't you!'

It wasn't a question, it was a demand. Moist was horribly aware of the whole refugee group clustered around him, their unprepossessing faces full of expectation and miscellaneous fragments of food. There were little ones, some no more than babes in arms. Moist could feel the pressure of their hope

---

* There was no point in speculating on what else they could have. Just the thought turned Moist's stomach.

which, alas, he knew was unfounded and probably misplaced. He was no leader. Not like Commander Vimes. But what would Of the Twilight the Darkness do if he just ran away? He could outrun any dwarf, make it back to the chateau . . . but could he outrun a goblin . . . ?

He shivered and shoved that thought to the very back of his mind just as a small goblin woman came up to him.

'Go into battle with nice cuppa tea!' she said. 'Special goblin tea! Very good for you! Boiled in sheep bladder! Excellent when always having to run! Got herbs! You drink! You drink *now*! Ain't nothing like a nice cuppa tea. Medicinal it is!'

Of the Twilight the Darkness handed Moist a large goblin club.

'Many, many ways to die today,' he said, with devastating humour. 'Trust elderly goblin, this one very much the best, hang! We hang together.'

Moist understood that last rather unfortunate suggestion. It was the traditional goblin-to-goblin greeting, as in, hang together or hang separately. He swigged the cold tea, which had a harmless accent of hazelnuts with a soupçon of wool, expecting at any moment either to be poisoned or to throw up. In fact, it was . . . pleasant and it also felt quite nourishing. If there were snails in it, like the wine, then, well, viva escargot! Although the secret ingredient, he was quite sure, was likely to be avec.

The potion appeared to work because a few moments later he felt ready for *anything*, full of beans, or possibly full of avec. Why, in the face of all the gods, had he been so apprehensive when there was absolutely nothing to be frightened of, oh dear no!

This cheerful state of mind continued right up until the moment they spotted the red lights of the railhead shining out like a beacon through the surrounding woodlands. Leaving the most elderly goblins with the twigs* hiding in the undergrowth as only goblins could hide, Moist and the rest crept forward.

The young men in the travelling work gang had crafted themselves cosy little shacks covered with oilskin. These were extremely portable and always a place where a friendly face could be certain of a hot drink, stirred with a spanner, of course. And if no gamekeepers were known to be about, a wild avec and rabbit stew might also be available for an al fresco meal.

Indeed, the pot of stew still bubbling over the embers of the camp fire smelled as good as any Moist remembered. He had expected to see the young lads he had met only that morning, cheerfully tucking in after a hard day's work. He had not expected to see corpses . . . but corpses were what he found. By the glow of the fire and the pale light of the lanterns, he could see that the workers had many things that could usefully have been employed as a weapon, but they had evidently been taken unawares. It had been a terrible encounter and most certainly they had lost. A quick assay of body parts indicated that there had been nine of them, cut down while having their meal outside their makeshift bothy.

* Any young goblin is thought of as being a twig.

Of the Twilight the Darkness was instantly on the case, sniffing the corpses and the ground.

'The damn dwarfs have been here, oh yes, can smell the naaaasty buggers! But some of them still here,' he added quickly, pointing to a small piece of woodland in the distance and dropping his voice to a whisper. 'Hiding in the wood' – *sniff* – 'over there' – *sniff* – 'several, one injured.' His beady goblin eye was glittering and Moist ... Moist had a sudden sensation of being on fire.

'Please,' he managed to say, 'please, tell me, what is the goblin for "Charge!"?'

Much, much later, Moist remembered that he had heard the goblin say at least the beginning of the word and then the whole world was a crimson haze full of shouting and the dark fog of war. He felt his arms and legs going about their terrible business, especially his arms, and he was aware of noises, *unpleasant* noises, cracking noises, splatting noises, but they came as a kind of incoherent memory, as did the screams ... Little parcels of recollection bobbing up and down like the bubbles in a bottle of home-made ginger beer, coming and going and never staying long enough to mean anything. But the bubbles were gradually drifting away now and, when he came to what was left of his senses, he was lying with his back up against a tree.

The railhead camp fire had been relit and to Moist's bemused amazement there were the signs of dawn on the horizon – but hadn't they been in this place for only a couple of minutes? Of the Twilight the Darkness was sitting on a lump of wood near by, smoking a pipe and occasionally blowing smoke rings into the early blue sky. It was a sight that a painter would love to paint, were it not necessary to paint it in various shades of blood, and, to do justice to the scene, with several tubes of gore and a splash of whatever colour you needed for guts. Moist's memory of the night before was now strewn with corpses.

'Well now, ain't you a dark horse, Mister Dripping!' grinned the goblin. 'Who ever would thought it? Tell you this: you ain't half going to be sore later. You done a man's job! Almost goblin job! Three! Count 'em! Well, count bits of 'em and work it out, but three dwarf crack fighters smash down like skittles. Two of 'em wearing first-class micromail armour, assassin grade, worth mint. Pillage. Here, take this as souvenir to show Miss Adora Belle. Good on mantelpiece!'

The goblin threw over what Moist had thought was a lump of wood and which he could now see was the head of a dwarf, still inside its helmet.

'That's right! Get it out of system! Throw it up, throw it up and throw it up again. Very good for tubes, does world of good. Better out than in.'

Moist staggered to his feet and said, through the winding mists, 'I couldn't have killed three dwarfs! I'm no fighter! Never! It plays havoc with your shoes.'

'Reckon dwarfs would disagree. Mind you, I show the one over there bit of goblin disapproval, as you may say! Especially when I got him on ground. Most time, everybody keep out of your way, just in case. You was getting a bit . . . *indiscriminate*, oh yeees. Still, no harms done.'

'No harm done?' Moist wailed. 'I just killed three dwarfs! Wouldn't you say that counts as a little harm?'

'Was fair fight, Mister Slightly Damp. One against many, like in best anecdote. Tell you already, most us lads climbing trees to get away from *you*. And you not a fighter. You said this, we all hear.'

'It was that drink! That's what it was! You've filled me full of goblin rot-gut! Who knows what it's done to me!'

'Me?' said Of the Twilight the Darkness, trying to look hurt. 'I keep you alive so you will see your very nice lady, who is always kind to goblins. Take from me, Mister Sopping, that drink just open up what's there already.'

'And what was here, may I ask?'

'Rage, Mister Dripping. You let something off leash. Now you can help us clean bloody mess and get us out of here.'

Moist looked at what remained of the railway workers who had just been doing their job, being no threat to anybody. Simple men who knew nothing whatsoever about politics and had wives and children and were now lying dead for a quarrel they had nothing to do with, and the rage swelled up again, almost lifting him off the ground. They hadn't deserved it, nor had those goblins whose fallen corpses he now saw here and there across the battlefield.

Of the Twilight the Darkness was staring at him and said, 'Amazing, what things we learn, that goblins can be people and you, Mister Damp, has a heart and crying because of death of men you don't know. World is full of miracle. Maybe I will see you singing in choir.'

In the misty light of morning Moist stared at the grinning goblin: as evil-looking as anything in a picture book that was designed to give the little kiddies all the nightmares they would ever need, and yet reading him a lecture on morality.

'What *are* you?' he asked. 'I've been listening to you for days, and you look like a goblin, no doubt about that, but every so often you come out with something I wouldn't expect to hear from a goblin. No offence meant, but you are a smart one.'

The goblin relit his pipe, which made him somehow more human, and said carefully, 'Are you saying goblins not ever clever, Mister Lipwig? Goblins not ever brave? Goblins not ever learn? Me, finest learner. All things to all men and all goblins.'

Moist looked at the little pile of micromail armour. It was treasure and a half. Light and strong. And easy to carry. And worth a fortune, lying there on the damp grass. He looked into the goblin's eyes.

'All yours, Mister Lipwig. To the victor the spoils,' Of the Twilight the Darkness said cheerfully.

'No. They can have it,' said Moist, indicating the Quirmian goblins.

'Don't need it,' said the goblin. 'Take your spoils, Mister Lipwig. You never know when useful.'

Moist looked at what remained of the dwarf fighters and thought, where's Mr Chriek when you need him? And that thought prompted another: a reliable witness was essential. He asked Of the Twilight the Darkness to fetch the Marquis or any of his workers from the chateau, with an iconograph if they had one. 'We need people to know about this.'

After the Marquis, trailed by goggling servants, had inspected the scene, exclaimed his horror, organized the taking of iconographs, and departed back to the chateau, promising to send the news by clacks at once, the decencies could be attended to.

The corpses of the railway workers and goblins who had fallen in the battle were carefully, even reverentially, placed on to the handcar. A few of the goblins disappeared into the scenery and returned with wild flowers to put on the bodies. It was one of those little observations that subtly turned Moist's universe around. Goblins believing that those who fell in battle had paid their dues.

After the solemn ceremony was over, the goblins took turns at pumping the lever of the handcar as Moist, the goblin band and their sad cargo headed back slowly along the track to the border, where they stopped to send out their own clacks. Moist arranged with the border guard for the bodies to be shrouded and put in a cold place until someone was sent to pick them up.

One of the guards took umbrage that the dead goblins were being left alongside the bodies of what he called 'real people'. And so Moist had a rather pointed little chat with him, after which the man was much better informed, although bleeding slightly from his nose. The memory of oh so many little bones hadn't had enough time to be forgotten. And perhaps some of the potion was still alive inside Moist. It was that kind of day.

That done, Moist looked at the ribbon of goblins trailing behind him and then looked up at the sign beside the Quirm turnpike which told the world that it was the well-known 'Fat Marie's'.

There could be no mistake about how the proprietor got her name and like so many roadside eateries she sold hot food quickly and served reasonable coffee to travellers and that was that. Her clientele hadn't even heard of cuisine, they just needed surety of carbohydrate and grease. However, she proved somewhat dubious about feeding goblins, and said, 'I might lose my regulars if I let them lot in.'

And once again Moist had to explain the facts of life, making it clear that refusing to serve goblins would very soon lead to her not feeding anyone else at all once Lord Vetinari had been informed. Fat Marie's was on Ankh-Morpork land and Vetinari was strict.

'After all,' Moist said, 'they'll sit outside, they really don't like rooms, and I'm paying, okay?'

Suitably chastened, Fat Marie shovelled out rather bad fish and chips and a fried slice to every goblin and was amazed at how fast they ate, especially the fried slice. That was one thing about the goblins, they weren't fussy.

After their meal, Moist arranged for the goblins to travel on to Harry's compound in the freight trucks of the utility engine that serviced the railhead, went to find the golem horse, still obediently rolling and galloping in the meadow, and headed back towards the city.

*　*　*

Harry King was close to incandescent at the best of times, but the state of mind he was in when he heard the news of the massacre could only be described as volcanic: one of those slumbering volcanoes that suddenly go off pop and the calm sea is instantly awash with dirty pumice and surprised people in togas. Moist tried to calm him down, but that was like trying to put a cap on a geyser, and you can't do that, especially not to a geezer like Harry King. Then the explosion became tears, the bubbling and sticky tears of a hard man who would never want anybody to see him cry.

Learning that Moist himself had got rid of a few of the dwarfs responsible helped, but even so Harry continued to dribble snot on to a very expensive tie while calling down the wrath of the gods on to the remains of the culprits, with a footnote that the gods had better get to them before Harry's curses did.

Moist offered to tell the workers' next of kin, but Harry declared that he would do the job himself. He set off on this doleful task immediately, leaving Moist with nothing to do but collect Of the Twilight the Darkness and the band of Quirmian goblins who had meanwhile arrived at the compound and were being entertained by Billy Slick and his grandmother.

When he arrived home in Scoone Avenue, Adora Belle opened the door herself. Moist, as ever, was impressed by her *sang froid* as she surveyed the motley group of Quirmian goblins he had in his wake. 'So good to see you again, Spike,' he said. 'I've brought you some little presents. Say it with goblins, as you might say.'

'How many are there, do you think?' she enquired.

'Two hundred or more,' said Moist. 'I haven't really been counting.'

'I suggest that Of the Twilight the Darkness takes them over to the Tump Tower where there's enough room in the basement for them to sleep.'

'You don't mind?'

'Of course not. Quite a lot of my best goblins are taking holidays to the Shires and elsewhere. We're very short. Well done, you!'

As soon as Moist had seen the goblins on their way, the Ankh-Morpork Watch metaphorically felt his collar. As collars go, Moist's was expensive, but a little the worse for wear after the fight with the dwarfs.

In this case, the hand doing the feeling belonged to Captain Angua, who asked him to accompany her to the Yard in tones that did not allow for an argument.

Once ensconced in an interview room, she took down his statement about the massacre in a deliberately methodical way, asking pointed questions, which was to say pointed at Moist.

'So you, Mister von Lipwig, took down a bunch of dwarf terrorists with the help of a number of goblins, yes? You must like goblins, then?'

'Yes, and so does Commander Vimes, captain,' Moist snapped. 'Tell me, where is Chuckles today?'

It was worth it to see the captain grimace; if you looked carefully you could see the outline of the fangs. It was a risky move, but he had a reputation to live down and cheeking the Watch was a pastime he cherished and was very good at. They were altogether too stuffy and Captain Angua, try as she might, looked stunning in her uniform, especially when she was angry.

'With the Patrician,' she growled. 'An attack on the railway is an attack on Ankh-Morpork. With delvers involved there is a possible connection with the attacks on the clacks. All of this needs to be investigated and it would have been *helpful* if one of the perpetrators had been left alive and available for interrogation.'

Moist almost choked, saying, 'Captain, when a lot of unpleasant people are trying to kill you, it's hard to remember that leaving one of them alive might be a spiffy idea. You have other things on your mind such as, maybe, not dying yourself. If it's any help, I think you'll find that the Marquis des Aix en Pains will by now have sent iconographs of the dwarfs who did this. The Marquis is a decent bloke and generally helpful and keen to have the railway, so I'm certain that you'll get your evidence.'

And as he thought that, mischief rose in Moist's mind and he said, 'And I know that you yourself can travel very fast, captain. They might still be fresh if you hurry.'

This time it was not a black look that Moist got. It was a look that said patience was about to crack.

Fortunately, the door opened just at the right time and Commander Vimes entered, his expression grim.

'Ah, Mister Lipwig, please follow me to my office, if you'd be so good. I always know when you're in the building.' He nodded at the simmering Angua and said, 'I'll deal with Mister von Lipwig, captain.'

Moist was unsure about how much Commander Vimes actually disliked him. After all, the man was so straight that you could use him as a pencil, whilst Moist, on the other hand, despite the success of the Post Office and the Royal Bank and even the wonderful new Mint, was still seen by Vimes and many others as bent as an old spoon and most certainly up to no good.

'Would you like some coffee?' Commander Vimes asked as they entered his office. 'The pot downstairs is *always* on and it doesn't always taste of mud.' He opened the door again and shouted down, 'Two coffees up here, please, Cheery, one black, and you can empty the sugar bowl into mine.'

Moist was somewhat disorientated, because Vimes was acting in a way that, if looked at forensically, might even have been somewhere within the circumference of friendly, rather like, he supposed, an alligator yawning. The commander was now back in his chair, and, yes, *smiling*.

The truth was that between Moist von Lipwig and Commander Vimes there was a certain . . . what they politely called a difference of opinion. Sam Vimes did *not* live in the same world as Moist von Lipwig. Did the man ever laugh, he wondered – the commander must have done something funny at some time. Probably he'd laughed at somebody falling over a cliff or suchlike.

At which point, to his surprise, Commander Vimes

cleared his throat and said slowly, like a man essaying something unfamiliar, 'Mister von Lipwig, it may be the case in recent years that I've given you the opinion that I consider you a cheat and a fraud and no better than a worm. However, the fact that you threw yourself in front of that train to save two kiddies suggests to me that the leopard can change his shorts.

'Theoretically, I'll be dressing you down for sorting out the murderous dwarfs involved in this latest atrocity and telling you that you should leave that sort of thing to the damn Watch. But I'm not stupid and I'm prepared to give credit where credit is due. The delvers are a vicious lot, a type of vermin that I'd very much have liked to see dance to Mister Trooper's tune just to show them how justice should be done. But knowing that at least some of the buggers are out of the way must suffice for now. So, on a personal note, which I'll certainly deny if you repeat this to *anyone*: Well done.'

And at this Vimes waggled, yes, waggled a finger, and in tones of a funeral bell and much louder said, '*Don't do it again!* That was an official reprimand, you understand, Mister Lipwig? And *this* is my hand.'

To Moist's amazement Vimes walked around the table and gave him the hardest handshake he had ever had. It was like shaking hands with a boxing glove full of walnuts. Nothing actually broke and there was no blood and Vimes hadn't even tried to squeeze, so it appeared to Moist that what had just been perpetrated must be Commander Vimes's everyday handshake. He decided it was probably the commander being a man who didn't believe in half measures.

And now the commander looked sombre, saying, 'If I were you, Mister von Lipwig, I'd make certain that my wife spent a lot of time out of the way in clacks towers for a while and I'd ask the Watch to keep an eye on my property. Those wretched delvers will stop at nothing, and I mean no offence when I say I'm surprised that you managed to take the bastards down.' He lowered his voice, almost to a whisper, and said, 'What did it feel like, son?'

There was an expression in Vimes's eyes that told Moist that now, if ever, it was time for the truth and so he too lowered his voice and said, 'To tell you the truth, commander, I had some unexpected back-up. You wouldn't believe it.'

And amazingly, Vimes's smile broadened and he said, 'Actually, Mister Lipwig, I just might. I know a little something of fighting dirty in the dark, don't I just. It was under Koom Valley a few years back and I had some back-up too, and I don't think I want to know where it came from. Just be careful now. The grags clearly have your number. You'd better go and see Vetinari, but I'm very glad we've had this little chat.'

'Why d'you think I'm going to see Vetinari next?'

'I *know*, because I've just come from the palace. He was sending for you and I asked his lordship if I could get a crack at you first.'

Moist walked to the door, turned round and said simply, 'Thank you, Commander.'

Outside on Lower Broadway, Moist hailed a one-troll

trolley bus* and he was not pleased when a dwarf jumped into the pannier beside him. He braced himself for a blow, but the dwarf just smiled at him.

'Mister Lipwig, how pleased I am to see you. I'd appreciate a moment of your time.'

'Look,' said Moist, 'I'm a *very* busy man with a great deal to do, and I'm expected at the palace.'

'The palace? Allow me.'

And the dwarf flipped the correct fare to said troll and gave him the destination in the troll's own language, much to the amazement of the troll. Oh my, thought Moist. Ankh-Morpork, the melting pot of the world, which occasionally runs foul of lumps that don't melt.

Moist looked down at the dwarf which was, of course, inevitable. He seemed to be more, well, streamlined than your traditional dwarf, although smiling in a confrontational sort of way: not unpleasantly, but with a kind of inner dedication to the smile. He realized that the dwarf reminded him of something . . . oh dear, what was its name? Oh, yes, a gyroscope, which he'd seen demonstrated in Unseen University's High Energy Magic building. In short, and of course this person *was* a dwarf, he did have the feel of a gyroscope about him, something spinning around an undeclared centre. The insight built itself in a matter of seconds, at the end of which, instead of insisting that his unwanted

---

* Which consists of a troll with a comfortable pannier on either side that can carry up to four people.

fellow passenger got out, Moist was paying a lot of attention to the smart little figure.

'Who are you?' he asked.

'I am merely a messenger,' replied the dwarf. 'I am here to tell you something that you cannot ignore. In a sacred place near Koom Valley your name is on the list of people to be summarily executed, *but* do not fret unduly, because—'

'Er, you mean I should just simply fret in a duly kind of way, then? So what the hell is that supposed to mean?'

The annoyingly grave face of the dwarf, with its curious essence of smile, was irking Moist, and the dwarf said, 'Well, Mister Lipwig, you are in a queue behind Lord Vetinari and Commander Vimes and, of course, so are a very large number of dwarfs considered to be un-dwarfish. It is a tiny war at the moment, it's burning underground like an abandoned coal measure, waiting to break out in unexpected places and soon, I suspect, to a place containing yourself.'

'Look,' said Moist, 'it may have escaped your notice, but I am not and never have been a dwarf, okay? I don't have a beard and I can't walk under a table. Human, you see?'

The composure of the dwarf was unshakeable, just like his smile, which now broadened a little as he said, 'You may not be a dwarf, my friend, but you are con- sidered a vector, a symbol of all that is opposed to real dwarfishness, a carrier, if you like, and also a central figure in a city that some dwarfs would love to see burned to the ground. The clacks were just the start.

Your railway will not succeed in tempting dwarfs from the true path of Tak. The commander and Lord Vetinari are surrounded by people who carry a large variety of useful weapons. You don't, though, do you, Mister Lipwig? You are not a warrior, you are a target, admittedly a remarkable and ingenious one. I suggest you remember how Albert Spangler watched his back and, above all, do not go into dark places.'

The dwarf shook his head and added, 'You have been warned, sir. I understand you have been known to say that a life without danger is a life not worth living, and frankly all I can say is, good luck with that. Tak does not require that you think of him, but he does require that you think, and I suspect that Tak will be requiring your services in the near future. There are things happening, political things, that you know nothing of, but Tak knows where to find you when Tak needs you.'

And with that the dwarf smiled, jumped out of the pannier and ran off at speed before Moist could react.

Taken by surprise, Moist continued the journey to the palace with his head in a whirl. Until the massacre at the railhead, he hadn't been doing *anything wrong*! Just trying to help everybody! And now he was apparently a target because he represented the wicked ways of Ankh-Morpork . . . which was not only unfair, but also untrue. Well, probably untrue, well, at least a bit. He assumed that the grags were hurt about the fact that he had just killed some of their number, even though it had been a fair fight. Well, probably fair and, anyway, they'd got what they deserved. Moist had

hardly done anything actually truly *wicked* in his life*
and now his new cleaned-up, hard-working, upstanding citizen persona was at risk.

Moist was seething by the time he arrived at the
Oblong Office.

'It seems I'm a damn target,' he began, 'and you knew
it, sir!'

In the following silence Lord Vetinari's head did not
move until he folded his newspaper. 'I assume the grags
found you, yes, Mister Lipwig? I thought you knew
that, along with myself, Drumknott, Commander
Vimes and many others, you are on what I believe is
called a hit list drawn up by radical grags. But if I were
you I wouldn't worry. After all, a life without danger is
a life not worth living, eh, Mister Lipwig?'

And Moist said, 'Well, yes, but what about Adora
Belle?'

'Oh yes, Mister Lipwig, I told her last week.'

'What! She didn't tell me!'

'I believe she wanted to surprise you, Mister Lipwig.
She knows how much you like surprises and you do
enjoy a quantum of frisson, she told me.'

Moist almost squealed, 'But you know I'm no
fighter!'

'Really, Mister Lipwig? But I already have reports

* Apart from occasionally going with a few clients down to the Pink
PussyCat Club to *appear* to have a good time and stick money down the
garters of the gyrating young ladies, which really was hardly evil at all in
the light of early-onset middle age, just rather sad, although extremely
enjoyable at the time and a death warrant if Adora Belle ever found out.

that say otherwise: thrilling tales of derring-do and, believe me, nothing was said about derring-don't.'

Moist, a long-time student of Vetinari and his moods, knew that you could never be sure of what he was thinking. But now the Patrician seemed carved out of stone, like a statue.

'Mister Lipwig, you know what they say about dwarfs?'

Moist looked blank. 'Very small people?'

'"Two dwarfs is an argument, three dwarfs is a war", Mister Lipwig. It's squabble, squabble, squabble. It's built into their culture. And in the squabbling, the grags hide and poison.

'The Koom Valley Accord, which I helped to broker with the Low King and Diamond King of Trolls, was hailed around the world as a fresh hope for the future. But now some of the senior dwarfs appear to be in thrall to a faction of the grags who are bent on destruction. Differences of opinion are one thing, but this sort of atrocity cannot be borne. Diamond King of Trolls and I are putting pressure on the Low King and we have every expectation he will deal with the matter.

'It has gone too far, Mister Lipwig. Once upon a time the grags were bold dwarfs who checked the mines for firedamp, hence the heavy clothing. Of course that gave them status but, in truth, they were just plucky miners . . . expert at mining, perhaps, but certainly not skilled in politics and thinking. After all, you don't negotiate with a lump of rock. With people, you negotiate all the time. The Low King knows it. The grags know it but don't like it.

'I am a tyrant and, if I say so myself, good at it, but I understand the ways of people and the way of the world. Everything is mutable. Nothing is unchangeable. A little give and a little take and a little negotiation, and suddenly the balance of the world is back on track again; that is what politics is for. But the politics of the grags consists only of "Do what you are told, we know best." And I find that rather tedious.'

'And I find it tedious when your men wake me up by prodding me,' said Moist.

'Really, is that all?' said Vetinari. 'I shall tell them not to prod too much in future.' He smiled and said, 'Mister Lipwig, Commander Vimes is a decent man and he spends much of his time telling people what to do and that is how the Watch works. It's not an area where freelancing is allowed. Things have to be seen to be done, in the proper manner. There is indeed a difference between tyranny and running a police force. There must be rules that everyone understands. Do you understand, Mister Lipwig?'

The Patrician stared at Moist, who said, 'Yes, I understand. The commander is Vetinari's terrier and I—'

'You, Mister Lipwig, are *useful* and a conduit for serendipity. For example, I understand you have just blessed us with more goblins at a time when we need them. Apart from that, I am told by Sydney, the head ostler, that one of our golem horses arrived here declaring "Give me livery or give me death". We had been given to understand that golem horses do not talk, but it would appear, Mister Lipwig, that you have introduced that one to the delights of speech. I am impressed.'

Lord Vetinari's smile was widening. 'What a little bundle of joy you are, Mister Lipwig.' He sighed and continued, 'To think I once fed you to Mister Trooper's capable hands. He often asks after your wellbeing. You know he never forgets a neck. Now off you go, Mister Lipwig . . . your audience needs you.'

The Low King's bellow of rage and betrayal when the news of the massacre at the railhead arrived echoed around the state quarters and into every corner of the great cavern. Bats dropped out of the ceiling, in the bakeries the dough refused to rise, and the silver on the decorative weaponry tarnished.

Rhys Rhysson sat down heavily on the Scone of Stone and waved the clacks flimsy he had just received.

'Dwarfs have killed railway workers!' he shouted. 'Ordinary men, going about their business in an enterprise that would be useful to dwarfs as well as humans.' The King looked almost in tears and thumped a fist into the palm of his hand. 'This after the clacks towers!' he said, with a groan of loss. 'This is a message from Diamond King of Trolls and he is trying not to upset me, but I think he feels sorry for me.'

He raised his voice and shouted, 'And this is the king of the trolls, our one-time arch enemy, but now a personal friend of mine! What will *he* think about the trustworthiness of dwarfs now? Thanks to intelligence gathered by the Ankh-Morpork Watch, including our own Cheery Littlebottom, we have the names of the idiots who did the deed. And now I know exactly who is behind it all.'

He paused and glared at the growing crowd. 'Where is Ardent? Bring him to me at once! I'll show him what his idiotic ranting has caused! I want him brought here in chains if possible. Good heavens, Tak gave us the Koom Valley Accord and now the little blister is trying to break it.'

The crowd was bigger now and the voice of the King was even louder. 'I repeat, I want him here. Now. Today. No excuses. No second chances. No redemption. Let it be known that the King will not let the benefits of the Koom Valley Accord be turned to dust by adventurers who believe that the past is still with us and belongs to them. All I see is its sterile echo.

'And I notice these days talk against goblins who are working in the human industries, such as the new railway and the clacks. I hear a lot of complaints that it is taking work from us dwarfs, but why is that? Because goblins learn quickly, work hard and are glad to be in Ankh-Morpork! And the dwarfs? We have factions that bring us down with every flaming tower . . . Who would trust us after that? Remember, if Tak teaches us anything, he teaches us to be tolerant of all sapient shapes. Let me tell you, the world changes with every generation and if we don't learn to surf on the tide then we will be smashed on the rocks.'

By the Low King's side, Bashfull Bashfullsson picked up the theme. He looked around at the assembled dwarfs and spoke.

'Tak did not expect the stone to have life, but when

it did, he smiled upon it, saying "*All Things Strive*".
Glaring at the onlookers, Bashfullsson continued,
'Time and again the last testament of Tak has been
stolen in a pathetic attempt to kill the nascent future at
birth and this is not only an untruth, it is a blasphemy!
Tak even finds it in his heart to suffer the Nac Mac
Feegles, possibly for their entertainment value, but I
wonder if he will continue to tolerate *us* . . . He must
look at us now with sorrow, which I hope will not turn
into rage. Surely the patience of Tak must find some
limitations somewhere.'

Bashfullsson bowed to the Low King and said, 'I am
your servant, your majesty. What would you have of
me?'

The King, still red in the face, said, 'I won't have you
bow to me, my friend, I rather think I should bow to
you. Your words are wise as ever and will be proclaimed
in every mine.'

At this point a dwarf arrived in the chamber at a run
and whispered something to the Low King's loyal
secretary, Aeron, who looked sombre.

'I regret to report, sire, that Ardent and his friends
seem to have disappeared.'

'So, the stupid troublemaker has run away,' hissed
the Low King in barely suppressed fury. He raised his
voice and announced to the crowd, 'They are banished.
All of them. No doubt the cowards will find a place to
hide, but anyone who helps them will be treated as
traitors, not to me but to the Scone.'

In the privacy of the robing room a little while later, the

King was pacing up and down when Aeron arrived with the latest report.

'They've caught some of the small fry, but the main players have indeed got away.' As he mentioned a couple of names, Rhys Rhysson's face went as cold as marble. Aeron placed a calming hand on his shoulder and continued, 'Albrecht and the folk of his mines are on your side, though many of the others appear to be wavering.'

'Wavering? That's not good enough. I need their full commitment,' said the King.

His secretary smiled. 'You'll get it, I'm sure. There may be some rogue elements still to be mopped up but we'll get them soon. But do be careful, Rhys, I can see this is taking a lot out of you and that's not good. And you do have another card to play.'

The King shook his head. 'Not yet, but perhaps some time soon, at a point of my choosing. I just have to find the moment.'

Aeron smiled again. And then there was the sound of a kiss.

The dwarf vandal had a stroke of luck. There was Engine One, right below him, the one they called Iron Girder, and there was no time to waste. He was an expert, and cunning, and the grags would pay handsomely if even one wretched locomotive was destroyed.

He dropped down silently from the roof and landed just behind the prestigious engine. It was a good time to throw a monkey wrench in the gears . . . There were guards, he knew, but they were stupid and sluggish and tonight they were on secondment and patrolling a long way away. He had checked and double-checked. And so he soundlessly approached the locomotive, alone in her cavernous shed.

There were so many things you could do to kill a railway engine and he had imagined them all. And so in the dark, ready to climb up again, out of the skylight, he unrolled his bag of implements, all carefully wrapped in hide so they didn't clink or rattle, and stepped up purposefully on to the footplate of Iron Girder . . .

. . . and in the gloom the locomotive spat live steam, instantly filling the air with a pink fog . . .

The dwarf waited, unable to move, and a sombre voice said, PLEASE DO NOT PANIC. YOU ARE MERELY DEAD.

The vandal stared at the skeletal figure, managed to get himself in order and said to Death, 'Oh . . . I don't regret it, you know. I was doing the work of Tak, who will now welcome me into paradise with open arms!'

For a person who didn't have a larynx Death made a good try at clearing his throat. WELL, YOU CAN HOPE, BUT CONSIDERING WHAT YOU INTENDED, IF I WERE YOU I WOULD START HOPING HARDER RIGHT NOW AND, PERHAPS, VERY QUICKLY INDEED. Death continued, in tones as dry as granite, TAK MIGHT INDEED BE GENTLE. STRIVE AS YOU HAVE NEVER STRIVEN. YES, TAK MIGHT BE GENTLE, OR . . .

The vandal listened to the sound of silence, the sound like a bell with, alas, no clapper, but finally the dreadful silence ended in . . . NOT.

Iron Girder had screamed the shrill whistling scream of

a lady in distress that had cut through the air like a knife, and by the time Corporal Nobby Nobbs and Sergeant Colon reached the shed, running extremely carefully and precisely,* all they found besides Iron Girder was some warm dampness, vaguely pink, a tool roll and a few fragments of bone.

'It looks like the locomotive fought back!' said Nobby. 'I know what this is, sarge. It's eldritch – uncanny, you could say.'

Fred Colon stepped forward and said, 'It don't look oblong to me, Nobby. Look at this crowbar and tool roll . . . You can't tell me that the engine lies awake at night like an old biddy keeping a poker beside her bed to fight off burglars. I reckon she was being coy. Live steam! It's a good job me and you were able to scare away all the other assailants!'

'And they was *very* heavily armed,' said Nobby, speaking very deliberately, to make things absolutely clear, 'but they didn't have the spunk to face us, that's what it was.'

Water was dripping from the stout girders high up in the shed. Colon looked around and said, 'Hey, Nobby, what's that white thing up there embedded in the roof?'

Nobby squinted and said, 'Er, it looks like half a skull if you want my opinion, sarge, and it's still steaming.'

In the distance were sounds of thudding feet as the

---

* Colon and Nobby had lived a long time in a dangerous occupation and they knew how not to be dead. To wit, by arriving when the bad guys had got away.

golem guards came at speed and quickly spread out.

Nobby raised his voice and said, 'We'd better tell them that the others'll be ten mile away by now, sarge, at the speed they were going, and I think old Vimesy might give us a day off in lieu for this night's work.'

'But look,' said Colon. 'We've been patrolling past that locomotive time and time again and nothing has happened to us.'

'We weren't proposing to smash her up, now, were we, sarge?'

'What? Are you saying Iron Girder knows who her friends are? Do me a favour . . . she's only a lump of old metal.' And in the silence something made a little clinking noise. Colon and Nobby held their breath.

'Wonderful machine, though, ain't she, Nobby! Look at those beautiful smooth lines!'

There was another pause as breaths continued to be held and Nobby said, 'Well, the golems are here now, sarge, and it's the end of our shift. I'll write a fulsome report as soon as we get back to the yard and that reminds me, you've got to give me my pencil back.'

The two of them perambulated away at impressive speed and for a while Iron Girder was alone; and then there was a very small sound that appeared to be half whistle and half giggle.

Sooner or later everything to do with the railway passed across Moist's desk and generally he hastened it all along its way. Today he was looking across the paperwork at a clearly embarrassed Dick Simnel.

'Now come on, Dick, you tell me what you think

happened last night. It seems as if the grags were setting about to put more than a dent in Iron Girder. This could be connected with the attack on the railhead, but there were some . . . significant differences. I expect there are a lot of ways of putting a locomotive out of commission, but the Watch was on the scene within minutes and according to them *she* fought back and got one of the murderous band. I know the two watchmen of old and every fight they have is always against much bigger forces, at least that's what they say if no one else is around, but it does seem that she got her retribution in first, you might say, and boiled him. They're still mopping the floor. How do you think that happened, Dick? Was it magic of some sort?'

Simnel blushed and said, 'Mister Lipwig, I'm an engineer. I don't believe in magic, but I'm wondering right now whether magic believes in Iron Girder. Every day when I come into work there're the train spotters, always there, and now they've got little sheds of their own . . . Have you noticed? They almost know more about 'er than I do, I tell thee, and I look at t'people who're still taking rides, I look at their faces and they're not the faces of engineers, they're more like the faces of people going to church, and so I wonder what's 'appening. No, I can't tell you how Iron Girder killed the dwarf who was trying to kill her and why she's never done it while everyday folk are around. That looks like thinking to me and I don't know how she thinks.'

Dick was glowing red now and Moist felt sorry for the engineer who lived in a world where things did what they were told, all the little numbers adding up, all the calculations dancing to the rattle of the sliding rule just as they should. But now he was in a conceptual world where the authority of that sliding rule held no sway.

Dick looked desperately at Moist and said, 'Do you think it possible that an engine like Iron Girder has a . . . soul?'

Oh, dear, thought Moist, he's really having problems here. Out loud he said, 'Well, I see you move your hands over her once she's stopped and it seems to me that you're petting her, and I notice that all the other drivers do that too, and although the Flyers have numbers I notice that the drivers give them names and even talk to them – in expletives, occasionally, but nevertheless they're talking to a mechanical thing. I do wonder if life is catching somehow, because I also notice that every time people go for joyrides on Iron Girder they pat her too and they would swear they don't know why. But what do *you* think?'

'Ee, I know what you mean. In the early days when I were just getting started I remember I spoke to Iron Girder all t'time and shouted often enough and occasionally swore as well, especially if she were truculent. Aye, you might have a point. There's a lot of me in her; a lot of me blood and buckets of me sweat and many, many tears. I've lost the end of one thumb to her and most of my fingernails are blue and I suppose, when you think about it, there really is a lot of her in me.'

He looked ashamed when he said that and so Moist quickly jumped in with, 'I think you're right, Dick, it's one of those times when you have to stop thinking about how and why and just remember that whatever's happening is working and it just might not work if anyone gets smart and tries to find the soul of what's happening. There are times when a sliding rule just doesn't cut the mustard and if I was you this morning I'd get her all sleek and shiny and let her *see* her worshippers and *feel* their worship. They're yearning for something and I don't know what it is, so drink up the gravy and don't spoil things with too much thinking or too much worrying either. And I promise you I won't mention a word of this conversation to anyone.'

And then he brightened up and said, 'Come on, Dick, life is good! Has your sliding rule allowed you to come to an arrangement with Miss Emily?'

Simnel blushed. 'Aye, we've been doing some talking, mostly about Iron Girder, and her mam's letting me come to tea wi' 'er tomorrow.'

'In that case, I suggest you get yourself a new shirt . . . you know, one that isn't greasy, and clean your boots and your nails and everything else, and now you're getting loaded up with money you must get yourself a sharp new suit. I know a few places that'd give you a good deal.' He sniffed and added, 'And have a bath, why don't you, for the sake of Miss Emily.'

Dick blushed further and grinned. 'Right you are, Mister Lipwig. I wish I could be deb on air like you are.'

'It's easy, Dick, you've just got to be yourself. They can't ever take that away from you.'

* * *

And when Moist left his desk for another look at where last night's excitement had taken place, he met Harry King, dressed to the nines and distressed to the maximum.

Harry flourished a bow tie at Moist and said, 'I hate these damn things, I mean, what's the point?' He growled. 'Got another bloody civic thing on tonight, Effie just thrives on them. I told her I'm busy, what with dealing with the railway, but she's determined to make a better man of me. And all this business about what knife and fork you eat from, it's a deliberate puzzle set out to make a simple bloke like me feel like a stranger. Whatever you pick up isn't going to change what the food tastes like, but Effie presses my knee hard if I gets it wrong.

'She wants me to have electrocution lessons, gods be damned, and I'm putting my foot down about that one. Knobs or not, I'm still Harry King and I'm still going to sound like Harry King. And I told Effie that I don't mind giving the money away to orphanages and suchlike – I like to see the faces of the little kiddies light up like daisies – it's the swank I don't like and all the incessant chattering when I could be doing good work in my office. Effie says it's knoblyess obligay, but just because I've got a lot of knobs I don't have to accept it, right? It's a terrible thing when a man can't be himself, knobs or no knobs.'

Fifty miles turnwise of Ankh-Morpork lies the Effing Forest, a source of laughter for some, but nevertheless, throughout the year, full of birdsong and, surprisingly, the occasional logger, as well as the family-run coal mines that are too small for the dwarfs to covet but just about big enough to scratch a living.

On this fine morning in the Wesley family forge, Crucible Wesley was arguing with his brother.

'Okay, you're a blacksmith, granted, but that engine looked complicated to oi. Jed, you're a good smith and a big lad, but I can't see you hammering out a whole locomotive on your own. You need a bit more of the book learning, say oi. You saw those boys at that there compound in the smoke with their sliding rulers, although you couldn't quite work out what them was for.'

The aforesaid Jed, dripping perspiration and stink, looked up from his anvil. 'Look, it's simple, you boils up the water, you boils it up *really* hot, and that drives the pistons and it's them as turns the wheels. There ain't really that much to it, apart from the oiling and the greasing. Oi reckon that stopping it once started'll be the 'ardest thing to do.'

Crucible Wesley, considered by locals as the brains of the outfit, in so far as the outfit had any brains, was nervous about this and went on, 'I know you were Blacksmith of the Year in Scrote three years running and got the silver cup that our mam's so proud of, but oi dunno . . . Oi reckon there's summat more to it'n that. Trade secrets and whatnot.'

Jed appeared to commune with the spirits for a while and then he announced, 'Well, oi've got the boiler half done and that's a fact. And oi reckon that if we takes it slowly there shouldn't be nuffin' to worry about. After all, oi seen steam coming out of Mam's kettle, 'tis only wet air after all.'

He thumped the boiler standing on its makeshift pedestal next to his work bench with one enormous hand.

'Come on, help me outside with this and us'll give it a go ... We can always shut her down if she looks like she's turning on us and oi reckon oi can outsmart a bloody kettle.'

They carried the huge vessel outside, although, truth to tell, Jed proudly picked up most of the weight on his own. His brother watched in admiration and a certain amount of trepidation, or it would have been trepidation had he known the word existed. As it was he could feel sweat trickling down his back. He started edging away backwards and once again he tried to remonstrate with his elder brother.

'Well, oi dunno, Jed, they was doing all those measurements and things like that with levers and suchlike and when it was hissing, it damn well hissed.'

'Yeah, and it cost we a dollar to see it! Don't 'ee worry about a slipping stick ... like I said, oi reckon oi got more brains than a boiler! And if it gives oi any problem then I'll hammer it out into horseshoes. Come on, I'll get the fire going and you can help oi pump the bellows.'

After Crucible had managed to help his brother set the boiler up in the clean open air amongst the trees, he had one last stab at trying to crowbar some sense into the dialogue.

'Oi reckon it's too difficult, otherwise us'd hear about other folk doing it as well.'

But to his dismay this suggestion only served to make his brother even more determined to tame the steam, because the man said, tapping the side of his nose, 'That's because oi reckon they weren't as clever as oi!'

There is something vaguely worrying about the word '*reckon*' that leaves the ear, for many hard to understand reasons, wishing it was something else a little more certain and a little less frightening. And as bad luck would have it, some twenty minutes later an ear was exactly what spiralled down out of the settling steaming fog and through mangled trees that looked as if they had been scythed by dragons, and the birds that were coming down cooked . . .

Moist was, by inclination, a stranger to the concept of two in the morning, a time that happened to other people. He didn't object to a certain amount of early alfresco when he was on the road, especially on the rail road, which was more like camping and therefore fun, but to be awakened in his own bed in the small hours was an abomination. That cried to the heavens for justice, although he did not cry at Sir Harry, who had just arrived in Scoone Avenue with all hell following him.

Crossly the butler rushed to get in front of Sir Harry as etiquette required, but Sir Harry swarmed up the stairs waving a clacks flimsy at anyone he could see, and burst into Moist's bedroom, booming, 'Someone has been buggering around with a steam contraption and has managed to kill two people, including himself, down in the Effing Forest. And you know what? Clacksmen on the Scrote tower spotted the explosion then went out and found the carnage, and you know the clacksmen! The news is already all over the bloody place! And so, apparently, are bits of the poor buggers! Two people dead, Mister Lipwig. The press'll have our guts for garters.'

By this time Moist had managed to get his pants on the right way up. He spluttered, 'But Harry, we aren't doing anything in the Effing Forest at the moment. There's going to be a little branch line that goes to Scrote and that'll be a very good earner, but this is nothing to do with us. Crossly, please get Sir Harry a stiff brandy and a soft chair.'

'Nothing to do with us or not, Moist, you know the press will be round us like flies on a midden.'

Moist said, to the annoyance of Harry, 'Trust me, Harry. Trust me. It wasn't us and I see no reason to worry. I'll deal with the press. I imagine they'll all be going to the Effing place as soon as it gets light, so if you don't mind I'll head there right now and be ahead of the game.'

'It's no bloody game!' Harry boomed.

And over his shoulder, Moist said, 'I'm sorry, but it helps to think of it like that, Harry.'

Just as Moist was heading down the stairs with Harry simmering behind him, Adora Belle arrived home. She sometimes worked nights on the Grand Trunk; she told Moist that it was to keep people on their toes, but he knew that she actually loved the quiet watches of a clear night when messages would twinkle from hill to hill like fireflies.

That was the spell of the clacks, and it wasn't only goblins who felt it. Adora Belle knew and didn't mind that the clacksmen and clackswomen would fraternize along the wonderful scintillating lines of light. After all, quite a few marriages had been brokered through the unsuspecting ether in the small hours of the night and sooner or later little clacksmen and women would be born.

Adora Belle had once told Moist, 'You know that it takes a special kind of person to be a clacksman and especially a clackswoman, and it's important that they marry and have children with the right kind of blood. They're our future, and heaven help them if their spouse doesn't also work on the clacks. Clacks people are a type and like attracts like.'

When Moist told her the news of the accident in the Effing Forest she disappeared into her office, and Moist could hear the goblins stampeding towards it and then a rattle of the clacks on the roof. Before long she sent down another goblin with a flimsy that said, 'News from Scrote. Stop. It's a boiler that burst. Stop. Not a train. Stop. Horrible deaths of two people, but no engine as such. Stop.'

That latest discovery made Moist doubly sure of himself and he clamped his hand on Harry's shoulder and said, 'Please, don't worry, Harry. I know how this one is going to go. All I need is for you and Mister Simnel to meet me in the Effing Forest as quickly as you can. And, oh, I think we might need Thunderbolt.'

* * *

It was time to talk to the golem horse once more. Moist was rather concerned about taking it on another long journey so soon, but the horse said, 'Sir, I am a horse. Being a horse is my passion in life, and getting to the Effing Forest will be a breeze. Saddle up, please, and let's be off.'

Moist had found something like a sweet spot in the gait. No muscle and bone horse could possibly gallop at this speed without legs getting tangled, but even so he covered the fifty miles to the Effing Forest by sunrise without much in the way of groinal sprains.

He immediately sought out the nearest pub to the accident, which was the premises of Edward Forefather, purveyor of fine beers, stouts and ales. At least that's what it said on the rather large plaque behind the bar and Moist was not going to argue.

The publican, already up and dressed, looked him up and down and said, 'I've been expecting somebody like you. You're from the city, aren't you? It's about the explosion, isn't it? Are you one of them reporters? Only I wants money if you're a reporter.'

Moist said, 'No, I'm not, I'm with the railway. I heard about the explosion and came to see what had happened.'

Forefather looked him up and down again and said, 'We know all about it. It was them Wesley brothers. How good is your stomach, young man? Of course, I'd leave the bar to help you, but that means I'd have to get my wife up to start on the early shift for the miners. They'll be coming up for their breakfast soonish.'

Moist understood the unspoken request and handed the man a reasonable sum, then followed him outside where he was led along a path into the forest. This part of the forest was quite pleasant, not too dark, the kind of place where people would go for a picnic, but as they got in further, Moist could see that whatever they were going to find next, it wasn't going to be a picnic.

In a clearing just a short walk from the pub the trees were stripped of their leaves, tangled wood was everywhere and the remains of the forge were embedded in various trunks. And there were fragments of the stricken boiler, too, some of them driven so hard into mighty oaks that Moist couldn't pull them out. The haze in the clearing sent a chill down his spine.

He took a deep breath and said, 'What happened to the bodies, Mister Forefather?'

'Oh, yes, sir. I've got them back in my cellar, it being quite cold down there. They're in a bucket. It isn't a big bucket, either. It was two brothers, strapping great lads. Crucible was the brains and Jed was the blacksmith. Although in the bucket I couldn't tell you which bits were whose. Jed was boasting about building a railway engine one day, and to tell you the truth, sir, he was a very good blacksmith, but what he knew about loco-motives I wouldn't dare think of. But he thought he could do it and all his mates were egging him on.'

He hesitated for a moment and then said, 'I was the first one to arrive here and mostly all there was was a mist, and I didn't like that at all. It was clammy and hot and made you want to puke. And that's it, sir. Not much more to be said, sir.'

Moist looked up and said, 'Should there really be an anvil up in that tree?'

The publican looked at him and then at the tree and said, 'You're a man with his eye on the business, aren't you? Generally speaking, the anvil has always been on the ground, by and large, but it was a most powerful bang.'

Moist brightened up as best he could and said, 'Thank you, Mister Forefather. Pretty soon there'll be a lot of journalists coming to see all this and I'm sorry about that, but they turn up like flies.'

'That's all right, sir. Good for business. Journalists drink twice as much as anyone else and for twice as long. We had them around when the mine fell in and they really can take their liquor.' Mr Forefather was rubbing his hands in anticipation.

In fact, it was mid-morning before most of the journalists put in an appearance. But well ahead of the pack was Otto Chriek of the *Ankh-Morpork Times*, who was always first on the scene.*

As for the rest of the press gang, they arrived at cross purposes, all of them expecting the others to tell them what was going on.

Mr Forefather was making hay by making bacon butties while his wife was frying eggs and the obligatory slice.

---

* It would be impolite to ask Otto how he got around so quickly. Of course, everybody knew that he was a vampire, but he was a fervent black ribboner and so whatever anybody thought they knew about him, they didn't talk about it.

Moist put the word out that, while of course the railway was in no way involved, the owners were coming to see the accident site for themselves and would be happy to answer questions. By the time Harry King, Simnel and Thunderbolt arrived, Moist could see Forefather carefully raising the prices on his beers as, gradually, the pub filled from across the Sto Plains.

Moist had already gleaned from Mrs Forefather that the brothers' old mum was being comforted by friends back in her own home, a short walk from the pub, and he was careful to see that no mention of this or the current whereabouts of the unfortunate Wesley brothers was made to the gang of journalists. And he surprised himself by realizing that this was a sensible and humanitarian thing to do, some of the press gang being the sort who would most definitely say things like, 'Well now, Mrs Wesley, how did you feel when you found out that both of your sons had been melted?'

As the press seized on the new arrivals, Moist, like a chess grandmaster, tried to keep his king, that would be Sir Harry King, away from the worst questions and instead played his shining knight, Mr Dick Simnel. He was learning a lot from Mr Simnel. They faced him with questions like, 'What do you say to people who think that live steam will kill everybody in the end?'

To which Dick's answer was, 'I don't know, sir, I've never met anyone who thought that. Steam is *very* dangerous if you don't know what you're doing and I feel sorry for them poor boys.'

Hardwick of the *Pseudopolis Daily Press* said, 'I hear

your own engine killed someone the night before last. What do you have to say about that, Mister Simnel?'

Before Dick could speak Thunderbolt came down like a judge and said, 'The person in question was clearly trying to sabotage the locomotive and while we naturally regret the fatality he was in a place where he shouldn't have been, doing something that he shouldn't have done. It is evident that he entered the engine shed through a skylight, which seems to show lawful business was not on his mind. His death, alas, was self-inflicted.'

'And what about Mister Simnel senior?' said Hardwick. 'Was *his* death self-inflicted?'

Simnel took the floor once again. 'It just goes to show you have to treat steam with respect, and yes, I learned t'hard way when me dad died and that's why I measure and test and measure again. It's all about t'little numbers. It's all about taking care. It's all about getting the knowledge. Steam has its rules. After all, we call it *live* steam for a reason. It's dangerous in t'wrong hands, but my hands, sir, have spent a long time building boilers and static engines, just to see 'ow far I could go. That generally meant me hiding behind a stone wall while bits of engine whistled over me 'ead. You learn by your mistakes, if you're lucky, and I tried to make mistakes just to see 'ow that could be done, and although this is not the time to say it, you 'ave to be clever and you 'ave to be smart and you 'ave to be 'umble in the face of such power. You have to think of every little detail. You have to make notes and educate yourself and then, only then, steam becomes your friend. Like Iron Girder, you've all seen her. Yes, miss?'

Moist recognized Sacharissa Cripslock. She said, 'You speak so caringly of your locomotive, Mister Simnel, and so I have to ask, do you have a sweetheart?'

There was a certain amount of tittering from the hacks, but Simnel barely blinked. 'Why, thank you for asking and yes, there is indeed a young lady who is looking at me kindly.'

Simnel turned towards another waving notebook and said, 'Yes, sir?'

'Grievous, sir, Grievous Johnson from the *Big Cabbage Gazette*. Is it your intention to share your knowledge with others trying to build their own engines? That might save a lot of lives.'

Simnel glanced at Moist and Moist looked at Harry King, who dropped an eyebrow, which Moist knew he could take as a yes.

Simnel knew it too and had spotted the signal. He said, 'Oh, yes, sir, we will do. At least the basics, safety and so forth. But it'll cost. Research and development has to cost. But I'll tek apprentices, show them t'ropes, and generally make them safer workers. In fact we're planning regular classes, a Railway Academy, you might call it.' His smile dropped as he continued, 'O'course I'm reet sorry about those lads, sir, but learning is hard and failure is sharp. I'd hate that kind of thing to happen again, but it's got to be done proper like. No scrimping. No cutting corners.'

Mr Simnel had won again. The press couldn't deal with a straightforward man. The certainty in his face simply disarmed them and possibly, thought Moist, made them wish they were better people. There wasn't an inch of politics in him and that stunned them.

Simnel was still beaming at them. 'Aye, if any of you'd like to come back to t'works at Ankh-Morpork at any time I'll gladly show you around. I'll show you *everything*.'

Far away from Moist and certainly from common sense, the grags took counsel, if it could be called that. Things in the outside world were changing so fast.

'We are losing, you do know that?' said a voice in the darkness.

'It can't be helped. It's the zeitgeist, it's in the air,' said another voice, sounding somewhat more cracked.

'And what do we care about the air, or any kind of geist? We are the justified, the stalwarts, the kings and servants of the darkness. Our people *will* come back.'

'No, they're leaving! Burning clacks towers was stupid! I say stupid! Everybody wants their news and it makes us look like criminals, which we are. And that's *not* justified.'

A dwarf who had been silent during the conclave in the cavern was remembering the old Djelibeybi legend about the way to get an ass down from the minaret, and of course the answer was you first have to teach it *not* to be an ass. But in what world could that ever happen when you're dealing with grags? It was, she thought, time to see for herself just how life was in the lands of the Troll King. She had been very careful, oh dear, so very careful and so she had survived, she hoped, to be the jackass that got out of the minaret, but alas, the idiots were still encouraging impressionable young dwarfs to attack the clacks towers. Whoever had had that idea had doomed them without dialogue.

Rhys Rhysson was right, she thought. We've lost all balance. We have to get out of here, out of everything that is *here*, out into the light. Surely, she thought, they wouldn't suspect her. She had been forensic in her search for unbelievers.

Nevertheless, when at last she ran the knives got her before she stumbled. And then there were eight left in the cavern and those watching in the darkness watched more closely to see who would be next. The time would be coming when the purity of darkness could not be mocked!

The terrible fact was that when dwarfs schism, they *schism* . . . every deviation from the norm was treated as an attack on all that was truly dwarfish.

Others had already fled and died, and who could say they knew how many more were left, not only in this cavern but in other caverns all the way to Uberwald. And the trouble with madness was that the mad didn't know they were mad. The grags came down heavily on those who did not conform and seemed not to realize that this was like stamping potatoes into the mud to stop them growing.

Everywhere one looked there were committees nowadays, mostly because, by arrangement and with the blessing of Lord Vetinari, other principalities, large towns and city states saw no reason to wait for the completion of *their* slice of the magic of the train, and, seizing these opportunities, new companies were entering the railway business with rather more success than the Wesley brothers. Drumknott was in his element as the paperwork mounted and his files multiplied; he contrived to be everywhere and into everything, ably supported by Mr Thunderbolt.

There were committees discussing industry standards, public safety, passenger welfare, whether one company's freight truck could be hitched to another company's train to complete its journey without need to offload* – and all the knotty financial and legal arrangements that would entail.

The whole proposition of other businessmen launching their own railways had made Harry call for Thunderbolt.

After hearing Harry's complaints, the lawyer said, 'It's a matter of patents, Sir Harry. You know, all that fiddly stuff that you said you paid other people to get their heads around? Well, Mister Simnel and I have filed applications for every one of his innovations. But I am sure there is more than one way of building a machine to run on rails. You cannot patent the idea of a railway as such, and if you take a walk down the Street of Cunning Artificers you will find someone quite bright enough to discover how to make a train that will run on rails without infringing any of the patents I have been able to obtain for you.

---

* A development that proved fatal to the Brassica Carriage Company, which had elected to construct its engines and tracks to a gauge based on the horse-drawn cabbage delivery carts.

'The idea of steam locomotion as such has been there for all to see and we all know that a boiling kettle will try to lift its own lid. Being clever, some young man watching the fire will work out that if he builds a bigger kettle he will be able to lift a bigger kettle lid. Although, as we saw at Effing Forest, he soon learns that it's not as simple as that. They're not all as bright and clever as Dick Simnel.'

Harry snorted. 'Stupid hayseeds. Not a patch on our Dick and his lads. All they've done is leave their old mum bound for the poorhouse.' And Sir Harry harrumphed. A full-blown harrumph.

Unaware that his client was temporarily distracted by the thought of a destitute lady living in the Effing Forest, bereft of her boys, her pride and joy, Thunderbolt continued. 'Take Mister Simnel's pressure gauge. Once the principle is proved and understood, the Cunning Artificers, extremely cunning as they are, might well find some way of achieving the same results without breaching patent. It's what they do. Cunning by name *and* nature.'

Thunderbolt had got Harry's attention now. 'And before you explode, Sir Harry, it is all within the law.'

'What? After all I've done and the money I've put in!' Harry's face was as red as a beacon. He looked as though he needed one of Dick's pressure gauges himself.

Moist decided to intervene. 'Harry, the whole point of trains is that they're universal. Put them on the tracks and away they go.'

In his mellifluous tones, the lawyer continued. 'If I

were you, Sir Harry, I would simply leave it to me to keep an eye on such things as patents and licences and regulation whilst you and Mister Simnel fill the world with steam. And remember, Sir Harry, the important thing is that you were the first. Nobody can take that away. You, Sir Harry, are on what I believe is called the hog's back, the top of the heap, the founder of the railway. The Ankh-Morpork and Sto Plains Hygienic Railway Company is as solid as the bank.'

The troll smiled and said, 'Or, indeed, as me – and I am diamond.'

Business for the Hygienic Railway Company was indeed booming, and the workforce ever expanding. The goblins from the Quirmian maquis had passed news back to their friends about the opportunities in the Big Wahoonie, which they seized with alacrity. And once Dick's announcement of his Railway Academy had been splashed across the papers, in the wake of the Effing Forest incident, there were queues of people every day wanting to be taken on as apprentices. Simnel was heavy on the lads he accepted, telling them they had got to let the iron into their soul. And it was not unknown for him to kick someone straight out again if he felt they weren't up to scratch.

Returning from another trip to review progress on the Quirm line, Moist paused to take in the latest changes to the compound. There were the apprentices . . . engrossed in their own little mechanical world with Wally and Dave tutoring them and making sure they had got their caps sufficiently flat. Moist watched them in their blissful mechanical dream and he could not help but notice that they were surrounded by goblins, most definitely paying attention, seriously so, as if their lives depended upon it, and gathering up any discarded greasy rags, which to goblins were like *haute couture*, and the mark of a real swell back in the burrows. And near by the train spotters were comparing numbers. And there was Mr Simnel, equally engrossed in his latest contraption.

As Moist crossed the compound towards him, Mr Simnel, with his greasy hat and his grubby shirt, the sleeves of which were rolled up to his elbows, wiped his grinning face with a rag, leaving a greasy smear on the grease.

'Mister Lipwig! Grand to see you! I have something to show you! We brought this beauty down from Sto Lat yesterday and built it last night!' He was shouting even louder than normal. 'Essential equipment! It's my design! I built it and I call it t'turning table!'

Moist almost had to put his hands over his ears as the engineer stepped closer. It's because he works with the trains all day, he thought, he has to be heard among all the hissing and clanking, but I wonder how he talks to his Emily?

And as for the turning table, it was, well, it was a table and it turned: a huge metal table with a pair of rails running across the centre, which was turned around by means of a large handle attached to a ratchet mechanism being wound by a troll with a look of intense concentration. Moist watched while Dick gave his demonstration.

'Great! That's brilliant, Dick, but . . . for the sake of the hard of thinking, what in hell's name is it for?'

Dick looked at Moist as if he was an infant and said, 'Can't you see it, Mister Lipwig? You drives your engine on to t'turning table and, here's the clever bit, you turn the whole thing around and it's now facing t'other way!'

And then Mr Simnel danced on the circular iron table in his clogs as it slowly revolved, and shouted, 'Grand! Gradely! We're nearly there!'

The triumph was emphasized with a hiss like Iron Girder at the end of a long run, which would have been a fitting end to the experiment, except that it took some time to get the troll to stop turning the handle so that Dick, who was starting to look a little green from the continued revolutions, could get off.

Happy that the tussle of wills between the other companies operating on the Sto Plains was being ably managed by Thunderbolt and Drumknott, no doubt with assistance from the dark clerks, Moist was looking forward to a period of domestic harmony, when he was summoned to the palace.

He was not surprised to see his lordship staring at the day's crossword puzzle. Drumknott whispered from behind Moist, 'There's a new compiler, you know, and I'm sad to say that it looks like an improvement. However, his lordship is doing his best.'

Lord Vetinari looked up and said, 'Mister Lipwig. Can it be that there is a word *quaestuary*?'

Actually, Moist knew exactly what it meant because of his misspent youth and so he girded his metaphorical loins and said, 'I think you might find, sir, that it means someone doing business simply for profit. I remember coming across the word once upon a time and it puzzled me because I thought profit was what business is all about.'

His lordship's face didn't move a muscle until he said, 'Quite so, Mister Lipwig.' And he pushed the paper aside and stood up. 'I hear that the line to Quirm is all but completed . . . If the Quirm Assembly is still dragging its feet I shall have to have a word with Monsieur Jean Némard . . . one of my special words. I have to say, Mister Lipwig, that your contribution to the development of the railway has been most gratifying to observe and I am sure we are all in your debt.'

'Oh,' said Moist. 'Does that mean I can get back to my day job and see my wife more than once every week or so?'

'Of course you may, Mister Lipwig! You have, after all, been acting in an entirely voluntary capacity. However, *my* business now concerns the railway to Uberwald. So I have to ask you, how soon can we have a locomotive run all the way there? Non-stop.'

Moist was taken aback. 'You couldn't do it, sir. Not non-stop. You have to take on water and coal and it must be more than a thousand miles up there!'

'Twelve hundred and twenty-five miles *exactly* from Ankh-Morpork to Bonk by coach, although I am aware that the train would have to take a different route.'

'Yes sir, but non-stop—'

'Mister Lipwig. If you're going to tell me that it's impossible you will be down with the kittens in short order. After all, you are the man who gets things done.'

'What's the hurry, sir? The lads are doing a great job, but it would be a rare day if they could lay more than three miles of track, even with all the money Harry King is throwing at it. And then, of course, there's all the unforeseen obstacles along the way and on top of that you know that every city along the Plains wants to be a part of the network. We're spread wide, sir. Any further and we'd split down the middle.'

Vetinari walked around his desk at speed and said, 'Good, then you could both work more efficiently! It appears, Mister Lipwig, that you do not understand the nature of our relationship. I ask, very politely, for you to achieve something, bearing in mind that there are other ways I could ask, and it is your job to get things done. You are, after all, a man who can apparently do *anything*, the great Mister Lipwig, yes? And my advice to you is to cease all the work that does not assist in getting from here to Uberwald in the quickest possible time. Everything else can, and will, wait.'

He held up his hand. 'Do not tell me what the problems are, just tell me the solutions. Indeed, you do not need to tell me the solutions, you merely have to achieve them.'

Moist said, 'Do you mind if I sit down, sir?'

'By all means, Mister Lipwig. Do get the man a drink, Drumknott. He looks a little hot.'

'I have to ask, sir . . . Why does it have to be done like this?'

Vetinari smiled. 'Can you keep a secret, Mister Lipwig?'

'Oh, yes, sir. I've kept lots.'

'Capital. And the point is, so can I. You do not need to know.'

Moist tried. 'Sir! Even now the trains are part of life to a lot of people, especially to those on the Plains who commute! We can't just drop everything, sir!'

'Mister Lipwig. Is there something in the word "tyrant" you do not understand?'

In desperation Moist said, 'We don't have enough workers, sir! Not enough people to man the foundries! Not enough people to dig the ore! We've probably got enough stock now to get halfway, but it's all about the workers.'

'Yes,' said Lord Vetinari. 'It is. Isn't it. Think on that, Mister Lipwig.'

'What about the wizards? Can't they get up off their fat backsides and help their city?'

'Yes, Mister Lipwig, and you know and I know it will rebound on us. Live steam is friendly compared with magic going wrong. No, Mister Lipwig, we will not look to the wizards. You just need to get the train to run to Uberwald on time.'

'And what time would that be, sir?'

'As I say, Mister Lipwig, any time soon.'

'Then I haven't got a prayer. It's going to take months, a year . . . or more . . .'

And suddenly the atmosphere turned to ice and his lordship said, 'Then I suggest you get going.' Vetinari resumed his seat. 'Mister Lipwig, the world lives between those who say it cannot be done and those who say that it can. And in my experience, those who say that it can be done are usually telling the truth. It's just a matter of thinking creatively. Some people say "Think the unthinkable", but that's nonsense – although in your case, sir, I think you have the nerves for it. Think about it. Now, don't let me detain you.'

The door closed behind Moist and silence enveloped the Oblong Office as the Patrician returned his attention to the crossword. Eventually he frowned, filled in a line and laid down the paper.

'Drumknott,' he said, 'how's Charlie's Punch and Judy business going these days? Is he doing well? I wonder whether he might consider a short holiday. Just a short one, that is.'

'Yes, sir,' said Drumknott. 'I'll go and see him this afternoon.'

'That's the way to do it,' said Lord Vetinari.

While he was still reeling from the Patrician's latest demand, Moist found himself riding back to the Effing Forest on a mission for Harry.

'Go and see the old girl and send her my sympathies,' Harry had said. 'Tell her I was impressed at how her boys tried to harness steam and I salute them as pioneers. Have a look around and see what she's got and since it would seem as if I have got gold coming out of my ears then I reckon we can give her a little pension, though for heavens' sake don't let anyone else know. Oh, and tell her that I'll make it certain that her lads will be up frontline when the history of the railway is written down, and say she can call on me at any time.'

The old homestead in the forest was all that Moist had expected, and Mrs Wesley burst into tears when he told her about Harry's offer. She was determined to think of Sir Harry as a saint or angel and if Moist knew anything about the ways of the world Harry's gesture would be all over the forest within hours; and because news spreads, it would get as far as Ankh-Morpork by the end of the day. Moist knew Harry the man as he was: extremely sharp with a heart of gold and tears of soppy. Harry's gesture was entirely Harry, with no ulterior motive, but nevertheless once the news had got around, he would be in all the papers as a benefactor of the poor and therefore a celebrity. Not for the first time Moist deplored his own tendency to see the angles in whatever happened, good or bad.

'*How much?*'

The simple question sounded like a declaration of war, which it almost was, as Harry was presented with the costings for the express line to Bonk.

Moist stood his ground. 'Dick says there's iron everywhere, Harry, but it needs digging out and then it's the making of the steel that uses up the money,' he put in hastily, before Harry could throw anyone down the stairs.

'You've got to put the gold in to get t'steel out, Harry,' said Simnel calmly. 'We've been getting a good deal from the lads down at the smelters, but it's twelve hundred miles to Uberwald, and that's a *lot* of steel.'

'Harry,' Moist said patiently. 'I know very well that

when you and your lady first married you used to cut the matches in half to make them last longer. But you are not that man any more. You *can* afford this.'

They watched Harry's face. In truth, Moist knew Harry had kicked his way up from the gutter and was proud of it, but he had made his money cheaply – since minions, on the whole, don't incur much of an overhead – and looked at every suggestion that he should pay for anything as evidence that something was wrong in the world.

Dick Simnel had got the measure of the man and said, 'If I was you, sir, I'd look at my money box and buy as much steel as I possibly could while I can, not making a big fuss about it, otherwise it'll suddenly get more expensive, if you know what I mean. Supply and demand.'

Harry still looked as if he thought people were trying to get something of a move on him, which was his ground state of being, and Moist thought, well, what *does* Harry spend his mountains of money on?

And so he plunged on. 'Go on, Harry, as a customer in good standing, the Royal Bank'll definitely give you a loan, if indeed you ever need one. Though frankly, I know your balance is more than enough to get rails all the way to the moon and back and that's including a fleet of locomotives as well.'

There was a rumble from Mr Thunderbolt. 'Of course, Sir Harry, you could sell shares: that means you *share* some of the outlays but, alas, you also have to *share* some of the dividends. It's up to you.'

Moist saw his cue right there and said, 'You see, Harry, everybody who buys your railway shares would then be dead keen on *their* railway and on your side. It's what the trolls call a no-brain. When the smoke is making you rich, it's *your* smoke and you don't complain about it. And,' Moist took a deep breath, 'if you share the risks you can afford to build houses for the railway workers, too. That way they'll live close to the railway, right alongside it, so they'll always be ready—'

'I don't need any telling on that score, Mister Lipwig. The lads that work for me on the conveyor belts all live on the doorstep. Difference is they built their own.'

'The buildings don't have to be little palaces,' Moist said, 'just comfortable, with a bit of a garden, which is nice for the kiddies, and then everyone is happy and you've got it made. After all, who doesn't like to have a place close to their work? Nice and warm with all the coal you need thrown in.'

Harry King would probably punch anyone who called him a philanthropist, but beneath the grumbling there was an undercurrent of curious softness. Elderly employees, no matter their species, ended up with a pension, a rare beast in Ankh-Morpork as a whole, and Moist, as Harry's bank manager, was aware that expensive hospital bills had a habit of disappearing when he got to hear about them. And most certainly at Hogswatch, Harry, grumbling like an elderly troll with a headache, nevertheless made sure all employees had actual named meat on their tables, and lots of it.*

Moist, who knew his man, continued, 'Look at it like this: I know that as a self-made man, sharing would be anathema to your soul, and so you *could* take all the risk and become as rich as Creosote. However, it seems to me, Harry, that you're already as rich as Creosote and so, as a scoundrel, I'd suggest that another fortune is not exactly what you need right now! As your bank manager I'd like to suggest that sharing both the risks and the profits would be the most prudent and socially acceptable way.'

For a moment Moist saw the psyche of Harry King putting together a retort that social acceptability could go and get its hands dirty by doing a proper day's work rather than interfering with honest entrepreneurs who were working their guts out day and night. But Moist also saw the grin, and realized that Harry knew this was all part of the solution. After all, Lord Vetinari liked the people of Ankh-Morpork to feel they had a stake in *their* city.

'Anyway,' he said, to clinch it, 'Vetinari wants the Uberwald route and he's the ultimate boss. Who knows, the city might be very generous with its level of funding. The trains go round and round and so does the money.'

* * *

---

* And yet Harry was still a Titan, a humorous term meaning deep trousers and short fingers, owing to his tendency to look on the disgorging of money in much the same light as root canal surgery delivered by a troll dentist.

The main line to Quirm was completed with a ceremony at the Ankh-Morpork terminus in which, regrettably, alcohol played a major role. The new engine was launched and named *Fierté d'Quirm* with an especially good bottle of champagne smashed across its boiler by the Marquis des Aix en Pains and his wife who, Moist noticed, was now very cheerfully, as they say in Quirm, enceinte.

And amid all the celebrations, it seemed that it was only Moist who noticed that Simnel had wandered away from the party to wipe the engine clean of sizzling champagne with his handkerchief, which immediately became a greasy rag. He gave Moist a severe look.

'We can't have this kind of thing going on, Mister Lipwig, interfering with the engine . . . not when I'm determined to get us up to forty miles per hour across the flat of the maquis, just to show those lobsters what we can do.'

On the maiden journey, Moist rode with Simnel and the stoker on the footplate as the maquis passed away behind them at terrible speed, with goblins waving from every rock and ancient tree. He thought at one point that he had spotted Of the Twilight the Darkness, waving, but to his surprise found the egregious goblin waiting when they pulled into the Quirm city terminus. It seemed to Moist that the little bastard had channels through the world that weren't available to humans.

In the carriages behind, a good time was had by all, with avec galore and lashings of the famous entente cordiale. The smart new passenger carriages were much admired. A highlight for many was the dapper gentleman looking after the First Class gentlemen's facilities, who was adept at handling towels and explaining the workings of the glass cistern – which contained goldfish that appeared to revel in the rush of the flush but were, in fact, kept from going with the flow by a concealed sieve of some kind.

There was a big parade to greet them at Quirm Central, heralding another round of civic and political razzmatazz, all punctuated with more alcohol and ending with a huge dinner in the engine shed. And there were yet more toasts before the locomotive was turned around on the new-fangled turning table to take the Ankh-Morpork contingent home, where they had to be decanted from the train.

And so it was that one fine summer evening shortly afterwards, Moist and Adora Belle sat down to an excellent dinner of fresh lobsters from Quirm brought up on the new *Fruits de Mer* Express. They were good, and cheaper now than he ever remembered, and the dish went very well with the watercress, which burned all the way down as they ate it.

And afterwards there were fresh strawberries and a soft bed with fluffy pillows and somehow it made all the running around worthwhile.

It began in Higher Overhang in the Shires. People locally were saying they could hear noises in the night . . . metallic noises, clanking, and the occasional scream of metal straining in torment. Of course everybody said, Well, goblins, what can you expect?

And all this came to the notice of Chief Constable Feeney Upshot, attached to the Ankh-Morpork constabulary. Feeney liked the attachment. It meant that anyone getting stroppy with him would sooner or later have to deal with Commander Vimes or even Sergeant Detritus, whose appearance in this sleepy hinterland had caused such a big stir a couple of years before. So Feeney got on his horse and headed to the Overhangs, so called because in the flaming distant past the landscape had been twisted all over the place with unfathomable caverns and a jagged unforgiving terrain.

Feeney was a decent and sensible copper and such men made friends because they never knew when they would need one, especially when they were a copper all alone, although in theory Feeney had the support of Special Constable Of the Chimney the Bones. There had to be a law, and law applied to *everyone*, and now the law had decreed that goblins were people and therefore protected by the law in these parts, which, in fact, was made incarnate in Chief Constable Feeney and his constable. Amazingly, the constable allowed his superior officer to call him Boney on the sensible basis that if there was some mêlée or other and you needed help you'd want a simple word to scream.*

Feeney had been to Ankh-Morpork and was proud

---

* Feeney was privileged. To a goblin, the name is always the name, untouchable and part of the goblin itself.

to have undertaken his basic training in Pseudopolis Yard under Sergeant Detritus. He recognized that Boney was slightly more intelligent than the notorious Corporal Nobby Nobbs and so he didn't grumble. And now he was glad to see his constable waiting for him just outside the main goblin cave where he had an office, regarded by the local goblins as something of a shrine.

These days there was a flourishing colony of goblins in Overhang Minor. The goblins were purveyors of fine pots, and Feeney knew that the production of pots was generally a quiet pastime and didn't involve very much banging. The small cave that passed as an office was, and you have to be careful about this sort of thing, definitely not manned but goblined. And the sound coming from the great cavern beyond it was not about pots, that was certain. It was metallic, heavy metal. Well – and Feeney stumbled here slightly, mentally at least – goblins were free, and if people wanted to bang metal around in the privacy of their great caverns, then they could. He blinked. It was the new world. If you didn't get your head around it, it could turn you upside down.

Feeney was polite and had been smart enough to pick up some of the goblin lingo, which really helped. It was a sunny day and it was an easy trip to the Overhangs and, yes, on the hill above the cavern there was a clacks station, goblined by goblins. After delivering his papers and force orders, Feeney sat down for a quiet word with his fellow officer and broached, in a careful way, the subject of the goblins banging things around in a context of disturbing the peace.

Since there were very few humans living anywhere near the goblins' settlement, Chief Constable Feeney put the complaints down to the humans' residual dislike of goblins doing anything whatsoever anywhere, but he did advise that maybe moving whatever it was they were doing further into their caves might be a very good idea.

The crackling voice of Boney said, 'No worries, boss, hang. We are copacetic on this one. No problems here.'

'Well, that's good to know, but why all the banging and clanging, Boney?'

'Chief, you know plenty goblins go to Ankh-Morpork and work for Sir Harry King, the shit magnet, on the railway. Know how it is, yess? Comes back every month with wages. Never had wages before! Sometime they comes with diagrams . . . And ideas and scheming attics.'

Boney watched his superior officer with a certain level of concern, and heard Feeney say, 'They are stealing . . . *ideas*?'

There was silence and Feeney knew he had made a faux pas, but Boney laughed and said, 'Nosir, improving! We like Sir Harry, veeery good employer, but we plan to build own goblin railway. Quick to get around and easy-no-problem – has found best way to build railway is not build. Digging! Dig underground. Underground goblin-size railway, yess? Will bring all goblins together from every caverns. So many caverns in bowels of world. It's no fuss. Goblins needed all over. How would nice Miss Adora Belle Dearheart do, if no goblins on clacks? We can be trusted – well, as muches as we trust you stinking humans. Wonderful railways underground, narrow gauge, of course. You see? We even have lingo! No rain and no snow, no bothering donkeys, no frightening old ladies underground. Hang! At last goblins' own world in tunnels under big-man human world. We goblins up in the light now. No turning back.'

Feeney thought about this on the ride home as his horse trotted gently towards the sunset. He wasn't a philosopher and couldn't even spell the word, but the voice of the goblin officer rang in his head. He thought, what would happen if goblins learned everything about humans and did everything the human way because they thought it was better than the goblin way? How long would it be before they were no longer goblins and left behind everything that was goblin, even their pots? The pots were lovely, he'd bought several for his mum. Goblins took pots seriously now, they sparkled, even at night, but what happens next? Will goblins really stop taking an interest in their pots and will humans learn the serious, valuable and difficult and almost magical skill of pot-making? Or will goblins become, well, just another kind of human? And which would be better?

And then he thought, maybe a policeman should stop thinking about all this because, after all, there was no crime, nothing was wrong ... and yet in a subtle way, there was. Something was being stolen from the world without anybody noticing or caring. And then he gave up, because he was nearly home and his mum had promised him Man Dog Suck

Po with mashed carrots, and it wasn't even a Sunday.

Building the longest railway the world had yet seen was a matter of daily grind, and nightly grind too, and each week took Moist further away from the city. Visits home to enjoy the fruits of his labour* became even rarer.

Scattered along the thousand-mile route new railway yards were springing up, each one a constant hive of activity with wagons coming and going all hours of the day and night. And while the company made sure the workforce was well provisioned, since, as Harry King had told the *Ankh-Morpork Times*, railway workers seriously needed a good meal and a good sleep in a comfortable bed after a day of heavy labour, in the end whether or not the bed was warm or comfortable didn't in fact really matter because a lad would sleep the moment he fell into it, just as soon as the former occupant, waving his billy can, had hurried off for *his* shift.

It was all about speed and occasionally pure machismo, or whatever it was called in the languages of trolls, goblins and golems and, of course, the real hardcore steel men from the mountains who fought amongst themselves over nothing.

Where the new line followed the course of the River Ankh as it narrowed towards its source high in the Ramtops, barges came up or down the river with wood for sleepers, iron ore, coal and other supplies. The

* Or indeed, the *fruits de mer* of his labour.

smelters worked through the night casting rails and if you were lucky enough to be in the right place and sufficiently protected you could see them open their guts and spill the glowing liquid steel: dancing and living like a creature from the underworld. If you were not lucky and stood too close then quite probably you would end up in that underworld facing the deity of your choice.

And all was fuelled by money, money, money, eager investors turning gold into steel and coal in the hope that it would turn back into even more gold.

The company was building bunkers everywhere along the tracks and it truly came home to Moist that when it came to the railways the engines and carriages and so forth were just the show up front, the iron horse, which needed to be fuelled and watered. And all of this was done by people almost the same colour as the coal, momentarily spotted as you went past, and then forgotten. He knew, because he had attended all the meetings and *listened*, that running a railway was a lot of small puzzles which, if you opened them, presented you with another sequence, full of constraints, and lists of things that definitely had to be done before anything else could happen. In short, the railway was complexity on wheels. It was amazing that Mr Simnel's sliding rule didn't glow as red-hot as the furnaces he worked.

And in Swine Town the workshops were turning out more and more engines: little tank engines that trundled up and down the ever-growing compound, shunting trains and carriages together; night trains, slow and heavy, that picked up wagon after wagon from the watercress farmers and others who needed to get their produce to the cities by dawn; the new Flyer Mark II, which had a roof to the footplate and wonderful new green livery; all now with names such as *Spirit of Scrote* and *King of Pseudopolis**.

The scream of steam was no longer an intrusion, just one of the noises of Ankh-Morpork, like the explosions in the Alchemists' Guild, and, as one old man said to his wife, 'You don't need a clock to tell you the time when you know the sound of the seven o'clock to Quirm.' It seemed only weeks since Iron Girder had first puffed gently around Harry King's compound, but now, inside a year, branch lines were springing up all across the Sto Plains, connecting little towns and villages in every direction.

And near these little towns and villages spanking new houses for the new railway staff were beginning to appear. Houses with baths! And hot running water! Admittedly the privies were outside, but nevertheless the plumbing was well maintained.† You could say that for Harry: if something was to be done then it was to

---

* Moist suspected Vetinari had had some say in that coinage since Pseudopolis had never had a king and was beset by the curse of democracy, an affliction the Patrician couldn't abide.

† Around the Sto Plains, as in other places, it took a while for country people to come to terms with indoor . . . facilities. A privy in the garden with fresh air all around was considered much more hygienic and, if you were careful, the tomatoes you grew would be most excellent.‡

‡ If you don't know what this means, your grandparents will tell you.

be done properly, and doubly so if Effie was around.*

It was as if there had been a space waiting to be filled. It was steam-engine time, and the steam engine had arrived, like a raindrop, dripping precisely into its puddle, and Moist and Dick and Harry and Vetinari and the rest of them were simply splashes in the storm.

Then one day at the Ankh-Morpork terminus, as Moist was setting out yet again to the Sto Plains, a lady got into his carriage, introduced herself as Mrs Georgina Bradshaw and sat down, gripping her expensive-looking bag with both hands. When Moist got up to offer her his forward-facing seat as railway etiquette apparently demanded, she said, 'Oh, my dear sir, don't worry about me, but thank you. I know a gentleman when I see one.'

'Moist von Lipwig at your service, ma'am.'

'Oh – are you *the* Mister Lipwig? Mister Lipwig the railwayman? I've heard all about you.'

'Yes, I am, I suppose,' said Moist, 'when no other contender is available.'

'Isn't this fascinating?' continued Mrs Bradshaw. 'I've never been on a train before. I've taken the precaution of bringing some pills in case I feel nauseous. Has that ever happened to you?'

'No, madam, I quite like the rhythm of the railway,'

---

* On the Quirm line Harry had had to stop her from giving them a bidet.

said Moist. 'But tell me, where did you get those precious pills?'

'It was a gentleman called Professor Dibbler, a purveyor of nostrums against the railway illnesses. He was *quite* persuasive.'

Moist couldn't help his smile and said, 'I imagine he was. Madam, Mister Dibbler is at best nothing more than a charming scamp, I'm afraid. And I'm quite certain his nostrums will be nothing more than expensive sugar and miscellaneous substances. I fear he's in the vanguard of the pedlars of patent medications which tax my patience.'

She laughed. 'Well put, sir. I'll consider that tuppence ha'penny down the drain.'

'So may I ask what is your business on the railway?'

'None, really. I thought, well, you only live once, and when I was a little girl my mother said I was always following carts to see where they were going and now that my husband Archibald has passed on I thought that this should be the time to go and see the world . . . you know, faraway places with strange-sounding names . . . like Twoshirts and Effing Forest and Scrote. One imagines all manner of *exotic* occurrences must take place somewhere with a name like Twoshirts. So many places I've never been to . . . I have a whole world to experience before it's too late, and I'm keeping a journal of it all as I go, so I'll be able to enjoy the world all over again when I get back.'

Something struck in Moist's head, causing him to

say, 'May I ask, Mrs Bradshaw, if your handwriting is good?'

She looked down her nose at him and said, 'Indeed yes, Mister Lipwig. I used to write a beautiful cursive script for my dear late husband. He was a lawyer and *they* expect excellence in the writing and use of the language. Mister Slant was always very . . . *particular* about that, and no one appreciates the judicious use of Latatian better than dear Archibald did.

'And, may I add, I was schooled at the Quirm College for Young Ladies, where they are *very* solid on the teaching of foreign tongues, even though Morporkian rather seems to have become the *lingua quirma* of late.' Mrs Bradshaw sniffed. 'And in working for my husband I learned a lot about people and the human condition.'

'Mrs Bradshaw, if you *were* to go everywhere where the trains go and write about all those places, perhaps you could send me a copy of your notes? They could be useful to other intrepid passengers . . . People would know what to expect from the Effing Forest or Twoshirts before they'd even paid a penny for their ticket. Already so many people from Ankh are travelling to Quirm just for the sunshine. It's become our heaviest service! And some of them go just for the day! I'm sure they'd think about going on other trips too if they saw all the little details of every place you visit, and perhaps you could include notes on accommodation as well as other places of interest en route?' he added, on fire with his own imagination. 'All the things that *you* would like to see and would be interested in. Wherever your travels take you, you can address your manuscript to Moist von Lipwig and give it to the nearest station master, and they'll see to it that it gets passed on to me.'

Moist thought about the amount of gold accruing in the coffers of Harry King's accounts and added, 'And I'm sure we could arrange some remuneration . . .'

As Mrs Bradshaw settled into the journey and looked out of the window Moist took out his notebook and scribbled a memo to Harry King: 'Please allow Mrs Georgina Bradshaw to travel anywhere she wants, even those little branch lines we haven't fully opened yet. She went to one of the best girls' schools I know of and understands language, and she is writing notes on all our destinations which may come in very useful. My instincts say that she will do us proud. I have an inkling that she will be either meticulous or humorous or, hopefully, both. And a widow who wears the kind of gold and diamond ring that she is wearing to travel through Ankh-Morpork and is still wearing it when she leaves is not going to be a fool. She speaks as well as Lady Sybil; that's Quirm College for you. Up School! Isn't this what we're after? We want people to widen their horizons on the train, of course, but why not day trips? You know what, there are people in Ankh-Morpork who haven't even got as far as Sto Lat yet. Travel broadens the mind, and also railway revenue.'

A sample of the great work arrived on scented paper one week later.

High Mouldering, on the Sto Plains, boasts wonderful salt-water baths from a pleasantly warm spring, and the owner and his wife give hygienic massages to those who would like to enjoy the benefit. Ladies and gentlemen separately, of course; there is nothing here that could be considered insalubrious or that would shock the most delicate of sensibilities.

Near by, the Hotel Continental offers accommodation for trolls, humans, dwarfs and goblins; fifty rooms are available at present. People wishing to tour the area may be interested in the Sacred Glade of Shock Knee, which deserves to be noticed for its amazing echoes. A short distance away is a shrine to Anoia, patron goddess for people who have difficulty with things stuck in their drawers.

A welcome break for the tired at weekends, with excellent meals. Highly recommended.

Moist made a note to see Mr Thomas Goatberger when he could next get back to Ankh-Morpork. If he was any judge, the publisher would be ready to bite his hand off to get a share of the railway magic.

When Moist did next return to the city, the matter of the railway to Uberwald had to take priority. Pacing up and down in the big room where Harry and Dick Simnel presided over their charts and reports and blueprints, Harry was still clearly worried.

'Now then, Moist, between ourselves and these four walls I've got the heebie-jeebies. We've taken gangs off the other lines, we're putting in more and more work on the long haul to Uberwald. This is a hell of an undertaking. I'm more at home knee-deep in shit, which is what we're going to be in here in this office if this doesn't work, believe you me.'

'Yes,' said Moist, 'but what you have to remember is that getting to Uberwald will mean getting to a whole load of other places on the way, and all of them'll want the railway and that will help cover costs right there. It's the tunnels and bridges that are a problem, but the best of it is that they're old technologies. There are plenty of masons who can build good bridges for us, and as for tunnels, the trolls are just begging to do them if they can dig out a home near by.'

Harry's only response was a grunt.

'And the nice thing about the trolls,' Moist added, 'is that they bring the whole family with them, even their kids. It's their way. If you don't know your rocks, you're no good as a troll. They just love changing the landscape. One of them asked me the other day if he could be a surveyor and I was just opening my mouth to say no when I thought, why not? He seemed like a bright lad, slow, yes, but quite bright. So I've told the boys to give him a bit of tuition, on the job, as it were.'

'Are you going to give him one of Simnel's special sliding slabs?' said Harry, smiling.

Moist laughed and said, 'Why not, Harry? I might just do that! No reason why a surveyor shouldn't be strong enough to lift up a mountain to see what's underneath!'

He took advantage of the lightened atmosphere to steer Sir Harry towards happier subjects, asking to be brought up to date on all the latest developments.

Every morning now the desk of Harry King was inundated by letters from people wanting no trains, some trains, or seriously wishing to have trains available right now. And then there were all the other helpful comments and suggestions: a Mr Snori Snorisson had written to say so many other people had arranged to meet under the station clock that his friend had taken four hours to find him . . . Shouldn't the railway provide stepladders for the use of shorter citizens . . . ? Help was requested for passengers with heavy luggage, and for the elderly or undead . . . With all the dangerous machinery involved, shouldn't there be guards – not the City Watch, of course, but somebody with some sense – to act as guardian of the train and its passengers? And that meant uniforms, hats, flags, whistles and other exciting accoutrements.

And this excitement was presumably why the editor of the *Ankh-Morpork Times* had decided to employ a railway correspondent, Mr Raymond Shuttle, who was an unashamed and self-confessed train spotter. The glint in his eyes was unmistakable.

Alongside the main business of the railway, Harry confessed himself delighted to see the enthusiasts spending their dollars on railway souvenirs such as the little clockwork models that were even now being created under licence by those deviously cunning artificers who were making a small fortune from railway memorabilia.* And the cannier artificers, always on the

---

* This would have been an even bigger fortune had not Thunderbolt carefully made certain that the Hygienic Railway Company took its slice.

lookout for moneymaking opportunities, were constantly making additions to these playthings for children: a little shed and four tiny figures to wait for the train. A signal box with a waving goblin. And yes, a miniature turning table just like the one in the compound, and so it went on. A lad with a doting parent could get his own tiny Iron Girder and oval track with straights and curves; and even miniature railway workers including a miniature Harry King.*

And once again, Moist marvelled at the power of the dream.

And then it was out into the grease-filled world of the compound to see the latest engines the lads were testing, and find out what the ingenious Mr Simnel had been up to since Moist had seen him last.

One thing he was sure of: even though Dick Simnel was forever coming up with blueprints for the next locomotive, every day would have seen him still hard at work on Iron Girder, which was probably why on every visit she continued to look a little different: a different boiler here, different wheels there, different paintwork and quite probably a host of integral things that Moist couldn't see. She was Dick's pride and joy, his first locomotive love, thought Moist, taking care not to say it aloud, the first test bed for every new innovation. No

---

* Harry was thrilled; he'd tried to be nonchalant about it but when he heard the suggestion that he should be part of a toy railroad he grinned from ear to ear, although Effie complained that they had made him look too fat.

locomotive shone as brightly as Iron Girder. No locomotive got the next big improvement before Iron
Girder. She was, indeed, the iron stalking horse for the
railway and Simnel her willing slave.

Just as Moist was debating where first to look for
Simnel, Emily King, in a very fine white cotton dress,
came jauntily skipping through the compound
towards the sacred engine shed as if completely
unaware of the attendant muck and grease. But after
all, he thought, she must have grown up with her
uncle's *other* business, against which the railway was a
fragrant pleasure garden. And here she was, bouncing
along cheerfully, and here was Iron Girder, and
suddenly Moist's spine went cold, every sinew twang-
ing, and he was near to biting his nails as the girl
continued towards the locomotive in her pristine white
cotton dress.

Moist moved like lightning across the compound as
Emily skipped on and reached Iron Girder. He looked
at Simnel, whose face had gone curiously grey even
under the grease and grime, and he was ready for anything as Emily patted the engine and said, 'Hello, Iron
Girder, how are we today, you lovely girl?' And while
Moist was still gawping, Emily took out her handkerchief and buffed Iron Girder's brass nameplate
industriously until it sparkled to the heavens. And as
Emily was talking to Iron Girder about how good she
was looking today, Simnel turned to Moist and said,
very quietly, 'She wouldn't have, you know, not Iron
Girder.'

'Good,' said Moist. 'And now you have *two* ladies,

you lucky man.' But in his head a voice said to him, 'But you more than half expected it, didn't you, Mister Lipwig? Oh, ye of little faith.' And then there was a sigh of steam.

For the next two hours Moist sat at his desk in Harry's compound, feeling as if he were a locomotive speeding along watching the scenery blur past. Every so often a boy came up with another pile of paperwork from some part of Harry King's domain and towards the end of the afternoon he felt himself subtly drifting into a coma, quite a pleasant one at the start: he visualized himself in a pale pink mist and it didn't matter. Nothing mattered. And little by little Moist von Lipwig began to unravel, but just as he was sliding under Of the Twilight the Darkness dropped down in front of him out of the evening glow, though exactly where he had dropped *from* Moist couldn't work out.

'Must go to sleep, Mister Lipwig! Burning candle at both ends means man with egg on face and burning bum. When did Mister Lipwig last eat? Not snack! Serious munch! I have some dried mushrooms if you are feeling peckish. No? Acquired taste . . . more for me, but you must sleep if nothing else. Mister Lipwig can't do everything. If he can't eat, can't do anything. Making money is good, but there is no pockets in a shroud. Give it a rest, Mister Railway! And *this* will help you big time no mistake.'

The goblin handed Moist a little bottle on which a grubby label proclaimed the contents as 'RAT POISON'.

'Label one big lie, Mister Lipwig, bottle cleaned out

and rats eaten, yes indeed, and filled with special goblin potion for tired person. Guaranteed no worms and it will give you refreshing sleep and you feel a lot better *if* you wake up in the morning! Guaranteed! Pure quill. None finer!'

It had been a long day and the heat of the smelters had made him as dry as the smelters themselves and so, what the hell, Moist took a long swig.

'Well done, Mister Lipwig!' chuckled the goblin. 'It will make your hairs curl . . . everywhere!'

Later, after Moist had finished talking to the dancing toadstools and Mr Whoopee, the man who could amusingly eat his own face, it must have been Moist's feet alone that found his bed, plodding along like a couple of old donkeys via the good offices of Sergeant Colon and Corporal Nobby Nobbs, who apparently found him just outside his house talking to his knees. And, according to Nobby, listening intently to what they had to say.

He awoke lying on his bedroom floor. Somebody had put blankets over him and even tucked him up nicely. He grasped his head and thought Oh no! I drank *another* goblin concoction! His dismay dwindled when he realized that he felt absolutely fine and not just fine, either, but so full of beans that the world probably had no beans left. When he stepped outside on to the balcony for a breath of fresh air the birds were singing and the sky was a wonderful shade of blue.

The door opened behind him and Adora Belle said, 'I know we have what might be called an unconventional marriage, what with our jobs and the pressure of work and so on, but I wouldn't be doing my wifely duty if I didn't ask you whether you have been firkydoodling with fast and loose women? No pressure. Answer in your own time.'

More or less spinning with the ecstasy of being alive and, of course, all those beans, Moist said joyfully, 'Now then, just a minute, bear with me now, tell me, is it *loose* women or is it *fast* women? Is there a spotter's guide or does one, as it were, cancel out the other?'

'Moist von Lipwig, you are rascally drunk. Can you even walk?'

For an answer Moist jumped in the air, clicking his heels, and said, 'Fast or loose, my girl, or why not both at once?'

Dragging him back into their bedroom and closing the door behind them, Adora Belle said, 'Well now, husband of mine, in that case let's find out.'

There was a thunderstorm over Schmaltzberg, but that was ever the case. Thunder rolled around the mountains, like the marbles of the gods. And in the privacy of his office, the Low King was discussing progress with Aeron who was looking more cheerful than usual.

'Things appear to be calming down,' Rhys said. 'They argue and argue and then somebody remembers that he has business to deal with concerning his rat farms, or there's some trouble over in his goldmine, water coming in, pit props buckling and so on and so forth, things they can't leave to underlings, and then everything goes quiet.'

'I know you're worried,' said Aeron, 'but I think . . . no, I believe, that you have more friends than you ever thought possible. Even the goblins know that you were one of the first who signed up for goblin emancipation. They, whether we like it or not, are becoming the future, Rhys. It was the business with the clacks towers that made even traditional dwarfs angry. The clacks is needed: everybody wants news. People are furious everywhere. After all, they say, goblins and trolls are minding their own business, so why not the dwarfs?'

'No more news of Ardent?' asked the King. 'It's been months, hasn't it? No more towers down or idiots trying to destroy the railway? Can I believe that his firebrand has burned out?'

Aeron handed the King his coffee and said, 'I believe Lord Vetinari said never do anything until you hear the screams. However, Ardent is not one to come back, helmet in hand, to say "sorry". There is too much pride there by half.'

After a quiet moment while Rhys Rhysson considered the possibilities, Aeron continued.

'So you will accept the invitation to the summit in Quirm? In these circumstances, Rhys, it does seem to me that it is *very* important that you are there and seen to be there.'

'Of course. Diamond King will be chairing proceedings this year and I must mend fences. He's helpful but I'm in no mood to try his patience. He has always been a most understanding ally.'

'And the other . . . thing?'

'The other thing is satisfactory,' said the King. He

paused. 'Yes, we should go to Quirm, but I think it would be wise to leave Albrechtson in charge here, just to take care of any business.'

Without his quite knowing how it had come about, and regardless of how little he was actually at the compound, it appeared that Moist was now Mr Railway. If anyone wanted to know anything about it, they asked him. If they'd lost their little child in the queue for Iron Girder, the call went out for Mr Lipwig and if somebody had a new idea for the railway it was sent to Mr Lipwig and after a while it didn't seem to Moist to matter what time it was or, worse, where he was: the claims on his attention were never-ending.

He was pretty certain that he slept quite often, sometimes back at home, if at all possible, or saving that a mattress and blanket somewhere within the warm and ever enlarging foundries along the route to Uberwald, or, if all else failed, snuggled down under the tarpaulins of whatever railway gang was near by, having shared whatever was in the cooking pot. If you were lucky it was pheasant or possibly grouse, and if you weren't so lucky, at least there would be pot luck, which generally meant cabbages and swedes and almost certainly something that was protein, but you wouldn't want to see what it was in daylight. However, to give them their due, the railway gangs, including the vanguard now bearing down on Slake, were resourceful men, especially in the tradition of setting snares to fill their pots along the permanent way.

Slake was one of those places, Moist thought, that

you put on the map because it was embarrassing to have a map with holes in it. There was some mining, forestry and fishing and after a while you got the feeling that those people who chose to live in Slake and the surrounding area were people who didn't want other people to know where they were. And when you walked around Slake you were always certain that you were being watched. He put it down as a place to avoid unless you liked bad cooking and banjos. Nevertheless, it had a mayor and was nailed to the map as a coaling and water stop.

No longer did Moist wear the snazzy suits and hand-made shoes that, along with his collection of official-looking hats, were his calling card back in the city. They didn't stand up well to the regime of the railway worker and so now he wore the greasy shirt and waistcoat with rough trousers tied at the knee. He loved the huge boots and the flat cap that seemed to go with them, making you feel safe at both ends. But the boots, oh the boots . . . a troll could drop on your head and you'd be dead, but the boots would be still alive and kicking! They had hobnails and were more or less like tiny fortresses. Nothing could get past a railway worker's boots.

Messages found Moist wherever he might be, via train, goblin runner or clacks, since there were very few places these days where their towers hadn't found a niche in the landscape.

In the small hours of one morning in the Plains township of Little Swelling when it was pouring with rain that hammered on the makeshift lodgings, Moist pulled back the tarpaulin and wood door to see the face of Of the Twilight the Darkness, who couldn't be called soaked, because there was really very little of him to soak.* As soon as the goblin got inside the bothy, such water as was on him simply disappeared.

Almost automatically Moist looked up to see the lights of the local clacks tower and as he did so it flashed a familiar code: it was from Adora Belle. He recognized her code as easily as he would recognize his own. 'Quickly!' he said. 'Get up that tower and get that message back to me, *now!*'

He waited, and in the gloom the voice of Of the Twilight the Darkness said, 'Did I hear the magic word, Mister Little Damp?'

Moist was surprised at himself because, even though the goblin had a smell you could almost see, that was no reason for not minding your manners, so he said, '*Please*, Mister Of the Twilight the Darkness. Thank you so very much.'

And thus chastened, Moist kept silent as the little goblin scuttled back out into the rain and scampered towards the tower.

Moist finished his ablutions, gathered his things together – on the assumption that whatever the message it would require him to go somewhere else – and went out to where the golem horse was waiting

---

* With all goblins, the male ones especially, you got the impression of sinews but they mostly consisted of sinews tied together with other sinews. Surely, the mind protested, there must be muscles in there somewhere, but quite possibly they had to fight to find some room among all those damn sinews.

unregarding of the weather, just in case it needed waking up, because however hard he tried he couldn't think of it as anything other than alive. Admittedly, the horse was giving him incipient piles, no matter how much padding he put between himself and it. And although the creature could now speak, Moist still yearned for all those fussing little rituals that defined horsemanship. He was aware that there should be such things as nose bags and adjusting the straps and giving the beast some water. The lack of these rituals slightly unbalanced Moist. It was creepy. In the falling rain it was as if he was in two different worlds.

And while he was wondering whether he should give the horse a name, which somehow would have made things feel better, *Mister* Of the Twilight the Darkness arrived, clutching a damp and smudged pink clacks flimsy.

> *Vetinari wants to see you immediately. Stop. PS Any chance of bringing home some of that goblin potion with you. Stop. PPS If you pass a bakery we could do with a couple of sliced loaves. Stop. Your loving wife. Stop.*

And he thought, well, isn't it nice to be wanted?

No more than a few hours and a bumpy ride through pouring rain later, the door to the anteroom outside the Oblong Office was opened by Drumknott, replete in a very smart engine driver's hat, wiping his greasy hands on an equally greasy piece of ever-present engine driver's rag.

'His lordship will be with you presently, Mister Lipwig. You've been a very busy man lately, haven't you?'

Moist could now see that the little secretary was also looking tanned beneath the smuts and soot, and the hat was, gods forbid, jaunty, a term never before applied to Drumknott.

'Have you spent much time on the railway, Mister Drumknott? It looks like it's doing you some good.'

'Oh, yes, sir! His lordship allows me to take a few turns on the railway late mornings after he's finished the crossword. After all, *everything* is about the train these days, isn't it, and he was gracious enough to say that I'm keeping him in touch.'

At that moment, there was a shrill whistle from the other side of the door and Drumknott pulled it open to reveal Lord Vetinari, to Moist's total surprise, catching one of the new little steam engines just as it was about to plunge off the highly polished desk. The familiar straights and curves were surrounded by little toy people: guards, engine drivers, passengers, the portly controller with a big cigar and various engineers with tiny crafted sliding rulers. And the tyrant caught the falling engine in a gauntlet, leaving water and oil dripping down on to the expensive polished ebony floor tiles.

'Quite amazing, isn't it, Mister Lipwig?' he said cheerfully through the smoke. 'Though isn't it a pity that they can only run on rails? I can't imagine what the world would be like if everyone had their own steam locomotive. Abominable.'

His lordship held out his hand for Drumknott to clean it with a not-so-greasy rag, and said, 'Well, Mister Lipwig is here, Drumknott, and I know you can't wait to get back to your wonderful railway.'

And Drumknott – the Drumknott who thought the finer things of life were stored in manila folders – headed off down the stairs two at a time to get into the cab, shovel the coal, start the engine, blow the whistle and breathe in smuts and soot and be that most wondrous of creatures, an *engine driver*.

'Tell me, Mister Lipwig,' said Vetinari, as the door closed. 'It occurs to me that rocks on the line could easily derail a locomotive . . .'

'Well, my lord, away from Ankh-Morpork we give the engines cow-catchers, a kind of plough, if you will. And remember, sir, a locomotive running free has a considerable weight and the signallers and linesmen keep an eye on the track.'

'So, there has so far been no deliberate sabotage?'

Moist said, 'Not since the attack on Iron Girder months ago, unless you mean the little boys who put their pennies on the track just to get them flattened? That seems to be more of a pastime, and copper bends easily. It's gone quiet, hasn't it, sir? I'm thinking about the grags knocking down clacks towers and generally being difficult. It looks like they've given up.'

Vetinari winced. 'You could be right. Certainly the Low King appears to believe so, and Commander Vimes reports that his agents in Uberwald are not picking up any disturbances. Other sources indicate the same. But . . . I worry that extremists are like perennial weeds. They may disappear for a while but they don't give up. I fear they've gone further underground, waiting for their moment.'

'Which moment would that be, sir?'

'Do you know, Mister Lipwig, I wonder about that every night. I take some pleasure in the fact that the era of the locomotive has begun with care and thought and a scientific outlook instead of a lot of tinkering. Encouraging free-for-all simply encourages more episodes such as we saw in the Effing Forest. So . . .' Vetinari now stared directly at Moist. 'Tell me, how is the railway to Uberwald coming along?'

'Making very good progress, sir, but there is a shortfall . . . as it were. We were expecting to drive the golden spike halfway through next month. There's a lot of work still to do and we're driving the train underground around the Gruffies. We're tunnelling hard, but there are already a lot of cave formations up there.'

And there's the bridges, he thought. You haven't told him about the bridges. 'And, of course, once we get to Uberwald we'll eventually continue on to Genua.'

'Not good enough, Mister Lipwig, not good enough at all. You must speed up. The balance of the world could be at stake.'

'Er . . . with all due respect, my lord, why?'

Vetinari frowned. 'Mister Lipwig. I have given you your orders; how you execute those orders is up to you, but they *must* be obeyed!'

Moist's mood was not helped by finding the golem horse had been clamped, apparently by the Watch since he could see a watchman close by, laughing. The horse looked at him, embarrassed, and said, 'I regret this inconvenience, sir, but I must obey the law.'

Seething, Moist said, 'As a golem horse, are you as strong as any other golem?'

'Oh, yes, sir.'

'Very well,' said Moist. 'Then get yourself out of the clamp.'

The clamp cracked and split and the watchman ran towards Moist just as he leapt on to the back of the horse, yelling after him, 'Oi! That's public property, that is!'

And Moist shouted over his shoulder, 'Send the bill to Sir Harry King, if you dare! Tell him it's from Moist von Lipwig!'

Looking back as the horse galloped away down Lower Broadway, to his glee he saw the watchman picking up the pieces of the yellow clamp and he shouted, 'No one interferes with the progress of the Hygienic Railway!'

Moist always preferred to move fast – after all, in his previous businesses a turn of speed was essential – and he arrived at Harry's compound with the horse panting like a celestial runner.* Stepping down and, for nothing more than effect, tying up the horse, he said, 'Why were

---

* It is well known that it is possible to climb Cori Celesti. Many athletes have attempted to climb to the summit and most of them have failed, although history *does* admit that a posse of elderly gentlemen with arthritis and bandy legs did manage this feat but subsequently died like heroes which was, after all, what it was all about. Other aspiring and indeed perspiring athletes have managed to get at least a little way up by

you panting? Golems don't pant. You don't breathe!'

'Sorry, sir. You wanted me to be a more horse-like horse, so I am doing my best, sir . . . neigh, whinny, whinny.'

Moist burst out laughing and said, 'That'll do, Dobbin . . . No, not Dobbin! How do you fancy Flash?'

Reflectively the horse said, 'I've never had a name before. I've always been "horse". But it's a very nice feeling to know who you are. I wonder how I did without it for these past nine hundred and three years. Thank you, Mister Lipwig.'

Moist made his way to Harry's office and made certain that he spoke directly and in private to Harry, who stared at Moist for an eternity before saying, 'Surely you know that they've hardly started reinforcing the first of the bridges on the Uberwald line? No train can run on thin air!'

'Yes, Harry, I know. Gods bless me, I speak to the surveyors and inspectors all the time. But it's only the beds of the bridges that need lots of work. The uprights have stood the test of time.'

And while Sir Harry was drawing breath to protest, Moist told him what he had in mind if Simnel's engineers weren't ready in time for whatever Vetinari was cooking up.

It took some time for Harry to get to grips with Moist's plan, but finally when he'd heard it all he said,

using what is known as the Path of Lights, which it has to be said does not favour anyone who is not a *true* hero. Nevertheless many still attempt to run up Cori Celesti or at least break their femur in trying.

'You're breaking all the rules, my lad, and you can only do that once to Vetinari. I'm pretty sure about *that*.'

It took all of Moist's guile and self-control in the face of an angry Harry King, but he held his ground and said, 'Harry, in all my time working for Lord Vetinari I've learned to understand the words "plausible deniability".'

'Eh? What does that mean, smart boy?' said Harry.

'It means his lordship chooses to have little idea of what I do and certainly doesn't give me clear instructions, and it also means I have to guess a lot, but I've always been very good at that. Got a lot to do, Sir Harry, or shall I say *my lord* Harry or should I even dare to say *Baron King of Ankh-Morpork* . . . you can fill in that bit for yourself . . . and, if I remember correctly, when Vetinari makes you the first railway baron you'll be entitled to six silver balls on your coronet. A knighthood? Pah! You could be a Baron overnight. I imagine Lady King would be most impressed by a man with six balls.'

Harry snorted. 'That'd give the missus a surprise!' He considered the picture Moist had painted of the future and said, 'Actually, I reckon she'd be swanking like a . . . Duchess!' He sobered up a little and continued, 'Believe me, I thought I was the King of the Shit, but *you* are full of the stuff! Would you damn well tell me how much trouble it's going to get us both into? Baron, my arse. All right, mister, how do we get this thing done, scoundrels that we are?'

Even with the added pressure from the Patrician and

with every lad, troll and goblin that Harry could provide, it still took time to build a railway. 'Tsort was not built in a day,' was the mantra when anyone got impatient. Still, day by day the great new railway line to Uberwald got closer to its destination.

If building the railway was one thing, maintaining it was quite another. The railway was out there in the wind and the weather, and, in many cases, far from civilization. Moist looked every week at the complaints, breakdowns and miscellaneous problems book, his instinct always being to start with the miscellaneous and sometimes humorous: intoxicated troll on line, harpies nesting in coal bunker, woman in labour.* And then, of course, there were also the landslides, which played havoc with the schedules. People also didn't appreciate that to leave a huge truck full of pigs on a level crossing was actively to prevent any movement on the railway, and as for the people who believed that if they held out their palm to the oncoming locomotive it would stop for them immediately! As, in fact, it might, but a skidding locomotive was a matter of filling up a large number of forms afterwards.

As Moist was all too aware, ever since the maiden voyage the newspaper editors of the Sto Plains had been waiting for the first true railway disaster, which,

---

* Miss Daisy Snapes was officially the first person to be born on a moving train, thanks to a midwife who rushed the mother to the guard's van. Young Daisy was born at thirty miles an hour and her doting parents named her Locomotion Snapes, until Moist got to hear about it and gave her and her parents a free season ticket on the railway, along with the suggestion that Locomotion might sound better as a middle name.

for preference, would include at least one horrible death.

And they got one, although not on the Hygienic Railway Company's line. Instead, the first casualty happened in the back country of Quirm, where three entrepreneurs, Monsieur Lavasse the winemaker, Monsieur Croque the cheesemonger and Monsieur Lestripe, a purveyor of decorative onion-wreaths, had invested in their own small single-track line between their vineyards and farms.

They had called on Simnel for expert advice, in particular how to avoid a head-on crash between their two locomotives on the single track, a conundrum that Dick had solved with classic Simnel simplicity by providing them with signals that could not be changed without a special brass token, carried by whichever driver had right of way on the line.

Amid press headlines claiming SIMNEL SYSTEM FAILS and ARE PASSENGER LIVES AT RISK? Simnel and Moist were summoned to Quirm to investigate, where they discovered the terrible truth. A middle manager at Chateau Lavasse had looked to speed things up and had duplicated the safety token and explained to the drivers and the signalmen that they just needed to be sensible. Trusting them to get it right had worked well for a while and so everyone relaxed, and then one day Signalman Hugo was preoccupied and forgot a vital safety step, and there were two trains heading for each other at some speed along the single track, with each driver thinking he had the right of way. And they did indeed meet halfway. One driver died, the other was seriously scalded by runaway cheeses which flowed like lava when they reached the heat of the footplate, and there was a great disturbance of foie gras.

And the clerk who had seen fit to order a second token said, 'Well, I thought I would be saving time so I only—'

According to Raymond Shuttle's report in the next day's *Times*: '"I am very sorry about the gentleman who was killed, and the man who was injured," Mr Lipwig told me. "I'm sure none of us will ever look at fondue the same way again. However, Mister Simnel has made it clear that while it's easy to deal with stupid, bloody stupid is horribly difficult to erase. I wonder how many dreadful crimes have been perpetrated following a well-meaning person saying 'I only . . .'?"'

Damage limitation achieved, Simnel and Moist headed back to Ankh-Morpork. As the slow train on the coastal branch line left the rocky ground which was so good for the famous Quirmian vines and started to skirt the steamy world of the Netherglades,* Simnel slept and Moist pondered the many challenges ahead

---

* The swamps in this part of the world are famous for their birdlife but also notorious, because they move constantly and quickly. Dry land is hard to find. The human inhabitants live on large rafts that serve as both shelters and gardens. The older generations have splayed feet, which they try to encourage in their offspring because the webs show that the owner is a great hunter of the swamps. They have no known enemies, probably because most people don't *want* to step into a swamp. They are in fact helpful to travellers, and they distil extremely useful medications from the floating flora and fauna of the swamps, which include the twisting honeydew and the egregious flytrap, whose venom can be used in the making of delicate ironwork etchings, and which must be approached

while staring out of the window at the passing land-scape. Watching the swamps roll by, Moist felt faintly relieved that the train didn't stop until back in drier terrain at the small town of Shankydoodle, a great exporter of champion racehorses. That was fine, he thought: there was a long winding footpath from there to the Netherglades and if you couldn't find it you had no business being there.

The rain poured down on the Sto Lat terminus, water gushing off the roof as people scurried to get out of the downpour, seeking a respite from the deluge. The little coffee shop of Marjorie Painsworth was dry and as an extra attraction on this dreadful night she had warm buns on sale. It was a beacon of solace for the young troll lady, who stirred her cup of molten sulphur un-certainly while waiting. She watched people coming in and out, and was surprised when a dwarf gentleman indicated the chair next to her and said, 'Excuse me, is this place taken?'

Crackle had never had much to do with dwarfs, of

with extreme caution as the venom can be spat over several yards.

There clearly has been magic at work in the Netherglades and its future as the pharmacopoeia of the world is being tested by Professor Rincewind of Unseen University. A dispatch from him reveals that the juice pressed from a certain little yellow flower induces certainty in the patient for up to fifteen minutes. About what they are certain they cannot specify, but the patient is, in that short time, completely certain about *everything*. And further research has found that a floating water hyacinth yields in its juices total *un*certainty about anything for half an hour. Philosophers are excited about the uses of these potions, and the search continues for a plant that combines the qualities of both, thereby being of great use to theologians.

course, but since the whole Koom Valley business had been sorted out, it was surely in order for her to talk to a dwarf, especially since this one was very well dressed and, well, looked human; an Ankh-Morpork dwarf as they called them. So she smiled and said, 'By all means do take a seat, sir. Isn't the weather inclement for this time of year?'

The dwarf bowed, sat down and said, 'Forgive my intrusion, but I am so happy to hear you use a word like "inclement". The very word itself paints a picture, don't you think? A grey one, but nevertheless . . . Oh, where are my manners? Please let me introduce myself: Dopey Docson at your service, madam, and may I say you speak extremely good dwarfish?'

Crackle looked around. People were still coming in out of the rain and leaving as the trains came and went. Sto Lat was, after all, a hub of the railway and almost all traffic passed through there. She had one ear cocked for the porter announcing her own train, but she managed to say, 'Your grasp of troll is likewise also remarkable, if I may say so. May I ask where your travels have taken you?'

The dwarf smiled again and said, 'I'm a librarian in Klatch, but I've recently buried my father in Copperhead.'

And Crackle stifled a laugh and said, 'Do excuse me, I'm very sorry to hear about your father, but that's amazing! I'm also a librarian, in the service of Diamond King of Trolls!'

'Ah, the Diamond Library! Alas not available to us at the moment, even under the famous Accord. I'd give anything just to see it.'

And the two librarians ordered more drinks and talked about books while whistles blew and train after train left the station. Crackle told Dopey that her husband didn't like books and considered that mumbling should be good enough for trolls like it was in the old days, and the dwarf told her about his wife who even after the Koom Valley Accord still thought of trolls as a kind of animal, and they talked and talked and talked about the meaning of words and, indeed, the love of words. And Marjorie recognized the syndrome and kept the hot coffee and sulphur flowing, with the occasional warm rock cake.

Of course, it wasn't her business, she thought, it wasn't up to her how other people led their lives, and she definitely didn't eavesdrop, well, not much, but she couldn't help hearing the dwarf say, 'I've been offered a post as librarian at Brazeneck University and they've already told me I can bring my own assistant.'

And Marjorie was not surprised to find two empty cups and an empty table when she next looked: this sort of thing was bound to happen with the railway. It expanded horizons, inside and out, people went looking to find themselves and what they found was somebody else.

As coups went, the Schmaltzberg coup went slowly, dripping through the tunnels and mines like treacle, and just as sticky. A connoisseur of coups would recognize the form. Two would get up to impress on a third that this was what should be done because this was what everyone else was going to do, and there was no point in being on the losing side, was there? There were always the ones who had misgivings, but the pressure of the tide was strengthening. Underground Schmaltzberg was in many respects a beehive and the swarm was deciding that they needed a new Queen.

Ardent and the banished grags were, of course, at the centre of all this, and now having triumphantly* returned were settling down as if the place was theirs by right . . .

'Nobody has to be hurt,' they said, and it may have been too that people would murmur, 'After all, it's in his own interests,' and there were other little giveaways such as 'It's time for fresh blood,' and such things as 'We must preserve our most hallowed ordinances,' and if you were susceptible to atmospheres, you could see that dwarfs, perfectly sensible dwarfs, dwarfs who would consider themselves dwarfs of repute and fair dealing, were nevertheless slowly betraying allegiances they had formerly undertaken with great solemnity, because the hive was buzzing and they didn't want to be the ones that got stung.

The watchwords were 'restoring order' and 'going back to the basics of true dwarfishness'.

Nevertheless, there is always somebody who will not buzz with the swarm and in this case it was Albrecht Albrechtson, around whom there coalesced the dwarfs who were totally against the takeover and who

---

* In their minds, at least, although it has to be said that they had been too careful to attempt to overthrow the Low King until he was far away in Quirm.

remained loyal to Rhys Rhysson come what may. The air in the corridors thickened, and the unspoken question was who would be the first to sting?

Albrecht Albrechtson placed his hand on the Scone of Stone.

'My fellow dwarfs, I made an oath, and so did you. And as we all learned on our mother's knees, the Ginnungagap awaits all murderers and oath-breakers.' His smile was a grimace. He went on. 'Perhaps I misheard.'

'Circumstances have changed,' said Ardent. 'The King is far too friendly with the trolls and the damn humans and, for goodness' sake, he also signed the declaration that the goblins – goblins, I ask you – should be treated as well as dwarfs! I don't know about you, but I don't see a goblin as being *my* equal.'

In the ringing silence, Albrechtson almost whispered, 'And the Koom Valley Accord? The understanding that would maintain peace in our time? We were all party to it. How easily do we break *our* oaths these days?'

'I never signed,' said Ardent.

'No, you didn't,' said Albrechtson. 'It was signed by Rhys Rhysson on behalf of all dwarfs.'

'Not on my behalf,' Ardent countered. 'And I didn't believe that little tableau of the two kings in the cavern. You know how humans are? I wouldn't put it past someone like Vetinari to have had it placed there.'

This time the silence banged. They had all walked past that strange shining tableau in Koom Valley where the air was so chilly in the cavern and the two dead kings rode into history in a state of intentional stale-mate. And perhaps some of them might have wondered what the dead kings would do if their peace were disturbed. The moment was broken by Ardent.

'What we need is stability,' he said. 'No one need come to blows, nobody will be hurt. I give you my oath on that.'

'Excuse me,' said Albrecht. 'Would that go the way of the oath you gave your King, you traitor?'

The clang of weaponry being deployed at speed echoed around the halls, to be followed by the resounding silence of not wanting to be the one to take the first slash. It was a stalemate, so stale as to be stinking.

'I will not rise to idiotic taunts,' said Ardent. 'We must deal with the world as it is. We have to make certain that it becomes the world that we want, where the dwarfs take their rightful place at the table. Times have changed. We need someone ready to defend our interests. Everyone keeps talking about the world changing. I intend to see that it changes to the better-ment of dwarfkind.'

He walked over to Albrecht and held out a hand. 'You used to think like this, my friend. Won't you join me?'

The multiple intake of breaths went around the cavern.

Albrecht hesitated for a moment. 'You can stick that right up your jumper.'

There was silence. Apart from some dwarfs saying to each other, 'What does that mean?' and other more trav-elled dwarfs, who had dealt with humans, coming to the rescue with, 'It's rather like saying "Put it where the sun does not shine",' causing those dwarfs who did not know the ways of humanity to say, 'Isn't that the little valley over near Slice, rather nice?' until one of them said, 'As I understand it, it means shove it up your arse.'

'Oh, really?'

'May I suggest a show of hands?' said Ardent. 'All those *not* for me and a proper resolution to dwarf affairs as they have been since time immemorial should raise their hand and make themselves known.'

Albrechtson promptly sat on the Scone of Stone.

'Well,' said Ardent. 'Stay there long enough, my friend, and you will have piles.'

And there was laughter, but worried laughter. And unusually, for dwarfs, people were thinking first. Yes, the goblins were rising and so were the humans and the trolls, and on the playing board of the world the dwarfs surely had to keep some allegiances. So what if a king changes? When the King came back he would find a *fait accompli* and the world would be busy with its own occupations. Politics notoriously change all the time . . . The unseen, unheard point was that everybody knew that if a dwarf-against-dwarf fight happened now it would go the distance, and where would they all be then?

In the highest room in her castle over the deepest canyon in Uberwald Lady Margolotta was awakened by the duty Igor and was not happy about it.

She opened the lid of her casket and said, 'Vhat's this all about? It's not even dusk yet.'

'Theriouth thingth happening, my lady. I heard there'th a coup in Schmaltzberg and Ardent ith in the athendant.'

Igor looked carefully at his mistress, who appeared to be suddenly lost in thought. He stepped back a little in case of an explosion. To his surprise, Lady Margolotta merely said, 'That little veasel? Sometimes the black ribbon is sorely tested. How far has the news got around?'

'Hardly at all, my lady. The clackth ith down, on the orderth of Ardent.'

A sudden syrup in his mistress's tone worried Igor. If silk could speak it would sound like that.

'On his orders? Really? Ve'll see about that. Oh, yes, ve vill.'

Lady Margolotta walked over to the balcony and dropped into the canyon, gathering speed until she glided towards the first clacks tower outside Uberwald and landed softly on the little deck, so close to the superintendent that he nearly lost a year's growth. But he knew the ropes. Lady Margolotta was a black ribboner and generally quite a useful neighbour.

'Oh, it's you, Arthur,' she said. 'How's your vife? Sorry to upset you.'

Rather nervously, the superintendent said, 'Dolores is fine, m'lady, thank you for asking.'

'And the children?'

'Doing very well, thank you, m'lady, and thank you so much for helping with the tuition fees.'

'Not at all. Is your clacks still vorking?'

'Oh yes, m'lady, but something seems to have

happened up the line. We've got one hell of a backlog and we don't know what's going on. Looks like the grag militants have been up to their old tricks again.'

'Yes, I know, Arthur. Could you please send a clacks to Lord Vetinari and a copy to Diamond King of Trolls? Also to the major clacks office in Quirm for delivery to Rhys Rhysson. My usual codes, of course, and priority vun.'

She waited while the man set things in motion, tapping her foot on the floor, and was relieved when Arthur had finished.

'Thank you, Arthur. Vould you be so good as to have any messages brought over to me as soon as possible by vun of your goblin couriers, please? And oh, it's your son's birthday, isn't it?'

'Yes, tomorrow!'

A heavy gold coin dropped into the man's hand.

'Tell him not to spend it all at vonce,' said a voice in the distance and suddenly Lady Margolotta was no longer there. The man looked nervously at the shiny coin in his hand. But there, that was the gentry for you. It paid to be in with the gentry. She had been so helpful when his daughter was taken bad, as well. Yes, of course, she was a vampire. But she wasn't a bad person. And he was oh so very glad he could be of use to her.

It had been a long wait to get home, but a wait worth waiting for, and after a pleasant evening with Adora Belle, what could be better than being woken up at 3 a.m. by members of the palace guard? And of course, the answer was absolutely everything, thought Moist.

Crossly was so furious that they were backing away from him across the threshold and Moist heard him say, 'This is insufferable! What about *habeas corpus*?'

And the most senior of the guards said, 'What about *habeas corpus*?'

Moist sighed and pulled on his trousers. Nowadays he kept a pair at hand, ready for occasions such as this. He had had enough. And so, stepping into his shoes and buttoning his shirt, he more or less slid down the stairs to where the grinning guards were shouldering aside the still protesting Crossly.

He was aware of Adora Belle, at her spikiest, looking over the banister and he had one of those *to hell with it* moments . . . As the guards strode into the hallway, he walked up to them and said, 'Where's your warrant?'

'What? We don't have to have a warrant.'

'Okay,' said Moist. 'Then you should seriously consider, for your own sake, apologizing to my wife for disturbing us at this time of the morning. She gets very . . . unhappy if her sleep is interrupted.'

At that instant Adora Belle leaned over the banister and said, 'This is a most excellent crossbow, one of Burleigh and Stronginthearm's finest, and I can only fire it once, gentlemen, so which intruder will I hit? Because right now intruders are what you appear to be, and rude intruders at that. After all, a simple "Do you mind coming with us, sir?" would have done the trick.

'Moist?' Raising the loaded crossbow, Adora Belle continued, 'Is this the one with the dodgy hair trigger? I always get them confused.'

Moist held out his hands and said, 'This is how it's

going to go. You may think that Vetinari will be on your side, the majesty of the Patrician and what have you. On the other hand, my wife could shoot any one of you if she wanted to and quite possibly might hit me instead. And I suspect Moist von Lipwig is more important to the Patrician than you bunch of herberts.'

'Off you go, gentlemen,' Adora Belle chimed in from her vantage point. 'I'm sure my husband will attend on his lordship around breakfast time. It's always good to do business on a full stomach.'

Moist looked at the guards and said, 'Gentlemen, I have no intention of getting you into trouble, or indeed of allowing my wife to skewer any one or two of you. And so I think I'd like to have an early-morning stroll to the palace. If it so happens that you are walking that way at the same time, well, so be it. Although you might want to make that a brisk walk, because I fear my wife will be watching us go from the upstairs window and that *is* the dodgy crossbow she's holding in her hands.'

And as he sauntered after the suddenly very sprightly guards clanging against each other in their hurry to get away, Moist was surprised to see the impeccably ironed Crossly make a fist and whisper, 'Well *done*, sir! They don't even clean their boots when they step inside.' And the sedate little man's face was fierce and fiery.

Within the palace, Moist found Lord Vetinari in conversation with a stone-faced Commander Vimes. The normal calm of the Oblong Office had been replaced by a low hum of determined-looking clerks arriving with messages to hand over to Drumknott.

Vetinari looked up and said, 'Ah, Mister Lipwig. I'm so glad you could spare us a little time from your early-morning exercise routine.'

'Your guards can't run for toffee. You ought to do something about it, sir, and while we're on the subject, it would be a good idea to teach them some manners.'

The Patrician lifted an eyebrow. 'I understood it was the prodding you objected to, Mister Lipwig. Was there prodding?'

'No, sir, but—'

'I am glad to hear it,' said his lordship. 'So, if we may to business? As I suspected, the apologists for the grags and other dwarf malcontents have merely been lying low, and I believe that in the darkness scandalous undertakings are still sprouting like mushrooms. It appears that there has been a palace coup in Schmaltzberg, only the third one in the history of the dwarfs. Unfortunately, the Low King is, as they say, out of position in Quirm where he has been attending a summit with Diamond King of Trolls. Rhys Rhysson is a notable negotiator, as we all know well from the Koom Valley Accord, and he has held the fractious coalition of dwarf chief mining engineers together for many years. And he is no mean practitioner with the axe, I believe, but he needs to be back in Uberwald with his inner council if this . . . unfortunate turn of events is not to spread underground to other mines.

'Having considered the options,' continued the Patrician, 'it would seem that the railway route to Uberwald, presently under construction, would pro-vide the swiftest and safest and most comfortable method for transporting the Low King, his retinue and war councillors. Time is, as they say, of the essence. You, Mister Lipwig, will travel with all speed to Quirm and take charge of arrangements. Commander Vimes will provide watchmen as an escort and will join you himself as you pass back through Ankh-Morpork, with reinforcements as he sees fit. Be aware, Mister Lipwig, that this is *your* Koom Valley, on wheels.'

'And when you get to Quirm,' said Vimes, 'be sure to look for a dwarf called Bashfull Bashfullsson. Very useful and most definitely on the Low King's side.'

'But the line is nowhere near finished, sir!' Moist wailed.

'Mister Lipwig, you know already that it is not your job to tell me what the problems are. It is your job to tell me about the solutions. Do we have an understanding? I am sure that Harry King will have a high-speed locomotive he can spare – one of his Flyers, perhaps?'

'But, my lord, Harry might have a dozen or so locomotives to spare, but it's the laying of the tracks, that's the rub.'

'Mister Lipwig, I want . . . No, I am ordering you to make miracles by all means necessary,' said Vetinari. 'Do I make my point? I am sure I could make it somewhat pointier.'

Moist saluted and with no hint of sarcasm said, 'Exactly, sir! Action this day! Miracles are us, sir!'

And laconically Vetinari said, 'Try to make it yesterday, Mister Lipwig.'

And that, Moist knew, was that, as far as that conversation was concerned.

* * *

Drumknott had been busy. Even as Moist was being roused from his bed by the palace guard, messengers had been sent to Harry King and to Simnel's home. By the time Moist arrived at the compound, he found it even busier than it was in the middle of the day. There to greet him in the grey light of early dawn were Harry and Dick. They appeared to be having an argument and Simnel was looking rather unhappy.

'But it's the look of the thing, Dick,' Harry was saying. 'I mean, Iron Girder is wonderful, of course, but I'm sure the Flyers are classier and more suitable for royalty.'

'Sorry, Harry,' Simnel replied. 'I think it might be risky if Iron Girder weren't the engine. Don't ask me why, because I can't explain why, even with my sliding rule, but she is what we need. And to tell thee t'truth, sir, I've shined her up so much, polished her, greased this, checked that, she's fit for any king, or queen, come to that. Oh, the Flyers are good, and reet smart, too, but I'll say it again: my Iron Girder is the best locomotive in an emergency.'

The arguments chased each other through Moist's brain. Vetinari says this has to be top secret, and it would be Iron Girder's first trip beyond the compound in months. Everyone is bound to notice. But we'll be running an unscheduled train, so they're going to notice anyway. And if it's one of the usual Flyers all the regular passengers will want to know why they can't get on it. And there'll be the armed escort from the Watch, that'll really make us stick out a mile. And after all, if you're going to run a special train the locomotive should be special . . .

'You know what, Harry?' said Moist. 'I think Dick's right about this. There's something about that engine—'

Just then, from Iron Girder, a little way away, there came a perceptible hiss of steam. Even Harry noticed it.

And Simnel said, 'Steam's up, gentlemen. All aboard, those who're going to Quirm. I'm sorry, Mister Lipwig, but his lordship's orders are to send freight trucks only, to distract attention, like. And to tell t'truth it may be the only way we'll get some Watch officers to fit on board. I've to work on that before you get back. Don't worry,' he added hastily, seeing the others' horror, 'it'll be regular carriages hitched up for the return journey.'

'I hope those trucks are full,' said Harry. 'Can't afford to waste the journey when there's goods waiting to go.'

'Well, the front one is presently a bit full of Sergeant Detritus,' said Simnel, and indeed through its open hatch Moist could now make out the form of the troll watchman, patiently hunched against the far wall. 'But yes, we've loaded up the rest right and tight.'

Moist snoozed his way to Quirm, rocked in the cradle of Iron Girder. He was certain she gave a smoother ride than any of the new-fangled Flyers. Everyone said that was silly, but nevertheless, the thought didn't leave him. Somehow the Flyers looked like machinery, but Iron Girder always looked like . . . somebody. And the train spotters all seemed to think the same thing. It was as if she *was* the railway.

* * *

The chateau that had been put at the disposal of the Low King while he was in Quirm for the all-important summit had 'ridiculously grand' written all over it.

Moist was greeted at the main entrance by a dwarf who was neatly dressed but notably lacking in the usual weaponry.

'Bashfull Bashfullsson, Mister von Lipwig. I know your face. It's in the papers so often.'

As they hurried inside Bashfull said, 'Please let me, as they say, mark your card, Mister Lipwig. The King is furious. Furious with the rebels and furious with himself for not doing enough at the right time and I dare say he's also furious with me. But me, well, I look to the sky and I say to Tak, "Don't get mad, but when you made us dwarfs you had a bad day and couldn't find anything in the subtlety box." It seems that we'd sooner fight and argue than live.'

Inside the chateau there was a squad of heavily armed dwarfs on guard, heavily armed, that is, being more heavily armed than the average dwarf who, nevertheless, could generally look like a squad all by himself. They scowled at Moist, with the regulation scowl of all guards everywhere, which intimated that you were less than the dust on the dust on their boots, so watch out. Bashfullsson ignored them and led Moist into the Great Hall, which was buzzing with activity.

But then there was the question of *seeing* the Low King. It was a delicate matter, but Moist wasn't going to let courtiers and guards push him around. He knew

Rhys Rhysson was a sensible and powerful dwarf, moderate, the kind of person who looks facts in the face, knowing that it's the only way to survive.

Moist waited while Bashfullsson dealt with the protocols, and wondered how many of the glittering company in the hall were actually on the King's side. Suspicion floated in the air like a fine dust, settling on every shoulder. After all, this was the beginning of a clandestine dwarf war. Much better to fight the trolls. You could recognize the trolls as possibly the enemy, but who knew where the traitors were in this chattering throng?

One of the dwarf guards attempted to dispossess Moist of his treasured lockpicks and only let go when Moist had retrieved them using very non-diplomatic language and some clever misdirection. He hadn't actually made use of the lockpicks in years, his tongue generally being more effective at getting into places than some bent pieces of metal ever could be. Nevertheless, he was still fuming and was about to say something non-political when Bashfullsson grabbed him by the arm and took him to see the King.

The King's suite was, surprisingly, at the top of the building. In normal dwarf dwellings, the *lower* a dwarf, the more important he was, and so, Moist surmised, putting the Low King into rooms on the top floor might just be a ruse to thwart any traditionally minded enemies.

Kings don't travel lightly or quietly. There were dwarfish flunkies everywhere alongside the chateau staff, folding things and indeed shovelling things into cases with a sense of panic, as if the bailiffs were coming.

But at last Moist and Bashfullsson were ushered into a small antechamber where the Low King was planning his counter-coup with his inner council. Every so often a clacks arrived and was hurried to the King.

Rhys Rhysson was smaller and slighter than Moist had expected and was surrounded in this cramped room by generals and some of the rest of the circus that has to follow a monarch.

Moist noticed black looks from a few dwarfs, angry at the human trespasser. Bashfullsson bowed to the King as he introduced Moist. 'Mister von Lipwig, your majesty. An envoy of Lord Vetinari.'

'And killer of a number of renegade delvers,' said the King to Moist. 'And not least a bank manager.' Rhys laughed. 'It must be tough in the banking business, Mister Lipwig?'

Moist joined in the little attempt at laughter and said, 'You have no idea, sire; but the most important thing you need to know about me is that I was a crook and a scoundrel and a very clever one. What better man to run the Royal Bank of Ankh-Morpork and the Mint than a crook? I had the tendencies of a crook and many of the skills of a crook and because I look at things with a crooked eye, metaphorically speaking, I see the opportunities and the problems. I'm very lucky and I have the knack of finding friends easily.'

'But probably not with those delvers, eh?' said the King.

'I was lucky and I survived. I survived and, if I may say so, I wish survival to the Low King and his court.' All right, he thought, that was drawing the long bow and no mistake, but he couldn't avoid it . . . all that armament getting in one another's way, well, with all that milling about something would go wrong sooner or later.

'Mister Lipwig, as you know, I have sudden important business that requires my presence in Uberwald as soon as possible, and at the highest speed. I understand from the clacks I received from Lord Vetinari this morning that you have a plan to get me there. I'm curious to know what that plan involves.'

There were the usual murmurs and glances, but Moist was not going to be intimidated by a bunch of small people who were giving themselves airs. He was never one for protocol – it got in the way and often concealed nasty and dangerous things.

'I'm afraid, sire, that I'm not willing to divulge Lord Vetinari's proposal here. There are too many people in this room, any one of whom could be a traitor!'

Uproar ensued. Moist kept his face blank and totally unmoving until all protestations had been protested.

'I'm not here to be nice, and I have to tell you that, while on this mission, my allegiance is to you and only you, sire. Apart from Mister Bashfullsson here, I don't know *any* of the rest of these dwarfs. The opposition must surely be intelligent enough to make certain they have a sleeper in the palace, funnelling everything back to them.'

He had gone too far, he knew it, but the dwarfs had

not impressed him with their security. It was far too stiff . . . all front and pomposity.

'Mister Lipwig, I am the King, surely, and I am still alive because of whom I know and whom I can trust, see. I appreciate your thoroughness in this matter.' The King turned to the dwarf by his side. 'Aeron, some privacy, if you please.'

And the dwarf called Aeron, who seemed to Moist to be a trusted assistant, a dwarf version of Drumknott, cleared the room of hangers-on, leaving only himself, Bashfullsson and a few other obviously senior dwarfs.

'Thank you,' said the King. 'Now, Mister Lipwig, in this small room, I trust everybody. And, boyo, I might just trust you because you are Mister Lipwig and I know your reputation. You're a survivor, quite possibly a plaything of the gods or, perhaps, the most handsome bag of wind that there has ever been. You get away with it, and thus I hope I will too, because more than *our* lives depend on us getting me to Uberwald and the Scone of Stone before those bastards wreck everything I stand for.' He smiled and said, 'I hope that doesn't feel like pressure?'

'Your majesty, pressure is where I start,' said Moist.

There was a noisy party with lots of quaffing and dwarf songs in full swing as the Low King and his commanders left the chateau quietly from the servants' entrance a short hour later. Several coaches had come and gone already that morning and the departure of a few more was unremarkable.

'Tagwen Tagwensson is doing a grand job of playing

King today,' Rhys noted to Moist as their carriage swung down the long gravel driveway. 'That song has over a hundred verses. They can keep that up for days!'

When they arrived at the Quirm terminus they were met by the extremely large form of Sergeant Detritus of the Ankh-Morpork City Watch, who was standing guard by Iron Girder, hefting his piecemaker, which had what might be called a wholesale capability.

The Low King's eyes lit up when he recognized the sergeant and he exclaimed, 'Detritus! If you're on board, then perhaps I don't need any other bodyguards.'

This was said laughing, but Moist couldn't help thinking that it might just be true.

'Good to see you, King!' Detritus roared. He looked around sharply and said, 'Dere any grags here? If yes, please line up.'

Behind the King, always present, Aeron was carefully busying himself getting people and weapons on board. He opened the door and quickly ushered Rhys into the gleaming carriage.

Bashfullsson tapped Detritus on the knee. 'I am indeed a grag, sergeant, and lining up as requested. What next?'

Detritus scratched his head. 'But you is okay, Mister Bashfullsson. Der commander knows you, and his lady.'

'Ah, so I'm lining up to get on the train, then?' said the dwarf. 'It's pleasant to meet you again, sergeant, but please remember there are grags and grags.' And he turned to follow Aeron into the carriage.

Once the whole retinue was safely aboard, Moist stood watch while Detritus heaved himself into the guard's van, which gave a tremendous creak and groan; but everything seemed to hold, so with a signal to the footplate Moist scrambled up into the van and they were off.

The train pulled away with the usual jerk of the couplings and as the long journey back to Ankh-Morpork began Moist suddenly realized that he was, as it were, not required on this voyage.

In the coaches the Low King, his bodyguards and councillors huddled together and were speaking very quietly, their thoughts deep in planning. On the footplate, the driver was focused on getting his royal cargo to its destination and was in a world of concentration. You could see it dripping off him like snow; listening to the wheels, listening to the rails, watching the lights, checking the gauges and driving the train in such a positive way that possibly even without Iron Girder herself they might just get there on willpower alone. And the stoker made it clear he had no need of Moist's assistance. So Moist now had nothing to do except sleep and . . . worry *so* much.

If the King was a target, if the grags got to hear that he was on the train, then the train was bound to be a target although, as it happened, Moist hoped they had run some interference.

For his part Moist thought attacks would surely come out in the wilderness, later, on the long lonely haul up to Uberwald. Despite everything he'd said to Lord Vetinari, he knew it was oh so easy to derail a locomotive. The ever diligent Mr Simnel had told Moist that he'd tried it at low speed at the back of the compound in a place where Iron Girder couldn't see, with impressive effects. Once derailed, it required the combined efforts of several trolls and golems over many hours with a clever system of pulleys to get the engine back on the track. If it happened to an engine travelling at speed under full steam . . . And this, Moist thought, is a man who lives by the sliding rule and the sine and cosine, not forgetting the tangent. Moist never challenged Dick's proclamations regarding his sliding rule; he could make the numbers dance and Moist was yet to see him get things wrong. It was like . . . like wizardry, but without the wizards and all their mess.

And indeed, as Dick was finding out, you could even have a girlfriend . . . an intriguing thought that seemed to echo at the back of his mind. And it was common knowledge now that Dick and Harry's niece were, as they say, walking out. He had apparently one night driven Emily around the compound by starlight and that had to mean something, didn't it? And Dick had told Moist, in the voice of somebody having found a strange and attractive new world, that she was very good at handling the fire box, without ever getting her dress dirty. And he'd added, 'I reckon Iron Girder likes her. You never see a smut on her. I come out every time looking like a dustman and when we've finished she looks like she's one of them ballerinas or something.'

But right now there was so much else to think about. This most important of trains was moving its priceless cargo, and Moist knew that the whole business relied on fairly simple things being done properly, at the precise time and in exactly the right way. There were people who made certain there was coal in the coal bunkers along the route and by now he knew how much water would be needed and who would make certain that it would be there when and where it was required. But how did you make certain that the person who made certain actually did these things? It had to be someone's responsibility!

And these tasks seemed to Moist like a great big pyramid whose every stone had to be laid in place before one wheel turned. In some ways it frightened him. For most of his life he had been mostly alone and as for the Bank and the Mint, well, Vetinari had got it right. He did have a knack for finding and keeping people who liked their jobs and were good at them, and since everything was delegated, why, then he could be Moist von Lipwig, a catalyst in the world. And now he could see why people had anxiety attacks, the kind of people who would lock their door and halfway up the garden path would come back to see if they'd locked said door and unlock it to make sure and lock it again then set off up the path only to go through the whole terrible procedure once more.

The fact of the matter was you had to hope and assume that a lot of capable people had done lots of capable things in a capable way, and double-checked them frequently to make sure everything was right. So worrying was stupid, wasn't it? But worrying was never quite like that. It sat like a little goblin on your shoulder and whispered. And suddenly that kind of worried person, in the strange world of mistrust, was now entering the stuff of nightmares, and right now he, Moist von Lipwig, for heaven's sake, was worried, yes, really very worried. What had been left in? What had been left out? I can hear the wheels just down there and I know the journey is going to take four days, at least, not counting breakdowns, dreadful weather and the storms up in the mountains, they can be ferocious, and all this without mentioning some lunatic dwarfs hell-bent on ruining the party for everybody.

It has to be said that this was an inner monologue. Yes, it was an inner monologue's own personal inner monologue, but outside Moist's skin absolute stone-cold certainty reigned: nothing could possibly go wrong. After all, Dick would be dealing with the technicalities, and he was a genius. Not in the same way that Leonard of Quirm was a genius, but, Moist thought loyally, in a reassuring, solid, *Simnel* sort of way. Leonard would probably get distracted halfway through the journey by an idea for using cabbages as fuel, or using the waste from the fire box to grow better cabbages, or painting a masterpiece of a nymph clad in cabbage leaves and coal. But Dick had his flat cap on straight. Vimes would be coming too, and although part of Moist – the part that still thought of coppers as people to avoid even in your best disguise – got the willies when the commander looked him in the eye or any other part of his anatomy, the rest of him was very grateful that Blackboard Monitor Vimes would be on his side if the grags came calling . . .

In fact, Moist was full of little monologues, chasing

one another around, but afterwards, because they were *his* monologues, they decided that they would come together again as one whole Moist von Lipwig and would therefore maintain and get through no matter the circumstances.

Everything is going to be mar . . . vell . . . ous, he assured himself. When has it ever not been – you're the lucky Moist von Lipwig! Right in the centre the hypothetical goblin of uncertainty twisted itself into a tiny quivering mush. Moist wished it well, smiled and said goodbye.

Harry King's vast mansion was well protected and a perfect place for a private dinner where the Low King and Vetinari could meet while preparations were being made for the long haul to Uberwald. It was widely considered that Harry's . . . *undertakers* had the jump on your average soldier or policeman when it came to a scrap, because *those* people had been taught to have rules while most of Harry's boys couldn't even spell the word. Any intruder foolish enough to be found lurking in the shrubbery of Harry's extensive estate in the dark and the dripping rain would be pruned in no short order.

Even though this was a private dinner, Effie King was not going to let the side down. She had begun her preparations for the meal with a headache and then moved on to a dither before segueing into an organization of military precision and dimensions, bullying the cooks on the way and frantically looking up such things as what spoon you used with what soup.

Effie genuflected deeply to the Low King as he arrived in her oak-panelled dining room. And Effie was in a more expensive and acceptable version of hog heaven.

'How was your journey, sire? Safe and comfortable?'

The Low King hesitated for a moment. 'It's Euphemia, isn't it?' he said.

Effie was on fire. 'Yes, your majesty, but just Effie to you.'

The King smiled again. 'Very good, and I'm "your majesty" to you, Lady King.'

Effie looked somewhat challenged until the King of the Dwarfs held out his hand and said, 'Actually, you can call me anything you like. I was just trying to make an old dwarf joke, just like myself right now: a fugitive trying to avoid even more dangerous fugitives and reliant on the help of others, such as your noble husband and his friends.'

Moist smiled as the noble penny dropped on Effie.

The King now looked around the other guests. He smiled at Commander Vimes and Lady Sybil and shook hands with Adora Belle who was, Moist thought proudly, a real looker when she wasn't in her work clothes. And from what he could see, she had bought a most attractive and therefore expensive gown for the evening. It was still grey, of course, but with a kind of lustre to it that made it seem almost festive. This was grey letting its hair down. He couldn't possibly argue about it, she earned more than he did.

The King's eyes scouted the room and he continued, 'And Lord Vetinari . . . will be joining us? And Mister

Simnel, the technical genius behind your remarkable railway?'

Harry looked around, just as Lord Vetinari stepped forward from the shadows in the room* and got there first and rather more smoothly.

'Your majesty, welcome to Ankh-Morpork. Mister Simnel is overseeing the final preparations for the locomotive that *will* get you back to your home and throne in time. Nothing is being left to chance, I can assure you.'

'Ah, Lord Vetinari – I didn't see you, forgive me,' replied Rhys, and Moist nearly choked on his drink when he continued, 'But I understand there's still some track to lay and bridges that need to be completed.' He paused. 'Rather close to our intended destination, I believe.'

Moist felt the air chill instantly. He quickly scanned the faces of Harry and Vetinari and jumped in – after all, it was what he was there for – 'Excuse me, your majesty, but Mister Simnel has developed a concept called loggysticks, the nature of which is enshrined in the phrase "first things first". Of course, the trick is to know exactly what needs to be first and, right now, since you are many days away from Uberwald, the gangs still have time to complete the last few sections. You will get to Uberwald for the appointed time. I'll stake my life on that.'

---

* At least, that's where Moist assumed he'd come from. Vetinari was one of the greatest students of concealment the Assassins had ever produced, so it could simply have been a shadowy state of mind.

There was a silence that froze the air in the room and Moist counted down to the inevitable comment from a smiling Lord Vetinari.

'Most gratifying, Mister Lipwig, and you have made that promise in front of all of us. Good show! And all good people here with quite excellent memories.'

After that, the first person to speak was Adora Belle, who said, 'Oh, that's definitely my husband, but I'm sure he'll manage it at the last possible minute . . . He always does. And if he can achieve it while riding a white charger he'll be as happy as a clam.'

The King laughed in a rather strange way and said, 'Well, then let's hope that he is not unduly shucked.'

'Your majesty, Mister Lipwig always achieves his goals, I assure you,' said Lord Vetinari, in his best oiled voice. 'I find it amazing and, of course, annoying, but so far he has always succeeded, which is why, therefore, all of his extremities are in their rightful place.'

Everybody present laughed nervously, except Lord Vetinari, who just laughed. The King of the Dwarfs stared at Moist as if seeing him in a new light, and said, 'Is that really true, Mister Lipwig?'

Moist forced his face to go so deadpan that it might have actually been dead. 'Yes, your majesty, everything that ought to be attached still is, isn't that right, Adora Belle?'

His wife didn't say anything. She just looked the look of a wife who was putting up with her husband's funny little ways for which he would suffer in the boudoir later.

After *that*, Effie beamed anxiously and said, in a

voice that she considered posh people would use, 'Shall we take our seats for dinner, your majesty, ladies and gentlemen? All the spoons are in their rightful place, I do assure you.'

Conversation around the dinner table, in deference to Effie and the flapping ears of the staff, was . . . nice, and mostly about the new railway and the wonders of what might be achieved with it, and indeed the interesting fact that lots of rich people were buying seaside houses in Quirm now that it was so easy to get there. And there was also another careful conversation about how good the fish and the seafood was becoming now it didn't have to bake in the sunshine, which might have had something to do with the mountainous platter of prawns, monkey clams and unidentified tentacular things sculpted to resemble the lost citadel of Leshp, which Effie had given pride of place in the centre of the table. And this went on in various different ways until dinner was almost over and the staff had left the room, whereupon Vimes gave Rhys a quizzical look, stood up and left the room. He returned a few minutes later, nodded to the Low King and resumed his seat at the table.

'Ladies and gentlemen, preparations for our departures are in place. As I speak, the Low King is departing by fast coach for Uberwald.' And there was something in the way he said that that made Moist think, because the Low King, at that moment, was clearly still in the room shovelling down expensive ice cream.

Sure enough, there was the sound of a coach pulling

up outside, stopping for a moment and then driving away, surrounded by well-armed bodyguards.

Back at the table the King licked his spoon in a very regal way and chuckled. 'That should keep those scoundrels busy for a while.' He smiled at Vimes. 'Thank you for your help in this, commander.'

'Think nothing of it,' said Vimes gruffly. 'It's a good idea. And Harry and I have added some embellishments of our own.'

'So who was on that coach, commander?' Moist asked.

'The coach?' Vimes replied. 'This is a very dark night and the King is cloaked and it is almost impossible to see inside, but the dark-accustomed eye might see Sergeant Cheery Littlebottom accompanied by some of my most trusted dwarf officers. Anybody interfering with the coach and its contents will find their life difficult, nay extinct.'

The King coughed before saying to Vimes, 'I remember Sergeant Littlebottom when we met by the Scone of Stone eight years ago. Oh, yes, I remember her.'

'She volunteered for the job, sire,' said Vimes.

'She did, did she?' said the King. 'Well, none of us know what the future holds, but if my backside is still on the Scone when all of this is over then Sergeant Littlebottom and her colleagues will have earned any favours they want from me. A king's gratitude has to be worth something, wouldn't you say, Blackboard Monitor Vimes?'

Vimes smiled as if remembering an old joke and

said, 'Well, I hope she does, because she's one of the best officers I've got.'

'How many Cheery Littlebottoms can you afford?' The King looked sombre. 'I'd hate for someone to die, just to see that I don't. Now, if I am to get to Uberwald with all due speed, we should be leaving very soon, yes?'

'Soon, your majesty,' Vimes agreed. 'The rail traffic between here and Sto Lat runs throughout the night. At present it's mostly freight and perishables for the market and the Post Office parcel business, but people are always coming and going at the terminus. Nobody could keep track of everyone. We've set it up so that you'll be just another anonymous traveller on the platform, looking like any one of the Third Class passengers, although, should the need arise, you and your travelling companions would be found to be carrying an inordinately large amount of deadly weaponry. And that, your majesty, includes fangs.

'The Watch is not going to be outdone on this one, sire. If the sh— excrement hits the wossname, nearly every place you go we'll have people watching you. Now, if you and Mister Lipwig will accompany me to the side room over there, we'll make sure that neither of you looks like either of you by the time we've finished.'

Turning to Harry, the commander said, 'Harry, are you sure you can vouch for the discretion of all your people, even those in the kitchens?'

Harry almost saluted. 'Yes, commander. Some of them are scoundrels – well, you know – but they're my kind of scoundrel.'

'Ah, yes,' said the King. 'I'm used to that sort of scoundrel. They are all so very . . . *useful*.'

Moist knew a lot about the tricks of disguise, although he never bothered with makeup as such. Becoming another person was a subtle matter that was probably only understood by those wrinkled old men up in the very high mountains around Oi Dong who knew the secrets of the known universe, one of them being how to kick your enemy's spine all the way out of their body. *They* certainly knew that true camouflage came from within. And, oh yes, an occasional change of clothes was warranted, but mostly Moist just thought about the type of person he wanted to be seen as and it all came into focus. A false nose was definitely a no-no – inevitably, any nose designed to make you look like a stranger would be noticeably strange. And why risk it when his own features were so unmemorable that no one recalled their shape in any case? Of course, trying to look female had some built-in snags, but he'd managed it on a few occasions, back in the bad old days which were, in retrospect, so damn good. And he had lost track of all the clergymen he had been. If there was ever such a thing as redemption, they would have to open a magnum of the stuff for Moist. No, a brewery.

The King's party split up when they arrived at the station. Rhys, now disguised as a rather disorientated, elderly dwarf, was accompanied at a distance by three other disreputable-looking characters, while the rest of his party disposed themselves in small, innocuous-looking groups along the platform.

Bashfull Bashfullsson had gallantly volunteered as another bodyguard, but both Moist and Commander Vimes had considered him too recognizable to other dwarfs, here in his native Ankh-Morpork, and suggested his special skills could be made better use of elsewhere. The dark clerks, however, had been trained by Vetinari who, as he had so recently proved, could stand in a room full of people without being seen: it was a technique. And there were others. Quite probably overhead. Whatever happened, Commander Vimes was *not* going to have the Low King of the Dwarfs killed on his watch.

Moist sighed as he walked, dragging one leg pitifully, but not too pitifully, to the rear of the train. There he found a station guard berating a well-dressed man who had sat down firmly in the Third Class carriage among sleepy workers with greasy hands and bags of tools, and chimney sweeps with, of course, their sacks of soot, inevitably leaking. Moist was all for the common man, and most especially the common man who could have afforded at least one bar of soap over a lifetime, and possibly didn't spit all the time, great hawking globs of spit, the ones with a personality of their own. And the toff, who reeked and dribbled best brandy, was holding up the train while the guard was dithering, derailed by a haughty voice.

And so Moist put an arm around the wretched man and went straight into his infuriating-drunk routine, complete with explosive belches, a surefire winner guaranteed to work every time. First there was the spittle in the corner of the mouth, and a nasty smell, which Moist was king of, and the conversation in which every word was shredded and mistreated and misapplied unto death while Moist leaned inappropriately and spat and dribbled.

The wretch hurried for the sole First Class compartment at the front of the train after less than a minute. A personal best for Moist, who, still in dribbling and stinking character, staggered and weaved his way to a seat just before the whistle was blown and the train moved in the half-hearted way trains always did as the engine got its act together. He was very proud of it and he'd only used up half of his Boffo's best artificial vomit with lingering smell.

It was a cold night for travelling. The King was on board somewhere, but this wasn't the time to show any interest in him. Moist's ragged clothes had been, well, adequate, and everybody in the compartment with the wind whistling underneath them had wrapped themselves up and tried not to exist until the train had reached its destination. Somewhere, he thought, there should be a statue erected to Effie, who had clearly tongue-lashed her husband into making the lower class coaches at least waterproof.*

---

* The only carriages that were open to the weather were the ones for those extra-large passengers (mostly trolls) who couldn't fit inside anything else, and that was because they were in fact the coal cars. No one minded – trolls were impervious to rain, which helped them cultivate a

* * *

The leader of the delvers watching one of the main routes out of Ankh-Morpork smiled as the large coach bearing the Low King's insignia came into view. Rain splashed over the coach as the horses galloped hub-wards and the leader of the delvers smiled at the raindrops. How easy it was going to be. He gave the signal to the waiting dwarfs and within minutes they were grabbing harnesses and bridles and bringing the coach to a shuddering halt. He kicked the coach door open.

'Bring out the King and you will not be harmed,' he commanded.

There was silence inside the coach and then he heard a voice say, 'We ain't got no king apart from Harry King and we ain't the ones that are going to get harmed. Consider us as the King Preservation Society, and Sir Harry King don't like his friends being put to any trouble. And you, my son, you are a lot of trouble, but thankfully not as much as we are. Come on, lads!'

The fight was fast and methodical and the coach drove away with the victors singing and drinking in the storm and the water on the cobbles was tinged with red.

Meanwhile, a few miles away, another group of delvers was having a remarkably similar experience with a remarkably similar coach, which had turned out

better quality of lichen in any case, and the coal doubled as a welcome snack during the journey.

to contain amongst other horrors a very fierce, very female dwarf in a watchman's helmet . . .

The train pulled in to the station at Sto Lat Junction, and Moist watched as the guard helped a grubby and pitiful old dwarf down from his carriage. The Low King clearly had some skill as an actor. Moist noticed one of the old dwarf's equally decrepit companions in adversity take pity on him and give him a piece of dwarf bread, breaking it in half with his axe. To his horror, Moist saw the King dribbling his thanks to the bread giver.

As he came up to the King, Moist whispered, 'Excellent . . . Where did you get that stink? It's got a life of its own.'

The King put a finger to his lips and said, 'Not me, it leaked from the man in front. I don't think he could have washed for years. But remember, a king has to cope with a lot worse than a little stink.'

There were a few hours to kill before the fast train left Sto Lat for Zemphis, as yet the furthest point hubwards to enjoy a Hygienic Railway service. Getting the Low King out of sight was a priority; even in disguise, there was a risk.

Leaving Simnel and Vimes in charge at the station, Moist and the Low King limped their way outside. Moist looked around for people he knew had to be there because he couldn't see them. Suddenly one of them was right in front of him, so close that they were almost touching. He hadn't seen him until that moment. It was as if he had shot up from below.

'Godfrey, Mister Lipwig – dark clerk. Lord Vetinari has arranged for a safe house to be available to your party. Mister Simnel suggested his mother's house, which isn't far away. We've met the lady and she is a royalist through and through. *Any* royalty, and sensible, too. Nothing to worry about there. Clerk Mavis says the old girl is quick on the uptake and understands the position. She is a good cook and there will be clean sheets.'

Moist looked at the dripping King, who smiled and said, 'It sounds like a gift from Tak on a night like this.'

As they walked the short distance through the rain-drenched and deserted streets to Mrs Simnel's house, Moist was always aware of their escorts because the little hairs on the back of his neck were telling him they were there, showing them the way. Before long, they reached a cheerful little house near the centre of town, the kind that was always referred to as a 'little palace', the kind a lad might buy for his widowed mother so she could be close for doing the shopping.

A discreet knock at the door caused some shuffling within before a lady who could only be Mr Simnel's mother stood in the doorway quietly ushering them inside. Once they were in her small but immaculate house, she paused and looked down at the Low King, then curtsied.

'Thank you so much, my dear Mrs Simnel,' said the King, who had clearly dealt with these things many times before. 'No need for that from the mother of the genius engineer.' And Mrs Simnel was suddenly awash with maternal pride.

'Oh, yes, your majesty. He's a good lad, our Dick. Did you know that when he were quite young he made me an iconograph, caught the imp himself, so 'e did, and trained it with butter. They really like butter, do imps. And it's ever so useful, yes indeed.'

While Clerk Godfrey, on flannel feet, quickly checked the rest of the house, Mrs Simnel turned to Moist and said, 'I know you, too. You're Mister Lipwig. Dick speaks very highly of you. I saw your picture in the paper only yesterday and I've seen our Dick in there, too. Makes an old mum reet proud, so it does. Of course, I don't buy it, the Reverend Amusable comes round and reads the paper to me, what with that tiny print an' all. I don't get around as much these days, but now my lad is in the money he has all kind of food delivered up fresh every day on the train and sees his old mum all right. The other day, ooh, it were a lobster in a bag of ice. I 'ad to go all the way up to t'posh restaurant to find out how to cook it, but it were gradely and toothsome and so much on it there was enough for Mrs Pankweather who's bedbound and can't digest most things, but you should've seen her tooth light up when she saw a plate full of lobster. Well, you 'ave to, after all. Not every elderly lady has a good strong lad to see she's all right.'

Mrs Simnel suddenly looked sombre and said, 'But he sends me money every week *regular*, so much I don't rightly know what to do wi' it, so I give some of it to the poor. You *are* a friend of his, aren't you, Mister Lipwig?'

'Yes, Mrs Simnel,' said Moist. 'You can't imagine how much.'

At this point Clerk Godfrey said, 'We are now going back to the marshalling yard to assist Mister Vimes and other members of the Watch who will be travelling with us on the long haul to Uberwald. Clerks Columbine and Silkworm will remain outside and will escort you back to the station in time to catch the train to Zemphis.' And then he was gone.

Mrs Simnel looked again at the bedraggled King, and said with unconscious informality, 'You look famished, pet. I know it's late but I've got some pease pudding in t'pot . . . not much, but it keeps you going and it'll build up your strength when you most need it.'

As it turned out, Mrs Simnel's pease pudding was the queen of pease puddings and even though the dinner at Harry's had only been a few hours earlier Moist noticed that the King almost sucked it up. When they'd eaten, Mrs Simnel put the lid back on the pot.

'I've got to leave some for my lad,' she said, 'out in all this weather. Mind you, he likes his pease pudding cold.'

And then the King settled into a comfy chair for a snooze. While he slept and Mrs Simnel busied herself clearing the dishes, Moist looked around at the walls and noticed carefully arranged pictures of smiling babies, or was it just one baby taken over and over, because, he thought, at that age all babies look like, well, babies, and only mothers could fathom which one was which. It was amazing.

'My word, Mrs Simnel, what wonderful children,'

Moist commented when she returned to wish him goodnight. 'All yours?'

She laughed. 'Oh, dear me, no! Our Dick's my only one, but I were trained as a midwife before I met my late 'usband and you know 'ow it is, I were right good at midwifery and especially when events were going badly.'

And here she looked sternly at Moist and said, 'I'm sure you know what I mean, Mister Lipwig? I only ever lost one because they couldn't find my whereabouts until it were too late. Any road, ever since then people call me out and you know 'ow it is, my lad says I don't have to do it any more, but once you've got a reputation for something it clings. Especially when the young lass is desperate.'

The look of Mrs Simnel was that of the put-upon, but in her eyes pride flashed a fin.

Snoring heavily in the huge armchair, the King turned over. Mrs Simnel adjusted the deep cushions to make him more comfortable and then there was a fleeting stillness as her attention seemed to be caught by something. She sent a quick, surprisingly sharp glance in Moist's direction and gave the cushions a final pat before straightening up and smiling sweetly. The moment, whatever it was, most definitely had passed. Moist's brain was soggy with tiredness, and the natural ability to read tiny signals that had kept him alive on so many occasions had deserted him hours before. Even so, he had to ask.

'Mrs Simnel . . . Is something wrong?'

She cut him short. 'Nay, lad. I were just thinking how

strange it is that someone so small and, well, hairy could be . . . a king. But 'appen that's the disguise. I'm sure he'll look reet fine in his crown and glitter when he's back on his scone. Now, you need a bed, my lad.'

Tired though he was, Moist could recognize a deflection tactic, and carried on. 'Mrs Simnel, is there something you're not—'

'Nay, there's nothing, nothing for you to worry about at any rate.'

Moist's thoughts were in a whirl, but then further thoughts were blown away by the sound of the front door being blown open as Dick arrived with water streaming off his gabardine, and greeted his mother. He was carrying so many bundles and boxes that he had to deposit them all in the little hallway where a shiny clock told the time, the days of the week and quite possibly the phase of the moon for that night, but most of all it was there to show the world that Dick Simnel's mother got the very best things he could buy for her. She was in his arms immediately, scattering parcels, but he managed to shake her off, laughing.

Seated in the still warm kitchen of the little house, Dick scoffed the congealed pease pudding while she unpacked some of the parcels.

'That's gradely, our ma! It's blowing up something cruel out there.'

Moist suddenly realized he was dog tired.

Mrs Simnel said, 'I've made up a bed for you, Mister Lipwig. I had made up one for t'King, but he looks comfortable where he is and I don't want to disturb him now. Will you be stopping for the night, our Dick?'

'Sorry, Mother, no, too much to do. We're all on double shifts.'

Mrs Simnel looked at Moist proudly. 'That's my lad. He's a worker, my boy, what with his tiddling stick.'

'That's a sliding ruler, Mother,' Simnel said, grinning at Moist.

'Aye, well,' said the proud parent, 'he's making his way in the world, is my lad, working for that Harry King.' And she went to kiss Dick, who picked her up and kissed her in mid air, and put her back down again, leaving her slightly more wet and greasy than before.

'Oh, Mother,' he said, 'don't make me out to be some kind of saint, I'm just another working man with filthy 'ands. Any road, I 'ave to get going, you know 'ow it is.'

On his way out, Dick looked in at the King and said, 'Is he okay, Mother?'

Moist watched Mrs Simnel's face very carefully.

'He's gradely, lad,' she replied. 'He just needs his sleep, such a shame to wake him up.'

Dick flashed a glance to Moist as his mother said that and seemed to be entertaining a thought and then shrugged like a man who had thought better about it. He handed Moist a parcel of clean clothes for himself and the King and then kissed his mother again.

'You will see to it, won't you, Mother, that they leave in time for the Zemphis express?'

And she did, after a bowl of porridge, hot and sugary, just the kind Adora Belle totally disliked. Moist could feel it sticking to his bones as he and the King, smiling and rejuvenated after their nap, left the haven of Mrs Simnel's little house as the sun began to rise over Sto Lat.

In a cavern somewhere near the gloomy, somewhat twisted metropolis of Slake the grags were discussing the railway menace, and ways of stopping it. They had found an artificer who liked working iron, and since he was a dwarf from Ankh-Morpork he was in a position to explain matters to them.

Sitting nervously in the dimly lit cavern and trying to appear to be very much on the side of the grags while, of course, being on the side of the money, the artificer explained that locomotives are heavy, and derailing them might be best left to when a train was heading through gorges or near the mountains. And he suggested that an alternative would be to deprive the engines of the basic necessities – fuel and water – and then attack them when they were most vulnerable. He had fortuitously come across a map that showed the locations of all the coal bunkers and water cranes and towers, and this he now produced.

'And just supposing we set our sights on stopping a particular train . . . how many people do we need to take down these . . . water cranes?' croaked an anonymous grag in the darkness.

'You'll need plenty of you on this,' said the helpful dwarf. 'The opposition is probably bright enough to realize that you'll be focusing your efforts on disabling the engines, and will have the cranes and bunkers well guarded. Of course,' he added, 'when you're up high in the mountains you have the advantage on 'em.'

The artificer looked hopeful after this, in so far as he could be seen in the dark cavern, and said, 'Well, that's about it, sirs. It's not very difficult, but you know where to contact me if you need me.'

In truth, the cavern was giving him the heebie-jeebies, and he wanted to be out of there as soon as possible. He heard the voice of the leader saying, 'Well done, my friend. Please take this gold as a token of appreciation and, yes, we do know where to find you and every member of your family as well.'

The artificer looked into the heavy leather bag and was delighted. '*Very* kind of you, sirs. I hope to help you again at some time in the future.'

And he went away happy with such big wages for so little real work. The grags didn't know anything! It was like taking money off children, but he kept smiling and said goodbye and had his throat cut in the darkness by a delver before he'd even left the dripping chamber. After all, what grag would hand over gold to an Ankh-Morpork dwarf? To a grag they were all unbelievers.

Moist was aware, as he and the King made their way hurriedly from Mrs Simnel's house back to the station, of the dark clerks keeping an eye on them, invisibly tracking them on either side. Yesterday's clothing had gone, and after a quick wash and brush-up the King had the appearance of a dwarfish businessman while Moist was scruffier, looking like an engineer hurrying on his way to work.

The cry from the porter announced, 'Shortly to depart from platform one the Altiplano Express, stopping at Big Cabbage for Brassica World and Zemphis for Zemphis Falls. Sleeping compartments at the front of the train. All aboard, ladies and gentlemen!'

Moist whispered to the King, 'You know what to do, sire.'

The King showed his ticket to the guard, who looked at it very carefully before saying gruffly, 'Middle Class, middle of the train.' Moist walked off as fast as he could and didn't look around. Looking around pegged you as a nervous person. You had to rely on instinct alone. Everybody knew what to do.

He had to manoeuvre to get out of the way of crates of chickens and he thought, why are there always crates of chickens? By the sound of it they didn't really want to be there. And now it seemed that chickens were going everywhere. A mother with a child hurried past. A goblin waved to presumably his wife, although it was quite hard to tell with goblins, and Moist glanced at the guard and savoured, just for one moment, the silence before the train came alive.

He embarked via the guard's van and the first person he met was Detritus without his badge and therefore being, well, just another troll. He looked uncomfortable. Behind Detritus Moist found Commander Vimes dressed as a guard, apparently thoroughly enjoying himself, if Moist correctly interpreted his twisted grimace.

Vimes waved a clacks flimsy and said cheerfully, 'The idiots! They tried their tricks while they were still on Ankh-Morpork soil. Poor souls . . . I suppose they thought they were outthinking us, but Cheery and her lads had the measure of them in swift order – Sir Harry's men too by the sound of it – and now both lots are heading for the Tanty where the dark clerks will be engaging them in important discussions. Let's hope the news doesn't get out to the grag command just yet.'

It was going to be a long haul to Zemphis. And after Zemphis they'd be launching on to the new track, which no passenger train had yet travelled. Time enough to worry about that when they got there, Moist told himself firmly. For now disguise was crucial; he must *be* the engineer, the lucky man who got to ride the latest Mark II Flyer every day and *get paid* for it.

As Moist walked up and down the carriages he began to look at the passengers around him. Amongst the normal mix of Ankh-Morporkians and other folk from the Sto Plains and surrounding areas whom he would expect to see on the regular journey to Zemphis, there were some dwarfs, travelling both together and singly. A few he recognized as part of the Low King's entourage; others were, if he was any judge, Ankh-Morpork dwarfs. Mind you, there was more than one kind of Ankh-Morpork dwarf: one sort were *happy* at being Ankh-Morpork citizens, and others seemed to feel grumpy and nervous about their status, not realizing that in Ankh-Morpork nobody paid much attention to what you were – unless you looked wealthy, in which case you would definitely be the centre of attention.

And then there were the people trying a little too hard to present themselves as harmless members of the public. They always stood out and Moist wondered if they knew how obvious they were to the trained eye of the suspicious scoundrel. They were worried and trying desperately not to look worried and nonchalance, real nonchalance, is very difficult to fake. If you didn't have the knack it cried out . . . amateur.

One dwarf in particular had caught Moist's eye as he passed, so he came back a short while later and took the seat opposite. As Moist sat rocking with the rhythm of the train, he sensed some discordance. Not fear, exactly, but the pulse of fear squashed down so heavily that it was almost singing, and in the privacy of Moist's skull the tickertape of suspicion ticked away.

Moist had been clever so far, not staring and, indeed, trying to look like a person who was not trying not to stare, a professional nonchalant, but the dwarf who was under his eyes was sweating. Sooner or later something was going to break.

'Oh, I know who you are!' Moist said suddenly, keeping his voice low. 'You're one of those train spotters, aren't you? I never forget an anorak.'

'Oh, yes, I'm a very keen train spotter, sir,' said the dwarf, keeping his voice level while his beard dripped sweat and his eyes screamed *help*.

'Excellent. So you'd know the top speed of a Flyer, then, would you? No?'

Hardly anyone on the train had looked up as he subtly questioned the dwarf, as subtly as a sledgehammer; it had become an extraordinary* rule of

* In that it went against every instinct of a born-and-bred Ankh-Morporkian.

railway etiquette that other passengers' conduct and conversation remained their private business, however obtrusive it might be. The dwarf had visibly jumped in his seat when Moist first engaged him, but he was still grave-faced and, yes, still sweating, so Moist carried on like a friend who wants to borrow money.

'As I said, I never forget an anorak. Taking the long haul to Zemphis, are we?'

The dwarf nodded and said simply, 'Yes.'

'Did you see which engine we've got?' said Moist. 'I tell you what . . . I'm hearing some trunnion rattle. Can you feel it? Maybe she's a new one just out of the yard?'

'Er . . . yes . . . I suppose so . . .' spluttered the wretched dwarf.

As he considered his next move, Moist looked around. Ah, there was another dwarf, further away, surreptitiously watching him watch the ersatz train spotter. Thinking furiously, he turned his attention back to the sweating dwarf in front of him.

'Hang on, I've seen you before, haven't I, at the gates of the compound, with your little notebook? We all have our little notebooks, buddy, and mine's in my luggage over there and yours is the cleanest anorak I've ever seen. *Real* train spotters get covered in muck and smuts . . . it's their badge of honour to have a greasy anorak. But you, mister, know nothing about trains or train spotting, do you?'

As he said this, he saw the other dwarf leave his seat and start to walk nonchalantly to the next carriage.

'You! Wait here!' Moist barked at the dwarf in front

of him as he ran after and jumped on the perambulating dwarf. There were screams of consternation from the other passengers, finally jolted from their careful lack of interest, as Moist rolled off, scrambled to his feet and kicked the dwarf heavily with his plate-layer's boots, the ones with the metal toecaps; an invitation to lie on the ground in agony, even if you were wearing chainmail.

Moist reached up and pulled the communication cord,* hardly visible overhead, and as the train slid to a screeching halt, he shouted to the passengers, 'Nobody gets off this train unless they can fly. We'll soon have company, ladies and gentlemen. This will be something to tell your grandchildren about.'

Reinforcements were already coming from both directions: dark clerks from one and City Watch from the other . . . this particular portion of the City Watch being Commander Vimes, who took one look and said to everyone present, 'Nothing to worry about, ladies and gentlemen. This gentleman hadn't bought a ticket for his journey, and that kind of behaviour makes our railway staff very upset . . .'

---

* Some months before, Mr Reg Shoe, travelling in an otherwise empty compartment, had got his fingers trapped when the carriage window shot up unexpectedly fast, and by the time the train reached the terminus he had lost the top joint of one digit. Mr Shoe, being a zombie, though indignant was merely inconvenienced by this accident, but at Effie's insistence Simnel had devised the communication cord: a small rope that ran the length of the train, with a bell attached to either end. If there was a problem, a passenger could pull this rope and the driver or guard, alerted by the bell, would slam on the brakes.

A little later, in the guard's van, the nervous young dwarf and his saturnine minder were, amazingly, talking to old Stoneface, who was sitting at the guard's desk and listening intently.

'Now, gentlemen, something is going on here.'

He held up a large, four-sided knife. The weapon really meant business, not just business, but business with ignominy. The young dwarf was being held between two coppers as the commander spoke to him, smiling like a shark.

'This, sir, is what assassins call a roundel, and I must tell you that even the professional killers don't use them. I believe they think it's cruel and has no finesse. Frankly, I think I'll agree about that. And I'm wondering, sir, why you're carrying it on this train?'

Vimes turned to the other dwarf, presently chained to Sergeant Detritus.

'And you, sir. What was your part in all this? We're on a moving vehicle, travelling through wilderness where *anything* could happen. And, you know, anything might happen very soon if I don't get some answers.'

He turned to an officer and said, 'Fred. You and Nobby shackle the young one and drag him somewhere where he can be alone with his thoughts and then I'll continue my little chat with this old feller, who I suspect would very much like to talk to me in a clear, thoughtful, and expansive way, leaving nothing out. You, sir,' and this was to Moist, 'I suggest you go back to your seat. I'll talk to you later.'

Dismissed, and with nothing better to do, Moist

resumed his patrol of the carriages. There were long, long miles to Zemphis ahead of them and in some stretches the landscape was so monotonous that another term would have to be devised. To pass the time, he wandered along to the fabled First Class sleeping compartments. Effie had clearly had a hand in these. Whole families in Ankh-Morpork, including aunts and uncles, grannies and granddads and all the kids and possibly their donkey could have slept well in just one of the delightful part bedroom, part drawing rooms.

And when Moist came back to the guard's van after pacing the corridors and gave the not very secret knock, he found the door opened by Nobby Nobbs, a watchman who though technically human (with a certificate to prove it) was so much like a goblin that he had acquired a goblin girlfriend. Adora Belle had met her many times and she had told Moist that Shine of the Rainbow was throwing herself away on Nobby.

'Wotcher, Mister Lipwig. You should have been 'ere when Mister Vimes was interrogating that old suspect. He rolled up his sleeve and the dwarf went mental, and I mean proper mental. He saw that mark, you know, the one on the commander's wrist, and went, well, totally mental, promising absolutely everything. Never seen anyone so scared in all my life and Vimesy hadn't even touched him. He broke, sir, that's the only way I can put it. He broke. I mean, he's had a go at me on occasions, you know, about such things as what I found on the street and was hurrying to give back to their owner and suchlike. Nothing important. But that dwarf ... it was like he melted, sir. Melted! You wouldn't know Done It Duncan, not being in the Watch, sir, well, the poor bugger owns up to anything just to get a drink and a place to sleep in the cells and maybe a chat and a ham sandwich. But this lawn ornament, he's got it worse.'

Moist looked around. 'Where are they now?'

'In there. And Mister Vimes took the young 'un off somewhere else with Fred.' Nobby pointed towards the far end of the guard's van. 'Mister Lipwig, you know that great idea you had?'

Moist hesitated. 'Help me, Nobby, I have a lot of great ideas.'

'Right, sir – the one about sorting the mail on the train, sir?'

And Moist thought, oh yes, and it would work. But Nobby carried on. 'Well, there's a special carriage on this train. It has shelves and pigeon holes and everything.'

Inside the mail carriage Moist saw the commander and his new little friend, with Fred Colon. Vimes was talking quite cheerfully to the young dwarf and when he saw Moist he gave a quick gesture indicating that he could listen but shouldn't disturb the delicate process. There were no signs of fighting or nastiness of any kind and there were two cups of coffee nestling in the wire pigeon holes. The commander, as soothingly as a mother with a new baby, played a theme that put Moist von Lipwig, confidence trickster, liar, cheat, fraud, swindler and king of slyness, the sort that dripped like the venom of a striking cobra, to shame.

'Oh dear, those grags. Tell me now, which one was it? Come on, help me now.'

'I can't remember.'

'And they did what? Surely not? Oh, it was your chum that we have in the van next door, was it?'

'Well, it might have been, yes.'

Moist wanted to applaud, but the show – if that's what it was – kept on going.

And now, with the strange red snake glistening on his arm, the commander crooned oh so carefully that a grandmother's tea party would appear to be a smash-and-grab raid in comparison. And it finished with a sigh, as the commander said with magnificently sincere anguish, 'Of course, if it was up to me . . . but you see I have to deal with Lord Vetinari and the Low King. I could put in a good word for you, my lad, telling them how helpful you've been . . . Yes, I think I'll do just that, and I thank you for helping me and I can assure you . . .' and here the glowing snake moved as the commander did, 'I can assure you, young man, that no matter what happens to you, nothing will happen to your family. But I don't think I'll be able to persuade people of your innocence if you're caught like this at any future time or, indeed, if you turn out to be lying to me. And now, if you don't mind, I need to talk to your colleague again.'

Moist loved that 'If you don't mind'. As if the fool had a choice. And dark clerks whisked the young dwarf away and came back with the older dwarf, when the careful, methodical interrogation continued, but in a louder voice, considering that this dwarf was much older. The words that Vimes used had more menace in them now; but nevertheless he half suggested that everything would get better if the dwarf in front of him told the commander absolutely everything he knew about the grags and delvers and his fellow conspirators who had been duped into being the ones who got caught and thrown to the Low King's justice.

'You, sir, you'll be sent for trial before the Low King, but, as I said, I'll put in a good word for you. At the next station I'll send a clacks, if your one-time friends haven't burned down the tower.' And *that* made him flinch. Moist had to try hard not to applaud.

'Fred,' said the commander, 'please ask them to bring in this gentleman's accomplice, so that they can enjoy each other's company for the rest of their journey,' and when both dwarfs were in the mail coach under the watchful eye of the dark clerks, Vimes continued.

'Okay,' he said, in the same cheerful tone, 'I'm sorry about the manacles, but we can't have you running away now, can we? And the pair of you must remember – especially you, sir, at your age – it could have been so much worse. I'm afraid to say that it might still turn out that way anyway, but as I said, I'll put in a good word. You'll be looked after until I can arrange for you to be taken off under guard, and if anything jogs your memory don't hesitate to tell them, and I'll see what I can do. But I'm sure you'll agree that it'll be for the safety of all parties, especially your own, if in the meantime you are held in this sealed room where nobody can hurt you.

I'll see to it myself that you have regular meals and refreshments.'

He turned to Moist and said, 'A word with you, please, outside.'

Back in the guard's van the commander pulled a cigar from somewhere and lit it in flagrant defiance of every railway law, sat down on a bench and said, 'Mister Lipwig, you look quizzical. Feel free to speak.'

'Well, commander, I'm impressed you did such a number on them. They think that you're their friend, that you want to help them.'

This was met by another puff of smoke.

'But of course I'm their friend,' replied Vimes, straight-faced, 'and I will continue to be their friend, for now. You are a rascal and I am not. Oh yes, I could make their lives impossible, or even worse. The older one you introduced to the railway boot so adroitly, well, he's the brains of this particular outfit, and the little one is what they call a catspaw, an idiot, filled to the brim with lies, exciting lies, telling him that he is doing the work of Tak. I mean, he isn't even a good train spotter.'

Vimes patted his pocket and said, 'And now I have names, oh such names, such wonderful names, and when the facts of life are explained to their owners they'll undoubtedly lead to other names and we shall see the bunny rabbits run. Police work isn't all about kicking down doors, you know, it's about getting to the bottom of things, and once you're right on the bottom you see all the way to the top and the top is what I'm after here! We'll be stopping for coal and water at a place called Cranbury very soon and there should be a clacks tower.'

He smiled. 'I wonder what his lordship will say about my lovely list of names? I reckon he'll go right past acerbic en route to ironic and end up slap bang in sardonic without even taking a breath.' He slapped his pocket again. 'I know some of these, don't I just, all powerful dwarfs, such stalwart defenders of the Low King on the one hand and dealing happily with the grags on the other. Thank you very much, Mister Lipwig, you're a loss to crime prevention, but you recognized the process because you recognize yourself – isn't that right? How useful, so do I. The mark must always think of you as his friend and you yourself must be as a sorrowful yet loving father. The mark's shield from the dreadful darkness outside.'

The commander turned and said, 'Nobby, who's on duty at Big Cabbage station?'

'Sergeant Willard, Mister Vimes.'

Vimes said to Moist, 'That'll do. He's an old copper and he'll have his hurry-up wagon and he'll get them in front of his lordship in no short order. And with them still in shackles, he won't have any problems. You know, I almost feel sorry for them. Grags, delvers, whatever they call themselves, the modus operandi is to find some innocent dwarf with the right connections and let it be known to him or her that if they do not toe the line and do what they are told, then perhaps all of their family will simply disappear into the Gap.'

He smiled and said, 'Come to think of it, that's

exactly what I do, but I'm a teddy bear by comparison and on the right side.'

Vimes stood up and waved his arms a bit for the circulation and said, 'And now I think I need to go and see the King about my interesting findings. And don't worry, I'll put in a good word too. You pay attention to people and that's a skill in itself.'

The outside air was permeating the carriages now with the scent of the Sto Plains, which consisted of one scent and that was cabbage or cabbage-like and it was a sad smell, it drooped helplessness. Melancholy. Mind you, the cabbages themselves were excellent, especially the newer varieties.

The town of Big Cabbage, theoretically the last place any sensible person would want to visit, was nevertheless popular throughout the summer because of the attractions of Brassica World and the Cabbage Research Institute, whose students were the first to get a cabbage to a height of five hundred yards propelled entirely by its own juices. Nobody asked why they felt it was necessary to do this, but that was science for you, and, of course, students.

As soon as the train arrived at platform two at Big Cabbage several watchmen appeared alongside the guard's van. Moist looked on as Commander Vimes passed out the captives he had been so awfully kind to, and watched them whisked away under guard in the hurry-up wagon.

As it disappeared, Vimes said to Moist, 'We have the names and addresses of their families and they'll have bodyguards day and night until this damn thing is over. I know Vetinari will huff and puff about the bill but then whenever doesn't he?'

Right on schedule, the train pulled away from Big Cabbage, leaving the great dirty distant smog of Ankh-Morpork on the horizon far behind them. Moist had a constant feeling that he was going slightly uphill, which was at least moderately the truth. Things were running as they should, people were settling down for the long haul, and that gave him more time to think. Theoretically, he knew the time to worry was when things were going wrong, but his instinct had a tendency to worry when things were just too good to be true and right now a cumulonimbus of worry was again building over his head; the anvil of the gods was just waiting to drop on him. What had he missed? What had he forgotten? No, everything was going to be all right.

There was a bridge ahead, with the usual troll on guard. The troll railway families treated the bridges, shiny and new as they were, as their own. Oh yes, a tunnel to a troll was a delightful walk in the park, but a bridge, your own bridge . . . especially one with toilet facilities, courtesy of Harry King, and enough space to raise a family . . . Trolls, thought Moist . . . Who would have thought it, they keep their bridges sparkling. Indeed, Effie had announced a best-kept bridge contest for the troll bridges throughout the length of the Ankh-Morpork railway, with no fewer than twenty goats for the winner.

* * *

To travel by the railway was to see the world changing, as trees, houses, farms, meadows, streams, townships that Moist had never heard of before the railway and barely recalled now – like that one there, Much Come Lately according to the sign – whizzed past at railway speed. But who lived there and what did they do, Moist wondered?

The hamlets of the railway workers intrigued Moist. The wives, noticing that passengers got out of the train at the frequent stops for coal and water and showing a grasp of the mercantile world Lord Vetinari would have applauded, stood ready with clotted cream teas, home-made pies, hot and excellent coffee, and on one memorable occasion a small piglet.

But even this was eclipsed by the wheeze he'd encountered a month back, in the hinterland in deepest Twoshirts, considered by Ankh-Morpork the place that was nowhere. A simple slogan had been put up by two industrious ladies that said, 'We knit nighties for railway sleepers!'. The ladies, knitting away while their husbands were walking the tracks, were building up a small fortune from all those passengers who, like Moist, had laughed and dug deep into their pockets. He loved the fact that if you got your customer laughing then you had their money in your pocket.

There was another sign coming up now and he squinted to see the name on the board and – *whoosh* – he saw they were at Monks Deveril, or had been, since alas the speed of the train had shunted it into the past and – *whoosh* – here came – *whoosh* – Upper Feltwhistle, apparently. But the ever-moving train had passed on and he hungered for sight of the Lower Feltwhistle sign but the train sped past, sending the unexplored townships into oblivion. Strange-sounding places with strange-sounding names living in the moment of the triumphant train.

With a clatter another train passed them on the up line, but where from? And going where? Moist gave up. Too much travelling on the railway could turn you into a philosopher, although, he conceded, not a very good one.

There was another coal and water stop at Seven Bangs. The name meant nothing to Moist and even Vimes shook his head. It was one of those places where people got off the train and disappeared into the hinterland and, presumably, only the tax inspectors and the Post Office knew who lived where. And by the look of Seven Bangs, the tax inspectors would probably take a day off sick rather than go there and possibly the postman, too, if he had bad news to convey, such as overdue tax demands. But nevertheless, the people of Seven Bangs had been joined by four linesmen, with their houses and their families, all cosily close to the line.

Moist chatted with the man who operated the water crane and asked, 'Do you have any trouble sleeping up here with trains going past all the time?'

'Well, bless you, sir, but no, sir, not at all. Oh, it took a little time for us to get acclimatized,' and he giggled like a man using an unusual word for the first time and finding it funny. 'My wife sleeps like a baby and the only time she woke up was last week when the Flyer couldn't get through, and she swears that the silence in the wrong place unsettled her.'

Vimes never seemed to leave the guard's van, except for occasional journeys down the train to talk to the King and his bodyguards, and it was into the guard's van that the clacks flimsies were delivered.

There were always goblins in the guard's van, of course, but it didn't stop at that. You found them everywhere, adjusting screws, oiling, greasing and, well, tinkering and tapping. Moist had asked Simnel about that early on and had been told they greased everything that needed greasing and tapped what needed tapping, and generally stopped things getting out of kilter.

Of course, there was still the smell, but once you got used to it, as Adora Belle had long ago, you never even thought about it. And they ran errands when the train stopped at out-of-the-way places, and collected clacks flimsies for news of everything that might pertain to the journey.

The good old clacks, people called it nowadays. They used to call it unsightly, but now, quite likely, you would ask the clacks what the weather was like ahead of your journey. A little comfort but not necessarily necessary. Nevertheless, once you were bereft of the clacks you thought of yourself as a second-class citizen. Spike was always telling him how enraged clients got about their clacks bills, which were, he considered, not bad in the circumstances; but a kind of ratchet formed in people's minds: here is the new thing and here it is. And yesterday you never thought about it and after today you don't know what you would do without it. That was what the technology was doing. It was your slave but, in a sense, it might be the other way round.

After the excitement of the water crane, Moist was at a loose end and now, by habit, if he felt himself at a loose end he went to the guard's van. Detritus lay asleep on a pile of packing cases near by, snoring, surrounded by all the necessary debris of the place. It seemed that all the travellers who were not passengers treated the guard's van as their home. Possibly the coffee maker was the reason for that. And here was Of the Twilight the Darkness, who made very special coffee. Moist thought about that for a moment, as the grinning goblin handed him a bubbling mug.

'I've got it. You're a shaman, aren't you?'

The goblin's grin was wider. 'Sorry, mister. You is not on the money here. You could call me a shamegog. Unfortunately, dissonance, but can't have everything.'

Moist looked into his coffee and said, 'It smells lovely, but what'll it make me do?'

The shamegog thought for a moment and said, 'It make you wide awake, busy man! Maybe puts hair on chest. Slight tendency to make you piss more often.' Now he gave Moist a sideways look that really only a goblin can achieve and said, 'Guaranteed not to make you killer of dwarfs.' It was really very good coffee. Moist had to give the goblin that.

He peered out of the window. Perhaps it was his imagination, but the Forest of Skund seemed to get blacker the closer they came to it. The forest was worse than the maquis. From what Moist remembered, the trees stood shoulder to shoulder. And if you thought that trees didn't have shoulders, you hadn't been to the Forest of Skund. It was one of those places where the magic hadn't been cleaned out yet. And some of the old fears and fancies still hung around the place. Nobody went in there until they had to, the occasional woodcutter for a bet, perhaps. It was a dark place, staring out across the plain and biding its time. Not a place to go if you didn't want a wizard dropping on your head. If a landscape could growl, that was the Forest of Skund.

Moist took the opportunity to look at the instrumentation in the van. There were two guards on the rota for this journey, and though the train couldn't be driven from here, the guard could at least stop it – a fact worth knowing.

As dusk fell, the sound of Detritus's snoring lessened from somewhere in the vicinity of badgers fighting to the death to a low rumble, which caused the rest of the van to resonate. There was a fascination in watching a chest made of stone move. Not for the first time Moist marvelled: *They are stone and we are told that stone lives*; and once again his thoughts harked back to Iron Girder, and, to his amazement, he stopped worrying: horses, trolls, golems, engines, well, where was the downside?

He looked around him. Apart from the sleeping Detritus the guard's van was for once totally empty. The rest of the train's occupants were settling down for the evening elsewhere, busy with their own affairs;

Commander Vimes was making his rounds of the carriages.

Moist moved quickly, no longer able to fight the little devil inside him. After all, he reasoned, he'd waited long enough to do this, and he might not have another chance. It was still light enough. He opened the door of the guard's van, and, gripping the side of the carriage, climbed out, kicked shut the door behind him and clambered on to the top of the train. Once there he scrambled to his feet, and then, throwing caution to the winds, Moist danced on the top of the train, leaping from carriage to carriage, listening to the train's rhythm, moving his body to accommodate it and feeling the engine and the moods of the railway until it seemed that he could understand it. It was a benison, a gift. It was a thing that could be courted but, he expected, it wouldn't allow too much familiarity. It enthralled him and he thought: steam is not to be taken lightly.

Once, he heard a shout of 'Oi!' from below and Moist was no stranger to 'Oi!'. He leaned down and said, 'Moist von Lipwig. I'm doing a little test.' He could hear the 'Oi' voice grumbling, and let it grumble because this was what he had wanted as soon as he had seen the new Flyers.

Flushed with the thrill of the ride, Moist dropped back down into the guard's van, still empty except for the sleeping form of Detritus. He smoothed down his hair and wiped the smuts from his face, and wandered out of the carriage, a smile on his face.

* * *

Down the length of the train the lights were going out when Commander Vimes reappeared from his latest sortie and headed for the coffee.

'The King and his council of war are making their plans,' he said. 'Your latest clacks reports and what I hear from let's call them observers on the ground suggest that work on the rails is going ahead reasonably happily.'

He looked slyly at Moist. 'Pretty soon, it seems, Mister Lipwig, you'll have to put your money where your mouth is. Oh, and another thing. Here's a flimsy from your good wife. Even with the news of the Schmaltzberg coup spreading, there appear to have been very few attacks on clacks towers outside Uberwald.'

Taken aback, Moist said, 'Well, that is good news.'

But Vimes just frowned and said, 'Don't get excited. I'd wager that there are still some out there who'd knock over a clacks tower even if they saw Tak on the top of it. That's the trouble, you see. When you've had hatred on your tongue for such a long time, you don't know how to spit it out.'

Moist had made sure, oh bliss, right from the start that he would have a sleeping compartment of his own, but, unlike those in the First Class sleeper carriage, his was more utilitarian and using it was an exercise suited to people who like toying with twisty cubes and other notorious playthings. It had a folding bed, which folded down and hit him on the head, and a washbasin into which his toothbrush would just about fit. But there was a sponge provided, and since he was suitably athletic he made the best of it, ending up if not clean, not any dirtier either. And gods, he was tired, and whatever it was that drove him seriously needed a rest, but the mind was its own worst enemy and the more he tried to get himself lulled by the rhythms of the railway, the more his niggling thoughts seemed to burgeon like a cloud.

They had been lucky so far – only the two grag spies to deal with, and pretty poor spies at that – but sooner or later the rat would surely be out of the bag and the grags would know that Rhys was on board. Simnel's hope seemed to rest on the fact that they would be using Iron Girder by that time. But could she really make a difference, Simnel's little experiment, more used to giving children rides around the yard? I'm sure that when that locomotive of Simnel's first arrived, Moist thought, it was pretty small and I wondered how it could go the distance, even to Sto Lat. But now she seems so powerful. And the way Simnel keeps upgrading her and paying her attention, it's as if something bad would happen if she wasn't the queen of the yard. She never sleeps. There's always that little hiss. That little tinkle of metal. Mechanical susurration, whether or not she is ostensibly running.

Moist thought about whoever it was who had got into the compound to smash her up, who ended up dead, dead, dead. Wild steam from a train that wasn't running. Earth, fire, wind and rain all in one element of speed. And slowly Moist shut down, although a part of him was always listening to the rhythm of the rails, listening in his sleep, like a sailor listening to the sounds of the sea.

As Moist slept, the train barrelled like a very slow meteor through the night, climbing up through the Carrack Mountains. Almost the only light to be seen with the moon under a cloud came from the engine's headlamp and the glow from the furnace when the door was opened to shovel in more coal.

The engine stokers of the Hygienic Railway were a breed apart: taciturn, perennially grumpy, seemingly only willing to talk to the drivers. In the unwritten hierarchy of the footplate the drivers were at the top, of course, and *then* the stokers and after the stokers there would be the wheel-tappers and shunters: lesser beings but acknowledged as useful. At times it appeared that the stokers considered themselves the most important component of the railway, keepers of its soul, as it were. When off duty they all messed together, grumbling, puffing their wretched pipes, and talking to nobody else. But shovelling coal all day built muscles of iron, so the stokers were strong and fit, and sometimes between shifts there were sparring matches with shovels, with the combatants cheered on by their fellows.

In fact, one of the stokers on the train was a bit of a legend, according to the others, although Moist had not come across him yet. Stoker Blake was said to be death on legs if he was aroused. The other stokers were fierce fighters, but it was claimed that none of them ever got to touch Stoker Blake. A stoker's shovel, incorrectly used, was an illustration of Commander

Vimes's dictum that a workman's tool used cunningly could give the average watchman a real headache.

And so the stokers laughed and danced as they sparred with their shovels and got drunk – but not when they were going to be on the footplate. They didn't need telling about that.

Tonight, cocooned from the cool wind that flew around the cab, Stoker Jim said to the train driver, 'Here's your coffee, Mick. Fancy a fry-up?'

Mick nodded without taking his eyes off the track ahead and so Stoker Jim carefully reached out and fried a couple of eggs on the back of his shovel, courtesy of the fiery furnace.

The houses hastily built for the railway workers were close to the water cranes and coal bunkers so that an eye could be kept on the precious coal and water supplies. They were quite small, which put some strain on the accommodation when there were children and grandparents as well, but everyone said that it was twice as good as what might be found in the big city and, after all, you were out in the fresh air, at least in between locomotives.

On this night, Mrs Plumridge, mother of Jack Plumridge the linesman, realized that her chamber pot was overflowing and cussed herself for not emptying it before twilight. She didn't trust the gleaming porcelain in the ablutions. All her life she had gone outside to a designated private spot in the garden, taking care to remember which of her little plots to empty it in this time, and therefore things got rather receptacle-shaped when a dwarf jumped out in front of her, screamed, 'Death to the railway!' and tried to throw something at her.

In response, Mrs Plumridge hefted the chamber pot with a strength you might not have expected from such an old woman who, according to her son, was made out of teak. The pot was very large and remained regrettably very full and the scream woke up all the households near by . . . and when the miscreant delver came back to consciousness he was tied up and en route to Ankh-Morpork for judgement.

The railwaymen and their grannies were no-nonsense people, earthy, you might say, and they didn't even allow the delver to wash himself, and that was a terrible thing in the circumstances.

When Moist awoke the following morning, he realized that he was hungry and was pleased to discover that there was breakfast (all-day breakfast it turned out) in the dining carriage.

He found the dining car empty but for Bashfull Bashfullsson and the Low King, sitting chatting like businessmen with a deal to make, taking advantage of the cornucopia.

Quietly, the King welcomed him and said, 'Not seen much of the train so far, Mister Lipwig. Been in a planning session with Bashfullsson and the others since we boarded. Will you join us?'

As Moist sat down, Bashfullsson turned to him as if to an ally. 'I'm trying to get Rhys here to tell us what he's up to.'

The King merely smiled at this. 'I intend to take Schmaltzberg with you, my friend Bashfullsson, and do it with as little bloodshed as possible. Believe me, although it's vexing to remember it, I am the King of my enemies as well as my friends. There's a certain *noblesse oblige*, see. It's a bad king who kills his subjects. I would rather see them humiliated than dead.'

Bashfullsson said, 'Really? After all the things they've done? And the things they've caused to be done? Finding young dwarfs and filling them with excitement and idiotic revelations . . .'

'I have names,' said the King. 'Names of leaders, names of hangers-on. Oh yes, there will be a reckoning. Not an auto-da-fé.'

'I fear you were too understanding with them last time, sire,' Bashfullsson said, picking his words carefully. 'Sad to say, but I've come to the conclusion that if you keep turning the other cheek they'll go on slapping you in the face. I think there's nothing for it but to go in, cut out and have done. No point in knocking politely this time, saying can I have the Scone of Stone back, please.'

To Moist's surprise, the King said, 'However much we disdain the word "politics", one of its most useful aspects is the stopping of bloodshed. Oh yes, bloodshed there will be. But the generations stream away and people change and things thought of as totally impossible suddenly turn out to be everyday. Nay, essential. Just like the railway is becoming, see. Apropos of that, Mister Lipwig, how *is* the railway progressing? How are your loggysticks going?'

'Copacetic, sire. That's an engineer term meaning all satisfactory.'

The King gave Moist a look. It wasn't by the standard of looks a nasty one, but it was after all a King's look, and the gaze of the King was subtly quizzical and testing.

'We shall see, boyo, we shall see.'

And after breakfast, there was nothing for it but to watch the mountain scenery flow past as if on some endless winding belt: trees, rocks, more trees, bigger rocks, trees again, what was possibly a clearing where lumbermen were working, brief darkness as they reached a rock big enough to require a tunnel, and so on, and yet, Moist thought, behind all those trees and all those rocks and crags, there are homesteads and small villages that we don't know about and so one day we will have to have a stop here . . . here . . . and here. And then one day, some kid from the settlement high up in that last lot of rocks will catch the train and end up in Ankh-Morpork, full of hope, and why not? Station by station we are changing the world. And he allowed himself a little glow of pride.

Apart from the Falls,* the only place that was of any significance in Zemphis was Downsized Abbey. It was a ruin now, the monks long gone; these days it was more of a souk, a medina, a heaving bazaar which reminded

* Moist had seen the Falls before and that's just what they were . . . falls. Pretty good falls by the standard of falls, but once you'd looked at them for a few minutes undoubtedly someone would say: 'Where can we get a coffee around here?'

Moist of the Shades of Ankh-Morpork on their holidays. Nothing was still. Silence was a rare blessing. And everyone was a trader and it seemed that sooner or later everything and everyone could be bought and sold. And, if necessary, disappeared.

Of the trading routes in Zemphis, the Aglet Road stood out, as caravans of camels arrived on their way to bring the people of the Plains the tiny little things on the ends of their shoelaces without which civilized life would be unbearable and quite dangerous. There were spices from Klatch*, materials from the Counterweight Continent which had arrived by slow barge, other mysterious delicacies, and unfortunately many ways to become very happy in a short space of time and stone dead shortly afterwards.

Alongside the legitimate goods traded at the front of the stalls, without doubt there was some contraband, as many traders luxuriated in the semi-lawless landscape. Cages of undomesticated imps were available in the back rooms of some more unscrupulous shops, and after dark the occasional camel slipped in or out of the town carrying barrels of crude treacle.

And even though most sensible people wishing to hang on to their personal possessions, or indeed their lives, would follow the advice of those who had been there and give it a wide berth, some possibly foolhardy tourists did come to Zemphis on their way to see the

---

* And if you knew where to ask, the fabled Klatchian migratory bog truffle, which despite resembling the Klatchian bog toad in both taste and appearance was extremely rare and therefore a delicacy.

Paps of Scilla, a jagged mountain range which allowed the determined mountaineer an absolute smorgasbord of ways to be found upside down above a crevasse and hanging by one leg over white water that acted like the mother of all grinders. There were eight peaks in all, sharp and unforgiving, and if there were such a thing as the good ambushing guide it would be right up there with the winners.

Contemplating the Paps from a seat conveniently placed by the burghers of Zemphis as a lookout point for those admiring the view, Moist reflected that shortly their train would have to travel through those peaks. They didn't look so bad on the map, but up close and personal they were awesome. Scilla must have been very proud eight times over.

A mist hung over the greenery clinging to the steep foothills of the Paps. The terrain looked impassable for a train, but Simnel's sliding-rule boys had found a suitable way through. Track had been laid and Moist knew that they'd had trolls hanging around there all week, keeping guard.

Just then, there was a shout from Commander Vimes. 'Lipwig! Drop!'

Moist dropped, while whatever the commander had seen scythed overhead, and he was just picking himself up when Vimes tackled him back down to the ground as the missile whistled round for another slice before finally dropping somewhere near their feet.

'And there you have it,' said Vimes. 'Really nasty fellows, delvers, but you've got to admire their workmanship.'

Moist, still at ground level, said, as if it mattered, 'Was it really them?'

'Quite likely, but there are other nuisances in these hills. You must know that where there are tourists there are also people eager for their dollars. Don't touch it!'

Moist's hand flew back.

'It's a boomerang,' said Vimes. 'You find something like this all over the world. You have to wave it carefully and suddenly your opponent gets it in the back. I've heard that there's a lad in Fourecks who can throw a boomerang with such precision that it can get the morning paper and come back with it.'

Moist gave the commander a look of disbelief.

'Well, that's what they say, and you know those boys from Fourecks, they love to draw a long bow,' Vimes continued, picking up the boomerang gingerly with a handkerchief. He sniffed it, grimaced and said, 'The stuff the grags have put on this one might not kill you but you'll wish that it had for a day or two, if you're lucky. I'm going to have to talk to Vetinari about this place. They've got *something* like a government here, but their policing might just be adequate in a kindergarten. They're not exactly bent, just not organized in the right way. Good grief, I could even send Nobby up here and the quality of the policing would go comparatively sky high.'

'Surely Vetinari's remit doesn't stretch all the way out here? And you're well out of your jurisdiction, aren't you?'

To Moist's amazement Vimes laughed, and said, 'I couldn't speak for Vetinari, but we all know he has his

. . . ways and his means. I think he allows this place to exist so that it doesn't exist in Ankh-Morpork. And as for my jurisdiction, I wouldn't be surprised if there are a number of people in this place who'd like to see some law in the streets. So if that were the case, well, it might be my duty to assist. But not today.'

He patted Moist on the shoulder and said, 'Mister Lipwig, I'm sure there've been times in your life when you've seen a wonderful opportunity to steal something valuable and you've decided for various reasons not to? Well, I feel as you would then. This place is a sink. Who knows what dreadful things are happening behind closed doors.' He shrugged and went on, 'But you can't kick down every door in the universe. And we have more pressing matters to attend to.'

Moist accepted this sad explanation and after a fruitless hunt around for their assailant they turned their backs on the Paps to head back to the station. As they left the lookout point, they heard a train whistle in the distance. Far away, climbing into Zemphis on the main line from the Plains, there was a streak of scintillating sunlight with a trail of steam.

Vimes looked at Moist and said, 'What the hell is that? There isn't another train due today, is there?'

'Well, Dick said he was polishing up Iron Girder for the big event, and before we left he was talking as if his favourite locomotive had been getting a complete overhaul. That must be her.'

In fact, it wasn't just an overhaul. When Moist had shown Simnel the micromail he had received as spoils of the battle with the dwarfs at the Quirm railhead, the young engineer had smiled and said, 'Aye, I know what the secret is here. This is a metal stronger than iron, malleable and half its weight, and it never rusts. Its ore is rare but it's the base of a new alloy I've made. I call it sorortanium, which Mister Thunderbolt says means the sister of iron. It's stronger even than steel! What boilers I could make with it if only I could get 'old of enough of the stuff! Thank you. It's amazing and I know just what to do with it.'

As they watched the astonishing locomotive dealing with the steep haul into Zemphis, Moist noticed that the engine appeared to shrug off the load behind her. The Flyer they had come in on earlier had been creaking as it chugged up the last steep haul into Zemphis. This new train didn't even seem to notice the gradient.

Vimes smacked his head and said, 'Is that really Iron Girder? Last I saw of Iron Girder, she was providing a playground entertainment for grown-ups. If that's Iron Girder,' he said, pointing at the shimmering apparition, 'surely she's grown?'

'It *is* Iron Girder,' said Moist. 'Dick spends all his time tinkering with her, over and over again, improving her at every turn and opportunity. And at the end, well, she's still Iron Girder. She'll always be Iron Girder.'

'But she's so easily spotted, all that shining . . . People are going to see her coming for miles! No chance of an inconspicuous departure, then!'

'I know,' said Moist. 'But since you can *hear* her coming for miles, Dick said it won't make any difference. Everyone'll know we're coming.' Though the silver carapace in fact could make a significant difference in other ways, he thought.

'If you please, *ah grag nun**, we have lost track of two agents on one of the trains,' said the acolyte. 'Alas, we are no longer in touch with them.'

The grag commander looked up. 'Ah-ha!' he said. 'Where were they when we last heard from them?'

'On the regular service from Sto Lat to Zemphis. But they failed to report at Big Cabbage or earlier as the train passed through Cranbury.'

'Are you certain?'

The acolyte jumped. 'Well, my lord, we are in the dark, but I think so . . .'

'In that case,' said the grag, 'make it known that we are no longer bothering with the other routes. Our . . . package must have been on that train to Zemphis. And from there . . . The Paps await, and they take no prisoners! They, my friend, are coming to us. And the creatures that live in the Paps will be our allies! It's all about the railway now, and we know that it is in the compass of our agents to stop those blasted wheels turning. Be mindful of bridges, however. The enemy favours the dreadful stone people who love to guard them. And surely tunnels can also be made to fail . . . This wretched technology contains the seeds of fallibility.'

'Yes, *grag nun*, we know that the locomotive has to stop frequently for coal and water. Deprive it of either

---

* Dwarfish, trans.: my lord.

and there is no locomotive, just a lump of old iron. So, the coal bunkers and, yes, water cranes . . . There will be guards, of course, but they should be easy to overcome when stationary.'

The chief grag returned to his study of the words of Tak as annotated by Grag Hamcrusher.

'Let me know when the deed is done.'

Down at the Zemphis terminus, Iron Girder looked even more spectacular up close. Dick Simnel was dressed smartly and grinning proudly as he showed off the glittering engine and all the dials and gauges on the footplate. Seeing Dick wearing clothes that had no grease on them was astonishing, like seeing a lion without a mane.

Along with Cheery Littlebottom and other members of the City Watch who had been summoned by Commander Vimes, Moist was surprised to see the cheerful and homely face of Constable Bluejohn, the largest troll on the force. Bluejohn, whom even Detritus described as 'a big boy', was by nature as gentle as a breeze and wouldn't hurt a fly – at least not on purpose, although he could quite possibly tear a lion in half with his bare hands if needed. Nevertheless the sight of him on the scene of any fracas was an invitation to run a marathon in the other direction rather than face the megalith. He lived in a reinforced house somewhere in Sunink, a little town inadvisably nestling in the outskirts of Ankh-Morpork. They said that the sound of Bluejohn walking to work was better than an alarm clock.

Vimes marched off down the platform to greet the new arrivals. Cheery was looking very cheerful, as cheerful as any decoy could be who had been the winner of a battle and had come out more or less unscathed, except for a small scar which you had to have, didn't you, or no one would believe you.

The tour of the footplate finished, Simnel turned to Moist. 'According to our schedule, we ought to be going.' He blew his whistle and shouted down the platform, 'All aboard!'

There was no way of avoiding considerable attention as the King's party assembled to board the armoured carriages behind Iron Girder. The engine herself was spectacular and her passengers were unusual even for a city like Zemphis. There were the dwarfs: the Low King and his bodyguards, Aeron his secretary and Bashfull Bashfullsson; there were suspiciously deep shadows that suggested the continued presence of dark clerks; there were several specialist members of the Watch;* there were the goblins, who scrambled into the guard's van being coupled on at the rear; and just in front of the van was a flatbed carrying Constable Bluejohn along with equipment and baggage too bulky for the guard's van.

Iron Girder was fully in steam again now and the vapour surrounded everybody. Vimes went with the engineers as they walked right around the train for a

---

* Which didn't include Corporal Nobby Nobbs or Sergeant Colon, who were not precisely special but, as Moist knew, curiously useful, which was why Vimes put up with them.

final check. Then came the scream of the whistle and the little shunting dance that Iron Girder did before gaining speed. With someone staring from every carriage window, the special express train to Uberwald started to show what it could do.

The story told locally about the Paps of Scilla was that they were formed when one huge mountain fell apart, leaving a treacherous network of broken caverns – some full of water, always overflowing – topped by the eight forbidding peaks, which seemed to hang in the moisture-laden air, surrounded by rainbows. After the boomerang incident in Zemphis, Moist wasn't very keen on seeing the Paps up close and personal, but Simnel's surveyors had excelled themselves. The railway track insinuated itself up through the craggy gaps so that the train climbed majestically higher and higher, leaving the city of Zemphis and the heat shimmer of the sierra far below.

Halfway towards the gloom of the pass between the tallest peaks, the train emerged from a large natural tunnel into another kaleidoscope of rainbows, which were distracting even when people weren't throwing things at your head.

Without warning, a boulder smashed down in front of the train and rolled across the tracks, to shatter in the opposite gully. Then there was another crash from the rear. The train shuddered horribly, and carried on.

Moist looked up and saw dwarfs perched on the craggy cliffs on each side of the canyon, levering boulders down on to the train. Commander Vimes could be heard cursing and shouting orders down the carriages, his words drowned out as yet larger boulders fell, raining down on the locomotive, which was moving slowly forward like an old lady testing the water.

Surely, Moist thought, this is the end. Even if the tracks ahead remain undamaged, no normal engine could withstand this bombardment. But then he realized that Iron Girder, slowly and methodically, was actually steaming on despite the boulders continuing to pound the train.

Moist couldn't stop himself. He shouted to anyone who would listen, 'They're bouncing off! It's the sorortanium, it takes the punishment and throws it right back!'

Meanwhile, at the rear of the train, Constable Bluejohn, standing on his flatbed gently rocking with the motion, thundered a troll threat, reached out and plucked a miscreant from his foothold unwisely close to the track. When he was joined by Detritus, the assailants soon discovered that aiming boulders at the trolls was a fool's errand. The lads, who were quite literally in their element, just grabbed them and tossed them back with interest.

Looking out of a broken window, Moist saw a small swarm of goblins leave the train and at first he thought, ha! Trust the buggers to run away, and then he mentally corrected himself: that was storybook thinking and with clearer eyesight and a bit of understanding he realized that the goblins were scrambling up to the delvers on the rocks and beating the shit out of them by diving into the multiple layers of dwarf clothing. The delvers discovered all too rapidly that trying to fight while a busy goblin was in your underwear was very bad for the concentration.

Of the Twilight the Darkness suddenly appeared at Moist's elbow. He was wearing a helmet that was far too big for him and spun around on his head. He pushed one arm into the greasy nest he called a jacket and struck a pose.

'Marvellous, ain't they? Always going for the gonads.'

There were screams, sometimes high-pitched, as the delvers lost their hold and fell down either under the train or into the water, still fighting the speedy goblins.

As Iron Girder steadfastly steamed on round the next bend, she and her coal tender came into Moist's field of vision and he was horrified to see that a couple of delvers had gained a foothold on the tender. They were being held at bay by a soot-blackened stoker who was valiantly protecting access to the footplate by wielding his shovel to deadly effect. Moist caught a glimpse between the chaos of fighting bodies of the stoker dispatching one of the delvers, kicking him over the side. A massive blow with the shovel dealt with the other dwarf, and the stoker dropped out of sight. His sheer efficiency had been vaguely disturbing. Perhaps that's the legendary Stoker Blake, Moist thought, and then ducked back inside as another boulder crashed past.

Finally the bombardment ceased and Moist made his way down the train. He found the Low King in one of the armoured carriages with Bashfullsson and the rest of his party. There was blood on the King's beard.

'The foe is either fleeing or dead,' the King said. 'The wounded will be taken aboard under lock and key and undoubtedly the good commander will have them talking to him as if they were the best of friends. He has a knack for that sort of thing.'

A while later Moist went into the guard's van, where Commander Vimes was having little chats to grags and their fellow travellers. He was speaking in his very low, *understanding* voice.

'I do understand your position. It's such a shame, especially since the ones that started it all are likely to get away into the darkness.'

And yet again Moist was impressed. The grizzled commander was all honey as he continued, 'Of course, as a friend, you might give me certain names. I like collecting names, they sing to me.'

And Moist thought, they have the honey, here comes the sting.

Cheerfully, Vimes took names like a guardian uncle, while in various corners of the van people were being bandaged, cleaned and fed.

And so, battered but triumphant, Iron Girder blew her whistle and gently got up to speed on the track out of the Paps towards Uberwald with goblins every-where: panel-beating, tidying up, greasing, bending and cleaning and almost rebuilding her on the run, as it were, and Moist noticed that at no point did Iron Girder turn them into a pink haze with live steam. The queen of locomotion valued her courtiers.

Moist had lost all track of time after the excitement of the ambush, but what he thought must be teatime refreshment was interrupted by the squealing of brakes followed by a jerk that caused crockery to scatter all over the floor as the driver leaned on his emergency brake lever, which did little more than pit screaming metal against metal. And then the train came to an abrupt stop, overturning anything that was left upright, followed by the voice of Bluejohn from the rear of the train saying, 'I reckon it needed pullin'. Sorry if I was wrong.'

Moist hurried towards the troll's flatbed. 'You appear to have stopped the train all by yourself,' he said, and waited. You waited a lot when you were talking to Bluejohn.

And at last when Bluejohn had assembled his words to his satisfaction he said, 'Oh, sorry, Mister Lipwig, if I broke anythin' take it outta my wages if you like.'

Moist said, 'That won't be necessary.' He leaned out to look down the track towards the front of the train. Simnel had jumped from the footplate to investigate.

'It's a load of kids!' he shouted back.

Moist jumped down on to the track and ran towards Simnel.

'Leave it to me, Dick, I can handle this,' he said as he reached the engine. In the fading light he could see some children on the track a short way ahead, who, it appeared, had flagged down the train with their pinafores.

The eldest of the children was female and well dressed and almost in tears. She said, 'There's a landslide, mister.'

'Where?'

'Round the next bend, sir,' gasped the girl.

And sure enough, when Moist strode along the track and looked into the gloom beyond, he saw a load of old timbers and rocks surrounded by other debris. And then the situation dawned on him. He carefully set his face like thunder and said, 'What's your name, young lady?'

'Edith, sir,' she simpered, but not properly, and he could tell that she wasn't used to a life of crime.

Moist beckoned the girl to come closer. 'Edith, pardon me for being suspicious, but my instincts tell me that your charming little scheme was devised so that you brave young people could save the train from derailing and then be heroes, am I right?'

The girl and her smaller chums looked miserable, but the scoundrel in Moist urged him to say, 'Well, it's an ingenious idea, but if Lord Vetinari were to hear about this you'd be having the kitten treatment.'

And the girl smiled and said, 'Oh, that's nice. I like kittens.'

'I dare say you do, but I don't think you'd like Cedric who comes with them . . . Now, I admire the resourcefulness of your little plot, but people could have been hurt.' He raised his voice. 'Can you imagine a railway accident? The screaming of the rails and the people inside and the explosion that scythes the countryside around when the boiler bursts? And you, little girl, and your little friends, would have done all that. Killed a trainload of people.'

He had to stop there because the girl looked like death. And, if his instincts were right, somewhat damp around the legs, not weeping for effect this time but traumatized, her face white.

Moist lowered his voice and said, 'Yes, you've seen it in your head now, and probably, when you think about it again, you'll remember that you very nearly killed lots of people.'

Edith said in a small voice, 'I'm really very sorry, it won't happen again.'

Moist said, 'Actually, it hasn't happened once. Still, I'd like you to see to it that it *doesn't* happen around here or anywhere else. Have I made my message clear?'

Damp and scared, Edith managed a weak, 'Yes, sir.' And Moist recognized true contrition.

He looked into her hopeful face and said, 'I'll square this with the engine driver, but if I was you I'd get my pencil and turn any clever ideas you have like this into a book or two. Those penny dreadfuls are all the rage in the railway bookshops. I hear there's money in it, and you won't meet Cedric that way. Oh, and don't keep waving your pinafores at people. It could give quite the wrong idea in the dark. Now, where do you live, young lady? I haven't seen any settlements round here, it's all woodland.'

She curtsied. She actually curtsied. And still red-eyed, she said, 'We live in the railway houses, just back by the water crane and coal bunker.'

'And is your father likely to be at home?'

The girl went white again but gamely managed, 'Yes, sir, if you please, sir.'

'In that case, while the gentlemen back there are settling things down, I'd like to see him, please.'

And uncertainly Edith led him to, yes, the railway houses and introduced Moist to a burly but cheerful-looking man who was sitting at a table devouring bread and cheese with half a pint of beer in his hand.

'This is my dad.'

The man put down a large slab of cheese and said, 'Can't shake hands, sir, I'm all over cheese, apart from what's not all over grease. Nesmith is the name.'

'Well, Mister Nesmith, perhaps your children might go off and play while I have a little chat with you.'

When Edith and the others had made themselves scarce at the speed of sound, Moist said, 'You must have heard the squealing?'

'Oh, yessir, I did, and our Jake and Humphrey were sent off to see what was going on, what with me just home after a long shift.'

'Well, Mister Nesmith, I congratulate you for your clean and well-spoken children, but I'm sorry to say they came very close to at least disabling the new express to Uberwald.'

Nesmith's face went grey as he contemplated a future with no work and no pension and quite probably a criminal record. Greasy tears flowed out of his eyes and he said, 'Anyone hurt, sir? If anyone's hurt I'll tan their hides.'

'Some broken crockery, and there's work to be done to get the track cleared before we can leave.'

The big round face was contorted. 'I can help there, sir, I can help, but I'll tan their hides for them, you see if I don't.'

'No, you will not, Mister Nesmith, I'll see you pay for it if you do, indeed I will. Look, they could have caused a terrible accident, but the important thing is that they didn't. They wanted to appear brave, as far as I can see, and you can't blame kids for that. However, the railway isn't a playground. Do you understand me, Mister Nesmith? Now, if I were you I'd get out my jim crow, off shift or not, and help clear the rails. Oh, and treasure your eldest daughter: you might be grateful for her imagination one day.'

Ohulan Cutash beckoned. Moist knew it as a likeable kind of place: a little market town with the usual hinterland of farmers and lumberjacks. Some mining too, dwarfs and humans quite often these days working on the same mine and even the same seams. It was big enough to have a mayor and sensible enough to have a very good tavern called the Fiddler's Riddle. And apparently it was a place where the current unpleasantness had not yet reached.

What Moist hadn't expected to find, as they pulled up to the platform just past midnight, was the brass band and the flags and the Morris dancing and the funfair, which it appeared had been organized to welcome the first proper train to arrive at the newly constructed station and had been going on for hours.

And as soon as Iron Girder came to a stop with her last hiss, Mr Skiller, the landlord of the Fiddler's Riddle, who turned out also to be the town mayor, began an address offering the freedom of his little town to everyone on the train. Although of course it wasn't a little town, oh indeed not, to its mayor. It was chasing Ankh-Morpork. A little part of Moist's brain laid a bet with itself that very shortly the words 'on the map' were going to be uttered.

And indeed, the mayor, large and florid as a proper mayor should be, said as Moist stepped down, minding the gap, 'This will put Ohulan Cutash on the map and no mistake. We're already breaking ground for a much bigger tavern with facilities.' He looked at Moist solemnly and said, 'You have to have facilities, these days, you know. We paid for our own clacks tower. We're very modern here, that's for sure.'

Moist looked around at the cobbled town square that lay a short distance from the platform. It would have been better if it hadn't been the middle of the night, but the mayor saw no problem with this and cheerfully pointed out to the now clustering passengers the locations of the wonderful things they would be able to see when it was daylight.

And it nearly broke Moist's heart to say to the man, 'I'm afraid we have to go very soon. Schedules, you know.'

And indeed, he could see the water crane pumping and could hear the rattle of the coal being delivered to the engine, but nothing could stop the mayor in his rampant hospitality.

'But we've arranged for a mayoral banquet.'

'Ah ... will you excuse me for a moment, mister mayor?'

Moist had a private word with Simnel about arrangements for the next leg of the journey and then with Vimes, who nodded and said quietly, 'Sensible. I wouldn't mind eating off a plate that wasn't rattling. There's no harm in pandering to a little civic pride. The mayor is a decent cove and they've got a Watch of sorts. Two watchmen, not too bad in the circumstances, and I know that because I trained them.'

Moist came back to the reception committee, put his arm around the ebullient red-faced mayor and said, 'Well, sir, I'm sure we can spare the time for a modest banquet before the dreadful pressures of the timetable force us onwards.'

They left Simnel at the station with his fellow engineers to await the arrival of the back-up Flyer, which had left Zemphis a few hours after Iron Girder. The King and Aeron remained ensconced on the train, safely guarded in the armoured carriage, busy with paperwork and plans for their arrival in Uberwald. The rest of the party followed the mayor across the square to his hostelry.

The town really had tried. Something about the mayor's conviction that the world revolved around their town, or would do if it ever came there, had dribbled into the minds of his ratepayers, who now set to warming up marvellous dishes they had expected to be serving several hours before. And were very understanding, especially after Moist's description of the fight along the Paps. Admittedly he had put a certain amount of shine on the episode; surely that was what shine was for? And it permeated, even into the consciousness of those who had travelled, and at one point Of the Twilight the Darkness actually stood up and made a bow.

And Moist couldn't help himself and pointed at the goblin, saying, 'Of the Twilight the Darkness and his gallant fellows fought alongside Commander Vimes, with great courage.'

And then Moist glanced at the commander, who puffed his cigar and said, 'Excellent fighters, to a goblin.'

'Oh, we like goblins,' said the mayor. 'They run our clacks tower. And do you know, the snail infestation in my Porraceous Sprouter patch has completely gone since they moved in.'

And there was another toast to the clacks at this point with a side order of goblins. By the time they had all processed back to Iron Girder, she had been covered with petals by the virgins of the town.* The Flyer had been and gone some time before, with its crew of engineers supplemented by Cheery Littlebottom – once more playing decoy – and other good fighters. It was even now on the track to Slake, acting as a pathfinder for Iron Girder to confuse the enemy.

As Iron Girder steamed out of Ohulan Cutash, most people headed off to sleep. Moist had loaned the sleeping compartment assigned to him to two of those wounded in the battle and was now bunking down in

---

* At least they said they were virgins. There certainly were petals.

the guard's van, comfortable enough when you were dog-tired and Detritus wasn't snoring. All Moist's life he'd managed to find a way of sleeping in just about every circumstance and, besides, the guard's van was somehow the hub of the train; and although he didn't know how he did it, he always managed to sleep with half of one ear open. And now he savoured the familiar sounds of the journey, the rocking soothing him right up until somewhere down the line when he was catapulted into the real world by the screech once more of the locomotive's wheels in distress, and the squealing of brakes in torment.

It was still dark outside. Moist drowsily stumbled across the flatbed as doors were being opened and feet were running in the carriage ahead and reached the armoured compartment of the King. It was empty.

There was a dwarf guard, who said, 'The King went to the footplate.' The dwarf looked ashamed. 'I tried to persuade him to let me go with him, but what can you do? He is the King.'

Moist said, 'Don't worry, just keep this station. I'll go and see what's happening.'

There was a drill for this, he knew, and where *was* the King? That was the trouble with royalty. However decent they were, and understanding, they were also likely to think that such things as security arrangements were for other people.

Frantically searching, Moist finally dropped down on to the track and ran along to the engine, where he found the King talking to Dick Simnel on the footplate and getting covered in smuts.

Pale flames were visible ahead on the track and Simnel's expression was grave.

'It were just as well the King were 'ere because the decoy Flyer has been derailed ahead of us and so would we 'ave been if it weren't for 'im. He can see in t'dark!'

'Ah, Commander Vimes,' said the King to Vimes, who had arrived at speed. 'You should know about the dark-accustomed eye if any human does. There's a long straight ahead and Dick hadn't seen the derailment, but I did, just in time. Now, there may be injured people up there.'

And then the King was running towards the flames, adopting the traditional dwarf strategy of running at the enemy with as much weaponry as you could swing. But Vimes caught up with him and rolled him to the ground just as an explosion rattled the trees and bounced off the mountains. The Flyer's boiler had blown up. Ahead of them now was just a warm mist and the occasional clink of stricken metal.

Vimes got the King upright and said, 'Apologies for the lèse-majesté – though you must know that we Vimeses have gone a lot further than that in the past. You should have listened. The whole deal for the crew of the decoy Flyer was to run away as fast as possible if attacked, but not before making sure that the emergency bung in the boiler was strapped right down.'

'Ah, yes, Blackboard Monitor, how easily we revert to type in an emergency. I'm sorry to have put you to extra trouble.'

'That'll teach the buggers a lesson,' said Dick,

panting as he caught up with them. 'They'll think twice about messing with one of my engines again.'

The crew of the Flyer were up a little gully, into which they had dived for shelter. It had once been home to frogs. Regrettably, it still was, and several of the designated bodyguards rose from the little swamp with nothing more than torn clothing and a lot of mud, some of which was hopping, but Cheery Littlebottom was as cheery as her name suggested.

There seemed to be no grags, but even as Moist looked around, an arm dropped out of a tree, still holding a club in an iron grip. And hereabouts, if you cared to look, and frankly nobody cared to do so but did nonetheless, there were several signs that grags and delvers and many others of the dark underworld had passed away in this spot, resting at peace and, thanks to the exploding boiler, in pieces.

Detritus appeared out of the gloom, saying, 'One or two of dem was still out dere. Not any more.' He slammed down a breastplate with a resounding clang.

'You all right, lads?' said Simnel to the engineers. 'Shame about the Flyer. It hurts, killing a locomotive, and it means we've not got either a pathfinder or a back-up engine no more. We need to clear the track now, then we'll pick up the scrap when we come back, to go towards a new Flyer. After all, we're getting reet good at building these things. But any bits of micro-mail you find, like this here' – he pointed at the arm holding the axe – 'I'll have now, mind, call it tit for tat. It'll be another trophy for Iron Girder.'

* * *

In the grey light of dawn the trolls made quick work of clearing the track ahead. As Moist watched, he suddenly saw creatures moving in the shadows, and then a sad little voice in the vicinity of his foot said, 'Please don't hurt us, please! We live here, we're gnomes, we're cobblers, it's what we do in these woods. We make charcoal and other things for sale, turned wood, excellent wooden furniture, and we try not to be in anyone's way, but the dwarfs have been marching and we think the bad times are coming again and we're scared.'

There was a sigh, then the voice went on, 'You must know it's the little people who're the last to be thought of when great tribes go to war. My name is Slam, I'm the speaker for all the rest who are in hiding in these hills because we know how to hide. It's a skill we've perfected over the years. May we be of assistance?'

'Gnomes!' said the King at Moist's side. 'I haven't heard of them for ages. There used to be a lot of them once upon a time.'

And Moist thought, yes, these are the little people who get trodden on and left behind like the goblins! If they had a cheeky champion like Of the Twilight the Darkness, or Tears of the Mushroom and her wonderful harp, they'd become known gnomes. But the face of Slam suggested to him that the gnomes had been through the mill and come out as a very fine grist, and had been content to slip into obscurity and somehow were now drifting into a kind of sad oblivion.

He realized that the King was staring at the

spokesgnome. Rhys said, 'I knew you were around here, in the forests. What can I do for you?'

'You could leave us alone, your majesty. Your absence. That's what everybody needs. To be left alone. Left alone to get on with their lives and, indeed,' said the little gnome more sharply, 'to be allowed to live at all.'

The King stepped back along the track and put one hand on Iron Girder, still spluttering and steaming, and, like somebody taking an oath, which he possibly was, said, 'I've known of you people since my childhood and right now, boyo, you may live as you like in these woodlands, and I'll be the first to defend your right to do so.'

He looked around at the rest of the crew and said, 'We must continue. There're still a lot of miles between here and Uberwald.'

Dick, who had been in an urgent conversation with Wally by the water tender, grimaced. 'I'm sorry, your majesty, but we've got a problem. There were a depot here for coal and water, but it's been smashed, and the grags have smashed the water crane and emptied t'water. We've still got t'coal, but we've barely got enough water to get to t'next depot. The engine can't run without water. We need to refill t'tank.' He paused. 'Come to think of it, where are t'railway folk? The way I reckoned the schedules, there should have been people 'ere all ready and waiting for us.'

Slam cleared his throat. 'We heard noises . . . People fighting . . .'

Moist looked at Vimes meaningfully and the

commander said, 'Detritus? Think you could find them?'

The watchman saluted with a thud. 'Me an' Bluejohn will go lookin'. We are good at findin' humans. 'S a troll fing. We'll find dem. Dead or alive.'

The two trolls headed into the undergrowth and Moist was sensitive to the fact that a large amount of firepower had gone with them. The commander looked grim.

The little gnome by Moist's feet tugged at his trouser leg to get attention. 'We can help with the water,' he said. 'There's a good spring behind the rise, and there's hundreds of us and it's not far and we make excellent buckets and I reckon we can fill your tanks in an hour or so.'

And they did.

Slam brought out a whistle from his jacket and blew it, and about a hundred replicas of the little gnome appeared. Not walked up, not came out of the sky, not came out of the earth. Simply appeared, each one carrying two buckets. It was evident that, small as they were, the gnomes were tough. Simnel watched them dashing away to the tender and back again, looking very carefully at their boots, massive things.

'Ey up, mister gnome, do you make them boots? I'm not being funny . . . but they are the biggest boots I've ever seen on such little folk. And, you know, with all the walking on t'lines and cinders and all, our boots wear out too damn quickly. I mean, look at these. Worn in all weathers. You said you were cobblers. Can you work metal an' all? Because if you can, what we really need are lads who can make heavy boots for t'railway workers. I'd be dead chuffed if you could. Boots for lads on t'permanent way've got to be permanent boots.'

Slam beamed. 'If someone could send us the specifications as soon as possible we'll send a sample. And, for your interest, mister engineer, we are not little folk. We are big on the inside.'

He was interrupted by Detritus coming through the undergrowth like a creature from the dawn of time, followed by Bluejohn in his role as heavy weapon. Bluejohn carefully put down two corpses and a mangled water crane.

Rhys Rhysson swore when he saw the corpses and young Simnel wept, but it was now fully morning, and time was passing. After a quick consultation with Commander Vimes and the Low King, the decision was made to leave. As everyone reboarded the train, Moist and Simnel said farewell to the gnomes.

'Please look after this place and give these gentlemen a decent burial, with a stone,' said the red-eyed Simnel. 'And if possible can you do owt wi' t'water crane?'

Slam beamed again. 'It's only metal. Didn't I mention that we're tinkers as well? We can definitely fix it for you.'

'Well then,' said Moist, 'you and your people are now working for the railway and that means you are working for Harry King and Sir Harry doesn't like anything bad to happen to his employees, oh my word yes. You'll see trains a lot in the future and I think you'll find your lives considerably more busy. I'll send a clacks to Sir Harry about remuneration.'

'What's remuneration?' said the little tinker.

Moist said, 'You'll find out.'

As Iron Girder struck out for Slake, the gnomes lined up and waved tiny little handkerchiefs until long after the train was out of sight.

Fishing for carp in Lake Overshot that afternoon, Mr Geoffrey Indigo was quietly surprised when the water in the lake simply disappeared in a certain amount of bubbling, leaving some gasping fish, startled frogs and a rather attractive nymph, who was very angry and spat at him as if it was his fault. But the man who had written that well-known book *Out with my Flies in All Weathers* kept his calm and made a note to mention this phenomenon at the next meeting of the Overshot Fishing Society.

As he meticulously cleaned his gear and generally tidied up, he heard a liquid noise and was surprised for a second time to see that the hole in the landscape was now refilling with water. He watched amazed as the nymph spat at him again, leaving him feeling somewhat wronged. And on the way home, squelching a little, he wondered if anyone would believe him.

When he told his wife later about the strange day, she snorted.

'Geoffrey, you really shouldn't take your brandy flask with you!'

'I didn't take it with me,' he protested. 'It's still on the sideboard, where it always is!'

'Then just don't tell anybody,' his wife concluded. 'People will think you're strange and we can't have that.'

Geoffrey, the least strange person in the world, except possibly when it came to talking about fish, decided not to say anything. After all, you didn't want to become a laughing stock ...

Moist was starting to worry about Dick Simnel and his band of overworked engineers. What sleep they got was in sleeping bags, curled up on carriage seats, eating but not eating well, just driven by their watches and their desire to keep the train going. If you met them away from the cab, their conversation was about gears and wheels and timings, but it was clear to Moist that they were frazzled after days of living on the footplate and wrestling their locomotives through various little tantrums.

And so he confronted Mr Simnel, saying, 'Surely we can afford to slacken pace a little and let you and your lads get your heads down for a bit? As far as I can see, we're well on schedule.'

And he detected in Dick's eyes not madness but something else more subtle. He was sure it had no name. It seemed to be a sort of hunger for anything that was new and above all for proving that something could be refined to the point of perfection and kept there. In the goblins this was endemic, although it didn't seem to do *them* much harm. Humans, apparently, were another matter.

'People are going to die if we push them any further,' he said to Dick. 'You lot would rather work than sleep! I swear, sometimes you seem to be as mechanical as Iron Girder, and that's not right, you have to ... chill, get laid back before you are laid-back and laid down for ever.'

To Moist's amazement, Dick suddenly ripped out at him like a lion. He could almost hear the growl.

'Who are you to talk, Mister Moist? What have you made, built, fretted over? I see none of your fingernails are torn and you can talk well in a fancy way, but what is it you've made? What is it you are?'

'Me, Dick? Well, now I come to look at it I'm the grease that turns the wheels and changes minds and moves the world along. Or you might say that I'm a kind of a cook, but it is a special kind of cookery. It's a bit like the sliding rule; you just move things about at the right time and you get the answer you need. In short, Dick, I make things happen, and that includes your railway.'

The young man swayed in front of him and Moist's tone became gentle. 'And I now see that part of my job is to tell you that you need some rest. You've run out of steam, Dick. Look, we're well on the way to Uberwald now, and while it's daylight and we're out of the mountains it's going to be the least risky time to run with minimum crew. We're all going to need our wits about us when we get near the Pass. Surely you can take some rest?'

Simnel blinked as if he'd not seen Moist the first time, and said, 'Yes, you're right.'

And Moist could hear the slurring in the young man's speech, caught him before he fell and dragged him into a sleeping compartment, put him to bed and noted that the engineer didn't so much fall asleep as somehow flow into it. And that job done, he went to the guard's van where Vimes was drinking coffee and carefully going through the paperwork relating to the captive delvers, who in the pinch sang like most canaries.

'Commander Vimes, can you help me a moment?'

'Problem, Mister Lipwig?'

'The lads are working all the time and they seem to think it's the badge of a man never to go to sleep.'

'I have to teach that to young coppers. Treasure a night's rest, I always say. Take a nap whenever you can.'

'Very good,' said Moist. 'Now look at them here. Still working on the sliding rules and fretting themselves because they've spent too much time trying to put one over on the universe.'

'It seems like that,' said Vimes, getting up.

Together they wandered along the train forcing the engineers to at least lie down in their bunks or face the wrath of Sir Harry King. And in a few cases Moist suggested Of the Twilight the Darkness should dose them with one of his harmless little potions. Not all of them, of course, in case there was an emergency. You never knew when you might need an engineer.

In his cell Albrecht Albrechtson had had plenty of time to consider Ardent's tactics. Ardent was a mere stripling youth,* but was already revealed as a manipulative chancer, seeking advancement come what may and by any means he deemed necessary. He wormed his way

---

* A dwarf is not thought of as a youth until he is in his fifties.

into everything and in that sentence Albrecht thought the important word was 'worm'.

Being Ardent's prisoner was galling. The food was good and drink likewise, even if the small beer was smaller than he'd have liked. He was allowed some of his books, too, apart from those Ardent considered un-dwarfish – a terminology that told you everything about the arrogant young upstart, still wet behind the helmet, who was no doubt keen to get his paws on the whole of Schmaltzberg, 'un-dwarfish' fat mines and all.

And in his little dungeon Albrechtson had to endure Ardent's self-serving philosophy about the role of the Low King. What insolence! Lecturing *him*, the foremost scholar on the subject. But it didn't do to get angry, at least not yet. Anger was a weapon to be honed and treasured and used only at the moment yielding most premium. And that thought was followed by a noise on the stone stairs as the pompous fool came again to get him to change his mind.

Of course, Ardent would begin as if he was just an old friend coming to chew the rat, but as he talked, Albrechtson would glimpse the coils of a decent mind unfolding. After all, he was opposing his sovereign, something not done lightly, if ever. Ardent had to be aware of the penalty for those who took up arms against the Low King. Despite everything, there must have been a good mind there, one which could have been useful to dwarfkind as a whole and might yet be useful, even if right now it couldn't tell pyrites from gold. It was no secret that the most highly balanced minds sometimes, well, overbalanced.

The key turned in the lock. There was Ardent, and his expression seriously frightened his erstwhile mentor. You needed to be mature to sense this sort of thing but you could tell in a person's eyes if they were being driven by an idea. They had a clammy look about them, and so did Ardent.

Nevertheless, Albrechtson laid down his pen and said in a calm voice, 'So kind of you to come and see me. I understand the King will be here shortly, courtesy of the train. Won't that be nice?'

There was a little bloom of spittle on one side of Ardent's face and he snapped, 'You can't possibly know that!'

Albrechtson sat back convivially and said, 'It's probably true, that I taught you all you know, young dwarf, but I did not teach you all *I* know. I have some skills that I didn't impart.'

'Then they must include guesswork. *I* hold the key to information in Schmaltzberg. No clacks towers are standing.'

'Oh yes, so I hear.'

'Rhys Rhysson is betraying all that is dwarfish. And for the sake of our species you surely know that I must take the Scone of Stone. The majority of the dwarfs here are behind me.'

Albrechtson twiddled a pen in his fingers and said, 'Possibly in order not to have to look at your face, Ardent. You're shaken and the courage of your convictions will see you convicted, the moment the King steps into Schmaltzberg. From what I know of Rhys Rhysson, he *may* be merciful.'

'Yes, I thought you'd say something like that, but the deed is done.'

Albrechtson looked stunned. 'You have actually taken the Scone?'

For a moment Ardent looked foxed. 'Not as such . . . Everything is in place. It only needs me to take the final step and Rhys Rhysson can have a retirement somewhere out of the way, like back in Llamedos.'

'Then do it now. Go on. There's nothing to stop you, is there? But the Low King is elected, isn't he? How certain are you? How certain are you that all your fellow travellers are stalwart? Because I'm absolutely certain that many of them are not. Oh yes, they fawn on you and promise a lot, but as the train comes closer and we hear the whistle of change blowing, I think you'll find that suddenly they have other engagements and recall never talking to you about the Scone of Stone. That's happening now, and you don't know it.'

It was unfair really. Ardent said, 'I invite you to remember that you're locked in here and I have the only key.'

'Yes. And of the two of us you are the only one sweating. You'll be surprised at what I know. How many clacks towers have come back out of the ground like mushrooms? And I know what the Ankh-Morpork dwarfs are saying. You want to know? They say "Why don't we have the Scone of Stone in Ankh-Morpork? After all, there are more dwarfs in Ankh-Morpork than there are in Schmaltzberg."'

'You would countenance our Scone in that wretched place?'

'Of course not. But neither will I see you on the Scone of Stone. Your grags are losing their followers, not just because of the clacks towers and not because of Ankh-Morpork but because new generations arise and think what's all this about – how could our parents be so stupid? And you can't stop people any more than you could stop the train.'

Albrechtson was almost sorry for Ardent now. You could live in denial for a long time, but, like a snake, it doubles back and strikes.

'You should face facts, Albrecht Albrechtson. You will be amazed at my support. Dwarfs must remain dwarfs, not simulacrums of humans. To follow Rhys Rhysson is to become *d'rkza*, a half-dwarf, less than that even.'

'No, it is your kind of thinking that makes dwarfs small, wrapped up in themselves: declaring that any tiny change in what is thought to be dwarf is somehow sacrilege. I can remember the days when even talking to a human was forbidden by idiots such as you. And now you have to understand it's not about the dwarfs, or the humans, or the trolls, it's about the people, and that's where the troublesome Lord Vetinari wins the game. In Ankh-Morpork you can be whoever you want to be and sometimes people laugh and sometimes they clap, and mostly and beautifully, they don't really care. Do you understand this? Dwarfs now have seen liberty. And that's heady stuff.'

Ardent almost spat and said, 'You say that when

you're known to be one of the biggest traditionalists in all the mines?'

'I still am. And most of our traditions were to keep us safe, just in the way that the grags in their great, heavy clothing exploded the firedamp so that we wouldn't be burned alive. The rules of the mine. They learned the hard way and the traditions are there for a purpose; they work. But somehow, you and the others don't realize that outside the caverns the world is different. Oh, I keep the special days and knock twice on every door and follow all the tenets of Tak. And why? Because they bring us together, as did the clacks towers until your blessed delvers started to burn them. Burning words dying in the sky! Is that to be the legacy of the dwarfs?'

He stopped. Ardent had gone pale and seemed to be shivering. But then his eyes blazed, and he snarled, 'You won't be driven, Albrecht, and nor will I. Train or no train. It'll never get here anyway. The world is not ready for locomotion.'

He glared at Albrecht, who said, 'Yes, of course it isn't. But what you don't understand is that the world wasn't ready for the clacks but now it screams if they are burned down. And I believe that locomotion has not finished with us yet.'

The response was the slamming of the door and the turning of the key. And now the fool had locked him in for the night, just where he wanted to be.

There were guards, Albrecht knew, but like guards everywhere they tended to slumber or go off somewhere to smoke a pipe during the long hours of the night, and in any case very few of them came near to this particular dungeon since sensible guards didn't want to upset someone like Albrecht. Even if you thought you were on the right side, you never *knew* who the winner would be and in those circumstances smaller fry might be the ones to get fried . . .

After a while, Albrecht picked up the little spoon with which he had eaten his meal and there was the subtle scratching of rock dust which led to the appearance of a goblin, who grinned at him in the gloom.

'Here you are, squire, here's clacks flimsies, fresh from Commander Vimes. And bottle of oil for lamp. Oh, and toothpaste you asks for. Have been told to tell you that train is moving like no one business. Sure to be here on schedule.'

It was a kind of therapy to hear of the inevitable approach of the famous Iron Girder, day after day.

The aroma of a goblin, Albrecht thought, seemed to be a metaphysical one. After the initial shock, you had to wonder if the goblin smell was somehow arriving inside your head as much as through your nostrils. It wasn't even all that bad. It had the savour of old sculleries and southernwood.

He took the packages and scanned the flimsies with the speed of a dwarf who had learned to assimilate the written word quickly. And he spoke with interest to the young goblin, a caste he had hitherto dismissed as a waste of space at best and a nuisance otherwise, but they seemed to be more level-headed than most of his fellow dwarfs, especially that fool Ardent, and it was amazing how they could get about in the darkness of

Schmaltzberg and make use of every rat hole before making use of the rat.

And this one waited patiently while Albrecht sorted out some flimsies of his own to go back to the locomotive. And then the old dwarf did something else that surprised him.

He said: 'What's your name, young goblin? And may I beg your pardon for not enquiring earlier? Please forgive an old dwarf who hasn't kept up with the times.'

The goblin looked stunned and said, 'Well, guv, if it don't hurt anything, I am The Rattle of the Wheels. Railwaymen friends is calling me Rat for short name. That makes oldies very annoy.'

Albrecht held out a hand. The Rattle of the Wheels stepped back and then came forward sheepishly.

'Nice to meet you, Rattle of the Wheels. Have you any family?'

'Yes, your worship. My mother is Of the Happiness the Heart, father is Of the Sky the Rim and small brother is Of the Water the Crane.'

And after a moment the goblin said, 'Actually, sir, you can stop holding my hand.'

'Oh, yes. I suppose that my name should be Of the Moment the Stupefied. Good luck to you and your family. You know, in a way I'm jealous of you. And now I've finished my work for the day I'd like you to take my paperwork, such as it is, and hide it somewhere around here where no dwarf is going to look.'

'We cleans toilets, sir. Knows plenty-many places that not visited. Same time tomorrow?'

The handshake fulfilled, the goblin disappeared into

a hole that even a rat might find difficult to get into. And as the sounds of the goblin scrabbling through the hole faded away, Albrecht thought, I would *never* have done that before. What a fool I was.

Miss Gwendolyn Avery of Schmarm awoke in the middle of the night to the shaking and rattle of the multiple bottles of age-defying unguents on her dresser. And then she realized that the whole house was shaking to a rhythmic thudding.

When she described this episode in dramatic tones to her friend Daphne the following morning, she said that it was like the sound of a lot of men marching past. She put it down to the cherry brandy she had had before going to bed whilst Daphne, knowing Gwendolyn's regrettable spinster status, put it down to wishful thinking.

The Slake ranges were half tundra, half desert, mostly windswept. In short, a fossil of a landscape where nothing generally grew but stumbleweed,* and the occasional gregarious pine, the nuts of which were said to be an antidote to melancholy.

There was water, oh yes, but mostly underground, and prospectors and rock hounds were said to send down buckets to dredge water from the depths of the caves.

It was slightly easier to find water on the uplands

---

* Stumbleweed is like tumbleweed, but less athletic. This tells you everything you need to know about Slake.

hubwards of the tundra, where there were icy streams courtesy of the Everwind glacier, making it possible to raise goats there. And so goats were what young Knut's family had bred and milked and minded down the centuries. And when the goats were eating what passed as grass on these highlands, he would sleep and dream of not chasing goats over a near-barren landscape. He had liked it at first but he was growing older and something was telling him that there was a better life than watching goats eat their lunch ... once, twice and sometimes thrice. Sometimes the faces they made were an entertainment and sometimes he laughed. And yet a yearning in him told him that goats were not enough.

And so it was, when the long sound echoed across the tundra, that he hurried to see what was making the wonderful noise and saw a shining streak snaking its way over the landscape in the early morning light; and it was heading his way. He wondered if it was anything to do with the strange bars of metal laid carefully on the tundra below by the gangs of men some weeks before. He had run errands for them and sold them his mother's cheese, but he couldn't really understand what it was they were doing and since the goats stepped carefully over the metal strips without harm he had given up wondering. But as far as he could make out from what the men had said, it was all for a wondrous thing that could go around the world on a flash of steam, and now he wanted to know more about this singing beast coming over the tundra, occasionally spitting fire.

Knut scrambled down off the hillside to where the

air was warmer, leaving the goats, and ultimately traced the noise to a kind of big shed. And just as he got to it, the creature, carrying people inside it, broke out of the shed and hurtled away along the metal rails. He watched it until it had entirely disappeared. And later some of the townspeople told him it was what they called a 'locomotive', and in his heart the yearning started and began by degrees to grow. Yes, there truly were other things than goats.

Having spent a long afternoon and evening alert for anything untoward while Simnel and his lads lay dead to the world, Moist in his turn had slept soundly all night and now dozed right through the morning, rocked by the motion of the train as she steamed on from Slake across the valley of the Smarl, dreaming of the bridge over the gorge at the Wilinus Pass, never a picnic at any time, that was looming up fast like a tax demand.

Anything could happen before they entered that dry-land maelstrom of sliding rocks, falling rocks and, well, rocks full of bandits of all disciplines. To coin a term that might fit the circumstances: it was like running a gauntlet with no shoes – a gauntlet full of rocks. And even pebbles had bad attitudes at that altitude. Moist winced at the thought of the place.

The train hurtled on through the vast landscape. A huge amount of space, oh yes, but not many towns, just the occasional settlement. There was so much space everywhere and Iron Girder ate it up like a tiger, attacking the horizon as if it were an affront, stopping only if it was known that water and coal were available. You could never have too much of either.

By the middle of the day, the mountain ranges of Uberwald were getting closer and the air was getting colder and Iron Girder's pace had settled to a steady climb through the foothills towards their destination.

Lonely goatherds could be seen on the trackside, and amongst the people staring at this new mechanism there was a definite outbreak of dirndls. In every township they passed people were ready for them with flags and, above all, with bands that wheezed and oompah'd as the crowds cheered Iron Girder on her way. And, yes, as the train came past slowly and carefully you had to watch out for the little boys running after her, following the dream. It was a sight to yodel for.

And now Moist noticed that Simnel was looking increasingly worried and took the opportunity of one of the engineer's rare breaks from the footplate to speak to him privately.

'Dick, Iron Girder is the best locomotive you've ever built, right?'

Simnel wiped his hands on a rag that had already seen too many greasy hands and said, 'She surely is, Mister Lipwig, we all know that, but it's not Iron Girder I'm fretting about. It's that bridge over t'gorge. We've done everything we can, but we need more time. There's no way the bridge will hold with all the weight of the train an' all.'

'Well now,' said Moist, 'you have the loggysticks and the knowledge of the weights and the stresses and all the other sliding rule business and that's telling you one thing, but I'm telling you now that if the bridge is still not secure when we get there I propose that Iron Girder will fly across the gorge with you and me on the footplate. You might call it a sleight of hand, even a trick, but we *will* fly.'

The engineer looked like a man who has been challenged to guess under which thimble the pea is, and knows deep in his boots that it will never, ever be the one he selects.

'Mister Lipwig, are you talking about magic here? I'm an engineer, I am. We don't 'old wi' magic.'

And suddenly Moist's voice was as smooth as treacle. 'Actually, Mister Simnel, I think you're wrong in that. You believe in the sunshine, although you don't know how it does it. And since we're on or near the subject, have you ever wondered what the Turtle stands on?'

Dick was cornered and said, 'Ee, well, that's different. That's just how things are meant to be.'

'Pardon me, my friend, but you don't know that. Nevertheless you go to bed at night quite happy in the belief that the world will still be there when you get up in the morning.'

Once again, Dick tried to get a grip on the proceedings, still wearing the look of a man certain that whichever thimble was going to be picked up it wouldn't be his. A given in the scheme of things.

'So we're talking about wizards, then, Mister Lipwig?'

'Well ... magic,' said Moist. 'Everything is magic when you don't know what it is. Your sliding rule is a magic wand to most people. And I know some kinds of magic. And so I'll ask you, Dick, have I ever let you down in any way during our time on Harry King's business?'

'Oh no, Mister Lipwig,' said Simnel, almost affronted. 'I see you as what my old granny called full of fizz.'

Moist caught the fizz in the air and juggled it.

'There you are, Dick. I believe you when you say that the numbers on the sliding rule are telling you things. In return I'd like some trust from you. No, please don't use your sliding rule for this. It's the wrong tool for the job. I know something ... Not exactly magic, but extremely solid ... and with what I have in mind, by the time we get to the bridge you'll think we're riding through the air.'

Simnel once again looked as if he was about to cry. 'But why won't you tell me?'

'I could,' said Moist, 'but Lord Vetinari would have me dead.'

'Eee! We can't 'ave that, Mister Lipwig,' said Simnel, shocked.

Moist put an arm round Simnel and said, 'Dick, you can perform miracles, but I propose to give the world a spectacle that'll be remembered for a very long time.'

'Eh up, Mister Lipwig. I'm just an engineer.'

'Not just an engineer, Dick: *the* engineer.'

And as Simnel cherished that thought he smiled nervously and said, 'But 'ow? There just isn't enough time and there aren't enough men, neither. Harry King has brought out all his 'eavy-duty workers from the city and the plains and so I don't know where you'll get more support from.'

'Well,' said Moist, 'I'll have to be like Iron Girder. I'll just whistle.'

Simnel laughed nervously. 'Ee, Mister Lipwig, you're a sharp one!'

'Good,' said Moist, with a confidence he wasn't entirely feeling. 'We should be ready by dusk.'

Just then Iron Girder let loose a little bit of steam and Moist wondered if it was a good omen, or possibly a bad one, but it seemed to him to be an omen anyway, and that was enough.

That afternoon, in an attempt to distract his thoughts, Moist decided to tackle something that had been niggling at the back of his mind ever since they had left Sto Lat. And for that he needed to talk to Aeron.

The King's secretary was slim for a dwarf, almost nimble and quick, and decidedly ubiquitous, his long beard following him like a banner as he went about on the King's business. He carried a sword, not traditionally a dwarf weapon, and had acquitted himself well during the attack on the train at the Paps of Scilla.

Choosing his moment carefully, Moist waylaid Aeron in a place where they could talk privately.

'Mister Secretary, I have to ask whether all is quite as it seems with the Low King.'

Aeron's eyes narrowed and his hand went to the hilt of his sword. 'Of course it is. What a ridiculous question. Treacherous, too!'

Moist put his hand out placatingly. 'Look, you know I'm on your side! I have to ask because of something I saw at Mrs Simnel's house.'

Aeron looked startled and said, 'I believe the side you're on is your own, sir, and whatever you think you saw it's certainly no business of yours.'

'Indeed it is, my friend,' Moist replied. 'The gods, for my sins, gave me a nose for scenting when the metaphorical shit is about to hit the windmill, and I want to be prepared.'

Aeron stood frozen, and without looking directly at Moist he said, 'Your perspicacity does you credit, Mister Lipwig. Your silence even more!'

'Oh, come on. There's something going on here and I'm not in on it. Don't force me to draw my own conclusions. I do have a very big pencil.'

But Aeron clearly had nothing further to say. The appearance of a couple of engineers at the end of the carriage provided the excuse he needed for bringing the conversation to an abrupt close. He turned on his heel and marched smartly off down the corridor, leaving Moist with every suspicious nerve in his body jangling.

An hour or so later, a knock at the entrance to the guard's van heralded the King's secretary, who this time smiled strangely and said, 'The King would like to grant you an audience, Mister Lipwig.' And he smiled again and said, 'And that, I'm sure you're aware, means at once.'

The King was sitting at a little table doing paperwork

when Moist arrived, and beckoned him towards another chair in the carriage, saying, 'Mister Lipwig, I understand that following our visit to Mister Simnel's mother, you appear to be under the impression that I may be . . . hiding something. Is that the case, boyo?'

The King looked at Moist with a stern glare, almost as if daring him to utter what he was thinking.

'Well, she does have a lot of . . . feminine insight . . .' Moist let the rest of the sentence tail away and watched carefully.

The King sighed and looked at Aeron, who was standing on guard by the door. Rhys nodded and then turned back to Moist.

'Mister Lipwig, I'm sure you are aware that the sex of dwarfs is often a well-kept secret and there have been times when even to enquire about the sex of another dwarf was considered a terrible thing. I am the Low King of the Dwarfs, but if I can get to what I might call the bottom line, I am also female.'

And there it was. This was the thing that had been niggling at the back of his mind ever since Mrs Simnel had started making the sleeping King – *Queen* now, he reminded himself – comfortable back in Sto Lat. He coughed and said, 'Well, nobody's perfect, your majesty. And to tell you the truth, I think I've known for some time. I'm good at putting rumours, suspicions and instinct together and getting the right result, because I'm a scoundrel. I expect Lord Vetinari has warned you about me. You could say that I'm Lord Vetinari's scoundrel.'

'As if *he* needs one!'

'Scoundrels take a different look at people, just to get the measure of them: the way they walk, the way they talk, the way they sit. All the little details left unsaid in the wrong place.'

The Queen was silent for a moment and said, 'A *real* scoundrel?'

'Yes, m'lady, I would say one of the best, possibly *the* best,' said Moist. 'But these days you might say that I'm tamed and at heel, which means I'm a very trustworthy scoundrel.'

'At Vetinari's heel? You poor boy.'

And now the Queen looked as if something worrying had been chased away and she said, 'You must know, Mister Lipwig, there are only very few people who are aware of my secret and they are trusted. One of them is Lady Margolotta and another, of course, is Lord Vetinari.

'It has always seemed to me that the attitude of dwarfs when it comes to gender is curdling us. Dwarfs, we keep insisting, must be *seen* to be male – and what does it say about a species if they can't look their own mothers in the face? We live a stupid lie and play a stupid game and I don't want this state of affairs to continue. I am indeed the Low Queen, Mister Lipwig, and I thank you for your silence at this time.'

The Queen appeared as innocent as one of those mountains which year after year do nothing very much but smoke a little, and then one day end up causing a whole civilization to become an art installation.

'Mrs Simnel is a nice lady,' she continued, 'although perhaps not as discreet as she thought . . . Of course, I know I can depend on you to treat my secret as if it were your own. I'm sure Lord Vetinari would be upset if you didn't do so.'

Moist polished his best reassuring smile to sparkling. 'As I told you, ma'am, I'm a born scoundrel, so I've learned to be very, very discreet for the sake of keeping my own neck safe from people who take a dim view of scoundrelhood. And as for Mrs Simnel, she knew all about the secret of steam and never told anyone about it.'

The Queen stroked her beard and said, 'For a proud mother that must have been testing indeed . . . Very well, Mister Scoundrel, I will have faith in you both. And now I can see that Aeron is becoming restive, so I'd better return to my paperwork.' She sent what Moist would swear was a teasing glance in her secretary's direction.

Moist, for whom it was second nature to watch and listen carefully – most particularly to what was not said – now felt he knew another secret, a secret as yet un-acknowledged. The Queen and her secretary were, without doubt, lovers. Possibly you had to be married to notice this fact, but their body language shone through.

A meaning cough from Aeron recalled his attention. The secretary was holding the door open for him, in a clear signal that the audience was over. As Moist stepped out past him Aeron said, 'Thank you, Mister Lipwig . . . From both of us.'

Before he set off back to the guard's van, Moist stood for a while letting the revelations settle. The King being a Queen was looming in his mind. Oh yes, everybody knew that dwarf women looked very much like the dwarf men, beards and all, even Cheery Littlebottom – an Ankh-Morpork dwarf if ever there was one and a strict feminist; although she was adamant that beyond the beards dwarf females were not the same as dwarf men. And since she was now very big, as it were, in the Watch, her insistence on chainmail skirts and subtly altered breastplates didn't matter too much, but the Queen—? What would happen if the Queen declared it! It would be *iacta alea est* in spades! And there would be no going back from that.

Aeron had now disappeared back into the Queen's armoured coach, and Moist was left listening to the rattling of the train. The future, he thought, was going to be . . . incredibly interesting.

The everlasting fog that filled the vertiginous gorge created deep swirling shadows in the fading light as they approached the final bridge before the Wilinus Pass. And the fog itself seemed to be alive as it moved and twisted, leaving the watchers with the feeling that they were teetering at the edge of the world.

The far side of the bridge was barely visible as Simnel stood in earnest conversation with the head engineer in charge of the bridge works. A bit of darkness in the fog near Moist turned out to be Commander Vimes, grinning.

'A rickety bridge, a heavy train, a terrifying drop to certain death below, with a pressing deadline and no back-up plan?' said Vimes. 'You must be in your element, Mister Lipwig. I'm told the engineers say it can't be done. Are you really planning to risk the Low King and the future peace of this region on one throw of the dice?'

Behind them an engineer said, 'I wouldn't travel over that for a pension.'

As Rhys and Aeron joined them, the creaks and groans of the ancient bridge structure intensified, and seemed almost alive, like some demon daring them to chance their fate. The less fanciful of the engineers might talk of natural movement caused by the drop in temperature as night approached, but it was hard to ignore the ominous atmosphere of the place which was almost . . . eldritch.

Then Iron Girder snorted steam, panting like a dog ready to be unleashed. Moist took a deep breath, stuck his fingers into his jacket and smiled with a confidence which had blossomed just a second before when he had finally heard the subtle sound he had been waiting for.

'It's a little-known fact, my friends, that these fogs have remarkable solidity. Allow me to demonstrate.'

He stepped off the edge of the cliff beside the track and stood there with the fog swirling around his ankles. He heard gasps from behind. He turned and faced his fellow travellers with a huge grin and a silent sigh of relief before stepping back on to what might be called solid ground.

'You see. Would you like me to run to the other side and back again while this mystical phenomenon continues, as I believe it will, or shall we all go over now, while the time is ripe?'

'D'you mind if I try?' said Vimes.

There was a *twinkle* and Moist said, 'By all means, commander.'

And Vimes disappeared into the swirling fog, lighting his cigar, saying, 'Just like standing on a pavement. Amazing. I suggest you make steam, Mister Simnel! I'm in some doubt about how long such a, as you say, mystical phenomenon will last. So I think alacrity is our motto here, gentlemen.'

Simnel, resisting the natural temptation of a scientist to examine the phenomenon more closely, looked around and said, 'Oh aye. All aboard, everybody!' And after a moment, he added, 'Quickly . . . please.'

Moist looked at Simnel and said, 'Do you now believe, Dick?'

'Yes, Mister Lipwig.'

'But do you *really* believe?'

'I surely do, Mister Lipwig! I believe in the sliding rule, the cosine and the tangent and even when the quaderatics give me gyp, yes, I still believe. Iron Girder is my machine, I built 'er, every last rivet carefully forged by 'and. And I reckon if I could bolt rails on to the sky, Iron Girder would take us to t'moon.'

Moist whistled and heard a signal from below. He raised his voice and said, 'Forward, please, Mister Simnel!' And immediately there was the familiar chugging sound of a train anxious to be travelling and getting up steam. Moist loved the moment as the power built up slowly and by degrees until there was a rolling thunder, taking charge of the universe, and they were moving into the villainous fog and on to the bridge.

It was difficult to see anything from the footplate, but Moist could just make out Simnel's white face as the vibrations and swaying intensified. Despite Moist's dramatic demonstration earlier, he could tell that Simnel and his crew were terrified and even he began to doubt whether the bridge would in fact hold under the pressure. And then the vibrations suddenly ceased and there was a strange sensation as Iron Girder left the rails and she flew.

Down below, the fog curled into even stranger shapes, spiralling vortices, stirred up by the passage of the train, and after a strangled few minutes there was a thump of wheels on rails as Iron Girder consented to exchange flight for the sensible permanent way once more and then Dick blew the whistle and kept blowing, and she was bowling along again as if nothing uncanny, mystic or even eldritch had happened.

It wasn't until Moist found time to himself after all the back-slapping he had received that the enormity of what he had done hit him like a jack-hammer: a whole train under steam, full of passengers! And a king apparently flying through thin air! And he sweated again as the next thought said, 'So many things could have gone wrong.' In fact so many things *could* have gone wrong and he began to feel certain that history might just slam backwards to ensure that they did. And the sweat ran down his whole body but he wouldn't have been Moist if he couldn't recover from this sort of thing. Just as long as Vetinari *never* got to hear about it.

* * *

The thought of Vetinari was still proving hard to banish later that evening when Moist finally bunked down in the guard's van. As the motion of the train lulled him into a tired and relieved doze, an image of the Patrician swam into Moist's mind. He shuddered at the recollection of his recent encounter. Vetinari had been at his desk reading reports of what looked suspiciously to Moist like other people's clacks messages.* He had frowned when he saw Moist and said, 'Well now, Mister Lipwig, is the train already cleared for Uberwald, by any chance?'

Moist had assumed an expression that would not have deceived a child, which was, of course, part of the game. 'Not *quite* yet, my lord, but I think the prospects are getting rosier by the hour.'

'Long-winded. Very long-winded indeed. Come to the point, if such a thing exists, please? After all, I *do* have matters of state to deal with.'

'Well, sir, I'm sure you recall, we have buried within the city limits a number of very ancient golems, and you vowed that they would only be deployed in the event of a threat to national security, and right now I think I could use several dozen of them, sir, that is of course if you don't mind?'

'Mister Lipwig, you surely try my patience. I'm quite well aware that both you and your wife have the tools that would allow you to enter said vault and, indeed, give said golems instructions, but nevertheless I strictly

---

* Although this accusation has never been levelled by anybody at his lordship, which is to say, none have been found.

forbid you to try anything of the sort. This has to do with the railway, I am assuming.'

'Yes, my lord, a minor little problem on the train to success, as it were.'

'Let me make myself entirely clear. If I find any evidence that you have removed city golems from their proper place and moreover have taken them outside the city limits, you will be thrown to the kittens. Is that understood?'

Vetinari's expression was as flat and impenetrable and as placid as a sea of pitch, and Moist had bowed and said, 'I assure you, sir, no such evidence will ever be found.' While overhead, the words 'If I find' floated like a sly invitation.

Uncomfortably alert again, with Vetinari's voice echoing in his head, Moist drew out the clacks flimsy he'd had from Adora Belle about the progress of the golems. He tore it up and threw the pieces out of the nearest window, from where he watched them disappear in the wake of the wonderful train.

From the gloom of the guard's van behind him someone coughed, pointedly. Vimes emerged with a little smile and said, 'Plausible deniability, eh, Mister Lipwig? But well done, anyway. Just between ourselves: those golems that'll never be used ... What do you suppose they're doing right now?'

Moist opened his mouth to deny all knowledge of the golems, then thought better of it. Something in Vimes's eyes dared him to try. 'Digging their way back home, I trust,' he said. 'Rather more easily since they tunnelled their way up here in the first place.'

And in the distance behind the train, the rickety bridge was falling bit by bit into the valley in a curious kind of mechanical ballet. It would be some time before it could be used again, thought Moist – but now we've got Rhys this far we can throw everything into getting this damn bridge built properly.

And a few hours later, as the golems tunnelled under his tavern, the Grosszügig Stein, Herr Muckenfuss noticed the floor dancing and every glass and stein in the building shook rapidly. Plump though he was, he scooped up every falling stein and glass with great determination until there was a sudden settling in the air and the tavern was eerily silent. He looked at Herr Bummel, his solitary customer, who stared at the dregs in his stein of the new cask of Old Blonk they had been sampling before whispering in impressed tones, 'I think I'll have the same again.'

As Bonk came ever closer and the horizon was now eaten by the mountains – looming outlines visible against the night sky, steep slopes occasionally catching the moonlight – Commander Vimes called a council of war in the guard's van, the centre of operations. With the experience of the attacks at the Paps and the destruction of the Flyer to draw upon, careful plans were laid for the defence of the train and the King.

'Well now, look around, all of you. What you see is canyons and trees. If I was a grag I'd probably see this next stretch as my last available opportunity to derail Iron Girder.'

Vimes's face was grim as he outlined his proposals and Rhys nodded his approval, interrupting now and then to add a refinement.

'We must also take care of attacks from above,' the commander continued. 'As we've seen, Iron Girder is well protected. She has her corsets on now, thanks to Dick's new alloy, but we might have to fight on top of the carriages. I see you grin, Mister Lipwig. So, smart boy, if that happens I invite you to join me and the others on the roof when the time comes. Are you game, sir? It's likely to be very dangerous up there.'

The inner Moist patted himself on the back as he thought of his illicit adventure on top of the Flyer. He could dance on the train, jump and spin and twirl, because he had the measure of the moods of every part of the train.

'I've wanted to do something like this ever since I saw my first locomotive, commander,' he said to Commander Vimes.

'Yes,' said Vimes, 'that's what I'm afraid of. So I must tell you that we work as a team or we become separate corpses.' He pointed at the trees towering overhead in the deep cutting they were travelling through. 'There is very little space in this damn cutting. Trees? Nothing but stiff weeds – remember that!'

'I'm sure we could do it,' said Moist. 'Why not bring Detritus up top as well?'

'No, he's good on the ground, but he isn't limber. Anyway, with Detritus on top of it I'm afraid the roof would pretty soon become the floor.'

The commander looked around and said, 'The rest of you know your stations. Remember, we're on this train to get the King back again. Guard him! Don't bother about us on top.'

When he could speak to Vimes with nobody else listening, Moist said, 'I know the rhythm of the train, but I'm no fighter, commander. Why choose me?'

'Because, Mister Lipwig, you'd pay a king's ransom in order to say that you fought on the roof of a train and I've seen you, you're a bastard in close combat, worse than Nobby and he tends to bite their knees. I saw the corpses of the grags from that incident at the Quirm railhead. You can fight, if only in terror, but it's true that the coward can often be the best fighter of all.'

As the sky grew pallid in the pre-dawn, the atmosphere on the train changed. The whole crew knew that they were now heading at top speed right into unfriendly territory. On every crag in the mountains of Uberwald you could see the lights of the Igors twinkling and wobbling in the darkness of the canyons, and green lightning flashed from gargoyle to gargoyle like spectres.

Moist had generally always kept away from the place. You got the occasional werewolf or zombie in Ankh-Morpork, of course, but in Uberwald they were commonplace. This was their place, with their rules – and that included the black ribboners, the slightly weird types who had sworn to shun the temptation to drink people's blood and similar ... But they were still weird, possibly even more so, drinking only cocoa and marching with banners and drums on every possible occasion. Arguably that was better than being taken to the crossroads and staked . . . again. The hand of Lady Margolotta was visible everywhere, and Moist knew that where you found her hand you would also find the hand of Vetinari.

But now there was menace in the air. Although Moist was, in fact, okay with menace, it was the thought of dying that was uppermost in his mind, and his little internal demon was shouting, 'Hahaha! Remember that a life without danger is a life not worth living!' And valiantly he stood by that assertion . . . though quite frankly he would rather have been standing on a beach in Quirm, if possible eating one of those really nice ice creams they made with a wafer-thin cone that crunched so beautifully as you bit into it. With strawberry sauce. And sprinkles.

Moist stood in the middle of the guard's van letting his body understand the motions of the train. He rocked when it rolled and concentrated on staying upright. After all, he reasoned, if there was going to be a fight then your legs had to know what was waiting for them. Vimes was puzzled about what he was doing, but when Moist tried to explain, the commander snorted in derision.

'In general, Mister Lipwig, I try to disable those who're trying to do the same to me as quickly as I can. It's a simple little approach. Not very complicated, but it helps me stay alive . . . that and the understanding that almost everything has a groin and every foot has a boot.'

The sound of metal and stone bouncing off the carriages came as a relief. Like an expected shoe dropping.

The train was travelling through a cutting that had once been used by wagons, and Iron Girder almost touched the rocky sides as she passed through at less than half speed. The guard's van was in a state of siege and only later did Moist learn that grags had swung down from the sides of the cutting.

An unfortunate few dwarfs had landed on Bluejohn's flatbed and while the biggest officer of the City Watch was at heart a pussycat, two grags trying to hack lumps out of him was clearly causing him to become somewhat acerbic and so the pussycat was now fighting like a lion. He hurled curses in trollish which actually shone red in the air as they were cast.

Quelling his nerves, Moist grabbed a jim crow and opened the trap door on to the roof of the guard's van, to the initial amazement of the grag who had been trying to force his way in. But any sense of achievement the dwarf might have felt was knocked away by the vicious metal bar hitting his jaw with a satisfactory clang.

Moist wasn't surprised to hear Commander Vimes scrambling up after him. And now, surrounded by grags in a state of disarray, Vimes tore off his shirt and as other dwarfs approached him Moist saw them suddenly realize that their futures were in the hands of the legendary Blackboard Monitor. Once freed, the brilliant scar on the commander's wrist was almost throbbing in the half-light. The grags stared at it and that was the first of their many mistakes, because the commander went, as they say in Ankh-Morpork, totally librarian on them.

As Vimes charged towards the far end of the van he smacked away one distraught grag so that he landed on top of another, making it look almost balletic as they twisted and fell on to the rails below. And now the goblins joined in to make the grags' day just a little bit more interesting: goblins in your armour was definitely *not* an aid to fighting.

The trap door and an adjoining panel had been torn away from the top of the guard's van and, while battling a particularly ferocious dwarf,* Moist saw Detritus levelling his enormous crossbow through the hole and heard the troll shout, 'Piece Maker!', a signal to anyone of sense to take extreme cover immediately. When the thunder had died away, Detritus yelled up to him, 'Hey, Mister Lipwig! Dis van is goin' backwards! Der gritsuckers knew jus' where to take der engine off!'

Moist turned and saw, to his horror, Iron Girder pulling away at speed from the now stranded guard's van. He looked down at Bluejohn who was holding a grag in each hand and there was screaming as he banged their heads together and tossed them into the darkness between the tracks.

'We're going backwards, Bluejohn!' yelled Moist. 'Take us forward, could you!'

---

* The way that Moist fought was erratic, since he took the view that if you didn't know what you were going to do next, neither would the enemy. After all, it was a mêlée and nobody owns a mêlée. You might as well try to control a hurricane.

There was a jerk as Bluejohn stopped the guard's van dead, quite possibly with his feet, and Moist jumped down on to the shuddering flatbed.

'Nice work, Mister Bluejohn. Now get out that thing Mister Simnel's lads made for you, please.'

In his curiously childish voice, Bluejohn said, 'Oh yes, Mister Lipwig, I can do dat and I can tow der guard's van as well.'

Vimes dropped down from the roof where he had been making life difficult for the grags on top – who were now essentially on the bottom – shouting 'What the hell's going on! Why've we stopped and where's the rest of the train?!'

'Those buggers have uncoupled us!' yelled Moist. 'But it's no problem . . . there's a handcar on Bluejohn's flatbed . . . for emergencies!' And, indeed, when the pedals of the handcar started to turn, the guard's van accelerated and shot like an arrow towards the disappearing Iron Girder.

Bluejohn's big face was aglow as he pedalled like, well, Bluejohn, because nobody else could have made that flatbed fly along the rails. It rattled and screeched and complained, but the troll's huge feet oscillated up and down in a blur and the inner demon of Moist von Lipwig whispered to himself, 'A little treadle machine to help somebody travel fast? Might be an idea to remember that.'

The whistle of Iron Girder echoed around the canyons, and Vimes shouted, 'Get me up close to that train, officer!'

Trolls don't sweat as such. A kind of blooming takes

place instead. Bluejohn grunted, 'Gettin' a bit outta puff now, commander . . . but I'll do my best.'

Bluejohn's handcar, still dragging the guard's van, including the recumbent grags, slammed into the last carriage, and before it bounced away again he reached forward and grabbed a buffer in each hand. Immediately Vimes flew like a demon, running across Bluejohn's ample back and into the besieged carriage. Moist followed as best he could. Grags and delvers were everywhere, still trying to get into the armoured carriage ahead, and then it was just a matter of who was friend and who was foe, and there were far fewer friends, making it very easy to spot the foes.

'Come on, lads! No speeches, you sons of mothers!' Vimes shouted back to the others in the guard's van. 'You know who the enemy is and you know what to do . . . Get them before they get you and don't let them get anywhere near the King! I'm heading up on the roof!'

Up on the swaying roof of the armoured carriage, Vimes quickly started to take his toll on the enemy, who were swinging down from the canyon walls on to the moving train. Unhappily for the attacking dwarfs, the problem with swinging down was that the defender on the train could easily judge where you were going to land, which was precisely the place you then got hit mightily with a jim crow. While Moist and Vimes, well accustomed to the motion of the train, could keep their feet, the dwarfs, even with their low centre of gravity, simply couldn't fight on the rocking and rolling carriages, and the two men were able to knock them down like skittles. Moist couldn't help feeling sorry for them. Idiots with a cause and it had been such a stupid cause to begin with.

And as he was watching Vimes fend off an attack from two of the buggers, there came a blow out of the darkness that knocked Moist on to his back, taking the wind out of him. He looked up into the face of madness. That special kind of madness warped by idealism. The madness that gloats – which, in these circumstances, was a bad idea. The grag swung his axe, but with reactions born out of terror Moist managed to roll as the mighty blade struck the roof beside him, splintering the wood where his head had just been. The grag lifted the axe once again and Moist thought, well, this is it, then . . . a life without danger is a life not worth living . . . Maybe the next one'll be even better . . .

And then he saw it and grinned: the entrance to the tunnel. And so he winked, as only Moist von Lipwig could wink, and said, 'Goodbye.'

Sparks rained down and it took him a moment to realize what had happened. Or, indeed, what unfortunately had not happened. The tunnel was just too capacious – the grag had not been shortened as expected and his axe was scraping along the roof, making a rather impressive fountain of sparks in its wake, illuminating the scene just enough for Moist to kick up and find his target, hoping against hope that *this* dwarf wasn't a female. And fortunately luck was with him and therefore regrettably not with the grag, who dropped his axe, clutched at his groin and unceremoniously fell from the carriage on to the tracks below.

As the train emerged from the tunnel, it came to a grinding stop. Moist scrambled to his feet and clambered back down across the flatbed to find out what had happened to the rest of the gang. He was relieved to discover the crew of the guard's van all more or less unharmed, including Of the Twilight the Darkness and his group of goblins, Fred Colon, Nobby Nobbs, Cheery Littlebottom, Detritus and Bluejohn, who was still hanging on to the last carriage, keeping the train together. There were also a few rather bewildered engineers and train drivers, some of whom had been trying to catch up with their sleep when the attack came but had apparently done their best.

Moist hadn't noticed Nobby and Colon in the mêlée but decided that he would not be surprised to hear that they had acquitted themselves with great derring-do and, of course, it was such a pity that it would turn out everyone else had been too busy to see them doing it. Even so, looking around the few groaning grags still on the train, Moist acknowledged that Nobby and Colon, if given no alternative, could fight like tigers, especially tigers with the nasty weaponry of the streets where anything went and wherever it went it could be very, very painful. Colon, in particular, was master of the underhand, and some of the groaning was familiar to Moist as the famous Ankh-Morpork lullaby.

Moist never thought of himself as a leader of men, so he delegated in circumstances such as these. The chore of marshalling went to Fred Colon, known to all for his excellent shouty voice that turned his face an unusual shade of puce and was expelled at a volume that even Iron Girder would have envied.

Such grags as were alive or weren't definitely dead were trussed up before being taken to the guard's van, where, Moist suspected, Commander Vimes would have a little talk with them about this and that and names and places and who and when and what dreadful manners they had. Lovely.

And now a figure leaned out of the armoured carriage. It was Aeron.

'The King is safe! Thank you all! Iron Girder came in for a hammering but the grags that managed to get on to the footplate were shown the furnace by Stoker Blake.' Moist winced at that. He had been close to the furnace a great many times when it had been opened by the stoker and it was instant suntan time, but if you were standing in the wrong place at the critical moment it was instant fiery death.

The journey onward, with the couplings once more in place, was altogether a sombre ride, for the victors as well as for the surviving dwarfs awaiting their dreaded conversation with the Blackboard Monitor who, it was believed, could cause you and your family never to have existed. Rubbed away, as it were, in the chalk dust of the blackboard.

A little later Iron Girder gently kissed the buffers at the Bonk railhead, and the first person to step down on to the hastily erected platform was Rhys Rhysson. He was greeted by a very large and extremely agitated rotund man, who had the word 'burgomaster' stamped firmly into his demeanour. He was sweating cobs and a fat man can sweat just as much as an engine. He genuflected to the King, an achievement considering his shape which was, not to put too fine a point on it, a globe.

'Welcome back, sire,' he said, panting. 'The humans of Bonk have always had a good relationship with your countrymen and I sincerely hope that this amicable arrangement is going to continue.'

This invitation was uttered at a very high speed and Moist saw it for what it was: a plea saying, please don't hurt us, we are fairly decent people and have always accepted your highness's claim to the Scone of Stone. The unsaid codicil being, please don't hurt us and above all, don't interfere with the running of our mercantile activities. Please. Please?

Rhys gripped the proffered and rather sweaty hand and said, 'I'm so sorry if you have been inconvenienced by the recent unpleasantness, Humphrey.' A gesture which left the burgomaster all smiles.

'Oh, it wasn't too bad, Your Majesty. It was a bit of a nuisance when you ... I mean the others started knocking down the clacks and all that. But you know how it is, it's like a family squabble in the house next door where you know it's not your business so you're ready with tea, sympathy and possibly bandages and medicaments. And next time you meet the couple next door you don't look too hard and mind your business and are still friends on the morrow.

'And anyway, her ladyship got involved, and once she'd made a couple of examples ... Well, thank goodness, we had our clacks back. She's firm but fair is Lady Margolotta, and remarkably swift.'

The sweating Humphrey knew full well he was talking about the most influential vampire in the world whilst at the same time giving her the appearance of an elderly lady who only had to bang her walking stick on the floor to get total respect.

'Of course all families have their ups and downs,' Humphrey continued, 'those little spats so easily started and so quickly left behind with no real damage done.'

Behind the burgomaster the train was unloading its passengers while Iron Girder occasionally hissed or spat in the way a locomotive has of making it clear it is not entirely quiescent.

Moist could hear Vimes debriefing Captain Sally von Humpeding, the Watch's only vampire member, who had been seconded to the Bonk Watch. They came over to report.

'Sally tells me that even though all communication from within Schmaltzberg has been cut off, reports have been reaching the Watch that all is not well with the conspirators,' said Vimes. He looked to Sally for confirmation.

'Yes,' she said, 'our sources indicate that the grag known as Ardent—'

She was interrupted by a snort of rage from Rhys and a rattle of axes from his assembled compatriots.

'Him again!' snarled Rhys.

'Yes,' said Sally. 'Him and a few others we'd been trying to locate after the massacre in Quirm. Well, it seems that Ardent and his followers are losing support; they're not having it all their way. There is unrest—'

'Good,' said Rhys. 'We can use that.'

'And Albrechtson?' asked Aeron.

'Well,' Sally smiled, showing a hint of fang, this being the most appropriate place in the world to let them get some air. 'Well. And loyal to you, sire.'

A rather smart goblin messenger insinuated his way through the crowd and passed a message to Sally, who read it. 'Ah,' she said. 'It's a message from Albrechtson. It seems the opposition know you've arrived, sire. Albrechtson would like you to know that he's being well treated and has been able to follow the progress of Iron Girder, thanks to the goblins.'

Rhys turned and looked at Simnel and Moist and said, 'Thank you, and Sir Harry, for getting me here safely. And Iron Girder, too. At the appropriate time you will know my generosity and I'd like to talk to you further. But do excuse me. I have a kingdom to reclaim.'

Addressing the company of dwarfs now fully assembled on the platform and armed to the teeth, he proclaimed, 'Let it be known that the Low King has arrived and will take his place on the Scone of Stone. Anyone wishing to deny him that trivial pleasure should be prepared to back up their coherent and well-founded objections with weaponry. It really is quite as simple as that. This message will be carried into Schmaltzberg by Bashfull Bashfullsson, a highly respected and knowledgeable dwarf known to all, accompanied by my trusted secretary, Aeron. We should also include Commander Vimes, the

Blackboard Monitor, and one-time Ambassador, to see fair play. Remember that at all times tampering with the King's Messengers is a matter of treason. Be aware, I'm not going to be a nanny about this. Insurgent dwarfs will get their just deserts.'

The sound of Vimes loudly lighting his cigar broke the silence.

'Let the others go first, I'll go along in a minute or two,' he said.

Moist, of course, hadn't been at Koom Valley but right now he wondered if he was about to see the ghost of Koom Valley's second incarnation – except it would be dwarf against dwarf. He wanted to shout out 'This is nuts!', and realized that in fact he had said it aloud.

To his surprise, the King said, 'Certainly so, Mister Lipwig. It beggars all reason, doesn't it? But sooner or later there comes a time when you have to take names and crack skulls. I'm sorry, it's at the other end of the spectrum from the little chat and it's what happens when reason no longer holds sway.'

'But you're all dwarfs. What can you possibly achieve?' groaned Moist, who for the rest of his life would always remember the tone of the King's voice . . .

'Tomorrow. That, Mister Lipwig, is what we can achieve. *Tomorrow.*'

The arrival of the messengers sent an immediate buzz around the multiple caverns of Schmaltzberg, somehow the centre of the galaxy when it came to hubbub of all sizes and rumour mills that turned faster than the mills of the gods. Rumour flowed like quicksilver. The phenomenon might be called the dwarf clacks were it not for the fact that the clacks didn't scramble the messages on a whim, thought Moist as he followed Rhys and the main band of dwarfs down into the honeycomb that was Schmaltzberg. The myriad noises flowing up from below through every tunnel and cavern were merging into a kind of audible mist or, he thought, fog. It simmered around the earlobe. The terrible sounds and confusions of war.

But now individual sounds were getting through. Raised voices, screams and the clatter of weaponry, punctuated with the occasional yell and dwarfish curses, which are known to have a life all of their very own. Further down, they came across Aeron, who was waiting with blood dripping from his sword. He noticed Moist's look and shrugged.

'There was a grag. He fought hard but would not submit, preferring death to ignominy . . . and so I accommodated him.' That last phrase contained more emphasis than Moist had heard for a very long time. Aeron turned to Rhys and reported.

'There have been certain clashes of opinion, your majesty,' he said, pointing to several dwarfs being treated in what would have been an impromptu field hospital had it been in a field.

Swords, hammers and axes were being deployed below as the King carried on marching, until they came to what must be the great hall, the largest cavern of them all.

As they passed through the portal, Moist came to a halt, trying to get a grip on this subterranean landscape, lit by the enormous chandeliers of dribbling candles along with cressets and great vats of squirming vurms* writhing in the corners; so there was light, he thought, but a strange light that was somehow negotiating with the eyes. You could see but what you saw was the darkness.

'Well, it's not a war any more,' said Vimes, suddenly there beside him. 'And not too many serious outcomes, except for the grags. That's dwarf-on-dwarf war: a hell of a lot of shouting and accusing and spitting, a lot like cats really, but that's dwarfs for you. They're not that stupid. Bags of bravado and sabre-rattling, but no one really wants to get hurt. You fight hoping for a small wound that looks good afterwards. Something to show the grandchildren, but really, when it comes to it, dwarf against dwarf, it generally settles down.'

Vimes puffed his cigar and continued, 'Mind you, if it were dwarf against troll this place would be running with blood. On the whole, it's like the taverns in Ankh-Morpork on a Saturday night. Everyone is full of gumption and pissy bravery and beer. Much too much beer. And then afterwards it's just a lot of groaning until they see the light.'

In fact, what Moist could see near by was dwarfs in small groups, some of them bandaged, in positions which suggested that war as such, if not over, had been

---

* Vurms are somewhat like glow worms, but with a stink that illumines. They can be found in deep dark places, where they subsist on the effluvia of any creatures that may arrive there. They are very useful to tomb raiders and others of that kidney – who in turn are often very useful to the vurms, especially their kidneys.

set aside for a breather and maybe a decent quaff. And younger dwarfs were going between the hurt and wounded with flagons. And one by one the dwarfs got up, shook hands with the nearest dwarf and walked haphazardly to the next group, where perhaps they would sit and chat and make up stories of near misses and clever parries and similar boozy boastings. Little by little, dwarf normality was flowing through Schmaltzberg once again.

'Pissed as farts,' said Vimes. 'But at the bottom, not bad, just susceptible to rabble rousers.' He sighed again. 'Maybe this time they'll have learned. And on that day Nobby Nobbs will be a shining hero!'

And that was all it took? Moist found himself wondering. After all the adrenalin of the train journey, the ambushes, the attacks ... the bridge ... the sleepless nights ... expecting at every turn to hear the swish of a scythe and to find that this time his luck really had run out ... and then Rhys gave a fine speech and just walked in and took back the kingdom?

'I was expecting them to put up more of a fight,' he said. 'You know, more of a glorious battle that would become the stuff of legends.'

'That's a very foolish thing to say, Mister Lipwig,' said Vimes. 'There's nothing "glorious" about times like this ... People have died, not necessarily good people and not too many, but nevertheless the face you wear on a battlefield should be a solemn one until the time when things are cleaned up and the real world drips its way in.'

Moist felt the shame welling up from his boots and

said, 'Commander, I stand abashed, quite sincerely.'

And instantly Vimes's face was eyeballing his and the commander exclaimed, 'Really? It seems it's not just the railway breaking new ground here!'

For once short of a ready reply, Moist turned to see what had become of Rhys and his party.

Rhys Rhysson had entered the cavern at a run. He headed straight for its centre, where stood the Scone of Stone. Now he looked around and demanded, 'Where is Ardent? I want him brought here, and as many of his followers as still remain. Though doubtless most have run: this place is full of exits.'

Bashfull Bashfullsson shouted, 'I have the scoundrel here, sire!'

The assembly of dwarfs went into the usual seemingly endless dwarfish hubbub, followed by a deep intake of breath from all concerned when Ardent was brought forward. His expression Moist couldn't read. But Moist, the man for atmospheres, could tell that Ardent was already somewhere beyond sanity, whilst Rhys seemed as cool and calm as ever, however fearful he might have been on the inside. And Moist would have wagered the mint that the King wasn't actually fearful at all. There was something in his demeanour that suggested an absolute assurance that this day was his (or indeed, *hers*, as he finally allowed the thought to creep back into his consciousness).

Sitting on the hallowed Scone of Stone with Ardent in front of him, Rhys said, 'You were dealt with mercifully after the Koom Valley Accord and still you thought it was right to try to take this kingdom from me. You encouraged those who tortured families to get their own way. What would people think of me if I had even a most minute inclination to treat you kindly? You are clever and many dwarfs speak highly of you, but your cleverness has been used to undermine my rule and make dwarfs appear to be vicious and stupid criminals in the eyes of all other species. What have you to say, in front of me and your kin?'

Ardent was silent.

'Very well,' said the King. 'No answer. You leave me no alternative. In times gone by a dwarf king would execute someone like you as a matter of course.'

And then there was the sound of metal and the King stood up, axe in hand. At last the light of terror passed across Ardent's face.

The King said, 'Oh, I see. Then perhaps as I am . . . you know . . . a modernizer, as you always say with a sneer, perhaps I'll deal with you as a modernizer should. Therefore, you will go on trial. And I shall see to it that among the jury there will be the families of those the grags tortured and those surviving guests of the wedding in Llamedos and all the others whose lives have been unnecessarily troubled by your existence in this world. They may be merciful and I will accept their verdict.'

Ardent remained silent and the King said, 'Take him away in chains but keep him alive, if only as a reminder for me that being a King is not an easy job.'

As Ardent was led away to much applause Rhys turned to the assembled dwarfs. 'Now I suggest someone goes and brings me my friend Albrecht Albrechtson who, to our shame, has been shackled and stuffed into a dungeon. Then perhaps the people delegated to go and let him out might hand him a flagon of brandy and, if practicable, run away. He has a piquant sense of humour.'

Rhys sat down again on the Scone of Stone and said, in tones that echoed around the cavern, 'It is usual at this time for me to say "my fellow dwarfs" . . .' There was a sucking feeling in the air as the King went on, 'but today I'll say "ladies and gentlemen dwarfs" . . . I am here not only to reclaim *my* Scone of Stone, which over the years has seen many important and notable buttocks sitting on it. I wonder, how many of those buttocks down the years were female?'

The sharp intake of breath by the whole gathering now seemed to draw all the air out of the place as the Low King continued.

'Hear me out! It is well known that the gender of a dwarf is entirely their secret unless they decide otherwise. And I recall that in Ankh-Morpork, a few years ago, there was a fashion show for dwarfs only. I was there, incognito, and I recognized a few of you, quite possibly purchasing for use in the privacy of your own home? Shatta made a lot of money that day and I understand that Madame Sharn wants to open a new shop here. Here in Schmaltzberg! Does this thought frighten anybody? In these days, I think not. And all I am doing now, my friends, is to introduce to you something important: it is the truth! You know . . . that thing which remains when all the lies have been burned away.

And now I will tell you that I have decided to no longer be your King!'

There was an extra hubbub of indrawn breaths and sotto voce speculation from the populace at large, with all eyes focused on the King. The magic was broken or possibly enhanced by the tiny sound of a match being struck by Commander Vimes. And the fat cigar glowed like a beacon. Vimes smiled and nodded at the King, and in that moment Moist realized that Vimes had probably always known, or at least since the famous adventure several years before when he was Ambassador to Rhys's election as Low King.

There was a disturbance as the crowd parted to allow the venerable Albrecht Albrechtson to make his way to stand by the Low King, who greeted him warmly in the traditional dwarf manner of butting helmets.*

'Welcome, old friend. I'm sorry that you have been . . . inconvenienced by my absence. Those responsible will pay for that,' he said in a loud voice, glaring at the crowd. Then more quietly to Albrecht, Rhys said, 'You've arrived at a good moment. I'm in the middle of making an announcement.'

'So I heard,' said Albrechtson. 'What are you doing? You don't have to stand down. You won.'

The Low King laughed. 'Stand down? Oh, I don't think so, boyo. You'll see.'

---

* A part of dwarf etiquette that outsiders find near impossible to master, the traditional helmet butt is a little less vigorous than the manoeuvre known on the tougher streets of Ankh-Morpork as the 'Shamlegger Kiss', but it must also not be so gentle as to imply that either the giver or the receiver is a sissy.

Turning back to the crowd, Rhys took a deep breath and said, 'This will be surprising news to many of my subjects, but I am female, just like your mothers were, and therefore am in truth your Queen!'

There it was again. The famous dwarf intake of breath. Even Albrechtson seemed startled. Moist looked at Aeron and noticed the dwarf's mailed fist was resting, oh so lightly, on his sword. Bashfullsson was standing right behind Albrechtson, watching him closely. Next to Moist, Vimes carefully laid down his glowing cigar on a rock ledge and tensed. This could be very interesting, Moist thought.

'And if you think your Queen is not as good a ruler as your King, do you really believe your mother was inferior to your father?' The Queen laughed. 'I see embarrassment among all of you. That's good. The thing about being embarrassed is that sooner or later you aren't, but you remember that you were.'

There was a noticeable shift in atmosphere as the Queen carried on, saying, 'I have seen that in warm breasts there is a truth which is not to be denied, but we dwarfs seem to deny everything, building little worlds inside a big one. And one might ask what we are trying to escape from – unless it is ourselves. We are dwarfs, yes, but we could be better than our dwarf ancestors stuck in their holes.'

When she had finished the Queen looked around at the assembled dwarfs and said, 'Well? No dwarf man enough to challenge me?'

Several eyes turned to Albrechtson, who looked

thoughtful but did not move. Bashfullsson relaxed his stance.

And suddenly the Queen's finger was pointing and she said, 'Shod Orebreaker, I always thought of you as a level-headed dwarf with your head screwed on, although possibly against the thread.'

And Moist felt the exultation of those who hadn't been the one facing the finger and the misery of Shod Orebreaker, and he wondered: had the Low Queen's voice changed, or had it always been like that? She hadn't threatened, but a visible threat was in the air. She had them in her hand, and she was squeezing, and the dwarf stepped backwards as she pointed at him and she said, 'Where are your grags now, Shod Orebreaker?'

The said Shod became a picture of panic. 'Not my grags, my Queen!'

This was possibly because Aeron had passed the Queen a thick file. The Queen licked a finger and riffled through the pages, looked down and said, 'Really? Then I must have been misinformed.'

She turned to the rest of the dwarfs and said, 'I wonder if I have been misinformed about all of you?'

But the assembled company was watching the flicking pages, trying not to crane to see whether their name was on the list . . . It was laughable. She had them by the short and curlies, and she said, 'Strange, isn't it, that when the chips are down they take other chips with them. If anyone wants to test my claim then let them step forward now!'

There were murmurings, dwarfs turning round to other dwarfs and the traditional aforesaid hubbub of such occasions and then there was a hush as Albrechtson spoke.

'My queen,' he said, and the hubbub bubbled. It was the unexpected moment: the great defender of all that was dwarfish now having a stocktaking of his thoughts. 'My queen, we, fortuitously, live and so we should learn. I have always considered myself knowledgeable, a true scholar of the ways of Tak, but the past days have shown me that even I have lessons to learn. In my little dungeon, I heard my ways changing and understood the meaning of humility. In fact, I am prepared to admit before you all that some of those lessons were taught me by a goblin a fraction of my age, whom I am proud to call my friend.'

Moist saw that the old dwarf was crying. Albrechtson hesitated, then shouted, 'Tak save the Queen! And I will fight anyone who says otherwise.' And Moist thought, Oh blast, it's all going to start over again.

But the assembled dwarfs made no move to take Albrechtson up on his challenge. The sea of faces in the hall looked universally stunned, as if someone had announced that gold was, to be honest, not that interesting after all.

The Queen gracefully thanked Albrechtson, then pulled herself up and said, 'I am well aware that many of you have financed the grags and their entourage and I know the names, yes, indeed I know the names of those who'd kill for a curdled thesis. In the fullness of time there will be no redemption for them. We were generous after the mess of Koom Valley and those were the stupid days, but if the grags and their friends think they can take my Scone from me they will know me for what I am. Your Queen. I believe all of you will have heard of Queen Ynci of Lancre, yes? Well, I consider her my role model, but right now I'm looking for peace for all the world and specifically for myself and my child.'

And in the thundering susurration that followed this there was one dwarf suddenly standing next to the Queen. It was Aeron, and he drew his sword, not against anyone in particular, but nevertheless very ready to defend his wife and his unborn child.

Over the uproar the Queen said, 'And is there anyone here now who doubts that I am the Queen by right? It seems to me our ancestors thought their mothers were inferior. Well, as I say, I am soon to be a mother, so which of you gentlemen would like to try and take my Scone from me?'

Moist looked around. There were no takers. The Queen looked dangerous to touch and she didn't even have a weapon in her hands. It had to be game, set and whole boxful of matches.

'Very well,' the Low Queen of the dwarfs concluded. 'There will be a feast for all who come with goodwill and there will, of course, be much quaffing.' She smiled and added, 'That includes cocktails, for those who like them. Believe me, the world is upside down, as it was meant to be. Praise Tak! And praise Iron Girder and all those who built her, fed her and polished her.'

'Ardent was on a hiding to nowhere,' said Albrecht at

the banquet later that day. 'People broke away to avoid the inevitable. You're right, your majesty. We forgot what it was to be true dwarfs, but then people were getting hurt! There were too many threats against decent dwarfs. The little bits of mercury flow together and in the end his support turned out to be built of sand.'

Vimes gazed around from his place as honoured guest at the low table and said, 'Look at them there, the world has indeed turned upside down. There will be grumbling, but what are you dwarfs without grumbling?'

Albrecht snorted and said, 'There should have been more of a reckoning.'

'Oh, really?' said the Queen. 'I don't intend to start my new life with a bloodbath. Justice will be done. Everyone knows who the main players are, we always have done. We have names, depositions. It's a small world for dwarfs, with nowhere else to hide, and, frankly, the work is almost completed. The deep-down grags behind this lost a lot of their best fighters attacking Iron Girder on her peregrination across the landscape.

'What a voyage that was! And the wonderful discovery of loggysticks. The train is the future; bringing people closer together. Think about it. People *run* to see the train go past. Why? Because it's heading to the future or coming from the past. Personally, I very much want the future and I want to see to it that dwarfs are part of that future, if it's not too late.'

Vimes smiled and said, 'Well, your majesty, you have the opportunity right now. I understand from young

Simnel that the bridge at Wilinus will take several months to be repaired and strengthened sufficiently to be able to take the weight of a fully loaded train. That means that Iron Girder and her carriages will be stranded here until the line is rebuilt.'

He looked down the table to where Moist was in earnest conversation with Bashfullsson. 'Mister von Lipwig will no doubt be happy to advise on the ... commercial opportunities.'

Rhys smiled. 'Ah yes, I'm familiar with Mister von Lipwig's reputation, and have been impressed with his, ah, capabilities. However, I think it might be advisable to summon our lawyer, Mr Thunderbolt, to ensure that all is done fair and square, see.'

Vimes laughed. 'Very wise.'

'And no doubt there will be a need for workers to help with construction?' enquired the Queen. 'The young ones, in particular, who may not be so interested in staying in the mines, but nevertheless want a good solid job with plenty of metal and hammering involved? We are still dwarfs, after all.'

Afterwards the Queen walked among her quite possibly loyal subjects and it was a grand perambulation, with little outbreaks of mail skirts and elaborately coiffed beards amongst certain of the dwarfs rushing shyly over to assure her of their fealty. As Vimes said afterwards, for that day at least she had won hands down, especially since a great many of the dwarfs she was talking to were already openly declaring themselves females who had been waiting for this moment for a very long time.

* * *

The evening before they were to leave Bonk, Moist wandered down to the railhead, idly pondering recent events. Well, he thought, the world has seen the footplate of Iron Girder and the Queen has been given her crown back and according to Commander Vimes the worst of the grags are either dead or behind bars.

At the makeshift station Iron Girder was being guarded by Nobby Nobbs and Fred Colon, who were both sound asleep. Iron Girder, however, wasn't, although the kettle was barely simmering after a long day giving rides to the locals up and down the single track.

Moist tiptoed to the empty footplate and whispered, 'What are you, Iron Girder?' There was a moment of silence, then a shimmer as the wisps of steam drifted up into the night air above the locomotive and a voice breathed into his brain, soft and warm and somehow damp.

'My, oh my, Mister Lipwig, you are the smart one, just as they say. I am me. I am Iron Girder. But all it takes is for people to believe and I am no longer just an artefact put together by clever engineers. I am an idea, a something made of nothing, whose time has come to be. Some even call me "goddess".'

Moist's fleeting thought about traditional representations of goddesses in diaphanous nighties with maybe an urn or two was banished as the voice continued a little more sharply.

'Am I not beautiful? And I tell you, my children will be even better! More sleek and more handsome and more powerful! Even now Mister Simnel is making my children for me. In time I will become ubiquitous, part of the landscape which is ennobled by my fleeting passage. I hear the worship every day that tells me that I am power personified and those who think to oppose me and put out my fire will find themselves thwarted, and swiftly. I, Mister Lipwig, I will rule on the up line and I will rule on the down line.'

In the twilight Moist saw a skinny figure walk up to Iron Girder. Dick Simnel shut down some hissing mechanism or other and the voice, the beautiful voice, was silenced.

'Aye, she's gradely all right! Come to see her for the last time before we head back to the city, have you? I can't blame you. Everyone's been wanting to see 'er, and I won't lie, Mister Lipwig, it's a wrench to leave her behind, for all she's got good work to do 'ere. Iron Girder, she's turned out to be a great lass. She was the power and she was 'arnessed, by gum. Oh, yes! 'arnessed by the sine and the cosine, and even the tangent had its little 'and in there somewhere! But not least she was tamed by my sliding rule.'

Dick grinned at Moist and continued. 'People see Iron Girder and they're gobsmacked by what can be done with mathematics! Don't you go thinking she'll burn you with living steam because she won't. I've seen to it that she won't. She'll always be my favourite engine, Mister Lipwig, the queen of them all. She lives. How could anyone say she doesn't?'

Moist looked around and saw that they were surrounded by goblins sitting quietly in a big circle like worshippers at the shrine, and once again Dick Simnel said, 'Power, Mister Lipwig, power under control.'

Moist was seldom speechless, but this time all he could say was, 'Good luck with that, Mister Simnel. Good luck.'

And the driver made his magic and the fire box opened and spilled dancing red shadows all around the footplate. And then came the rattle and jerk as Iron Girder took the strain and breathed steam for one more turn around the track as the goblins whooped and cackled and scrambled up her sides. And then came the first chuff and the second chuff and then the chuff bucket overflowed as Iron Girder escaped the pull of friction and gravity and flew along the rails.

Dick Simnel lit his pipe from a hot coal and said to the night, 'Aye, gradely.'

When Drumknott entered the Oblong Office a few days later there was a familiarity to the silence, interrupted only by the scratch of a pencil as the austere figure behind the desk filled in a word on that day's crossword. Drumknott coughed.

'Yes?'

The face of the Patrician was forbidding. An eyebrow shifted quizzically, a characteristic known and feared by many. Drumknott smiled.

'Many congratulations! You have that expression down to a T and the accent never faltered. And, of course, the frown! You've always been very good at the frown. Quite frankly, if he was standing next to you I wouldn't know whom from which.'

Suddenly the face of the Patrician disappeared, leaving only Charlie the Clown in Lord Vetinari's clothes, looking embarrassed.

'It wasn't very difficult, Mister Drumknott, with you giving me those little signs and everything.'

'Oh no,' said Drumknott. 'Your performance was perfect. You've impersonated his lordship for two weeks and not put a foot wrong! But now to business. The sum we agreed will be deposited in your special account at the Royal Bank tomorrow.' Drumknott smiled again and said, like a cheerful uncle, 'How is your wife these days, Charlie?'

'Oh, Henrietta's fine, Mister Drumknott, thank you for asking.'

'And your little boy – Rupert? He must be out of school now, yes?'

Charlie laughed uncertainly and said, 'Not so little, sir, he's growing up like a weed and wants to be an engine driver.'

And Drumknott said, 'Well now, Charlie, you already have enough money to put him through a trade anywhere in the city and give your daughter a dowry fit for a queen. And, of course, you're still in the same house? Excellent!'

'Oh, yessir, and thanks to you we've got much better bedrooms for the kids now and are saving up for a granny flat for when we can afford a granny. And Henrietta is overjoyed at the amount of money I'm bringing in these days and can even afford to get her hair cut at Mister Fornacite's, just like the posh ladies do. She's over the moon about it.' He grunted and said,

'I don't earn that much from the puppet shows and clowning business.'

And now Drumknott beamed once again and said, 'I'm sure his lordship will be glad to hear that your family is so happy and . . . alive. Long may it continue. I'll be recommending to him that you could be promoted, as it were, to higher things. And now, since his lordship is expected back within the hour, if you don't mind I'll take you out through the back door. We really don't want to see two Vetinaris in one place, do we?'

Charlie went almost white and said, 'Oh, no sir, we don't want that.'

'Well, we shan't, shall we,' said Drumknott. 'Off you go and I'll lock the door behind you.'

When Charlie had disappeared, happy but in haste, Drumknott, after a moment's thought, said to Dark Clerk Ishmael, 'I'm sure his lordship will want to know that we've checked the location of this Mister Fornacite's salon and the school that our friend's children go to. Is it the same as last year?'

And the clerk replied, 'Yes, it is, sir, I checked again the other day.'

'Well done.'

As his lordship had pointed out: 'If you take enough precautions, you never need to take precautions.' It was just a matter of making sure that Charlie didn't get . . . well, creative about his future.

Never had Moist been more happy to see his front door than when he got home and his wife opened it before he did, saying, 'Oh, it's you. Not dead? Good. How did it go?'

'Pretty well. The golems were incredible. Sad that we've had to leave Iron Girder there until the bridge is repaired. Still, we've got so many of Harry's golems and workers on it now it's not going to be long before Vetinari can have a special train of his own, if he likes.'

'To make sure relationships between Uberwald and Ankh-Morpork proceed in a ... cordial fashion, no doubt,' said his wife with a smile.

Behind him, Of the Twilight the Darkness said, 'Already Uberwald goblins giving themselves railway name. Speaks funny, those ones, but quick clever, like all goblin.'

'Yes,' said Adora Belle, 'that reminds me. We got reports while you were away from clacksmen along the road from the Shires about some rather odd occurrences. Strange rumblings, steam coming out of molehills, that sort of thing. You wouldn't know anything about that, would you?'

Of the Twilight the Darkness reassembled his features into the closest approximation of innocence that a goblin can muster. 'No ideas, missus. Steaming molehill? Maybe cow eat bad grass. Course, maaany goblin interest in steaming things. Some even practises own little engine. Educational! Clever goblins.'

It was clearly a conversation for another day. Moist headed for the fluffy pillows with a grateful sigh. 'I'll have a rest and tomorrow I'll dally with the Bank. There must be some paperwork for me to sign.

It would be nice to have a simple job for a while.'

Adora Belle snorted. 'How long would that be?'

Moist hesitated. 'Maybe a fortnight? There might be a *lot* of paperwork.'

'Yes, and you won't do it,' said Adora Belle. 'You know Mister Bent keeps everything shipshape. All you have to do is go around being friendly to everybody.'

'And nobody's trying to kill me, Spike.'

And Adora Belle said, 'We can but hope.'

At breakfast, Lady Sybil said to her husband, 'It sounds quite an adventure, Sam. I hear the Queen has changed her name to Blodwen. It means "fair flower" in Llamedos. Isn't that nice? I must write to her.'

'She'll like that,' said Vimes, whose wife's capacity to remain in touch with everybody she had ever met was well known and sometimes quite useful. Especially in political circumstances. The commander looked down at his muesli and said, 'You know, that Lipwig character isn't quite as bad as I thought. Acts like a scoundrel, but reasonably helpful when the chips are down. Mind you, I'm not going to tell him so.'

He pushed the healthy fibre around his bowl, wistfully recalling the stoker's fry-ups. 'But he does like being the centre of attention, of course.'

'Yes, some men are like that, dear.'

Lady Sybil was silent for a moment, then said, 'Sam, I know you're going to be busy what with the backlog and everything, but can I ask a favour?'

'Anything, dear.'

'When they have the line to Uberwald running, I'd

love to go to visit the Queen, and most of all I'd like a holiday by the train. And Young Sam's mad about trains, you know. He's nearly filled up his first notebook already.'

'Well,' said Vimes, 'you know if I have a holiday I walk into a crime.'

Lady Sybil finished her egg and said, 'Jolly good, dear, you'll like that.'

Harry King was not entirely surprised when Drumknott arrived at the compound the following day and said, 'His lordship commands you and Lady King to present yourselves to him within the hour.' And the secretary winked uncharacteristically at Harry, and his wife when he told her was, according to her, all of a tizzy at the news.

'The palace in one hour! How can a girl look her best inside an hour?'

'Come on, Duchess,' said Harry. 'You look a treat as always and getting younger every day.'

'Oh, you teaser, Harry King!'

But Harry said, 'The coach is here and clean as a whistle and his lordship believes that punctuality is the politeness of Princes and that applies to you, too, young Emily. I expect your boy wouldn't want you to be late. That's not the railway . . . way.'

Harry hadn't told his wife what to expect, preferring to keep it as a surprise, and so as the coach arrived at the palace, his wife nearly had another tizzy to contend with because there were the great and good of Ankh-Morpork, and presumably some of the silly and nasty as well, just to see Harry King being turned into a Lord. *Lord King of the Permanent Way*. And in the wonderful ceremony that followed, Lord Harry's old Dutch did indeed become a Duchess.

Dick Simnel was made a knight, and a master engineer too, courtesy of the Chief Mining Engineer himself, and now stood hand in hand with the beaming Emily. Commander Vimes, resplendent in his ceremonial pantaloons and looking furious about them, was already burdened with every title it was his lordship's pleasure to bestow, but was given another medal anyway, struck in sorortanium and featuring Iron Girder herself. In fact there was a medal for every watchman who had been on the train, and every crew member, goblins included.

Later, there came the inevitable interview in the Oblong Office with Drumknott at a side table taking notes.

'I understand, Mister Lipwig,' said the Patrician, surveying the city below them from the window, 'that there were some remarkable events along the journey.'

Moist kept a straight face but around his neck he felt the prickle of a phantom noose.

The Patrician continued. 'A fog which became conveniently solid, a train which apparently flew across a gorge, and I'm still getting reports of subterranean phenomena all the way from the city to Bonk. The Archchancellor has assured me that no magic was involved in any of these events. You will recall, I am sure, Mister von Lipwig, that I expressly forbade the use of the buried golems in the railway enterprise, and that any evidence of their use would send you to the kittens?' He moved towards the fire, which was getting low in the grate, and gave it a prod with the poker – rather too pointedly, Moist thought.

'Excuse me, my lord, but did you find any such evidence?'

Vetinari turned to his secretary. 'Did we find any evidence, Drumknott?'

Drumknott looked at Moist. 'No, sir, we did not.'

'Well then, there is nothing more to say,' said the Patrician. 'After all, strange and inexplicable things turn up around here almost every week.'

Drumknott cleared his throat. 'Yes, sir. There was that fall of pianos in the Fish Market last week. It's just a part of being Ankh-Morpork.'

'Indeed, we are no strangers to strangeness. And frankly some things can be written down as phenomena without cause or issue,' said Vetinari, looking as benevolent as it was possible to do whilst holding a red-hot poker, and whilst being Vetinari.

'Incidentally, Mister Lipwig, your prowess in that fight on the train was excellent! Of course you needed a *little* assistance.'

Moist looked up at the Patrician, silhouetted by the flames behind him, and inside his head there was the horrible tinkle of a penny dropping. He gulped.

'You! You were Stoker Blake! That's impossible!'

'Really?' said the Patrician. 'As impossible as a train travelling on free air? Do you not believe that I could throw coal into the fire box? After all, what is that compared to dealing with Ankh-Morpork with its myriad demanding problems every day? I assure you of this, Mister Lipwig, I am a man of many talents and you should hope never to encounter some of them. Compared with them, Stoker Blake was a mere babe in arms.'

'What,' said Moist, 'fighting with shovels?'

'Dear dear, Mister Lipwig, you *are* easily impressed. You surely remember that I was schooled in the Assassins' Guild. After that experience, my predecessor on the footplate, Killer John Wagstaff, was, as they say, a pussycat in comparison. Indeed, I enjoyed my life as Mister Blake and all the new little skills it has taught me. Excellent implement, the shovel. And as for the other stokers, I think I made friends there, yes, there was a certain camaraderie among us. All said, a little holiday from the weighty business of the city, and I dare say I might be predisposed to travel on the footplate again when the mood takes me.'

'But why?'

'Why, Mister Lipwig? You of all people ask me why? The man who danced on the train roof, the man who actually looks for trouble if it appears to be the kind of trouble which is associated with the term derring-do? Though in your case a few more derring-don'ts might be a good idea. Sometimes, Mister Lipwig, the young you that you lost many years ago comes back and taps you on the shoulder and says, "This is the moment when civilization does not matter, when rules no longer hold sway. You have given the world all you can give and now it's the time that is just for you, the chance to go for broke in the last hurrah. Hurrah!'

Vetinari swung the poker against the fender, causing sparks to dance in the fireplace. He looked at the sparks and in whiplash fashion turned to Moist and said, 'And if you, Mister Lipwig, ever tell anyone else about this, Mister Trooper will be very glad to see you again. Do we have an understanding? Excellent.'

As if anyone would believe him if he did breathe a word about it! Moist was finding it hard enough to credit from the man's own lips. Then as he tried to process what he had been told, the Patrician's words about his own prowess sparked a renewed sense of grievance.

'You've given everyone else on that train a medal, even Nobby Nobbs. Is there nothing for me, then, my lord?'

There was a pause and Vetinari said, 'Oh, there is, Mister Lipwig, there is, and it's something wonderful: it's the precious gift of staying alive.'

And later, when he came to think about it, Moist thought that was, well, on the whole a good deal and, after all, he had *danced on the speeding locomotive.* That was living, all right!

A few weeks later, Drumknott persuaded Lord Vetinari to accompany him to the area behind the palace where a jungle of drain pipes emptied and several mis-matched sheds, washhouses and lean-tos housed some of the necessary functions without which a modern palace could not operate.*

---

* Frankly most palaces are just like this. Their backsides do not bear looking at.

There was a young goblin waiting there, rather nervous, clasping what looked like two wheels held together by not very much. The wheels were spinning.

Drumknott cleared his throat. 'Show his lordship your new invention, Mister Of the Wheel the Spoke.'

Vetinari's face was unmoving as he watched the goblin put a leg over his creation and pedal the little machine around the washerwomen, who threw up their arms saying things like 'Oh my! Whatever next?'

And the oldest washerwoman said, 'I reckon you could have a young lady on the pillion behind you.'

Lord Vetinari said, 'You're going to want one of these, aren't you, Drumknott?'

'Well sir,' said Drumknott, 'this is not a mechanism, really. All it does is simply extend the parts of the body and look, no steam, no soot, just sweat.'

'Interesting,' said the Patrician. 'One man, his own motor.'

When the goblin eventually stopped in front of Lord Vetinari, he looked imploringly at Drumknott, who waited patiently for his master to decide.

Vetinari finally did smile and said, 'A remarkable *velocipede*, Mister Of the Wheel the Spoke. I do believe that Leonard of Quirm had a similar idea, but now we are in a world of motion, I see no problem here. It appears that every man could be his own horse. I commend you. May I suggest, young goblin, that you take your prototype along to Commander Vimes. An instrument that doubles one's speed ought to be very useful to a hurrying watchman, or, indeed, an insufficiently hurrying one. Mister Drumknott, please write a note to the commander and I will sign it. After all, some of them could do with the exercise. And if I were you, sir,' he added to the goblin, 'I would make an appointment with a certain troll lawyer called Thunderbolt and do what he tells you.

'The world is changing and it needs its shepherds and sometimes its butchers. And in this case, I'm its shepherd. Your enterprise has been noted. And all that anyone can say now is: What next? What little thing will change the world because the little tinkers carried on tinkering?'

Acknowledgements

I was assisted in writing *Raising Steam* by the boiler-suited gentlemen of the Watercress Line in Hampshire, who showed me – well, they showed me everything, including their workshops, the footplate and the fire box of a travelling locomotive and, wonder of wonders, the signal box: a treasure in mahogany and brass. Champion!

And, of course, my grateful thanks go to Rob for keeping the whole show on the rails, and to my editor, Philippa Dickinson, who supplied advice and flapjacks and, above all, patience.

ALL ABOARD!

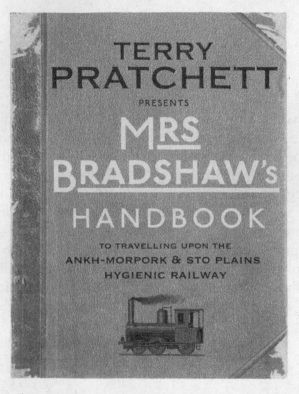

Mrs Georgina Bradshaw's invaluable illustrated guide to the destinations and diversions of the railway deserves a place in the luggage of any traveller, or indeed armchair traveller, upon the Disc:

★ Edifying sights – from souks to the seaside.
★ Respectable lodgings for all species and heights.
★ Practical hints – from travel sickness to
   transporting swamp dragons.

Don't leave Ankh-Morpork without it!

AVAILABLE NOW

A SLIP OF
THE KEYBOARD
COLLECTED NON FICTION

With a Foreword by Neil Gaiman

Terry Pratchett has earned a place in the hearts of readers the world over with his bestselling Discworld series – but in recent years he has become equally well-known and respected as an outspoken campaigner for causes including Alzheimer's research and animal rights.

A Slip of the Keyboard brings together for the first time the finest examples of Pratchett's non fiction writing, both serious and surreal: from musings on mushrooms to what it means to be a writer (and why banana daiquiris are so important); from memories of Granny Pratchett to speculation about Gandalf's love life, and passionate defences of the causes dear to him.

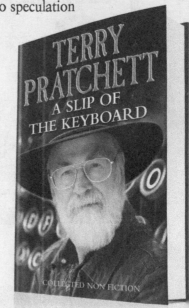

With all the humour and humanity that have made his novels so enduringly popular, this collection brings Pratchett out from behind the scenes of the Discworld to speak for himself – man and boy, bibliophile and computer geek, champion of hats, orangutans and Dignity in Dying.

Visit

www.**terrypratchett**.co.uk

to discover everything you need to know
about Terry Pratchett and his writing, plus all
manner of other things you may find interesting, such as
videos, competitions, character profiles and games.

 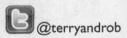